Titles in the Garrett, P.I., Series

Sweet Silver Blues

Bitter Gold Hearts

Cold Copper Tears

Old Tin Sorrows

Dread Brass Shadows

Red Iron Nights

Deadly Quicksilver Lies

Petty Pewter Gods

Faded Steel Heat

Angry Lead Skies

Whispering Nickel Idols

Cruel Zinc Melodies

Gilded Latten Bones

INTRODUCING
GARRETT, P.I.

•Sweet Silver Blues•

•Bitter Gold Hearts•

•Cold Copper Tears•

GLEN COOK

A ROC BOOK

ROC
Published by New American Library, a division of
Penguin Group (USA) Inc., 375 Hudson Street,
New York, New York 10014, USA
Penguin Group (Canada), 90 Eglinton Avenue East, Suite 700, Toronto,
Ontario M4P 2Y3, Canada (a division of Pearson Penguin Canada Inc.)
Penguin Books Ltd., 80 Strand, London WC2R 0RL, England
Penguin Ireland, 25 St. Stephen's Green, Dublin 2,
Ireland (a division of Penguin Books Ltd.)
Penguin Group (Australia), 250 Camberwell Road, Camberwell, Victoria 3124,
Australia (a division of Pearson Australia Group Pty. Ltd.)
Penguin Books India Pvt. Ltd., 11 Community Centre, Panchsheel Park,
New Delhi - 110 017, India
Penguin Group (NZ), 67 Apollo Drive, Rosedale, Auckland 0632,
New Zealand (a division of Pearson New Zealand Ltd.)
Penguin Books (South Africa) (Pty.) Ltd., 24 Sturdee Avenue,
Rosebank, Johannesburg 2196, South Africa

Penguin Books Ltd., Registered Offices:
80 Strand, London WC2R 0RL, England

Published by Roc, an imprint of New American Library, a division of Penguin Group (USA) Inc. *Sweet Silver Blues*,
Bitter Gold Hearts, and *Cold Copper Tears* were previously published individually in Roc editions.

First Roc Trade Paperback Printing, August 2011
10 9 8 7 6 5 4 3 2 1

Sweet Silver Blues copyright © Glen Cook, 1987
Bitter Gold Hearts copyright © Glen Cook, 1988
Cold Copper Tears copyright © Glen Cook, 1988
All rights reserved

 REGISTERED TRADEMARK—MARCA REGISTRADA

Set in Minion
Designed by Ginger Legato

Printed in the United States of America

Sweet Silver Blues.................1

Bitter Gold Hearts.............223

Cold Copper Tears.............465

INTRODUCING GARRETT, P.I.

•••Sweet Silver Blues

Bam! Bam! Bam!

It sounded like someone was knocking with a sledgehammer. I rolled over and cracked a bloodshot eye. I couldn't see a figure through the window, but that wasn't surprising. I could barely make out the lettering on the grimy glass:

GARRETT
INVESTIGATOR
CONFIDENTIAL AGENT

I had blown my wad buying the glass and wound up being my own painter.

The window was as dirty as last week's dishwater, but not filthy enough to block out the piercing morning light. The damned sun wasn't up yet! And I'd been out till the second watch barhopping while I followed a guy who might lead me to a guy who might know where I could find a guy. All this led to was a pounding headache.

"Go away!" I growled. "Not available."

Bam! Bam! Bam!

"Go the hell away!" I yelled. It left my head feeling like an egg that had just bounced off the edge of a frying pan. I wondered if I ought to feel the back to see if the yolk was leaking, but it seemed like too much work. I'd just go ahead and die.

Bam! Bam! Bam!

I have a little trouble with my temper, especially when I have a hangover. I was halfway to the door with two feet of lead-weighted truncheon before sense penetrated the scrambled yolk.

When they are that insistent, it's somebody from up the hill with a summons to do work too sticky to lay on their own boys. Or it's somebody from down the hill with the word that you're stepping on the wrong toes.

In the latter case the truncheon might be useful.

I yanked the door open.

For a moment I didn't see the woman. She barely came up to my chest. I eyeballed the three guys behind her. They were lugging enough steel to outfit their own army, but I wouldn't have been shy about wading in. Two of them were about fifteen years old and the other was about a hundred and five.

"We're invaded by dwarfs," I moaned. None of them was taller than the woman.

"Are you Garrett?" She looked disappointed in what she saw.

"No. Two doors down. Good-bye." *Slam!* Two doors down was a night-working ratman who made a hobby of getting on my nerves. I figured it was his turn in the barrel.

I stumbled toward bed with the vague suspicion that I had seen those people before.

I wriggled around like an old dog. When you're hungover there is no way to get comfortable, feather bed or creek bed. Just as I was getting reacquainted with being horizontal again, *Bam! Bam! Bam!*

I told myself I wouldn't move. They would take the hint.

They didn't. It sounded like the entire room was about to cave in. I was not going to get any more sleep.

I got up again—gingerly—and drank a quart of water. I chased it with skunky beer and clung to my temper precariously.

Bam! Bam! Bam!

"I don't make a habit of busting female heads," I told the tiny woman when I opened the door again. "But in your case I think I can make an exception."

She was not impressed. "Dad wants to see you, Garrett."

"Say, that's wonderful. That explains a gang of runts trying to break my door down. What does the gnome king want?"

The old codger said, "Rose, it's obvious this isn't a convenient time for Mr. Garrett. We've waited three days. A few more hours won't make any difference."

Rose? I should know a Rose from somewhere. But where?

"Mr. Garrett, I'm Lester Tate. And I want to apologize—on Rose's behalf—for bothering you at this hour. She's a headstrong child, and having been overindulged by my brother all her life, she's blind to any desires but her own." He spoke in the soft, tired voice of a man who spends a lot of time arguing with a whirlwind.

"Lester Tate?" I asked. "Like in Denny Tate's uncle Lester?"

"Yes."

"It's beginning to come back. The family picnic at Elephant Rocks three years ago. I came with Denny." Maybe I had laundered my memory because Rose had been an unspeakably nasty wench that day. "Maybe it was all the hardware that made me forget your faces." Denny Tate and I went back about eight years, but I hadn't seen him in months. "So, how is Denny?" I asked, maybe a little guilty.

"Dead!" barked sweet sister Rose.

Denny Tate and I were heroes of the Cantard Wars. That means we did our five years and got out alive. A lot of guys don't.

We went in about the same time, were barracked less than twenty miles apart but never met till later, here in TunFaire, eight hundred miles from the fighting. He was light cavalry out of Fort Must. I was Fleet Marines, mostly aboard the *Imperial Kimmswick* out of Full Harbor. I fought in the islands. Denny rode over most of the Cantard, chasing or running away from the Venageti. We both made sergeant before we got out.

It was a nasty war. It still is. I like it better now that it's much farther away.

Denny saw more of the worst than I did. The fighting at sea and in the islands was sideshow stuff. Neither we nor the Venageti wasted wizards on it. All the flash and fury of sorcery got saved for the struggle on the mainland.

Anyway, we'd both survived our five, and had done part of them in the same general area, and that had given us something in common when we met. It was good enough till we got to know each other.

"So that's why you're a walking arsenal. What is it? A vendetta? Maybe you'd better get inside."

Rose cackled like a hen laying a square egg.

Uncle Lester laughed, too, but it was a laugh of a different breed. "Shut up, Rosie. I'm sorry, Mr. Garrett. The weapons are here to feed Rosie's hunger for drama. She believes we don't dare enter this neighborhood unarmed, lest the local thugs ravish her."

It was not a good dawn for me. Few of them are. Without thinking, I cracked, "The thugs in my neighborhood have some taste. She doesn't have to worry." Blame it on the hangover.

Uncle Lester grinned. Rose looked at me like I was dog flop she wanted off her shoe.

I tried to gloss over with business. "Who did it? What can I do about it?"

"Nobody did it," Rose told me. "He fell off a horse and busted his head, his neck, and about ten other bones."

"Hard to believe a skilled horseman could go that way."

"It happened in broad daylight on a busy street. There's no doubt that it was an accident."

"Then what do you need me for? Especially before the sun is up?"

"That's for Dad to tell," Rose said. The shrew had a lot of anger in her, anger that was there before I gave her cause. "Bringing you in on it was his idea, not mine."

I knew Denny's old man modestly. Well enough to use his first name if I was the kind of snotnose who calls his friend's parent by name instead of Mister. He ran a very successful cobbler's business. He, Denny, and two journeymen handled the custom and commercial trade. Uncle Lester and a dozen apprentices made boots under an open-ended deal with the army. The war had been good to Denny's dad.

They do say it is an ill wind indeed that blows no one any good.

Well, I was awake. Hair of the dog and scintillating conversation had reduced the pounding in my head to the tramp of ten thousand legions. Still, there was a nagging guilt about not having made time to see Denny before the old gal in black climbed on his back. I decided to find out why the old man needed somebody in my line of work when there wasn't a doubt about how Denny checked out.

"Let me get myself put together and we'll be on our way."

Rose grinned wickedly. I realized I'd fed her a murderous straight line. I didn't stick around to hear her pounce on it.

●●●2

Willard Tate was no bigger than the rest of his tribe. A gnome. He was bald on top with tasseled gray hair to his shoulders on the sides and longer in the back. He was bent over his workbench, tapping tiny brass nails into the heel of a woman's shoe. Clearly he was at the top of his trade. He wore square TanHageen spectacles, and they don't come cheap.

He was engrossed in his work. Recalling his state since his wife died, I figured he was working off grief.

"Mr. Tate?" He knew I was there. I had cooled my heels for twenty minutes while they told him.

He drove one more nail with a single perfect tap and looked at me over his cheaters. "Mr. Garrett. They tell me you made mock of our size."

"I get nasty when somebody drags me out before the sun comes up."

"That's Rose. If she has to see you in, she'll see you in the hard way. I made a bad job of her. Keep her in mind as you rear your own children."

I said nothing. You tell somebody you look forward to blindness more eagerly than to having kids, you don't win any friends. Those that don't think you're lying think you're crazy.

"Do you have a problem with short people, Mr. Garrett?"

About six flip answers never saw the air. He was dead serious. "Not really. Denny wouldn't have been my buddy if I did. Why? Is it important?"

"In a sideways sort of way. Did you ever wonder why the Tates are so small?"

I had never dwelled on it. "No."

"It's the blood. The taint of elvish. On both sides, several generations before my time. Keep that in mind. It will help you understand later."

I wasn't surprised. I'd suspected it before, the way Denny got along with animals. Plenty of people have the taint, yet most cover it up. There is a lot of prejudice against the half elfin.

My hangover had improved, but not much. I had no patience. "Can we get to the point, Mr. Tate? You want me to do a job, or what?"

"I want you to find someone." He rose from his bench and shed his leather apron. "Come with me."

I went. He took me into the Tate secret world, the compound behind the manufactory. Denny never did that.

"You've been doing all right for yourself," I said. We entered a formal garden, the existence of which I'd never suspected.

"We manage."

I should manage so good. "Where are we headed?"

"Denny's apartment."

Buildings stood shoulder to shoulder around the garden. From the street they looked like one continuous featureless warehouse. From the garden I could not imagine how I'd ever thought that. These houses were as fine as anything up the hill. They simply didn't face the street and make temptingly dangerous statements.

I wondered if they killed the workmen when the job was done. "The whole Tate tribe lives here?"

"Yes."

"Not much privacy."

"Too much, I think. We all have our own apartments. Some have street-side doors. Denny's does." Tate's tone said "This is a Significant Fact."

My curiosity was definitely growing. Tate's whole attitude indicated indignation at Denny's having had secrets from his old man.

He took me to Denny's place. The air inside was stuffy and warm, the way closed places get in summer. Nothing had changed since the one time Denny had invited me in—through the street-side door—except that Denny wasn't there. That made a lot of difference.

The place was as plain and neat as a new cheap coffin. Denny had been a man of ascetic habits. He'd never hinted at the comforts enjoyed by his family.

"It's in the basement."

"What is?"

"What I want you to see before I start explaining." He collected a lantern and lit it with a long match, which he kept burning.

Moments later we were in a basement as spotless as the ground floor. Old Man Tate and his match went around lighting lamps. I made like a cat too lazy to lick his own paws and just hung around with my mouth open.

Tate wore a small, smug smile when he faced me again. "Well?"

The cat that had my tongue could have fought a couple weights heavier than a snow leopard.

The only place you even hear about that much precious metal lying around is in stories about dragon hoards.

Actually, when my mind started working, I saw it wasn't so much after all. Just more than I'd ever imagined I would see in one place. A few hundred robbers working double shifts for four or five years might pile up as much.

"Where . . . ? How . . . ?"

"I don't know most of the answers myself, Mr. Garrett. My knowledge is limited to the notes Denny left. They were all written to himself. He knew what he was talking about. There is enough to fill in the outlines, though. I expect you'll want to read everything before you start."

I nodded but did not hear him. My friend Denny, the shoemaker. With a basement full of silver. Denny, whose only mention of money had been about the share he had taken when his regiment had overwhelmed a Venageti treasure caravan fleeing the defeat at Jordan Wells.

"How much?" I croaked. I was not getting any better. The little guy that sits in the back row inside my head started catcalling me. I never thought wealth could have so much impact upon me.

"Sixty thousand marks in Karentine coined silver. The equivalent of eighteen thousand marks in coined silver of other states. Eight hundred four-ounce bars. Six hundred twenty-three eight-ounce bars. Forty-four one-pound bars. One hundred ten pounds in larger bars. Just under one thousand coined goldmarks. There's some billet tin and copper, too. A nice amount, but it doesn't count for much compared with the silver."

"Not unless a couple copper sceats would make the difference between eating and starvation. How did he do it? Don't tell me making ballroom slippers for fat duchesses. Nobody gets rich . . . working." I almost said "honestly."

"Trading in metals." Tate gave me a don't-be-stupid look. "Playing the changes in the shifting exchange rate between gold and silver. Buying silver when it was cheap against gold, selling it when gold was cheap against silver. He started with his prize money from the army. He switched back and forth at the best points in the cycle. That's what I meant when I said keep the elvish blood in mind. We people of elvish ancestry have a feel for silver."

"You're stereotyping yourself, Pop."

"You understand what I've said? How he came by it? I don't want you to think it's dishonest wealth."

"I understand." That did not make me think it was necessarily honest.

Anyone with a knack for reading the shifts could get rich the same way. Silver goes up and down violently according to the army's fortunes in the Cantard. As long as we are plagued by sorcerers, there will be an incredible demand for the metal.

Ninety percent of the world's silver is mined in the Cantard. Under all the excuses and historical claims, the mines are what the war is all about. Maybe if we could rid the world of magicians and their hunger for the mystic metal, peace and prosperity would break out all over.

"Well?" Tate asked.

"Well what?"

"Will you do the job for us?"

Good question, I thought.

looked at Tate and saw a momentary idiot, a fool trying to twist me into doing something he feared I'd turn my back on if I knew the whole story.

"Pop, would you make shoes if you didn't know the size? If you hadn't even seen the person who was going to wear them? Without knowing anything about getting paid? I've been real patient on account of you being Denny's old man. But I'm not going to play games."

He hemmed and hawed.

"Come on, Pop. Open the poke. Shake it out. Let's see if the little porker oinks or meows."

His expression became pained, almost pleading. "I'm just trying to do right by my son. Trying to carry out his last wishes."

"We'll put up a statue. When does the clam open up? Or do I go home and finish sleeping off this hangover?" Why do they always do this? They bring you in to handle a problem, then lie about it or hide it from you. But they never stop screaming for results.

"You've got to understand—"

"Mr. Tate, I don't have to understand anything except exactly what is going on. Why don't you start from the beginning, tell me what you know, what you want, and why you need me. And don't leave anything out. If I take the job and find out you have, I'll get extremely angry. I'm not a very nice man when I get angry."

"Have you had your breakfast, Mr. Garrett? Of course not. Rose wakened you and brought you straight here. Why don't we do that while I order my thoughts?"

"Because there's nothing guaranteed to make me madder quicker than a stall."

He went red in the face. He was not used to backtalk.

"You talk or I walk. This is my life you're wasting."

"Damn it, a man can't . . ."

I started toward the stairs.

"All right. Stop."

I paused, waited.

"After Denny died, I came here and found all this," Tate said. "And I found a will. A *registered* will."

Most people don't bother to register, but that didn't amount to anything remarkable. "So?"

"So in the will he names you and me his executors."

"That damned sawed-off little runt! I'd break his neck for him if he hadn't already done it himself. That's it? All the shuffle-footing and coy looks is because he rung in an outsider?"

"Hardly. It's the terms of the will that are embarrassing."

"Yeah? He tell everybody what he thought of them?"

"In a way. He left everything but our executor's fees to someone none of us ever heard of."

I laughed. That was Denny. "So? He made the money. It's his to give away."

"I don't deny that. And I don't mind, believe it or not. But for Rose's sake . . ."

"You know what he thought about her? Want me to tell you?"

"She is his sister."

"Not that he had any choice about it. The nicest thing he ever said about her was, 'She's a useless, lazy, whining, conniving freeloader.' The word *bitch* came up a few times, too."

"But—"

"Never mind. I don't want to hear it. So what you want is for me to find this mysterious heir, eh? And then what?" They want you to do some crazy things sometimes. I could guess why Denny registered his will. A Rose with thorns.

"Just tell her the bequest is here for the claiming. Get a statement of intent we can file with the registry probate. Already they're harassing us about showing them that we're doing something to execute the terms of the will."

That figured. I knew those jackasses. Before the brewery gave me the consulting job, I did investigations for them, freelance, to make ends meet. "You said 'her.' This heir is a woman?" Denny never mentioned knowing any women all the time I knew him. I had him figured for a complete asexual.

"Yes. An old girlfriend, from when he was in the army. He never fell out of love, it seems, and they never stopped writing letters, even though she married somebody else. You'll find your best leads in those letters. You were in the Cantard, too, so you'll know the places she talks about."

"The Cantard?"

"That's where she is, yes. Where are you going?"

"I've been to the Cantard once. I didn't get a choice that time. This time I do. Find yourself another patsy, Mr. Tate."

"Mr. Garrett, you're one of the executors. And I'm too old to make that trip."

"Won't hold a shot of legal water, Pop. An executor don't have to do squat if he didn't say he would and sign to do it up front. Good-bye."

"Mr. Garrett, the law allows the executors to draw up to ten percent of the value of an estate to recompense themselves and to cover their expenses. Denny's estate will go on the upside of a hundred thousand marks."

That was a stopper. Something to make me think. For about two winks. "Five thousand ain't to die for, Pop. And I don't have anybody to leave it to."

"Ten thousand, Mr. Garrett. I'll leave you my side. I don't want it."

I admit I hesitated first. "No."

"I'll pay your expenses out of my own purse. That makes it ten thousand clear."

I stayed clammed. Was the old coot in training for a devil's job?

"What will it take, Mr. Garrett?"

"How come you're so hot to find this frail?"

"I want to meet her, Mr. Garrett. I want to see the sort of woman capable of making a monkey of my son. Name your price."

"Even rich don't do you any good if the wild dogs of the Cantard are cracking your bones to get at the marrow."

"Name your price, Mr. Garrett. I am an old man who has lost the son he expected to follow him. I am a wealthy man with no more need to cling to wealth. I am a determined man. I will see this woman. So again I say, name your price."

I should have known better. Hell, I *did* know better. I'd been saying so for ten minutes. "Give me a thousand on account. I'll look over the stuff

Denny left and do some poking around at this end, just to see if it's feasible. I'll let you know what I decide."

I went back up the stairs and pulled up a chair behind the desk where Denny's letters and notes were piled.

"I have to get back to work," Tate called. "I'll have Rose bring you some breakfast."

As I listened to Tate's tiny footsteps fade away, I couldn't help but weigh the possibility of dear Rose slipping something poisonous into my food. I sighed and turned to my work, hoping this next meal wouldn't be my last.

The first thing I did was look for the stuff Denny's family had missed. Misers always have something they think they have to hide. A basement like that, plain as it looked, had a thousand crannies where things could be squirreled away.

Just as I spotted it a little dirt fell from the underflooring overhead. I cocked an ear. Not a sound. Somebody was doing a passable job of cat-footing around up there.

I had my feet on Denny's desk and was expanding my literary horizons when Rose and my griddle cakes sneaked onstage. I checked her over the top of the first page of a letter that somehow had a quality of déjà vu. But I didn't pay much attention. The smell of griddle cakes with wild honey, tea, hen's eggs, hot buttered bread, and steamed boodleberry preserves was a bit distracting to a man in my condition.

Rose was distracting, too. She was smiling.

Snakes smile that way before they strike.

When her sort smile you had better check over your shoulder for a guy with a knife.

She placed the tray before me, still smiling. "Here's a little of everything we had in the kitchen. I hope you'll find something to suit."

When they're nice to you, you had better get your back against a wall. "Your feet hurt?"

"No." She gave me a puzzled look. "What makes you ask that?"

"The look on your face. It has to be pain."

Not a flicker of response, except, "So the old man talked you into it, did he?"

I raised an eyebrow. "Into what?"

"Finding that woman of Denny's." Plenty of vitriol pent up behind that smile.

"Nope. I told him I'd go over Denny's papers and look around town a little. I would tell him what I thought. That's all."

"You're going to do it. How much did he offer you to find her?"

I put my best blank card-playing face and stared into the starved ice marbles of her eyes. I don't believe that stuff about windows of the soul. I've seen too many lying eyes. But beyond hers lay nothing but shatter-sharp flint and frosty iron.

"I'll give you twenty percent if you don't find her. Twenty-five if you find her dead."

Blank-faced, I started on my breakfast. There was ham and sausage, too. The tea was so good I drained half the pot before I touched anything else.

"I could be very generous," she said, turning sideways, posing to show what she had.

She had the equipment. All of it, and plenty of it. A prime little package, but a package filled with rot. "Denny said that you like small women."

Some better than others, I thought. "I make a point of trying not to be cruel to people, Rose. The best I can do here is speak plain and say I'm not interested."

She took rejection well. She ignored it. "I'm going with you, you know."

"With me? Where?"

"To the Cantard."

"I've got a flash for you, lady. I'm not doing any dirty work for you, and you aren't crossing the street with me. I do thank you for bringing breakfast. I need it, and appreciate it. Now go away and let me see if there's any reason I should be fool enough to get into this at all."

"I'm a stubborn woman, Garrett. I usually get what I want. If you won't help me, you'd better walk away from the whole thing. People who get in my way get hurt."

"Unless you're out of here by the time I finish this cup of tea you're going over my knee and getting what your old man should have given you while you were still young enough to have some sense pounded into you."

She retreated to the stairway. "I'll claim you raped me."

I grinned. Last refuge of the female scoundrel. "I'm not rich like you, but I can afford a truthsayer. Go ahead. Let's see how your dad takes losing two kids in one week."

She started upstairs. End of that game.

I went back and dug the dark package from the shadow between two floor joists anchored on the outside foundation. It was not hidden. Every space along that wall was stuffed. But the wrapping of this bundle was a cavalry saddle blanket. Denny's service meant a lot to him. He kept every memento. What he would wrap in his saddle blanket would be important, too.

I dropped my seabag into the harbor as I strutted down the gangway the day I mustered out. Tells you how thrilled I was with the life of a Royal Marine.

The bundle contained a stack of military maps of the Cantard, most ours, a few Venageti. Both kinds are dangerous to have. You could get arrested for spying. The people who ask questions for the court don't stop till you confess.

With the maps were overlays of skin scraped transparently thin and several slim, expensive, bound journals.

I took the lot to Denny's desk.

Each of the overlays examined a critical battle of the past six years. The names of captains, commanders, and outfits were noted. One journal examined each battle commander by commander and unit by unit.

What the hell? Denny wasn't any war buff.

Reading gave me a glimmer, though. For instance, the table of royal officers:

1: Count Agar: Impulsive. Overly aggressive. Prone to act on inadequate intelligence.

9: Margrave Leon: Timid. Wants sure thing before offering battle. Easily rattled during engagement.

14: Viscount Noah: Vacillator. Excessively ferocious when engaged. A spendthrift of men and matériel.

22: Glory Mooncalled: Best all-around commander under Karentine colors. Excellent tactician. Able to train slowest and most uninspired men. Handicapped by low birth, mercenary status, and role in Seigod Mutiny while serving Venageti side. Weakness is a consuming hatred of Venageti warlords.

There was a Venageti list, too, and an analysis of potential matches and mismatches. If you were in the business of shuffling gold and silver, it would be handy to know who would control the silver mines a few months down the road. Denny had been serious about trying to outguess fortune.

I smelled an old dead carp, though. Denny drew forty-eight marks prize money and mustering-out pay. You don't turn forty-eight marks into a hundred thousand without cutting corners.

Denny's business log contained some hints.

Note from V: An agent of Stormlord Atto inquired the cost of 50 pd silver. First tremor of preparation for new offensive?

Z reported verbally: *Harrow* made port with 200 pd silver in ballast. Must sell before Mooncalled takes Freemantle.

Harrow southbound with 1000 pd granulated inside hollowed ballast billets. Biggest deal yet. Pray for fair weather.

Letter from K. Warlord Ironlock, 20,000 men, 3 firelords of the Eastern Circle, Third Rite, ordered to Lare. Attack through the Bled? Viscount Blush defending. Buy coined silver.

V, Z, and several others could be the cavalry cronies Denny hung out with. There were hints it was a tight group operation. But K was no old army buddy.

I turned to the heir and lover's letters last, about the time a cousin dropped in to ask what I wanted for lunch.

"Whatever the rest of you are having. With a quart of beer. And tell Old Man Tate I need him."

That was when I started the letters. That's when the guy in the cheap seats decided I was going back to the Cantard. The rest of me fought the valiant fight for a long time.

"You look like you saw a ghost," Tate said.

I looked up from the letter I'd been staring at for five minutes. "What? Oh. Yeah. Almost. Mr. Tate, you told me it was honest money."

He did not say anything. He had suspected it was something shady.

"You had any unusual visitors? Sudden old friends of Denny's asking questions?"

"No."

"You will. Soon. There's too much here for them to let it go. Be careful."

"What do you mean?"

It seemed an honest question. So maybe he did not know the world well enough to read what Denny had written. I laid it out for him.

He did not believe me.

"Doesn't matter what either of us thinks. The point is, so far I'm interested enough to keep on. I'll need that thousand. There are going to be heavy expenses from the start. And a box. I need a big box."

"I'll have Lester bring the money from the office. Why do you want a box?"

"To pack all this stuff."

"No."

"Say what?"

"You're not taking it out of here."

"I'm taking it or I'm taking me away. You want me to do a job, you let me do it. My way."

"Mr. Garrett . . ."

"Pop, you're paying for results, not the right to mess with me. Get me a box, then go pound nails in a shoe. I don't have time for whining and games."

He hadn't recovered from what I had said about Denny. He did not have any fight left. He took off.

The funny thing was he left me feeling guilty, like I had been giving him a hard time just to puff up my own ego. I didn't need that guilt. So I ended up giving in and just letting everything go the way Tate wanted.

Strange how you can manipulate yourself when somebody outside can't.

I leaned back and watched dust fall from the underflooring as a pair of sneaky feet stole after Tate.

I was still that way when the cousin brought lunch and beer. I was busy inhaling that when Uncle Lester appeared with a fat moneybag and a big wicker chest. I finished my beer in one long draft, belched against the back of my wrist, asked, "What do you think about all this, Uncle Lester?"

He shrugged. "Ain't my place to say."

"How's that?"

"Eh?"

It began to sound like hogs-at-the-trough time—all grunts and snorts. "Did you read any of this stuff?" I asked.

"Yes."

"Care to comment?"

"Looked like Denny was dipping his toes in the shadows. You could tell that better than me."

"He was. And he was an amateur. A damned lucky amateur. You ever have any hints that he was into anything?"

"Nope. Unless you count that woman's letters. Them writing back and forth like that all this time seemed a mite odd to me. Ain't natural."

"Yes?"

"The boy was kin, and he's dead, and you don't want to speak ill of either one. But he was a bit strange, that boy. Always a loner 'fore he went off to the war. I'd bet that woman is the only one he ever had. If he had her. He didn't look at one after he got back."

"Maybe he crossed?"

Lester snorted and gave me his best look of disgust, like I didn't know about the Tates and the elves back when—though the cartha are the inter-species rage these days.

"Just asking. I didn't think so. He seemed to be a guy who just wasn't interested. I've been in brag sessions when he was around. He never had a story to tell."

Lester smirked. "Listened polite like, way you might if'n I started telling stories about when I was a kid."

He had me.

It is not often Garrett gets caught with nothing to say.

He grinned. "On that note I'll be goin'."

I grunted at his stern. Then I leaned back and closed my eyes and surrendered to the haunt that had me so distracted. To the coincidence so long the devils themselves must have pulled it in.

Kayean Kronk.

Maybe Denny *could* spend all those years in love with a memory. I gave it three hard ones before I broke the spell.

There was only one thing to do. Go see the Dead Man.

•••6

He's called the Dead Man because they killed him four hundred years ago. But he is neither dead nor a man. He is a Loghyr, and they don't die just because somebody sticks a bunch of knives into them. Their bodies go through the motions—cooling out, rigor mortis, lividity—but they do not corrupt. Not at any rate mere humans can detect. Loghyr bones have been found in the ruins on Khatar Island; they are very similar to a human's when they are dry.

"Hey, Old Bones. Don't look like the diet is working." The Dead Man is four hundred fifty pounds of mean, a little ragged around the edges, where the moths and mice and ants have gotten to him. He was parked in a chair in a dark room in a house that pretended to be both abandoned and haunted. He smelled. The corruption process is slow, but it goes on. "You need a bath, too."

A psychic chill set me shivering. He was sleeping. He isn't easy to get along with at his best, and he's at his worst when newly awakened.

I am not sleeping. I am meditating.

The thoughts hammered at my brain.

"Guess it's all a matter of perspective."

The psychic chill became physical. My breath clouded and my shoe buckles frosted over. I hurried with a little propitiations that are necessary when dealing with the Dead Man. The freshly cut flowers went into the big crystal bowl on the filthy old table before him. Then I lit candles. His sense of humor insists there be thirteen of them, all black, burning while he is in consultation.

To my knowledge he is the only Loghyr ever to allow his genius to be commercialized.

He does not need the candlelight to see visitors or flowers. But he likes to pretend that he does.

Aha! I see you now. Garrett. You pestilence. Can't you leave me alone? Every other day you're in here, worse than the moths and mice.

"It's been five months, Chuckles. And from the looks of this place you've been meditating the whole time."

A mouse that had been hiding beneath his oversized chair made a break for it. The Dead Man snatched it with his mind and sent it flying out of the house. Moths exploded away from him. He was incapable of doing malicious harm to bugs, who wanted to eat him, but could make life unholy hell for people with the effrontery to ask him to work.

"You have to work sometime," I told him. "Even a dead man has to pay the rent. And you need somebody to give you a bath and clean the place up. Not to mention getting the vermin out again."

A big, shiny black spider crawled out of one piglike nostril on the end of his ten-inch trunk. It did not like my looks. It ducked back inside.

Cheap flowers.

They were not. I had given him absolutely no legitimate cause for complaint. He couldn't banish me because he didn't want to work. I knew the state of his finances. His landlord had come to me about his last month's rent.

Must not be much of a client you have, Garrett. You sneaking around after cheating wives again?

"You know better." I was out of all that, thanks to him.

How much?

"You owe me for a month's rent already."

You have the smug, content look of a man whose expenses have been guaranteed.

"So?"

How much can you soak your client before he squawks?

"I don't know."

Enough, I think, the way you look. Which is like a man who has a good fix on the pot at the end of the rainbow. Start reading.

"What?"

Stop playing the idiot, Garrett. You're too old. You dragged that crate of stuff here so you could bore me. That is the worst of being dead, Garrett. It is damned boring. You cannot do anything.

"Loghyr don't do anything when they're *alive.*"

Read, Garrett. Your welcome is wearing thin.

I won. Sort of. He listened while I gave him every word, showed him every map. A smooth, professional report. I stumbled only twice, once over the name Kayean, once when he set a squeaking mouse whizzing playfully around my head. It took a couple of hours and I got very dry. But I'd prepared for that, having been through it before.

As I downed a long draft of beer, my head rang to, *Very thorough. As far as it goes. What did you leave out?*

"Nothing. You got the whole show."

You are lying, Garrett. And not very convincingly. Though perhaps you are lying more to yourself than to me. You tripped on the woman's name. It has meaning to you.

Well, if you will lie to your best friend, you will lie to yourself. The Dead Man doesn't tell any tales. "It has meaning."

Continue.

"I knew a Kayean Kronk when I was in the Cantard. Her father was one of the Syndics of Port Fell. I was nineteen when I met her. She was seventeen. I fell hard. I thought she did, too. But the campaign in the islands came up and I only got to see her maybe two days a month because we spent most of our time at sea. After about six months of that she started getting cool. Then I came in and there was a very kind letter asking me not to come see her, she was in love, the usual sort of thing. I never saw her again. I heard she was going with a cavalryman, and her father disliked him even more than he had disliked me. That was the last I heard of her till today.

"I had a rocky few years after that. It hit me pretty hard."

End of confession.

A long silence.

Your friend never mentioned that woman's name?

"He never mentioned a woman."

An odd coincidence, and a long one, but not impossible. It would be illuminating to know if he was aware of the identity of the woman's previous lover. How did you meet?

"We met in a tavern where veterans hung out. We had liked one another. Not one detail I could recall implied that he had knowledge of me through a third party. I don't think he was the kind of guy who could stay around somebody who had been his lover's lover. I'd bet his whole fortune that he didn't realize that I was the Marine she'd been seeing."

You may be betting it. You realize that the amount of money involved is going to have a lot of people interested in this business?

"That's why I came to you. I need your advice."

My main advice you would ignore.

"What's that?"

Leave it alone. Stick with the brewery work. This could get you killed. Especially on the Cantard end. Some very dangerous people have to be involved there, if only peripherally.

"How so?"

Who did the woman marry? the Dead Man countered.

"I don't know. Why? Do you think it's important?"

I will hazard to opine that it may become the crux of the affair.

"Why?"

It is evident from the woman's letters that she has access to information very restricted in nature and extremely dangerous to possess. She passed along data not only on the present movements and future plans of your armies, but on those of the Venageti as well. The implication is that she is in a unique position. Among you humans, females are not permitted to assume the responsibilities of such a position as a career. Thus, the further implication that she is mated to a man in such a position.

The Dead Man's mind speech has all the nuance of verbal communication—once you learn to do without gestures and facial expressions. He was crowing. "I could have figured that out soon enough."

About the time someone cut your throat. You count upon your ability to bluff or battle your way through obstacles, rather than thinking your way around them. It is a failing common to your race. All of you seem to believe that exercising your minds is shameful or painful, and prefer instead to snatch up a sword at the first hint of . . .

He was off on his favorite crusade. Soon he would begin the paeans to the infinite superiority of Loghyr reasoning and logic and wisdom. I shut him out.

That can be done if he is distracted by musing upon his own magnificence, if you're subtle and don't draw attention to what you're doing. I hid behind my beer and counted silently. Having heard it all before, I knew how long he needed to get it out of his system.

Garrett!

So I miscalculated by a few seconds. He probably cheated. He knew me pretty well, too. But he was abnormally mellow. He employed none of his usual childish devices. Maybe I had given him enough to crack the boredom of being dead.

"Yes?"

Pay attention. I asked if you are determined to go ahead with this.
"I'm not sure."
Your body calls your mouth a liar. I have this advice for you, inasmuch as you mean to go ahead despite all reason. Do not go this one alone. And do not permit emotion to get in the way of your usually strong instinct for your own best interest. Whatever else this woman may be or may have been, she is not the girl you loved when she was seventeen. No more are you that callow Marine of nineteen. If ever, for a minute, you allow yourself to believe that those days can be restored, you are lost. They are dead. Take it from an expert on being dead. There is no way to get your health back. You live on memories of what was and fancies about what might have been. Both can be deadly to the man who loses sight of the demarcation between them and reality.
"End of speech?"
End of speech. Were you listening?
"I was listening."
Did you hear me?
"I heard."
It is well. You are a pestilence upon my waning centuries, Garrett, but you keep me amused. I do not want to lose you yet. Be careful in the Cantard. You will not have me there to lift you out of the consequences of your folly. It grates, but I fear I would miss you, insolence, disobedience, and all.

Which was about the nicest thing he ever said to me. I had to get out before we started getting maudlin.

I made a beer run before going back to give him his bath and his place a bit of cleanup.

It was past suppertime when I left the Dead Man's place. The shadows were long and indigo. The sky was turning colors you usually see only in elvish portraiture. It had been a long day, and there was a lot of it yet to go.

The first order of business would be to see the Dead Man's landlord and get him a few months ahead on his rent.

I'll buy the place for him if I ever make the big strike, though he could do that for himself if he wanted. It would, however, take several months of concentrated work for him to earn enough money. The very thought sends him into psychic spasms.

Next step would be to look up Morley Dotes, which I'd had in mind even before the Dead Man admonished me against following my usual lone-wolf course. He was right. The Cantard is no place to go alone.

A massive hand hurtled out of an alley mouth, snagged my arm, and yanked.

Sometimes the city isn't so safe, either.

I slammed into a wall and slid away from a fist I sensed more than I saw. I threw a feeble right that was just a distractor while I unloaded a girlish shin kick. The mountain of muscle and gristle before me waltzed back far enough for me to take in its true dimensions. They were awesome.

"Saucerhead Tharpe."

"Hey, Garrett. Man. If I'd knowed it was you, I'd never have taken this job."

"Shucks. I bet you say that to all the boys."

"Aw. Don't be that way, Garrett. We all got to make it the best way we know how."

I caught a glimpse of a familiar short person watching from across the street.

I dragged out a fat purse containing part of the largesse her uncle had bestowed upon me earlier.

"Hey. Come on, Garrett. You know you can't bribe me to lay off. I'm really sorry this's got to be you and me. But I got paid for the job. Where would I be if it got around that I could be bought off? I'd be out of work. I'm very, very, sorry, Garrett. But I got to do what I got paid to do."

I had expected no luck, but it had seemed worth a try.

I said, "I'd be the last guy to ask you to welsh on a deal, Saucerhead."

"Gee. I'm glad. I was scared you wouldn't understand."

"I want you to do a job for me, Saucerhead. There's five marks in it."

"Yeah. I'd feel a whole lot better about this if I could do something for you. What is it?"

"That woman across the street. The one that sicced you onto me. When we're done here I want you to take her down to the Bazaar, strip her down naked, bend her over your lap, and give her thirty good whacks on the backside. Then turn her loose and let her walk home."

"Naked?"

"Naked."

"She wouldn't get out of the Bazaar, Garrett."

"There's another five in it if she gets home all right. But without finding out you're looking out for her."

Saucerhead grinned. "It's a deal, Garrett." He stuck out a palm the size of a snowshoe. I dropped five marks into it.

Saucerhead's hand dipped into a pocket.

I hit him upside the head with the purse. I put everything I had behind it. Then I ran like hell for two steps.

He gave Rose her money's worth, fulfilling his contract to the letter.

I tried to defend myself, of course, and actually did pretty well. Not many hang in there a whole minute against Saucerhead Tharpe. I even gave him one he might have remembered for the next ten minutes.

Always thoughtful, is Saucerhead Tharpe. After he put my lights out he tucked my purse underneath me, just in case somebody came along before I woke up. Then he went along to the next job on his agenda.

hurt everywhere. I had about two acres of bruises. Saucerhead had found places to hit that I didn't know I had. All body and soul wanted was to go lay up for a week. But mind knew it was time to find Morley Dotes. Not even Saucerhead Tharpe would have messed with me if I'd had Morley Dotes along.

Morley is the best at rough and tumble. And, by his own admission, the best at most everything else. Some people would like him and Saucerhead to square off, just to see how it would come out. But neither of them will swat a fly without getting paid first. And Saucerhead isn't dumb enough to take a job on Morley. Nor is Morley vain enough to contract on Saucerhead. Neither cares much about who might come out best. Which says something about their professionalism.

The obvious place to look for Morley was a place called Morley's Joy House.

The name is one of his bad jokes. It is a hangout for the elfin, the cartha, and breeds. The fare is vegetarian and nonalcoholic. The entertainment is so impenetrable and dull that the existence of a dead Loghyr might be exciting by contrast. But Morley's kind of people enjoy it.

The place went silent when I stepped inside. I ignored an arsenal's worth of death-looks as I limped to the alleged bar. Morley's barman gave me the once-over. He grinned, revealing pointy darkelf teeth. "You have a knack for making people mad at you, Garrett."

"You ought to see the other guy."

"I did. He came in for some sprouts. Wasn't a scratch on him."

Conversations picked up behind me. The barman was being as friendly as darkelves ever are. That made me a marginally acceptable lower life-form, presence tolerated. Like that of a beer-drinking dog in a human tavern.

"Word's around already, huh?"

"Everybody who ever cared about you one way or the other already knows the whole story. Slick the way you evened things up."

"Yeah. That's out, too? How'd it go?"

"She made it home. I figure that's one quail that won't ever mess with you again, Garrett." He cackled in that way they have that gives you chills and makes you wonder if you will ever wake up from the nightmare. "Next time she'll get somebody to cut your throat."

The possibility had occurred to me. I'd made a mental note to rummage up some of my more interesting gimmicks and armaments. In the general course of business I find being fast on my feet protection enough, so I load myself down with hardware only in special cases.

This case looked like it was getting pretty special.

The Dead Man had warned me.

"Where's Morley?"

"Up." He pointed. "He's busy."

I headed for the stairs.

The barkeep opened his mouth to yell at me, then thought about it. That might start a riot. In his friendly voice he said, "Hey, Garrett, you owe us five marks."

I turned around and gave him the fisheye.

"Saucerhead said you'd knock it off his tab."

"A grin like that ought to be bronzed and saved for posterity."

It got bigger.

"That big goof isn't as dumb as he looks, is he?" I dug down carefully, my back to the crowd. No point in showing what I was carrying and having the boys who were high on lettuce getting fancy ideas.

"Nope."

I flipped the five coins and headed upstairs before he could get back to trying to stop me.

I hammered on Morley's private door. No response. I pounded again, rattling hinges.

"Go away, Garrett. I'm busy."

I shoved through the door, which was not locked. Somebody's wife squealed and dove into another room, a fistful of clothing trailing. Otherwise, I caught nothing but a flash of fancy tail. It was not one I recognized.

Morley did his best to look elf-haughty in nothing but his socks and a snarl. He could not bring it off, despite being half darkelf.

"Your timing is lousy as usual, Garrett. Not to mention your manners."

"How did you know it was me?"

"Magic."

"Magic, my ruddy red. You have trouble making food disappear. If you call that silage you eat food."

"Ah-ah. Watch your mouth. You owe me one apology already."

"I don't apologize. My mother makes excuses for me. How did you know it was me?"

"Voice tube from the bar. You look awful, boy. Saucerhead must have sold that gal his top of the line. What did you do to her?"

"Wouldn't lie, cheat, and steal for her. And turned her down when she tried to bribe me with the big bribe."

He laughed. "You never learn. Next time diddle the gal and walk. She'll sit around wondering what went wrong instead of sending cutthroats after you." His grin vanished. "What do you want, Garrett?"

"I've got a job offer for you."

"Not something foolish involving Saucerhead Tharpe, I hope."

"No. I've got a job I need some backup on. I can thank Saucerhead for reminding me that if I don't get it soon my health might suffer."

"What's in it?"

"For me, ten percent of a hundred thousand marks, plus expenses. You're expenses."

He whistled soundlessly, his pucker bringing his dark hatchet features to even more of a point. "What do we have to do? Take out one of the Venageti warlords?"

"You're closer than you think. I have to go into the Cantard and find a woman who just inherited on the upside of a hundred thou. I have to talk her into either coming here to claim it or waiving her claim in favor of whoever is next in line."

"That doesn't sound so tough. Except for the part about the Cantard."

"There are some people around who might feel that the money was not the deceased's to bequeath. There are some in the deceased's family who feel a strong reluctance to let so large a fortune go to a stranger. There is the possibility of similar difficulties on the legatee's end. It's possible her relationship with the legatee was, shall we say, imprudent."

"I love it when you talk dirty, Garrett. And I love what money does to you humans. It's the only thing that saves you from being totally tedious."

I did not have anything to say to that. People do get silly about money.

"I take it your principal has his own ax to grind in this, or he'd be with the keep-it-in-the-family faction."

"Could be."

"Is he as nebulous as you are?"

"Could be. You interested?"

"Could be."

I winced.

He grinned. "Suppose I just follow you around for a while? You're a chatty sort of fellow. I'll let you know when you've said enough to let me make up my mind."

"Oh, happy day! The pleasure of his company without having to pay for it. All right."

"Who said anything about not paying for it?"

"I did. No play, no pay."

"You got an attitude problem, Garrett. All right. What are you going to do now?"

"Go wrap myself around a couple of pounds of steak."

He turned up his nose. "All that red meat is why you people have such a peculiar odor. Where should I meet you?"

I raised an eyebrow.

"Matter of some unfinished business," he said evenly.

I glanced at the door to the other room. "I see. I'll be back."

9

Morley had pecked around the edges till I'd about lost the restored good humor brought on by beer and a full belly. "You have a basic character flaw, Garrett. I think it's a self-image problem. Ninety-nine people out of a hundred will say any damned fool thing that pops into their heads and not worry about how other folks will see it. With you every damned word is a contract with the gods."

I scowled up the street. There were lights inside my place.

"You can talk without feeling you've committed something, Garrett. Hell, you should do like me. Believe every word you say like it was God's mouth when you say it, then forget it in the morning. The appearance of sincerity counts for more than actual truthfulness. People only need to believe for a few minutes at a time. They know the name of the game. You take that lady I was with tonight. Am I in love with her? Is she in love with me? Not bloody likely. She wouldn't be seen in public with me. But I still had to say all the words."

I don't know how he got onto that. He rambles. I ignored it, mostly. "You on the payroll or not?"

He looked at my place. "Company?"

"Looks like."

"Could it be friendly?"

"My friends have better manners."

"I thought you'd admit you don't have any friends. Are you going in?"

"Yes. You behind me or not?"

"Temporarily, anyway. My cash position isn't what it should be. I've suffered several financial setbacks lately."

"D'Guni races again."

"You want to get rich quick, Garrett? Come down to the pond and see how I lay my bets. Then bet the other way. No matter what bug I pick, it zips out to the middle, then skitters in circles while the plodders head straight for the other bank. Either that or it gets eaten."

"The race is not always to the swift." Only elves would bet on the near-random results of water-spider races. "Ready?"

"Go ahead."

The door was unlocked. How thoughtful. There were four of them. Two sat on my bed. The other two occupied my only two chairs. I recognized three as cavalry veterans from Denny's crowd. The one called Vasco might be the V of Denny's notes. They were trying to look tough.

I guess they *were* tough, inside their heads. They had survived the Cantard. But they did not have the tough look that comes from growing up on the streets.

"Come on in, guys," I said. "Make yourselves at home. Fix yourselves a drink. My place is your place."

Vasco said, "See if he's armed, Quinn."

"He's armed," Morley said behind me. "Take my word for it."

One of my guests chuckled. "Look, Vee. A darko breed in man's clothing."

"Amateurs," Morley said.

"Amateurs," I agreed. "But the pros all start out as amateurs."

"Some have to learn their business the hard way."

What he meant was, anybody on the shady side of the law who knew what they were doing should know who he was.

Vasco made a gesture that restrained the character with the intemperate mouth. He said, "I figure you have some idea why we're here, Garrett. But there're a couple points I want to make sure you understand."

"Amateurs," I said again. "Pros know when to take their losses."

"That money didn't belong to Denny, Garrett. Not more than a third of it, anyway."

"Pros don't put all their eggs in one basket. And they don't put the basket where they can't get at it. If I was you boys I'd find a new line of business. Without Denny's contacts your old one is going to turn into a crapshoot."

Vasco winced. I knew too much. "We've got that angle covered, Garrett.

All we need to do is get hold of Denny's papers and study up on his style. There weren't any secret codes or anything. The other end doesn't have to know that he's gone."

Might be workable at that. Maybe they were not so dumb after all.

Those records and notes and letters might be a silver mine.

"What did you do with them, Garrett?"

"So we get to the crux, eh?"

"Yes. I'll lay it out. We can take the loss on the silver if we get the papers and you stay away from the Cantard end. We ain't going to like it, but we can take it. My recommendation to you is, pocket your retainer and walk. Next best thing, if you think you have to make a show, is leave town for a while, then come back and say you couldn't find her. Or fake up a waiver and forge her chop."

"Sounds good," I said. "A practical solution to all our problems."

They looked relieved.

"Trouble is, when I got out of the Marines I decided I wasn't going to let anybody else run my life ever again. You guys were in the army. You know how it is."

It stunned them momentarily. Then Vasco said, "You look like you've had a bad day already, Garrett. I wouldn't want to give a man bruises on his bruises. Maybe you could reassess your position."

"You had your say. I made my position clear. You'd better be leaving. I'm not usually this tolerant of uninvited guests."

Vasco sighed. My old drill sergeant used to sigh that way when a recruit was particularly stubborn about learning. "Quinn, watch the breed."

I set myself. I'd picked my first move already.

"Stand aside, Garrett." That same sound of exasperation filled Morley's voice. "It's time for a little of that old elfin magic."

"Vee?"

"Take him, Quinn."

When Morley goes into action he seems to grow about six extra limbs. He uses them all so fast you hardly see them move. And when he isn't kicking or punching he's biting, head-butting, hip-jugging, or knee-dropping.

He opened by leaping up and giving Quinn the heels of both feet, *bap! bap!* right between the eyes. He flew to another victim without touching down. Quinn folded his cards and went to dreamland.

Vasco came after me.

I learned that you do not duke it out with a guy almost as good as you are when your whole body is stiff and sore from the last whipping you took.

He got me into a clinch that turned into a giant bear hug on the floor. He kept trying to bang his forehead off my temple. I got my teeth into his ear and chomped. That discouraged him. He threw himself away from me. From flat on my back I flicked out a heel and clipped him at the base of the skull. He went wobbly.

I jumped up, seized the moment by the scruff of the neck and seat of the pants, and ran him out the door to the accompaniment of appropriate old-time remarks about seedy little army types who failed to acknowledge the natural superiority of their overlords, the Marines.

A great glassy crash sent me hurtling back inside to help Morley.

He had polished off his share. He was eyeballing Quinn. "Grab the other end and help me throw him out."

"You broke my window."

"I'm charging you double rate for this one, Garrett. You provoked them."

"I'm not paying you squat. You threw somebody out my window."

"You never heard a word I said about truth and sincerity. You had a perfect chance to close it all down when Vee suggested you take the retainer and run. But no! Bad Garrett has got Morley Dotes behind him. He can run his mouth like a fool and provoke them all to hell."

"I would have said the same thing if you weren't here."

He cocked his head and looked at me like a bird looking at a new kind of bug. "Death wish. Suicidal tendencies. Know what causes that, Garrett? Diet. That's right. Your meat-heavy human diet. You need more roughage. You don't get enough roughage, your bowels tighten up. When your bowels tighten up you get these dangerous, self-destructive mood swings . . ."

"Somebody is going to get his bowels loosened up. You had to go and throw somebody through my window, didn't you?"

"Will you quit with the damned window?"

"You know how much that window cost? You got any idea?"

"Not a candle to what this job is going to cost you if you don't stop complaining. All right! Next time I'll ask them pretty please to go out the door like nice little boys. Come on. Let's run it off."

"Run? Run where? Why?"

"To work off this nervous energy. To get rid of the combat juices flowing inside us. Five miles ought to do it."

"I'll tell you how far I'm running. I'm running all the way over there to my bed. Then I'm not moving except to breathe."

"You're kidding. The shape you're in? If you don't stretch those muscles, then cool them outright, you're going to wake up so stiff you won't be able to move."

"Tell you what. You run my five miles for me. I'll consider forgiving you for the window." I crashed onto the bed. "I could use about a gallon of ice-cold beer."

Morley didn't answer me. He was gone.

10

*B*am! Bam! Bam!

Morning is wonderful. Its only drawback is that it comes at such an inconvenient time of day. A time when the early birds of the world are aflame with their mission of bringing the joys of dawn-watching to the nations. And to me in particular.

Bam! Bam! Bam!

Two mornings running. I wondered if I had offered unwitting insult to the Seven Grand Devils of Modrel.

I went through all the usual cursing and threatening. None of it helped.

Morley would crow when he saw me. I was as stiff as he wanted. It took me three minutes to put my feet over the side and sit up.

The first thing I saw was a mottled green face half a yard wide staring through the broken window. I said something intelligent like, "Gleep!"

The face grinned.

It was a groll, a hybrid of human, troll, and the Beast That Talks that is never named in polite company. I grinned back. Grolls are slow of wit and often quick of temper.

Its giant toad mouth opened and spilled some of that hair-raising bass which is their excuse for speech. I did not catch what it said. It was not meant for me, anyway.

The banging on the door stopped.

"Hello yourself," I croaked, and dragged myself up onto my feet. I figured I'd better open up before his patience went and he let himself in through the wall.

There was another one outside the door. It looked exactly like the other one—big, wide, and ugly. I guessed it would stand twenty feet high in its socks—if it ever wore socks. It didn't wear much else, except a loincloth, a utility belt, and an empty pack harness.

The loincloth did not do much to preserve modesty.

So from here on I have to call them both He with a capital H. Mules would go gibbous with envy.

Both grolls noted my amazement and grinned. That's the sense of humor such creatures have.

"I'd invite you in if you'd fit," I said. One is polite to grolls at all times, irrespective of one's prejudices. Otherwise one finds oneself reassessing one's attitude while being squished between warty green toes.

A short one stepped around the big one. "I expect I'll fit," he said. "And I could use a drink, actually."

"Who the hell are you?"

"Dojango is the name, actually. These are my brothers, Marsha and Doris."

"Brothers?"

"We're triplets, actually." He responded to my unspoken question, "But with different mothers, actually."

Triplets with different mothers. Right. I didn't ask. Making sense out of the things human folks tell me is brain strain enough.

"What the hell are you doing here?"

"Morley Dotes sent us, actually."

"What the hell for? Actually?" One of the big grolls growled at me. I used my fingers to sculpt a friendly smile.

"To help in the Cantard."

The villain himself, Morley Dotes, had sneaked onstage. "So you decided you want the job, eh?"

"At the moment there are certain advantages, where my creditors are concerned, to my being both employed and being out of town," Morley replied.

"And you thought you'd gather all your friends under the umbrella of that advantage? Like maybe my principal wouldn't think of putting a bottom in my expense pot?"

"If you would use half that vaunted detective brain of yours, you would bless my vision."

"It's too early in the morning for me to remember my name. Enlighten me, O Illustrious One."

"Consider mules."

"Mules? What the hell do mules have to do with it?"

"We're going into the Cantard. No one will risk loaning or renting us mounts or pack animals. We'll have to buy. On the other hand, wages for Doris and Marsha will run about what it would cost for a brace of good mules. And they can carry twice the load twice as long. And they're a hell of a lot more use in a fight."

That made sense. Good sense. But . . . "What about friend Dojango?"

Morley sighed. "Yes. Dojango Roze. Well, Garrett, they won't break up the set."

I do believe I scowled. "You sticking me with deadwood?"

"Dojango can lift a blade. He can sniff out water and find firewood. He can understand Doris and Marsha. If you keep an eye on him, he can cook an edible meal without burning anything too badly."

"I'm trying not to slobber in anticipation." I scanned the triplets who had different mothers. They grinned groll good-fellowship. They figured Morley had sold me.

Dotes said, "Keep Dojango away from the juice and he'll do all right."

Everyone knows breeds cannot handle their booze. Dojango's grin became apologetic.

"How much is this road show going to burn me?"

Morley tossed out an outrageous figure. I slammed the door and went back to bed. He had one of the big triplets lift him so he could yell numbers through the broken window. I faked a mean snore till some interesting integers began rattling around behind me. In fact, Morley was so pliable I began wondering how bad his creditor situation was. I did not need more complications than I already had.

"It's your diet that makes you so stubborn, you know that, don't you, Garrett? All that red meat filled with the juices stirred by the terror of the murdered beast, and you never exercising so you sweat them out of your own body."

"I figured it was something like that, Morley. That, too much beer, and not enough green, leafy veggies."

"Cattails, Garrett. The white hearts down near the roots of the young plant, diced into a tossed salad. Not only tasty, but informed with an almost mystical capacity for lightening the burden of guilt lying upon the carnivore's soul."

"Horsepucky." When I was in the Marines we raided an island where the Venageti promptly cut us off from our ships and drove us into a swamp. Cattails were a mainstay of our diet till the fortunes of war shifted. I don't recall them doing anything remarkable for the temperaments of our sergeants and corporals, who seemed carnivorous enough to eat their own young. Rather the opposite, in a geometric progression.

I know we all took it out on the Venageti when the time came.

Maybe I did not start eating cattails young enough. "Morley, I did a job for a professor at the university one time. He was always spouting who-cares facts. Like one time when he said there are two hundred forty-eight different kinds of fruits, vegetables, greens, and tubers that people eat. Hogs will only eat two hundred forty-six of those. They won't touch green peppers and they won't touch cattail hearts. Which goes to show you that hogs have more sense than people."

"No point trying to salvage you, is there? You're determined to suicide the slow way. Are the boys hired?"

"They're hired." I hoped I would not be sorry.

"How soon can we leave?"

"You in a hurry, Morley? You need to get out of town fast? That why you're being so agreeable about going into the Cantard?"

Dotes shrugged.

A shrug was answer enough.

Considering Morley's talents and reputation, it would take somebody heavy to have enough clout to scare him. In my mind, somebodies that heavy narrowed down to a crowd of one. The big guy himself. The kingpin. "Since when is Kolchak into bug racing, Morley?"

He popped down out of the window. His voice lingered behind him. "You're too damned smart for your own good, Garrett. It's going to catch up with you someday. I'll be in touch. Come on, you lummoxes. Dojango! Put that back. Doris!" He sounded like a muleteer trying to get a wagon started.

I went back to bed thinking I'd better use some of Tate's money to get a new window put in. Maybe a flashy piece with my name leaded in colors.

11

This old universe hasn't got one notion of the meaning of the word *mercy* where I'm concerned. I just got to snoozing when the door began shivering like a drumhead again.

"Going to have to do something about this," I muttered as I hit the floor. "Like maybe move and not tell anybody."

I opened up and found Uncle Lester and the boys outside. "You guys decide to forget the whole thing, I hope?" I noticed that two of the kids had gotten into something rough. They showed plenty of bruises and bandages and one had an arm in a sling. "What happened?"

"Unfriendly visitors. Willard wants to talk to you about it."

"All right. I'm on my way." I took just long enough to make myself presentable, gulp some water, and pick up the lead-weighted head thumper.

Willard Tate was in a state. He waited, wringing his hands. All my life I have heard that expression. Except for a maiden aunt whose every breath was an act of high drama, I'd never seen it before.

"What happened?" Uncle Lester was a clam. Maybe he was afraid if I knew too much I'd turn around.

Tate pumped my hand with both of his. "Thank you for coming. Thank you. I didn't know what else to do."

"What happened?" I asked again as he clung to my hand with one of his and dragged me like a stubborn child. Uncle Lester and the boys tagged along. I spotted a pale-faced Rose watching as we crossed the garden, headed for Denny's apartment.

Tate did not tell me. He showed me.

The place was a wreck. The apprentices were still cleaning up. Several of them wore bandages and bruises. Some wise soul had barred entry from the street by nailing boards across the doorframe.

Tate pointed.

The body lay in the middle of the room, belly down, one hand stretched toward the door.

"What happened?" I asked again.

Third time was a charm.

"It happened around midnight. I had the boys in watching, just in case, because you made me nervous the way you talked. Five men broke through the street door. The boys were smart. Odie came and woke everybody up. The others hid and let the burglars go downstairs. So we ambushed them when they tried to leave.

"We just wanted to capture them. But they panicked and started a fight, and they weren't shy about trying to hurt us. And now we're stuck with *that*."

I knelt to look at the dead man's face. He had started to puff up already. But I could still see the cuts and scrapes he had picked up flying through the window at my place.

"Did they get away with anything?"

"I did a count," Uncle Lester said. "The gold and silver is all there."

"They weren't after gold or silver."

"Huh?" All the Tates are brilliant. But they hide their light under a bushel. Maybe it's a business reflex.

"They were looking for Denny's papers. His letters to the woman. I took care of hiding most everything, but there could have been something I over-looked. Those papers might be worth more than any amount of metal they could haul out of here."

Old Man Tate looked dumbfounded, so I told him about my little chat with Denny's partners. He did not want to believe me. "But that's—"

"Trading with the enemy when you take the costume off it and look it straight in the face."

"I know my son, Mr. Garrett. Denny wouldn't betray Karenta."

"Did you hear me say anything about treason?" I thought it, though. Mainly in the context of what happened to folks foolish enough to get caught trading with the Venageti. I have no moral reservations about that. The war is a struggle between two gangs of nobles and wizards trying to grab control of mines likely to give their possessors near mastery of the world. Their motives are no higher than those displayed in squabbles between street gangs right here in TunFaire.

Being Karentine, I would prefer the gang running my country to win. I love being with a winner. Everybody does. But it doesn't hurt my feelings if somebody besides the lords makes a little profit from the squabble. I explained that to Tate.

"The problem is, the connection is still alive," I said. "And some pretty tough boys want to keep it that way. Meaning they don't want you and me meddling. Do you follow me?"

"And they want Denny's papers and letters and whatnots so they can keep contact with the woman?"

"You catch on fast, Pop. They'll let their claim to the metals go for the papers. And Denny will live on forever in letters he never wrote."

He thought about it. There was a part of him that wanted to grab the big score while it was there for the grabbing. But there was a part of him that was crazy stubborn, too. Maybe if he had been a little poorer . . . But somewhere along the way he had made up his mind and set it in concrete. Changed circumstances would not budge him. "I *will* meet this woman, Mr. Garrett."

"It's your neck," I said. And tried to time a meaningful pause. "And your family's. That could be one of the boys on the floor, attracting flies."

I got to him that time. He puffed up. His face got red. His eyes bugged out, which is a sight in the half elfin. His mouth opened. He began to shake.

But he did not let it get hold of him. Somehow, he turned it off. After half a minute, he said, "You're right, Mr. Garrett. And it's a risk due more consideration than I have given it. If, as you say, those men were army friends of Denny's who survived the Cantard, it's damned lucky several of the boys weren't killed instead of that poor fellow."

"Like you said, they panicked. They just wanted to get away. But next time they'll be looking for trouble."

"You're sure there'll be a next time? Coming so close to getting caught already?"

"You don't seem to understand the stakes, Mr. Tate. In eight years Denny and those guys built a handful of prize money into a hundred thousand marks." Plus whatever fun they took along the way, but I did not mention that. The old boy did not need all his illusions stripped. "Think what they could have done with another eight years and that kind of capital."

Gotten into a crunch, probably. Too much wealth draws attention—though I suppose Denny knew that and planned accordingly.

"Perhaps I do not, Mr. Garrett. I'm only a shoemaker. My interest is fathers and sons and a family tradition that goes back more generations than can be counted. A tradition that died with Denny."

He was an exasperating old coot. I think he understood plenty. He just didn't give a damn anymore.

"You're certain they will return, then?"

"Breathing fire, Pop."

"Then it behooves me to take steps."

"The step you ought to take is to come to an accommodation."

"Not with those swine. They—and that woman—seduced my son away . . ."

I shut him out and gave my whole attention to the basement. As far as I could tell, nothing had changed. It seemed likely, then, that they had found nothing I might have missed. "Huh? I'm sorry. I missed that."

He gave me a look that said he knew why. But you could not get him to talk nasty at spear's point. "I asked if you knew someone I could retain as a guard for the premises."

"No." I did know someone. Me. But I was up to my nostrils with long cold lonely nights waiting for something that never happened, or that was really lethal when it did. "Wait." A thought. "Maybe I do. The people who are supposed to make the trip to the Cantard with me. I could do us both a favor by parking them here." Morley, too, if it put him out of the heat.

Tate looked startled. "You're going to go? You sounded so dead set against it."

"I'm still against it. I think it's about as smart as raiding a roc's nest. I don't even see any point to it. But I told you I'd look into it. I haven't really made up my mind yet either way."

He smiled. He grinned. I was afraid he would try to slap me on the back and maybe loosen one of my kidneys. But he restrained himself. A very restrained kind of guy, Old Man Tate.

He got very serious.

"What can you do about that man's body, Mr. Garrett?"

I figured we were going to get to that. "Nothing."

"What?"

"Nothing. He's not my problem."

The old boy gulped air. Then the sly merchant came tippy-toeing forward. "You want to hold me up for a bonus? All right. How much?"

"Don't bother. You don't have enough. I'm not putting a finger on that stiff. It's not my responsibility, and I don't do that kind of work. My advice is, call the magistrates and let them handle it. You'll be clear. He was killed during a break-in."

"No. I don't want anyone nosing into family business."

"Then have your boys take him and dump him in the river or an alley somewhere down the hill." There are bodies in the river most mornings. In the alleys, too. Unless they were someone important, they caused little comment.

Tate saw that he could not reach me through my lust for wealth. He gave that up. "You go ahead here, then. Send those men here as soon as you can. I have work to do. Keep me posted." He ducked out.

I poked around and wondered if the evil gleam in Tate's eye meant he thought he could put the corpse off on Morley and the triplets.

12

The flooring did its dust drop. I had noticed it several times before Tate left. I figured my sweetheart Rose was eavesdropping again. I ignored her.

Look as I might, I could not find anything missing. I settled back to give the whole business a think. It was obese with potential trouble. And I was getting near the point where I had to make a real decision.

The local end of it would take care of itself. There was nothing to investigate at this end. At the other end . . .

I did not want to think about that end yet. It would be unpleasant no matter how smooth it went. It would be unpleasant just traveling to and revisiting the Cantard.

A door opened and shut overhead. A moment later women began talking. The one with the quarrelsome voice had to be Rose. I wondered who the other one was.

A delightful aroma preceded her down the basement stairs. She proved to be a fiery little redhead with long straight hair, jade green eyes, a few freckles, and high, firm breasts that thrust boldly against a ruffled silk blouse. There was nothing between that blouse and her but my daydreams.

"Where have they been hiding you?" I asked, jumping up to take the tray she carried. "Who are you?"

"I'm Tinnie. And you're Garrett. And the last time you saw me I was just a spindle-legged kid." She looked me right in the eye and grinned. Her teeth looked sharp and white. I wanted to stick out a hand and let her take a bite.

"Could still be on spindles for all a guy can tell from that skirt." It fell to her ankles.

Her grin got sassy. "You could get lucky and get a look sometime. You never know."

My kind of luck came down the stairs right then. "Tinnie! You've done your job. Get out."

We ignored Rose. I asked, "You're not Denny's sister, are you? He never mentioned you."

"Cousin. They don't talk about me. I'm the one who causes trouble."

"Oh? I thought Rose took care of that."

"Rose is just obnoxious. That doesn't bother them. I do things that embarrass them. Rose just makes people mad or disgusted. I make the neighbors whisper behind their hands."

Rose simmered and reddened. Tinnie winked at me. "See you later, Garrett."

Yeah. I wish. That little bit was enough woman to make a man sit up and howl at the moon. She had a sway as she sashayed past Rose and started up the stairs.

When you got down to it and ignored the personality of a black widow spider, Rose was not something the dogs barked at, either. She was another small package with its contents all in the right places, and only prime materials had been used.

Rose could move with a sway that promised fireworks—if she wanted. But her fireworks were the kind that blow up in a man's face.

We eyed each other like a couple of tomcats about to square off. We both decided what she had in mind wouldn't work any better this time. She got flustered because she didn't know what else to do.

"Ought to have a backup plan when you jump in on something," I told her. "Like Saucerhead Tharpe."

"You're right, Garrett. Damn you, anyhow. How did you get so old being as stubborn as you are?"

"By guessing right most of the time. You wouldn't be a bad kid if there was room for anyone else in your world."

For a few seconds, there, I got the feeling she wished there *was* someone else in her world. Then she said, "Too bad we couldn't have met under other circumstances."

"Yeah," I said, not feeling it. She would be trouble no matter what the circumstances. That was how she was made.

"We don't have any common ground at all, do we?"

"Not very much. Not unless you had some feeling for your brother. I was fond of Denny. How about you?"

I had touched something. At last.

"It isn't fair. Him dying like that. He was about the nicest guy I ever knew. Even if he was my brother. That Cantard bitch—"

"Easy!" I snapped it, which gave me away enough to make her gawk and wonder.

"What's in this for you, Garrett? Besides a chance to line your pockets? Nobody goes to the Cantard without more reason than money."

I thought about Morley Dotes when she said that. I thought about me. I wondered about me. Garrett, tough guy. Can't reach him. No emotional handles. But I was on the brink of doing something no moron in his right mind would do.

Like Old Man Tate, I wanted to see this woman who could put a halter on Denny.

Rose and I traded stares. She decided I wasn't going to give her a thing. "Be careful, Garrett. Don't get yourself hurt. Look me up when this is over."

"It wouldn't work, Rose."

"It could be fun giving it a look."

She sashayed up the stairs.

She did look good from that perspective. Maybe . . .

Seconds after the door slammed, while common sense was fighting for its life, a copper-wreathed face peeped at me from the head of the stairs. "Don't even think about it, Garrett. I wouldn't love you anymore."

Then Tinnie vanished, too.

I gulped some air and said "Duh!" a few times, then got my dogs under me and went galumphing off on the trail.

She was gone when I got upstairs. I was alone with the dead guy. Denny's friend. There was no sign of Rose or Tinnie when I looked into the garden. I closed the door and took a quick look through the dead guy's pockets.

Some vulture had beat me to it. There wasn't a thing left.

●●●13

Old Man Tate got the body out somehow. Dropped it in the river, I guess. I didn't ask, and didn't hear a thing about it. A lot of people never heard from again take that one last swim.

I got Morley and the triplets installed at Denny's place. Morley thought it was a great idea. That being the case, I spent the evening hanging around his place, nicked by dagger looks from the breeds, hoping I would catch a flash to illuminate his eagerness to join a fool's quest.

I didn't catch anything brighter than candlelight.

All I found out was that I wasn't the only guy watching.

You get a sixth sense after enough years. Mine pegged two heavyweights in the first fifteen minutes. One was human and looked like he could give Saucerhead a fight. The other was so ugly, and stayed in his shadowed corner so deep, that I couldn't tell what he was. A breed for sure, probably with some troll and kobold in him, but more than that. He was as wide as he was tall. His face had been rearranged several times, probably for the better.

The bartender knew I had something going with Morley. He stayed civil. I asked about the men I had picked out.

"Don't know them. The ugly one was in here last night. First time. Sat in that corner all night nursing a beer he brought with him. I would've thrown him out if he hadn't bought a meal."

"That would've been a show to see." I took a pint of the water that passed for beer there and tipped him to take the sting out of the crack. "Think they're the kingpin's boys?"

"Not unless they're from out of town."

That was what I thought. I didn't recognize them either, but they looked like trouble on the hoof.

Well, no skin off my nose. As long as they were not interested in me.

I gave it up at Morley's place after the pint. There were better places to put an ear to the ground. I went and hung out in some of them. I didn't find out a thing.

Curious.

I headed for my place wondering if the glazier had gotten started yet. I felt no shame at all charging the replacement window to Tate.

The new window was in place and lettered as pretty as a blonde in her birthday suit. But I strolled by without admiring it, putting a slouch in my shoulders and a shuffle in my walk.

Maybe I wouldn't go home after all.

There were problems. One was that somebody was waiting in the breezeway beside the ratman's; even without seeing the glow of his pipe I could smell the weed he was smoking. The other was that there was somebody waiting inside. Whoever that was had all the lamps burning, using up oil at a rate to curdle my liver.

I knew a heavy weed smoker. Another friend of Denny's. Another old soldier, name of Barbera, who smoked so much that most of the time he didn't know if he was in this world or the next. A pathetic case, he was always in trouble because folks could talk him into anything. He had been one of Denny's charities.

No doubt Denny's other pals thought it would be a giggle to hop him up and sic him on me.

I faded into a shadow down the block and took a seat against a wall that needed tuck-pointing. The view of my place was as scenic as a garbage dump.

A lot of nothing happened for a long time. Unless you count the flares as my lurker lighted up, or the passing of drunks so far gone they were unafraid of the nighted streets. Only after we started getting some aromatic moonlight did anything interesting happen. And that was just a couple guys checking in with the weed man.

They passed me by without seeing me. But I got a look at them.

Vasco and Quinn, my old pals.

So they meant to do me dirty, eh?

I didn't move, though I thought about knocking some heads. I was beginning to wonder about that lamplight. Vasco and Quinn had made no effort to talk to whomever was inside. So maybe that whomever wasn't one of them.

Who, then?

My friend the ratman came home from his shift at the graveyard, drunk as usual. In my less charitable moments I've wished he would get lost in one of the graves he digs.

He shuffled up to my new window, glanced inside.

Whatever he saw, it was interesting. He watched for a minute. When he moved on he cast furtive looks around. He didn't see anyone watching. That must have given him courage. He slipped over and tried the door.

It opened.

Barbera came blazing out of the shadows. He climbed all over the ratman. When he had him pounded down to about three feet high, he took off, headed my way. A little message for me from Denny's pals. Misdelivered.

I reckoned they needed an answer.

I stepped out of the shadows as Barbera lumbered past. He caught me from the corner of his eye. I said, "Hi, there," and smacked his ear with my sap as his eyes grew big and he tried to turn.

He did not go down. But his knees got wobbly and his eyes glazed. I kicked him low, punched him high with my left, bounced the sap off his forehead.

He wobbled a little more.

They need a lot of pounding when they're hopped.

I gave him all he needed, and then some, and when he no longer knew what planet he was on, I snagged the seat of his pants and walked him into an alley, where I gave him a few more taps with my sap. Then I took his pouch of weed. A while later I paid a half-dwarf half-goblin wino to deliver it to Vasco with the word that he had not gotten his money's worth.

That taken care of, it was time to see about my intruder.

I didn't do any seeing. When I got back to where I could see my place, a troop of Tates were going inside, stepping over the groaning ratman like he was something that fell behind the horse. In a moment they marched back out with an angry Tinnie.

So there you go. Exactly my kind of luck. If I found the pot of gold at the end of the rainbow, I'd break my leg running toward it and have to lie there watching some other clown walk away with it while I did my groaning.

I let the street clear. Then I went and got a bucket of beer and locked myself inside. Nobody disturbed me.

'd planned to surprise everybody by showing up at the Tate place at the crack of dawn, ready to travel. But I had a dream about Loghyr bones.

Maybe it was the beer. That beer was green. But I knew better than to ignore it. It could be a summons from the Dead Man.

The worst thing about going out in the morning is that the sun is there. It slaps you right in the eyes. When you go back inside you can't see squat.

Squat was what I saw when I went into the Dead Man's place. It was as dark as a crypt in there.

About time, Garrett. Did you come via Khaphé?

"That wasn't a dream, eh?"

No.

"What do you want?"

I do not have the resources to follow all your adventures from afar. If you want my help and advice, you have to report to me occasionally.

I figured that was as near as he would get to saying he owed me. I would take what I was given. "What do you need?"

Details of what you have seen and learned since your last visit.

So I gave it to him, without leaving anything out.

He pondered awhile. *Buy yourself some poison rings, Garrett. Carry a boot knife.*

That was not the advice I expected. "Why?"

Are you known for such things?

"No."

Do the unexpected.

"I hiked all the way over here for that?"

It is the best I can do given the information you make available.

Make it my fault. Just like him. I did him a few odd jobs, cleaned the place up some, and burned some sulfur candles to make the vermin's lungs more robust. I wondered what Morley thought about breathing air. It's kind of hard to inhale green, leafy vegetables.

Then I took the Dead Man's advice. I stocked up on lethal hardware. I even picked up a few sneaky-petes I recalled from my Marine days. Let them come after me now, I thought. I'm ready for anything.

Horses. They are one of the little unpleasantnesses to be endured during any lengthy journey. Unless you want to walk. Morley Dotes had high praise for that sort of exercise, which meant it hurt. Personally, I have very little interest in voluntarily inflicting pain or discomfort upon myself.

I went to an outfitter I knew, a black giant they called Playmate. He was human, but must have had a little mixed blood somewhere. He stood nine feet tall. The color-impregnated clan scars on his cheeks gave him a ferocious look, but he was a sweetheart, as gentle as a human being could be.

Those gruesome features brightened when he spotted me crossing the yard of his place. He came at me with arms spread wide, grinning like I was going to rig out a battalion. I ducked his hug. He could crush you in his enthusiasm. Had he possessed the killer instinct, he would have made one hell of a professional wrestler.

I had done him some good on a skip trace a while back. My getting the guy to pay up saved Playmate from bankruptcy. So he owed some good fortune to me, but this greeting was not that much more warm than what he gave strangers who wandered in off the street.

"What can we do for you, Garrett? Name it and it's yours. On me. Long as you need it."

"I need a couple of horses and camping gear for five for three or four months."

"You got it. Going out to try your hand at trapping? Business that bad?"

"I have a job. It's taking me out of town."

"Three, four months is a far piece out and back. Where you going?" He was headed for his stable, where a whole clan of four-legged assassins awaited my advent with malice bubbling in their blood.

"The Cantard."

Horses and I do not get along. I can ride, but just barely, when I have to.

I'm a city boy and never saw much need to hang around with beasts that have it in for me.

Playmate slowed down. He gave me one of those looks you save for your crazy cousin when he says something totally stupid. "The Cantard? Garrett, you're a great man, and I have complete faith in you. If any civilian could get into and out of the Cantard alive, it would be you. But I'm not so confident of my animals."

"I don't want you to give me anything, Playmate. I'll buy what I need. No risk to you."

"Don't give me that tone of voice, Garrett."

What tone? I didn't intend the guy any grief.

We entered the digs of their satanic majesties the horses. Twenty pairs of big brown evil eyes turned my way. I could almost hear them sizing me up in their secret language, plotting misery.

"This is Thunderbolt," Playmate said, indicating a big black stallion with wicked teeth. "A spirited animal. Partly battle-trained."

"No."

Playmate shrugged, moved on to a roan. "How about Hurricane, here? Fast and smart and a little unpredictable. Like you. You should get along great. Complementary personalities."

"No. And no Storm, no Fury, no nothing with a fire-breathing name to live up to. I want an old mare on her last legs with a name like Daffodil and a temperament to match."

"That's disgusting, Garrett. Are you a man or a mouse?"

"Squeak. Me and horses don't get along. The last time I rode one he tricked me by turning around while I was getting on. Then he stood there laughing at me behind my back."

"Horses don't laugh, Garrett. They're very serious creatures."

"You hang around me, you'll see them laugh."

"If you have a problem with animals, why make the trip overland? Catch a river barge down to Leifmold, then take a coaster south. It would save you six hundred hard miles."

Why not? It never occurred to me, that's why not. Sometimes you stumble into a rut so deep you can't see over the edges. I didn't want to go to the Cantard, really, so I'd developed the habit of thinking about getting in and out fast. The quickest way from one place to another is usually the shortest. The shortest haul from TunFaire to the Cantard is straight overland.

A ham of a hand slapped me on the back. "Garrett, you look like a man who's just had a religious revelation."

"I have. And the first saint of my new church is going to be Saint Play-mate."

"As long as the job don't call for a martyr."

"Have faith, my friend. And make lots of donations. That's all this church will ask."

"Most of them only ask for the offerings. I tell you I almost started my own church once?"

"No."

"I was scoping it out when I thought I was going to lose the stable. I figure a man my size, tricked up in the right outfit, would make a hell of a prophet. And in a city as god-ridden as TunFaire, people are always looking for something novel."

"Wouldn't have thought you so cynical."

"Me? Cynical? Perish the thought. Come back when you need a horse, Garrett."

Morley and the triplets were sitting around looking smug when I showed up at the Tate place with my travel bag on my shoulder. "You guys earned your keep? Or are you just in practice for the next time the Grinning Death comes through?"

Morley stopped gnawing a carrot long enough to say, "We thumped some heads this morning, Garrett."

Doris bobbed his head and chortled something in dialect. Morley said, "He just claimed he broke twenty heads himself. He's exaggerating. There weren't more than fifteen guys involved. I recognized some of them. Second-raters. Whoever hired them was trying to get by on the cheap. He got what he paid for."

I wondered if any of them had recognized Morley. "Did they get away with anything?"

"A lot of bruises and a few fractures."

"I mean anything physical."

"That isn't physical enough for you?"

"Damn it, you know what I mean."

"Testy in the morning, aren't we? You didn't pay a bit of attention when I explained about fiber."

"Morley!"

"No. Nothing."

"Thank you."

"What's in the bag?"

"My travel gear. We're headed out."

"Today?"

"You have some reason to hang around?"

"Not really. You just caught me by surprise."

That was the idea. "The arrangements are made. You guys are ready to go. We'll head for the boat from here and hide out there till we pull out."

"Boat? What are you talking, boat?"

Morley was ghost-spooked pale. The triplets looked green around the gills, which was something for Doris and Marsha, who were a lovely shade of pale lime to begin.

"Boat?" Morley croaked again.

"Boat. We'll barge down to Leifmold, then catch a coaster headed south. We'll stay with it as far as we can. Then we'll put ashore and finish what we have to overland."

"We mix with water worse than oil does, Garrett."

"Nonsense. All the great navigators were elvish."

"All the great navigators were crazy. I get seasick watching the water-spider races. Which may explain why I can't bet them worth squat."

"Probably not enough starch in your diet."

He looked at me with hurt puppy eyes. "Let's take it overland, Garrett."

"Not on your life. I don't get along with horses."

"So we walk. The triplets can carry—"

"Who's paying the wages, Morley?"

He did nothing but scowl.

"Right. The boss says we take boats as far as we can, *then* we do it the hard way. You have your boys pick up and pack up. We head out in fifteen minutes."

I went and hunted up Pop Tate and told him I'd be doing the job and would be leaving the city shortly. We dickered awhile about expense money. To end up with what I wanted I had to give him what he wanted, a pretty complete outline of my plans.

I could change them, of course.

I don't like letting people in on everything. It subverts my reputation for being unpredictable.

●●● **16**

T he river barge *Binkey's Sequin* reminded me of a shopkeeper's wife. She was middle-aged, middle class, a little run down, a little overweight, extremely stubborn and set in her ways, needing masterful coaxing and cajoling to get her to give her loving best, but also faithful and warm and unsinkably optimistic in her care for her children. Morley hated her at first sight. He prefers them sleek, lean, taut, and fast.

Master Arbanos, her skipper, was an oversize gnome of that ethnic minority the ignorant sometimes confuse with hobgoblins (though any idiot knows hobgoblins don't come out in the daytime because the sunlight would broil their eyeballs). After he got us settled in what, with a smile of self-mockery, he called the cabin, he pulled me aside and told me, "We won't be able to sail till morning. Hope that don't throw you off schedule."

"No." But being naturally nosy and suspicious, I wanted to know why.

"Cargo's late. Best part, that is. Twenty-five cask of the TunFaire Gold, that they don't trust nobody but me and my brother to get down the river unbruised."

TunFaire Gold is a premium wine with a reputation for traveling poorly.

"So here I sit," he complained, "with eight ton of potato, two ton of onion, three ton of pig-iron billet, and forty hogshead of navy salt pork turning to mold while I wait for them to baby that spoiled grape juice down from TagEnd. If I didn't get paid more for hauling that than the rest put together, I'd tell them what to do with their TunFaire Gold poison! You bet I would."

Cargo manifests. How thoroughly exciting. "No problem for us. As long as we get there in a reasonable amount of time."

"Oh, won't be no problem with that. We'll get there almost the same time we would have."

"We will? Why?"

"We'll be going out with the tide, with an extra five knot of current running where the river is usually slowest. I just thought you might be in a hurry to move at this end, what with the way your friends are keeping out of sight down with the codfish smell. The way I hear tell, you landsider don't favor fish odor too much."

I had not mentioned the stench, being the naturally courteous guy that I am. But, "Now that you bring it up . . ."

"What?"

"Wait."

One of the Tate cousins or nephews was limping down the dock, checking ships with mad eyes. He was covered with dried blood. People stepped out of his way and stared after him.

He spotted me, staggered faster. I went to meet him.

"Mr. Garrett! They got Tinnie and Rose! They said if we don't give them Denny's papers—"

He collapsed. I caught him, lifted him up, and carried him aboard *Binkey's Sequin*. Master Arbanos gave me an appalled look. Before he started complaining, I tossed him a couple of marks. His personality shifted like a wolfman's under a full moon. You would have thought he was the boy's mother.

A draft of brandy bubbling in the gut got the kid into a state to tell his tale.

Rose and Tinnie, as was their custom, had gone out to do the afternoon marketing. Lester and the usual cousins and nephews and some kitchen help had accompanied them, again as was customary. When they were returning with the servants and two boys lugging vegetables and whatnot, disaster had struck, in the form of Vasco and a half dozen thugs.

"They grabbed Rose and Tinnie before we could drop the groceries and get our weapons out. Uncle Lester was the only one who was able . . . They killed him, Mr. Garrett."

"You all do them any damage?" The kid wouldn't have been in such bad shape if they hadn't tried. I needed to know how much blood was in it to tell if the women had a chance.

"Some," he admitted. "I don't think we killed anybody. We had to back off first. That's when they said we could have them back if we gave them Denny's letters and notebooks and stuff."

Well, they had no real reason to commit murder. The blood was balanced. One of their lot for Uncle Lester. A trade could be made. The problem was, they would find out I was headed south if I had much to do with the exchange.

I grinned.

"Sounds bad to me," Morley said.

"Thought you were staying out of sight." I wondered how long he had been sitting on that sack of onions listening. Not that he had heard anything he shouldn't.

He shrugged.

"They tell you where to get in touch?" I asked the kid.

"Yes. The Iron—"

Old Man Tate himself materialized. I thought he never left the family compound. He stormed aboard, shaking all over. He was winded from his hike and so damned mad he couldn't do anything but sputter.

"Sit down, Pop," I said. "I'm working on it already."

He plopped onto another bag of onions, giving Morley a curt nod. Master Arbanos winced but kept his yap shut.

"Here's the lay," I said. "We've got to make the trade."

Tate sputtered but nodded, then wheezed, "If it was just Rose, I'd be tempted to tell them to go to hell."

"Right. Look, I put the papers and whatnot in a box and moved them out of your place so those clowns wouldn't get them when they broke in. I didn't figure them for this. Anyway, what we have to do now is set the exchange up in such a way that we get the women back in one piece. I think I can do that, but you'll have to trust me on it."

Tate started sputtering again.

Morley said, "He's the expert, Mr. Tate. Permit him to exercise his expertise." His tone was more diplomatic than what I usually manage.

"I'm listening." Tate glared at me.

"Master Arbanos. What time are we going to take off tomorrow?"

"Five minutes after the seventh hour."

"Right. Mr. Tate, you go over to the Iron . . ." I snapped my fingers at the kid.

"Iron Goblin," he said.

"The Iron Goblin. Tell whoever meets you there that he's to deliver the women here at five after the seventh hour tomorrow morning. Or no deal.

I'll tell them where they can get the papers when the women look like they'll get back to their own people okay. In fact, if Master Arbanos will provide me pen and paper, I'll write the instructions."

Tate wanted to argue. He always wanted to argue. The old goat would disagree if you said the sky was blue. I let him simmer while I scratched a note. Master Arbanos was going to get rich selling me favors.

"Just pretend you're me," I told Tate when I finished. I folded the note and handed it to him. "Don't argue with them. Tell them that's it, take it or leave it."

"But—"

"They'll take it. They won't expect me to trust them. They would know I'd try to set up something so they can't mess us around. And they'll check around about me. They'll find out that I've done a couple of these things before and held up my end every time."

That was true. As far as it went. But this time a snatch and switch was not the whole story. This time the snatch was part of something bigger.

I was starting to take things personally, too.

Tate got his spleen out, and yakked his fear into submission, then took my note and marched off. We got the kid cleaned up and bandaged and sent him home.

Vasco didn't want to play the game my way, though he brought the women when he came to argue. He came on time, too, which told me that he would do it my way if I didn't bend.

He left Rose and Tinnie fifty feet up the dock, guarded by a half dozen men, and marched aboard. "Still in there pitching to get your throat cut, aren't you?" I asked.

His lips tightened but he refused to be baited. The sergeants teach you to control your temper, down in the Cantard. He looked around, did not see anything to disturb him.

He should have been disturbed. It had been all I could do to restrain Morley, who wanted to bushwhack the bunch and leave them floating in the river.

"Before you start," I told Vasco, "you'd better realize that I've got no special need for those women. I don't have any for Denny's papers, either. Which is why I'll make the trade."

"Where are the papers, Garrett?"

"Where are the women?"

"Right there. You can't see . . . ?"

"I don't see them on the boat. You don't get squat till I think it's too late for you to screw me over."

"Why would I do that?"

"I don't know. You haven't shown a lot of sense so far."

"You won't needle me into doing something stupid, Garrett."

"I don't have to. You do fine without me. Get those women over here." Master Arbanos was ready to cast off.

"What guarantee do I have that you're not cheating us?"

I ticked off points. "One: I always play these things straight. You know my reputation. Two: I don't need the papers for anything. Three: I know who you are, so I don't have to mess with you now. I can come for your head whenever I want it."

"Keep talking tough, Garrett. You'll get burned."

"Maybe you'll send Barbera after me?"

His mouth tightened even more. He jerked around, jumped to the wharf, gestured at his goons. They released the women. I waved them toward *Sequin*.

They came forward slowly. I guess they thought blood would fly any second.

Vasco stopped a few steps from the edge of the wharf. "So where are the papers, Garrett?"

I didn't have anything to say. He was still between me and the women. I just sort of looked around like a bored sightseer.

That's when I spotted the two guys from Morley's place, Big One and Ugly One. Not together, but both hanging around, relaxed, just part of the crowd eyeballing the goings-on.

I backed up a couple of steps like I was giving the gals room to jump aboard. I whispered down to Morley, who was crouched between onion sacks, "Take a peek at the guy sitting on the cotton bales."

"Give, Garrett," Vasco said.

I ignored him. The women had a few yards to go yet. Even Rose's sour face had begun to show some hope.

Master Arbanos began letting lines go.

Morley whispered, "I see him. What about him?"

"Who is he?"

"How the hell should I know? I never saw him before."

"I did. Once. The other night. Hanging around with the big guy over there leaning against those navy pork barrels." I started to tell him where and when, then decided it might be wise to save a little something for my old age.

"I don't know him, either," Morley said.

"Give, Garrett." Vasco had just about decided I was going to cheat him. He started after the women.

"Run!" I yelled at them. And to Vasco, "They're in a box in an abandoned house on the Way of the Harlequin, half a block west of Wizard's Reach."

"It's your ass if they aren't, Garrett."

"Anytime you think you can take a piece of it, Vasco. Anytime."

The boat began to drift away from the wharf. The women took my advice, sprinted and jumped. A delectable bundle of goodies plopped into my arms. Morley popped up and caught Rose, making suitable purrs at the advent of unexpected treasures. I tossed him a sneer.

Vasco trotted away, barking orders at his troops.

I couldn't restrain a chuckle.

"What's so funny?" Tinnie asked. She made no effort to peel herself from me. I thought about pushing her away—sometime next week.

"Just imagining what might happen when they try to collect those papers."

"You mean you lied to them?"

The wharf was fifteen feet away now. Ugly One got down off the cotton bales. He paid us no special attention. And I had trouble paying him any, either. Tinnie would not hold still.

"Oh, no. I told him the truth. I just didn't tell him all of it."

"Amateurs," Morley said, taking a break from Rose, who was doing to him what Tinnie was to me. "They had any professional smarts at all, they'd know that's the Dead Man's place. Slick, Garrett. Remind me not to get on your wrong side. You're so slick you'd slide uphill."

I glanced at the two men on the wharf and wondered.

"I told you I was going with you, Garrett," Rose crowed, as if she had planned the whole thing. She got over her frights fast.

"You might think," I told her. "You might think." I figured to have Master Arbanos put in a mile or two down and get shut of those females.

Damn! That Tinnie was merciless.

I decided I liked her.

About then Old Man Tate came charging out the dock, too late for anything but the bye-bye. "Master Arbanos, where are you going to put in so we can get rid of these women?" I figured I'd yell the news across to Tate.

"Leifmold."

Leifmold. All the way down to the coast.

He would not relent. He was deaf to offers of money on this. He had a reputation, a schedule, and a tide, and he would waste none of them for any puny bribe I could pay.

Rose grinned wickedly while I argued.

Tinnie's smile was more promising.

The trouble with that damned boat was that there was no privacy. You started a little hand-holding and ear blowing and there was Doris or Marsha or Dojango or some damned crewman exercising his eyes. It nearly drove Morley and me crazy. Rose seemed plenty willing to be friendly with him. Of course, he had the authentic golden touch.

I guess eating your vegetables is good for something.

Leifmold was not that long a journey. The first chance I got I pulled Morley aside and asked, "How are we going to ditch those two?"

"Bad choice of words, Garrett. Though I understand your frustration. Does our principal have reliable associates in Leifmold?"

"I don't know."

"Why not?"

"I never had any reason to ask."

"Too bad. Now we have to try to charm it out of those girls." He did not sound optimistic.

Rose laughed at us when we tried to get some word out of her. Tinnie just pretended she was deaf.

Morley and I went off to the stern and brooded together alone.

"Can't do it, Garrett," he grumbled after a while.

"Uhm," I grunted.

"No way."

"Uhm."

"Skirts in the Cantard. Worse than poison, what I hear. We go in there with women, we're dead. Guaranteed."

"I know. But we can't just run off on them, either."

He gave me a look. "If it wasn't poor business sense in this case, I'd say you were too romantic. Baggage is baggage. There isn't anything any one of them is sitting on that you can't get from another one."

There was a lot of traffic on the river, most of it taking advantage of the tide. And most of it faster than *Binkey's Sequin*. But there was one gaudy yachtlike vessel back upstream that seemed to have us on a leash. "I don't know how a guy with your attitude has your luck."

The yacht boasted a sail of red and yellow stripes. It had sleek lines. It smelled of wealth, which meant power. It could have passed us easily, but it just hung back.

"They want to be treated that way, Garrett. If you don't treat them like rats, they have to admit that they're responsible for their own behavior. And you know women. They never want to admit they get a kick out of messing around."

"How about trying this angle—if Master Arbanos is willing."

"I'm listening."

"We tie them up just before we make port. He hides them out while he's loading and unloading, then he takes them back to TunFaire. Just part of the cargo."

"Sounds good to me. When you talk to him, ask about that boat with the striped sail."

I had wondered if he'd noticed.

Master Arbanos held me up. The man was a buccaneer. But I was between a rock and a hard place, and he knew it. I paid. In the end it all came out of Tate's pocket, anyway.

I asked about the striped sail ship.

He looked at me like I was a moron. "Sorry, I forget you are not a riverman. That is *Typhoon,* personal vessel of Stormlord Thunderhead. Everyone on the river knows it. It runs to Leifmold and back all the time, showing the Stormlord's colors."

"Oh my, oh my, oh my," I murmured.

"The Stormlord never sails her himself. She is just for show. Her master is a bitch cartha with the temper and moral of an alley cat. She has had trouble with everyone on the river. Some say will strike the striped sail and hoist the black one by night."

"What does that mean?"

"That some think she turn river pirate when no one is looking."

"Is it just talk? Or is there something to it?" Bless me, but wouldn't it be my kind of luck to be aboard a barge pirates were stalking. The gods have a fellow especially assigned to complicate my life.

"Who knows? There are pirate. I have seen their leaving."

"And?" He wanted coaxing.

"They don't leave any witness. Which is why I never accept any cargo they find attractive."

Little wheels and gears clicked in my mind, like the works in a water-clock. A clock running a little slow, perhaps. What sort of cargo might attract a pirate working from a vessel belonging to one of the Stormlords? What was this whole business about?

Silver. Sweet silver. The fuel of the engines of sorcery.

One more complication?

Why the hell not? Every other angle had been covered, hadn't it?

I gave Master Arbanos a generous portion of the metal sugar. He assured me my will would be carried out where the women were concerned. They would be treated like royalty, and on *Sequin*'s return to TunFaire he would deliver them to Old Man Tate personally.

I could ask for nothing more.

Master Arbanos's crewfolk—all of them his relatives—moved the night before we were due to reach Leifmold. They caught the gals asleep.

Such caterwauling and cursing! I never. Rose I expected to be less than polite, but Tinnie I'd had pegged as at least half a lady. She turned out to be the louder of the two.

At least that went off without hitches.

The sea lay on our left. Leifmold climbed steep hills a mile to our right. We were waiting to pick up a pilot, whose expertise would be needed if *Binkey's Sequin* was to negotiate the traps laid for Venageti raiders. Morley was loafing in the bows. "Come here," he said, beckoning languorously. He was nibbling a raw potato stolen from the cargo. I gave it a disgusted look.

"Not bad if you sprinkle a little salt on," he said.

"And good for you, no doubt."

"Of course. Take a gander round the harbor there."

I did. And saw what he meant.

The striped-sail yacht was warping into a dock. She had passed us in the night and had pulled rank to get the first available pilot. "Needs keeping an eye on," I admitted.

"You read that guy Denny's papers. Did he mention Stormlord Thunderhead anywhere?"

"No. But a couple other wizards got memorialized. I'm willing to look for an indirect connection." When you consider the possibility of wizards being involved in anything, the smart thing to do is to assume the worst.

So chances were striped sail had nothing to do with us. But I would take the paranoid approach on the off chance.

The women raised all kinds of holler when we tied up, but nobody paid them any mind. Morley and Doris and Marsha and I went off looking for one of several coasters recommended to us by Master Arbanos. Morley left Dojango to watch the Stormlord's yacht. No one there ought to recognize him even if they were up to no good.

Our luck was in. We found a ship called *The Gilded Lady* planning to put out next morning. Her master was amenable to our buying passage. Morley started looking gray around the edges.

"You handled the river all right."

"No waves on the river, Garrett. Lots of waves along the coast, and the ship running parallel to them." His eyes bugged. "Let's not talk about it. Let's find someplace to put up, then get out on the town. There's a place down here even better than mine—don't you ever tell anybody I admitted that—that you've really got to try."

"I'm not in a roots and nuts mood, Morley. Looking a long voyage in the eye, I need something with more body."

"Body? Don't you care what you're doing to your body? I promise, you'll like this place. Give you a little something different. All that red meat is going to kill you, anyway."

"We did red meat the other day, Morley. But since you bring up self-abuse, let's do some calculating. Who is more likely to die young? Me eating what I want or you messing around with other guys' women?"

"You're talking apples and oranges now, buddy."

"I'm talking dead is what I'm talking."

He did not have a rejoinder for fifteen seconds. Then he said only, "I'll die happy."

"So will I, Morley. And without hunks of nut stuck between my teeth."

"I give up," he said. "Go ahead. Commit slow suicide by poisoning yourself."

"That was my plan." A tavern sign caught my eye. It had been a dry trip down the river. "I'm going to tip a few."

Doris and Marsha recognized a beer joint when they saw one, too. They grunted back and forth. Morley started trading gibberish with them.

Oh, my. Did all the triplets have an alcohol problem?

I said, "As soon as we find a place for the night somebody better check on Dojango. At least so he knows where to find us."

Morley reached a compromise with Doris and Marsha. "They can have one bucket each. That's all."

"*Bucket?*"

"They're big boys, Garrett."

"So I noticed." We marched into the tavern. It was early yet, so there was no crowd. Still, a silence fell and grew so deep I knew we had walked in where we were not wanted.

I've never let that stop me. I tossed a coin on the bar. "A mug of brew for me and a bucket apiece for the big boys. And my buddy here will have whatever you can stomp out of a parsnip."

Cold-eyed stare. "We don't serve their kind."

"Well, now, they don't speak Karent very well. So when you look at them there, they're still smiling. But I don't think they'll keep on smiling if I have to translate that for them. You know how grolls are when they get mad."

He thought about arguing. He might have had there been forty or fifty more people to back his play. But Doris and Marsha had begun to get the drift. Their smiles vanished and their faces grew mottled.

"We want beer," I said. "Not your women."

He did not laugh. He headed for the tap. Not many people are fool enough to make a groll mad.

They do get mean.

"Not bad beer," I said, quaffing my third while Doris and Marsha nursed their milk pails. "And serving it up didn't break one bone, did it?"

The barman wasn't interested in bantering.

Most of his regulars had deserted him.

We followed their example.

About fifty sullen men had gathered outside. Their mood looked ugly. I told Morley, "I ought to pay closer attention to what neighborhood I'm in."

"I like the way you think, Garrett."

Half a brick thrown by somebody named Anonymous arced toward us. It had some arm behind it. Doris—or maybe it was Marsha—stabbed a paw out and snagged it. He looked it over for a second. Then he squeezed it and let the powder dribble between his fingers.

That impressed me, but not the mob.

So he snapped off the timber from which the tavern's sign hung. He stripped the sign off and flailed the timber around like a switch.

That got the message across. The mob began to evaporate.

Morley asked, "Could a mule do that?"

"No."

We were more circumspect in selecting a place to spend the night.

19

"So where the hell is he?" I demanded. There wasn't a shadow of Dojango. Morley looked bleak. He had been looking bleak for a while. I thought maybe I should buy him a bunch of carrots or something. He muttered, "Guess we'll have to scout the alleys and taverns."

"I'm going to take a gander at that ship. Catch me on the pier when you find him."

Morley said something to the two remaining triplets. They grunted and moved out. I marched on down to where I could get a look at that striped-sail ship.

There wasn't much to see, a few men lugging things off, then lugging other things on. It wasn't hard to understand why Dojango bugged out. Watching is boring work. It takes a patient guy to lurk for a living.

A man came out on the rear deck, leaned on the rail, hawked, spat into the harbor.

"Interesting." He was Big One from Morley's place and the pier.

He began scanning the waterfront almost as if he had heard me. Then he shrugged and went into a cabin.

Curious.

Maybe Dojango would have stayed on the job if he had seen that guy before.

I lazed in the shade, wishing I had a keg to nurse and wondering what was taking Morley so long. Nothing else happened except that the stevedores finished loading and unloading.

I heard a soft scuff behind me. Maybe at last . . .

But when I looked I saw Big One. He was not in a friendly mood.

I dropped off the bale where I'd been loafing. Did this call for lethal instruments?

He walked right up and whacked the bale with a short club. No accusations. No questions. Nothing but business. I leaned out of the way and let him have one in the gut.

It did as much good as gut-punching a barrel of salt pork.

That club was meant to scramble my brains, I feared. I hauled out a knife.

I did not get to use it. The cavalry arrived in the guise of Doris or Marsha. The groll picked Big One up by one arm and held him out like a doll. A slow grin spread over his green face. Then he casually heaved him over the bales into the harbor.

Big One never made a sound.

They would have heard me cussing fifty miles away.

Doris—or Marsha, as the case may have been—beckoned me to follow. I did, grumbling. "I could have handled him." Probably about like I had handled Saucerhead, by pounding my body off his club till it broke.

This case was doing wonders for my self-esteem.

Dojango was not falling-down-drunk. He was climbing-the-walls-and-howling-at-the-moon-drunk. Marsha kept him under control while Doris explained what happened on the waterfront. Or Doris did while Marsha did. I passed my thoughts afterward.

"Bad business," Morley said. His sense of humor had deserted him.

Bad business indeed. But I had gone up against wizards before. You can handle them if your footwork is deft. They have more handles than your ordinary street thug. The big thing is, they're all as crooked as a hen's hind leg. They are in the middle of every stew of corruption. But they go for a squeaky-clean public image. It's smart to keep some tarnish in your trick bag and be ready to spread it around.

"We'll be out of here tomorrow. Our worries will be over."

"Our worries will be over about the time I learn to handicap the D'Guni races."

"Meaning never?"

"Or maybe a little longer."

"I'm beginning to wonder if we ought not to reexamine your diet, Morley. Such unrelenting pessimism must have some deficiency at its base."

"The only deficiencies bothering me are of good luck, financial where-withal, and female companionship."

"I thought you and Rose—"

"As you said, she wants something for nothing. She had a chance at a once-in-a-lifetime experience and she tried to sell herself to me! As if she had something special. As if a woman with her attitudes could ever develop whatever talent she did have. I'll never understand you people. What you do to your women . . ."

"What I do to them isn't any different from what you do to yours. Rose's problems are hers. I do get tired of hearing folks blame their faults on everybody else."

"Whoa, Garrett. Come on down off your stump."

"Sorry. I was just thinking how I was going to spend tomorrow."

"Say what?"

"Listening to Dojango groan and moan and heave his guts over the side while he blames his drinking problem on his mother or somebody."

Morley grinned.

20

Dojango gripped the rail and made an awful noise as he sacrificed to the gods of the sea. A soft whimper followed.

"What did I say?" I asked.

We were twenty feet from the quayside.

Morley was a little green himself. His trouble was all anticipation. The ship wasn't even noticeably rolling.

The ship's master approached. He had time for us now that the vessel was turning toward the channel. He said, "I spoke to the harbormaster this morning. The war situation is quiet. We're clear all the way to Full Harbor if you want to stay with the ship that far."

"Of course we do."

Morley groaned. Dojango whimpered something about throwing himself overboard and ending it all. I grinned and set to dickering for the extra passage.

Halfway out of the channel the groll portion of the triplets began gabbling at Morley. When we went to see what they wanted, we found we were overhauling *Binkey's Sequin.* The Tate girls were out on deck. They spotted us as we slid past on the starboard side.

"I get the feeling they're upset about something," Morley said. He smiled and waved.

"Women have no sense of proportion," I said. I grinned and waved, too. "Wag a little tail at you and you're supposed to eat out of their hands." I looked at Tinnie and wondered if it might be worth it.

They blistered the air. I wondered if my personal sacrifices could be parlayed into a bonus from Old Man Tate.

We swooped past *Sequin* and dashed for the mouth of the channel. Master Arbanos's vessel was a dark lump in the distance as we began our turn to the south.

"I'll be damned!"

It was a morning for meeting old friends. A river scow entering the Leifmold channel carried Vasco and his buddies. "That damned Dead Man," I muttered. "He could have banged them around a little, at least."

They hadn't spotted us. I got everybody out of sight so it would stay that way.

I had counted on the Dead Man to stall them longer than he had. Now I worried. Had they done something I would regret?

"Keep an eye on these pirates," Morley grumped. "They might murder us while we're laying in the scuppers puking our guts out." The ship had completed her turn. She was rolling in the offshore swell.

Morley had no call to worry. The ship's crew treated us perfectly. The journey was almost without event. Once, the Stormlord's striped sail passed us, wallowing and struggling through seas she was not designed to face. She did not seem interested in us, and was not to be seen in the harbor at our first port of call.

Once we saw a royal man-of-war farther out, and another time a masthead lookout yelled down that he had a Venageti sail in sight. Nothing came of either sighting. We entered Full Harbor eight days after departing Leifmold. No striped sail was to be seen there, either.

For once I felt a little optimistic.

21

"We're here," Morley growled the next morning. "What now?" He had stoked up on biscuits baked with lard and served with greasy gravy. It was the nearest he could get to a vegetarian breakfast.

"Now I try to pick up the woman's trail. Her family should still be here. They ought to know something."

It sounded too simple even to me. But sometimes things go your way. It would be sweet if I could find her at her dad's place, make my pitch, and head out with her yea or nay.

Full Harbor had changed and not changed. New buildings. New naval facilities. New streets laid out after the cleanup from the big Venageti attack three years ago. Same old whores and stews and pawnshops and overpriced inns and tailors preying on the loneliness of young sailors and Marines far from home and in the shadow of death. The gods know I wasted enough of my own time and pay in places like that. Reformers keep talking about shutting them down. They won't. The boys would have nothing left to fill their time.

I expected commentary from Morley Dotes. He disappointed me in a pleasant way. "You humans are a despair, that this is the best a soldier can expect."

Maybe it was his human side talking.

We are the only race that goes in for war habitually, in a big way. The others, especially the elves and dwarfs, have the occasional brawl, but seldom more often than once a generation, and then usually only a single battle, not much sorcery, winner take all.

Plenty of them get in on our doings as auxiliaries. They can be useful but are unreliable. They have no concept of discipline.

"You're right. Let's find ourselves a base, then get to work."

We drew plenty of stares, being civilians, and them being what they were. I didn't like the attention. Mine is a business where I don't want to be remembered.

We found a place that would accept civs and breeds without devouring the income of ten years. It was about as sleazy as a place could get. I bribed the owner to keep alcohol away from the triplets, then Morley and I hit the streets.

Full Harbor, on the map, looks something like a lobster's head lying between its arms. The city proper, and its naval facilities, sits at the end of a fortified neck of land. The arms reach out and shield the bay from the worst storm-driven seas. The city's location makes it very defensible. The Venageti have managed to penetrate it only twice, each time losing the entire force committed. The farther you get from the waterfront and naval facilities, the more "civilized" the city becomes. There are some low, wooded hills just inside the neck of the peninsula, right behind the Narrows Wall. They harbor the homes of the city's well-to-do.

No lords reside in the city. They refuse to risk themselves or their properties where the Venageti might show up with the unpredictable suddenness of a tropical storm.

They're funny that way—plenty willing to trek all over the Cantard risking themselves for glory and personal gain, but . . .

I don't understand them any more than I understand frogs. But I'm handicapped by my low birth.

Kayean's father had been one of the Syndics who dwelt in the hills, with a wife, four servants, and eight kids. Kayean was the oldest.

Memories returned, bringing a certain nostalgia, as I guided the rented carriage up and down pacific lanes.

"What're you looking all moony-eyed about?" Morley demanded. We had left the triplets at the inn, an action the wisdom of which I still doubted, though Morley assured me he had not left a farthing between them.

"Remembering when. Young love. First love. Right here in these hills." I had not filled him in on every little detail. A bodyguard did not need to know all the sordid angles.

"I'm a bit of a nostalgic romantic myself, but I never figured you for one, Garrett."

"Me? The knight in rusty armor always clanking out to rescue undeserving maidens or to do battle with the dragons of some lunatic's imagination? I don't qualify?"

"You see? Romantic images. Though why should you mind working for nuts if they have money to spend? You can milk a man with an obsession like a spider milks a fly."

"I don't work that way."

"I know. You really *want* to rescue maidens and champion underdogs and lost causes—as long as you get enough grease to keep the joints in the armor from freezing up."

"I like a beer sometimes, too."

"You've got no ambition, Garrett. That's what's wrong with you."

"You could write a book about all the things you've found wrong with me, Morley."

"I'd rather write one about the things that are right. It'd be a lot less work. Just a short little fable. 'He's kind to his mother. Doesn't beat his wife. His kids never have to go in the snow barefoot.' "

"Sarky today, aren't we?"

"I'm off my feed. How much longer are we going to be looking for the ghosts of might-have-been?"

Not only sarky but a little too perceptive. I supposed I might as well confess. "I'm not being romantic. I'm lost."

"Lost? I thought you said you knew these parts like the back of your hand."

"I did. But things have changed. All the trees and bushes and stuff that were landmarks have grown or been cut down or—"

"Then we'll just have to ask somebody, won't we? Yo!" he shouted at a gardener clipping a hedge. "What's the name of the guy we're looking for, Garrett?" The gardener stopped working and gave us the fish eye. He looked like a real friendly type. Poison you with his smile.

"Klaus Kronk." The first name was pronounced *claws* with a soft sibilant, but Morley took it for a nickname.

He climbed down and approached the gardener. "Tell me, my good fellow, where can we find the Syndic Claws Kronk?"

The good fellow gave him a puzzled look that turned into a sneer. "Let's see the color of your metal, darko."

Morley calmly picked him up and chucked him over his hedge, hopped over after him and tossed him back, thumped on him a little, twisted limbs and made him groan, then said, "Tell me, my good fellow, where can we find the Syndic Claws Kronk?" He wasn't even breathing hard.

The gardener decided that at least one of us was a psychopath. He stammered directions.

"Thank you," Morley said. "You have been most gracious and helpful. In token of my appreciation I hope you will accept this small gratuity." He dropped a couple of coins into the man's palm, closed his fingers over them, then rejoined me aboard our conveyance. "Take the first left and go all the way to the top of the hill."

I glanced back at the gardener, still seated beside the lane. A glint of mischief sparked in his swelling eyes.

"You think it's wise to make enemies out here, Morley?"

"We won't get any comebacks from him. He thinks I'm crazy."

"I can't imagine why anybody would think that about you, Morley."

We had only one turn left to make. A cemetery flanked both sides of the road. "You know where you are now?" Morley asked. "A landmark like this ought to be plenty memorable."

"More memorable than you know. I think our gardener friend got us. We'll see in a minute." I turned between the red granite pillars that flanked the entrance to the Kronk family plot.

"He's dead?"

"We're about to find out."

He was. His was the last name incised in the stone of the obelisk in the center of the plot. "Got it during the last Venageti incursion, judging from the date," I said. "Fits what I remember about him, too. He would get out and howl for Karenta."

"What do we do now?"

"I guess we look for the rest of the family. He's the only one who's established residence here."

He lifted one eyebrow.

"I can find my way from here. Kayean and I used to walk up here at night to, uh . . ."

"In a graveyard?"

"Nothing like tombstones to remind you how little time you have for the finer things in life."

"You humans are weird, Garrett. If you want an aphrodisiac, there's one that the sidhe tribes of the Benecel river basin make from the roots of something like a potato plant. It'll keep your soldier at attention for hours. Not only that, but when you use it you're guaranteed there's no way you're going to become a papa."

Vegetarian sexual aids? Some people take good things too far.

22

S tarting from the cemetery I was able to find the Kronk place with only one miscue. From the lane the place next door looked more like the one I remembered than the correct one. We were partway up the flagstones when I spied the peacock cages under the magnolias.

"About-turn and march," I said. "One house shy of our mark." I recalled how, if Kayean was not very careful sneaking in and out, those peafowl would raise six kinds of hell and there went the evening if it happened on the sneak-out side. Her old man knew what was going on but was never quick enough to catch her. She had been fast on her feet.

I explained that to Morley as we retreated to the lane.

"How the hell did a slob like you ever meet a quail living in a place like this?"

"I met her at a party for bachelor officers the admiral put on. All the most eligible young ladies of Full Harbor were there."

He gave me an overly dramatic look of disbelief.

I confessed, "I was there waiting tables."

"It must have been animal magnetism and the air of danger and forbidden fruit surrounding an affair with a member of the lower classes." He said it deadpan. I could not decide whether I should be irritated or not.

"Whatever it was, it was the greatest thing that had happened in my young life. Hasn't been much since to eclipse it, either."

"Like I said, a romantic." And there he let it lay.

•••

"Lot of changes since I was here," I said. "The place has been completely done over."

"You sure it's the right one?"

"Yeah." All the memories assured me that it was. We had walked these grounds under the watchful chaperonage of a patient and loving mother who had seen the whole romance as a phase and would not have believed her eyes if she had walked in on us in the cemetery.

Morley took my word for it.

We were still fifty feet from the door when a man in livery stepped outside and came to meet us. "He don't look like he's glad we dropped by."

Morley grunted. "He don't look like your average houseboy, either."

He didn't. He looked like a Saucerhead Tharpe who was past his prime but still plenty dangerous. The way he fish-eyed us said that, fancy clothes or not, we were not fooling him.

"Can I help you gents?"

I'd decided to go at it straight ahead, almost honest, and hope for the best. "I don't know. We're down from TunFaire looking for Klaus Kronk."

That seemed to take him from the blind side. He said, "And just when I thought I'd heard all the gags there was."

"We just a little bit ago found out he was dead."

"So what are you doing here instead of heading back where you came from if the guy you want is croaked?"

"The only reason I wanted to talk to him was to find out how I could get in touch with his oldest daughter. I know she's married, but I don't know who to. I thought maybe her mother or any others of the family who were still around might be able to point me in the right direction. Any of them here?"

He looked like it was getting too complicated for him. "You must be talking about the people who used to live here. They moved out a couple years ago."

The changes all seemed recent enough to support his statement. "You have any idea where she is?"

"Why the hell should I? I didn't even know her name till you told me."

"Thank you for your time and courtesy. We'll have to trace her some other way."

"What you want this machuska for, anyway?"

While I considered his question, Morley said, "Throw it in the pond and see which way the frogs jump."

"We represent the executors of an estate of which she is the principal legatee."

"I love it when you talk dirty lawyer," Morley said. He told our new buddy, "She inherited a bundle." In a ventriloquist's whisper, he told me, "Hit him with the number so we can see how big his eyes get."

"It looks like around a hundred thousand marks, less executors' fees."

His eyes did not get big. He didn't even bat one. Instead he muttered, "I thought I heard every gag there was," again.

So I repeated myself for him. "Thanks for your time and courtesy." I headed for the lane.

"Next stop?" Morley asked.

"We ask at the houses on either side. The people who lived there knew the family. They might give us something."

"If they're not gone, too. What did you think of that guy?"

"I'll try not to form an opinion till I've talked to a few more people."

We had a less belligerent but no more informative interview at the next house down the lane. The people there had only been in the place a year and all they knew about the Kronks was that Klaus was killed during the last Venageti invasion.

"You make anything of that?" I asked as we turned the rig around and headed for the peacock place.

"Of what?"

"He said Kronk was killed *during* the Venageti thing. Not *by* the Venageti."

"An imprecision due entirely to laziness, no doubt."

"Probably. But that's the kind of detail you keep an ear out for. Sometimes they add up to a picture people don't know they're giving you, like brushstrokes add up to a painting."

The peacocks raised thirteen kinds of hell when they discovered us. They crowed like they hadn't had anything to holler about for years.

"My god," I murmured. "She hasn't changed a bit."

"She was always old and ugly?" Morley asked, staring at the woman who observed our approach from a balcony on the side of the house.

"Hasn't even changed her clothes. Careful with her. She's some kind of half-hulder witch."

A little man in a green suit and red stocking cap raced across our path cackling something in a language I didn't understand. Morley grabbed a rock and started to throw it. I stopped him. "What're you doing?"

"They're vermin, Garrett. Maybe they run on their hind legs and make noises that sound like speech, but they're as much vermin as any rat." But he let the rock drop.

I have definite feelings about rats, even the kind that walk on their hind legs and talk and do socially useful things like dig graves. I understood Morley's mood if not his particular prejudice.

The Old Witch—I never heard her called anything else—grinned down at us. Hers was a classic gap-toothed grin. She looked like every witch from every witch story you've ever heard. There was no shaking my certainty that it was deliberate.

A mad cackle floated down. The peafowl answered as though to one of their own.

"Spooky," Morley said.

"That's her image. Her game. She's harmless."

"So you say."

"That was the word on her when I was here before. Crazy as a gnome on weed, but harmless."

"Nobody who harbors those little vipers is harmless. Or blameless. You let them skulk around your garden, they breed like rabbits, and first thing you know they've driven all the decent folk away with their malicious tricks."

We were up under the balcony now. I forbore mentioning his earlier response to a gardener's bigotry. It wouldn't have done any good. Folks always believe their own racism is the result of divine inspiration, incontestably valid.

My dislike for ratpeople is, of course, the exception to the rule of irrationality underlying such patterns of belief.

The Old Witch cackled again, and the peafowl took up the chorus once more. She called down, "He was murdered, you know."

"Who was?" I asked.

"The man you were looking for, Private Garrett. Syndic Klaus. They think no one knows. But they are wrong. They were seen. Weren't they, my little pretties?"

"How did you . . . ?"

"You think you and that girl could sneak through here night after night, running to that cemetery to slake your lusts, without the little people noticing? They tell me everything, they do. And I never forget a name or a face."

"Did I say they were vermin?" Morley demanded. "Lurking in the shadows of tombstones watching you. And probably laughing their little black hearts out because there is no sight more ridiculous than people coupling."

Maybe I reddened a little, but otherwise I ignored him. "Who killed him?" I asked. "And why?"

"We could name some names, couldn't we, my little pretties? But to what purpose? There is no point now."

"Could you at least tell me why he was killed?"

"He found out something that was not healthy for him to know." She cackled again. The peafowl cheered her on. It was a great joke. "Didn't he, my little pretties? Didn't he?"

"What might that have been?"

The laughter left her face and eyes. "You won't be hearing it from me. Maybe that machuska Kayean knows. Ask her when you find her. Or maybe she doesn't. I don't know. And I don't care."

That was the second time that day I'd heard Kayean called machuska, and only the second time I'd heard the word since I had gotten out of the Marines and the Cantard. It was a particularly spiteful bit of Venageti gutter slang labeling a human woman who has congress with members of other species. A word like our own kobold-knocker is a like nickname.

"Can you tell me where she is?"

"No. I don't know."

"Could you tell me where I might find some of her family?"

"I don't know. Maybe they all went to join her. Maybe they went somewhere to escape their shame." She cackled but she didn't put much heart into it. The peafowl didn't, either. Their feeble response was pure charity.

"Is there any way you can help me?"

"I can give you some advice."

I waited.

"Watch out who you play with among the headstones. Especially if you do find Kayean. She might show you one with her name on it."

"Time to get out of here," I told Morley. "In case it's catching."

He agreed. I thanked the Old Witch. We backed away in spite of her efforts to cling to our company.

"Was that worth it?" Morley asked.

"Absolutely."

A little fellow in green and red jumped into our path. He removed his cap and bowed, then rewarded Morley with a grandiloquent obscene gesture. He raced into the bushes giggling.

This time I didn't interfere with Morley's rock throwing. Lurk behind tombstones, would they?

The giggles ended with an abrupt "Yipe!"

"I hope I broke his skull," Morley growled. "What're we going to do now?"

"Go back to the inn and eat. Check on the triplets. Guzzle some beer. Think. Spend the afternoon trying to turn something up in parish or civil records."

"Like what?"

"Like who she married if she was married here. She was a good Orthodox girl. She would have wanted the whole fancy, formal show. It might be easier to trace her through her husband if we knew his name."

"I don't want to be negative, Garrett, but I have a feeling the girl you knew and are looking for isn't the woman we're going to find."

I had the same sad feeling.

23

"**W**here the hell are they?" Morley roared at the innkeeper.

"How the hell should I know?" the man roared right back, obviously used to rough trade. "You said don't give them anything to drink. You didn't say nothing about nursemaiding them or keeping them off the streets. If you ask me, they looked like they was growed up enough to go out and play by themselves."

"He's right, Morley. Calm down." I didn't want him getting so stirred up he'd need to run ten miles to work it off. I had a feeling it would be smart if we stuck together as much as we could. Assuming the Old Witch knew what she was yakking about, somewhere there was a killer who might get unnerved by our poking around.

I repeated myself. "Calm down and think about it. You know them. What are they likely to be doing?"

"Anything," he grumbled. "That's why I'm not calm." But he took my advice and sprawled in a chair across the table. "I've got to find some decent food. Or something female. You see what's happening to me."

I didn't get a chance to put in my farthing's worth. Dojango came ambling in looking like a rooster on parade. He had his hands shoved into his pockets, his shoulders thrown back, and he was strutting.

"Calmly," I cautioned Morley.

Doris and Marsha each had a hide with the look of old, scuffed shoes, but they were grinning, too. Strutting was too much for them. The ceiling was only twelve feet high.

Morley did very well. He asked, "What's up, Dojango?"

"We went out and got in a fight with about twenty sailors. Cleaned up the streets with them."

"Calmly," I told Morley, hanging on to his shoulder.

From the looks of Dojango, compared to his brothers, his part in the fight must have been mostly supervisory.

Morley suggested, "Maybe you'd better tell it from the beginning. Like start with what made you go out there in the first place."

"Oh. We were going down to watch the harbor in case anybody interesting came in. Like the guys on that striped-sail ship or the ones that snatched Garrett's girlfriends, or even the girls themselves."

Morley had the good grace to look abashed. "And?"

"We were headed back here when we ran into the sailors."

Doris—or maybe Marsha—rumbled something. Morley translated. "He says they called them bad names." He kept a straight face. "So. Besides making the streets safe from marauding, name-calling sailors, did you accomplish anything?"

"We saw the striped-sail ship come in. One guy—the one Marsha threw in the drink in Leifmold—got off. He hired a rickshaw. We figured we would be too obvious if we tried to follow him, so we didn't try. But we did get close enough to hear him tell the rickshaw man to take him to the civil city hall."

Full Harbor has two competing administrations, one civil, one military. Their feuding helps keep city life interesting.

"Good work," Morley grouched.

"Worth a beer?" Dojango asked.

Morley looked at me. I shrugged. They were his problem. He said, "All right."

"How about two?"

"What is this? A damned auction?"

Morley and I mounted the rig. He asked, "Where to now, peerless investigator?"

"I figured on hitting the civil city hall next, but Dojango changed my mind. I don't want to run into that guy again if I can help it."

"Your caution is commendable if a bit out of character. Keep an eye peeled for a decent place to eat."

"Get up," I told the horses. "Keep an eye out for a pasture where Morley can graze."

• • •

I don't understand it. We went into the church and there was nothing going on. Every day seems like a holy day of obligation for the Orthodox from what I've seen.

A priest in his twenties with a face that did not yet need shaving asked us, "How may I help you gentlemen?" He was unsettled. We weren't ten feet inside the door, but already we had betrayed ourselves as heathen. We had overlooked some genuflection or something.

Earlier I'd decided to deal straight with the church—without telling everything, of course. I told the priest I was trying to locate the former Kayean Kronk, of his parish, because she had a very large legacy pending in TunFaire. "I thought somebody who works here, or your records, might help me trace her. Can we talk to your boss?"

He winced before he said, "I'll tell him you're here and why. I'll ask if he'll see you."

Morley barely waited until the kid was out of earshot. "If you want to get along with these people, you should at least try to fake the cant."

"How do you do that when you don't have the foggiest what it is?"

"I thought you said you and the gal used to come here for services."

"I'm not a religious guy. I slept through them most of the time. The Venageti must not have made it this far during the invasion."

"Why do you say that?"

"Look at all the gold and silver. There aren't any Orthodox among the Venageti. They would have stripped the place and sent the plunder out on the first courier boat."

The priest came hustling back. "Sair Lojda will give you five minutes to argue your case." As we followed him, he added, "The Sair is accustomed to dealing with unbelievers, but even from them he expects the honor and deference due his rank."

"I'll be sure not to slap him on the back and ask if he wants a beer," I said.

The Sair was the first to ask for my credentials. I made my pitch while he examined them. He did not give us the full five minutes allotted. He interrupted me. "You will have to see Father Rhyne. He was the Kronk family confessor and spiritual adviser. Mike, take these gentlemen to Father Rhyne."

"What are you grinning about?" I asked Morley as soon as we were out of the presence.

"When was the last time you had a priest take less than three hours even to tell you to have a nice day?"

"Oh."

"He was a dried-up little peckerwood, wasn't he?"

"Watch your tongue, Morley."

He was right. The Sair's face had reminded me of a half-spoiled peach that had dried in the desert for six months.

Father Rhyne was a bit remarkable, too. He was about five feet tall, almost as wide, bald as a buzzard's egg, but had enough hair from the ears down to reforest fifty desert craniums. He was naked to the waist and appeared to be doing exercises. I have never seen anyone with so much brush on his face and body.

"Couple of minutes more, men," he said. He went on, sweating puddles.

"All right. Throw me a towel, Mike. Trying to shed a few stone," he told us. "What can I do for you?"

I sang my song again, complete with all the choruses. I wondered if I would run out of bottles of beer on the wall before I picked up Kayean's trail.

He thought for a minute, then said, "Mike, would you get the gentlemen some refreshments? Beer will do for me."

"Me, too," I chirped.

"Ah. Another connoisseur. A gentleman after my own heart."

Morley grumbled something about brewing being an unconscionable waste of grains that could be stone-ground and baked into high-fiber breads that would give thousands the bulk they desperately needed in their diets.

Father Mike and Father Rhyne both looked at him like he was mad. I didn't contradict their suppositions. I told Father Mike, "See if you can't track down a rutabaga. If it doesn't put up too fierce a fight, squeeze it for a pint of blood and bring that to him."

"A glass of cold springwater will be sufficient," Morley said. Coldly. Sufficiently. I decided not to ride him so hard.

Once our guide stepped out, Father Rhyne confessed, "I wanted Mike out of the way for a while. He has a tendency to gossip. You don't want this spread around any more than need be. So you're looking for Kayean Kronk. Why here?"

"The Kronks were a religious family. This was their parish. I know she was married some time ago, but I don't even know her husband's name. It would have been in keeping with her character to have had a big parochial wedding. If she did, and it was here, then the groom's name would be on record."

"She was not married in the church. Not this parish or any other." There was something very odd and ominous about the way he said that.

"Is there any chance you could give me a useful lead or two, either toward her or a member of her family who might be willing to help?"

He eyed me a full half a minute. "You seem like an honest enough fellow, if not entirely forthright. But I expect our trades are a little alike in that respect. You satisfied the Sair, who has the eye of a buzzard when it comes to judging character. I'll help however I can as long as I don't have to violate the sanctity of the confessional."

"All right. How can you help me?"

"I don't know. I can't tell you where to find her."

"Is that privileged knowledge?"

"No. I don't know."

"What about the name of the guy she married?"

"I can't tell you that, either."

"Privileged? Or don't know?"

"Six of one, half dozen of the other."

"All right. I'll worry about getting a dozen out of that later. Can you tell me where I can get in touch with any of her family?"

"No." Before I could ask he raised a staying hand and said, "Ignorance, not privilege. The last I heard of any of the Kronks was about two years ago. Her brother Kayeth had been decorated and brevetted major of cavalry for his part in the victory at Latigo Wells."

Morley stirred just the slightest. Yes, another cavalryman. It might or might not mean something. Kayeth was younger than Kayean, which meant he was younger than Denny and me, which meant their periods of service might not have overlapped at all.

Idiot! They didn't need to overlap for them to have met if Denny was her lover after me.

"Do you recall what unit he was with?"

"No."

"No matter. That should be easy to find out. When was the last time you saw Kayean?"

He had to think about that. I figured he was having trouble remembering. I was wrong. He was debating proprieties. He gave me an exact-to-the-minute time and date slightly more than six years ago, and added, "That is when she ceased to exist in the eyes of the church."

"Huh?"

Morley said, "He means she was excommunicated, Garrett."

Father Rhyne nodded.

"What for?"

"The reasons for excommunication are revealed only to the soul to be banished from grace."

"Wait a minute." I was confused. "Are we talking about the same woman?"

"Take it easy, Garrett," Morley said. "Excommunication don't necessarily mean she turned into some kind of religious desperado. They do you in because you won't let them extort your whole fortune. Or, if you're a woman, because you won't come across."

That was a deliberate provocation. Father Rhyne took it better than I expected. "I have heard that sort of thing happens up north. Not here. This is a church militant, here in this archdiocese. The priest who tried that would find himself staked like a vampire. The reasons for Kayean's excommunication were valid within the laws of the church."

I stepped in before Morley rendered his opinion of laws that judged him to be without a soul and therefore beyond the protection of its golden rules. "That's not really the sort of information that's likely to help me, Father. Unless the reasons for her excommunication have some bearing on where she is now."

Father Rhyne shook his head, but with just enough hesitance to show he was not sure.

"My job, and my only job, is to find the woman so I can tell her she has inherited a hundred thousand marks. Once I tell her, I'm supposed to ask if she wants it. If she does, I'm supposed to escort her to TunFaire because she has to claim it in person. If she doesn't want it, I have to get a legal deposition to that effect so that others down the list can benefit from the legacy. That's it. That's all."

"Nevertheless, you have a personal interest."

Glass Door Garrett, that is what they call me. See right through me. "The guy who died was a good friend of mine. I want to see what kind of woman would get him to leave her everything when he hadn't even seen her for seven years."

A twitch of a smile worked one corner of Rhyne's month. I stopped, confused. Morley said, "In the shadows behind the tombstones."

That did it. Of course. Rhyne had been Kayean's confessor. He'd never say a word, but he remembered sins confessed that included a Marine named Garrett.

"All right. We know where we stand. We know what my job is. I've asked the questions I think are pertinent—and a few that weren't and some that were probably impertinent—and I think you've answered me fairly. Can you think of anything you could volunteer that might be helpful?"

"Hang on a second, Garrett," Morley said. He drifted to the door as soundlessly as a cloud and jerked it open. Father Mike almost fell over.

I'd wondered what had been keeping him.

"Ah! That beer at last!" Father Rhyne had on a big, jovial host's grin, but his eyes were not smiling. "Just put the tray down and go about your duties, Mike. I'll talk to you later."

Father Mike went out looking like he hoped later would never come.

Rhyne chose to pretend that nothing untoward had happened. He poured beer from a monster of a pitcher into enormous earthenware mugs. Morley's water was in a blown-glass tankard of equal size. I'd barely taken my first sip before Father Rhyne parted from his mug and said, "Ahh!" He wiped his mouth with the fur on the back of his forearm, then belched like a young thunderhead. He poured himself a pint chaser.

Before he hoisted it, he said, "What information can I volunteer? I can tell you that you won't find her in Full Harbor. I can tell you to walk very carefully because I can infer, without absolute certitude, that there might be people who wouldn't want you to find her. I can tell you not to look for the image that lives in your memory because you will never find *her*."

I finished my brew. "Thank you. Good beer."

"We make it ourselves. Will there be anything more?"

"No . . . Well, something from off the wall. I've heard her father was murdered. Any comment?"

He got a very evasive look. "It's possible."

His expression told he would clamp his jaws on that cryptic statement. I returned my mug to the tray. Morley followed my lead. He had downed enough water to show he appreciated the stuff in quantities too small to rock a boat. We headed for the door. I said, "Thanks for everything."

"Sure. If you do find her, tell her we haven't stopped loving her, even if we can't forgive her. That might help."

Our gazes locked. And I knew that fat little hairball did not mean "we" at all. I also knew the whole thing was as chaste and courtly as any perfect knight's affection for his lady in an old *roman*. "I'll do that, Father."

"Another one," Morley said when we got outside. "I've got to meet this woman." There was not an ounce of sarcasm in his tone.

•••24

"**A**re we making any headway?" Morley asked as we climbed aboard the rented rig.

"Oh, yes. We've eliminated some legwork, like making the rounds of every Orthodox parish in Full Harbor. We've added a visit to the army office at the military city hall to see if they will help us locate Major Kayeth Kronk."

I did not look forward to that. They'd probably assume we were Venageti spies.

"What now?"

"We can try that. We can try the civil city hall, too, though I don't think we'd get much there. Or we could go back to the inn and I could lie around staring at the ceiling and wondering what a sensible young woman can do to get herself excommunicated."

"That doesn't sound productive. And butting heads with the army, even to get them to tell us to get out and leave them alone, is likely to be an all-day job."

"The civil city hall it is, then."

We were headed up the steps when a voice roared, "Hey! You two."

We stopped, turned. Near the rig stood a city employee, the type who carries weapons and is supposed to protect citizens from their neighbors' villainies, but who spends most of his time force-feeding his purse and sparing the reputations of the wealthy and powerful. "This yours?"

"Yes."

"You can't leave it here. We don't want no horse apples tracked all over the hall."

Despite his friendly way of putting it, his position had merit. I marched down the steps. "Have you a suggestion what I can do with it?"

He did not know who we were. We had come in a fancy rig. We were well dressed. Morley looked a bit like a bodyguard. I wore a look of cherubic innocence. A suspicion slithered through his slow wit. I had handed him that straight line so he would stick his foot in his mouth. Then I would choke him on it.

"We usually ask visitors to leave their conveyances in the courtyard behind the hall, sir. I could move it back there for you, if you like."

"That's very thoughtful of you. I'd appreciate that very much." I dug out a tip about one and a half times the going rate for such a task. Enough to impress, not enough to arouse resentment or suspicion.

"Thank you, sir."

We watched him drive into a narrow passageway between one end of the hall and the city jail.

"Slick, Garrett."

"What?"

"You should have been a con man. You sold him using nothing but intonation, bearing, and gesture. Slick."

"It was an experiment. If he'd had two ounces of brain to rub together, it wouldn't have worked."

"If he had two ounces of brain he'd be making an honest living."

I think Morley's attitude toward so-called civil servants is as cynical as mine.

The next public employee we encountered—on a more than which-way-do-we-go? basis—had two ounces of brains. Just barely.

I was digging through what passed for vital statistics in Full Harbor and finding that four of the Kronk children were not listed at all. Morley, in pursuit of an inspiration of his own, dug through the property plats and brought one over. He sat on the floor reading it.

Two-Ounces appeared out of nowhere and bellowed, "What the hell do you think you're doing?"

"Research," I replied in my reasonable voice.

"Get the hell out of here!"

"Why?" Reasonable again, of course.

That got him for a moment. Both ounces went stumbling after something with more authority than a bottom-rung city flunky's "because I said so."

Morley dealt himself a hand. "These are public records legally open to public inspection."

That left Two-Ounces armed only with bluster because he didn't know for sure. "I'm going to call some guards and have you wise guys thrown out on your asses."

"That won't be necessary." Morley closed the plat book. "No need for a scene. The matter can wait till after you've explained to the judge tomorrow morning."

"Judge? What judge?"

"The judge who's going to ask you why a couple of honest investigators like ourselves, sent down from TunFaire, can't look at documents any vagrant off the streets of Full Harbor has a right to see." He went off to return his plat book.

Two-Ounces stared at me while I neatened up after myself. I think he saw nothing but potential disaster. There is no man so insecure as a bottom-level functionary in a sinecure he has held for a long time. He's done nothing for so long that nothing is all he can do. The prospect of unemployment is a mortal terror.

"Ready?" Morley asked, returning.

"When you are."

"Let's go. See you in the morning, friend."

The man turned slowly to watch us go, his face still drained. But the poison had begun to creep into his eyes. It was the hatred and power greed that make vicious liars out of people who tell you they're public servants.

25

"How'd I do?" Morley asked as we pushed out the front door. He was grinning.

"Not bad. Maybe one slice too much ham."

He wanted to debate but I cut him short. "You learn anything?"

"Not unless you care that the house was sold by Madame Kronk, a decent interval after the date on that memorial obelisk, to a character with the unlikely name of Zeck Zack, for what seems like a reasonable market price. You ever heard of him?"

"No."

"You find out anything?"

"Only that the civil city administration keeps pretty loose track of who's dying and being born."

"Oh. So with those Kronks being prominent, imagine what they've got on ordinary, real folks."

I shrugged. "You leave no stone unturned till you find a trail. Where's that clown who took the carriage?"

"Probably at the nearest swill pit guzzling your tip."

"Then we'll just get it ourselves. We're big boys. We can handle it." We turned into the alley between the hall and the jail. It was clean for a city alley—probably because of where it was—but gloomy because of the hour.

Morley said, "We could probably find a judge we could bribe to back us with that guy."

"I don't think Old Man Tate would buy it when it showed up on my expense sheet."

A large somebody stepped out of the wall a dozen feet ahead. His appearance was vague in that light. Morley said, "Behind you," let out a screech, and flung himself through the air.

I whirled, ducking. Just in time. A club whipped the air where my head had been. I gave the guy a kick in the root of his fantasies, then clipped him on the cheek as he bent to pray. Behind him was a guy who was more surprised than me. I jumped and grabbed his arm, tried giving him a knee. He tried to pull a knife while he stared over my shoulder, a big wad of fear in his eyes.

I figured Morley was about finished behind me.

My man tried to knee me and I tried to knee him again and sometime during our dance he decided he really ought to get the hell out of there. He twisted away and started hiking.

I was satisfied. I turned to check behind me.

Morley's man was out. Morley himself was bent double, holding up a wall, puking his guts out. His man must have gotten in a good one.

My first was down, thrashing and twitching and making disgusting handsaw noises. The light was too poor to be sure, but I thought his color looked bad.

"What did you do to him?" Morley croaked.

"Kicked him."

"Maybe he swallowed his tongue." Morley went down on one knee. He moved gingerly.

The guy finished up with one wild convulsion, then he was done. Literally.

Morley trailed fingertips over the corpse's cheek. One of my rings had cut him. The cut had a nasty color.

I looked at my hand.

So did Morley.

The poison chamber on one of the rings had been torn open by the force of the blow.

"We'll have to get rid of him," Morley said.

"Fast. Before somebody stumbles in here."

"I'll get the rig. You drag them to the side so they don't get run over." He ran away as fast as he could.

I wondered if I would see him again. It might be in his interest to find a back way out and just keep on going.

He returned but it seemed like he'd been gone for about twenty hours. He tied off the traces and clambered into the back of the rig. "Hoist him up here."

I hoisted. Morley pulled. When the cadaver was in, Morley set it up with its back against the driver's seat.

"People will see him."

"You just worry about driving. I'll handle this. I've done it before."

I had done my share of driving that day. Horses and I can enjoy an armed truce while they are in harness. But this was too grand an opportunity for that devil tribe to revert to the war rules. "You'd better handle the traces."

"I'll be busy back here. Get moving before somebody comes or the other one wakes up."

I climbed up and took the traces.

"We're just a bunch of guys out on the town. Don't hurry. But get us out of this section fast."

"Make up your mind!" I snapped. But I knew what he meant.

At first Morley sat back with his arm around his buddy slurring some song so thickly that Garrett could only understand about every third word. Later he started cussing the corpse out, telling him what a fool damned no-good he was for getting blasted before the sun even went down. "You ought to be ashamed of yourself, what am I going to tell your old lady, how're we supposed to have any fun dragging you around? You ought to be ashamed."

Later still, once we were in an area where a bunch of drunks in a carriage were as unusual as eggs under a hen, Morley stopped rambling and asked, "Who were those guys, Garrett? Any idea?"

"No."

"Think it was a robbery?"

"You know better. The place, the timing, the behavior of that clerk, the disappearance of the guard from out front, all say it wasn't."

"Off the striped-sail ship? One of them went to the hall."

"I doubt it. Only a local could set up something like that so fast. We've obviously stepped on a toe somewhere."

"Why?"

"My guess is it was a warning whipping, a Saucerhead job. Pound us around awhile, then tell us to take the next boat home. But we blew up in their hands."

"That's what I figure. Then the real questions are who sent them and why do we make him nervous?"

"Him?"

"I don't think we need to count the Old Witch. Do you?"

"No. Nor the church people, probably. I guess we'll have to find out who Zeck Zack is."

"Too bad we can't ask this guy here."

"You checked him?"

"Dry as a bone. It's time we started thinking about how to break up the party."

"We can't dump him in the drink here. After dark, Marines watch the shores like hawks in case Venageti agents try to sneak in. They never catch anybody, but that doesn't stop them." I did my share of watching in my time. I was very young and very serious about it.

My successors would be just as young and just as serious.

Morley said, "Find the busiest, sleaziest cathouse you can. We go in drunk with him between us. We find a dark corner in the waiting room, squat, order drinks for three, tell the madam not to bother our buddy because he's dead drunk, take our turns at the trade, then get out. They won't bother him till the crowd thins out because they'll want to roll him. By then they'll have forgotten us and he'll be their problem."

"Suppose we run into somebody who knows him?"

"There are risks in everything. If we dump him here in an alley, whoever sent him will know what happened. My way he'll have to wonder. That was blockshaush in the ring, wasn't it?" He used the elvish name for the poison. On our side of the line we call it black sauce.

"Yes."

"Good. By the time his boss finds him it'll be too late for even a master wizard to tell he was poisoned." He sounded very thoughtful. I knew what he was thinking. He was wondering what other uncharacteristic surprises I had in store. He was thinking I was tight with the Dead Man, and that was probably why I was carrying poison. He was wondering just how much and what kind of advice the Dead Man had given me.

I figured a little worry would do him good. It might take his mind off his stomach for a while.

We ditched our friend Morley's way. I expected tribes of his buddies to swarm, but it came off smooth. The guy's boss would never really know what had happened.

Who *was* his boss? Why did he want to discourage me from doing my job?

packed a lunch, knowing it would be a long day of runaround at the military city hall. Because they would not let Morley in, I told him to go find out what he could about Zeck Zack. The triplets I sent to watch incoming harbor traffic again.

"But be careful," I told Dojango. "They might decide to take you in to ask if you're Venageti spies."

"Actually, that possibility occurred to us yesterday," Dojango told me. "We've lived on the fringes of the law long enough to know when we're pushing our luck."

Maybe so. Maybe so.

I hefted my picnic basket and went to work.

First there was a clerk, then a senior clerk, then various sergeants followed by a couple of lieutenants who gave me to a captain who admitted he did not think I would have much luck before he dropped me in the lap of a major. One and all checked my bona fides before sending me on. Sometimes twice.

I kept a smile on my mug, stayed polite, and kept my tongue on a tight rein. I could play the game.

I figured I would earn every mark I would gouge from Tate for that day. Besides, it was all part of the plan.

Outlast the bastards.

The major was halfway human, and he even looked like he might have a sense of humor. He apologized for the shuffle and I offered to share my lunch.

"You packed a lunch?"

"Sure. I've dealt with the army before. If it was something complicated, I would have brought a blanket and an overnight bag. You get in the craw of the system and stay there, disturbing routine, somebody is going to go out on a limb, take a chance, tell you what you want to know or make a decision to throw you out, just to get you out from underfoot. I get paid exorbitantly for letting people give me the runaround, so I don't mind."

For a moment I thought I had misjudged him. He was not pleased. Knee-jerk response. Give him credit. He gave it a think before he came back. "You're a cynic, aren't you?"

"Occupational hazard. The people I meet leave my faith in human nature mostly negative."

"Right. Let's try again, with the understanding that I'll be the man who ends your quest with an answer or by having you booted out. You want?"

"Some way of getting in touch with Major Kayeth Kronk, cavalryman, the only one of the woman's family of whom I have been able to catch wind. I want to ask if he knows where I can get in touch with his sister. The simple, obvious thing for the army to do is tell me he's out at Fort Whatever. I'd go interview him. But it won't work that way. The army will act on the perfectly reasonable assumption that the entire Venageti War Council has been holding its collective breath for years, waiting to discover the major's whereabouts. So any communications will have to be managed the hard way."

"You are a cynic."

"I'm also right. Not so?"

"Probably. What's your hard way?"

"I write him a long letter explaining the situation and asking him to meet me here or, if that's impossible, to respond to a list of questions. The weakness of the method is that I end up having to trust the army both to deliver the letter and to get the reply back to me. My cynical side tells me that that's too much to expect."

He looked at me from a face of stone. He knew I was setting him up for something and was trying to figure out how I was boxing him in. "That's probably the best you'll get. If that. It isn't the army's problem. But we do help with family matters where we can."

"Any help I get will be appreciated. Even if it isn't much help."

He had not figured any angles yet, which might mean that he did not know how a headquarters really worked. "I'll check with my boss. You check with me tomorrow morning. Just to be safe, bring your letter with you, unsealed but ready to go."

That took care of the aboveboard.

I figured I'd been around long enough—and had explained my problem to enough people—for the word to have spread throughout the headquarters. So I thanked the major, shook his hand, and said I would be heading back to my inn. Did he want to keep the rest of the lunch?

No.

I dawdled through hallways. I loitered in corners. Finally, he found me. *He* being the first staffer to convince himself that I was not a Venageti agent, and therefore safe, and therefore maybe he could pick up a small gratuity by telling me where I could find the man I wanted.

That had been the whole point of taking the runaround.

"Fort Caprice?" I asked back. He nodded. I crossed his palm with silver. We both got out of there.

I went off disappointed. Major Kronk did not, at least now, belong to the same outfit that Denny and his buddies had.

Dojango and his brothers got back to the inn before I did. When I arrived they were eating like they meant to use up my expense money before the end of the week.

Dojango reported, "Nothing to report, actually. Nothing came in today. But we did bribe a piermaster to let us go down there mornings and wait for the rest of our family to arrive. Quite a coup, I thought, actually."

"Quite a coup," I agreed. I forbore asking where they had gotten the wherewithal to grease a piermaster. Nothing about those boys was going to surprise me anymore.

And I have yet to report half their tricks.

Morley wandered in an hour after I did. "Any luck, Garrett?"

"I found out where her brother is stationed. You?"

"Some."

"Zeck Zack?"

"An interesting character. Nothing secretive about him, supposedly. Everybody knows him. Nothing obvious to connect him with your Kronk people. He's a centaur, an auxiliary veteran who was given citizenship for his service. He's some sort of middleman between the centaur tribes and the merchants of Full Harbor. The darkest rumor about him is that he indulges in a little night trading. He likes to play with human women. The bigger and fatter, the better."

"Can't hang a guy for that," I said, demonstrating my vast tolerance.

"Lucky me."

As proven by the prevalence of accidents like Morley and his buddies, cross-race contact is a sport too popular for us to go lynching the players.

Morley went on, "He does own the house, but he's never there because he's never in the city."

"But there's more."

"Oh?"

"You have a gleam in your eye."

"Probably because I finally found a decent place to eat and got a wholesome meal inside me."

"No. It's more an 'I know something you don't' kind of gleam."

"You've got me." But he sat on it till I threatened to take him for a boat ride.

"All right. Yesterday somebody decided we were too snoopy and deserved a thumping. Had those guys onto us before we started. We bumped a sore tooth somewhere. Unless our friends from the striped-sail ship were behind it."

"Or Vasco is in town without us knowing it," I added.

"That, too. But I thought I'd start with the folks we'd talked to. The down-lane neighbor and Old Witch: no chance. The guy at Zeck Zack's: surly as hell, no help, maybe, but I couldn't be sure. I bribed the vermin to keep an eye on the place. So?"

"Come on! You went to the church?"

"I asked around before I dropped in. You remember what you said about the gold and silver?"

"Yes."

"That church was inside Venageti lines for thirteen days. Afterward, the Sair was praised for talking the Venageti into sparing the church. Then he and his flock talked the army into releasing a hundred twenty prisoners of war as a counter gesture. Everyone thinks he's a great man, full of compassion for the enemies of his church."

I already knew, but he wanted me to ask. So I did. "But you know different, eh? What do you know, Morley?"

"A third of those soldiers he sent home, all supposedly common infantry, were Venageti officers who could have been ransomed or put to the question. They surrendered at the church after exchanging uniforms with dead soldiers. At the order of the chief Venageti undercover agent in Full Harbor."

"The Sair?"

"You got it."

"You go on like you were there."

"I talked to somebody who was."

I raised an eyebrow. I do that very well. It's one of my outstanding talents.

"I took Father Mike for a walk. After I assured him that I have no interest in politics, and would not use what he told me against him, he told me about it. He's the old boy's helper."

"Are all the priests in on it?"

"Just the two. The old boy sent the others to safety when the Venageti began closing in. I guess you can figure why."

"Fewer witnesses. So the old boy sicced the dogs on us because he thought we might dig something up on him."

"No."

"Wait a minute . . ."

"Father Mike was very positive."

"Who, then, if you eliminate everybody?"

"Always room for another player in the game. I didn't get to talk to the hairy priest. Nor to anybody the others mentioned us to, and everybody admitted they did, though they couldn't remember to who—except that crazy witch. And at her place we had the vermin listening in. There's no telling who *they* reported to."

"Yeah." This needed some thought. "You've still got the gleam in your eye. You must have gotten around like a bolt of lightning."

"Us breeds can move when we need to. Hybrid vigor."

"So?"

"Your friend Kronk died at that church the day it was liberated. Father Mike was vague about details. Kronk was one of the dozen partisans the Venageti took prisoner. Father Mike didn't think he knew about him and the Sair, but he could have. He doesn't think Kronk was killed while the Venageti were still in control. The body wasn't found till six hours after the army moved in. But two others died at the same time. I have the names of the surviving prisoners if you decide to go howling off down that path."

"That's not what I'm here to do. But give me the names and we'll keep them in mind. In case we keep stumbling over some of them. I see the gleam has gone out. Does that mean the well is dry?"

"Yes. What now?"

"Now I write a long letter to Major Kronk for another major's benefit, while all this information simmers."

"Marinates, you mean. I'm sure you'll soak your brain in a few gallons of beer."

I did not feel up to repartee. Too much to digest. "Tomorrow morning I see my major. Then we do a few more interviews. If we don't strike something hot, the day after we're off into the Cantard."

"Maybe we can bribe a priest to pray for a break," Morley said. "I'm here, but I'm not thrilled about going out there."

"And I am?"

here were breaks. They were mixed to say the least.

    I went to see my major right after I breakfasted, three eggs gently fried in the grease of a half pound of bacon slowly cooked to a crisp, a mountain of griddle cakes on the side, heavily buttered and buried in strawberry jam. Morley was despondent. He began holding a wake for my health.

He went out when I did, on the trail of roots and berries, barks and grasses, that would hold still long enough for him to prey upon them.

The triplets headed for the waterfront to wait for their relatives. I sincerely hoped they had none anywhere. I figured my luck was running so hot a platoon would descend on me like orphans left on the church steps.

I didn't have to wait long or put up with much before I was told I could see the major. My outlook began to improve.

The major took my message after a rudimentary greeting, checked it for messages to the Venageti War Council, said, "This looks acceptable. It will go out in the next courier pouch headed the right direction."

"Not going to test for invisible ink?"

He gave me one of those good hard stares they practice in front of the mirror when they're shavetails. I let it slide off. "You're cocky today, aren't you?"

"It's a personality defect. I spent five years on the inside of the service. It's hard to take it seriously when it doesn't have a noose around your neck."

"Do you really care if your letter gets delivered?"

I didn't tell him I never expected it to get beyond the nearest trash receptacle. He gave me a reassuring pat on the shoulder and said, "Don't bother us anymore. We'll let you know when there's an answer." I couldn't tell him I'd brought it in only for form's sake.

But he could figure that out for himself.

"I see that you don't care about this letter. Someone on the staff obviously took pity and told you. For a suitably warm expression of gratitude."

I remained silent.

"I see," he said. "I thought so. You needn't be surprised. Not only can a few of us think, there're some—mostly majors and colonels—who can figure out how to lace their own boots in the morning. But I won't ask you about it if you'll answer a few questions about something else."

"Why?"

"Say I'm looking for a fresh viewpoint on something."

"Shoot."

"I'll start with a list of names. When you hear one you know, tell me what you know about him or her."

"That's all?"

"For now."

"Go ahead."

I scored three and a half out of maybe thirty. One was Zeck Zack. One was a Venageti commander my outfit had fought in the islands who later participated in the attack upon Full Harbor. The third was a dwarfish sharpie who had been executed for misappropriation, fraud, and profiteering, which basically meant he had gotten caught stealing from the army without paying kickbacks to the right officers. The half was a name I knew I had heard somewhere sometime but could not remember where or when or in connection with what. As far as I knew, Zeck Zack was the only character there who was still alive.

I lied about recognizing one more name, that of a man who had been imprisoned with Klaus Kronk the day he had died.

"Is that all?" I could see no connection among the names on the list. Maybe there was none, really. Or maybe it would have been obvious to someone who knew who the hell all those people were.

"Just about. You seem to be what you pretend. You've been doing a lot of poking around. Have you stumbled across anything that might interest a man in my position?" He assumed I knew what his position was. I did, now.

"No," I lied. I had figured to do my patriotic duty by reporting the Sair. Sometime after arriving I had made an unconscious decision to pass.

"Would you consider doing a little work for Karenta while you're doing the job you have already? Wouldn't cost you much time and shouldn't take you out of your way."

"No."

He looked like he wanted to argue.

"I did my so-called patriotic chore," I declared. "Five years of my life making sure their gang of thieves didn't get one up on our gang of thieves. There is no way I'm getting onto that treadmill again."

A thought occurred to me. That happens occasionally. He saw it spark.

"Yes?"

"I might work a trade." I had the priest to sell. "If you tell me where to find Kayean Kronk."

"I can't."

"Oh?"

"I never heard of her till you came in yesterday. She's no one who's ever interested this office."

"I guess that's that, then. Thanks for your time and courtesy." I headed for the door.

"Garrett. Drop by when you get back from Fort . . ." He glared at me like I'd almost tricked him into revealing the Emperor's secret name. "Drop by when you get back. We may have a story or two to swap."

"All right."

I got out before he decided to look at me a little closer.

It was too nice a morning just to head for the inn to pick up Morley so we could visit the civil city hall again. It seemed a day made for lying around sniffing a clean sea breeze. I headed for the waterfront.

The triplets probably needed help watching for their relatives, anyway. They would be so hard to spot.

I found them doing exactly what I planned to do, sprawled in the sun atop a mountain of army grain sacks awaiting transport to the forts in the Cantard. I'd never have spotted them from the harborside. I clambered up with a cold keg under my arm. I sent it around once before I asked, "How's it going, Dojango? Any sign of the family?"

The keg was half weight by the time it got back to me. I took a good long guzzle before I passed it on.

"Actually, Garrett, your timing is perfect. Come here." He drew on the keg before he moved.

They had shifted a few sacks so they formed a parapet of sorts. They could watch from concealment yet could claim the shifted sacks made pillows for the grolls if anybody asked.

"Some of your cousins, I think."

"Actually."

A ragged old coaster lay about thirty feet in the lee of the only pier space available. Lee was the very operative word. The ship was taking the breeze on her beam. About fifty guys were pulling on hawsers, trying to haul her in.

She was not coming.

In fact, she was winning the tug-of-war.

"Why don't I go trade this empty in on a full keg?" Dojango asked.

"Yeah. Why don't you?" I gave him some money.

A guy could work up a powerful thirst watching that much grunting and cursing and sweating and yelling for help.

The ship was interesting because Vasco, Quinn, and some other old friends were stomping around her deck in a storm of frustration.

I thought about canceling Fort Caprice and just watching them instead, on the chance they would lead me to Kayean. I looked at that from a couple of angles, then rejected it. They had not come to Full Harbor to see Kayean. They had come to keep me from seeing her.

I studied the striped-sail for a while. It seemed deserted except for the short and wide thing, who was napping in the shade cast by the low sterncastle. Dojango arrived with the keg. We soon had another dead soldier. Dojango ventured the suggestion that we send for reinforcements again.

"I sadly fear we have to go to work. Do your cousins know your brothers?"

"Not by sight, actually. But they must know you're traveling with grolls."

"They aren't the only grolls in the world." I stripped down while I explained what I wanted to do.

"I think it's insane, actually. But it might be fun to watch." His part would be to observe and guard the valuables.

"Tell the boys."

Below, a gust caught the coaster. She heeled. Men yelled. Four or five went into the water.

"They know what to do."

"Let's go." I tumbled down the front of the pile. Doris and Marsha tumbled after me, grinning their great goofy groll grins. They trotted to the ends of a couple of hawsers and started heaving. I grabbed another. I wish I could say my strength made the difference.

That coaster fought like a granddaddy trout, but in she came.

Vasco and Quinn must have gotten my stage directions. They spotted me as the dockhands started swarming around Doris and Marsha, trying to slap their backs. Somebody yelled. I faked big eyes as men came leaping onto the wharf.

I lit out.

I did not see Dojango atop the sack pile as I raced past. That meant nothing had changed at the striped-sail ship. I whipped that way with a herd of boots pounding behind me.

Hard right turn onto the yacht's gangway.

Short, Wide, and Hideous opened his eyes and hit his feet. I made the deck before he could head me off. Then he spotted the pack behind me.

He stopped.

I did not. I pulled straight ahead and dove over the far rail. I groaned on the way down.

The water was so slimy I'd be lucky if I didn't bounce.

We joined up again back at the inn. After I ordered a keg to celebrate, Dojango told me what he had seen.

Vasco, Quinn, and four others had chased me. That I did not need to be told. They had started up the gangway when they had spotted Short, Wide, and Hideous. They had stopped dead. Then they had scattered like roaches surprised by a sudden light.

"They didn't even go back to their boat for their stuff," Dojango said. He laughed and drew himself another beer.

"What about the guy on the yacht? What did he do?"

"He ran inside."

"And?"

"And nothing, actually. Nothing happened at all."

"Something will," I prophesied.

We killed the keg while we waited for Morley.

28

Morley was a long time showing. When he did, I knew he had not been running *from* anything—unless it was himself. He wasn't scared of anything else.

"A little trot to settle your meal?" I asked.

"Started out that way. I came back here, you weren't in yet, so I thought I'd get in five or ten miles while I had time. I've gotten out of training since we left TunFaire."

He seemed a little pallid for Morley Dotes. "Something happen? You get yourself into trouble?"

"Not exactly. Let me catch my breath. Tell me what you did."

I did. He seemed mildly amused by my gambit on the waterfront.

"Your turn," I said.

"First a conclusion, then two sets of facts which may support it. My conclusion is, you're in over your head, Garrett. We keep cutting the trails of people with big clout. And they're starting to notice."

"And the facts?"

"My run took me out near the Narrows. I decided to see if my tribute to the vermin had earned me anything but scorn. Wonder of wonders, they had something. Zeck Zack is back in town. He arrived early this morning. The comings and goings started an hour later. I gave them a bonus and told them to keep an eye on him."

"One set of facts, Morley. How about the set that has you spooked?"

He did not argue, which was proof enough that he was nervous.

"I decided to drop in on Father Rhyne. I figured I'd go in the back way so I wouldn't inconvenience anybody, what with a rowdy service going on in the main hall."

He was stalling getting to the point, which meant it was something that did not please him.

"He came up dead, Garrett. Sitting at his writing table, dead as a man can get, still not cold."

"Killed?"

"I don't know. I didn't see any wounds, but that leaves plenty of room."

Plenty of room for sorcery or poison.

"He didn't seem like the kind of guy who drops dead coincidentally after people come around asking questions that only he can answer. Especially when you consider the fact that his boss and Father Mike have turned ghost."

He meant they had vanished. "When?"

"Sometime after breakfast. The prune was at first services. Father Mike was at breakfast. When I mentioned to somebody that Father Rhyne didn't look too healthy neither of them could be found. Nobody saw them leave."

"Maybe they decided they couldn't trust you not to be a tattletale."

"Maybe. Father Rhyne did try to leave a message, however he died. I don't know who he meant it for, but since you're looking for a married woman, I grabbed it."

He gave me a wad of paper. I smoothed it out on the table. There were just two words on it, printed big in a very shaky hand.

BLOOD WEDDING

"Blood wedding? What does that mean?"

"I don't know, Garrett. I do know this. Rhyne was number four. They're dropping like flies around us."

He was right. Four deaths. Three of them on the manslaughter level: the burglar in Denny's apartment, Uncle Lester, and the thug from the alley beside the civil city hall. And now one unexplained. "It does seem that way."

"Any change in plans?"

"No. Let's go see the boys at city hall."

Inspired by a silver memory-jostle, the guard outside frankly admitted that he had been paid to disappear for an hour. He gave us an excellent description of an ordinary guy who could have been right there on the street with us. I suspected he was the guy who had gotten away in the alley.

The clerk was not pleased to see us. In fact, he tried to take a sudden, unauthorized leave of absence. Morley was on him like a wolf on a rabbit. We took the committee into the records room to confer.

He claimed almost as much ignorance as the guard. But he said they had come to see him again a while after we busted up the ambush to ask about us. The clerk said they talked it over and decided we were not the people they had expected, confederates of a man who had been there earlier. They had jumped the wrong people.

So who the hell were we?

The words *investigators from TunFaire* had done nothing to cheer them up.

We turned him loose, then, and headed for the inn.

"He wasn't coming across with everything," I said.

"He's on somebody's pad. He's more scared of them than he ever could be of us."

29

W e roomed in what could hardly be classified as a room. It was a converted stable attached to the inn. It was not elegant, which was why we spent a lot of time in the common room. We took it because it was the only place the grolls could quarter comfortably.

That night we retreated there earlier than usual, none of us being in the mood for the jostle of the evening trade, when all the neighbors came to guzzle and swap lies. Besides, I wanted to get an early start in the morning.

I still had to turn the carriage in and pick up mounts.

The rest of our outfitting we had managed to get in whenever we were not off chasing chimeras.

It looked like a quiet evening. Not even Dojango felt much like talking. He had a hangover and Morley wouldn't let him near any hair of the dog.

Breeds just don't handle their alcohol well.

A subtle change in the roar from the common room caught my ear, though I couldn't pin down exactly what it was. Morley caught it, too. He cocked an ear, frowned. "Dojango, see what's happening."

Dojango went out. He was back in about four blinks. "Six guys rousting the innkeeper. They want you and Garrett, actually. They look plenty bad, too, Morley."

Morley grunted. Then he grumbled and growled and snarled and barked in grollish. Doris and Marsha sat down on either side of the door, several feet away. Dojango came over and got behind Morley. Morley told me, "Let's get as far from the door as we can. Give them plenty of room to come in if they come."

The grolls' skins began changing color. They faded into the landscape.

"I didn't know they could do that."

"They don't brag about it. Ready, Dojango?"

"I need a drink, actually. I need one bad, actually."

"You'll be all right."

Ka-boom! The door exploded inward and a couple of Saucerhead Tharpe types came mincing after it. Their fearless leader followed. A rear guard of three more muscle wads came in after him. The storm troops spread out so the boss could eyeball us from between them.

He stopped.

He didn't like what he saw.

We were waiting for him.

Morley said a few words. Doris and Marsha growled back. Our guests looked around. One of them said, "Oh, shit."

Morley smiled at the head invader and asked, "Shall we go ahead with it, then?"

"Uh . . . we just dropped in to deliver a message."

"How thoughtful," I said. "What was it, so long you each had to memorize a whole word? And don't you guys find all that wood and iron a little encumbering?"

"The streets aren't safe at night."

"I'll bet they aren't. It isn't that safe inside some places, either."

"Don't overdo it," Morley told me.

"What's the message?"

"I doubt there's much point my delivering it, considering the circumstances."

"But I insist. Here I am visiting a strange city, where I didn't think I knew anyone, and someone is sending me greetings. It's exciting, and I'm curious. Dojango, go get a keg and some mugs so we can entertain properly."

Dojango gave our visitors a wide berth leaving. They did nothing after he left. I guess the shift in odds wasn't encouraging.

I rescued a small philter packet from my duffel. "What was that message again?"

The voice seemed small for the man when he said, "Get out of Full Harbor. If I have cause to get in touch with you again, you're dead."

"That's not what I'd call neighborly. And he doesn't bother to say who he is or why he's concerned for my health. Or even if I've done something to offend."

He began to simmer despite the situation. Morley was right. A slice too much.

Dojango came with the keg and mugs.

"Tap it. Friend, I'd like to talk to a man so interested in me he'd send you around. Just to find out why, if nothing else. Who sent you?"

He set his jaw. I'd expected that. I opened the packet I'd gotten and tapped bits of its contents into the heads of the beers Dojango drew. "This is a harmless spice guaranteed to put an elephant out for ten hours and a man for twenty-four." I gestured.

Dojango got hold of his nerve and took a mug to a man near one of the grolls. The thug refused to take it. Morley barked something. Marsha—or Doris—snagged man and mug and put the contents of one inside the other with less trouble than a mother getting milk down a toddler. Then he stripped the thug to the altogether and tossed him out our only window.

If the man had any sense at all, he would get himself hidden fast, before the drug took hold. Folks in Full Harbor have very strong feelings about public nudity. Caught, he could end up spending the rest of his life in the Cantard mines.

The rest of the muscle decided it was time to go. The other groll held the door until his brother came to help. After things settled down, I asked, "Who sent you?"

"You're a dead man."

"A thought which will comfort and warm you during those long nights in the mines." I gave Dojango another mug. This time the other groll took a turn feeding baby. "I keep going till I get that name. You're last. If I have to do you, you get a short dose. Just enough to make you forget who and where you are, but not enough to put you down so you don't go wandering into trouble."

"For heaven's sake, Switz," one of the thugs said as I handed Dojango another mug. "We aren't getting paid enough for this. He's got us by the balls."

"Shut up."

Another said, "You ain't going to see me in no mines."

"Shut up. It can be fixed."

"Bull. You know damned well he wouldn't bother. He'd say we deserved it. He don't have that kind of pull, anyway."

"Shut up."

One of the grolls snagged the loudest complainer.

"Wait a goddamned minute!" he yelled at me. "It was Zeck Zack that sent us."

I was startled. I made use of my reaction. "Who the hell is Zeck Zack?"

Fearless leader groaned.

Morley gestured. The grolls put our man down but did not turn him loose. I said, "We won't be sending the rest of you after all. But I'm still going to need you sleeping. Set yourselves down someplace comfortable. We'll serve up the brew."

The leader said, "You're dead meat, Trask."

"I bet I'll last longer than you," the other thug replied.

While they bickered I got everything settled. I got the three to drink their beer. We settled back for a listen to our songbird.

"One thing," he said. "The first guy you threw out. He's my brother. You get him back in here or I don't say nothing."

"Morley?"

Morley sent Dojango and Doris.

Trask was able to tell us almost nothing we didn't already know. He had no idea why Zeck Zack wanted us thumped and run out of town. He had not seen the centaur. Only Switz saw or heard from Zeck Zack. He didn't know if the centaur was in town or not. Probably not, because he almost never was.

I asked a lot of questions and got almost nothing more. Zeck Zack shielded his infantry from troublesome knowledge about himself.

"You kept your part of the bargain, with one proviso that benefited your brother." The brother was back inside and redressed, sloppily. "So I'll keep mine, with a proviso that will benefit me. Dojango is going to tie you up just tightly enough so it will take you a couple of hours to get loose. When you do, take your brother and get lost."

Dojango did the honors. He had been sneaking some off the keg and was getting braver by the minute.

"Not bad for improvisation," Morley said.

"Yeah. Thought so myself."

"What now?"

"We strip the other three and dump them where they're sure to get got, then we go see a centaur named Zeck Zack."

Morley didn't like it, but he went along. He was making top money and staying out of the hands of his creditors, and what more could a guy want? Cabbages and cattail hearts?

Morley led the way down the old path from the cemetery to the house. I knew the trail but he had the night eyes. Each fifty paces he stopped and asked the darkness, "Hornbuckle?"

He didn't get an answer until we neared the waking radius of the peafowl.

I was amazed by the grolls. For all their height and mass, they moved through the woods with more stealth than a human.

"Sit," Morley said when tittering answered him at last.

We sat.

Diminutive forms pranced around and among us. Morley gave each a piece of sugar candy, the most certain bribe there is. They wanted more. He promised it. If . . . They scattered to do our scouting for us.

I'll bet Morley hated himself. He certainly looked disgusted as he tucked the rest of the candy inside his shirt.

I asked, "Can we trust them?"

"Not much. But they want the rest of the candy. I don't plan to run out till we're on our way again."

After that we stayed quiet, waiting. I got itchy between the shoulder blades, that feeling you get when someone is watching. Or you think someone is.

That scalawag Hornbuckle flipped Morley a mock salute.

"How many?"

"Four. Two humans. Very nervous. One centaur. Worried and grumpy. One *other*. They're awaiting a report from someone and that someone is late. Sugar?"

"Not yet. Are there wardspells? Alarms? Booby traps? Dangerous guard animals?"

"None."

"Any reason for us to fear?"

"They are wicked creatures. All."

"Silence the peafowl so we can pass."

"Sugar?"

"All the sugar I have when we come out."

"You might not get out."

"Why not?"

Titter. "They are wicked creatures. Very wicked. Especially one."

"All right." Morley took out his candy. "One piece for you. A half piece for each of your friends. The rest if we come out. Tell me the best way to get to them."

Their boy Switz did it to us, so we did it to them.

Kaboom! One groll after another went through the huge double doors of the ballroom. Then Morley. Then me. Then Dojango to guard our rear.

It was thoughtful of them to have waited in the only room where the grolls would have space to maneuver. The ceilings were eighteen feet high.

They scattered like squeaking mice when the cat pounces.

Doris and Marsha each snagged a man. Morley streaked between them, pursuing a shadowy something that crashed through a window at the far end of the ballroom.

Where the hell was the centaur?

There he was, a one-critter cavalry charge. I managed a leg whip that tangled some fetlocks or forelocks or whatever they're called. It was a sin, what his hooves did to the carpets and flooring.

Impetus flung me against something made of mahogany or teak, very hard and very immovable. I practiced exhaling a bushel more air than any human being normally inhales. Somebody was hollering.

"Help, Morley! I got him, Morley! Help!"

I staggered to my feet.

Dojango had him all right.

Zeck Zack was about average for his tribe, about the size of a small pony. He was not built to carry a hundred thirty pounds of Dojango on his back.

His problem was complicated by Dojango having his arms and legs wrapped around his skinny chest. He couldn't breathe. He staggered around, banging into things, then went down on his knees.

I got a choke rope on him, pried Dojango loose, then looked around.

The grolls had their men subdued. Morley was coming back from the window empty-handed and looking puzzled.

I caught my breath, straightened my clothing, and led Zeck Zack into a better light, where Morley patted him down for hardware and other lethal surprises. The centaur remained glassy-eyed.

"What happened?" I asked Morley.

"I don't know. I got there three seconds after it went through the glass. And there was nothing. Not a sign of it."

"What was it?"

"I can't even tell you that. I never got a good look."

The grolls brought the two men over and plunked them down on the floor. They were in a playful mood after events at the inn. They had plucked these birds, too.

"Did you see me, Morley?" Dojango bubbled. "Did you see me? I mean, actually, I took the damned thing down. Did you see me, Morley?"

"Yes. I saw. Shut up, Dojango."

Morley seemed troubled.

He kept looking toward the broken window.

"Well, you've got him, Garrett. Are you going to do something with him?"

"Yeah. All right." I looked at Zeck Zack. "I have a problem, Mr. Zeck." Centaurs stick their family names up front, figuring their antecedents are more important. "People keep trying to whip me and I can't figure out why."

Zeck Zack had nothing to say. He'd heard me, though.

"All right. I'm going to tell you a story. Then you can tell me one. If I like yours we can part as friends."

Still no reaction. I had a feeling Zeck Zack was tough, and had been through the narrow passage before. He was cool enough. He would do what had to be done.

"Once upon a time up north a guy died. He left everything to a gal he knew when he was in the army. His father hired me to come find her and see if she wanted the legacy. A simple job. A kind I do all the time. Only this time I get people ambushing me and sending thugs to work me over, and nobody anywhere giving me a straight answer. So you might say I'm a little fussed."

I gave him a chance to comment. He did not. I hadn't thought he would.

"People are trying to push me. So now I'm pushing back. I'm asking questions. I want answers. What's with this woman Kayean that's worth knocking heads?"

He had nothing to say.

"What's in this to die for? Are you ready to die for it?"

I got a reaction that time. Just a flicker around the eyes. He didn't think I looked the killer type. But he didn't know me so couldn't be sure.

"He's starting to listen, Garrett," Morley said. "But we ought to convene this somewhere else. The one that got away could bring reinforcements."

"I have faith in sugar as an alarm potential. You know anything about centaurs? I've never dealt with one."

"A little. They're vain, avaricious, mean in most senses of the word, miserly. Overall, not much to recommend. Did I mention that most of them are thieves and liars?"

"Where are their pressure points?"

"Did I mention cowardly? You're on the right track with that rope. Strangle him slowly. He'll come across."

"I don't want to do it the hard way. Nobody's been hurt yet. I'd rather talk, work something out where we could get off each other's backs, and get on with finding the woman. I'm tired of this job. Too many people are interested in us and I don't know why."

Zeck Zack sort of nibbled at the bait. He spoke for the first time, piping. I almost laughed at his voice. "Can you prove you're what you say you are? If you were nothing more, there would be no difficulty between us."

A wedge!

Morley told Dojango, "Tie up those guys so Doris and Marsha can have their hands free." One of the two was the greeter who had thought we were hilarious gagsters. He looked the worse for wear.

The grolls helped form a circle around Zeck Zack once they were free of their babysitting chores. I handed over every piece of documentation I had. He examined it all minutely. Meanwhile, Morley got antsy.

Zeck Zack said, "This is all silly enough to be true. I'll give you the benefit of the doubt. For the moment."

Morley said, "Garrett, we're running out of time. Choke him."

"That would do you no good," Zeck Zack said. "I might tell you many interesting things but I would tell you nothing of value. My position is exposed. Therefore, I am allowed to know nothing of importance. However, I do know one thing of value to you. If you are what you say you are."

I waited.

"I know someone who knows someone who could bring you face-to-face with the woman."

"Yeah?"

"Did I mention treacherous?" Morley asked.

"One more test, of sorts," Zeck Zack said. "I will recite a list of names, phrases, places. You tell me if you know or have heard of them. I have an ear for the truth."

I've lied successfully to men who thought that. Many times. "Go ahead."

I scored a mere one half on this one. The same half I scored on the army list. Zeck Zack was amazed by what he heard with his ear for the truth. "You could just be what you say." He gave me a squint-eyed look. "Yes. It might even make sense . . . I think I know what is happening. It should be put to the test."

He did some thinking. The rest of us did some waiting, Morley with very poor grace.

Zeck Zack asked, "Where can I leave you a message?"

I used my best raised eyebrow.

"Not trusting me, you will, of course, remove from your present lodgings. I will not possess sufficient manpower to locate you again quickly. I am going to attempt to arrange for you to see the woman and complete your mission. If I am successful, I must be able to get that word to you."

I had a strong feeling he meant to do just what he said, though not out of any inclination to make my life easier. He had motives I couldn't fathom. Everyone but me seemed to have shadowed motives.

"The innkeeper where we're staying now. We'll leave him feeling kindly toward us." I removed the choke rope. "I'm going to play a hunch, a long shot, and take a chance on you, centaur. Maybe because I'm getting desperate. If you've been bullshitting me to get your behind out of a bind, or if you're planning on taking another crack at me, you have a problem."

"Indeed I do. As I said, I am exposed. And vulnerable, as you have demonstrated tonight."

I thought I would leave everything on that very unsatisfactory note.

Morley, who had been eager to evacuate some time ago, now jumped all over me for wasting half a night.

"Come on, Morley. It's time to go."

31

We sat on a patch of grass not far from the witch's house, surrounded by little folk stoned on sugar. Only a couple were sober enough to titter occasionally.

Morley had turned from argumentative to reflective. "You know what made it interesting, Garrett? That list. Sixteen items. But six of them were the same thing: a name, translated into six different languages. Curious. Especially because it isn't a name either of us recognizes in any of its forms."

"What was that?"

He rattled off a jawbreaker. "I'd give you the Karentine, but it wouldn't make any sense."

"Try it anyway. Karentine is all I speak."

"There're two possible translations. Dawn of Night's Mercy. Or Dawn of Night's Madness."

"That doesn't make sense."

"I told you it wouldn't."

"What language uses the same word for *mercy* and *madness*?"

"Dark elfin."

"Oh," I glanced toward the centaur's house. Not a thing had happened since our departure. I looked at the witch's place. A light burned in an upper-story window. It hadn't been burning when we'd come down the path. "Why don't you guys head on up to the cemetery? I'll catch up in a few minutes. There's something I want to check out."

I expected Morley to give me an argument. He didn't. He just grunted, got to his feet, got the triplets moving, and vanished into the night.

Somebody small with a man-sized grin had passed out leaning against me. I tilted him over gently, patted his shoulder when he mumbled something, rose, and headed for the house. I prowled around looking into windows.

"I'm up here, Private Garrett."

"Good. I was hoping to see you. But I was a little leery of waking you." I couldn't see her.

She laughed. Her laughter was mostly merriment, but it also carried a trace of mockery. She didn't believe me. But she knew I didn't expect her to.

"How can I help you, Private Garrett?"

"You could start by not calling me Private Garrett. I'm out of the Marines. I'd just as soon forget them. Then you can tell me if you know anything about somebody named Dawn of Night's Mercy or Dawn of Night's Madness."

She was silent so long I feared she had deserted me. Then she threw down the dark elvish *gobblewhat* Morley had used, applying a distinctly interrogative inflection.

"That's right."

"*Gobblewhat* is not a person, Mr. Garrett. It is a prophecy, and an unpleasant one from your point of view. The name *Gobblewhat* is dark elfin, but the prophecy is not. It is an echo, a rumor, an aspiration, out of a deeper night."

Being what she was, she naturally stoked the drama on her declamation, then clammed up, leaving her answer obscure.

I tried asking questions. That was a waste of time. She was done talking about *gobblewhat*. She closed the subject by saying, "That was spur of the moment. What did you really want?"

There was no point playing games. "Are you still in business? I'd like to buy a few of your special tools."

She ripped off a first-class witch's cackle. It was hilarious. I grinned. The peafowl even got into the act, though their mirth was confused and sleepy. "Go around to the front door," she told me. "You'll find it unlocked."

When I rejoined Morley and the triplets, I carried five tiny, folded pieces of paper. I had hidden each carefully. Each bore a potent and potentially useful spell. I was still repeating the witch's instructions to myself. Basically, all I had to remember was to unfold the papers at the appropriate moment, though a couple required a whispered word at the right time.

Morley said, "So. You survived the trail. I was about to go looking for you. What now?"

"We go back and get what sleep we can. Then early tomorrow we hit the road for Fort Caprice."

"I thought you were going to let the centaur do the finding for you."

"Contrary to the false notion formed earlier, I don't trust him to do anything. If he comes through, fine. Meantime, I go on looking. He expects us to hide from him. I can't think of a better place than out in the Cantard. Two birds, one stone."

Morley was as thrilled as I might have expected. "I had to ask, didn't I?"

ort Caprice was a bust.

It was four days out of Full Harbor, pushing hard all the way, shielded every step by more luck than any five fools deserved. Not only did we not encounter one of our own Karentine patrols, but we didn't fall in with Venageti rangers or representatives of any of the nonhuman races of the Cantard, most of which are at least marginally involved in the war. Their loyalties shift like a chameleon's color, according to where they think the most profit lies.

Fort Caprice was not in the heart of the cauldron, though. The richest silver country lay a hundred miles farther south.

Major Kayeth Kronk proved to be brevet-Colonel Kronk now, at the tender age of twenty-six. I did not remind him that we had met before, though I'm sure he remembered me before we reached the end of our short interview. I told him I was looking for his sister Kayean, and told him why. And he told me that he didn't have a sister Kayean.

And that was all he would say about it. When I kept after him he got stubborn. Then he got mad and had a couple of soldiers show me the street.

We poked around among the hangers-on Fort Caprice had acquired— like fleas, ticks, and worms to a hound—and found out nothing more interesting than which men were watering their wine and which women would send you away with something you hadn't had when you arrived. So we made the four-day journey back to Full Harbor, with fool's luck cleansing the way ahead of us again.

It was a lovely time to visit the Cantard.

I hoped the centaur would come through so I wouldn't have to do it again.

That would he tempting fate a bit too far.

We were out of Full Harbor nine days, all told.

T he major from the military city hall was waiting at the gate through the Narrows Wall. There was nothing magical about it once I realized that without sorcery, a trip to Fort Caprice takes a predictable amount of time. He cut me out of my herd.

"Any luck?" he asked.

"Zip. Zero. Zilch. What can I do for you?"

"I have another list of names."

"And getting my reaction is important enough for you to lay in wait for me out here?"

"Maybe."

"Fire away."

He did.

I knew five of the twelve names this time. Father Mike. Father Rhyne. Sair Lojda. Martello Quinn and Aben Kurts, of Denny's old crowd. I admitted knowing the latter two only as friends of a friend, saying I thought they were in shipping. Then I asked, "What ties this together? What's up?"

"All these people, and three more for whom we have no names, have died or disappeared during the last eleven days. I'm certain you would recognize more if you saw them. Imelo Clark was a guard at the civil city hall. Egan Rust was a clerk there. You interviewed them. I was not sure you had any connection with Kurts and Quinn, but since you did, then I assume there's also one with Laught and the three unknowns, all of whom seem to have come off a yacht from TunFaire."

"What the hell are you trying to say?"

"Don't get your hackles up, Garrett. You're safe. You were out of town during the excitement. In fact, the only time I place you or yours near anyone at a critical time is Father Rhyne. I'm satisfied your associate found him dead."

I didn't say anything. My thoughts were pounding off in twenty directions. What the hell was going on?

"It seems apparent that, in most of these cases, someone is cleaning up after you. It's a wonder you haven't been turned invisible yourself."

Thoughtlessly, I admitted, "It's been tried a couple times."

He wanted details. He demanded details. I gave him some without mentioning centaurs or dead men or much else that would do him any real good. He thought it was crafty of us, setting the one group up for a career in the mines.

He observed, "I have a feeling that there are a lot of things you wouldn't tell me no matter how nicely I ask. Like where the others from TunFaire fit in."

"I wouldn't be even a little shy about telling you that if I knew. What's the story on them, anyway?"

Kurts and Quinn had died the evening we left Full Harbor. They had been found in an alley on the far south side. At first it had looked like they had fallen foul of robbers. Laught—identified because his name and that of the yacht were stitched on the inside of his jumper—died later that night in the graveyard where Kayean and I had played when we were kids. At almost the same time a tremendous explosion and fire had consumed the yacht. No one knew how many had died in that. The unburned remains of the yacht had sunk. It was a miracle the whole waterfront hadn't gone up.

"That's pretty rough stuff," I said. "The stakes must be big. I don't want to sound dumb or impertinent, but what's your interest? Seems to me it's a civil problem, gaudy as it is."

"Full Harbor's reason for existing is military. Anything gaudy could affect the city's military situation. Garrett, I'm convinced you know things I want to know. But I'm not going to press you. When you feel like baring your soul, drop in. And I'll trade you the name of the man she married. Meantime, I'll just use you as a stalking horse."

"Yeah." I waved bye-bye, but my heart was not in it. I was pondering that equine-derived chestnut.

Morley and the triplets joined me. "Who was that?" Morley asked. I told him. He asked, "He have anything interesting to say?"

I told him all that, too.

"Gang warfare and vampires," he mused. "What a city."

"Vampires?"

"Several people claim they were attacked this week. It's all the talk. You know how those stories get going. People will see vampires in every shadow for a month."

● ● ● 34

We slept at the same inn. We couldn't be safer elsewhere, and the quarters were the best available for grolls.

The innkeeper had five messages for me. They were from Zeck Zack, had come at a rate of one daily, and had become increasingly strident. I got the impression he wanted to see me.

"Tomorrow is soon enough," I told Morley. "Tonight I'm going to lie around and ruminate and drink beer to get the Cantard dust out of my throat. I'm not much closer to the woman but I'm starting to see the outlines of the other stuff. Except for Vasco and his crowd, I don't think it has anything to do with silver. I think three or four conspiracies with completely alien or only marginally overlapping goals have collided here, maybe with the woman being the link. I don't think I'm the only one going around wondering, Who the hell are those guys? What do they want?"

I let it go there. Morley could chew on it if he wanted. I snuggled up with my beer and tried to let my mind go blank.

Some might say I did not have to work very hard.

Zeck Zack turned up next day. He got righteous with me.

"Do I work for you?" I asked.

He looked around. A lot of unfriendly faces were turned his way. Centaurs are not popular, which is probably why Zeck Zack spent so little time at his city house. He desisted, though he kept simmering. He handed me a sealed letter. "Your instructions are in there. You are to come alone."

"Have you been smoking weed?"

"What?"

"I don't go anywhere alone. People have been dying around this town. Four of them right out around your place."

"You will go alone or they will not let you see her."

"Then I'll find her my own way."

Morley walked in then, coming back from grazing. He slapped Zeck Zack across the rump, a familiarity and indignity that almost sent him into paroxysms. Morley said, "There was another vampire thing last night, Garrett. Sounded like the real article."

"Remind me to wear my high-collar shirt when I go barhopping tonight." His pursed lips told me he had something more on his mind but wouldn't say what until I got rid of the centaur.

I told Zeck Zack, "You see? It's dangerous to wander the streets alone."

"I will put it to them. They are going to be very irritated with both of us. They have gone to a great deal of trouble to make the woman available. But, perhaps, for that reason they will accede to your petition."

I did my eyebrow trick. My petition? "Right. Check it out. You know where to find me."

He extended a hand. "The instructions? They will have to be changed."

I gave them back. He left, giving me a couple of dark looks.

"He wanted me to come to the meet all by myself, on the lonesome," I told Morley. "Just me face-to-face with 'them,' whoever 'they' are."

"Whoever, they have him peeing down his leg. And he has a reputation for being a tough bastard."

"I noticed he had a case of nerves. What's up?"

"The place is being watched. Somebody followed me out and back. I didn't give it a good scout because I didn't want them to know they'd been made, but I spotted two more. I figured that's iceberg."

"Damn! The works. A whole crew. And now they know I'm dealing with Zeck Zack."

"Spilled milk. Who do you figure for it?"

"That army bastard. I don't know why. Vasco or the striped-sail crowd wouldn't have the resources. The centaur doesn't need to know every breath we take. He hopes he has us on the hook."

"Maybe the major needs a closer look."

"Maybe. Though I don't even know his name. And I'd rather not. I'd just as soon get on with the job I'm getting paid to do."

Morley nodded. "It's getting thick. I find myself looking forward to the trip home—in my more insane, impatient moments."

I slouched in my seat. "I guess we spend the day on in-and-out, getting a scout on how many and how good they are. We can make like we're getting ready for another trip out of town. We can eat the food on the way home if the meet goes down and I get what I need."

"We'll have to work a way for all of us to shake them, too."

"Yeah. This thing couldn't get any more complicated if you hired three wizards to knot it up."

●●●**35**

I was wrong, of course. It could get more complicated. And it did.

Morley, the triplets, and I spent the day running the bird dogs, and scoped out both daytime and nighttime routines for shaking them, though it looked like there would be at least twenty of them on us around the clock. It isn't hard to shake watchers when you know they're around, especially in a city as crazy as Full Harbor.

Morley had gone out for supper. I was having mine with Dojango in the common room. His brothers were in our quarters, where they felt more comfortable.

Dojango wasn't a bad sort to pass the time with, if you made allowances. He knew more crude stories than anyone I'd ever met, though he didn't deliver them very well. Actually.

Further complication waltzed through the door.

"Saucerhead Tharpe!" I groaned.

"And Spiney Prevallet," Dojango said of the guy who was the last of the four to enter. "Doris! Marsha!" He could put a snap in his voice when he wanted. It carried over the common-room noise.

The two in the middle need no introduction. My old flames, Tinnie and Rose. Tinnie stomped past Saucerhead, who was giving the grolls the once-over and not liking what he saw. I said, "I see the Venageti didn't get you. And I thought their sailors had an unfailing eye for the finest."

She halted in a widespread stance within slapping range, but her fists settled on her hips. "You're a brass-balled son of a bitch, Garrett. You know that?"

"Yeah. I've heard that talk, too. And it's true, so don't think you can flatter me. Have a nice trip? How long you been in town?" I kept one eye on Rose who looked as vicious as an entire pack of wolves circling in for the kill. Saucerhead and Spiney, with better sense and no emotional investment, put their hands in their pockets and kept them there. "Had supper yet? Sit down. My treat. It isn't the Unicorn Gambit, but the food sticks to your ribs."

"You . . . ! You . . . !" Tinnie stammered. "Don't you sit there and act like you didn't do anything. Don't treat me like one of your flapping old army buddies, you bastard." The fire was fading from her eyes. She had become conscious of the silence surrounding us, of all the staring eyes and knowing smirks.

"You're not being very ladylike," I noted. "Sit down, my one true love. Let me ply you with food and spirits."

"Bought with Uncle Willard's money?"

"Of course. It's a legitimate business expense."

A smile flirted with her lips despite her determination to be angry. She plopped into the chair Morley usually inhabited.

"Dojango, would you scare up enough seats for the rest of our guests?"

He looked at me like I was crazy, but he did it.

"You're lucky you got here when you did. An hour from now this place will be standing room only. Hello, Saucerhead. I paid your fee against your account at Morley's place. All right?"

"Yeah. Sure. That's what I wanted. How you doing, Garrett?" He was embarrassed to be seen in the company of two real live women. What was it going to do to his reputation?

"Not so good. I've fallen right into the middle of the damnedest thing I ever saw."

Civilized behavior begets civilized behavior. Rose decided to play the game and was the perfect lady as Dojango held her chair. "Rose," I said. "You're looking lovelier than ever."

"It must be the sea air. And a change of diet."

I looked at Tinnie. "Not roots and berries, I hope."

Tinnie winked.

I faced Spiney Prevallet. "Mr. Prevallet. I've heard of you but don't think we've ever met."

"Garrett. No, we haven't. I've heard of you, too." And that was all he had to say for the evening. It was enough to set my teeth on edge. His voice was neutral but as cold as the bottom side of a coffin.

If Morley and Saucerhead are the best at what they do, Spiney Prevallet is crowding them. And he's said to be less squeamish and less choosy about the jobs he takes.

The landlord himself came to take orders. Men like him have a sixth sense. He wanted to size up the trouble before it happened. I smiled at him a lot.

"You've had trouble?" Rose asked. She sounded hopeful.

"A little. More, you'd say I've been trouble. Everybody I talk to turns up dead."

That got their attention. I gave them an edited and censored account of my adventures. Somehow, I forgot to mention Zeck Zack.

I was still talking and wondering how to get rid of them, in case the centaur showed, when Morley walked in.

He never batted an eye. He walked up behind Rose, who had her back to the door, and trailed his fingertips lightly up the side of her neck. "A miracle. I would have sworn the pirates would have—"

Tinnie cut in. "Garrett already used that line. Only with him it was Venageti sailors."

"Then add plagiarism to his list of sins." Morley placed a small box on the table before me. "That four-legged wonder of a cook sent you this kelp salad. Since you've already eaten, maybe you should save it for a snack."

I peeked despite his warning. Kelp salad, all right. "He gave it to you?"

"To bring over. He knew we had company and didn't want to intrude."

"I don't have much use for kelp, but since he went to all the trouble . . ."

Morley kept stroking Rose's neck and shoulders. He nodded once to Tinnie, ignored Spiney and Saucerhead completely. If, as I suspected, the kelp concealed Zeck Zack's instructions for making the meet, we had a problem. I expect that had Morley's undivided attention.

"Did you bribe Master Arbanos somehow?" I asked Tinnie.

"That little water rat? He did exactly what you told him to. He handed us over to Uncle Willard personally."

"I'm sorry I missed that."

"You're going to get your chance to take part in a reenactment."

"How did you manage—"

Rose said, "Our good Uncle Lester bestowed a small legacy on each of us."

"I see." Women with their own money do tend to get independent, don't they?

That box of salad sat there staring at me, begging to be opened, and I hadn't one idea how to get rid of them.

"Why are you here, Tinnie? Rose I understand. A hundred thousand marks makes for a big greed." Morley was over talking to the grolls, now. I hoped his mind was more fertile than mine.

"I have a grudge to settle with a certain bastard who had me tied up and shipped like a sack of turnips."

"After he had the brass-balled gall to get you out of the hands of kidnappers. What can you do with a churl like that?" I countered.

She had the grace to redden.

Morley came over and begged Dojango for his seat, which was next to Rose. With bad grace Dojango gave way and joined his brothers.

I saw it then, and Morley knew when I knew. He gave me the ghost of a smile and went to work charming Rose.

Dojango ducked through the door to our quarters.

Five minutes later I developed an irresistible need for the loo. I grabbed my box and promised to be right back. I trickled fingers through Tinnie's hair. She slapped my hand but it was only a pat.

Dojango was waiting. "Out the window. Night course. Morley says you'd better read your instructions and dump them down the loo first."

I had that much sense. I didn't figure he needed reminding, though. "Who's next?"

"Morley. He comes to see why you're taking so long. He's worried. Then Doris goes, then me. Marsha stalls and distracts them by keeping them from getting through the door."

"Sounds good. If it works."

ambled up the lane toward the Orthodox cemetery, where we were to meet at the Kronk family plot. Convenient, that. Zeck Zack or his messenger was supposed to take us to the meet from another plot just two hundred yards away, come midnight.

I reached the place where the first man to arrive was supposed to lie in the weeds for anybody following the rest. "Morley? I'm clean."

Dojango came out of the darkness, not Morley. "What took so long?"

"I had more tails than an Uighur. All pros. Took a while to shake them. Where's Morley?"

"Pushing sugar."

"Doris and Marsha?"

"At the plot. They just got here, too. They almost forgot. They were having fun trotting around town watching the humans huff and puff trying to keep up."

"The ladies?"

"You and Morley better forget those two and take up kicking beehives."

"Mad, huh?"

"Furious, actually."

Morley came back from his pandering. "Just in time, Garrett. Let's go check something out." He marched off through the graveyard.

His destination proved to be a decrepit mausoleum. He examined its door. I couldn't see what he saw. He grunted. "Huh. Maybe they knew what they were talking about. Marsha. Open it up."

The groll obliged. There was no sound of seals breaking. There was almost no sound at all. Curious in a door that should have been unmoved for generations.

Then the stench rolled out.

I considered a crack about ducking the stampeding buzzards, but desisted. Death is no joke.

"We need a light, Morley," Dojango said.

"I figured we would. I borrowed a lucifer stone from my bitty buddy Hornbuckle." He removed it from its protective sack. It was a young one, burning bright.

I didn't want to go inside, but I did. I stayed only as long as I could hold my breath, which was long enough to get an education. It was pretty bad, but I did recognize what was left of Father Mike, the Sair, and the clerk from the civil city hall. I had no idea who the others were.

Marsha closed it up. We walked to the Kronk plot in silence. Finally, Morley said, "Somebody's garbage dump."

"Who put them there?"

"Soldiers. I quote Hornbuckle: 'Soldiers without livery.' "

"I see." I saw a great deal. It had nothing to do with finding Kayean, but a lot to do with a nameless major.

Morley said, "On no evidence at all I'll bet you fifty marks your major was part of the outfit that liberated the church the day your girlfriend's father died."

"No bet. Not even at ten to one."

A man in the major's position wouldn't quietly dispose of the top Venageti agent in his territory. Not when he could bring him in and harvest all sorts of rewards. Not unless that agent could name some very interesting names, like maybe that of an agent even better placed than he.

"Investigators from TunFaire, you had to say. He thinks we're the King's men and we're looking for him. What other reason for the interest in people named Kronk?"

"Or the Emperor's men." I shook my head. "My poor sweet, silly Kayean. She had to make the worst choices in fathers and husbands."

Morley frowned. "Husbands? You don't even know who he is."

"I don't have to know he's somebody Zeck Zack and his bosses want to keep us away from. It can't be her. There's no evidence that she's anything but a woman carrying on a profitable correspondence with an old flame."

Morley grunted. "What about your major?"

"You know me. I'd rather negotiate, like with the centaur. Or I just let them ride and hope for the best, like with Vasco and his bunch. I've only killed two men since I got out of the Marines, and one of them was by accident. But I think somebody is going to have to chop the head off this snake before it crushes us all."

We scouted the terrain thoroughly. There was no sign the centaur planned anything cagey, but that wasn't especially reassuring.

Zeck Zack came for us himself, which said something about his relationship to the shadow folk behind him. "You're early," he accused.

"So are you."

"I told them I needed time to scout you for treachery. In truth, I wanted time to talk."

"You trust us, then?"

"As much as one dares, given the circumstances. Your claims received independent corroboration from persons who had no wish to further your mission."

"Who?"

"I believe they called themselves Quinn and Kurts."

So. I had to reorganize my notions about who had done what to whom that bloody night.

"Mr. Garrett, I've gone to a great deal of trouble on your behalf. For myself as well, I admit, for it could mean my neck if the knowledge of the movement of certain letters reached the wrong persons. But still, on your behalf I have saved your lives by convincing them that the surest way to handle you is to let you get your affidavit. You might also note the removal of two deadly enemies, which improves your odds."

"You want something."

"Sir?"

"Besides me not mentioning any letters—a subject I wouldn't mind chatting about, just to satisfy my curiosity—there must be something else. Call it a hunch."

"Yes. I might as well be direct. There is so little time."

"So?"

"In my youth I was guilty of, shall we say, a mortal indiscretion. A certain gentleman acquired proofs sufficient to place me in extreme jeopardy should they come to the attention of either my employers or the Karentine military. He used the threat to compel me to perform tasks that only worsen my chances of living to old age. The whereabouts of the evidence is known only to him. He does not allow me to get anywhere near him. You, however, could walk right up to him."

"I get the picture." I had no intention of scragging anybody for him, but I played the game out. I wanted him to stay my buddy. "Who?"

He wanted to get cagey.

"Come on. I don't agree to anything till I hear a name."

He had made up his mind to tell me if I pressed. He did. "A priest named Sair Lojda. At the Orthodox church at—"

"I know him." Morley and I exchanged glances. So the centaur didn't know that the Sair had gone invisible. Far be it from me to respect a dead villain so much I failed to profit from him. "You've got a deal, buddy. He's dead meat right now. If I see the woman, get what I want, and leave in one piece, I'll show you the body before the sun comes up."

"Pact?"

"Pact and sworn."

"Good. Let's go. They'll be getting impatient."

●●●37

Z eck Zack led us down the trail to his house. The peacocks raised twelve kinds of hell. "I'm going to roast the lot someday," the centaur said. "Every damn night they wake me up with that whooping."

He took us in through the tradesmen's entrance Kayean used to sneak out. Then it was through servants' corridors to the front antechamber.

"Dark as hell in here," Morley complained. "What have you got against light, centaur?"

If it was bad for him and the triplets, it was worse for Zeck Zack and me. We had no night eyes at all.

There was a ghost of light in the antechamber. It leaked in from the ballroom. It was just enough to betray the form of a man awaiting us.

The centaur said, "At this point you must shed all your weapons. Indeed, everything you're carrying that is made of metal. Past this point you may go armed only with the weapons given you by nature."

I started shucking. I could smell the end of the chase. I would give Zeck Zack the benefit of the doubt.

"Damn, it's cold in here," Dojango muttered.

He was right. And here I'd thought my teeth were chattering because I had to go in there armed only with the weapons given me by nature. I announced, "I'm ready."

Zeck Zack said, "Step up and let the man double-check, Mr. Garrett." He made no apologies.

I stepped forward. A pasty face the color of grubs appeared before me for a moment. Eyes of no color stared into mine. They were filled with an old hopelessness.

He patted me down smoothly and efficiently. Professionally. He did only one thing unprofessional.

He slipped something into my pocket.

It was done slickly. He touched me just heavily enough to make sure I noticed. Then he went to frisk Morley.

One lone candle illuminated the ballroom. It sat, with a quill and ink-well, on an otherwise barren table at the chamber's geographical center. The table was four feet wide and eight feet long, long side toward me. Two chairs faced one another across it. I went and stood behind the one on my side, dropped my credentials and all the legal stuff on the table. Shivering, I shoved my hands into my pockets and waited.

I hadn't imagined anything. I palmed a folded piece of paper.

I checked the disposition of my troops. Morley was to my left, my weak side, two steps out and one back. Dojango was the same to my right. The grolls were behind me. Morley's nose twitched and pointed three times. Three beings shared the room with us, all in front.

One came floating out of the darkness.

She was beautiful. And something else. Ethereal, a poet might have said. Spooky is good enough for me.

She moved so lightly she seemed to float. Her gown whispered around her. Gauzy and voluminous, it was as white as any white ever was. Her skin was so colorless it almost matched her apparel. Her hair was the blond called platinum. Her eyes were ice blue and without expression, except they narrowed as she neared the light, as though it was too bright. Her lips were a thin wound vaguely purpled by the cold. She wore no makeup.

"You're Kayean Kronk?" I asked when she halted behind her chair.

She inclined her head in a barely perceptible nod.

"Let's sit, then. Let's get it over with."

She pulled her chair back and drifted into it.

I glanced at Morley and Dojango as I settled. They were staring into the darkness, as rigid and fierce as trained wolves on point. I didn't know Dojango had it in him.

I looked across the table. She waited, her hands folded.

I gave her the whole thing, Denny dying, leaving his bundle, her having to come to TunFaire with me if she wanted to claim the legacy, or having to execute a sworn and sealed affidavit that would renounce and abjure, in perpetuity, all claims upon the estate of Denny Tate.

While I tried to talk what Morley called dirty-lawyer talk I shuffled and referred to my papers and used that to cover unfolding the thing that had been deposited in my pocket. It was a note of course.

It said:

Come take her out. Soon. Please. While there is still a chance for her redemption.

I shivered and tried to convince myself that it was the cold.

I read on, and under the guise of jotting notes jotted a note:

Open the enclosure only in her presence. Do so elsewhere and all hope dies.

I folded in one of the charms I had obtained from the Old Witch. Hands-at-the-door had not removed those, if he had detected them at all. I got the paper into a pocket and concentrated on concentrating on that spooky woman.

I tried to sound incredulous. "Are you honestly rejecting one hundred thousand marks? Less fees, of course. In *silver?*"

A ghost of a hint of revulsion feather-touched her eyes as she nodded. It was the only emotion she betrayed during the interview.

"Very well. I won't pretend to understand, but I'll draw up the affidavit." I began scratching slowly on a piece of paper. "One of my associates will witness my signature. One of your companions will have to witness yours."

Again she nodded.

I completed the thing, signed. "Morley. I need your chop."

He came and gave me it. He was still as taut as a drawn bowstring.

I pushed the paper, ink, and pen across. "Is that satisfactory?"

She considered the paper just long enough, then nodded, collected everything, floated up, and drifted away into the darkness.

I put my papers and such together, rose, waited behind my chair. Soon enough the apparition drifted back. She placed the signed affidavit on the table, just beside the candle. Thus there was no possibility of physical contact, as there might be if she offered it to me directly. I gathered it up and tucked it away.

"I thank you for your time and courtesy, madam. I will trouble you no more." I headed for the anteroom.

I noted that neither Morley, Dojango, nor the grolls turned around to retreat. There are times when not having night eyes can be a blessing.

Slipping my counternote to my correspondent was easy. Zeck Zack was so anxious to get us out of his house, and so eager to get himself out, too, that he was blind. In half a minute he was fussing unmercifully, trying to get us moving down the dark halls before we had recovered half of our hardware.

38

The peafowl carried on like wild dogs had them surrounded and help would come only if they yelled loud enough to rattle the clouds. I sympathized. Lately I felt the same way. But if I yelled, *they* would know where I was and start closing in.

As we approached the witch's house, the air quivered. A cackle fluttered down like gaunt, soggy snowflakes. Out of everywhere and nowhere, she asked, "Did you enjoy your taste of the prophecy, Mr. Garrett?" More soggy cackle.

Morley and the boys might not have heard. Zeck Zack glanced at the house, puzzled. I just put my head down and marched, not wanting to think about it.

The centaur was determined to stick with us. I expected him to press on the matter of Sair Lojda, and he didn't disappoint me. He started in halfway to the graveyard. I told him, "Wait," and refused to listen.

Morley picked the spot to squat, the one we had used before keeping our date with Zeck Zack. Morley sat down. So did I. Morley said, "We need to talk."

"Yeah."

Zeck Zack grumbled, "This is where you tell me how sorry you are, can't keep your half of the bargain?"

"No," Morley said. "We can deliver on that fast enough to make your head spin. The problem is, *you* didn't deliver."

I looked at Morley. He explained, "You gave her the paper upside down. She didn't turn it. She couldn't read. It's reasonable to assume that your Kayean could."

"She could. You're right. That wasn't her. Didn't begin to resemble her. They just plain didn't know I knew her."

Zeck Zack looked upset. I didn't bother to ask. I did say, "One question, old horse. When you bought that house, was it your idea, theirs, or the priest's?"

"The priest's."

"One cycle of coincidence unmasked. Did he find what he was afraid might be hidden there?"

"No."

"Did you? I'm sure you looked."

He was regaining his balance. He grinned. "I took that place apart. I needed some back leverage."

"I can take that as a no?"

"Right."

"Garrett," Morley said, "is that paper going to satisfy you? It'll get you your ten percent."

"That's not what I said I'd do. I haven't found her yet."

He grunted. I couldn't be sure in that light, but thought he seemed relieved and pleased. "Then we have plans to make, things to do, and our butts to cover." He rose. "Your pal there jacked us around, but maybe he didn't have any choice. I say we deliver our half. Maybe he'll suffer a fit of gratitude. Come on."

There was an edge to his voice I didn't like.

I'm not sure Zeck Zack followed Morley. Maybe he just didn't want to go back down to that house. Or maybe he thought he would get to watch the priest die.

Morley hiked straight to the mausoleum we'd visited earlier. "Open it up, Marsha."

Marsha obliged.

Zeck Zack noted the little giveaway details that said the tomb was in use. "You already did it? Before . . . you dumped him here?"

Morley gave him the lucifer stone. "See for yourself. Pardon us if we don't join you. We've been in there once already tonight. We don't have your iron stomach."

Their gazes locked. Right then Zeck Zack would have murdered him cheerfully. The odds didn't favor him. He spun, raised the stone, stamped inside.

Morley said something in grollish.

Marsha slammed the door.

"Morley!"

"A little night trading, I told you the first time I reported on him. Like a little innocent smuggling, I thought. What do you want to bet he procures for them?"

I had known Morley a long time, though not well. I'd seen him angry, but never out of control. And never eaten up with hatred.

"You know what we walked into down there, don't you, Garrett?"

"I know." And Father Rhyne's last message and Kayean's excommunication made sense. Of a sort. So did the attacks and rumors of attacks.

Morley calmed down. "Something had to be done. He could have trotted straight down there and told them we weren't taken in. He'll be all right for a while. We already know he has a strong stomach. We can turn him loose later, if you want. Anyway, a few days in there might incline him to tell us how to find her."

"I'll know how to reach her soon enough." Though Morley gave me the fish eye, I didn't elucidate.

"You sure you know what you're doing? There wasn't anything in your deal about digging her out of a nest of the night people."

"I know." I knew only too well. And I am cursed with an imagination capable of conjuring up the worst possibilities.

"If we blow it and get taken, me and the triplets are just dead. We don't have enough human blood to be any use to them. But you . . ."

"I said I know, Morley. Back off. We have the major to worry about. He knows we were in touch with the centaur. I expect he knows the priest was blackmailing Zeck Zack. With the priest gone that leverage is gone. So are we. Meaning we might have learned something that made us run for cover. He's going to tear this town apart. He's going to have guys sitting on every way out. We can't stay here. When the sun comes up the sextons will start planting the day's crop of stiffs. They'll wonder what we're doing hanging around. We can't go back to the inn. Everybody will be watching that."

"Don't get yourself in an uproar. We've got the woods to hide in. We've got ourselves a night trader who knows ways to get people and things in and out of town. I say let's worry about our friends of the nest and let your major worry about himself."

Morley had a point of sorts, though he didn't realize it. The more the major scurried around looking for us, the more likely he was to draw the attention of superiors who might want to know what was going on. And few if any of the men he commanded would be Venageti operatives. Their suspicions dared not be aroused.

He had to juggle carefully.

wakened to an itchy nose, tittering, and the *harrumph-harrumph* of grollish laughter. I opened my eyes. Something brown and fuzzy waved in my face. Behind it was one of the little folk, seated in the crotch of a bush. I controlled my temper and got my forequarters upright, leaning against a tree. I was stiff and sore from sleeping on the ground.

No doubt Morley would argue that it was good for me.

"Where the hell are Morley and Dojango?"

The only answer I got was some big grollish grins and titters from the undergrowth.

"All right. Be that way."

"Sugar?" A tiny voice piped.

"If I'd had any, you would have swiped it while I was sleeping."

"With those great beasties watching over you?" the one in the bush asked.

I didn't feel like arguing. Morning is always too early for anything but self-pity, and even that's usually too much trouble. "Is there anyone in or around the centaur's house?" You have to strive for precision with those folk. "Human or otherwise?"

"Sugar?"

"No sugar."

"Bye, now."

So. No pay, no play. Little mercenaries. I considered going down and burglarizing the centaur's kitchen. But I wasn't hungry enough to bet that

Zeck Zack's masters had done the rational thing and gotten the hell out the minute my affidavit and I departed. Besides, I didn't feel like getting up and doing anything.

I sat there trying to reconcile the Kayean who dwelt among the nightmares with the Kayean I had known. I shuffled through what I remembered from her letters to Denny. Nothing there but the occasional hint that she was not happy. Never a word about her whereabouts or circumstances. She hadn't been proud of herself.

No sense worrying about it. That would give me nothing but a headache and the heebie-jeebies. She could explain when I got to her.

Morley showed up around noon, staggering under a load of junk. "What's all that?" I demanded. "You planning an invasion? Where's Dojango? What the hell have you been up to?"

"Taking bids on your butt from Vasco, Rose, and your major. It was hot going till they got up to a quarter mark. Here." He dumped half his load beside me. I noted a sack that looked like it might contain comestibles. I hit it first.

"What is all this stuff?"

"Raw materials. For the arsenal we'll need if we're going into a nest after your lady. They'd smell metal hardware ten miles off. You any good at flaking stone arrow points?"

"I don't know. I've never tried."

He looked exasperated. "Didn't they teach you anything practical in that Marine Corps of yours?"

"Three thousand ways to kill Venageti. I'm a tool user, not a toolmaker."

"I guess the load falls on Doris and Marsha again." He gobbled grollish, and gave the big guys a bunch of stuff. Two minutes later, snarling and rumbling, they were chipping out arrowheads with a touch as delicate as a mouse's. They were good, and they were fast.

Morley said, "They're put out. They say it's dwarf's work. They want to know why they can't just make themselves some ten-foot clubs and go in and break skulls. Grolls are slow sometimes."

I could whittle a bit so I set to making myself a sword from an ironwood lath. It's a good hard wood that will almost take an edge, but won't hold one the way steel will. So I gave myself only one. The backstroke side I channeled and set with waste from the arrowhead flaking. That gave me a vicious tool.

Time rolled by. I shed my troubles in my concentration on my craftsmanship.

"Have mercy, Garrett!" Morley snapped. "Do you really have to put in the blood gutters?"

I looked at the thing in my hand. I sure was doing it up purple. I tried it for balance. "Close. Needs a little more work. A little more polish to lessen the drag during the cut."

"And you call me bloodthirsty."

"I'd rather carry a saber."

"Come off it. One time we're going to use this stuff. Finish it up. I cut some bolts, there. Fletch them and sharpen them. I'll harden and poison the tips when I'm done here." He was removing metal parts from crossbows and replacing them. The reworked weapons wouldn't hold up, but, like he said, it was just the one raid.

"Old Man Tate is going to pee blue vinegar over the expenses. Why poison? It won't do you any good." I dragged bolts, glue, feathers, and thread together and started in.

"Because not everybody we meet is going to be immune."

True. The bloodslaves would fight ferociously to defend their chances of someday joining the order of masters.

"You know anything about the nests in the Cantard, Garrett?"

"Who knows anything about any of them anywhere?"

"True. They wouldn't survive. But?"

"There are rumors. Because of the military situation, they don't have to be as circumspect in the Cantard. Plenty of easy prey, too. Nobody misses a soldier here or there. The nests are supposed to be bigger than usual because of that. When I was stationed down here, there were supposed to be six nests. That got reduced when some Karentine agents snatched a Venageti warlord's daughter and let it out that she had been carried off to a nest. The warlord forgot everything else, went off to the rescue, found the nest and cleansed it, and got himself killed for his trouble. While his army was busy hunting night people, one of ours was sneaking up behind them. And that's all I know. Except to guess that they're happy to see so much silver leaving this part of the world."

"They would know everything about silver, wouldn't they?"

"They would know everything about what everyone was doing, that's for sure. Which explains how Kayean was able to make Denny rich."

Silver is as poisonous to the night people as cobra venom is to humans. It kills them fast and makes it stick. Not much else does. Other metals bother them to a lesser degree.

"Speaking of sneaks," Morley said.

Dojango appeared, burdened with poles and bow-staves and whatnot. He was tipsy. He said, "It's set for tomorrow night."

"How much did you have?" Morley demanded.

"Don't worry, cousin. I came here clean. Actually. They'll have the horses and gear waiting at an abandoned mill they said is three miles up something called North Creek. They said they'd only wait one night. They said they would take the animals and stuff out tomorrow morning and bring them back the next day if we don't show. They seemed a little nervous about being out in the countryside, actually."

"Guess we'll have to resurrect our centaur. Sit down and start turning those dowels into arrows. Garret. You know this North Creek?"

"Yes." I was tempted to ask who he thought was in charge, but kept my mouth shut. Morley had taken care of things that needed doing.

Dojango started making arrows. "Some interesting news started going around just before I came back up. About the time we were taking a peek into that tomb last night, Glory Mooncalled, *unsupported,* actually, attacked Indigo Springs."

"Indigo Springs?" I asked. "That's a hundred miles farther south than the army's ever gone. And he tried it without wizards?"

Dojango smirked. "He not only tried it, he pulled it off, actually. Caught them sleeping. Killed Warlord Shomatzo-Zha and his whole staff in the first assault, then wiped out half their army. The rest ran off into the desert barefoot, wearing nothing but their nightshirts."

"Good hunting for the night people," Morley grumbled.

"And unicorns, centaur slavers, wild dogs, hippogriffs, and any other kind of critter that wants a piece of them," Dojango added. "This is going to mean problems, Morley. If we have to spend much time out there."

"How come?"

"If it's true, it's an unprecedented disaster for Venageti arms. When Glory Mooncalled changed sides, he swore vengeance on five warlords. For years he's been waltzing them around the Cantard, making fools of them. Now he's struck deep into traditionally safe territory and stomped one of the five the way I'd stomp a bug."

"So?"

"So the Venageti are going to start flailing around like a boxer with blood in his eyes, hoping they hit something. Karentine forces will begin to move, trying to take advantage. Every nonhuman tribe in the Cantard will be out trying to profit from the confusion. In a week it'll be so hairy it'll be worth your life to squat to poop if you don't have somebody to stand guard."

"Then we'd better move fast, hadn't we?" Morley asked.

A sentiment with which I agreed wholeheartedly. But my sneak to the bloodslave guarding the things in Zeck Zack's ballroom had paid no dividends yet and I doubted that my revelation would come for days—if at all.

•••40

Zeck Zack was as cooperative as a centaur could be after his sojourn with the dead. He didn't balk until having led us from the city via an underwall smugglers tunnel, he discovered that he had been enlisted in our enterprise for the duration.

Morley was in a puckish mood.

"But sir, surely you see all your caterwauling is without foundation. If you will reflect seriously you cannot help but confess the rectitude of our position. If we were to release you, as you so unreasonably insist, you would dash back through the tunnel and instantly set about wreaking evil upon us, imagining us to be the authors of your ill fortune rather than assuming that onus yourself, as is the fact."

I had arrayed my army in squad diamond, with a groll out front, another behind, Dojango on the right and Morley on the left. Night-blind, I marched at the heart of the formation, ready to rush to any quarter suddenly threatened. Zeck Zack stumbled along between Morley and me.

It wasn't long before the centaur surrendered to the inevitable. He betrayed a hitherto sequestered facet of character and began arguing with Morley in the same florid language and overblown, overly polite formulations.

The men who had brought our horses and gear were thrilled to see us. Our advent meant they couldn't just take everything back and sell it again. Nor, they decided after eyeballing the grolls, could they murder us and do the same.

We parted ways immediately upon delivery. They were of the school that maintains wandering around at night could get you killed. We kept moving on the hypothesis that the wise man puts ground between himself and people who want to kill him.

Not a lot of ground. Those horses had heard of me and just to make trouble they insisted that the sensible thing to do was stay put.

Nobody was out to kill *them*. Nobody behind them, anyway.

Their attitude didn't improve when the sun rose and they found themselves headed into the Cantard.

Morley accused me of anthropomorphizing and exaggerating the natural reluctance of dumb beasts to go into unfamiliar territory.

It just goes to show they had him fooled. They're crafty in their malice, unicorns under the skin.

Having had no revelation, I set a course due west. Thither lay the most barren territory in the Karentine end of the Cantard, the desert of colorful buttes and mesas people in TunFaire picture when they think of the Cantard. I decided to head there because it seemed a logical place for the night people to have established a nest. It was so inhospitable as to be repugnant to most races. There were no discovered resources to bring exploiters with their guardians. Ample prey existed close by—especially when there were Zeck Zacks to do the rounding up.

Our second day out Morley began to suspect that I was not sure of my course. He went to work on the centaur.

"There's no point to it, Morley," I said. "They wouldn't be stupid enough to trust him."

Doris grumbled something from behind us. I could now tell the grolls apart. I had made them wear different hats.

"What?" I asked.

"He says there's a dog following us."

"Uh-oh."

"Trouble?"

"Probably. We'll have to ambush it to find out. Watch for a place where the wind is toward us."

Three possibilities suggested themselves. The dog could be a domestic stray seeking human company. Damned unlikely. It could be an outcast from a wild pack. That meant rabies. Or, most unpleasant and most likely, it could be an outrunner scouting for game.

Marsha found a likely bunch of boulders on the lower slope of the butte we were rounding. He headed up a steep, twisting alley between, into shadows and clicky echoes. Morley, Dojango, and I dismounted and followed, rehearsing the balky animals in the vulgates of several languages.

"What did I tell you about horses, Morley?"

Doris hunkered between rocks and started blending in.

"Keep going, Morley. They're sight as well as scent hunters. It'll need to see movement."

Morley grumbled. Marsha grumbled back, surly, but continued climbing. A bit later there was one brief squeal of doggie outrage from below, canceled by a meaty smack.

The horses were not reluctant going downhill. Lazy monsters.

Doris had squashed the mongrel good. He stood over it grinning as though he had conquered an entire army troop.

"Yech!" I said. "Looks like a rat run over by a wagon. Lucky he missed its head." I squatted, examined ears. "Well, damn!"

"What?" Morley asked.

"It was an outrunner. A trained outrunner. See the holes through the ears? Punched there by unicorn teeth. There's a hunting party somewhere within a few miles of us. They'll track the dog when he doesn't turn up. That means we have to leave enough nasty surprises to discourage them, because we aren't going to outrun them if they take our scent."

"How many?"

"One adult male and all the females of his harem that aren't too pregnant or cluttered up with young. Maybe some adolescent females that haven't run away yet. Anywhere from six to a dozen. If they do catch up, concentrate on the dominant female. The male won't get involved. He leaves the hunting and heavy stuff to the womenfolk. He saves himself for giving orders, mounting females, killing his male offspring if they stray from their mothers, and trying to kidnap the most attractive females from other harems."

"Sounds like a sensible arrangement."

"Somehow, I figured you'd feel that way."

"Wouldn't killing the boss break up the harem?"

"The way I hear, if that happened they'd just keep coming till they were dead or we all were."

"That is true," Zeck Zack said. "A most despicable beast, the unicorn. Nature's most bankrupt experiment. But one day my folk will complete their extermination. . . ." He shut up, having recalled that the rest of us held a different view of the identity of nature's most bankrupt experiment.

We hurried on. After a while Zeck Zack resumed talking so he could explain some of the nastier devices his folk used to booby-trap their back trails. Some were quite gruesomely ingenious.

He had contributed nothing but carping before. His sudden helpfulness suggested the proximity of unicorns scared the tail feathers off him.

••• 41

After pausing at a brackish stream to water and gather firewood, we scrambled up several hundred feet of scree around the knees of a monster monolith of a butte and made camp in a pocket that couldn't be approached in silence by a mouse. The view was excellent. None of us, with our varied eyes, or even with the spyglass, could see anything moving in the twilight.

We settled down to a small, sheltered tire. Being in the mood myself, we broached one of the baby kegs and passed it around. It held only enough for a good draft each for me, Zeck Zack, Dojango, and sips for the grolls. "Yech!" was my assessment. "Drinking that was the second mistake I've made in this life."

"I won't be so forward as to ask what the other might have been," Morley said, "suspecting it might have been being born." He smirked. "I presume beer jostled on the back of a pack animal in the hot sun loses something."

"You might say. What possessed you, Dojango?"

"A slick-talking salesman."

We sat around the fire after eating, mostly watching it die down, occasionally assaying a story or a joke, but largely tossing out notions about how we might deal with the unicorns if it came to that. I didn't contribute much. I'd begun to fret about my revelation.

Something must have gone wrong. There had been time for them to reach the nest, I felt. Had the bloodslave betrayed himself? Had he been found out?

Without him prospects were poor. We could wander the Cantard looking until we were old men.

At some point I would have to admit defeat and head north with my false affidavit. I supposed we'd give up when our stores were depleted to just enough for the overland journey to Taelreef, the friendly port nearest us after Full Harbor. Going back into the shadow of the major's claw seemed plain foolhardy from there in the desert.

One of the grolls was telling Morley a story. Morley kept snickering. I ignored them and began drowsing.

"Hey. Garrett. You got to hear this story Doris just told me. It'll tear you up."

I scowled and opened my eyes. The fire had died to sullen red coals casting little useful light. Even so, I could see that Morley's words didn't fit his expression. "Another one of those long-winded shaggy-dog fables about how the fox tricked the bear out of berries, then ate them and got the runs and diarrheaed himself to death?" That had been the most accessible of the grollish stories so far, and even it had lacked a clear point or moral.

"No. You'll get this one right away. And even if you don't, laugh a lot so you don't hurt his feelings."

"If we must, we must."

"We must." He moved over beside me. In a low voice, he said, "It starts out like this. We're being watched by two of the night people. Laugh."

I managed, without looking around. Sometimes I do all right.

Doris called something to Marsha, who responded with hearty grollish laughter. It sounded like they had bet on my response and Marsha had won.

"Doris and Marsha are going to jump them. Maybe they can handle them, maybe they can't. Don't look around. When I'm done telling the story, we're going to get up and walk toward Doris. Chuckle and nod."

"I think I can manage without the stage directions." I chuckled and nodded.

"When Doris moves, you follow him and do whatever needs doing. I'll go with Marsha."

"Dojango?" I slapped my knee and guffawed.

"He watches the centaur."

Zeck Zack had backed himself into a tight place where nothing could come at him from behind. His legs were folded under him; his chin rested upon his folded arms; he appeared to be sound asleep.

"Ready?" Morley asked.

I put on my hero face that said I was a fearless old vampire killer from way back. "Lead on, my man. I'm right behind you."

"Big laugh."

I hee-hawed like it was the one about the bride who didn't know the bird had to be cleaned before it went into the roaster. Morley pasted a grin on and rose. I did so, too, and tried shaking some of the stiffness out of my legs. We walked toward Doris.

Doris and Marsha moved with astonishing swiftness. I had run only two steps when I glimpsed a dark flutter among the rocks. Doris hit it. A great thrashing and flailing started. Another broke out behind me. I didn't look back.

When I got there, Doris had the vampire in a fierce bear hug, facing away from him. Sinews popped and crackled. Strong as he was, the groll was having trouble keeping the hold. Blood leaked from talon slashes on his hide. The blood smell maddened the vampire further. His fangs ripped the air an inch from the groll's arm.

Let that devil sink one and Doris was done for. It would inject a soporific venom capable of felling a mastodon.

I stood with a knife in one hand and silver half mark in the other, wondering what to do. Whenever a foot flailed out at me, I tried to cut the tendon above the heel.

Suddenly there was a flicker of light. Dojango was feeding the fire.

Doris pushed the vampire's ankles between his knees. I flung forward, trying to drive my blade into one of the devil's knees, to hobble it. It twisted half an inch. My point hit bone and cut downward through flesh harder than summer sausage.

A wound to the bone, a foot long, and when I was done about three drops of liquid leaked out. The vampire loosed one flat, shrill keen of pain and rage. Its eyes burned down at me, trying to catch mine with their deadly hypnotic gaze.

I slammed the half mark into the wound before it could start healing.

It was done so quickly, deftly, and instinctively that even now it amazes me.

The vampire froze for many seconds. Then dead lips peeled back and loosed a howl that terrified the stones and must have been audible twenty miles away; immortality betrayed. I clamped both hands on the wound to keep the coin in place. The night beast bent back like a man in the last throes of tetanus, hissed, gurgled, shook so violently we barely held on.

The flesh beneath my hands began to soften. Around the coin it turned to jelly. It oozed between my fingers.

Doris threw the thing down. The fire painted his great green face in light and shadow patches of hatred. The vampire lay among the rocks, still hissing, clawing at its leg. It was a very strong one. The poison should have finished it sooner. But they're all strong, or they couldn't be what they are.

Doris snagged a boulder twice as long as me and smashed the thing's head.

For several seconds I watched flesh turn to jelly and slide off bones. Then, as though the vampire's end was a signal, my revelation came.

I knew a direction.

When daylight came . . .

If daylight came. Morley and Marsha were embattled still. Doris was on his way to help. He collected his ten-foot club as he went. I shook all over and went to help myself.

Somehow, as we approached, the second vampire broke loose. It hit the ground, then hurled itself through the air in one of those hundred-foot bounds that have led the ignorant to believe they can fly.

The leap brought it straight toward me.

I don't think it was intentional. I think it jumped blind, with the fire in its eyes. But he saw me as he came. His mouth opened, his fangs gleamed, his eyes flared, his claws reached. . . .

"He" or "it"? It had been male when it was alive. It could still sire its own kind. But did it deserve . . . ?

Doris's club met him with a solid *whump!* The vampire arced right back the way he had come and fell at Marsha's feet. Marsha bounced a boulder off him before he could move—if he could have moved.

I didn't go on. I headed for the fire and another of those skunky kegs and hopefully some unsober reflection.

Dojango was shaking worse than I was, but he was on the job, feeding the fire with one hand, keeping a crossbow aimed at Zeck Zack with the other. He didn't look up to see who or what was coming toward him.

Another twenty-mile shriek shredded the fabric of the night.

"I make it twelve," I said. "One lame. If I stare through this glass any more, my eye is going to fall out."

Morley took the spyglass, studied the unicorns playing around the watercourse and pretending they didn't know we were nearby.

Morley handed the glass to Dojango. He told Zeck Zack, "One of your traps worked."

The centaur wasn't talking to us this morning.

I retreated to higher ground, a better view, and contemplation of last night's revelation, which remained with me.

It amounted to a direction, a line on which Kayean and I were points. The trouble was, the line ran through me, so I had no certain idea which of the two ways pointed toward Kayean and which ran away.

The Old Witch hadn't mentioned that problem.

I favored going southeast. That would put the nest nearer Full Harbor and the roads toward the war zone. It also put a large, promising mesa astride the line.

"Hey," I called down. "Somebody bring me the glass."

Morley came grumbling up. "Who was your butt boy yesterday?"

"A genie. But somebody threw his beer keg on the fire last night." I trained the glass on the mesa, asked, "What took you so long with that thing last night?"

"I was trying to get it to talk. It was a new one, barely up from being a bloodslave. Not born to the blood. I thought it might crack. Hey! The stallion and two of the mates are taking off."

So they were. They headed up our back trail at a grand gallop. The other unicorns moved out of sight behind the scruffy trees lining the watercourse. I swung the glass. "Did you learn anything we can use?"

"Nothing you'd find interesting. What is it?"

"Somebody coming right up our back trail. Too far to tell for sure, but it looks like a big party."

He took the glass. "Fortune, thou toothless, grinning bitch. Here we are treed by unicorns and there—I'd give you odds—comes your major friend."

"No bet till they're close enough to show faces."

"You want a sure thing, don't you?"

"I've never had a gambling debt hanging over my head."

He scowled and returned the glass.

The male unicorn was back. He and the trained dogs lurked behind the living screen bordering the creek, waiting for us to make a break. The females had moved to a tributary dry wash a mile away.

Answering a question, I told Morley, "They'll jump out and try to panic the horses, which isn't hard unless the horses are well trained. If they succeed, they'll pick off a few, eat the horses where they fall, and carry the riders back to those who missed out on the hunt. If the horsemen regroup and come back at them, they'll just scatter and wait. People aren't going to bother carrying off dead horses."

"They ought to be close enough to see something."

I raised the glass. The riders were close enough to pick individuals from the dust but not close enough to distinguish features. "I'd guess fifteen horsemen and two wagons. See what you think."

He watched awhile, grunted. "They ride like soldiers. Looks like we trade bad trouble for worse. At least *they* seem to know where they're going."

"I know where I'm going, too. That mesa."

"Back the way we traveled for an entire day? When were you struck by this marvelous revelation?"

I ignored him. He didn't need to know.

The riders passed the female unicorns' hiding place. "Going to hit them from behind." I took the glass back. "Well. What do you know. Did you check that lead wagon?"

"No."

"Can you think of two women who might be roaming the Cantard with Saucerhead Tharpe?"

"What? Give me that damned thing." He looked. "That stupid bitch. Hell. Your pal Vasco and his boys are there, too. Regular reunion of the Garrett Appreciation Society. Looks like they're prisoners. I count ten soldiers and one officer."

My turn at the glass showed me he was right. "That's my Major No-Name. This puts me in a moral bind."

"Yeah?"

"I can't let those women get hurt."

"The hell. They asked for it. What would they do if they were up here and you were down there?"

I didn't get to answer that one. The unicorns burst out of the dry wash. At first it seemed their strategy was perfect. The soldiers' horses darted every direction. Then suddenly they were all facing the rush. The soldiers held leveled lances.

The groups crashed together. The unicorns broke first, running for the wash. One soldier and two horses were down. The unicorns had lost no one, but they had collected the majority of wounds.

An arrow smacked into the shoulder of the slowest. She stumbled, went down on her knees. Before she could rise, soldiers with lances overtook her. Major No-Name called something taunting. He sent five men to plink arrows into the wash. Angered, the unicorns came roaring out. In another brief mix-up, another soldier, another unicorn, and two more horses died. No-Name held his ground and mocked the attackers. The soldiers who lost their mounts took replacements from their prisoners.

"He do have a hate for unicorns, I think," Morley said.

"Here comes the boss female after orders."

"I'm going back down. Give me the high sign if he tells her to take the dogs with her."

"Will do."

The major was expecting a fight. He made a makeshift fort of his wagons and baggage off his pack animals, put all the extra animals inside the barricade, armed his prisoners, and had them wait on the wagons. I wondered what he told them.

The male unicorn was either stupid or had lost a favorite. They do become mercurial when that happens.

I signaled Morley. I thought I knew what he had in mind. I didn't like it but I could see no alternative.

• • •

So. The dogs went howling toward the major's group. The unicorns charged behind. A fine, merry dustup got started.

The male unicorn didn't want to watch. Morley proved that by racing from the foot of the scree to the watercourse unchallenged.

Zeck Zack was after him before he was halfway across. There is nothing on four legs faster—in the short run—than a motivated centaur.

The unicorn heard hoofbeats. He popped up to see what was happening.

It was too late. Zeck Zack was all over him, and showed us he had handled a unicorn one-on-one in younger days. It didn't last long.

All the while I was bounding down the slope. It was move-out time.

••• **43**

verything and everyone was ready when I got down. I scrambled aboard my horse. For once we agreed on absolutely everything. We were a team with a single mind. That mind said, "Make tracks."

I got out ahead of the crowd so I could lead by example. I steered around the base of the butte so we were headed east again, until we reached a point where I could see the battleground. That journey took an hour and a half.

We halted. I raised the spyglass. Nothing moved except the vultures. From that lower angle of vision it was hard to tell how great the disaster had been. I could distinguish one wagon on its side. A vulture perched on a wheel.

"Somebody ought to take a closer look," I said, staring at Zeck Zack.

He nodded. Without comment he borrowed a couple of javelins and trotted off. The morning had wrought marvelous changes in him. "He might be back in the army," I told Morley. Dotes just grunted. I added, "Don't forget, somebody thought enough of him to get him Karentine citizenship."

"It isn't what you were, it's what you are, Garrett. And that creature is the worst kind of night trader. The kind that sells your kind to *them*."

Yeah.

Zeck Zack circled the mess a few times, closing in, then he raised a javelin and beckoned, knowing I had the glass on him.

"Let's go."

It was grisly. The dogs were all dead. So were most of the unicorns and a dozen horses. But there was not a human cadaver to be seen.

"They went on," the centaur said.

I told Morley, "For a Venageti he sure sticks tight to Karentine field doctrine. Challenge unicorns when you can. Carry away your dead. Poison the flesh of the animals you leave behind." Every dead animal had been cut dozens of times. Each cut was stained a royal blue where crystalline poison had been rubbed into the wound.

No one was going to profit from dead army animals.

I counted eight slain unicorns. They had kept at it until the dominant female had been killed. The survivors would be in bad shape.

Unicorns in that part of the Cantard would seek easier prey for a while.

I raised the glass and searched the base of the butte. There they were, looking back at us.

"See them?" Morley asked.

"Yeah. Burying their dead. Can't make out anybody special except Saucerhead."

Zeck Zack took a cue from that and galloped off toward the butte shadow where the major was returning the earth's children to her.

"Trying to ingratiate himself," Morley said. "So you'll be a little loose on the rein when the time comes."

"When do you figure he'll run?"

"When we start into the nest. We won't dare waste time chasing him. And with us keeping them busy, his chance of making it would be good. This is his country and he can still pick them up and put them down when he wants."

I watched Dojango for a minute. He was collecting souvenirs. He had cut the dewclaws off a unicorn, had knocked out some of its razor teeth, and was trying to figure how to take its horn. That would bring fifty marks bounty in Full Harbor and more as a curio in TunFaire.

"What are you going to do about it?" Morley asked.

"Let him run. I won't have any more use for him."

Zeck Zack came prancing back. He reported that four soldiers and the major had survived, and four other men as well. I knew about Saucerhead. One of the others sounded like Vasco. The remaining two could have been anybody.

"Survived don't mean unscathed, either," the centaur said. "They got cut up pretty good."

"What about the women?"

"Not much scathing there. A little frayed around the edges, as anyone would be after that."

Morley muttered, "Bet we can thank that dope Saucerhead for that."

Zeck Zack went right on. "One of them kept screaming at me to tell you she going to crack your eggs, fry them, and feed them to the unicorns. When the boss soldier tried to shut her up, she bit him and gave him a knee in *his* eggs."

"My lovely little Rose. What a wonderful wife she'll make some poor sod. Well. Let's go." I urged my mount to face east. Our unity had begun to unravel.

"She does bounce back, doesn't she?" Morley said in a tone that sounded suspiciously like admiration. "You just going to ride off?"

"Yes. The major isn't going to make prisoners of anybody again. That's going to turn into a three-way marriage of convenience that'll be as rowdy as those marriages get. But they'll take care of each other. Do you think you could get Doris and Marsha to pull a wagon? We might have a use for it."

The one wagon was not damaged, just overturned and lacking a team.

"It's army. We wouldn't want to get caught with it."

"We won't."

He spoke to the grolls. They responded in what sounded like impolite terms. He told me, "They want to collect unicorn horns. Those could be more use than any wagon. Stick one of *them* in the heart with a horn and it's all over, sure as silver. And they can't smell horns coming."

"Deal, then. Wagon for horns. Those people back there are going to be burying and bickering for a long time."

The grolls took the deal. *Crash!* Down went the wagon onto its wheels. The grolls scampered from unicorn to unicorn, perhaps dreaming of buying a brewery.

A pair of adolescent females, outraged by the trophy taking and not too badly injured, charged out of the wash. It was disconcerting, watching the absentminded way the grolls clubbed them to death.

44

We didn't try for the nest mesa that day. I wanted to go in early, when they had settled for the day, not late when they were about to awaken. Once they were soundly asleep, while the sun was high, it was almost impossible to wake them. Even the elder bloodslaves would have trouble responding.

So legend went.

We got out of sight of our pursuers, then went to work hiding our trail and laying false scents. Zeck Zack worked hard making himself useful. He knew all the tricks. He even had the grolls hand-carry the wagon two miles off to leave false wheel marks.

We set up for the night atop the copse of a small butte not more than two miles from the face of the nest mesa. My head throbbed with the nearness of Kayean. From that vantage I could see most of the scrap facing the mesa and our back trail.

"No fire tonight," Zeck Zack said as I crouched behind the spyglass trying to tell what kind of luck the major was having. "Also scatter a little and stay near the stones that got the hottest during the day. That is how they find their prey from a distance. Through their warmth. It would be wise, too, to keep too much metal from accumulating in one place."

"You wouldn't give them a holler, would you? To score a few points?"

"I've never been known for an inclination toward suicide. I am known to be quick-tempered, rash, foolish, sometimes even stupid. But not suicidal.

I enjoy the good things in life too much." Wearing a distant look, he echoed himself, "Too much."

"You might remember that the major wants you as much as he wants me. Your blackmailing priest was a buddy of his and you know it," I added.

"He has to get out of the Cantard before he can cause me any grief. He has to get through tonight. Last night he was too strong for them. Tonight he won't be. Especially if they haven't fed for a while. And they have not. The two who came to Full Harbor could not restrain themselves, though their attacks put them at great risk."

"Why would they spot him more quickly than us?"

"Eleven humans are easier to find than one."

"Oh." The day was getting on toward failing. Those who were tracking us were having no luck and seemed now to be more interested in settling for the night.

"There." The centaur pointed. A darkness was rising from the mesa face.

I shifted the glass. "Bats. A billion bats." And coming up from a point right on the line through my head, my mystical connection with Kayean.

Morley came in from scouting around. For a city boy he caught on fast. I repeated the centaur's advice. He gave Zeck Zack the fish eye, then nodded curtly. "Makes sense. Don't sleep too soundly tonight, Garrett."

Right. With us here on the lip of it, I'd be lucky to get the old forty winks. You never admit it to the guys you're with, but you get scared. Damned scared. And this time there might be a bigger stake than just death. I could be dead and have to keep walking.

If you ask me, the difference between a hero and a coward is that a hero finds some damn-fool way to con himself into going ahead instead of doing the sensible thing.

They never did give me much credit for sense.

I did sleep, because a hand shaking my shoulder woke me up. Morley.

I heard it before he told me. A hell of a row over by the foot of the mesa. Gods, how I had wanted to run over and warn them when they had chosen to camp less than a mile from the gate to the nest. But, like Zeck Zack, I am not renowned for my suicidal tendencies.

As Morley said, the women were at little risk, and they were the only ones we had to give a damn about. Still, I had a soft spot for Saucerhead Tharpe. Saucerhead was implausibly romantic. He deserved preservation as the last of a knightly breed.

I got up where I could see just as the last of two campfires yonder died.

Not two minutes after that the screaming and banging stopped. And about two minutes after that somebody finally said something. Dojango: "Guess we don't have to worry about the army anymore."

No. I guess not.

Nobody got any more sleep. I stared at the stars and wondered about the size of certain mouths, and about how much Rose, Vasco, and the major had yakked it up among themselves. Between them they had enough to work out what I meant to do. Did they have guts enough to stay buttoned up on the chance I might get them out?

"Going to have to be careful work over there tomorrow," Morley said sometime in the wee hours. He didn't have to ask if I was awake. He knew. Just as I knew that he and the others were awake and hanging on to something silver.

45

We started the crossing two hours later than I'd originally planned. That gave the sun two more hours to get up and glare at the gate to the nest. Two more hours for the night people to sink more deeply into slumber. Two more hours for us to prepare and two more hours for us to get crazier with fear. Every instinct screamed, "Get out of there!"

Morley spent that time rechecking every damned thing we would carry: flares, firebombs, spears, crossbows, swords, knives, unicorn horns—the list was endless. I watched the gate through the spyglass, looked for secondary outlets, and helped the triplets polish off the last few kegs of beer. Zeck Zack mapped a convoluted route across that would be out of sight of spying eyes. The grolls, once the beer was gone, amused themselves by bringing enough water to do the horses for a couple of days. Dojango rigged up hitches they could pull if we didn't come back. Not much was said. The few lame jokes that were told got roll-on-the-ground laughs. Anything to ease the tension.

Morley distributed the lethal instruments and flares and rehearsed everyone on using them. We packed it all up, filled canteens, drank too much water, and finally the sun was high enough to suit me. "Let's go."

Morley muttered, "Wish I knew if they knew we were coming. Then we might not have to leave all the metal hardware. Especially the silver."

He was talking to no one but himself. My own contribution to nonconversation was, "I haven't been so loaded down with junk since we landed on Malgar Island." I'd been scared witless that day, too. Now those Venageti looked like friendly puppies.

••••

The centaur's route took us to the wasted camp. He knew we wanted to know.

We had an idea, of course. We'd watched the vultures circle for hours.

We heard them squabbling first. Then we heard the flies. Out on the Cantard those side fliers of death get so thick they sound like swarms of bees.

Then we pushed between boulders and saw it.

I guess it was no more gruesome than any other massacre. But the bodies were so badly torn by attackers, vultures, wild dogs, and whatnot, that we had to count heads to find out that only four of the major's party had been left for the carrion eaters. Two pasty-skinned, black-clad bloodslaves had been left, too, but they remained untouched. Even the flies and ants shunned them.

Nobody said anything. None of the dead could be identified; there was nothing to say. We went on, fear perhaps tempered by the rage that makes men hunt down the man-eater, be it wolf, rogue tiger, or one of *them*.

Nearer the gate we spread out, Morley and I flanking the hole and doing a cautious scout for surprises. Nothing seemed untoward. We assembled closer to the cave. Bat reek rolled over us. There was no sign of vampires, but I had a bit of red hair twisted around my finger. It had come off a thornbush nearby.

Morley and I went in first, each with a sword and unicorn horn. Dojango followed with flares and firebombs. The grolls backed him with spears and crossbows. Zeck Zack was rear guard because we expected him to turn ghost on us anyway. He wouldn't have to stumble over anybody when he decided to leave.

We would change up on weapons and tactics if we reached the nest proper.

I gave a signal. We all closed our eyes, excepting the centaur. He counted a hundred silently, snake-hissed. Eyes barely cracked, we mouse-footed into the mouth of hell.

We advanced a few steps, stopped, listened. Morley and I knelt to let the triplets have more freedom to support us. We continued in that fashion. The deeper we sank into the darkness, the more frequently we paused.

By right of better eyes Dojango should have been in my place. But Morley feared his nerves weren't up to it. I agreed. Dojango had buckled down and tightened up a lot, but he wasn't ready for the front line.

Gods, the stench in that hole!

The first hundred feet weren't too bad. The floor was level and clean. The ceiling was high. There was daylight at our backs. And there was no sign that anyone was waiting for us.

Then the floor dropped and turned right. The ceiling lowered until the grolls had to duckwalk. The darkness tightened and filled with the rustle and flutter of bats disturbed. Within a few yards we were saturated with the filth that was the source of the stench. The air grew chill.

Zeck Zack hissed.

We stopped. I was amazed that he could move so quietly on hooved feet. I'd assumed he was hell-bent for wherever already.

The hiss was the only sound. The centaur handed something forward. It gleamed through Dojango's fingers as he passed it.

It was the lucifer stone Morley had given the centaur before shutting him in that tomb.

An iron chill dragged its claws up my back. By the stone's light I saw Morley entertaining the same question: was the centaur announcing payback time? Burying us here would solve several of his problems.

I watched Morley struggle with the urge to kill Zeck Zack. He put it down. Barely. He gave me the stone because I had poorer eyes. I folded it into my right hand, under my fingers, against the grip of my wooden sword. I could lift a finger or two and leak light when I needed it.

Onward. Already the sun, freedom, and fresh air seemed a thousand years and miles behind us. Progress slowed as we examined every cranny for ambushers.

It looked like a dried-out corpse. Mouth open. Eye sockets empty. Hair gray and wild. One buzzard claw came reaching out of a crack at me. I fell away, throwing a wild backhand stroke with the stone-set edge of my sword. Bone parted like dry sticks.

The thing that had pushed those old bones leaped out.

A groll's spear drove through it. Dull eyes stared into mine as it pitched forward onto the unicorn horn I raised to meet it. Cold, stale, awful breath washed my face. Again I saw that look I had seen on that butte about a century ago: immortality betrayed.

It tried to sink fangs into my throat. They weren't yet well developed. Its disease was not far advanced.

I was terrified anyway.

A Dojango toe connected with its head.

I grabbed the lucifer stone and got up. Neither old bones nor the blood-slave did. But brothers of the latter had come for the party, too.

They had no weapons but tooth, claw, ferocity, and a conviction of invincibility. None of that did them any good.

Morley and I held them. Dojango retreated behind his brothers and lit a flare. The night people made little squeaks and pawed at their eyes. A moment later it was over.

There were only four of them, plus somebody who had been dead for years. It had seemed like a battalion.

Morley and I inspected each other for wounds. He had one shallow gash but waved off attention. He wasn't human enough to have to worry.

The enemy had been met. He had been overcome in the opening encounter. Our nerve solidified. Our fear came under control. Dojango was proud of himself. He had proven he could think despite his terror.

We regained our breath and went on. Without the centaur Zeck Zack. There was no telling when he had deserted. Probably during the excitement, when he was sure no one would notice him going.

Behind us, the flare burned out. The bats began to settle down. The air grew colder.

46

The second bunch were more difficult than the first, though they were no more successful. They were bloodslaves farther along the scarlet path, harder to kill, but as vulnerable to blinding and more sensitive to the power of the unicorn horn. They did make us work up a sweat.

The third bunch was bad.

They let us know we were near the nest. They were bloodslaves who had slipped past all the perils of snares and pitfalls and were so far advanced in the disease that they were on the verge of joining the masters. Which meant they were almost as fast and strong and deadly as the two we had destroyed on the butte. After we skewered one with a horn it was almost impossible to touch the other three, even with them flare-blind. In the darkness where they dwell, they had little use for sight. They ignored their pain and used their ears.

One got past me and Morley. The grolls pinned him with their spears, then finished him with unicorn horns. Dojango's fear-fevered arm gave us the other two. He hit them swith firebombs. We finished them while they thrashed in the flames and screamed.

"And that's it for the element of surprise," Morley said. "If ever there was one."

"Yeah."

They were the first words spoken since our entry underground, save a soft grollish curse from Doris on breaking a unicorn horn pinning a blood-slave.

The fires died. We readied ourselves. "Not far now," I guessed. Morley grunted. "The odds have got to be better," I said. Morley grunted again. Some conversationalist. He looked odd in the glow of the lucifer stone. Was he going to flake out?

He got himself organized inside, stepped forward, whacking the flat of his sword with his horn and listening to the echo. After about fifty steps there was no echo.

I let light leak between my fingers.

No cave wall. No ceiling. "Dojango. Give Doris a flare."

The groll knew what to do. They threw for height and distance.

We were on the platform overlooking a floor about forty feet below. Man-made stairs ran down a widening sweep. Below, nearly a hundred ... creatures ... faced us and started screaming, pawing at their eyes. The dozen or so in white made me think of maggots on a dead dog.

Marsha snapped a spear down the stairs. It hit a youngster who had been rushing up when the flare ignited. He tumbled.

"How do you figure chewing it now that you've bitten it off?" Morley asked. He shivered in the cold.

"Sure won't do any good to change our minds. We have to keep pushing, keep them panicked."

He growled at the grolls. I looked out along the line that began in my head, and saw a half dozen women in white, some leading children born to the blood. I couldn't pick her out.

Morley seemed to be looking for someone, too.

"There they are." Dojango indicated cages to one side. A score of prisoners stared at us, most of them forlornly.

The flare was almost out, but the grolls had shed and opened their packs and were pasting the crowd with firebombs. Dojango was assembling a powerful lamp. Morley and I snatched bows and scattered arrows wherever it looked like the panic was fading.

I told Morley, "Like the pregnant lady told her guy, it's time we took steps." I started down the stairs, again armed with sword and unicorn horn, straining against the weight of my pack of lethal confections. Morley elected the same weapons and snuggled his pack a little tighter. Dojango chose to bear horn and crossbow. His pack was empty, so he left it. The grolls shrugged their packs back on but didn't arm themselves with anything but their clubs, which they had dragged in through all the difficulties of the entry cave, tied to their belts and trailing like fat, stiff tails.

"Prisoners first?" Morley asked.

"I wouldn't. Even if they could be trusted they'd get in the way. Straight ahead. Where the women are going. That will be where the masters hole up."

We reached the cavern floor. The grolls went ahead, swinging their clubs. Muttering to himself, Morley minced around an ankle-deep pool of filth. He flicked a toe at a night creature. Some were trying to fight back now.

Tinnie and Rose added shrieks to the uproar. In a free second I saluted them with my sword. They didn't appreciate the gesture.

Morley kicked a human thighbone out of his path. "You ever wondered what bloodslaves feed on while the disease is running its course?"

"No. And I don't want you to tell me."

We climbed toward the gap through which the females had fled. It was a hole maybe four feet tall and three wide. It was clogged with bloodslaves trying to reach the protection of their masters.

The grolls hammered them with all the passion of miners who'd hit a gravel reef.

"And you wanted to bring mules," Morley crowed.

Dojango's crossbow thunked, creaked, thunked again as he sniped at a hero with designs on the lamp we had left at the entrance.

The night people began to press in. Not good. Armed or not, there is only so much that can be done against such numbers.

I still had a few tricks folded up my sleeves and tucked into my boots, but I wanted to hoard those as long as I could.

The grolls opened the hole.

Morley spoke to them. They threw once-human trash aside and wriggled through. I followed with the lucifer stone. Morley came last.

Nothing tried coming through after us.

"Well. We made it to the heart of the nest. Just like the heroes in the old stories. Only that was the hard part for them. The hard part is just beginning for us."

The brides of blood had ranged themselves before the stone biers of their lovers, who had not awakened. There were fifteen of them. In only four had the disease run its full course. One of those I had faced across a table in Full Harbor, in a house where I had loved another in whom the disease was only a few years along and still reversible. Beside her stood a man whose face betrayed him as he who had passed me a note. She shuddered when she met my gaze, slipped her hand into his.

Well. Did you ever want to cry?

From the hole behind us Dojango said, "They've got the lamp. And the fires are out. Don't look like they're up for breaking in here, though."

"Figure we got troubles enough already. She here, Garrett?"

"Yeah."

"Cut her out of the herd and let's get on with it."

I beckoned Kayean.

She came, eyes downcast, towing the man. The other brides, and the eight or so bloodslaves with them, hissed and shuffled.

The tip of Morley's unicorn horn intercepted Kayean's man and rested on his throat. "Where is he, Clement?"

"Kill him here, Dotes. Don't take him back."

"If I don't take him back, they'll kill me. Where is he?"

Which was all very interesting.

What the hell was going on?

"Back there." The bloodslaves pointed past the brides. "Hiding with the children. You won't get him out without waking the masters." He stared at me, eyes filled with appeal. "Take her out. Before they wake up."

An excellent suggestion, and one I would have loved to have put into effect. Except that, though unspoken, we had come in knowing that if we went out again we would be leaving *them* dead behind us.

It had less to do with emotion than necessity. If we left them alive, they would be after us as soon as the sun went down. There would be no outrunning them. And they dared not let us go. They would have the Karentine army all over them as soon as we reported the location of the nest.

"We need to talk, Morley."

"Later. Come out of there, Valentine."

Something stirred, hissed, back among the biers. The hissing formed words, but just barely. "Come get me."

I said, "Folks, things are going to get nasty in a minute. Some are going to die the real death. You don't want it to be you, I'm taking volunteers to sneak out to the big cavern. We pull this off, you can migrate to another nest." And if we didn't we would be their midnight snack.

After a few seconds one of the newer females started toward us, eyes downcast. Most male bloodslaves become what they are by choice. Few women do. They are selected and collected for the masters by night traders like Zeck Zack.

One of the old females objected. She tried to stop the deserter.

Dojango's bolt hit her square in the forehead, driving four inches into her brain.

She fell and flopped around. The bolt wasn't enough to kill her, but plenty to scramble her mind.

I let the volunteer through. "Anybody else?"

The old females looked at the fallen one, listened to the creak of the crossbow rewinding, hissed back and forth, and decided to leave us to the mercy of their masters. One by one, the crowd departed. The little ones, too.

They have no loyalty to one another at all.

47

"**K**ill that thing," Morley snapped. He repeated himself in grollish.

Marsha thumped the flopping woman till she stopped.

"Valentine. Come out."

Hissing again. I raised the lucifer stone overhead so I could look at this creature who so interested Morley Dotes.

Then a lot came together.

I knew that face. Valentine Permanos.

Six years back the kingpin's chief lieutenant, one Valentine Permanos, and his brother Clement had vanished with half the kingpin's fortune. There had been rumors about them running to Full Harbor. Morley would have to come across with more numbers to make it all add up, but I saw enough of the edges to relax with my allies.

"Let's do it, Garrett," Dotes said, getting a two-handed grip on his unicorn horn.

Valentine Permanos began shaking one of the still forms.

His face was a horror. They say the swiftness of the disease's progress depends a great deal on the will of its victim. This one was much further gone than his brother. He *wanted* to become one of *them*.

I recalled old rumors that he had been dying a slow death when he scooted on the kingpin.

Morley drove his horn straight into the heart of the first vampire he reached. So did I. The body shuddered. Its eyes opened for a moment and filled with that look of betrayal, then glazed over.

Morley did another one. So did I. He got a third. I lined one up. Morley cursed. "Dojango. Throw me another horn."

"That's a hundred marks, Morley. What's wrong with the one you got, actually?"

"It's stuck in his goddamn ribs! Now throw me another horn."

I moved to my fourth victim. My shakes were going away. Six more after this one. Over the hump. We would be headed out in a few minutes.

I drove the horn down.

With no warning, the one Valentine was shaking flung itself toward me.

I twisted away. Dojango's hasty bolt ripped its face open. Morley whacked it with his horn. The ceiling was so low the grolls had to stay on their knees. Still, Doris managed to bounce his club off the vampire's chest.

The monster leaped back from whence it had come, eyes burning, amazed, hissing something we weren't meant to understand. I noted the huge ruby pendant it wore, then grabbed Morley's shoulder and kept him from pursuing it. "Get back here! Now!" I backed up. "That's the bloodmaster himself. Touch me. Everybody touch me."

"What the hell?"

"Do it!"

Hands clasped onto me. "Close your eyes." I palmed a sweaty slip from my sleeve, ripped it open. I counted to ten, expecting claws and fangs to rip me with each beat.

I opened my eyes.

They were all up now. They had their hands to their temples and their maws open in soundless screams. They swayed back and forth with the madness.

"Two minutes!" I yelled. "Less than two minutes to finish it! Let's go!"

I admit I did less than charge headlong. I didn't completely trust the Old Witch's magic. And the bloodmaster looked like he was less than incapacitated.

It was gruesome work, work in which I take no pride even though it was *them* we slaughtered and threw behind us so the grolls could hammer their heads to a pulp. We didn't get through it easily, either, for even in their two minutes of madness, they knew they were being attacked. I picked up a dozen shallow claw gashes that would require careful attention later. Morley nearly got his throat ripped out because, out of some weird nobility, he tried to leave the bloodmaster for me.

Groll clubs hammered that old monster's skull, and not a second too soon. Dojango was yelling about goings-on in the big cavern, where the crowd had decided to get involved after all. Morley was busy trying to get his prisoner sewed up. I yelled at the grolls to turn around, then threw Kayean and her guy out of the way so they wouldn't get stomped. Doris chucked Dojango back, started stabbing with his club, driving the bloodslaves back.

I heard a sharp whine, turned.

Morley was pulling a unicorn's horn out of Clement's chest.

I snarled, "That wasn't necessary." I glanced at Kayean, wondering if she was going to go now. She sank down beside Clement and held his hand again. I faced the hole, shucked my pack, and pitched a few firebombs past the grolls. That drove the bloodslaves back.

"Let's go!" I ordered. I glanced back. Morley was on his way, dragging his prisoner. Kayean was rising reluctantly, her face as cool as the death she'd nearly become. But Dojango . . .

"Damn you, Dojango, what the hell are you doing?"

"Hey, Garrett. You know what a genuine bloodmaster's bloodstone is worth? Look at this sucker. It must be three or four thousand years old."

Three or four thousand years. For that long the monster had preyed upon humanity. I hoped they had a special place for him where they stoked the fires especially hot.

I dove through the hole behind the grolls and scattered the rest of my firebombs and arced a couple of flares into the crowd. The screaming picked up again. I dropped to one knee, wooden sword ready, while the grolls flailed around with unprecedented fury.

A hand dropped onto my shoulder. I glanced up into sad, gentle, possibly forgiving eyes.

Morley plopped pack and prisoner on the other side of me and started flinging his bombs. I heard Dojango's crossbow thunk. Morley asked, "What the hell did you do in there, Garrett?"

"Later."

"I know sorcery when I smell it. What else do you have up your sleeve?"

"Let's free the prisoners and start hiking." The denizens of the pit had faded back, but they were gathering before the steps of the tunnel to the world. They had not given up. If they stopped us, their way of life would remain secure. They could wait until one of their born-to-the-blood children was old enough and tough enough to make himself bloodmaster.

An arrow arced down out of the gloom and thunked into Marsha's shoulder. Someone had gotten to the gear we had left at the entrance to the cavern. What was merely a nuisance to a hide-thick groll could be lethal to the rest of us.

"Move it!" I snarled. "Your meat up top, Dojango."

Rose and Tinnie howled like an alley full of cat-fights. We pushed over to the cages. Most of the captives were as colorless as their captors. The night people didn't drain them quickly, like a spider. Most were too far gone to realize what was happening. I was surprised they were even alive. As somebody had said, the Cantard had been too quiet for the hunting to be good. "Hello, Saucerhead." I ignored the women's cage. "Are you going to be as stubborn as usual? I don't want to leave you here."

Give it to Saucerhead. Not much brains but plenty of spunk. He worked up a grin. "No problem, Garrett. I'm unemployed. I got fired on account of I couldn't keep us from getting into this fix."

He had enough wounds to show he'd damned well tried. He was blue with the cold, the arctic chill I'd hardly noticed in my frenzy to get in and get out.

"You're free to take a job, then. Consider yourself on retainer."

"You got it, Garrett."

"How about you, Vasco? Still think you can get rich by stopping me? Look here. This is Denny's girl. How much longer you figure she would have been good? A year? Maybe. If you were lucky. All your buddies died for nothing."

"Don't preach at me, Garrett. Don't push. Just get me out of here. I'll bury my own dead." His teeth chattered.

"How about you, Spiney?"

"I never had any quarrel with you, Garrett. I got none now."

"Good enough." There were two Karentine soldiers in with them. They were the worse for wear, too. I didn't think it worth my time to ask if they would give me any grief.

Meantime, Morley chatted up the ladies. They were in a separate cage. Rose was ready to deliver the moon if we would just get her out. *Me* was the word I heard, not *us*. Lovable, thoughtful, family-oriented Rose. Tinnie behaved with as much decorum as the circumstances allowed. I decided to give her a closer look if we ever got out of there.

"Think we ought to turn them loose?" Morley asked.

"Up to you. They might slow us down."

It takes longer to tell than it took to happen. Even so, Dojango decided he'd had enough. "You guys quit jacking around or my brothers and I walk without you." He had the bloodstone and several unicorn horns, and though he was feeling wealthy, he was also worried about living to enjoy his gains.

His crossbow thunked. An instant later an arrow hissed overhead.

"He's got a point, Morley."

Morley spoke to the grolls. They opened all the cages with a few well-placed club strokes. Over Dojango's protests, Morley and I passed out unicorn horns. The grolls tossed our last few flares onto the steps and we headed for freedom.

•••**48**

Freedom was a coy bitch.

Our first charge looked like it would carry through. But they swarmed, threw everything at us, utterly determined to keep the secret of the nest. And I mean threw everything: filth, bones, rocks, themselves. And some were almost as tough as their masters. We lost every one of the older prisoners who had tagged along. They were unarmed and as slow as men in a syrup bath.

One of the soldiers fell. Vasco took a wound but managed to keep his feet. I collected another assortment of scratches. Saucerhead went down and had trouble getting up. When Doris grabbed him and started carrying him, the monsters swarmed all over him. I thought he was a goner for sure. When I saw he was still alive, I had to overcome self-disgust for momentarily wishing he'd died so we wouldn't have to drag him out.

Then the night people fell back and were silent. I wondered why, noting there were only about thirty of them left willing to fight. Then I noticed that the last two flares were about to die.

In moments they would have us in their element: darkness.

Time, then, for another one from up my sleeve. One I had expected to have to use earlier than this. "Everybody get in close, here. Leave something sharp-pointed out, face uphill, and close your eyes."

There were those who wanted to ask questions and those who wanted to argue. I lied, "Those who don't do what I say are going to end up blind."

Morley snapped orders in grollish. The triplets did what I wanted. That damned Doris was up and lugging Saucerhead again.

The last flare died.

Rustle and scrape as the night people began moving.

This one was actually in my boot, not up my sleeve. I said, "Close your eyes!" and ripped the paper open.

A blast of sulfurous air overrode the stench of the cavern. Light slammed through my eyelids. Night people shrieked. I counted to ten slowly. "Eyes open. Let's move." The enveloping light had waned to a tolerable glare. The Old Witch had said it was good for several hours. The light was much like that of the sun. The night people found it excruciating. If they didn't get out of it quickly, it would destroy what served them as sanity.

We went up the steps. I ripped rags off a fallen bloodslave, threw them over Kayean to shield her from the light. She was already in pain. Morley and Dojango wanted to stop and play with the bows we had left.

"Get out while you can!" I snarled. "Our luck has been too damned fantastic already. Let's not push it."

Marsha grabbed Dojango and started dragging. Everybody else started hiking. When he saw he would have to play alone, Morley grabbed his booty and joined the retreat.

There was no respite. The tunnel was one place the night people could escape the light. And once free of its maddening influence they became rabid, terrible enemies again.

Nevertheless, we outran them to the mouth of the world.

"**W**hat the hell is this stuff?" Morley growled as we struggled through the webbing or netting or wire that had materialized in the mouth of the cave during our time below.

"How the hell should I know? Just get through it." I was fussing over Kayean. She hadn't spoken a word yet. But she was whining like a baby. At first I thought it was fear of going out into a world she hadn't seen in years. Then I realized it was because the tangle we were in was wire and the metal's touch hurt.

Who put it there?

My money was on Zeck Zack. But where had he gotten the wire? And what did its presence mean to us?

We broke out. It was broiling, summer hot out there.

"Midnight." Morley groaned. "We were down there longer than I thought."

"Keep moving. Lots to do yet."

We were halfway down to the desert floor when the screaming started behind us. There was pain in it, but it was mostly frustration and rage.

Dojango gasped. "They say those things can recover from almost anything. You think any of the masters will come around?"

I told the truth. "I don't know. We'll tell the army first chance we get."

We hustled across to our camp. There was a three-quarter moon, so the going was quick, though Kayean kept whimpering at the brightness. So did Morley's prisoners. As we climbed to our camp, Dotes said, "We'll have to pack them in moist earth and wrap them up good to protect them from the sun."

"We have to do some talking, too."

"I suppose so."

"What happened to the major? Tinnie, do you know?"

She was sticking as close to me as Kayean was. "The one who arrested us? I don't know. I guess he got killed when the vampires attacked."

"Vasco. Did you see what happened to him?"

"I was too busy."

"Anybody?"

Rose said, "I thought I saw them carry him away. But maybe I was wrong. He wasn't in the cages when you showed up."

"Maybe they ate him," Dojango suggested.

"We have the right number of bodies," Morley said. Then he gave me a sudden, odd look, as though he suspected me of knowing something I hadn't shared.

I did, but I hadn't shared it only because it had hit me just minutes before. I whispered, "That name that kept turning up on those have-you-heard-of lists. The one I'd heard but couldn't remember? I remembered."

"And?"

"A legendary Venageti agent. Supposedly a shape-shifter. Also supposedly caught and killed. But if he was, why are some folks—with Venageti connections—so interested in him?"

"I don't know and I don't think I want to know. All I'm interested in now is moving myself from this godforsaken here to there where I can sit down to my first healthy meal in a month. But I suppose we have to protect ourselves. You think we rescued him?"

"There's a chance."

"Which one?"

"Take your pick."

"Not the women?"

"No. One would know the other had changed. I'd vote for someone about his size."

"Always assuming he's still with us."

"Always assuming that."

We were pleasantly surprised to find our camp as we had left it, unplundered and the horses uneaten and patiently waiting. Morley sent Marsha off for a load of moist earth. He assumed the job of sentinel. The rest of us doctored one another. When I was satisfied that I wouldn't succumb to the disease through my wounds, I hunted for Dotes. He was perched on a boulder contemplating the desert between our camp and the mesa. He said, "You haven't said a word to her."

"I'll talk to her when she wants to talk. For now I'm satisfied with her letting me bring her out after what you did to Clement. It's time you explained the latest moves in Morley's Game."

"I suppose. Otherwise you'll badger me incessantly. You knew that six years ago the kingpin's number one walked with half his plunder."

"Old news. I also heard that he and his brother ran off to Full Harbor."

"It took them a couple of years to find that out. The kingpin sent some men down. They must have stirred things up the same way we did. Something happened to them. They only got one report back. It said Valentine wasn't in Full Harbor anymore, and that after a fast romance, his brother had married a local girl named Kronk. She had gone off with her husband when he followed his brother wherever."

"Then you knew all along who she married."

"Yeah. But telling you wouldn't have helped you find her. His trail was already covered."

I controlled my anger. "So the kingpin sent you down here."

"Not exactly. I volunteered. When you asked me to join up with you, it was like the answer to a virgin's prayer. An honest-to-god miracle. The kingpin was ready to list my name with those sleeping among the fishes. It was an out. I went and told him the story and said I would get Valentine if we could call it even. He bought it. He wants Valentine a lot worse than he ever wanted me. So I went ahead and hooked up with you, betting the longest odds I ever played, hoping you could find the woman and she would have lasted longer with Clement than she did with you or your buddy."

For a while we stared at the desert. Shapes moved there, but none came our way. They didn't have the fully developed senses of their masters. Finally, Morley started talking again.

"I didn't have the foggiest where it was going till we walked into that place of Zeck Zack's and found those vampires waiting. Then it clicked. The evidence was there all along. I knew Valentine back when. He was dying a slow death and he had no more conscience than a shark. For him it was the logical way to dodge death. He probably took the money in case he needed to buy his way in. Knowing him, he probably figured on being bloodmaster within fifty years."

"So. The loose ends begin to come together. But there's still one big one hanging out. Who were the people on that ship with the striped sail? What were they doing? Why were they interested in us?"

I had an idea and I thought Morley's confessions lent it strong circumstantial support. But I meant to reserve that. It might prove useful. I wasn't convinced that those people were out of the game.

"Why take Valentine back?" I asked.

"For the kingpin's peace of mind. And mine. I don't want him doubting for a minute."

I glanced out at the desert. "What are they doing?" Those who had come out of the nest behind us were scampering around like blind mice.

"I don't know. But I'll give you another loose end. Zeck Zack."

"Not much we can do about him."

"I should have cut his throat."'

"And you criticize me for what red meat does to me?"

"Marsha's back. Let's pack our prizes."

"What are we going to feed them?"

"Let them get hungry. They'll eat what we give them." He dropped off his boulder. "Where do we go now?"

"Back to Full Harbor. Take a peek through the centaur's tunnel. See how much excitement there is about us. I hate to leave our stuff if we don't have to. Buying new would stretch the budget too far."

"That innkeeper probably sold everything already."

"We'll see. Keep a watch on our friends. Just in case the major is with us." I had a couple tricks up my sleeve yet, one of which would probably give me the major, but I didn't want to use them if I didn't have to. Magics of the sort I had gotten from the Old Witch were too precious to squander.

We packed our prizes, as Morley dubbed them, in the earth Marsha brought, wet them down, bundled them up, and loaded them on the wagon. Tired though we were, I wanted to be traveling with first light.

Before I folded my blanket over Kayean's face, she met my gaze directly for the first time and rewarded me with a feeble smile.

The nineteen-year-old Marine was still alive. He could be touched.

50

Vasco and Saucerhead also went into the wagon, with a moderately carved-up soldier in the driver's seat. Doris insisted he was capable of helping Marsha pull. Fine. Let him if he wanted. Let him bleed to death. I wasn't his mother.

Mrs. Garrett taught her boys never to argue with grolls.

We put the women on horseback. Everyone else would walk, like it or not.

We were ready to head out when Morley summoned me to his boulder. "Bring the spyglass."

When I got there I heard it. It came from the direction of the cave. I trained the glass. There was barely enough light. "The ones who came out can't get back inside."

"Oh, my. Isn't that sad." Then he muttered something else, and pointed.

"Oh, my twice or thrice," I said. "I guess this means we slip out the back door."

"Yep. Papa's coming home. Jodie goes out the window and keeps moving fast. It won't take him long to figure we got out again."

I could hear them now as well as see them. "I never saw so many in one mob before. He must have rounded up his whole tribe." I guessed there were at least five hundred centaurs. Their advance was a movement of precision to be envied by any cavalry commander. They changed directions and formations as easily and quickly as a flock of birds, and with no more apparent signaling.

"Let's not sit here talking about it while they just prance up and grab us."

"Good thinking." We got moving.

Zeck Zack and his people didn't interfere with us at all, though I'm certain their scouts knew where we were. We hastened eastward as fast as we could hoof it, with me sort of hanging around the rear, staring at backs, wondering which, if any, was the major.

News of Glory Mooncalled's adventure had reached every cranny of the Cantard. The land was coming to life. Three times we went into hiding while soldiers passed. They were all headed south. The smallest lot were Venageti rangers. No telling what they were up to when they heard and decided to head home. I didn't care as long as they didn't want to include me in their game of kings.

Morley and I both watched our companions more closely than we did the rangers. The major, if he was with us, didn't give himself away. Not that I expected him to, but I wasn't missing any chances.

We kept on until everyone was stumbling, and kept on still. What Zeck Zack might want to do with us we had no idea, but he had no cause to be friendly. And there were the other perils of the Cantard, which Glory Mooncalled had conjured to life like a shower livens the plants of the desert. It seemed we couldn't go five miles without some sort of alarm. The nights were more friendly than the days.

We reached the abandoned mill without falling into misfortune. I began to feel optimistic. "We'll rest here a day or two," I announced.

Some of my comrades by circumstance wanted to argue. I told them, "Take it up with the grolls. If you can whip them, go do what you want." I wasn't feeling a bit democratic.

The only would-be sneak-off was Rose.

I had to give the little witch credit for being stubborn and determined. No matter what, she was going to keep after Denny's legacy until she got it. She worked on Morley, but he had reached a state where he had nothing on his mind but watercress sandwiches. She worked on Saucerhead, but he had signed on with my squad and the gods themselves couldn't have moved him until I released him. She worked on Vasco, but he was completely introspective, interested only in going home. She worked on Spiney Prevallet, but he said he'd had his fill of pie in the sky by and by and told her to go to hell.

She decided to take the future by the horns herself.

I caught her with a sharpened piece of firewood trying to decide the best place to stick it into the bundle containing Kayean. I'm afraid I lost my temper. I sprawled her across my lap and applied the stick to her posterior.

Morley said, "You should have left her with her spiritual family."

She gave him a look to sear steel.

I think his remark hurt her more than the spanking, though a person of her temperament was the sort to turn the thrashing into a grudge worth nursing for years. It sent her off to sit alone and reweave her skein of self-justification. Come the next night, while we were waiting for Dojango to come back with a report on our standing in the city, she decided to go her own way.

Morley reported her defection. "Shall we let her go?"

"I guess not. Chances are she'd get herself enslaved or killed, and I have an obligation to her family. We know she won't learn from experience, so there's no point letting her suffer for education's sake. And if she did get through, she'd just set us up for something unpleasant."

Tinnie was sitting beside me, her shoulder half an inch from mine. We'd been rehashing those things men and women talk about when they have other things on their minds.

"You really ought to ditch her, Garrett." Morley sighed.

Tinnie said, "His conscience wouldn't let him. And neither would yours, Morley Dotes."

He laughed. "Conscience? What conscience? I'm too sophisticated to have one and Garrett is too simple."

I said, "Go get her, Morley. And put hobbles on her."

Once he had gone, Tinnie asked, "Would he really let her . . . ?"

"Pay him no nevermind, Red. We talk that way. But it's just talk."

Rose was not fighting when Marsha lugged her back into the circle of light cast by our fire. The fight was out of her. Morley came to report, "She ran into something out there. We scared it off. She won't say what it was, but you might consider a double watch and maybe a prayer for Dojango."

"Right." I took care of it and resumed my seat, considering Rose across the fire, feeling moody.

Tinnie touched my arm and said, "Garrett, when we get home . . ."

"If we get home is soon enough to talk about when we get home." It came out more curt than I'd intended. She fell into a silence as sullen as my own.

51

Dojango waited until afternoon to return. His report was exactly what I wanted to hear. Nobody in Full Harbor was the least interested in a band of nosies from TunFaire. Nothing unusual had taken place while we were away. All the talk was about Glory Mooncalled and the epic dustup taking shape down south. Our things were still at the inn, being preserved by an innkeeper who felt kindly disposed because we had left him the clothing and possessions of those thugs we'd thrown into the streets mothernaked.

"Or so he says," Dojango editorialized. "Actually."

"We'll watch him. Let's get it packed up. I want to hit that tunnel as soon after dark as we can. Did you make the other arrangements?"

"No trouble. They'll be delivered to the back door of the inn. They should be waiting when we get there."

"What about shipping complications?"

"Shouldn't be any, actually. It's done all the time. Every ship headed north carries a few for families that can afford it. Strictly routine, actually."

"Good. Morley. One problem left, and tonight would be the time for it to make itself apparent." We wandered away from the others slowly, keeping our backs toward them.

"You have any candidate in mind?" he asked.

"Pressed, I'd have to call Vasco's name. But he's the only one I know well enough to know he's not acting normal. And he's got good enough reasons."

"You have a move in mind? A test?"

"Right after we come out of the tunnel. I want Dojango, Marsha, and Saucerhead to go through first. You and me and Doris will bring up the rear. If we load the rest down with what has to be carried, they'll be surrounded and have their hands full when it happens."

"You could go to work for the kingpin, scheming like that."

"I've got to bring it off before it's any good. This isn't some stupid kid we can pluck like some ripe pear. He's going to have moves and plans of his own."

"We wouldn't have it any other way, would we?"

We ventured back. During the afternoon's course we passed the word on the night's festivities. Though some were not pleased with my dispositions, they were all realistic enough to understand that I would put people I trusted most where they would do the most good.

That was the disposition we assumed when we broke camp, except for having the grolls take turns pulling the wagon. I told Saucerhead he could ride until we neared the wall, but he insisted that he had healed enough to hike. Vasco and the wounded soldier also hoofed it, saying they wanted to keep loose. Morley and I trudged along eating everybody's dust.

A time or two I moved up to make sure Kayean's wrappings were holding. After the second check I dropped back and said, "I've noticed you haven't done anything to keep your prize from starving."

Kayean threw up almost everything I gave her. When I unwrapped her, I had to make certain her hands and feet were bound. I had clipped her claws first chance after we had come out of the nest. She still had her teeth and the hunger was upon her, though when she was rational she was game enough in battling the disease.

"You also notice he's gone into the long sleep that gets them when they're starving. He'll last till we make TunFaire. And that's all I need."

Much as I disliked the deed itself, I now suspected that Morley had done the best thing by killing Clement. Clement's death had freed Kayean.

Without a word having been exchanged I somehow understood that she had marched through the doorway to hell only because that was the pathway her husband had taken and she was a whither-thou-goest kind of lady. For his part, I think Clement made his move sixty percent out of conscience and remorse, forty percent out of spite. Kayean wasn't wearing white because she was his bride. One of the masters had taken her from him.

I hoped she hadn't been forced to bear one of their soulless brats. I didn't believe any woman could recover from that.

••••

It all went perfectly, with rescuees carrying our prizes into the tunnel. It was spacious enough for the wagon, but I didn't want to be found roaming the streets with army property I couldn't explain having. We could hire something on the other side.

Morley and I were fifty feet from the tunnel's end, with Doris behind us, when it happened.

Up ahead Marsha started booming his lungs out.

"Damn it!" Morley swore. He translated, "Ambush. Nine men, one woman. Striped-sail bunch. They must have made Dojango while he was in town."

"I wanted to hold on to this forever," I said, dipping into a boot. "Grab on to me. Tell Doris, too."

Beyond the tunnel's end Rose started yelling. "Garrett! Help! Morley!"

Morley muttered, "Shut up, you stupid bitch."

"Stupid? She figures she just solved her whole problem for nothing."

Rose's yelling stopped with a smack so loud we heard it back in the tunnel.

"Against the wall," I said. They held on to me. I ripped the paper spell open. Two seconds later four guys with swords galloped into the tunnel, ready for anything. They looked around and didn't find it.

One yelled, "Ain't nothing in here."

I didn't hear the reply. They withdrew.

"What now?" Morley breathed.

"As long as we move slowly and don't make any noise or any sudden moves, they won't see us or know where we are. We'll slide out and see what's going on."

What was going on was that the two thugs I knew from the striped-sail ship, with a woman who appeared to be in charge, and seven other men, had my folks lined up against a wall in the storage basement where the tunnel began. Marsha they kept contained with a ballista almost as heavy as a field piece.

In half a minute their questions made it obvious they were after a specific person, but didn't mind trampling a few others along the way. My folks just looked at them, baffled, except Rose, who put on a great crying act. I gathered that Tinnie's was the hand that had reddened her cheek.

"Well?" Morley whispered. "We can take them if Doris gets that ballista."

"We don't need any blood in it. We'll bluff. You go over there and yell for everybody to freeze when Doris busts up the ballista. I'll put a knife to the lady's throat. Take these." I gave him a couple of throwing stars from my collection of un-Garrett-like weapons.

He needed no further explanation. He told Doris what to do. We parted. I drifted toward the lady commander, no doubt the woman about whom Master Arbanos had been so dubious. Dojango had begun yammering at her, explaining that everyone else in the several parties that had gone out of the city had been killed by unicorns or vampires.

"What the hell was that?" asked one of the men at the ballista, whirling around. "Skipper, is this place haunted?"

A ballista went up in the air and shattered against the joists supporting the floor above.

Morley yelled, "Everybody freeze!"

I laid the edge of my knife on the woman's throat and whispered, "This is your friendly spook. Don't even breathe fast. Good. Now, I suggest you have your boys put down their tools."

Doris pounded three or four men out of sheer youthful exuberance. Morley tripped and head-kicked Ugly One when he took a notion to turn on me.

The lady gave the order. And added, "You're interfering with royal business. I'll have your—"

"Not at all. I have a damned good idea what you're looking for and I'll be happy to help you find it. I just don't want my people getting chewed up while you're getting your man. Do you have some way to pick him out of a crowd?"

"Pick who out?" Oh, she wanted to play coy.

"Are you the only person ever born with a brain? This is your stalking horse talking. I figured your crowd out a month ago," I lied. I backed her up a careful five steps and in plain voice vented the moment's inspiration. "I also figured out that Big One there is on the other side. He tried to kill me in Leifmold, which would have just ruined your whole scheme."

Big One started moving toward the nearest weapon.

Two throwing stars hit him, followed in an instant by a grollish fist.

The woman said, "That explains one hell of a lot. I thought we were snakebit. All right. What do you want, Garrett?"

"For me and mine to be left the hell alone. Take your man if you can pick him out. I'm all for that because I don't like what he's got planned for me. Hell. I'll narrow it down for you. I've been working on it. I know who he's not. If he's anybody. He could have been killed out there. A lot of men were."

I gave orders. The women, Saucerhead, Dojango, and Marsha, the latter three lugging Kayean and Valentine, moved to one side. I said, "Do your shopping among what's left."

"Will you let me go?"

"Why not? You don't seem to be a suicidal lady."

"You're going to find out if you call me lady one more time."

Morley snickered. "You've made a friend for life, Garrett."

What she had to say to him does not bear repetition. She asked me, "What's in those bundles?"

"What I came after." I turned her loose.

Morley was flickering around the edges because of too many hasty movements. So was Doris. I had stayed slow, though, so I figured I was still good. I tiptoed after the woman who was not a lady.

She examined the crop, dipped a hand into a pocket, brought out an amulet built around a piece of amber with an insect embedded.

Spiney Prevallet went from somnolent indifference to explosive fury so suddenly I would have been astounded if I'd had time. He knocked the amulet away with one hand and seized the woman's throat with the other.

I pricked the wrist of that hand with my knife, sliced his cheek, then got back out of the way because that—pardon the expression—lady was going to work.

I found a part of me glad the villain had not been Vasco.

Spiney ran for it. The woman snagged her amulet and raced after him. Her minions—those still upright—did nothing because they weren't sure what we would let them do.

"Fade," Morley suggested.

"Yes."

Dojango was many things, some of them things I didn't like, but he was not stupid. The moment he saw some folks preoccupied, he started getting other people out of there.

Spiney tried for the exit himself and ran head-on into a grollish fist. The woman jumped him immediately, forced the amulet into his mouth while he was still groggy.

He began to *change*.

I have heard that a shape-shifter has no true shape of its own. That it does not even have a sex as we know it, but just splits into unequal masses when it comes time to reproduce. I don't know.

Spiney changed into the major, then into a character who looked vaguely piratical, then into a woman vaguely familiar, apparently regressing through identities assumed in the past.

Everyone else was out. I wasn't curious enough to stay to see the ultimate form the Venageti agent assumed. I had no reason to presume any excess of goodwill on the part of the striped-sail people.

52

I t was a dawn-threatening hour when we reached the inn. I had let the soldiers go their ways, betting they would be so happy to get back alive that they'd cause no immediate grief. Morley and I had an argument. He thought we should have fed them to the striped-sail gang, who would have kept them busy answering questions while we got out of town.

A brief interview with the innkeeper confirmed my suspicions in that direction. He had kept our quarters open and had maintained our gear intact at the behest of the striped-sail crowd, who had hoped we would come back so they could catch our trail again. Which they had done with Dojango's visit.

I slept like the dead for five hours, then went out looking for transportation home. My luck was limited. I went back and announced, "First ship with room enough for all of us doesn't leave till day after tomorrow. The Glory Mooncalled situation has the fainthearted civilians heading north. The scow I did find is a garbage pail, but the next best chance means waiting more than a week." I did not mention that even this sleaziest of transports had stretched my remaining expense money to its limit. We'd all get hungry if it was a very long passage home.

I sat beside Morley. "I'll never take another job that takes me out of TunFaire, even if there's a hundred thousand in it for me."

"Speaking of money, when are we going to get paid? It's not critical to me because I didn't sign on for the pay. But the triplets did and they're starting to wonder."

"It'll have to wait till I can corner Tate and gouge him again. I committed what I had left to getting us home."

"They're trusting you, Garrett. Don't disappoint them."

"You know me better. I'll get my money out of Tate, one way or another, and you guys will get yours. Dojango! Where are those boxes?" He'd just come in. "You didn't drink up that money I gave you, did you?"

"Actually, I just came to tell you they're here, on a wagon out back. The landlord is having a fit that they might upset his customers if we bring them inside."

Morley grumbled, "I'll go have a fit of dancing on his head."

We put our prizes into their caskets that night. They were the standard, cheap shipper coffins folks from up north bought to bring their sons home from the war. Dojango admitted that he had gotten some drinking done. He had gotten a buy on the coffins because the long quiet spell in the Cantard had caused a depression in the Full Harbor casket industry.

I was irritated but didn't press.

After dark I took my prize out and got her cleaned up before I installed her in her coffin. Tinnie helped with the trickier parts and Kayean wasn't too much trouble. She didn't do any screaming.

I wondered what sorcery went into the creation of those white gowns. Kayean's refused to be damaged and soil would not cling.

Morley was less fastidious. He put some fresh dirt in the other box, unwrapped his prize, dumped it in, began nailing the lid down. He had to ask Marsha's help when the pounding wakened Valentine and he started screaming and trying to break out.

We'd just gotten him quieted down and the landlord off our backs again when Zeck Zack came calling.

The centaur came alone and started out friendly enough. He pranced in, looked us over, asked, "Did you bring her out, Mr. Garrett?"

"Yes."

"May I see her? I haven't seen her since she followed her idiot husband into shadow. Her and her damned twisted sense of what is right. I should have stopped her somehow."

"Might have been nice."

Morley and Saucerhead gave him ferocious scowls. Tharpe didn't know him at all. I feared there would be sparks. But he disarmed them by saying,

"I never laid a hand on her and I never would. Despite my reputation. And not just because her father was a friend of mine."

As Morley had observed before, another one.

I opened the casket. She was sleeping. The centaur looked for a while, then backed off. "That's enough. Close it. Can she be cured, Mr. Garrett?"

"I think we reached her in time. She fought it all the way. I think she's got enough left."

"Good. Then we can get down to business. Someone among you took something from the nest that rightfully belongs to my people."

That drew some puzzled looks.

"The bloodmaster's amulet. His symbol of power. The nest's bloodstone."

I don't know who started laughing first.

He gathered his dignity like a cloak. "Gentlemen, I went through years of hell and humiliation in order to find that gateway so my folk could cleanse that nest and gain enough booty and bounty money to migrate out of the Cantard. You can have your two bloodslaves. One of them I owe, and the other isn't worth enough to make a difference. But everything else in that hole is mine!"

We exchanged looks. Dojango was getting nervous. I didn't want to start anything, but I wasn't going to tolerate the centaur's tone, either. "You've got more balls than brains if you think you can walk in here talking like that. You could get yourself hurt."

"I don't have any swords hanging over my head now, Mr. Garrett. And I have friends in town who will be happy to help me recover my property."

"Now that's an interesting coincidence," I said. "Just yesterday I made a new friend, a lady down from TunFaire rounding up the Venageti priest's friends. I wasn't going to mention your name."

He stared at me a moment, decided my bluff needed calling. "Go ahead. Meantime, get that bloodstone out to my place before sundown tomorrow or find Kayean a new guardian."

"He's insane," Morley said. "You should have let me kill him when I wanted to. It's going to be trickier doing it here."

Zeck Zack said, "A large group of my friends are waiting in the street. They'd rather not disturb anything in such a public place, but they will come in if I'm not out in a reasonable time."

"Go on," I said. "Get out. Before I call *your* bluff."

He went, but left an admonition to get the bloodstone to him by next sundown. Or else.

Dojango asked, "You're not going to give it to him, are you, Garrett?"

Morley snarled, "We're going to give it to him, all right. Only it ain't going to be what he wants."

I said, "Take it easy, Morley. Think. He's trying to set us up."

"I know. And it's going to be a shame to abort his scheme because it's a wowser for a creature as mentally handicapped as a centaur. We've got plenty of time. Let's get some sleep and worry about it tomorrow."

woke up very late, and what dragged me from dreamland was Saucerhead Tharpe and the grolls stomping in. I popped up. I'd been left alone with the women and Vasco. I checked myself for knife wounds.

"Where're Morley and Dojango? What have you guys been up to?"

"Around somewhere," Saucerhead said in his slow way. "I think Morley said something about getting something decent to eat. We took the coffins and most of our stuff down to the ship so we'd be ready to go tomorrow morning."

I grumbled a bit and went for a breakfast of my own. I didn't worry much until afternoon rolled around and still there was no sign of Morley or Dojango. I started fish-eyeing Saucerhead, who had something on his conscience and was doing a poor job of hiding it. Then I found the bodies.

Actually, they weren't bodies. They were Kayean and Valentine, bundled up and concealed under some odds and ends and junk and straw left from when the place had been a stable. Then I knew what Morley had done.

Saucerhead looked relieved. He told me, "He said just sit tight and pretend they're around somewhere if anybody asks."

Two minutes later I noticed that my last paper spell fold was missing. I couldn't guess what Morley planned to do with it since there was no way he could know what would happen when he opened it. I tried fifty lines of reasoning but fixed on none of them. There was no predicting a darkelfin breed like Morley.

When afternoon gave way to evening I started prowling. The grolls got restless, too, and might have gone off if they hadn't the strictest of orders. My game of tease with Tinnie lost its savor. Rose got nervous because everyone else was, though she didn't know what was going on. Only Saucerhead was able to relax. I have to fight the temptation to say that it was because he wasn't smart enough.

Nothing happened until just before midnight, when one of Zeck Zack's "friends" came to chide us for not having delivered. I told him, "We're right here waiting whenever he wants a piece of us. Tell him he'd better bring a box lunch because it's going to take a while to get the job done."

The messenger departed a little flustered.

I wondered how the centaur's nerves were doing, out in the graveyard or wherever he was planning to take us when we tried sneaking up on him. I was willing to bet he'd planned for every contingency but us sitting tight. I hoped Morley hadn't walked into any of his plans.

Two hours later the handful of people left in the common room began buzzing. I went to find out why. Rumors were flying about a large fire out in the Narrows Will. One of the mansions there.

Morley's opening move, I presumed.

There was nothing more for another three hours, then Dojango stumbled in, wounded, pale, barking in grollish. He flopped down as Doris and Marsha stamped out.

"Well?" I demanded.

"They're going to pick up the coffins."

I looked him over. Tinnie helped. She had a fair touch with wounds.

"That all you have to tell me?"

"Morley sent me back 'cause I got hurt, actually. He's still out there working them. If that critter gets out of this alive, it sure won't be on the cheap." And that was all he would say.

A while later the grolls came tramping back in with the coffins. The landlord was right behind them raising hell about our bunch stomping back and forth through the common room during quiet hours. "I'm never leaving TunFaire again," I promised myself once more, and snarled. "Quit your bitching. You've made a bundle because of us, playing all the sides, and we'll be out of your hair in an hour anyway. Do us all a favor and make yourself disappear."

I looked so nasty he had no trouble getting the hint.

We refilled and sealed the coffins and gathered what remained of our possessions. For Tinnie and Rose and Vasco and Saucerhead Tharpe that meant no work at all. Their adventures had left them with nothing but the clothing on their backs. I wondered if I ought to put a burr under Dojango's saddle, recalling how meticulously he had gone over the ruins of their last encampment, salvaging coins and jewelry the night people had discarded. I decided the wiser course was to keep everyone dependent upon my charity.

We marched out to the sighs of the landlord and his crew.

We reached and boarded our ship without suffering misadventure.

Time passed. The tide turned. The sailors prepared to cast off. And still there was no sign of Morley.

"Where the hell is he, Dojango?"

"He said don't worry. He said go ahead. He said don't hold up anything on his account." Dojango said it, but he didn't feel it. He wanted to do something.

I didn't believe it. Morley Dotes wouldn't sacrifice himself for anyone.

"Here he comes," Saucerhead said. The deck crew was paying out the last lines, fore and aft.

He was coming for sure, in that sort of wild sprint only elfin can manage. Zeck Zack was thirty yards behind and gaining fast.

"Perfect," Dojango whispered.

Perfect, like hell. Morley wasn't going to make it without help. I looked around for a weapon and couldn't find anything.

"Now!" Dojango said. And, "Actually!"

The striped-sail woman and her crew materialized from amid the freight on the pier. They all carried ready crossbows. Morley whipped past. Zeck Zack skidded to a halt, stood there shuddering. Morley leaped from the pier to the ship, teeth glistening in a grin.

"Is this the one?" the woman called.

"The very one, darling," Morley gasped.

The gang closed in on the centaur.

"You damned fool!" I yelled at Morley. "You could have been killed."

"But, if you'll notice, I wasn't."

••• 54

T he passage north was slower than it had been going south. The winds were less friendly. But it was almost as eventless. There was a spot of trouble one night when Rose tried pushing Kayean over the side, but she collected only bruises for her trouble. There were no encounters with pirates, privateers, Venageti, or even Karentine naval vessels. Leifmold and I almost believed the gods had decided to lay off me for a while.

Rose's assault on Kayean was due to my lack of foresight.

I was taking her out of her box at night, giving her the chance to breathe real air and face the real light of the stars. Foodwise I had gotten her to where she could keep down small amounts of lightly browned chicken flesh. I'd left her on deck to fetch some, and had gotten into an argument with Tinnie, who felt I should be apportioning my time somewhat differently. Rose made her move and took her lumps in my absence. I found out what was happening only when one of the ship's night watch told me Rose needed saving.

I got there in time, though Kayean almost crossed the line and surrendered to the hunger. Rose crawled away, into the comforting arms of a Morley getting back to his cynical ways.

I calmed and fed Kayean and we sat in the starlight awhile, watching the wake luminesce and the flying fish leap. She finally spoke. "Where are you taking me?"

Her words were barely intelligible. Down in the nests, it is said, they don't allow their brides to talk. She was rusty.

No one had told her what was going on. I'd just snatched her and dragged her along, giving her as much control of her destiny as she'd had while she was in the pit.

So I told her the story, and I wound up saying, "I think you ought to grab it. Denny wanted you to have it, and right now it's the only thing you've got going in this whole world."

She gave me a look that took me back in time. I had to take her down and put her away before I did something foolish. I returned to the deck to watch the sea unscramble my brain.

Morley came out of the darkness and settled beside me. After a while, he said, "I have a statistic I want you to consider, Garrett. Of all the guys who have loved her, only one is still alive." Then he was gone. The superstitious half-breed.

Later I took advantage of Tinnie's conciliatory mood to lay my haunts for a while.

Fate had us overhaul *Binkey's Sequin* running up the Leifmold channel and I cut a deal with Master Arbanos even before we made the quay. He was vastly amused to see me saddled with Rose and Tinnie again.

We laid over three days in Leifmold, waiting for Master Arbanos to off-load a cargo of army supplies and take on twenty-five tons of smoked cod. Morley split his time between getting fat eating green leafies and keeping Rose too busy to get into trouble. The triplets sold one of their unicorn horns and went on a toot. I think Vasco spent his time thinking about doing himself in. The rest of us just waited, with me lending a thought or ten to my routine once we reached TunFaire.

I still had to get myself and my associates paid.

55

We tied up at *Sequin*'s place on the TunFaire waterfront late in the afternoon, which pleased me to no end. Eager as we were to escape the smell of fish and visit old haunts, there were things Morley and I had to get done before our return became known. Keeping control until sunset was less difficult because it was only for a short time.

After hard dark fell, we all trooped off and slithered around the city's back ways to the back door of Morley's place, where everyone and everything, willing and unwilling, went into temporary hiding. I sneaked off to get some advice from the Dead Man while Morley worried about how he was going to consummate his arrangement with the kingpin.

He had asked Saucerhead and me to be his bodyguards when the meet went down, for which he would "gladly pay your standard fees—as soon as Garrett delivers me my wages for the last couple of months." I figured he had delivered above and beyond the call, if mainly to save his own hide, and I could do him a favor in return. Saucerhead signed on because he'll do any damned fool thing as long as he's getting paid.

I swear I did *not* know what he was going to pull.

The Dead Man acted like I'd just stepped out half an hour ago and had just given him time to work into a comfortable snooze before I came clanging and banging. After having fulfilled his reputation for being cranky, he asked for my story. For five hours I gave it to him. He didn't interrupt often as he didn't need more information for anything. He thought my precau-

tions against getting stiffed by Willard Tate would prove needless, but supposed they would hurt nothing.

We talked tough at each other a little while I cleaned up around there,
then I hightailed it back to Morley's to grab thirteen winks before I walked
into the Tates' den.

News from the Cantard was all the talk when I got back. You miss a lot
when you're traveling.

It seemed that when all the armies and half armies and whatnots had
turned up at Indigo Springs for the big soirée that would determine who
kept the water hole, Glory Mooncalled was gone. Without a trace except a
friendly note to the Venageti warlords on his list.

I liked the guy's style.

I was grinning when I went to work on the Tate gate by dawn's early
light. "I'll get a little of my own back here."

A sleepy apprentice finally opened up. He was too addled to recognize
me.

"How's the arm? Looks good. I need to see the old man."

"It's you!"

"I think so. Last time I looked it was world-famous me, back with the
goods from the wars."

He dashed away, which is something people don't ordinarily do, yelling
all the way. I closed the gate behind me and waited.

I have to admit that Willard Tate was a lot sharper at that hour than I
will ever be. By the time the kid led me in, there were steaming cups of tea
set out. His first words were, "Sit down. Breakfast will be ready in ten minutes." He looked at me expectantly.

I set my accounts down beside my tea, got comfortable, took me a sip,
and said, "I've got her. Tinnie and Rose, too. If you want them."

That old man was downright spooky. He glanced at what I'd placed on
the table, considered my choice of words, gave a nod that said he understood
the situation, and asked, "What is she like?"

"Like nothing you ever imagined. Like nothing I ever dreamed, either,
even in a nightmare."

He reached for the accounts. "May I?"

I pushed them toward him.

"Tell me about it while I'm looking at these."

The version I gave him was more tightly edited than the one the Dead

Man had gotten, but I didn't leave out anything he needed to know. To say he was surprised would be putting it mildly. To say he took it all well would be understating. The short version took two hours and skirted the worst behavior of females surnamed Tate. I think he caught wind of what I left out, though.

When I finished, he said, "I've checked and you have a reputation for being honest with your expenses. Bizarre and substantial as these are, I suppose they're justified. Considering."

"The advance covered almost everything but salaries," I informed him. "Between us we're maybe a hundred out of pocket, mainly because of the cost of bringing the girls home."

Tate grunted, shoved the accounts back. "You'll have the balance before you leave."

"And my executor's fees?"

"That's in the hands of the probate. When can I expect delivery?"

"Tonight. But very late. Probably after midnight. I have to help Morley with something first." Morley's business had gotten lost in the editing.

"All right. I guess it will have to do." Then he let me in on why he was being so understanding. "Would you be interested in taking another job? After you've recuperated from this one?"

I raised an eyebrow.

"You know the major portion of our business is army boots. The most expensive component of a boot is sole leather. Army specs require thunder-lizard hide for soles. We have our own contract hunters and tanners, trust-worthy men all. I thought. But of late the shipments have been short."

I saw where he was going and shut him out. I had turned out to be crazy enough to go into the Cantard, but I will never be the screaming sort of psychotic who goes into thunder-lizard country. Besides, I'd made myself a promise never to leave TunFaire again and I never break a promise to myself without my self's prior permission.

I let him talk. When he ran dry I said I would give it a think and got the hell out with my expense money, knowing I would shriek a big "No!" the second I had my executor's fees in hand.

56

Morley had set his meet on wooded creekside ground at the boundary between the real world and the high city of the dukes and barons and stormwardens and whatnot. It was a place often employed for such encounters. Any uproar, as might be caused by treachery, would bring an army of high city protectors down on everyone.

Over the years the formula and etiquette of a "brookside" have become fixed. As proposer, Morley set the time of the meet and the size of each party. He picked an hour after sundown and four people. It would take four of us to lug Valentine's coffin. Dojango, Saucerhead, and I would back him.

The kingpin, on agreeing, got to pick which end of brookside was his, and could come early if he wanted, to check the grounds for signs of treachery. Morley was not permitted an early survey.

The kingpin agreed to meet. An hour after sunset I was helping carry a coffin uphill, into a situation that seemed to me to be of no special value to either of the principals. The kingpin's reputation said he was good for his word. If he'd made promises to Morley, he would keep them. I couldn't understand why he had agreed to the meet—unless his hatred for Valentine had overcome his good sense.

Morley Dotes was a tough and tricky independent, known to be in need of money, and TunFaire boasted a dozen men willing to pay large sums for the kingpin's life.

We went up with Morley and Dojango in front, me and Saucerhead in back, so we bigger guys got most of the weight. We parked the coffin carefully. Morley stayed beside it. The rest of us fell back ten steps and kept our hands in plain sight.

After a while a shadow left the poplars opposite us and came over to Morley. "He's in the box?"

"Yes."

"Open it."

Morley lifted the lid carefully from the foot end.

"Looks like it could be him. Hard to tell in this light."

Morley slammed the lid shut. "Go get a torch, then." He kicked the coffin. "This guy isn't going anywhere."

The kingpin's man went away. I hoped Saucerhead and I were back far enough not to be recognized. I was getting a bad, bad feeling.

There was some talk in the woods. Then somebody struck a spark. A torch flared.

Saucerhead said, "Let's get out of here, Garrett," and began backing up. I noted that Dojango had already vanished. Morley was easing away from the coffin. I drifted with Saucerhead, got myself behind a nice bush. Tharpe kept going. Morley held up about five feet from my side of the box.

The kingpin and his troops marched up. "Open it," said the boss of bosses. One of his boys got the job done.

"Gods. He looks weird," another said.

The kingpin asked, "What did you do to him, Dotes?"

Morley replied, "Nothing. He did it to himself."

"Right." The kingpin tossed Morley a bag. Major gold, from the sound when it hit Morley's hand. "We're quits, Dotes." And then the boss of bosses just had to do it. He just had to bend down for a closer look.

"You're right," Morley said. "You're absolutely right."

A bone white arm shot up. Unclipped claws closed in the flesh of an exposed throat. A fanged mouth rose to feed, the smell of blood bringing the fever on the monster so powerfully it could think of nothing for the hunger.

The kingpin's bodyguards started to do their jobs.

I started to make tracks.

Morley passed me before I'd gone a hundred yards. He was chuckling, which made me even angrier.

We had one hell of a blowout about it, and it might have gotten violent if Saucerhead hadn't been there agreeing with everything I said.

• • •

It was the talk of the morning, the vampire found surrounded by four dead men, feeding, so gorged it couldn't defend itself when the uphill protectors arrived. They hacked it to pieces, then burned the pieces and coffin on the spot. They threw the victims into the fire, too, just to make certain the infection didn't spread.

We were in the clear. But that didn't alter my attitude toward Morley. Meanwhile . . .

57

Meanwhile I made a delivery of females to the Tate compound, as fine-looking a set as ever I have seen. A pity they had so many nonvisual defects between them—though I meant to see Tinnie again.

Tate at the gate, mate. Actually, as Dojango would say, Tates at the gates, mates. About fifteen of them, including the old man himself. Such huggings and kissings and tear-sheddings and backpattings. "I am amazed, Red," I said when a lull in the action gave me a chance to get a word in to Tinnie. "You'd think they were glad to see you guys." Tinnie was getting two-thirds of the attention, but that left plenty for Rose.

Only the old man remained aloof. When the crest of the storm passed, he forced his way to me and asked, "Where is she, Mr. Garrett?"

"On the wagon."

He looked. He saw nothing but the box. "You've got her in a *coffin*?"

"Did you pay any attention at all last night? She can't go wandering around in her condition."

"All right. All right." Suddenly he was a very nervous, irresolute little man.

"Come on, Pop. You're doing all right. Get some muscle to do something useful. You did get a place ready?"

"Yes." Now he was my old aunt, wringing hands. Kayean had become an important bridge to the son he had lost.

When you looked at it up close, you kind of had to feel for Rose, the living child whose return he hadn't bothered to acknowledge. Maybe she thought if she got her hands on all that money he would notice her.

"Don't expect a lot, Pop. She can't do much but sit and stare at things nobody else sees. And probably just as well." He didn't know about Kayean and me before Kayean and Denny. I was not the boy to clue him, but I did admit, "I've got an emotional investment here, too. I want you to know something. You try any fanciness, you treat this woman less than perfectly, and you won't have to worry about boot soles and thunder-lizard hides anymore."

I got a little too intense. He backed off and gave me the look you give the nut on the corner preaching that pixies are the secret masters and if we don't do something they're going to run off with our sisters and daughters. Then he formed a crew of cousins and apprentices and got the coffin moving.

He had done a room, all right. Nary a window, and as light-proof as you could get. One very pale, consecrated candle burned on a mantel over a fireplace before a large mirror. A very black, very huge, very fat, very wrinkled, and very old woman sat to one side, the tools of her trade on a table beside her. I recognized her. The Mojo Woman. Mama Doll. TunFaire's leading authority on the diseases of the undead.

Maybe I owed somebody an apology.

A couple of the boys got in ahead with sawhorses. The pallbearers deposited the coffin. Mama Doll moved her bulk like it was all the work in the universe. First this part of her, then that, then another, got under way, like the sailing of a ship of a thousand parts. Before anyone could mess with the coffin lid, she slapped a hand down right above where Kayean's would be folded over her heart. She rolled her eyes and mumbled to herself for a minute, then backed away and nodded.

While the boys unfixed the lid, she grabbed protective amulets from the table. A big lead-up to a big anticlimax. When they lifted the lid, Kayean did nothing but keep on sleeping.

I had to go shake her to wake her up.

It was evident Kayean was in control and safe to be near.

"Out!" Willard Tate ordered. "Everybody get out!"

Relatives and apprentices hurried. Mama Doll moved at her usual lugubrious drift. Garrett stayed where he was.

The boss turned on me. "Out!"

"Move me, Pop."

"I can call the boys."

"I can break both your legs before they get here."

"That's enough," Kayean said, her voice little more than a whisper. She touched my arm. "Wait outside." A ghost of a smile touched her lips, light as a moth's kiss. "I can break his legs if he asks for it." Her touch was slightly heavier, her voice softer. "Thank you for still caring."

And the boy Marine was alive again.

Only two things you can do in a situation like that. Be a goof or get the hell out.

I got.

There was light outside when Tate left. He was a wrung-out, exhausted old man. He found me blocking his path. In a hurried mumble meant to get it over, he told me things.

Kayean was going to stay where she was for a while. Part of her inheritance would be used to buy a home and part invested to create a living so she would be free of worries when Mama Doll declared her cured. Of the rest of the fortune she wanted ten thousand given to Vasco and the remainder divided among Denny's other heirs.

So Rose would make out after all.

"She is in and of the family, Mr. Garrett, by virtue of my son's love for her. You need not be concerned for her. We Tates take care of our own."

"I guess you're all right, Mr. Tate. Thanks." I stepped aside.

He limped off to his bed.

She was lying on the bed, cold and corpselike in the light of the lonesome candle. But at least she was in a proper bed and not laid out in that goddamned coffin. I collected the room's only chair and positioned it silently.

I stared at her for a long time, wrestling with the kid Marine. I touched her hair, which had begun to show a hint of color. When I could stand no more, I rose, bent, and brushed those cold lips with mine for the last time.

I headed for the door.

I heard a sigh. When I glanced back, she said, "Good-bye, Garrett." And smiled a real smile.

I never slowed down.

I went and wrapped myself around a barrel of beer.

Each year, on the anniversary of the day I brought her out of the nest, a courier brings a package. The gift is never niggardly.

I know where she lives. I never go up that way.

58

The probate coughed up my fees four days after I delivered Denny Tate's heir. I got in touch with Tinnie. The redhead and I did some celebrating. She was along when I went to visit the Dead Man.

She invited herself and she made it stick. Redheads are stubborn witches.

She looked at his place and said, "It's a dump, Garrett."

"It's his home."

"It's still a dump. How do you feel?"

"Almost broke. And kind of good about myself."

"Smug self-satisfaction, I'd call it."

"Come on. Try your witchcraft on him. See how far it gets you."

He woke up the way he always wakes up. Cranky. *Garrett. Again. I demand that you cease your infernal pestering.* Then he noticed Tinnie. *What is that creature doing here?* He has no use whatsoever for females of any age or species, an attitude I find too parochial. But there's no convincing him, and I doubt there would be even if he was still alive.

I tolerate too much from you, Garrett. I reap the gall-ridden harvest of my indulgence.

"You're going to have to indulge me a lot more now, Old Bones. Or you might find yourself camped in the street. You're talking to your new landlord here."

After half a minute, he asked, *You bought this place? You spent the money from the Tate business on it?*

Ah. That genius still worked. "Yes. Call it an investment in my future. The pestering has just begun."

For the first time in our acquaintance I had caught him without a comeback. The silence stretched.

I started the housekeeping while he stewed.

•••Bitter Gold Hearts

•••1

There was nothing to do after I wrapped up the Case of the Perilous Pixies. Two weeks of living with the Dead Man's grumblings and mutterings would try the patience of a saint. A saint, I'm not.

Worse, Tinnie was out of town indefinitely and the redhead refused to share me with anyone she didn't know. It was a trying time to be alive. Nothing to do with my evenings but keep the breweries from going into receivership.

It was early and a devil was doing some blacksmithing in my skull, so I wasn't at my best when somebody came pounding on the door of our battered old house on Macunado Street.

"Yeah?" I snapped when I yanked the door open. It didn't matter that the woman was wearing a thousand marks' worth of custom cloth or that the street was filled with guys in flashy livery. I've seen too much of the rich to be impressed.

"Mr. Garrett?"

"That's me." I lightened up a little. I'd had a chance to give her the up and down, and she was worth a second look. And a third and a fourth. There wasn't a lot of her, though nothing was missing, and what was there had been put together quite nicely. A phantom smile crossed her lips as my gaze drew north again.

"I'm half fairy," she said, and for a moment music broke through the gravity of her voice. "Can you stop gaping long enough to let me in?"

"Of course. Can I ask your name? I don't recall you being on my appointment calendar. Though I'd love to jot you in as often as you want."

"I'm here on business, Mr. Garrett. Save that for your bar girls." She pushed past me a few steps, then stopped and glanced back with mild surprise.

"The outside is camouflage," I told her. "We leave it looking like a dump so we don't strain the honesty of our neighbors." It wasn't the best section of the city. There was a war on, and it was hot, so there were plenty of jobs available, but some of our neighbors hadn't yet given in to the silly notion of personal gain through honest employment.

"*We?*" she repeated icily. "I wanted to consult with you on a matter that requires the greatest discretion."

Don't they all? They wouldn't come to me if they thought they could solve their problems through the usual channels.

"You can trust him," I replied, nodding toward the other room. "His lips are sealed. He's been dead for four hundred years."

I watched her face go through a series of changes. "He's Loghyr? The Dead Man?"

So she wasn't such a lady after all. Anybody who knows the Dead Man has roots solidly anchored in the downhill end of TunFaire. "Yes. I think he ought to hear it."

I get around and hear a lot of things—some of them true, most of them not. I'd recognized the livery of the Stormwarden Raver Styx outside and thought I could guess what was eating her. It would be fun springing her on the heap of moth-eaten blubber who had become my permanent houseguest.

"No."

I started toward his room. The routine is for me to wake him when I have a business caller. Not everyone who visits is friendly. He can provide powerful backup when the mood hits him. "What did you say your name was, miss?"

I was fishing and she knew it. She could have skipped right around it, but she hesitated in an odd way before confessing, "Amiranda Crest, Mr. Garrett. This is a critical matter."

"They always are, Amiranda. I'll be with you in a minute."

She didn't walk out.

It was important enough that she would let herself be pushed.

He was indulging himself in what had become his favorite pastime, trying to outguess the generals and warlords in the Cantard. No matter that the information he got was scanty, out-of-date, and mostly filtered through me. He did as well as the geniuses who commanded the armies—better than most of those stormwardens and warlords whose main claim to the right of command was heredity.

He was a mountain of rigid yellow flesh sprawled on a massive wooden chair. The works had been moved several times but the flesh hadn't twitched since somebody stuck a knife in it four hundred years ago. He was getting a little ragged. Loghyr flesh doesn't corrupt quickly, but mice and whole species of insects consider it a delicacy.

The wall facing his chair had no doors or windows. He'd had an artist paint it with a large-scale map of the war zone. At that moment he had hosts of bugs trooping up and down the plaster landscape, re-creating recent campaigns, trying to discover how the mercenary Glory Mooncalled had evaded not only the Venageti out to destroy him, but our own commanders, who wanted to catch and leash him before his string of triumphs made them look more foolish and inept than they already did.

"You're awake."

Go away, Garrett.

"Who's winning? The ants or the roaches? Better watch out for those spiders down in the corner. They're sneaking up on your silverfish."

Quit pestering me, Garrett.

"I have a visitor, a prospective client. We need a client. I want you to hear her outpouring of woe."

You brought a woman into my house again? Garrett, my good nature has limits wider than the ocean, but it does have limits.

"Whose house? Do we have to go back to talking about who's the landlord and who's the squatter?"

The bugs scattered. Some of them jumped on others. That's life in the war zone.

I almost had the pattern.

"He does it with mirrors. If there was a pattern, the Venageti War Council would have spotted it months ago. Finding Glory Mooncalled isn't a hobby for them. It's life or death." The mercenary was picking them off one by one. He had an old score to settle.

I take it this one is not that redheaded witch of yours?

"Tinnie? No. This one works for the Stormwarden Raver Styx. She has fairy blood. You'll love her at first sight."

Unlike you, who loves them all at first sight, I am no longer the victim of my flesh, Garrett. There are some advantages to being dead. One gains the ability to reason. . . .

I'd heard this before—several dozen times. "I'll bring her in." I stepped out, returned to the front room. "Miss Crest? If you'll come with me?"

She glowered. Even angry she was a gem, but there was a quiet desperation in her stance that gave me all the handle I needed. "Amiranda, haunter of my dreams. Please?"

She followed me. I think she knew she had no choice.

●●●2

amiranda Crest started shaking when she saw the Dead Man. I'm used
to him and tend to forget the impact he has on those who never have
seen a dead Loghyr. Her cute little nose wrinkled. She whispered, "It
smells in here."

Well, yes, it did, but not much, and I was used to that, too. I ignored the
remark. "This is Amiranda Crest, who comes to us from the Stormwarden
Raver Styx."

*Please pardon me for not rising, Miss Crest. I am capable of mental prod-
igies, but self-levitation is not among them.*

Meantime, Amiranda blurted, "Oh, no. Not from the Stormwarden.
She's in the Cantard. Her secretary, the Domina Willa Dount, sent me. I'm
her assistant. She wants you to see her about something she wants you to do,
Mr. Garrett. For the family. Discreetly."

"Then you're not going to tell me what it is?"

"I don't know what it is. I was told to give you a hundred marks, gold,
and tell you there is a thousand more if you'll do the job. But the hundred
is yours if you'll just come to see her."

She lies, Garrett. She knows what it is about.

He wasn't paying the rent with that.

She had changed strategies while I was alerting the Dead Man. "That's
all? Nothing to tell me why I'm sticking my neck out?"

She had begun counting ten-mark gold pieces into her left hand. I was
startled. I'd never met anyone with fairy blood who was right-handed.

"Save yourself the trouble, Miss Crest. If that's it, I'll stay here and help my friend hustle cockroaches."

She thought I was joking. A man of my class turning his back on a hundred marks gold? A man in my line? I ought to be sprinting uptown to find out who they wanted killed. Chances were *she* had run uptown, bartering her good looks for the pretty things she wore.

She asked, "Couldn't you just take me on faith, and for the gold?"

"The last time I trusted somebody from up the Hill I got stuck in the Marines. I spent five years trying to kill Venageti conscripts who didn't know any better than I did what we were fighting about. I didn't figure that out till I came back home, and then I liked your lords and ladies of the Hill even less. Good day, Miss Crest. Unless you'd be interested in some more personal business? I know a little place that serves seafood you could kill for."

I watched her think it over, looking for angles she could use. Finally, she said, "Domina will be very angry with me if I don't bring you."

"How sad. But that's not my problem. If you don't mind? Your boys out front are probably baking in the sun, anyway."

She stomped out of the room, snarling, "You're throwing away the easiest hundred marks of your life, Mr. Garrett."

I followed her to make sure she used the door for its intended purpose. "If your boss wants to see me so bad, tell her to come down here."

She paused, opened her mouth to say something, then shook her head and slipped outside. I caught a glimpse of the sweltering guards jumping to their feet before the door closed. I went back to the Dead Man.

You were a little stubborn, were you not?

"She'll be back."

I know. But what temper will possess her?

"Maybe she'll be ready to lay it out straight, without the games."

She is a female, Garrett. Why do you persist in such unreasonable optimism where that alien species is concerned?

This was one of our running arguments. He was a misogynist to the marrow. This time I refused to play. He gave up.

Are you interested in the job, Garrett?

"My heart won't be broken if it doesn't develop. You know I told the truth when I said I don't have much use for the lords of the Hill. And I particularly have no use for sorcerers. We don't need the money, anyway."

You always need money, Garrett, the way you drink beer and chase skirts.

He exaggerated, of course. His envy was talking. His single greatest regret about being dead was his inability to guzzle beer.

Someone is hammering on the door.

"I hear it. It's probably old Dean, early for work."

The Dead Man would not endure a female housekeeper, and my tolerance for housework is minimal. I'd only been able to find one old man—who moved with the flash and style of a tortoise—willing to come in, pick up, cook, and clear the vermin from the Dead Man's room.

I was surprised to find Amiranda back already. "Quick trip. Come in. I didn't know I was so irresistible."

She strode past me, then turned, hands on hips. "All right, Mr. Garrett. You get it your way. The reason Domina wants you is because my . . . because the Stormwarden's son Karl has been kidnapped. If you insist on getting more than that, we're both out of luck. Because that's all I've been told."

And you certainly are worried about it, I thought.

She started for the door.

"Hold it." I squinted at her. "Give me the hundred."

She handed it over without a smirk of triumph. One point for Amiranda Crest. I decided she might be worth liking.

"I'll be back in a minute."

I took the gold to the Dead Man. There was no safer place on earth. "You heard?"

I did.

"What do you think?"

Kidnapping is your area of expertise.

I rejoined Amiranda Crest. "Let us fare forth, fair fairy lady."

That failed to put a smile on her face.

Not everyone appreciates a great sense of humor.

We marched off like a parody of a military outfit. Amiranda's companions were clad in uniforms. That seemed to be the limit of their familiarity with the military concept. At a guess I would have said their only use was to keep their livery from collapsing into the dust.

I tried a few conversational sallies. Amiranda was done talking. I was one of the hired help now.

The Dead Man was right. Kidnapping is my area of expertise, mostly by circumstance. Time and again I get stuck doing the in-between. Each time I deliver the ransom and bring the body home alive the word gets around a little more. Both sides in a swap know where they stand with me. I play it straight, no tricks, and heaven help the bad boys if they deliver damaged goods and my principals want their heads. Which they always do in that case.

I loathe kidnapping and kidnappers. Abduction is a major underground industry in TunFaire. I'd as soon see all kidnappers sent down the river floating facedown, but sound business practice makes me play the game by live-and-let-live rules. Unless *they* cheat first.

The Hill is a good deal more than a piece of high ground looking down its nose at the sprawl of TunFaire, the beast upon whose back it rides. It is a state of mind, and one I don't like. But their coin is as good as any down below, and they have a lot more of it. I register my disapproval by refusing jobs that might help the Hill tribe close their grip even tighter on the rest of us.

Usually when they try to hire me it's because they want dirty work done. I turn them down. They find somebody less morally fastidious. So it goes.

The Stormwarden Raver Styx's place was typical of those on the High Hill. It was huge, tall, walled, brooding, dark, and just a shade more friendly than death. It was one of those places with an invisible "Abandon Hope" sign over the gateway. Maybe there were protective spells involved. I got a strong case of nerves the last fifty feet, the little watchman inside telling me I didn't want to go in there.

I went anyway. One hundred marks gold can shout down the watchman anytime.

The inside reminded me of a haunted castle. There were cobwebs everywhere. Amiranda and I, after shedding our escort, were the only people tracking the shadowed halls. "Cheerful little bungalow. Where is everybody?"

"The Stormwarden took most of the household with her."

"But she left her secretary behind?"

"Yes."

Which told me there was some truth in the things I'd heard about the Stormwarden's husband and son, both named Karl. Put charitably, they needed a shepherd.

At first glance Willa Dount looked like a woman who could keep them in line. Her eyes could chill beer, and she had the charm of a stone. I knew a little about her from whispers in the shadows and alleys. She arranged dirty deeds done for the Stormwarden.

She was about five feet two, early forties, chunky without being fat. Her gray eyes matched her hair. She dressed, shall we say, sensibly. She smiled about twice as often as the Man in the Moon, and then without sincerity.

Amiranda said, "Mr. Garrett, Domina."

The woman looked at me like I was either a potentially contagious disease or an especially curious specimen in the zoo. One of the uglier ones, like a thunder lizard.

There are times when I feel like I belong to one of the dying breeds.

"Thank you, Amiranda. Have a seat, Mr. Garrett." The "mister" left her jaws aching. She wasn't used to being nice to people like me.

I sat. So did she. Amiranda hovered.

"That will be all, Amiranda."

"Domina—"

"That will be all."

Amiranda left, furious and hurt. I scanned the clutter on the secretary's desk while she glared the girl from the room.

"What do you think of our Amiranda, Mr. Garrett?" Again she got a jaw ache.

I tried putting it delicately. "A man could dream dreams about a woman with her—"

"I'm sure." She scowled at me. I had failed some test.

I didn't care. I'd decided I wouldn't like the Domina Willa Dount very much. "You had a reason for asking me to come here?"

"How much did Amiranda tell you?"

"Enough to get me to listen." She tried to stare me down. I stared back. "I don't usually have much grief to spare for uptown folks. When the fates want to stick them I say more power to them. But to kidnapping I take exception."

She scowled. I give the woman this—her scowl was first rate. Any gorgon would have been proud to own it. "What else did she tell you?"

"That was it, and getting it took some work. Maybe you can tell me more."

"Yes. As Amiranda told you, the younger Karl has been abducted."

"From what I've heard, there aren't many more deserving guys around." Karl Junior had a reputation for being twenty-three going on a willful and very spoiled three. There was no doubt which side of the family Junior favored. Domina Dount had been left to keep it civilized or to cover it up.

Willa Dount's mouth tightened until it was little more than a white point. "Be that as it may. We aren't here to exercise your opinions of your betters, Mr. Garrett."

"What are we here for?"

"The Stormwarden will be returning soon. I don't want her to walk into a situation like this. I want to get it settled and forgotten before she arrives. Do you wish to take notes, Mr. Garrett?" She pushed writing materials my way. I figured she supposed me illiterate and wanted to enjoy feeling superior when I confessed it.

"Not till there's something worth noting. I take it you've heard from the kidnappers? That you know Junior hasn't just gone off on one of his adventures?"

By way of answering me she lifted a rag-wrapped bundle from behind the desk and pushed it across. "This was left with the gateman during the night."

I unwrapped a pair of silver-buckled shoes. A folded piece of paper lay inside one. "His?"

"Yes."

"The messenger?"

"What you would expect. A street urchin of seven or eight. The gateman didn't bring me the bundle till after breakfast. By then the child was too far ahead to catch."

So she had a sense of humor after all.

I gave the shoes the full eyeball treatment. It never works out, but you always look for that speck of rare purple mud or the weird yellow grass stain that will make you look like a genius. I didn't find it this time, either. I unfolded the note.

We have yore Karl. If you want him back you do what yore told. Dont tell nobody about this. You be told what to do later.

A snippet of hair had been folded into the paper. I held it to the light falling through the window behind the secretary's desk. It was the color I recalled Junior's hair being the few times I had seen him. "Nice touch, this."

Willa Dount gave me another of her scowls.

I ignored her and examined the note. The paper itself told me nothing except that it was a scrap torn from something else, possibly a book. I could go around town for a century trying to match it to torn pages. But the handwriting was interesting. It was small but loose, confident, the penmanship almost perfect, not in keeping with the apparent education of the writer. "You don't recognize this hand?"

"Of course not. That needn't concern you, anyway."

"When did you see him last?"

"Yesterday morning. I sent him down to our warehouse on the waterfront to check reports of pilferage. The foreman claimed it was brownies. I had a feeling *he* was the brownie in the woodpile and he was selling the Stormwarden's supplies to somebody here on the Hill. Possibly even to one of our neighbors."

"It's always reassuring to know the better classes stand above the sins and temptations of us common folks. You weren't concerned when he didn't come home?"

"I told you I'm not interested in your social attitudes or opinions. Save them for someone who agrees with you. No, I wasn't concerned. He sometimes stays out for weeks. He's a grown man."

"But the Stormwarden left you here to ride herd on him and his father. And you must have done the job till now because there hasn't been a hint of scandal since the old girl left town."

One more scowl.

The door sprang open and a man stomped into the room. "Willa, has there been any more word about . . . ?" He spotted me and pulled up. His eyebrows crawled halfway up his forehead, a trick for which he was famous. To hear some tell it, that was his only talent. "Who the hell is that?" He was renowned for being rude, too, though among people of his class that was a trait the rest of us expected.

●●●4

illa Dount spoke up. "There hasn't been anything yet. I expect we won't be contacted for a while." She looked at me, her expression making that a question.

"They like to let the anxiety level rise before they come after you. It makes you more eager to cooperate."

"This is Mr. Garrett," she said. "Mr. Garrett is an expert on kidnappers and kidnappings."

"My god, Willa! Are you mad? They said don't tell anybody."

She ignored his outburst. "Mr. Garrett, this is the Stormwarden's consort, the Baronet daPena, the father of the victim."

How he twitched and jerked! Without changing her tone or expression, Domina Dount had hit him with a fat double shot, calling him consort (which labeled him a drone) and mentioning his baronetcy (which wasn't hereditary and purely an honor because he was the fourth son of a cadet of the royal house). She may even have gotten in a sly third shot there, if, as you sometimes heard whispered, Junior wasn't really a seed fallen from the senior.

"How do you do, Lord? He has a good question, Domina." I'd been working up to it when he burst in. "Why bring me in when the kidnappers said don't tell anybody? A man with my reputation, and you sent out what amounted to a platoon of clowns, with the girl dressed flashy enough to catch a blind man's eye. It's not likely the kidnappers won't hear about it."

"That was the point. I want them to."

"Willa!"

"Karl, be quiet. I'm explaining to Mr. Garrett."

He turned white. He was furious. She'd made it clear who stood where, who was in charge, in front of a lowlife from down the Hill. But he contained himself. I pretended blindness. It isn't smart to see things like that.

Willa Dount said, "I want them to know I've brought you in, Mr. Garrett."

"Why?"

"For young Karl's sake. To improve his chances of getting through this alive. Would you say they're less likely to harm him if they know about you?"

"If they're professionals. Professionals know me. If they're not, chances are they'll go the other way. You may have moved too soon."

"Time will tell. It seemed the best bet to me."

"Exactly what do you want me to do?"

"Nothing."

She blindsided me there. "What?"

"You've done what I needed you to do. You've been seen coming here to confer with me. You've lent me your reputation. Hopefully, Karl's chances have been improved."

"That's it?"

"That's it, Mr. Garrett. Do you think a hundred marks adequate recompense for the loan of your reputation?"

It was fine with me, but I ignored the question. "What about the payoff?" Usually they want me to handle that for them.

"I believe I can handle that. It's basically a matter of following instructions, isn't it?"

"Explicitly. The payoff is when they're most nervous. That's when you'll have to be most careful. For your own safety as well as the boy's."

Senior snorted and huffed and stamped, wanting to get his hand into the action. Willa Dount kept him quiet with an occasional touch of her icicle eyes.

I wondered what the Stormwarden had left her in the way of leashes and whips. She sure had the old boy buffaloed.

Karl Senior was still a handsome man though he was running away from forty—if he had not already sneaked past fifty. Time had dealt him a few wrinkles but no extra pounds. His hair was all there, curly and slickly black, the kind that might not start graying for another decade. He was a little short, I thought, but that didn't hold him back. He looked like a fancy man, and word was that he did night work best.

Age had apparently not slowed him down. Those looks, a smooth tongue, his toy title, those magical eyebrows, and soulful big blue eyes all conspired to drop into his lap the sort of soft morsels we ordinary mortals have to scheme and fight just to get near.

It was a certainty he was no use in a crisis. He danced and twitched like a desperate kid awaiting his turn at the loo. He would have panicked if Domina Dount would have let him. He was a member of the royal house, those wonderfully firm and decisive folks who had blessed the Karentine people with their war against the Venageti.

Natural son or not, Karl Junior was a seed that had not fallen far from the tree. He was the image of Karl Senior in body and character, and to that menace to feminine virtue, he had added a generous helping of arrogance based on the fact that his mommy was the Stormwarden Raver Styx and he was her precious one and only, whose misdeeds would never be called to account.

Senior didn't like my being there. Maybe he didn't like me. If so, the feeling was mutual. I've been busting my butt since I was eight and I don't have any use for drones of any sort, and those from the Hill least of all. Their idleness got them into the kind of mischief that resulted in sending a whole generation south to fight over the silver mines of the Cantard.

Maybe Glory Mooncalled would turn on his Karentine employers once he polished off the Venageti Warlords. It wouldn't hurt.

I said, "If you've had your way with me, then I'll be running along. Best of luck getting the boy back."

Her expression said she doubted my sincerity. "You can find your way to the street?"

"I learned scouting when I was in the Marines."

"Good day, then, Mr. Garrett."

Karl Senior exploded the second I closed the door. It was a good door. I couldn't decipher his yells even when I put my ear to the wood. But he was having a good time working the panic and frustration out.

●●●5

Amiranda caught me just before I reached the gate. I caught my breath, then chewed on my tongue a little so I could still fake being a gentleman. She'd changed from the show ensemble she'd worn to fetch me and now, in her everydays, looked like something I find only under the covers of midnight fantasies.

She looked good, but she also looked worried. I told myself this was no time for one of my routines.

My sometime-associate Morley Dotes tells me I'm a sucker for a damsel in distress. He tells me many things about myself, most of them wrong and unwelcomed, but he has me on the damsels. A good-looking gal turns on the tears and Garrett is a knight ready to tilt with dragons.

"What did she say, Mr. Garrett? What does she want you to do?"

"She said a lot of not much at all. What she wants me to do is nothing."

"I don't understand." Did she look disappointed? I couldn't tell.

"I'm not sure I do, either. She said she wanted the kidnappers to see me around the edges of the thing. So my reputation will shade him and maybe give him a better chance."

"Oh. Maybe she's right." She looked relieved. I wondered what her stake was. I'd formed a suspicion and didn't like it. "So do you think he'll be all right, Mr. Garrett?"

"I don't know. But Domina Dount is a formidable woman. I wouldn't want her on my back trail."

A black-haired looker of the late teens or early twenties variety left a doorway about thirty feet away, caught sight of us, gave me a once-over she followed up with a come-and-get-it smile, then walked off with a sway to still the tumult of battles.

"Who was that?" I asked.

"You needn't pant, Mr. Garrett. You'd be wasting your time. You don't dare touch her with your imagination. That's the Stormwarden's daughter, Amber."

"I see. Yes. Hmmm."

Amiranda placed herself in front of me. "Put your eyes back in, mister. You made a big show of wanting to see me outside of all this. All right. To-night at eight. At the Iron Liar."

"The Iron Liar? I'm not from uptown. How could I afford . . . ?" I had to put that excuse away. This was the same little gem that had counted the hundred gold marks into my paw a couple hours ago. "Eight, then. I'll spend the rest of the day breathless with anticipation."

I smiled smugly after I hit the street.

I wandered down the Hill wondering why I'd never heard of daughter Amber when the Stormwarden and her family played such a big part in TunFaire's news and gossip. We had obviously been missing the best part.

••• 6

Strange noises were coming from the Dead Man's room. I went into the kitchen, where old Dean was cooking sausages over charcoal with one eye on an apple pie that was about ready to come out of the oven. When he saw me, he began hoisting a pony keg out of the cold well I'd had installed with the proceeds of the Starke case. By damn, I was going to have cold brew whenever the whim hit while I could afford it.

Dean asked, "A good day today, Mr. Garrett?" as he drew me a mug.

"Interesting." I tipped my head back and swallowed a pint. "And profitable. What's he up to in there? I've never heard him make such a racket."

"I don't know, Mr. Garrett. He wouldn't let me in to clean."

"We'll see about that after I wrap myself around another one of these." I eyed the sausages and pie. If he expected me to eat that much, he was more optimistic than I thought. "Did you invite a niece over again?"

He reddened.

I just shook my head and said, "I have to go out this evening. Part of the job."

There was a little troll blood on all sides of his family. I don't have any particular prejudices—who was going out with a part-fairy girl?—but those poor women had gotten a double dose of the troll ugly from their parents. Like they say, personality plus, but horses shied and dogs howled when they passed. I wished old Dean would stop matchmaking. I had given up hope that he would run out of eligible female relatives to parade past me.

Three sausages, two pieces of the world's best apple pie, and several beers later I was ready to beard the Loghyr in his den. So to speak. "Food fit for the gods as usual, Dean. I'm going in after him. If I'm not out by the weekend, send Saucerhead Tharpe to the rescue. His skull is so thick he'd never know Old Bones was thinking at him." I thought about recommending Saucerhead to Dean's eligibles. But no, I couldn't. I liked Saucerhead.

The Dead Man sensed me coming. *Get away from here, Garrett.*

I went on in.

It was war in the Cantard again, and this time the god of the wall had all the hordes of bugdom enlisted in his enterprise. It was the combined racket of their creepy little feet and wings that I had been hearing.

"Caught him yet?"

He ignored me.

"That Glory Mooncalled is a tricky bastard, isn't he?" I wondered if he meant to clean up the entire bug population of TunFaire. For a service like that, we should find some way to get paid.

He ignored me. His bugs got busier. I sat in the only chair available to me and watched the campaign for a while. He was experimenting, not re-creating. It was no campaign I recognized.

Maybe he was even making war upon himself. The Loghyr can section up their brains into two or three discrete parts when they want.

"Had an interesting day today?"

He didn't respond. He was going to punish my impertinence by pretending I didn't exist. But he was listening. The only adventures he truly had were the ones I lived for him.

I gave him all the details, chronicling even the most trivial. Somewhere down the line I might have to call on his genius.

I finished and watched him play general for a while. I got the feeling there was a hidden pattern that I was too dense to see.

It was nearing time to meet Amiranda. I pried myself from the chair and headed for the door. "See you when I see you, Old Bones."

Garrett. If you get lucky, don't you bring her back here. I will not endure such foolishness in my house.

I seldom did, though occasionally circumstances insisted. It seemed too much like mocking his handicap.

In life the Loghyr are as randy as a pack of seventeen-year-old boys. It was my suspicion that his misogyny was his way of compensating.

I was almost out the door when he sent, *Garrett. Be careful.*

• • •

I *am* careful. Always. When I'm paying attention and when I figure I have something to worry about. But how do you get into trouble just walking up the block to buy a bottle of stink-pretty from the neighborhood chemist?

Believe me, it can be done.

It was my lucky day in more ways than one. I smelled weed smoke and that got me curious. Not many in the neighborhood use weed, and this was less of a cloud than a minor storm. I started looking for the source.

Source was five breeds, all with a lot of ogre in them. Ogres are not fast at the best of times and these boys had spent their take getting so high their pointy heads were bumping the belly of the sky. Their professional sins were legion. They hadn't done their homework, either.

One asked me, "Your name Garrett?"

"Who wants to know?"

"I do."

"It's him. Let's do it."

I did it first.

I kicked the nearest in his daydreams, spun and punched another in the throat—then tripped over my own damned big feet. The first guy bent over and started puking. The second lost interest and wobbled away holding his throat and sucking air.

I rolled and leg-whipped another one, catching him by such surprise that he fell on his back without trying to break his fall. His head bounced off the street. Lights out.

It was a good start. I began thinking I might make it without getting hurt.

The other two stood around trying to get their muggy brains untangled. I got in the finishing licks on the two I had hit already. A crowd began gathering.

The last two decided to get on with the job. They closed in. They were more careful. I was faster but they took advantage of superior numbers to keep me boxed. We waltzed for a while. I got in a few hits but it's hard to hurt guys like that when you can't get in a sucker punch. They got a few in on me, too.

The third such blow murdered my optimism. It left me seeing double and concentrating my considerable intellect on the age-old question: which way is up?

One of them started saying something about me staying away from the Stormwarden's family while the other wound up to finish me off. I grabbed a big gnarly walking stick from an old bystander and smacked the one between the eyes before he could unwind. I went after the talker while the fighter was seeing stars and his hitting arm was flaccid. Yakety-yak did a good job holding me off, stick and all, until I got in a whack that broke his arm.

He was ready to call it quits. So was I. The bystanders were scattering. I returned the old guy's stick and scattered myself. What passed for minions of law and order in TunFaire were coming. I didn't want to get hauled in and charged with intent to commit self-defense, which is about the way the law worked when it worked at all. I left the ogre boys trying to figure out what had happened.

My lucky day indeed.

The Dead Man was all enthusiasm when I told him about the incident. He gave me a good mental grumble about wishing the ogres had been a little more competent. But when I was about to leave, to get washed up and changed, he sent, *I told you to be careful.*

"I know. And I'm going to keep that a little more closely in mind. Watch the cockroaches. They're about to flank the silverfish at Yellow Dog Mesa."

He detached a part of his attention from his war and used it to levitate and throw a small stone Loghyr cult figure. It smacked the other side of the door as I shut it.

I decided to ease up. When he gets that irritable, he's hot on the spoor of a solution to a problem that has been bugging him for a long time.

7

Amiranda was waiting and looking uncomfortable when I got to the Iron Liar. I wasn't late, she was early. In my experience a woman on time is a rarity to be treasured. I didn't remark on it.

She asked, "What happened to you? You look like you were in a fight."

"First prize to the lady. You should see the other guys." She seemed excited by the idea of my getting into a fight. Point taken away from Amiranda Crest. I tried the story on her just to see how she would react.

She appeared befuddled and frightened, but got control quickly. "Why would the kidnappers do that?"

"I don't know. It doesn't make sense." Then I turned to more interesting subjects, notably Amiranda Crest. "How did you get hooked up with the Stormwarden?"

"I was born to it."

"What?"

"My father was a friend of her father. They worked together sometimes."

The brain had to run some numbers before I could say anything more. The Stormwarden's father had died before I was born. Fairy folk lived a long time and aged slowly. Could this morsel be old enough to be my mother?

"I'm twenty-one, Garrett."

I gave her the famous Garrett raised eyebrow.

"I've gotten too damned many of those glassy-eyed stares when human men suddenly realize there's a chance I might be older, more knowledgeable, and more experienced than they are. Sometimes it turns into panic or terror."

I apologized where I was guilty, then told her, "You jump to too many conclusions. I suspect the reactions you get don't have anything to do with how old you might be. You're Molahlu Crest's daughter. Even though he's gone, his reputation lingers. And it's got to hang on you like a shroud. People have to wonder if the wickedness is in the blood."

"Most people have never heard of Molahlu Crest."

I didn't answer that. If she wanted to believe it—which she did not for a moment—let her. It could be her way of coping with a difficult ancestry.

The Stormwarden's father (who had taken the name Styx Sabbat), and Molahlu Crest had clawed their ways up from the bottom of the Hill, the former riding a talent for sorcery, the latter an absence of conscience or compassion. A corduroy road of bodies was their route to the heart of the circles of power. They had been takers and breakers and killers, and the only good thing anyone ever said about either was that they had remained true friends from beginning to end. Neither greed nor hunger for power had come between them.

Which is something. How many friends do any of us have that we can count on forever?

Molahlu Crest, they say, had a small talent for sorcery himself, and that had made him doubly deadly. In the old days everyone in TunFaire was scared of him, from the richest and most powerful to the least of the waterfront bums. No one knows what happened to Molahlu Crest, but the conventional wisdom is that the Stormwarden Raver Styx got rid of him.

I wondered if Amiranda knew differently. After a while in my business, professional curiosity becomes habitual curiosity. Then you have to watch yourself so you don't stick your nose in everywhere.

You can get it mashed and have nothing to show for your trouble but a cauliflower schnoz.

We talked of light things and she began to relax. I splurged and ordered the TunFaire Gold with our meal. It helped.

It's a cynical device, but I have yet to encounter the woman who won't loosen up if you buy the Gold. The wine's reputation is such that your buying it makes them feel they're something special.

I like the Gold better than any other wine, but to me it is still spoiled grape juice with a winy taste. I'm a beer man born. I don't begin to pretend to understand wine snobs: to me even the best is nasty.

When the mood was better, I asked, "There been any more word from the kidnappers?"

"Not when I left. I think Domina would have let us know that much. Why are they waiting so long?"

"To get everybody so worried they'll do whatever it takes to get Junior back. Tell me about him. Is he really the kind of guy they say he is?"

Her expression became wary. "I don't know what they say about him. His name is Karl, not Junior."

I pecked at her from a couple directions. She gave me nothing.

"Why are you asking so many questions, Garrett? You did what you were paid for already, didn't you?"

"Sure. Just curiosity. It's an occupational hazard. I'll try not to be a nuisance."

I wondered about her. She was a woman with troubles, very much turned inward. Not my usual sort. But I found myself interested in her for her own sake. Odd.

The meal ended. She asked, "What now? Evil plans?"

"Me? Never. I'm one of the good guys. I know a guy who runs a place you might find interesting, since you're slumming. You want to give it a try?"

"I'm game for anything but going back to that . . ." She was trying to be pleasant company and to have a good time, but she was having to work at it. Thank heaven for TunFaire Gold to support my naturally irresistible charm.

Morley's place was jumping—as much as it ever does. Which means it was packed with dwarfs, elves, trolls, goblins, pixies, brownies, and whatnot, along with the curious specimens you get when you crossbreed the races. The boys looked at Amiranda with obvious approval and at me with equally obvious distaste. But I forgave them. I would be sullen and sour, too, if I was in a place where the drinks were nonalcoholic and the meals left out everything but the rabbit food.

I went straight to the bar, where I was known and my presence was tolerated. I asked the bartender, "Where's Morley?"

He indicated the stairs with a jerk of his head.

I went up. Amiranda followed, wary again. I pounded on Morley's door and he told me to come in. He knew it was me because there was a speaking tube running from the bar upstairs. We stepped inside.

For a rarity Morley did not have somebody's wife with him. He was doing accounts. He looked worried, but his beady little eyes lit up when he saw Amiranda.

"Down, boy. She's taken. Amiranda, this is Morley Dotes. He has three wives and nine kids, all of them locked up in the Bledsoe mad ward. He owns this dump and sometimes he acts like he's a friend of mine."

Morley Dotes was a lot more to those who knew the underside of the city. He was its top physical specialist, meaning for enough money he broke heads and arms, though he preferred ladies' hearts. He did that for free. He was half human, half dark elf, with the natural slightness and good looks of the latter. He wasn't what I would call a close friend. He was too dangerous to get close to. He had worked with and for me a few times.

"Don't you believe a word this thug tells you," Morley said. "He couldn't tell the truth if he got paid for it. And he's a dangerously violent psychotic. Just this afternoon he whipped up on a bunch of ogres who were minding their own business hanging out on the street smoking weed."

"You heard about that already?"

"News travels fast, Garrett."

"Know anything about it?"

"I figured you'd be around. I asked some questions. I don't know who hired the ogres. I know them. They're second-raters too lazy and stupid to do a job right. You might keep a watch out over your shoulder. You hurt a couple of them bad. The others might not consider that a simple hazard of the business."

"I have been watching. You could pay back a favor when we leave by taking a look at the guy who's following us."

"Somebody's following us?" Amiranda's question squeaked. She was frightened.

"He was with us from the Iron Liar here. He wasn't on me before that. Maybe he picked us up there. But the implication is that he was on you all along."

She got pale.

"Get her a chair, dope," Morley said. "You have the manners and sensitivity of a lizard."

I got her into a chair, not without a glare for Morley. The man was bird-dogging, making his points for the time Amiranda and I went our own ways. Not that I blamed him. I was developing the feeling that she was worth it. On mainly intuitive evidence I'd decided she was a class act.

"What are you into this time, Garrett?" Morley retreated to his chair, came up with a flash of brandy from somewhere behind his desk. He held it up questioningly. I nodded. He produced a single cup. He knew I preferred beer. He didn't touch alcohol himself. I was mildly surprised that he would have it in his place. For his ladies, I supposed.

I took the cup and passed it to Amiranda. She sipped. "I'm sorry. I'm being silly. I should have known it wouldn't be as simple as . . ."

Morley and I exchanged glances while pretending we hadn't heard her murmur. Morley asked, "Is it a secret, Garrett?"

"I don't know. Is it a secret, Amiranda? Might be worth telling him. It won't go any farther if that's what you want, and he might do you some good down the line." I raised a fist to Morley's smirk, silently cursing myself for that brilliant choice of words.

Amiranda pulled herself together. Not a girl for the traditional water-works. I liked that. I was liking Amiranda more all the time. Damsels in distress were fine, and good for business, but I was tired of the kind who clung and whined. Much better the woman who got up on her hind legs and stood in there punching with you after she put you on the job.

Though in this case I didn't have a job, strictly speaking. I had a dispute with somebody who sent ogres around to thump on me.

Amiranda thought a bit and made a decision. She told the kidnapping story.

She told it so damned good I smelled a rat. She told Morley exactly what I knew, and not an iota more or less.

"It's not a pro job," Morley said. "Have you gotten yourself into something political, Garrett?"

Amiranda looked startled. "Why do you say that?"

"Two reasons. There's nothing shaking in the kidnapping business right now. And the pros wouldn't touch *that* family. Raver Styx may not look as nasty as her father and Molahlu Crest, but she is. In her own quiet way. Nobody who lives on the underside of TunFaire society would think the potential payoff worth the risk."

"Amateurs," I said.

"Amateurs with enough money to hire head crackers and tails, Garrett. That means uptown. And when uptown does dirty deeds, it's always political."

"Maybe. I'm not so sure. It don't have that stink. I'll wait before I make up my mind. There's something cockeyed in the whole mess. But I can't see where the profit lies. That would clear it up. But I'm not on a job and looking. I'm just trying to watch out for me and Amiranda."

Morley said, "I'll peek in the closets and look under the beds and get back to you tomorrow. Least I can do after the stunt I pulled in that vampire business. You still living with the Dead Man?"

"Yeah."

"You're weird. Let me get back to work." He grabbed his end of the tube connecting with the bar. "Wedge. Send Blood and Sarge and the Puddle up here." I shepherded Amiranda toward the door.

"See you." We went down and out, easing past three high-class bone crushers headed up. I call them high-class because they looked smart enough to be trusted with work more intellectually demanding than skull busting.

My old buddy Saucerhead Tharpe had come in downstairs while we were up. He wanted me to join him for a pitcher of carrot's blood and some yakking up old times, but I begged off. We had to keep moving if Morley was going to do us any good.

I told Amiranda, "You ever feel like you need protecting, you come down here and hire Saucerhead Tharpe. He's the best there is."

"What about the other one? Morley? Do you trust him?"

"With my money or my life but never with my woman. It's getting late. I'd better get you home."

"I don't think I'm going home, Garrett. Unless you insist."

"All right." I do like a woman who can make up her mind, even though I may not understand what she is doing.

The Dead Man would have fits. But that was all right. What did he live for but to chew me out and to march his bugs around the walls?

Only one thing further about that night needs to be reported. When we were slipping into bed, I noted the absence of a gewgaw worn by every woman who doesn't want to hear little voices piping, "Mommy!"

"Where's your amulet?"

"You're a gentleman in your heart, aren't you, Garrett? Most men would have pretended not to notice."

I don't often get caught without something to say. This was one of those rare times. I kept my mouth shut.

She slipped in beside me, warm and bare, and whispered, "You don't have to worry. I can't make you a father."

And of that night nothing more need be said.

She was gone when I awoke the next morning. I never saw her again.

8

Morley himself stopped by to let me know what he'd learned. Old Dean let him in and brought him to the overconfident closet I call an office. I didn't rise and I didn't offer the usual banter. Dean went off to the kitchen to get Morley some of the apple juice we keep in the cold well against those millennial moments when I don't feel like having beer.

"You look glum, Garrett."

"It happens. The strain of being Mr. Smiles catches up."

"Well, you may have good reason. Even though you don't know it yet."

I showed him my eyebrow trick. He wasn't impressed. Everyone knows what familiarity breeds.

"I put out feelers that touched everybody in the snatch racket. Nobody has gone underground. Nobody is scoping out a job on the Hill. I got the personal guarantee of some of the best and the worst that there's nobody in this burg crazy enough to go for the Stormwarden's kid. Not for a million in gold. Gold don't do you any good when you're getting your toes roasted in the sorceress's basement."

"That's what's supposed to give me a sour puss?"

"No. You get that when I tell you about the guy who was tailing you last night. Or your lady, actually. You should have told me she was Amiranda Crest, Garrett. I wouldn't have made remarks about her father."

"She's used to it. What about the tail?"

"He trotted right down here after you, not even thinking somebody might be following him, too. Fool. He hung around watching the place for a couple of hours. About the time even a moron would have figured out that she was spending the night he took off and headed—"

Dean stuck his head in through the doorway. "Excuse me, Mr. Garrett. There's a Mr. Slauce here to see you, representing somebody he calls the Domina Dount. Will you see him?"

"I can wait," Morley told me.

"Out that door." I indicated the closet's second exit, which opened on a hallway leading past the Dead Man's room. "Bring Mr. Slauce in, Dean."

Slauce was a blustery, potbellied, red-faced little man who was way out of his element. I think he had me pegged for a professional killer. He worked hard at being polite. It was obvious he wasn't accustomed to that.

"Mr. Garrett?"

I confessed that I was that very devil.

"Domina Dount would like to see you again. She said to tell you she's received another letter from her correspondent and would like further professional advice. I assume you understand what she means. She didn't explain to me."

"I know what she meant."

"She authorized me to offer you ten marks gold for your time."

I wondered what she really wanted. She was throwing one hell of a lot of money around. A laborer, if he got paid in a lump for the time, wouldn't draw ten marks gold for three months of his life.

And right now gold was strong because Glory Mooncalled's successes in the Cantard had put several more silver mines into Karentine hands, meaning all their production came north.

Willa Dount might want to climb my leg about Amiranda. For ten marks I would take what she wanted to hand out. There is never enough money around our place because of the endless fix-ups.

"Leave word at the gate that I'm on my way. I'll be there as soon as I take care of a few details and have lunch."

Slauce's ruddy face got redder. The nerve of me! I was supposed to frog when uptown said jump. He wanted to drag me off by the heels. But his instructions held. "Very well. I'm sure she would appreciate your taking as little time as possible. She did seem distracted." He counted five two-mark pieces onto my desk.

"I won't be more than a half hour behind you. Dean? Will you see Mr. Slauce to the door?" We like to know that our guests are out when they head out. Some of them are so slow they might not remember which side of the door they're supposed to be on when it shuts.

Morley returned to the room. "Better bite those things to see if they're real, Garrett. Somebody's running a game."

"How so?"

"That's the guy who was tailing your lady last night."

"Yeah? He looked taller in the dark."

"Maybe he was wearing platforms. I think it's time you thought about getting out of this."

"I'm not in it."

"I know you, Garrett. You're going to get into it up to your ears if you don't turn your back now."

Morley is usually not much shakes as a prophet. I paid him no mind, thanking him and telling him the favor was a chunk off the account he owed from the vampire business. I saw him out, then let Dean serve me lunch.

Then I ambled off to earn my ten gold marks.

•••9

illa Dount was piqued by my churlish failure to bounce when she hollered but she hid it well. Everybody but the Dead Man was hiding irritation with me. I decided I'd best keep my hands covering my pockets.

"Thank you for coming, Mr. Garrett."

"Your man said you'd heard from the kidnappers."

"Yes. Another letter. Delivered much like the first." She passed it over.

The same hand, with the same poor spelling, told her that Junior's market value was "200000 Markes gold." Instructions for delivery would follow.

"Two hundred thou? The kid's in trouble, isn't he? The Emperor himself might not go for that much."

"The sum can be raised, Mr. Garrett. It will be paid. That isn't the problem."

"What is?"

"I face a twofold dilemma. Part is that I won't be able to conceal an outlay of that magnitude from the Stormwarden. That's my problem and I'll deal with her displeasure when the time comes. She won't like the expense but she would like to lose her son far less."

"I gather your own balance scale might not tilt the same way."

"My opinions are of no moment, Mr. Garrett. This is the Stormwarden's household and here the Stormwarden's will and whimsy alike are law."

"What do you need me for?"

"Advice on overcoming the mechanical difficulties of delivering that much gold."

"You'll need a big pocket to carry it."

"I'm paying handsomely for your time, Mr. Garrett. Don't waste it on witticisms. I have no sense of humor."

"If you say so."

"Two hundred thousand marks in coined gold weighs four thousand pounds. To move that much weight will require a heavy wagon and at least a four-horse team. Can they possibly expect me to get that someplace where the payoff can't be seen?"

"With a payoff that big they'd set it somewhere way out in the country, after running you along a route they could watch to make sure you aren't being followed."

"They will insist on coined gold; won't they? Bar would be easier for me to get together and handle but harder for them to dispose of. Right?"

"Probably."

"I thought so. I've already started exchanging our bar stock for coin. What else should I know?"

"Don't improvise. Do whatever they tell you, when they tell you. They'll be very nervous and likely to panic and do anything if they see one little thing going different from what they prescribed. If you've got to get some paybacks, wait till everybody is home safe. That much money will leave tracks. Bloody ones, probably."

"I'll worry about that when the time comes. Most probably it'll have to wait till the Stormwarden returns. Thank you, Mr. Garrett. Your expertise has confirmed the soundness of my own reasoning. I would say that we've had an amicable and productive relationship. But there is one thing you could do to make it perfect."

"What's that?"

"Stay away from Amiranda Crest."

"It's been twenty years since I let anybody pick my friends, Domina. You're a sweetheart, but if I make an exception for you—"

"I'm not accustomed to disobedience."

"You ought to get out into the real world more. You'd get in practice real fast."

"Get out of here before I lose my temper."

I figured that was good advice. I headed for the door.

"Stay away from Amiranda."

I supposed Amiranda had gotten similar advice regarding Garrett.

• • •

I nearly trampled the Stormwarden's daughter Amber. I pulled the door shut behind me. "Eavesdropping?"

"She's right."

"About what?" Her ears were sharper than mine if she could make out anything through that door.

"You should forget Ami. I'm much more interesting."

In that instant I decided she was wrong. Amiranda Crest was a woman. This one wore a woman's body but the creature inside was spoiled, vain, snobbish, and probably not very bright. At a snap judgment. "We'll have to talk about it sometime."

"Soon, I hope."

I think I grunted.

"Let me know when."

Persistent little devil.

The office door opened. "What are you doing here, Amber?"

"Talking to Mr. Garrett."

Willa Dount put on a fierce scowl and pointed it my way. It was my fault that the women in the Stormwarden's house tracked me down. "Go back to your apartment, Amber. You know you aren't permitted in this wing."

"Stick your elbow in your ear, you old witch."

The Domina was absolutely astonished. I feared she would begin sputtering. But her footwork was good. "If you wish to contest my authority in your mother's absence, we'll refer the dispute to your father."

"Naturally. He'll say whatever you tell him to say, won't he?"

Domina Dount remained painfully aware of my presence. "Amber!"

"How did you get a hold on him? It can't be because you're a woman. You freeze bathwater when you sit in it."

"That will be quite enough, Amber."

"Excuse me, ladies. I never feel comfortable in these hen sessions. I'll just be running along."

If looks could kill. Domina Dount wanted me deaf to her humiliation. Amber wanted my support.

I walked. I watched for Amiranda, but there was no sign of her.

● ● ● 10

The Dead Man remained engrossed in his war games. He was feeble company at the best of times. When he was like this, with his genius totally committed, he was no company at all. I consoled myself with the suspicion that he was onto something overlooked by the commanders of the many armies in the Cantard. I was spared his irascibility, too.

Old Dean was worse company. Each meal came with its pitch for some deprived and homely female relative who, he hinted, had just the touch the house really needed. Amiranda did not come to visit as I'd hoped. After a few days of that I got to feeling wretchedly sorry for myself and decided to go spend my recent gains buying a few barrels of beer retail, for on-site consumption.

I couldn't get my heart into it. They ran me out of the first two places for doing nothing but taking up space while I nursed a single brew.

The kidnapping kept nagging me. I should have been happy to have my hundred ten marks for doing nothing. But I wasn't. There was a wrongness about the thing, the ring of bad crystal. Look at it as I might, though, I couldn't root out the source of the bad odor.

There wasn't much I could do about it. I didn't have a client. Nobody goes digging around on the Hill just to satisfy a personal curiosity. There was too much potential for pain and none at all for profit.

In the third bar, nearer home, they let me sit and brood. I'd done well by them in the past and would again. When the man sat down opposite me, I presumed they were trying to make the best use of table space. I didn't look at him till he growled, "Your name Garrett?"

I looked. He was a big one, broad, thirtyish, with the air of a tough and clothes you don't find anywhere but on the Hill. But no livery. A hired hand who did his work in the shadows. Nothing gave away who owned him. "Who wants to know?"

"I do."

"I got a feeling you and me aren't going to get along. I don't recall inviting you to sit."

"I don't need an invite from a crumb like you."

He was off the Hill for sure. Their heads swell when they get connected up there. "I know we're not going to be pals."

"Break my heart, smart boy."

"I was thinking more along the line of an arm or leg. What do you want, Bruno?"

Bruno is a derisive generic for a dumb pug. A quick glance around told me he had a couple of buddies along but they were too far away to give him a hand quickly. They were at the bar trying to blend in.

"Word is going around that you been hanging around Raver Styx's place. You got a rep for mixing in where you're not wanted. We want to know what you're up to."

"Who is we?" He was so rude he didn't answer, so I suggested, "Why don't you ask the Stormwarden?"

"I'm asking you, Garrett."

"You're wasting your time. Go away, Bruno. You're interfering with my drinking."

He jabbed a hand out and got hold of my left wrist, started to squeeze. He had a good grip but my right hand fell on his. I buried my thumb in the flesh just behind the root joints of his middle and forefingers. I pressed hard. His eyes got big and his face turned white. I smiled a friendly smile.

"All right, Bruno. You were just going to tell me who you work for and why you're down here trying to convince people that you're somebody scary."

"You go to hell, you cheap—unh!"

"You've got to learn to think before you speak. With a mouth like yours it's a miracle you've lived this long."

"Garrett, you're going to be sorry you were ever—unh!"

"They say pain is the fastest educator. In your case it looks like even that won't help. Yes?"

Someone had come to the table, approached unnoticed because I was watching Bruno's pals slowly develop the suspicion that all was not well with their buddy.

"Mr. Garrett?"

The daPenas were a polite bunch. "Junior. Have a seat. Bruno was just leaving." I let go his hand. He flexed it as he rose, trying to leave me with his best deadly look.

He wanted to pop me one, just to remember him by, but when he went to cock it, I let a foot fly under the table and got him in the shin. His eyes got big again, he made one little whimper of a sound, and decided to go away while he was still fit to limp.

"I see Domina Dount pulled it off and got you back in one piece."

"Yes."

"Congratulations on your good fortune. So how come you're down here slumming?"

The son was the image of the father without the marks of age and dissipation. How had the question of paternity risen? Maybe when he was a baby he hadn't looked so much like his immediate male ancestor. Those notions hang on forever.

"I wanted to thank you personally."

"Thank me? For what? I didn't do a damned thing." The kid had one of those apologetic, whiny voices that made you suspect he wanted to be excused for being alive.

"But you did. At least you appeared to. The kidnappers . . . I overheard them talking. They had somebody watching our place. When they saw you, they talked it over and decided they had to play the whole thing as straight as they could. Because of your reputation. So you see, I owe you a debt of thanks. I might not be here if you hadn't . . ."

In addition to his other charms Junior was a rocker. Whenever he spoke, he jerked back and forth, staring into space. It must have been a joy growing up in the Stormwarden's household.

I got a strong feeling that he had much more on his mind, that gratitude was just an excuse for seeking me out. But you don't have much luck pressing guys like him when you don't have a hold on them. They tend to break for cover. So I leaned back and tried to look pleased with his praise and interested in anything else he might want to tell me.

In a moment it was obvious he was working himself up to something. He started stammering. But he never got the chance to open up.

"Here you are, my lord." And here he was, the Domina's florid flunky, Slauce, wearing an ingratiating smile belied by eyes in which the humor had been extinct for years. "I've been looking everywhere."

I doubted that. He had to have been following Junior to pop up so quickly and inconveniently.

"Courter. I was just telling Mr. Garrett how grateful I am for his help." He rocked.

His eyes gave him away. He was terrified of this character Courter, who had used the name Slauce when he had visited me.

"The Domina needs you right away, my lord." A command cautiously couched for my benefit. Junior flinched.

Across the room Bruno and the boys had been huddled together for a while. Apparently they decided the presence of Junior and his keeper meant there was no more percentage for them there. They went away, though Bruno left me a final dirty look.

Junior got up and Courter took hold of his arm, not heavy-handed but definitely like he thought his man might try to run. He passed close enough to trip. I thought about giving it a shot to see what would happen, but I left it as a thought.

"See you later, Karl."

His look of despair brightened as he took the notion seriously.

Courter looked at me for the only time during his visit. He had visions of bloodshed echoing through his eyes. I smiled and gave him a big friendly wink. It did nothing for his ulcer.

I gave it the old try but I couldn't get involved in my drinking. I held a caucus with myself, took a vote, and decided to go home and purge my soul by either subjecting it to the torment of old Dean's recitation of the encyclopedia of his eligible relatives, or simply dosing it with a generous helping of the Dead Man's poisonous humors.

They disappointed me. Both of them. I think they had discussed it while I was gone. Dean was whistling when I walked in. "What happened? Your females ambush a troop of hussars and take them prisoners for life?"

He was in too good a mood to take offense. I couldn't get a pout from him. I demanded, "What's going on around here? Why are you grinning like a fox with goosefeathers in his whiskers?"

"It's his nibs. He's ebullient. Exultant. Positively ecstatic."

"All that, huh? This I've got to see."

"It is one for the books, Mr. Garrett."

"What's that you're working on there?"

"A lamb roast."

"Lamb is mutton. I don't like mutton." I had more mutton than I ever wanted while I was in the Marines. We ate it every meal except when we had to make do with rocklike chunks of salt pork or circumstances forced us to eat our horses or, worse, we had to subsist on roots and berries.

"You'll like this. You'll see." He talked cooking technique.

I walked, grumbling, "Mutton is mutton is mutton," figuring I would have to eat the stuff with a big show of appreciation because whenever I get critical of Dean's cooking and he takes umbrage, the next meal is sure to include green peppers. There is no foodstuff in this or any other world quite so hideously nauseating as the green bell pepper. A pig—even a hungry pig—has better sense than to eat green peppers. But not people. It positively astounds me what people will eat.

In such a humor I shoved into the Dead Man's room.

Ah. Garrett. Good afternoon. Good of you to stop in. How is that kidnapping business going?

"The kid came home in one piece." I stepped out of the room, looked around, stepped back inside.

Congratulations. A job well done. You will have to tell me all about it. What was that little dance step?

"Just making sure I was in the right house with the right Dead Man. No congrats due. I didn't have anything to do with it." I went ahead and brought him up to date, leaving out none of the details but Amiranda's overnight vacation from the household of the Stormwarden.

An interesting situation, infested with anomalies. Almost a pity you have no concern in it. A challenge to crack its shell and lay open the meat within.

"Feeling our genius today, are we?"

Indeed. Yes indeed. The mystery of the magic of Glory Mooncalled is a mystery no more. Subject to observational confirmation, of course.

"You figured out how he does it? When the Venageti War Council can't do better than stumble over their own feet?"

Indeed.

"How?"

Ratiocination, my boy.

My boy? He *was* in a mood to crow.

Cogitation. Induction. Deduction. Repeated experiment manipulating the possible course of events within the known parameters. And from this came a hypothesis bearing the weight of near certainty. I know how Glory Moon-

called did what he did, and with just a bit more information I could predict with some degree of certainty what he will do next.

"So how does he do it? Does he turn invisible? Does he run through secret tunnels to sneak up and sneak away?"

I have to reserve the how for now, Garrett. The hypothesis is insufficiently tested, based as it is on one assumption not yet validated. A bit more observation should confirm it, though, and you will be the first to know.

"No doubt." He would crow like a herd of roosters watching three suns rising. If he was not already. "Why don't you—"

"Mr. Garrett?" Dean had his head in the doorway. "Excuse me. There's a young woman here to see you."

His nose was up and his choice of the word "woman" over "lady" told me he thought her a floozy and probably some playmate of mine not nearly as worthy of me as any one of a dozen of his nieces.

"Who is she?"

"She wouldn't say. She seemed perfectly familiar with you, though." Again with the nose up.

I excused myself and headed for the door expecting Amiranda. They just can't stay away from you, Garrett.

It was Amber. She gave me her big teasing smile as I let her in. Dean had instructions to let no one in without consulting me or the Dead Man first.

I scanned the street as Amber brushed past. I didn't see Courter Slauce but assumed he was out there watching.

Amber did some posing, showing off her best features, of which she had several. "Aren't you dressed for the kill today? What's the occasion?" I gave the street another scan. Nothing. But women from the Hill don't wander my end of town unchaperoned. Not unless they're so severely unaware of personal danger that the bad guys shy off as if they were holy madmen.

"A hunt. Of sorts." She did have a promising smile.

"I see. How old are you, Amber?"

"Twenty." She lied. My immediate guess was eighteen going on thirty.

"Uh, this way." I stalled for time while I led her to my office. There is a side of me that is very fond of women. There is also a side that's wary of those who bring gifts without being asked. When they stand near a center of power and are as changeable and spoiled as this one probably was, I want to play it very carefully. I thought I saw a way.

"I'm a charming scamp, I know. Hurt me to the quick though it does, I'm old enough, plain enough, and poor enough to suspect that maybe my profession has more to do with you being here."

"Maybe." She went on trying to flirt. I had a bad feeling she might be one of those who couldn't deal with a man until she proved to herself she could lead him around by his hopes and fantasies. That kind regards consummation as something to avoid at all costs. She was young but she knew her men well enough to know actually giving in would dilute her power.

I assumed she was playing that game, so I did my best to let her think she might get what she wanted without stretching her virtue.

She did appeal. A whole damned lot. But I'll have to know a Stormwarden's daughter a lot better before I take the risks inherent in such a situation.

"There is one thing you could do," she admitted. "But that can wait. Don't you feel crowded in here? Isn't there somewhere else? That old man could walk in anytime."

At which point I made the mistake of sitting down. My sitter was barely in place when a hundred pounds of potential parked *her* sitter on my lap.

So much for Garrett's infallible estimates of members of the female species.

She had me going for a minute—until she giggled. I don't like my women to giggle. It makes me doubt their maturity.

Still, when the culprit is sitting on your lap, wagging her tail . . .

"Mr. Garrett." It was that old man. "Mr. Dotes is here. He says it's important."

Saved!

Damn it.

11

"**D**o you have to, Garrett?"

"You don't know Morley Dotes. If he comes here, it's important."

I had Amber about half pried loose when Dotes blew in. He stopped and gawked; then that sparkle flashed in his eye. I'm going to throw pepper in there someday just to get tears to wash it out.

"Down, boy. What's going on?"

Amber made a show of neatening herself up. I guess she knew she had it and couldn't help flaunting it.

"Your pal Saucerhead. He's in the Bledsoe carved up bad enough to kill a mammoth."

"Bound to happen in his line of work." Which was pretty much the same as Morley's less public line, so he gave me a sour look when he could steal a second from appreciating Amber. "How did it happen?"

"Don't have much yet. He staggered in from somewhere way the hell out in the country. They say he shouldn't have made it, but you know him. Too stubborn and stupid to die. They don't think he'll make it."

"Who does, down there? What the hell was he doing out in the boondocks?"

Morley gave me a funny look. "I thought you'd know. He left the place early last night because he had a job. Said you recommended him."

"Me? I never . . . Oh. Damn. I'd better get down there." I had butterflies the size of horses. Amiranda. Had to be.

"I'll stroll along with you, then. I haven't had my exercise today." Far be it from Morley Dotes to admit he had a friend anywhere in the known universe.

As he turned to leave, Amber whispered, "Wait, Garrett." The music was out of her voice.

"Is it critical?"

"To me it is."

"Wait for me at the front door, Morley. So. Tell me."

"My brother came home this morning. They let him go."

"Good for him."

"That means Domina paid the ransom."

"Seems likely. So?"

"So there's two hundred thousand gold marks out there somewhere that belong to my family, that somebody couldn't yell about if it got taken away. Do you think you could find it?"

"Maybe. If I wanted to bad enough. A chunk like that, in the hands of amateurs, would leave a trail like a rogue mammoth. The trick would be getting to it before all the other sharpshooters in town."

"Help me find it, Garrett. You can have half."

"Whoa, girl. That's asking for big trouble with no guarantee of any—"

"This may be my first, last, and only chance to make a hit big enough to get away from my mother. If I could get that money before she comes home, I could disappear so thoroughly she couldn't find me with an army. You could do pretty good with a hundred thousand, too."

"That I could. That I could."

She posed. "And there are ancillary benefits, too."

"Yes. Yes indeed. I'll need some time to think about what I'd need and what I'd have to do. In the meantime, I've got a friend in the infirmary trying to die. I want to see him before he goes."

"Sure." She didn't sound thrilled to hear about obligations imposed by friendship. "I'll come back tomorrow if I can get away from Courter and his bullies. Next day for sure. Maybe you could give that old man the day off." She turned on the smile.

"Maybe I'll think about that, too."

She giggled. "You do that."

I patted her fanny. "Come on. Off with you. My friend Morley will be getting impatient." I followed her to the front door. There is nothing I can say to disparage the view from that perspective.

Dean was waiting to bolt up after me, which meant he had been eavesdropping again. I shot him an ugly glare, but it ricocheted like water off the proverbial duck.

Morley was waiting outside. While I stood listening to Dean shoot the bolts, we appreciated Amber's departure.

"Where do you find them, Garrett?"

"I don't. They find me."

"Bull feathers."

"It's true. I just sit here like a big old trapdoor spider and nab them when they walk by. Then I turn on the Garrett charm and they swoon into my arms."

"That one is no swooner, Garrett. The one the other night wasn't, either. High Hill fluff, both of them. Right?"

"Off the Hill. I wouldn't call them fluff."

"No. Probably not." He sighed. "Why doesn't something like that ever turn up at my place?"

"You're doing all right from what I see. Don't get your heart set on this one. You'd be asking for a visit from the whirlwind. Her mother is a Storm-warden."

"Another dream shattered by bitter reality. Still, it's a pity. A pity—that's sweet. Let's go see Saucerhead and find out which way to lay our bets."

12

The Bledsoe infirmary is an imperial charity, meaning it's supposed to provide medical care for the indigent. If you're in the place, though, your chances improve a hell of a lot if you or a friend happen to come up with some cash. Human nature, I guess. I'm not always the biggest fan of my own species.

They weren't going to let me near Saucerhead at first. He was supposedly in real bad shape and would be checking out very soon. Then somebody saw the flash of gold between my fingers and heard a hint or two about metal changing hands if the prognosis improved, and first thing you knew the whole infirmary had a new attitude. Zip! Morley and I were in Saucerhead's ward watching a gang of physicians and healers do their stuff.

Saucerhead looked terrible when they started, paper pale after losing what appeared to be several gallons of blood. He didn't look much better when they finished, but his breathing was steadier, less inclined to the characteristic sighs. I scattered a few marks and showed that I had a few more that might want to keep the others company.

Saucerhead didn't do anything but breathe for a couple of hours. Good enough by me. That put us a few points up on Death.

Morley spoke only once the entire time we were waiting, in a tiny whisper. "If I ever get so desperate I come in here, you come cut my throat and put me out of my misery." The remark illuminated the side of Morley Dotes with a morbid dread of sickness. After this visit he would be on double rations, stoking up on green leafies and whatnot, for weeks.

Not that the Bledsoe was *anybody's* idea of heaven. One look around was enough to curdle a vampire's bones. And this was just a ward to die in. The insane wards are supposed to be ripped straight out of the dungeons of hell.

I couldn't figure why Saucerhead had picked the Bledsoe. He was no tycoon but he wasn't a pauper, either.

We saw only one other vertical human being after the staff left, a priest who was probably the only decent human being working the Bledsoe. I knew him vaguely. He was one of the bigger names in one of the more obscure and bizarre of the several hundred cults hag-riding TunFaire. He came over and stared down at the huge slab of muscle that was Saucerhead Tharpe. There was a nobility about Tharpe even in his extremity. It recalled the nobility of the lion or the mammoth. A good guy to have on your side, a bad guy to have for an enemy, simple, trustworthy, and as tough as they make them.

"Has he had his rites?"

"I don't know, Father."

"What gods did he have?"

I put temptation aside. "None that I know about. But we don't need sacraments. This is a life watch, not a deathwatch. He's going to make it."

The priest checked the name chalked on the wall above the head of Saucerhead's cot. "I'll say a prayer for him." Small smile. "It never hurts, even with a sure thing." He went on to those who needed him more, leaving me with the suspicion I had been one-upped.

Saucerhead must have been awake awhile before he let us know. His first remark, a hoarse croak, was, "Garrett, remind me to stay the hell away from your women."

I grunted and waited.

"Getting that one out of the Cantard got me half killed. I thought this one did me all the way."

"Yeah. What the hell did you come *here* for? If you had go-power enough to make it this far, you could have got yourself to somebody who could have done you some good."

"I was born here, Garrett. I had it in my head I was done for and it seemed right it should end up where it started. I guess I wasn't thinking too good."

"Yeah. You big dumb goof. Well, you're going to make it in spite of yourself and these jackals. You got enough energy to tell me what happened?"

"Yeah." His face darkened.

"So? What happened?"

"She's dead, Garrett! They killed her. I got five or six of them but they was too many and they got past me and cut her . . ." And he started, by god, getting up off that cot.

"Hold him down, Morley. What the hell are you doing, Saucerhead?"

"I got to go. I never blowed a job like that before, Garrett. Never."

Morley put him back down with one hand. Saucerhead was running on spirit alone.

There were tears in his eyes. "She was just a little bit of a thing, Garrett. Sweet as a sugar bun and cute as a button. They shouldn't ought to have done that to her."

"You're right. They shouldn't have." Part of me had known the worst all along, but the part that wishes and hopes was just getting the word.

Saucerhead tried getting up again. "I gotta, Garrett."

"You gotta heal up. I'll take care of the rest. I've got an interest that came before yours. After you give me everything you've got, Morley is going to get you out of here and take you wherever you want to stay. And I'm going headhunting."

Morley gave me a look. He didn't say anything. He didn't have to.

"Don't you start playing devil's advocate, Morley Dotes, telling me there's no percentage in getting involved. You'd do the same damned thing even if you dressed it up as something else. Come on, Saucerhead. Give it to me. Start from the beginning, the first time you laid eyes on her."

Saucerhead may not be speedy mentally, but his mind gets where it needs to go. And he sees what goes on around him and remembers it.

"The first time I seen her was with you at Morley's place. I thought to myself, How come a runt like Morley Dotes or a homely geek like Garrett always comes up with all the jewels?"

"He isn't dying," I said. "A sick sense of humor is the first thing that comes back. Imagine. Calling me homely. Never mind that night, Saucerhead. When did you see her again?"

"Yesterday afternoon. She tracked me down at my place."

She found him there and told him that I'd recommended him for any bodyguarding she needed done. She had a thing she wanted to do that night but she was nervous and scared and even though she was sure there would be no trouble, she thought it wouldn't hurt to have somebody along. Just in case. Just to make her more comfortable. After Saucerhead agreed to stick with her until she felt she didn't need him anymore. She went away until shortly before dusk, when she came back with a small open carriage.

"She have anything with her?"

"Bunch of cases in the back. The kind women stuff with clothes and things. She wasn't planning on coming back."

"Uhm. She say anything about what she was doing?"

That was the only time he was a little uncertain about what he ought to tell. He decided I needed everything. "She never said what she was up to. But she was going to meet somebody. And she wasn't planning on coming back."

"Then if you hadn't been along, she would've disappeared and nobody would've known what really happened." Gods. I blind myself with my own brilliance sometimes.

"Yeah. You going to let me tell it? Or should I catch a nap while you're jacking your jaw?"

"One more thing, then you can get on. Your payment. How and when?"

"Up front. I always make them pay up front . . . well, I almost made an exception for her. I took every coin she had, and then she was still half a mark short. I forgave her that and told her she should hold out part of the fee so she wouldn't short herself. But she said there was no problem, and when we got where we were going, I'd get my other half mark and maybe a nice bonus for being such a sweetheart."

"Yeah. That's Saucerhead Tharpe all over. A real sweetheart. All right. Go on."

They had moved out in the twilight, Saucerhead on horseback behind the carriage. He was lightly armed, but that wasn't unusual. He preferred to rely on his strength and speed. I didn't have to ask if he had seen anyone watching or following. He was looking for that and saw nothing. They left the city after dark and headed north at a leisurely pace, not doing any fancy switchbacking, not hurrying, and not drawing any special attention. Because he rode behind the buggy most of the way, they didn't talk much. But there was a three-quarter moon and a clear sky, and he was able to tell she was getting more worried and nervous as the night wore on. She was thoughtful of him and the animals, pausing for several rests.

About three in the morning they came to a woodland crossroad a couple miles from the famous old battleground at Lichfield, where some say the old imperial bones still sometimes get up and stalk around in search of the man who betrayed their commander.

As is customary at important crossroads, there was a central grass diamond with its tutelary obelisk. Amiranda stopped next to the obelisk where her team could crop grass. She told Saucerhead they would wait there. As soon as the person she was meeting showed, he could head back to TunFaire.

Saucerhead dismounted. After working the kinks out he just stood leaning against the buggy, waiting. Amiranda had little to say. An hour dragged past. She became more worried by the minute. Saucerhead's feeble attempts to reassure her foundered on his ignorance. She believed her worst fears were coming true.

The moon was about to depart the heavens and the east was lightening when Saucerhead realized they were no longer alone. An absence of the gossip of birds awakening tipped him off. He just had time to warn Amiranda before they charged out of the woods.

The moment he saw them he knew they weren't just road agents.

"There was at least fifteen of them, Garrett. Ogres. Some of them with the pure blood, like you don't hardly never see no more. They had knives and sharp sticks and clubs and big bones and you could tell they was bent on murder. They was cussing in ogrish on account of me being there. They wasn't expecting me."

Saucerhead wasn't clear himself on how it went after that, except that he got himself between the ogres and Amiranda, with his back against the buggy, and went to work with a knife and club of his own, and when he lost those, with bare hands and brute strength.

"I killed five or six, but there just ain't a whole lot any one man can do when he's outnumbered so bad. They just kept piling on me and hitting and cutting me. That girl, she didn't have enough sense to run. She tried to fight, too. But they dragged her down and cut on her . . . I thought I whipped them for a minute 'cause they all ran off. To the edge of the woods. But then I went down and couldn't get up again. Couldn't even move. They thought I was dead. They dragged me over and dumped me in the brush, then they dragged everyone else over, then they started going through the girl's stuff, cussing 'cause there wasn't nothing worth nothing, but they squabbled like sparrows over every piece anyway. And not once even thinking about helping their buddies that was hurt."

Then they heard someone coming. They scurried around cleaning up after themselves, then took off down the road with the buggy and Saucerhead's horse.

About that time Saucerhead got himself together enough to get on his feet. He found Amiranda, scooped her up, and headed out.

"I wasn't thinking so good," he said. "I didn't want her to be dead so I didn't believe it. There's this witch I know that lives about three miles from there, back in the woods. I told myself if I could get the girl to her everything would be all right. And you know me. I get my mind set . . ."

Yeah. I tried to picture it. Saucerhead half dead, still bleeding, stumbling through the woods carrying a dead woman. And after that, he walked all the way back to TunFaire so he'd be in the right place when he died.

I asked a lot of questions then, mostly about the ogres and what they'd said when they'd thought him dead. He hadn't heard anything I could use. I got directions to the witch's hut.

Saucerhead was getting weaker then, but he was working himself up again. I told him, "You just relax. If I don't get it straightened out, you can take over when you're well again. Morley, I want you to get him out of here. Come on. Morley will be back to get you, Saucerhead."

Morley finally spoke when we hit the street. "Nasty business."

"You heard of anybody getting rich since yesterday?"

"No." He gave me a look.

"Got any contacts in Ogre town?" If you aren't part ogre, you can't get the time of day down there. I had a couple of people I knew there but none I knew well enough to get any help on this.

"A few. But not anybody who'll tell me anything about a deal that has Raver Styx on the other end of it."

"That's my problem."

"You going out there to look around?"

"Maybe tomorrow. Got some loose ends to knot up around here first."

"Use some company when you go? I'm way behind on my exercise."

He pretended he was interested in anything but what interested him. "I don't think so. And somebody has to stay here and keep reminding Saucerhead that he's hurt."

"It got personal, eh?"

"Very."

"You be careful out there."

"Damned right I will. And you keep your ears open. I'm interested in news about ogres and news about anybody with a sudden pocketful of gold."

We parted. I went home and wrapped myself around a couple gallons of beer.

●●● **13**

The Dead Man's mood hadn't soured by the next morning. I got worried. Were we getting to the beginning of the end? I didn't know enough about the Loghyr to be sure what sort of symptom persistent good humor might be. I told him about Saucerhead, leaving out none of the details. "That give you any ideas?"

Several. But you have not given me enough information to form more than one definite opinion.

"A definite one? You? What is it?"

Your little overnight treat was involved up to her cute little ears in the kidnapping of the Stormwarden's son. If not a part of the conspiracy itself, she did at least have guilty knowledge.

I didn't argue. I had formed that suspicion myself. It was good to know I had a mind nearly as agile as his, if not so absolute in its decisions. But him being a genius exempts him from the doubts plaguing us mere mortals.

"Would you care to run through your reasoning?"

It would appear simple and obvious enough for even one of your narrow intellectual focus to unravel.

I gave him a big grin. That was his way of zinging me for having dared entertain overnight in my own home. He couldn't shake his good humor completely, though.

He added, *Troublesome as females are when they step out of their proper roles as connivers, manipulators, gossips, backstabbers, and bearers and nurturers of the young, slaughtering them is not an acceptable form of chastise-*

ment. I urge you to persist in your inquiries, Garrett. With all due caution. I would not care to see you share the woman's fate. How would I attend the funeral?

"You're just a sentimental fool, aren't you?"

Too often too much so for my own welfare.

"Ha! Dirty truth gets caught with its nose sticking out. If I get scrubbed, you might have to get off your mental duff and do some honest geniusing in order to keep a roof over your head."

I am an artist, Garrett. I do not—

"And I'm a frog prince under a witch's spell."

"Mr. Garrett?"

I turned. Dean was at the door. "What?"

"That woman is here again."

"The one who was here yesterday?"

"The same." You would have thought he smelled spoiled onions in his pantry the way his face was puckered.

"Take her into the office. Don't let her touch you. It might be communicable." I let him get out of hearing before adding, "You might carry it to your nieces and suddenly have them all turn desirable."

You ride him too hard, Garrett. He is a sensitive man with an abiding concern for his loved ones.

"I let him get out of hearing, didn't I?"

I would not want to lose him.

"Me, neither. I'd have to go back to cleaning up after you myself." I got out then, ignoring him trying to come up with the last word. We could kill a whole day that way.

Amber was looking her best and sensed that I saw and felt it. She tried starting up where she left off. I told her, "I've decided to find that money for you. I think we're going to have to stick to business and move damned fast if we want to catch the trail before it's cold. I did a lot of legwork yesterday, poking under rocks. I came up with a sack full of air. I'm starting to think the whole thing was an out-of-town operation."

"Garrett!" She wanted to play. But she could accept two hundred thousand marks gold as a good reason for not, for the moment. I figured her for the type who could get hooked on the challenge. That might be my next problem.

"What do you mean, out-of-town operation?"

"Like I said yesterday, a thing involving two hundred thousand and snatching Raver Styx's kid is going to take big planning and leave big tracks, even when the best pros are working the job. One way to give the tracks a chance to disappear in the mud is to do your design work, recruiting, purchasing, and rehearsal somewhere far away. Then you might take the gold somewhere else, still. In fact, with so much gold involved, you might want to tie up loose ends by erasing any connection between yourself and the kidnap victim."

"You mean kill off the people who helped you?"

"Yes."

"That's horrible. That's . . . that's terrible."

"It's a terrible world. With a lot of terrible people in it. Not to mention things like ogres and ghouls. Or vampires and wolfmen, who see the rest of us as prey, though they used to be human themselves."

"It's horrible."

"Of course. But it's the kind of thing we may run into. You still game? We're partners, you're going to have to carry your half of the load."

"Me? How can I help?"

"You can get me a chance to talk to your brother and Amiranda."

She looked puzzled. Not too bright, my Amber? But decorative. Definitely decorative. "I haven't dug up but one clue yet, and it's not worth squat by itself."

"What is it?"

"Uh-uh. I keep my cards to my chest till I get a better picture."

"Why do you need to talk to Karl and Amiranda?"

"Karl because he's the only one who had any direct contact with the kidnappers—except maybe Domina Dount, when she delivered the ransom. Amiranda because she works for the Domina and might have picked up something useful. I can't go grill Willa Dount. She'd want the gold back herself if she knew we were looking for it. Wouldn't she?"

"Yeah. But Karl would want a cut if he knew what we were doing. He wants out of that house as bad as I do. Amiranda, the same way."

"You get me a chance to talk to them. I'll think of some reason for it."

"All right. But you'd better be careful. Especially with Amiranda. She's a little witch."

"You don't like her?"

"Not very much. She's smarter than me and when she wants she can make herself almost as pretty. Even my own mother always treats her better than me. But I don't think I hate her. I just wish she'd go away."

"And she wants to get away as badly as you and your brother do? When she gets better treatment?"

"Better than awful is still bad, Garrett."

"How soon can you fix it so I can see Karl?"

"It'll be hard. He won't be able to sneak out right now. Domina has Courter watching him every minute. She says the kidnapping won't stay a secret and when the news gets out how much the ransom was, somebody else might try it again. Would they?"

"That happens. There are a lot of lazy, stupid crooks who try to get by imitating success. Your family will be at risk till your mother takes some action to make it plain that folks who mess with her live short and awful lives."

"She probably wouldn't even care."

She would care even if she had no use or love for her offspring, but I had no inclination to illuminate Amber about the symbols and trappings of power and what the powerful have to do to keep them polished and frightening. "The next step has to be your brother. If he can't come to me, I'll go to him. You arrange something. I'll follow you home about a half hour behind you. I'll hang around outside somewhere. You give me a signal when it's all right to come in. Might as well set it for me to see Amiranda, too. What will the signal be?"

I had chosen a conspiratorial tone. It worked. She got into the spirit of doings shadowed and sinister. "I'll flash a mirror out my window. Give me five minutes after that, then meet me at the postern."

"Which window?"

While she explained, I reflected that she had this gimmick too pat to have come up with it on the spur of the moment. I hoped it was a device she used to sneak lovers inside. If she had been getting away with that, the notion might be marginally workable. If she was setting me up . . .

But she had no reason that I could see. It was plain that her only interest was laying hands on her mother's gold.

You get paranoid in this business. But maybe paranoids get that way because of all the people out to get them.

"Better scoot along now," I told her. "Before they miss you up there and start wondering."

"A half hour wouldn't make any difference, would it?"

"A half hour might make all the difference."

"I can get real stubborn when I really want something, Garrett."

"I'll bet you can. I hope you're as stubborn about the gold if we find things getting tight." I guided her toward the front door.

"Tight? How could it get dangerous?"

"Are you kidding? Not to be melodramatic"—like hell!—"but it could get to be a long, dark, narrow valley between your mother and the kidnappers before we get that gold socked away."

She looked at me with big eyes while that sank in. Then she turned on the smile. "Keep that golden carrot dangling out front and this mule won't even see the brooding hills."

So. A little slow, maybe, but gutsy.

Old Dean was watching from down the hall, exercising his disapproving scowl. I patted Amber on the fanny. "That's the spirit, kid. Remember. I'm half an hour behind you. Try not to leave me standing in the street too long."

She spun around and laid a kiss on me that must have curled Dean's hair and toes. It did mine. She backed off, winked, and scooted.

went back and got a big cold one to fortify myself for the coming campaign. I had to draw it myself. Dean had been stricken blind and could
hear nothing but ghosts. He was exasperated with me.

I downed the long one, drew another, lowered the keg, then went to tell
the Dead Man the latest. He growled and snarled a little, just to make me
feel at home. I asked if he was ready to reveal Glory Mooncalled's secrets.
He told me no, and get out, and I left suspecting cracks had appeared in his
hypothesis. A cracked hypothesis can be lethal to the Loghyr ego.

After depositing my empty mug in the kitchen, I went upstairs and
rooted through the closet that serves as the household arsenal, selected a
few inconspicuous pieces of steel and a lead-weighted, leather-wrapped
truncheon that had served me well in the past. With a warning to Dean to
lock up after the ghosts left, I hit the street.

It was a nice day if one doesn't mind an inconsistent hovering between
mist and drizzle. Comes with the time of year. The grape growers like it
except when they don't. If they had their way, every stormwarden in the
business would be employed full-time making fine adjustments in weather
so they could maximize the premium of their vintages.

I was moist and crabby by the time I reached the Hill and started looking
for a place to lurk. But the neighborhood had been designed with the incon-
siderate notion that lurkers should not be welcome, so I had to hoof it up
and down and around, hanging out in one small area trying to look like I

belonged there. I told myself I was a pavement inspector and went to work detecting every defect in the lay of those stones. After fifteen minutes that lasted a day and a half, I caught Amber's signal—a candle instead of a mirror—and started drifting toward the postern. A day later that opened and Amber peeked out.

"Not a minute too soon, sweetheart. Here come the dragoons."

The folks on the Hill all tip into a community pot to hire a band of thugs whose task is to spare the Hill folk the discomfitures and embarrassments of the banditry we who live closer to the river have to accept as a fact of life, like dismal weather.

Not fooled for a minute by my romance with the cobblestones, a pair of those luggers were headed my way under full sail. They had been on the job too long. Their beams were as broad as their heights. But they meant business and I wasn't interested in getting into a head-knocking contest with guys who had merely to blow a whistle to conjure up more arguments for their side.

I got through the postern and left them with their meat hooks clamped on nothing but a peal of Amber's laughter. "That's Meenie and Moe. They're brothers. Eenie and Minie must have been circling in on you from the other side. We used to tease them terribly when we were kids."

A couple of remarks occurred to me, but with manly fortitude I kept them behind my teeth.

Amber led me through a maze of servants' passages, chattering brightly about how she and Karl used the corridors to elude Willa Dount's vigilance. Again I restrained myself from commenting.

We had to go up a flight and this way and that, part through passages no longer in use, or at least immune to cleaning. Then Amber shushed me while she peeked between hangings into a hallway for regular people with real blue blood in their veins. "Nobody around. Hurry." She dashed.

I trotted along behind dutifully, appreciating the view. I've never understood those cultures where they make the women walk three paces behind the man. Or maybe I do. There are more of them around arranged like Willa Dount than there are like Amber.

She swept me through a doorway into an empty room and rolled right around with her arms reaching. I caught her by the waist. "Tricked me, eh?"

"No. He'll be here in a minute. He has to get away. Meantime, you know the old saying."

"I live with a dead Loghyr. I hear a lot of old sayings, some of them so hoary the hills blush with embarrassment at his flair for cliché. Which old saying did you have in mind?"

"The one about all work and no play makes Garrett a dull boy."

I should have guessed.

She was determined to wear me down. And she was getting the job done.

Whump! The edge of the door got me as I was bending forward, contemplating yielding to temptation.

The story of my life.

I let my momentum carry me several steps out of orbit around Amber. She laughed.

Karl came into the room spouting apologies and turning red. He might have gone into a hand-wringing act if he had not had them loaded.

"I smell brew," I said. "The elixer of the gods."

"I recalled you were drinking beer in that place the other day. I thought it would be only courteous to provide refreshments, and so I . . ."

A chatterer.

I was amazed. Not only had he managed to come up with an idea of his own, he had managed to carry it out by himself, without so much as a servant to lug the tray. Maybe he did have a little of his grandfather in him after all. A thimbleful, or so.

He presented me with a capacious mug. I went to work on it. He nibbled the foam on a smaller one, just to show me what a democratic fellow he was. "Why did you want to talk to me, Mr. Garrett? I couldn't make much sense out of what Amber told me."

"I want to satisfy my professional curiosity. Your kidnapping was the most unusual one I've ever encountered. For my own benefit I want to study its ins and outs in case I ever get into a similar situation. The success of the kidnappers might encourage somebody to pull the same stunt again."

Karl looked very uncomfortable. He planted himself on a chair and gripped his mug in both hands. He pressed it into his lap in hopes of steadying it so I wouldn't notice it was shaking. I let him think he had me fooled.

"But what can I tell you that would be of any use, Mr. Garrett?"

"Everything. From the beginning. Where and how they laid hands on you. All the way through to the end. Where and how they turned you loose. I'll try not to interrupt unless you lose me. All right?" I took a long swig. "Good stuff."

Karl bobbed his head. He took a swig of his own. Amber sidled to the tray and discovered that Karl had brought wine, too, though he hadn't bothered to offer her any.

Junior said, "It started five or six nights ago. Right, Amber?"

"Don't look at me. I still wouldn't know about it if I didn't eavesdrop."

"Six nights ago, I guess. I spent the evening with a friend." He thought about it before telling me, "At a place called Half the Moon."

"That's a house of ill repute," Amber said, in case I didn't know.

"I've heard of it. Go on. They got you there?"

"As I was leaving. Going out the back way so nobody would see me."

That didn't sound like the behavior of the hell-raiser he was supposed to be. "Why the sneak? I thought that wasn't your style."

"So Domina wouldn't hear about it. I was supposed to be out working."

That puzzled me. "The word is that she has everyone on a tight leash while your mother is in the Cantard. Yet you two seem to come and go when you want."

"Not when we want," Amber said. "When we can. Courter and Domina can't be everywhere watching all the time."

"I thought you said you wouldn't interrupt, Mr. Garrett."

"So I did. Go on. When last seen you were making a getaway out the back door of Lettie Faren's place."

"Yes. I stopped to say good night to someone, right in the doorway, with my back to the outside. Somebody put a leather sack over my head. It must have had a drawstring sort of thing on it because before I could yell I was being strangled. I was scared to death. I knew I was being murdered and there wasn't any way I could stop it. And then the lights went out." He shivered.

I set my mug down. "Who were you saying good-bye to?" I tried to keep it casual but he wasn't a complete dummy. He didn't answer. I stared him straight in the eye. He looked away.

"He doesn't want to believe it," Amber said.

"What's that?"

"That his favorite little tidbit was in on it. She had to be, didn't she? I mean, she would have seen whoever it was over his shoulder. Wouldn't she? And she would have had time to warn him if she wasn't part of it?"

"That's certainly worth a few questions. Does the lady have a name?"

Amber looked at Karl. He tried divining the future from the lees of his beer. Maybe he didn't like what he saw. He grabbed the pitcher off the tray and poured himself a refill, mumbling something as he did so.

I collected the pitcher and pursued his fine example. "What was that?"

"He said her name is Donni Pell."

Put a point down for the kid. If she had wanted, she could have stuck it to him anytime, but she held back until he was ready to surrender the name himself.

Karl started working himself up a case of the miseries. He said, "I can't believe Donni was in on what . . . I've known her for four years. She just wouldn't . . ."

I reserved my opinion of what people in Donni's line would and would not do for money. "All right. Let's move on. You were strangled unconscious. When and where did you wake up?"

"I'm not sure. It was nighttime and in the country. I think. From what sounds I could hear. I was bound hand and foot and still had the bag over my head. I think I was inside a closed coach of some kind but I can't be sure. That would make sense, though, wouldn't it?"

"For them it would. What else?"

"I had a bad headache."

"That follows. Go on."

"They got me where they were taking me, which turned out to be an abandoned farmhouse of some sort."

I urged him to get very detailed. It was in moments of transfer when kidnappers were most at risk of betraying themselves.

"They lifted me out of the coach. Somebody cut the ropes around my ankles. One got me by each arm and they walked me inside. There were at least four of them. Maybe five or six. After they got me inside, somebody cut the rope on my wrists. A door closed behind me. After a long time standing there I finally got up the nerve to take the bag off my head."

He paused to unparch his throat. He could pour it down once he got started. Being a naturally courteous fellow, I matched him swallow for swallow, though I hadn't been working my throat nearly so hard. "A farmhouse, you say? How did you discover that?"

"I'll get to it. Anyway, I took the bag off. I was in a room about twelve feet by twelve feet that hadn't been cleaned in years. There were some blankets to sleep on—all old and dirty and smelly—a chamber pot that never did get emptied, a rickety homemade chair, and a small table with one leg broken."

He had his eyes closed. He was visualizing. "On the table was one of those earthenware pitcher-and-bowl sets with a rusty metal dipper to take a drink with. The pitcher was cracked so it leaked a little into the bowl. I drank about a quart of water right away. Then I went and looked out the window and tried to get myself together. I was scared to death. I didn't have any idea what was going on. Until I got back here and found out Domina had ransomed me, I had my mind made up that some of Mother's political enemies had grabbed me so they could twist her arm."

"Tell me about that window. That sounds like a big lapse on their part."

"Not really. It was closed with a shutter and the shutter was nailed from outside. But the place was old and there was a crack in the shutter big enough to see through. As it turned out, my seeing what was outside didn't matter."

"How so?"

"The way they let me go. They just walked off and left me there. I figured it out when they stopped feeding me."

"Did you ever see any of them?"

"No."

"How did they get food to you, then?"

"They made me stand facing the wall when they brought the food in and took the old platter out."

"Then they talked to you?"

"One did. But only from outside the door and then all he ever said was that it was time to get against the wall. But sometimes I could hear them talking. Not very often. They didn't have much to say to each other."

"Not even about how they were going to spend their shares of the money?"

"I never heard any mention of money at all. That was one of the reasons I decided the whole thing was political. That and the fact that, after the strangling, they treated me pretty gently. That isn't what I would have expected of kidnappers for profit."

"It isn't customary."

He had his eyes closed and his mind on the past. I don't think he heard me. "The only thing I ever heard that might have had anything to do with the situation was the last afternoon. Before they vanished. Someone came running into the place and yelled, 'Hey, Skredli, it's coming through tonight.' I never heard what, though."

"Skredli? You're sure?"

"Yes."

"You think it was a name?"

"It sounded like one. You think it might have been?"

I knew damned well it was. Skred is the ogre equivalent of Smith, only it is twice as common. Skredli compares with Smitty. Half the ogres in the world are called Skredli, it seems like. So much for the lucky break.

We let it sit that way for a minute while we split the remaining contents of the pitcher. It was a good brew. I wish its like befell me more often. But I usually can't afford the price of a sniff on my own hooks.

"So. We're almost to the end. What happened after Skredli got yelled at?"

"Basically nothing. As far as I know, for those guys that was the end of it."

I waited for him to expand upon that.

"They didn't bring me any supper. By midnight I was hungry enough to bang on the door and complain. That didn't do any good. I tried to sleep. I did a little, then when breakfast didn't come, I got up and pitched a real fit. I pounded the door so hard I broke it open. Then I got so scared they would beat me that I hid in my blankets. But nothing happened. Eventually I worked up enough nerve to go look out the door, then to slip out and explore."

"They were gone?"

"Long gone. The ashes in the kitchen weren't even warm. I ate some scraps they left behind. After those hit bottom I felt braver and decided to do some exploring."

Karl paused to look into his mug and curse because he could see the bottom and there were no reserves to rush into the fray.

I waited.

Karl told me, "That's why I know all about the farmhouse. A pretty substantial place before it was abandoned." He gave me an exhaustive description, not a peasant hovel but not a manor house, either. "After I'd looked around awhile I finally got up enough nerve to follow the coach tracks through the woods. After a mile or so I came to a road. A passing tinker told me it was the Vorkuta–Lichfield Road, a little over three miles west of the battlefield."

Amazing. Karl had been sequestered within two miles of the place where Amiranda had bought hers and Saucerhead almost took a slice too many. I was so astonished I may have blinked. "So you just walked on home?"

"Yes. I think I'll go fill this pitcher again. This is taking longer than I thought."

"No need. I'm almost done. Just a couple questions more."

"What do you think? Was it an unusual kidnapping?"

"In some ways. But it went off smooth and you can't criticize success."

"I don't know much about this kind of thing. I was so damned scared while it was happening I didn't study it or think about it. How was it remarkable?"

He had a hook out and wanted to see if he could pull in the name of his friend Donni Pell. Amber had a similar notion. She was alert for the first time in half an hour. I disappointed them both because I had ideas of my own and wanted to save Donni for myself.

"Two peculiarities pounce at you like ogres from ambush. The one that bothers me the least is that they locked you in a room you could break out of without bothering to keep you tied or blindfolded. But that could be explained several ways. No, the big croggle is the way Willa Dount handled her end. She turned over a lot of gold to proven crooks without doing anything to make sure the merchandise she was buying was in good condition. The custom is for the purchaser to insist on delivery at the point of sale. Otherwise there's nothing to keep the kidnappers honest."

Karl mumbled something that sounded like, "I wondered about that, too."

He was in a declining mood and getting restless. I supposed it was time to attack. I went after him hard about timing and movements, and when I noticed Amber looking at me odd and Karl frowning angrily as he stumbled over his answers, I decided I'd gotten too intense. "What the hell is this? I'm doing a professional exercise and I get going like it's the real thing. Thanks, Karl. You've been a lot more patient than I would have been if the roles had been reversed."

"You're done?" He considered the bottom of his mug.

"Yes. Thanks. Drink one for me and think a kind thought while you're at it."

"Sure." He got up and out, trailing one curious glance at his sister.

•••15

"**Y**ou got to pressing there at the end, Garrett. Were you onto something?"

"Apparently not. Unless I missed something that was right under my nose, your brother was a waste of time."

"Then why did you spend all that time on him?"

"Because I didn't know what he could tell me. Because you never know what little thing will turn out to be the critical clue. I went hard on the timing because I want to have it pat when we see what Amiranda has to say so we can look at it from the Domina's side."

"I couldn't find Amiranda."

"What?"

"I couldn't find her. She didn't answer her door. When I asked around, nobody had seen her. I finally sneaked into her rooms. She wasn't there. And most of her stuff was gone."

I did me what I hoped was a convincing show of perplexity. "Did she have a maid? Did you talk to her? What did she say?"

"I talked to her. She didn't know anything except that Amiranda is gone. Or so she said."

"Damn! That knocks hell out of everything." I got up and stretched.

"What are we going to do?"

"Start somewhere else. You just keep picking till you pull a thread loose. You're the inside man here. You find out what you can about Willa Dount's end of things. The how, the where, and the when of the payoff in particular, but anything that sounds unusual or interesting. Keep trying to get a line on Amiranda. And while you're doing all that, try not to attract too much attention. We don't want anybody knowing what we're doing. There's two hundred thousand marks gold at stake and the price is going up. My resident genius says we're about to hear from Glory Mooncalled again."

Her eyes glittered. Each time Glory Mooncalled acted, the Venageti position in the Cantard weakened, the Karentine flourished, the price of silver plunged and that of gold soared. "We're getting richer by the minute!"

"Only in our imaginations. We have to find the gold."

She started toward me with that look in her eye, ready to celebrate. "What will you be doing?"

"The outside stuff. Picking at threads. Talking to this Donni."

"I'll bet. I'm much prettier than she is, Garrett. And maybe just as talented."

"Then I'm going to have my supper, consult the genius, and get on the road so I can be at that farm tomorrow morning. I'll have a whole day to poke around and pick up the trail."

She had gotten in close enough to force a clinch. My resistance was going the way of the dodo. Suddenly, she stiffened and backed away.

"What is it?"

"I just had an awful thought. My mother is going to be home any day. If we don't have the gold found and me out of here before she does . . ." She backed away. "We have to get to work."

Poor little rich kid. Somehow, I couldn't work up a lot of sympathy. If she wasn't miserable enough to walk with nothing but the clothes on her back, she wasn't miserable enough.

The sparkle came back to her eyes. "But once we do, look out, Garrett."

There is a limit to how much you can kid people and still live with yourself, but also a limit to how much you can kid yourself. "I admire your confidence. *If* we find it."

"*When*, Garrett."

"All right. When we find it, look out, Amber."

We exchanged idiot grins.

"Do I go out the same way I got in?"

"That would be best. Don't let the servants see you. And watch out for the dragoons."

I gave her a kiss meant to be a businesslike sealing of our compact. She turned it into a promise of things to come. I finally peeled her off and fled.

•••

I was distracted. The little witches do that to you. I zipped around a corner and almost plowed into Karl Senior and Domina Dount.

Fortunately, they were distracted, too. Very distracted. If they noted a third presence at all, they probably assumed it was a wayward servant. I backed up to consider alternate routes.

Amber had it wrong. Willa Dount didn't freeze bathwater.

Now I knew what hold she had on Daddy. If it turned out to matter.

Reason didn't do me a bit of good trying to get out of there another way. In two minutes I knew I would get lost if I kept on. I found a place where I could look into the real people's world between curtains. I recognized the hallway.

Nothing for it but to march and look like I was about honest business.

It worked fine until I started hiking across the front court headed for the main gate.

Pudgy Courter came in from the street. He started to say something to the gateman, then spotted me. His eyes got big, his face got red, and he started to puff up like an old bullfrog about to sing. "What the hell are you doing in here?"

"Hell, I might ask the same of you. Little out of your class here, aren't you? Guy like you ought to be slicing vegetables—"

I was close enough. He took a swing. I'm not sure why. I don't think I trampled him hard enough to set him off. I caught his wrist and kept on walking, pulling him along in a stumble. "Tsk-tsk. We should be more friendly to our betters."

I let him go as I stepped outside. He was past the flash point now. He retreated, cursing under his breath, while I glanced around for the four clowns who had been stalking me before Amber let me inside. They were gone.

It was a piece of bad luck, getting spotted like that. I could only hope it would balance out and not get things all stirred up inside. Amber could deal with Willa Dount, especially motivated by visions of gold, but I had my doubts about Junior. He had no strong reason to hide having talked to me.

I figured I'd best get down to Lettie Faren's place right away.

didn't get there as quickly as I'd planned, though the delay lasted only a few seconds. Going down the Hill, I realized that I'd picked up a tail. It didn't take long to discover it was my friend Bruno from the tavern.

Why was he on me?

Five minutes later I knew he was alone. It was personal. I had hurt his feelings and now he felt a need to hurt mine.

I stepped into an areaway when I came to one I knew would suit my purpose. I found a shadow and got into it. He came charging in a few seconds later, apparently wanting to take advantage of my stupidity. But when he got there, he saw nothing. He started cursing.

"But you mustn't blame the gods. All is not lost, Bruno. I'm right here." I stepped out of the shadows.

He was too mad for preliminaries. He tucked in his chin and came after me.

I was in no mood for ego games myself. His first swing I tapped his wrist with my weighted stick. Then I whacked an elbow, putting one arm out of commission. Then I let him set himself up and dropped a couple of good thumps on his noggin. After he was down I put him in the shadows so the street kids wouldn't find and strip him before he woke up. I doubted he would appreciate the courtesy. I hoped he wasn't so stubbornly stupid one of us would have to get killed to end whatever was going on.

• • •

Lettie's place was into the lull that comes between the businesslike gentlemen of the afternoon and the revelers of night. I got past the thug at the door without trouble. He didn't know me.

I found Lettie where you always find her, in the back room counting the take. She was a grotesquely obese female of mixed but uncertain antecedents who made the Dead Man look slim, trim, and able to run like a deer.

"Garrett. You son of a bitch. How the hell did you get in here?"

"The sorcery of feet. I put on my magic boots and walked. You're looking as lovely as ever, Lettie."

"And you're just as full of camel guano. What the hell do you want?"

I tried to look hurt by her remarks.

"All right," she snarled. "Out you go."

I clinked coins and showed the face of a dead king on a gold double mark. "I thought the motto of the house was no paying customer is ever turned away."

Gold was talking big talk in TunFaire these days. She eyed the coin. "What do you want?"

"Not what. Who. Her name is Donni Pell."

Lettie's eyes narrowed, hardened. "Shit. You would. You can't have her."

"I know you don't like me, and we'll never run off to become shopkeepers and raise babies together, but when did you ever let personal feelings get in the way of making money?"

"When I was thirteen years old and in the middle of my first big love affair. That's got nothing to do with it, Garrett. I can't sell you merchandise that I don't have in stock."

"She's not here?"

"You figured it out. With a brain like yours, why do you keep that heap of blubber in your front room?"

"Sentiment. And it keeps him off the streets. Where did Donni go?"

"You want her bad, don't you?"

"I want to see her. Don't try to hold me up, Lettie. You've got employees who'll tell me for silver."

"Goddamned human nature. You would, wouldn't you? Give me one good reason why I shouldn't have Leo come in here and twist your face around so you're looking out the back of your head."

"This little crumb that fell from the sun." I flashed the double mark.

"All right. You win, Garrett. What do you want?"

"She's gone, so the why, the when, the how, and the where. Then tell me about Donni Pell the person."

"The why is she got hold of a bunch of money. And that's the how, too. She came in here three, four nights ago and bought out her contract. Not that she was in very deep. She said a rich uncle up north died and left her a fortune. Bull. If you ask me, she got her hooks into some half-wit off the Hill. She had the looks and manners and style for it. She claimed she was off to take over managing the uncle's manor. More bull. She couldn't survive without platoons of men around."

I raised the old eyebrow. Lettie liked me when I did my trick. I used it as often as I could.

"That woman was a freak, Garrett. Ninety-nine out of a hundred of them hate men. She *loved* what she was doing. If she hadn't been selling it, she would have been giving as much away for free."

"A working girl who enjoyed her work? Unusual. She must have brought the clients in."

"In herds. I wish I had a hundred like her. Even if she was a pervert."

I gave her a glim at the other eyebrow.

"You know in this business you got to be tolerant and understanding, Garrett. But it stretches tolerance and surpasses understanding when a perfectly beautiful young human woman prefers ogres for playmates. Even ogre women don't want anything to do with those creeps. I'd let a vampire or wolfman in this place before I'd open my door to an ogre."

She was going good so I let her rant, using up her hostility on a target other than me, just once throwing in, "Well, there *are* the sexual myths," just to make sure she got all the venom spent.

"Bullshit. That's all bullshit, Garrett. You're talking to an expert, Garrett." And on she raved.

She wound down. I placed the double mark squarely in front of her. "That about the ogres was worth this. Come up with something more and you might get to see some of the old king's ancestors."

Her eyes narrowed. "It's murder, isn't it, Garrett? And a heavyweight client. I know that look. The paladin look. You're after somebody's head. You dumb boy, you keep playing with the lifetakers."

"I'm after a hooker named Donni Pell who might be able to tell me something I need to know."

"You got the works already, Garrett. All I can give you for your money now is a kiss for luck."

"Background her. Her people. You know them all. How long was she here? Where did she come from?"

"She don't have any people. They died in the plague four years ago. That's why I didn't believe the story about the uncle. She was here for about three years. Sometimes more trouble than she was worth on account of stunts she pulled on her johns. She didn't tell a lot about herself but lies, like all the rest, but I usually get their real stories out of them on the bad nights."

"I know you do."

"Her people were country folk with a good-sized freehold up around Lichfield somewhere."

I muttered, "I'll bet I could go right to it without missing a turn."

"What?"

"Nothing. That chip looks lonely sitting there by itself. What more can you tell me about Donni?"

"You got the load, Garrett." She reached for the coin.

"What about Raver Styx's menfolk? The two Karls."

Her eyes glazed. "Somebody killed one of them?"

"Not yet." I saw she needed to see some color to keep her momentum. I showed her another double.

"The kid was one of Donni's regulars. She said she felt sorry for him. I think she halfway liked him. He treated her like a lady and he wasn't bashful about being seen with her. The father visited her sometimes, too, but with him it was strictly business. I don't think I want to talk about that family anymore, Garrett. That woman is poison."

"She's out of town, Lettie."

"She'll be back. You got what you came for. Get out. Get out before I start remembering and yell for Leo."

I put the second double mark down beside the first. "We wouldn't want to interrupt Leo's nap, would we?"

"Out, Garrett. And don't show your ugly phiz around here anymore. You'll get it broke."

She loved me, that fat old Lettie.

17

I went by Playmate's stable and smithy yard and told him to send a buggy to the house in a couple of hours, and to load it down with one of every kind of tool he had. He gave me a look but knew better than to ask. I might tell him something he wouldn't want to know.

Old Dean thought he was going to bribe me. He still wasn't talking but he laid on the best spread I'd seen in months. I did right by it. When I went in to see the Dead Man, I was waddling.

I didn't expect another decent meal for days.

Garrett! Dismiss that creature at once! Get him out of my house.

"Good to see you back to your normal cheerful self. What creature? Why?"

That Dean. The fiend brought not one, not two, but three women in here. Get rid of him, Garrett. Throw him out.

So. A fantasy meal explained. Dean wanted me to see what I didn't have to be missing. Him and me, we were going to have to have a little talk, man to man, and get things straight. Real soon now.

I settled in my visiting chair, sipped some beer, then cut loose. The Dead Man sulked and pretended to ignore me, but he took in every word. He had to have something to distract himself while he waited for Glory Mooncalled to prove out his hypothesis. I talked for two hours nonstop, with good old Dean keeping my mug topped. He enjoyed a little vicarious adventure. And his coming and going showed just how little depth there was to the Dead Man's animosity.

I finished my report, having spared no detail.

There is something missing, Garrett.

"I know that. Either that or I know too much and I'm getting distracted."

You are not getting distracted.

"I keep thinking I've got the kidnap side figured out. Three different times I've decided that Junior kidnapped himself. Then I find myself up to my ass in ogres again, with them perfect for the villains. And if the kid did kidnap himself, why did he come home? He and his sister want out of there so bad they can taste it. The way it went down, with no direct exchange, all he had to do was take the gold and hike and leave his mommy wearing weeds."

The ransom money was paid?

"Willa Dount scrounged two hundred thousand and delivered it to somebody. Junior came home next day. Amber is digging on that for me. The deep-down root thing that bugs me can be tied up in one bow. Why did Amiranda have to die? Real kidnapping or fake, with her in on it or not, why did she have to be killed?"

I am certain you will unmask the reason. You have allowed yourself to become emotionally entangled. Again.

I saw him sizing up one of his favorite hobbyhorses, getting ready to mount up and ride. Dean had gone to answer the door a minute before. I got up. "My transportation is here. You mull it over while you're killing time. Maybe you'll spot a connection I've missed."

I didn't doubt that he had seen one or two already but didn't feel obligated to point them out. Neither of us had a real money interest here, and he had no emotional investment, so whether he saw something or not he would just let me exercise my own genius.

I visited the armory. Unlike Saucerhead I don't figure my hands are my best defense. I tossed a bundle into the buggy, under the seat, and was about to flick the traces when Dean came stumbling out of the house with a hamper.

"Mr. Garrett. Wait."

"What's this?"

"Provender. Victuals. Rations."

"Leftovers?"

"That, too. A man has to eat something. What were you going to do out there?"

Hell. I'm a city boy. I don't think about food. "I was going to borrow a page from Morley Dotes and live off roots and bark, but rather than injure your feelings I'll just park that hamper up here beside me and suffer."

He smiled smugly as I pulled away. For however long I subjected myself to this rustication, every bite would remind me that I needed a feeder and a keeper, and the fodder would, for certain, be the best of the best cooked up by his nieces.

The man was obsessed. That is all I can say. He had worked for me long enough to know I wasn't the kind of catch you'd want your female relations stuck with. But he persisted.

Karenta is a kingdom at war. You'd expect some sort of watch to be kept on the entrepôts to one of its most important cities, in case some enterprising Venageti commander decided to try something imaginative. But the war has been going on since my generation were kids, seldom spilling out of the Cantard and the adjoining seas. Any guards who were awake when I left were too busy playing cards to step out and check my bona fides. But our lords from the Hill want the ordinary folk to seethe with fervor against the enemy.

It's a lot easier to seethe against Raver Styx and her ilk. They profit no matter how the fighting goes.

I used the route Saucerhead and Amiranda had followed. The moon was now full. The team didn't mind night travel, even with me at the traces. And the nation of horses has been out to get me ever since I can remember.

It was a smooth, quiet ride with very little to see. The only traffic I encountered was the night coach from Derry, half an hour ahead of schedule and just lumping along with its two or three somnolent passengers and load of mail. Guard and driver tossed me friendly greetings, which showed how worried they were about the night.

I suppose, theoretically, that I should have had one hand on a silver blade at all times. There *was* a full moon. But there hadn't been a confirmed wolfman incident this close to the city since before I went into the Marines.

Once I did unravel a murder that had been dressed up to look like a wolfman's work. It's a hell of a way to make sure your old man doesn't get the chance to write you out of the will.

I reached the dire crossroad about the same time Saucerhead had. I gave it a look around as it stood, considering the fact that there was more moon than there had been that night. I didn't see or get a feel for anything, so I loosened the horses' harnesses, made sure they couldn't run off, climbed onto the buggy's seat, and napped.

I did a good job of snoozing, too. I thought first light would waken me, but the honor went to a ten-year-old who shook my shoulder and asked, "Are you all right, mister?"

I counted my hands and feet and purse and discovered that I hadn't been murdered, mutilated, or robbed. "I am indeed, son. Except maybe for a case of premature senility."

He looked at me funny and asked a few kidlike questions. I tried giving reasonable answers and asked him a few in turn. He was on his way somewhere to help somebody with farm chores, but he let me buy him breakfast. Which goes to show how tame it really is around TunFaire these days, for all we city people put down the country. No city boy would have risked hanging around with a stranger. The real monsters of today live in the city's shadows and cellars and drawing rooms.

He didn't tell me one thing even remotely useful.

Acting on the premise that it is never wise to put temptation into the path of an honest man, I led my team into the woods opposite the area I intended to explore. I made sure the beasts wouldn't have the pleasure of deserting me, returned to the diamond, and checked to make sure they and the rig were invisible, then went across and started looking through the bushes.

It wasn't hard to find where the dead and wounded had been thrown into hurried concealment. The brush was torn and trampled. The corpses had been cleared away but their drippings had been ignored, at least by the cleanup crew. The flies and ants had come and gone. The bloodstains were now the province of a gray-black, whiskery mold that described perfectly every spot and spill. Which didn't tell me anything except that a lot of people had done a lot of bleeding.

My woodcraft was no longer what it had been in my Marine days, but it took no forest genius to follow either of the trails leading deeper into the woods. The first I tried split after about a third of a mile, heavy traffic having turned eastward suddenly. It looked like four or five ogres had been on Saucerhead's trail when they were recalled by their buddies. The other trail ran down into the woods east of where I stood.

I didn't need to follow Saucerhead to know where he'd gone. I turned east.

Five hundred yards along I paused, planted the back of my lap on a fallen tree trunk, and told my brain to get to work. I knew what I would find if I went on a little farther. I could hear the flies buzzing and the wild dogs bickering with the vultures. Much closer and I would smell it, too. Did I *have* to look?

Basically, there was no getting out of it. There was maybe one chance in a hundred that I was wrong and the centerpiece of that grisly feast was a woods bison. If I was right, chances were ten to one against me finding anything that would split things wide open. But you can't skimp and take shortcuts. The odds are always against you until you do stumble across that one in ten.

Still, dead people who have been lying around in the woods for days aren't particularly appealing. So I spent a few minutes considering a spiderweb with dew gems still on it before I put my dogs on the ground and started hoofing it toward a case of upturned stomach.

Five years in the Marines had brought me eyeball to eyeball with old death more times than I cared to remember, and my life since has provided its grisly encounters, but there are some things I can't get used to. Consciousness of my own mortality won't let me.

The conclave of death was being held at the downhill end of an open, grassy area about twenty yards wide and fifty long. Patches of lichened granite peeked out of the soil. I collected a dozen loose chunks of throwing size and cut loose at the wild dogs. They snarled and growled but fled. They have grown very cautious around humans because bounty hunters are after them constantly. Especially farm kids who want to pick up a little change for the fair or whatever.

The buzzards tried to bluff me. I didn't bluff. They got themselves airborne and began turning in patient circles, looking down and thinking, *Someday, you, too, man.* In the pantheon of one of the minor cults of TunFaire, the god of time is a vulture.

Maybe that's why I hate the damned things. Or maybe that's because they've become identified with my military service, when I saw so many circling the fields of futility where young Karentines died for their country.

So there I stood, a great bull ape, master of the land of the dead. Instead of pounding my chest and maybe forcing myself to inhale some tainted air, I moved as upwind as I could and started looking at what I'd come to see.

There wasn't a woods bison in that mess.

I muttered, "I ought to remember Saucerhead's tendency to exaggerate."

I counted up enough parts to make at least seven bodies. Four or five he said he'd taken. Even torn apart they remained ogre ugly. They'd been buried shallow beneath loose dirt, leaves, and stones. The lazy way, I might call it, but I look at comrades differently than ogres do. They don't form bonds the way humans do. For them a dead associate is a burden, not an obligation.

No doubt they were in a hurry to quit the area, too.

You do what you have to do. I got in and used a stick to poke around, looking for personals, but it took only a minute to figure out that the living hadn't been in too big a hurry not to loot the dead. Even their boots had been taken.

That wasn't the behavior of a band expecting to be in the big money soon. But with ogres you never know. Maybe their mothers had taught them the old saw, "Waste not, want not."

I circled the burial site three times but could find no sign of comings or goings other than by the route I'd followed, and that the second group had taken down from the road.

In places the soil was very moist from groundwater seepage. Such places sometimes hold tracks. I started looking those over, trying to cut the trail of a guy on crutches or one who wore his feet backward; something that would stick out if I happened to be hanging around with a bunch of ogres and one of the bad guys showed up. I didn't expect to find anything, but luck doesn't play for the other side all the time. Got to keep looking for that ten to one.

I found the nothing I expected, though not exactly because there was nothing to be found. It was one of those cases of suddenly deciding you ought to be investigating something somewhere else.

I heard a stir in the woods behind me. Not much of one. Thinking some of the dogs had gotten brave, I turned with the stick I still carried.

"Holy shit!"

A woolly mammoth stood at the edge of the woods, and from where I was it looked about ninety-three hands high at the shoulder. How the hell it had come up so quietly is beyond me. I didn't ask. When it cocked its head and made a curious grunting noise, I put the heels and toes to work according to the gods' design. The beast threw a trumpet roar after me. Laughing.

I paused behind a two-foot-thick oak and gave it a stare. A mammoth. Here. No mammoth had come this close to TunFaire in the past dozen generations. The nearest herds were four hundred miles north of us, up along the borders of thunder-lizard country.

The mammoth ambled out of the woods, laughed at me again, cropped some grass a couple of bales at a time while keeping one eye on me. Finally convinced that I was no fearless mammoth poacher, it eyeballed the vultures, checked the dead ogres, snorted in disgust, and marched off through the woods as quietly as it had come.

And last night I'd been unconcerned because no wolfman had been seen since I was a kid.

Like I said, luck is not always with the bad guys.

It was time to stop tempting it with the one out of ten and hike on back to my rig before the horses got wind of that monster and decided they would feel more comfortable back in the city. Too bad Garrett had to ride shank's mare.

I sat on the buggy seat, beside the crossroads obelisk, and watched a parade of farm families and donkey carts head up the Derry Road. I didn't see them. I was trying to pick between Karl Junior's farm prison and Saucerhead's witch.

The decision had actually been made. I was putting the thumbscrews on myself trying to figure if I was going to the farm first just to delay the pain skulking around the other place. No matter that I had to head the same direction to reach both and the farm was nearer.

You don't alter the past, turn the tide, or change yourself by brooding about your hidden motives. You will surprise yourself every time, anyway. Nobody ever figures out why.

"Hell with it! Get up."

One of the team looked over her shoulder. She had that glint in her eye. The tribe of horses was about to amuse itself at Garrett's expense.

Why do they do this to me? Horses and women. I'll never understand either species.

"Don't even think about it, horse. I have friends in the glue business. Get up."

They got. Unlike women, you can show horses who is boss.

The bout with introspection rekindled my desire to lay hands on the people responsible for the human equivalent of sending Amiranda to the glue works.

The exit to the farm was up on a ridgeline where the ground was too dry to hold tracks, and hidden by undergrowth. I passed it twice. The third time I got down and led the team, giving the bushes a closer look, and that did the trick. Two young mulberry trees, which grow as fast as weeds, leaned together over the track. Once past them the way was easy to follow, though it hadn't been cleared since Donni's departure.

I had to go through a half mile of woods, not a mile. It was dense in there, dark, quiet, and humid. The deerflies and horseflies were out at play, and every few feet I got a faceful of spider silk. I sweated and slapped and muttered and picked ticks off my pants. Why doesn't everybody live in the city?

I ran into a blackberry patch where the berries were fat and sweet, and decided to lunch on the spot. Afterward I felt more disposed toward the country, until the chiggers off the blackberry canes started gnawing.

The track through the woods showed evidence of recent use, including that of the passage of at least one heavy vehicle.

I had a feeling that, no matter what suspicions haunted me, I wouldn't unearth one bit of physical evidence to impugn Junior's version of what had happened.

I kicked up a doe and fawn near the edge of the wood. I watched them bound across what once had constituted considerably more than a one-family subsistence farm, though now the acreage was wild and heavily spotted with wild roses and young cedars. The grass was waist high and some of the weeds were taller. A trampled path led downslope to what had been a substantial house. There were no domestic animals in sight, no dogs barking, no smoke from either chimney, nor any other sign that the place was occupied.

Still, I remained rooted, giving the wildlife time to grow accustomed to my presence and return to business.

The Boga Hills loomed indigo in the distance. The most famous Karentine vineyards are up there. This country was close enough to have some of the magic rub off, but hadn't been turned into vineyards. I wondered if someone hadn't gotten that idea and had abandoned the place when they found out why. Then I recalled Donni Pell.

A girl who came from some kind of money who went to work for Lettie, on contract, supposedly because she liked the job. A girl who now supposedly owned a place that, a few years ago, had been in satisfactory shape for a quick sale to TunFaire's land-hungry lords. I doubted it was part of the problem at hand, but it might be interesting to unravel the whys.

Ten minutes of pretending I was scouting for the company left me impatient to get on with it. I tied the horses, got down low, and started my downhill sneak.

The place was as empty as a dead shoe. I went for the buggy, turned the team loose to browse while I prowled.

Junior's report was accurate down to the minutiae. The only things he hadn't mentioned were that the well was still good and his captors had equipped it with a new rope and bucket. The horses awarded me a temporary cease-fire after I drew them a few buckets.

There was no doubt that a band of ogres—or a mob equally unfastidious— had spent several days hanging around. Days during which they must have eaten nothing but chicken to judge by the feathers, heads, and hooves scattered around. I wondered how they had managed to pilfer so many without arousing the ire of the entire countryside.

I did a modestly thorough once-over, with special attention to Karl's lockup. That room had the rickety furniture, cracked pitcher, filthy bedding, overburdened chamber pot reported. The chamber pot was significant. I concluded that its very existence meant I must surrender my suspicions of Junior or radically alter my estimate of his intelligence and acting ability. If he had put together a fake, he had done so with a marvelous eye for detail, meaning he had anticipated a thorough investigation despite his getting home healthy and happy, which meant . . .

I didn't know what the hell it meant, except maybe that I had my hat on backward.

Why the hell did Amiranda have to die?

The answer to that would probably bust the whole thing open.

Conscious that I had a passing duty to Amber as a client, I went over the place again with all due professional care to overlook nothing, be that the tracks of a four-hundred-pound ogre with a peg leg or two hundred thousand marks gold hidden by throwing it down the well. Yes. I stripped down and shimmied down and floundered around in the icy water until I was sure there would be no gold strike. My curses should have brought the water to a simmer, but failed. I guess I just don't have the knack.

Four hours and the risk of pneumonia turned up just one thing worth taking along, a silver tenth mark that had strayed in among the dust bunnies against the wall where Junior's blankets were heaped and hadn't been able to find its way home. It looked new but it was a temple coin and didn't use the royal dating. I'd have to visit the temple where it had been struck to find out when it was minted.

But its very presence gave me an idea. It also gave me a bit of indigestion for not having thought to ask a few more questions while I'd had Junior on the griddle. Now I would have to get the answers the hard way—on the trip home. The hard way, but the answers I got were likely to be square.

The sun was headed west. It wasn't going to rebound off the hills out there. I had a call to make, and if I wanted to get it handled before the wolf-men came out to stalk the wily mammoth, I had to get moving.

The horses let the armistice stand. They didn't even play tag with me when I went to harness them up.

Saucerhead's directions to his witch friend's place hadn't included the information that there was nothing resembling a road near her home. In fact, any resemblance to a trail was coincidental. That was wicked-witch-of-the-woods territory and anybody who managed to stumble into her through that mess deserved whatever he got.

I had to do most of it on the ground, leading the team. The armistice survived only because they realized they would need me to scout the way back. When we hit the road again all deals would be off.

The last few hundred yards weren't bad. The ground leveled out. The undergrowth ceased to exist, as though somebody manicured the woods every day. The trees were big and old and the canopy above turned away most of the remaining light. Lamplight pouring through an open doorway gave me my bearings.

A rosy-cheeked, apple-dumpling-plump little old lady was waiting for me. She stood about four feet eight and was dressed like a peasant granny on a christening day, right down to the embroidered apron. She looked me over frankly. I couldn't tell what she thought of what she saw. "Are you Garrett?"

Startled, I confessed.

"Took you long enough to get here. I suppose you might as well come on inside. There's still a bit of water for tea and a scone or two if Shaggoth hasn't got into them. Shaggoth! You good-for-nothing lout! Get out here and take care of the man's horses."

I started to ask how she knew I was coming, but only managed to get the old flycatcher open before Shaggoth came out. And came out. And came out. That doorway was a good seven feet high and he had to crouch to get through. He looked at me the way I'd look at a decomposing rat, snorted, and started unhitching the horses.

"Come inside," the witch told me.

I sidled in behind her, keeping one eye on friend Shaggoth. "Troll?" I squeaked.

"Yes."

"He's got jaws like a saber-tithed tooger. Soober-toothed teegar. The god-damned growly things with the fangs."

She chuckled. "Shaggoth is of the pureblood. He's been with me a long time." She had me in the kitchen then and was dropping a tea egg into a giant mug that I wished was filled with beer. "The rest of his folk migrated because you pesky humans were overrunning everything, but he stayed on. Loyalty before common sense."

I forbore observing that she was human herself.

"They're not a very bright race. Come. By the by, you'll have noted that he isn't sensitive to sunlight."

No. That hadn't registered. Teeth had registered. "How come you know my name?" Great straight line to a witch. "How did you know I was co—geck!"

Amiranda was seated beside a small fire, hands folded in her lap, staring at something beyond my right shoulder. No. Not Amiranda. The essence of Amiranda had fled that flesh. That wasn't a person, it was a thing.

The pain would be less if I thought that way.

"Excuse me?" I glanced at the witch.

"I said Waldo told me you would come. I expected you sooner."

"Who's Waldo? Another pet like Shaggoth? He can see the future?"

"Waldo Tharpe. He told me you were friends."

"Waldo?" There must have been a little hysteria edging my giggle. She gave me a frown. "I didn't know he had a name. I've never heard him called anything but Saucerhead."

"He's not enthusiastic about being Waldo," she admitted. "Sit and let's talk."

I sat, musing. "So Saucerhead jobbed us. The big dope isn't as dumb as he lets on." I kept getting drawn back to the corpse. It did look very lifelike, very undamaged. Any moment now the chest would heave, the sparkle would come back to the eyes, and she would laugh at me for being taken in.

The witch settled into a chair facing mine. "Waldo said you'd have questions." Her gaze followed mine. "I worked on her a little, making her look a little better, putting spells on to hold the corruption off till she can be given a decent funeral."

"Thank you."

"Questions, Garrett? I went to a good deal of trouble on Waldo's behalf. What will you need to know?"

"Anything. Everything. I want to know why she was killed and who ordered it done."

"I'm not omniscient, Garrett. I can't answer that sort of question. Though I can surmise—which may not stand scrutiny in the light of what you already know—why. She was about three months pregnant."

"*What?* That's impossible."

"The child would have been male had it seen the light of day."

"But she spent the last six months practically imprisoned in the house where she lived."

"There were no men in that house? Hers was a miraculous conception?"

I opened my mouth to protest but a question popped out instead. "Who was the father?"

"I'm no necromancer, Garrett. The name, if she knew it at all, expired with her."

"She knew. She wasn't the type who wouldn't." I'd begun to get angry all over again.

"You knew her? Waldo didn't. Nothing but her name and the fact that you sent her to him."

"I knew her. Not well, but I did."

"Tell me about her."

I talked. It eased the pain a little, bringing her to life in words. I finished. "Did you get anything out of that?"

"Only that you're working in a tight place. A stormwarden's family, yet. Did Waldo tell you that the assassins were ogre breeds?"

"Yes."

"A curse on the beasts. Waldo hurt them, but not nearly enough. I sent Shaggoth to find them. He caught nothing but graves. There was nothing on the bodies to betray them."

"I know. I saw them myself. Tell Shaggoth to watch his step in the woods. There's something out there that's bigger than he is."

"You're making a joke?"

"Sort of. A mammoth did sneak up on me while I was looking at those ogre bodies."

"A mammoth! Here in this day. A wonder for certain." She rose and went to a cabinet while I sipped tea. She said, "I've been considering your situation since Waldo left. It seemed—and does more so now that I know who she was—that the best help I could offer would be a few charms you might use to surprise the villains."

I looked at Amiranda's remains. "I appreciate that. I wonder why you'd commit yourself that way, though."

"For Waldo. For the woman. Maybe for your sake, laddie. Maybe for my own. Certainly for the sake of justice. Whatever, the deed was cruel and should be repaid in coin equally vicious. The man responsible should be . . . But your tea is getting cold. I'll put another pot of water on to boil."

I got fresh tea, this time with fire-hardened flour briquettes that must have been the scones mentioned earlier. I gave them a try. One should show one's hostess the utmost in courtesy, especially when she is a witch.

Shaggoth stuck his head in and grumbled something in dialect that sounded suspiciously like, "Where the hell did my scones go?" He gave me a narrow-eyed look when the witch replied.

"Don't you mind him," she told me. "He's just being playful."

Right. Like a mongoose teases a cobra.

She sat down and explained how I could use the tricks she'd prepared for me. When she finished, I thanked her and rose. "If you can get Shaggoth to help me without breaking any bones in his playfulness, I'll get out of your hair."

She looked scandalized at first, then just amused. "You've heard too many stories about witches, Garrett. You'll be safer here than out in the moonlight. Shaggoth is the least maligned of those creatures who haven't yet emigrated. Consider the moon. Consider her ways."

Those who survive in this business develop an intuition for when to argue and when not to argue. Smart guys have figured out that you don't talk back to stormwardens, warlocks, sorcerers, and witches. The place for reservations is tucked neatly behind the teeth. "All right. Where do I bed down?"

"Here. By the fire. The nights get chilly in the woods."

I looked at what was left of Amiranda Crest.

"She doesn't get up and walk at midnight, Garrett. She's all through with that."

I have slept in the presence of corpses often enough, especially while I was in the Marines, but I've never liked it and never before had I to share my quarters with a dead lover. That held no appeal at all.

"Shaggoth will waken you at first light and help you get her into your buggy."

I looked at the body and reflected that it would be a long, hard road home. And once I got there I'd have to face the question of what to do with the cadaver.

"Good night, Mr. Garrett." The witch went around snuffing lights and collecting tea things, which she took to the kitchen. She started clattering around out there, leaving me to my own devices. I asked myself what the hell the point was of having nerve if I didn't use it, rounded up a small herd of pillows and cushions, and tried to convince myself they made a bed.

I tossed a couple logs on the fire and lay down. I stared at the ceiling for a long time after the clatter in the kitchen died and the light went with it. The flicker of the fire kept making Amiranda appear to move there in the corner of my eye. I went over everything from the beginning, then went over it again. Somewhere there was some nagging little detail that, added to the maverick coin from the farm, had me feeling very suspicious about Junior again.

Sometimes intuition isn't intuition at all, but rather unconscious memory.

I finally got it. The shoes Willa Dount had shown me first time I went up the Hill.

Those shoes. They deserved a lot of thought from several angles.

In the meantime, I had to rest. Tomorrow was going to be another in a series of long days.

B reakfast with Shaggoth was an experience. He could eat. Three of him could lay waste to nations. No wonder the breed was so rare. If there were as many of them as there are of us, they would have to learn to eat rocks because there wouldn't be enough of anything else to go around.

He brought the buggy around front and put the horses into harness with an ease that awakened my envy. Those beasts trotted out docilely and cooperatively and stood there smirking because they knew I would be irked by their easy acquiescence.

Damn the whole equine tribe, anyway.

The witch came out with a lunch she'd packed. I thanked her for that, for her hospitality, and for everything else. She ran through the instructions for using the spells she'd given me. Those instructions were as complicated and difficult to recall as instructions for dropping a rock. But specialists think the uninitiated incapable of falling without technical assistance.

I offered to pay for the help again.

"Don't start up, Garrett. Let me do my little piece for justice in an unjust world. Somewhere out there, there is somebody with the soul of a crocodile. Somebody who ordered the murder of a pregnant woman. Find him. Balance the scales. If you don't think you can handle him alone—for whatever reason—come see me again."

She was quietly furious about Amiranda. And she hadn't even known the woman. It was curious that Amiranda could find so many allies by getting herself murdered. And a pity none of us had been around when she needed us most. Though Saucerhead had done everything he could.

I didn't argue anymore. "I'll let you know how it comes out. Thanks for everything." I exchanged glares with the horses, putting on a good enough snarl to get my bluff in.

"Watch yourself, Garrett. You're playing with rough people."

"I know. But so are they."

"They probably know who you are and might know you're poking around. You don't know who they are."

"I've had plenty of practice being paranoid." I swung up onto the seat, glanced back at the bundle I'd be taking home, and hollered at the horses to get going. Good old Shaggoth trudged through the woods ahead of the horses, showing them the easy way to get back to the road—the way I'd completely missed coming in. The beasts kept glancing back, silently accusing me of being a moron.

I started with the first farm beyond the road to the place where Junior had been held. No, nobody there had seen a young man on foot the day Karl claimed to have started home. Certainly no one of any breed had come there looking to rent or buy a buggy or mount.

It was what I expected to hear. He wouldn't have done it so close, but the chance had to be covered. It was donkey-work time, grasping for straws. I had nothing concrete to affirm or deny my suspicions.

I got the same response house after house. Some talked easily, some not, the way people will, but the end was always the same. Nobody had begged, bought, borrowed, rented, or stolen transportation of any sort. Lunchtime came and went and I began to consider restructuring my assumptions.

Maybe Karl Junior *had* walked home. Barefoot. Or maybe he'd hitched a ride or had flagged down one of the day coaches running into the city. Or the ogres might have left him some way to get home.

That seemed damned unlikely. Walking, stealing, flagging a coach presented difficulties, too, for reasons of character and obvious traceability. Coachmen remember people they pick up along the road.

Hitching looked like the best and most logical alternative. It's the way I'd have gotten myself to town. But I doubted that a resort to the charity of strangers would even occur to a spoiled child off the Hill.

But had he gotten home that way, my chances of discovering the people who had helped were even more remote than they were by my present, most-favored course. So I stuck to what I was doing. I reasoned that if he had hitched, he would have mentioned it. He'd been careful to mention such details.

I now had a strong attachment to the assumption that Junior had participated in his own kidnapping. I had to caution myself not to get so attached that I began discarding contrary evidence.

The vision sent me back to wartime days. The farmer and his sons and a dozen other men were advancing through the hayfield in echelon, scythes rhythmically swinging. They looked like skirmishers cautiously advancing. I pulled up and watched for a few minutes. They saw me but pretended otherwise. The paterfamilias glanced at the sky, which was overcast, and decided to keep cutting.

All right. I could play it their way.

I slid down, walked to the edge of the field where the hay was down already—just to show how thoughtful a fellow I am—and approached the crowd from the flank. The women and kids raking the hay into piles and getting it onto the backs of several pathetic donkeys were much more curious than their menfolk. I gave them a "howdy" as I passed, and nothing more. Anything more would have been considered a heavy pass by many farm husbands.

I parked myself a cautious distance from the guy who looked like he was the boss ape in these parts and said "howdy" again.

He grunted and went on swinging, which was all right by me. I was trying to be accommodating.

"You might be able to help me."

This time his grunt was filled with the gravest of doubts.

"I'm looking for a man who passed this way four or five days back. He might have been looking to rent or buy a horse."

"Why?"

"On account of what he did to my woman."

He turned his head in rhythm and gave me a look saying I had no business going around asking for help if I was not man enough to rule my woman.

"He killed her. I just found out yesterday. Got her over in the buggy, taking her to her folks. Want to find that fellow when I get that done."

The farmer stopped swinging his scythe. He stared at me with squinty eyes that had looked into too many sunrises and sunsets. The other scythes came to rest and the men leaned upon them exactly like tired soldiers lean on their spears. The women and kids stopped raking and loading. Everybody stared at me.

The boss farmer nodded once, curtly, put his scythe down gently, hiked over to the buggy. He leaned against the side, lifted the cover off Amiranda.

When he returned, he stood beside me instead of facing me. "Pretty little gal."

"She was. We had a young one coming, too."

"Looked like. Wadlow! Come here."

One of the older farmers came to us. He planted his scythe and leaned. He looked even more laconic than the first one.

"You sold that swayback mare to that smart-ass city boy what day?"

The second farmer considered the sky as though he might find the answer written there. "Five days ago today. About noon." He eyed me like he was suspicious I might want the money back.

I knew what I wanted to know but had to play the game out. "He say where he was headed?"

Wadlow looked to my companion, who told him, "You tell him what he wants to know."

"Said he was going into the city. Said his horse got stole. Didn't say much of nothing else."

"Hope you took him good. Was he wearing shoes?" It was an off-the-wall question but about the only thing left I had to ask. Except, "Was he alone?"

Wadlow said, "Didn't have no shoes. Boots. Pretty rich-boy boots. Wouldn't last a week out here. He was by his lonesome."

"That's that, then," I said.

The older farmer asked, "That tell you what you need?"

"I reckon I know where to look now." And that was true. "Much obliged." I checked the sky. "Thank you, then." I turned to go.

"Luck to you. She was a pretty little thing."

My shoulders tightened and I shuddered in a sudden wash of emotion. I raised a hand and marched on. I had a man's work to do. Those farmers understood better than anybody I knew, except maybe Saucerhead Tharpe.

By the time I settled on the buggy seat, the skirmishers were on the move again and the women and children were back to work. Maybe they would find the time to talk about me over supper.

21

I t was late when I entered the city but a sliver of light still remained. I had a brainstorm. It was a long shot but it might stir something.

I had Amiranda's body propped up beside me. The witch's spells were holding their own and the light helped with the illusion. Maybe somebody who knew she could not be alive would see her and think she was.

To that end I made a few cautious forays into the outskirts of Ogre Town, then went up and circled Lettie Faren's place because a lot of the Bruno types from the Hill came there to waste their wages.

The wages of sin is that you get cheated out of them.

Then I headed home, going around to the back so no one would see me take the body inside.

Dean was there despite the hour. He helped with the door and gawked. "What's the matter with her, Mr. Garrett?"

I wasn't in one of my better humors. "She's dead. That's what's the matter with her. Murdered."

He stammered, apologized, stammered some more, so I apologized back and added, "I don't know why. Maybe because she was pregnant. Maybe because she knew too much. Let's take her in to his nibs. He might be able to sort it out."

The Dead Man isn't always as hard and insensitive as he pretends. He read my mood and saved the usual act. *That is the one who spent the night.* It was the first he admitted knowing about that.

"The same. Let me tell it while I'm in the mood."

He let me run through it up to the moment I carried her in there. Dean ran me mug after mug and hovered solicitously in between. I knew I was doing a good job reporting and had done a good one poking around because he didn't interrupt once and his only questions afterward were about the mammoth. Purely personal curiosity.

Let me mull it over, Garrett. You go get drunk. Watch out for him, Dean.

"Watch out for me? Why?"

You are working yourself up toward a quixotic gesture. You are unreasonable and irrational when you fall into such moods. I caution you to restraint. The information you have gathered is mainly circumstantial and there is not enough to point an accusing finger accurately. Tomorrow I will suggest some courses that may, possibly, produce evidence more concrete.

"More concrete? It's plenty hard enough for me."

You expect to tackle the favorite and only son of the Stormwarden Raver Styx on the basis of a pair of shoes and a horse? When you know there is a high probability that she would shield him even if he were caught cutting the hearts out of babies in the public streets? Further, you may have chosen the wrong villian to be the target of your wrath.

"Who else?"

That is what you will have to discover. It is true, I believe, that there is a reasonable probability that the young daPena and the dead woman were involved in a contrived kidnapping. But that is not a certainty. One simple fact could explain away all the evidence you have adduced as indicting the younger Karl.

"Here you go playing games with my mind again. How are you going to explain everything away?"

Two hundred thousand marks gold. A payoff of that magnitude could waken charity in the heart of a beast as foul as an ogre, perhaps. Perhaps they saw no need to plunder their hostage of pocket money.

Damn him. He could be right. The problem with this thing was that there were too many answers instead of not enough. "I don't believe it," I insisted.

Take this and reflect upon it in your cups, then. What became of the gold?

"Huh?"

Insofar as you know, the gold was turned over. Correct? By the woman Amber's direct statement, and by implication from others, all the young people wanted out of the Stormwarden's household. But the younger daPena returned. Would he have done so if it had been he who had received the gold? Or would he have run? You may have to attack it through the money after all.

Or, possibly, through the entertaining girl Donni Pell, who looks like the candidate for the connection with the ogre community.

This time I said it aloud. "Damn you."

He let me have a dose of the mental noise that passes as his chuckle. *Come back in the morning, Garrett. I will suggest an approach.*

I started to go, but there was the thing that used to be Amiranda staring at me with empty eyes. "What about this?"

Leave it. We will commune.

"What's this? Are you a necromancer as well as a mental prodigy? Have you been hiding some of your lights under a bushel?"

No. I expressed myself figuratively only. Go away, Garrett. Even my boundless tolerance has its limits, and you are pressing them.

I went off and got myself rather sloppily wrapped around a few gallons of beer. Faithful to his orders, old Dean hung around and shoveled the pieces into my bed when it was time. Damn the Dead Man, anyhow. Why did he have to complicate things?

22

Old Dean knew how to get me going on the morning after. He bullied me into eating a good breakfast. When he thought I was slackening, he started banging pots and pans until I yielded to the lesser evil and resumed eating.

A good big breakfast with plenty of apple juice and sweets really knocks the edge off my hangover, but food always looks and smells so ghastly I just can't believe it will do any good.

Once I'd stoked up to Dean's satisfaction, he presented me with a huge steaming mug of a smoky-flavored herb tea that had come to us courtesy of Morley Dotes sometime back. It had a mildly analgesic nature. "His nibs is ready anytime you are, Mr. Garrett. You may take the mug along with you."

He was going to trust me carrying something out of the kitchen myself? I gave him a look that he interpreted correctly. He grumbled, "That room was creepy enough with one corpse in it. He can clean up after himself if he's going to keep the other one in there with him."

I rose. From the kitchen doorway I said, "Maybe they'll get married." Feeble, but it wasn't my best time of day.

Dean gave me a black look and reached for the biggest pot he could find.

The Dead Man was trying to sleep when I stepped into his room. He was long overdue for one of his three-week naps, but now wasn't the time. "Wake it up, Old Bones. You're supposed to have some suggestions for me this morning."

He had several, but none of the first few was fit to record. I observed, "I take it you're sure enough of your Glory Mooncalled theory that you can indulge in a little smug snoozing."

The latest from the Cantard contains nothing contradictory.

"You going to break down and tell me?"

Not yet.

"What about the suggested approach you promised me last night?"

I would have thought that you would have seen the best chance already. You had the night to reflect on next moves.

"I took the night off. Give."

You are allowing yourself to become dependent upon my genius. You should be exercising your own, Garrett.

"We human types are bone lazy. Come on. Pay the rent."

Get the younger Karl. Bring him to me. He appears to be the weakest link in the chain of circumstance. If there is a tumor of guilt in him, I will open him up and expose it. One glimpse of that poor child there should be shock enough to leave him pliable.

"That's all I have to do, eh? Just go drag him out of that fort he calls home and bully him into coming here where you can work him over."

I cannot do your legwork for you, Garrett.

"Bah!" He was getting a sarky tone on him, Old Bones was. Maybe he'd stub a toe on his Glory Mooncalled theory and get dragged down from the heights of conceit.

Oh, how he loves to strut.

There was a foreign object just inside the front door. "Dean!"

He came at a run. "Yes, Mr. Garrett?"

"What the hell is this?"

Actually, I knew what *this* was. It was my old pal Bruno frozen in mid-stride two steps inside the front door and leaning against the wall. His expression was one of terror and one hand grasped the air before him. Dean had used that to hang up the sweater and knit cap he wears when he comes in early mornings. That showed me a side of him I hadn't suspected.

"He came to the door while you were out in the country. When I answered he just busted in past me. His nibs must have heard the uproar."

Better than a watchdog. "And nobody bothered to tell me."

"You had things on your mind."

"How'd he get against the wall?"

"I pushed him out of the way. I have to get in and out to do the marketing."

I stepped over in front of Bruno. "What am I going to do with you? You just keep coming back. Maybe drop you in the river to see how fast you swim? I'll have to think about it, because you're getting to be a nuisance." I turned to Dean. "Maybe we ought to get a chain so things like this don't happen."

Dean admitted, "His nibs could have been asleep."

The problem of Bruno's ego slipped my mind as I trudged up the Hill. I had a bigger problem. How the devil could I get to Junior, let alone pry him out? Considering the attitudes of some up there, I might not get close to the Stormwarden's place. The hired guards might be waiting for me.

They weren't. Not obviously. I tramped around the daPena place three times, hoping maybe Amber would spot me before Eenie, Meenie, Minie, and Moe started closing in and I had to show the Hill the flash of departing heels. It didn't work. I had to go. I decided to take a long walk. Sometimes getting the blood moving vanquishes the gloomier humors and the brain will come up with a thought.

The best I could manage in three hours of marching was the notion of sending Junior a letter saying I knew where the gold was and if he would come down to my place we could talk it over. The trouble with that was it might take a lot of time I didn't have.

He might dither a couple of days. Or he might not be able to slip his leash. Or the letter might not get to him at all, with highly unpredictable results. And Amiranda's body wasn't going to keep forever.

For want of something more constructive to do, I went around to Saucerhead's place to see how he was mending. A girlfriend I didn't know said he was keeping just fine and I should get the hell away before I got my eyes clawed out. She was no bigger than a minute but she had her back up and looked like she would give it a damned good shot.

So much for Saucerhead. Maybe something had fallen into Morley's lap. Besides somebody's wife or an eggplant steak dinner.

Morley wasn't eager to accept visitors that early in the day, but he was awake, so I was allowed to go upstairs. He greeted me with a scowl and no banter.

I said, "You look like a guy who isn't getting enough fiber in his diet. What's the matter? Was there a crop failure in the okra forests?"

He grumbled something that sounded like, "Goddim fraggle jigginitz."

"Would you want your virgin daughters to hear language like that?"

"Snacken schtereograk!"

Aha! He was cussing, all right, but in one of the Low Elvish dialects. I've learned that when he goes to grumbling in Elvish he's usually having money troubles. "Been playing the water spiders again, have we?"

"Garrett, are you a curse upon my house?" He actually used a dwarfish idiom equally capable of being translated as "mother-in-law." But I'm such a nice fellow nobody would ever accuse me of mother-in-lawing. "You're the reverse blackbird, you know that? The backward harbinger. Every time I have some bad luck, I have some more because you turn up right afterward. I can count on it."

"You don't want me hanging around, stop betting on the bugs. There's a simple cause-and-effect relationship there—very much like the one between betting on the bugs and losing your boots."

He repeated his curse-upon-the-house remark. "What do you want, Garrett?"

"I want to know if you've heard any news I might find useful."

"No. Ogre Town is as quiet as a crypt. Those guys came from somewhere else. And they took the gold with them when they went back. There hasn't been a whiff of gold around town. If there was a hint of a pile that size, you know the hard boys would be as busy as maggots. Saucerhead is doing all right."

"I know. I found out the hard way. He's got some little she-devil standing gate guard. I thought I was going to get gutted before I got out of there. Who the hell is she?"

He gave me the first flash of teeth of the visit. "His sister, maybe?"

"Horse pucky. Nobody's sister carries on like that."

He grinned. "Actually, I did hear one thing you might want to know, but I don't see how it would be much use."

"Well?"

"A drunken sailor off a night boat staggered in here right before we closed this morning. The gods know why he came here."

"I was just thinking that myself. Only they know why anybody does." "Night boat" is a euphemism for smuggler. Smugglers account for a third of TunFaire's river trade.

"You want to hear this or do you want to wisecrack your way to ignorance?"

"Speak to me, Oracle of the Lettuce."

"He mentioned that Raver Styx's ship entered the harbor at Leifmold the afternoon they left for TunFaire. She's on her way home, Garrett. She'll be here in a few days. If that will make any difference in the way you do what you think you have to do."

"It might. I figure Junior deserves special attention because of Saucerhead and Amiranda. Having Mom around might present difficulties."

"That's the whole barrel, then. Go away so I can feel sorry for myself."

"Right. Next time you got to bet on the bugs, let me know so I can get down the other way and clean up."

"There won't be a next time, Garrett."

"Good for you, Morley." I left the room thinking I had heard it before. He might hang in there awhile, but sooner or later he'd hear about a sure thing and the fever would get him.

I told the barman downstairs, "Send him a couple of turnip tenderloins smothered in onions and a double shot of your high-proof celery juice, straight up. On me."

He didn't crack a smile.

I headed home, my head filled with visions of a steak so rare Morley would die to look at it.

23

Dean had the place sealed up tight. Good for him. Sometimes he forgets. I pounded away. He came and peeked through the peephole. He made a production out of checking to see if I was there under duress. Then he started clinking and clunking as he unlatched latches. He flung the door open.

"Am I glad you're finally here, Mr. Garrett." He did sound glad. He retreated. I went in after him, started to pull the door shut.

"What the hell? What's this?"

We had gained another hall ornament. This one went by the name Courter Slauce when it wasn't in the home-furnishings racket.

"Dean!"

But he was headed for the kitchen at a high-speed shuffle and dared not battle the momentum he had developed. He tossed an answer over his shoulder but it didn't have enough oomph behind it. It fell on the floor before it got to me.

I paused beside Slauce. "Finances take a turn for the worse? You'll never make ends meet housebreaking."

Funny. He didn't answer.

He could hear well enough, though. And I could almost hear the nasty thoughts slithering round inside his head. I told him, "You'll make great company for Bruno. He's been dying for a shoulder to cry on."

I stepped past Bruno. Such a quandary. Drop in on the Dead Man and let him know I hadn't yet found a way to lure Junior into his lair? Or track Dean down and find out why we had another statue in the hall?

Dean won the toss. He was closer to the beer.

As I pushed through the door I heard Dean saying, "There. There, now. It'll be all right. Mr. Garrett is here now. He'll take care of everything."

Sure he would. He stepped on in to get a better idea of where to start.

Dean had his arms around an Amber who was shaking and looked like eighteen going on a terrified ten instead of thirty. Dean was patting her back and trying to still her tears. The same Dean who had stamped her with his scarlet seal of disapproval.

Something had shaken her badly. And the soft heart inside the old crab's shell had melted to her terror.

"Well?" I asked, sidling to the cold well. "Somebody want to give me an idea what's going on?"

Amber let out a growl, tore herself away from Dean, charged into me, opening the floodgates as she came. So much for having a beer.

Dean had the grace to look embarrassed as he drifted to the cold well.

I let Amber get the tears out. There is no point interrupting a woman when she is crying. If you don't get it over in one big chunk, you have to take it in a lot of little ones that come at unexpected and inopportune times. Meantime, Dean got me a mug.

When Amber was down to the sniffs and quivers, I sat her in a chair and told Dean to break out the brandy we keep for special occasions. I settled opposite her, in hand-touching range, and went to work on my mug. The first half went down quick and easy.

When I thought she was ready, I asked, "Can you talk about it now?"

She took a big bite out of her brandy before she nodded. "I have it under control. It was just . . . the circumstances, I guess. Domina and my father having a screaming argument that had everybody running for cover. Then the news about Karl. Then when I finally managed to sneak out so I could come talk to you, Courter caught up with me down the street, and when I wouldn't go back home, the look he got made me think he wanted to kill me, too. I went kind of crazy and ran away screaming. But if the whole world has gone crazy, don't I have the right to get a little crazy myself?"

The words tumbled out of her, tripping over one another in their haste to dance in the open air.

"Hold it! Halt! Stop! Good girl. Now take a deep breath. Hold it. Count to ten, slowly. Good. Now tell me what happened. Start from the beginning so it makes sense."

Dean took my mug, which needed filling, and at the same time interrupted. "If you'll pardon me, Mr. Garrett, the most important point comes out of order. Her brother is dead."

I stared at Amber. She shivered, nodded. She was counting well past ten. "How?"

"They say he committed suicide."

That caught me flat-footed. I didn't know what to say. Before I got my mind in order, my permanent motionless houseguest broke all precedent and reached out beyond the bounds of his demesne.

Garrett. Bring them in here.

Dean caught it, too. He looked to me for instructions. "Do what he says, I guess. Amber, come with me. My associate wants us to talk it over in his presence."

"Do I have to?"

"Keep thinking two hundred thousand marks gold."

"I'm not sure I want to keep on . . . Of course I do. I want out of that place more than ever, now. I'll never feel safe there again."

"Let's go, then. Don't worry about him. He's harmless to those who intend him no harm."

I'd forgotten one thing.

24

Amber let out a squeal that was half pain, half horror. I thought she would faint. But she was made of tougher stuff than I suspected. She hung on to my arm a bit while she stared at Amiranda, then got hold of herself, stepped back, looked at me. "What's going on, Garrett?"

"That's what I found instead of the gold."

She stepped over to the corpse.

Bring Mr. Slauce, Garrett. It may be helpful to present him with the same shock.

"What about the other one?"

Dispose of him once we are done here. He should have learned his lesson.

"Want to give me a hand, Dean?" I didn't doubt that I could manage Slauce by myself. If nothing else, I could tip him over and roll him. But why strain myself?

We dragged him inside and per instructions sat him down facing Amiranda. Amber seemed in control again. She said, "You have some things to tell me."

"I'll tell you my story if you'll tell me yours."

About then the Dead Man loosed his hold on Courter Slauce. I went to the door to make sure he didn't use it before we were done with him. He shook all over. There wasn't much bluff in him when he looked around. He didn't say anything. That disappointed me. I'd expected some bluster and the invocation of the Stormwarden.

"I want to know some things," I told him. "I think Miss daPena has a few questions, too. It's even possible Miss Crest might want to know why she was killed."

His eyes darted to the corpse. "I don't know nothing about that. Where did that come from? I thought she run off. Domina has been chewing my butt for days because she managed to get out of the house with her stuff. Never mind that I was halfway across town delivering a letter to one of the Baronet's girlfriends when she did it. That wouldn't have done for an excuse anyway, since I couldn't tell her."

He is telling the truth he believes, Garrett.

"Then he wasn't in on it?"

Not wittingly, though I did not say that, Garrett.

"All right. Slauce. Who kidnapped Junior?"

"What the hell? How should I know? What the hell are you doing sticking your nose in, anyway? You got paid. You're out of it."

"That supposes nobody but Willa Dount would hire me. Slauce, I think you know the answer to the question. Just in case, though, I'll tell you the answer. Nobody kidnapped him. Unless a man can kidnap himself. My main interest, though, is why did Amiranda have to be killed? And who said the word that made it happen?"

Amber opened her mouth. I raised a hand, cautioned her to silence. Slauce didn't need to know her angle.

You are getting ahead of yourself, Garrett. No interrogation or manipulation of this man can be soundly founded—until we have heard everything Miss daPena has to tell us. Have you forgotten what brought her here? Or is her brother's demise too trivial for consideration?

I hadn't forgotten. I was stalling, having to deal with Amber's grief and hysteria and hoping for a breakthrough with Slauce that would give me the answer to my own dilemma. But I wasn't thinking soundly. Not to hear Amber out would be stupid.

Since I'm one of the smartest guys around, it wouldn't do for me to tarnish my image by doing something dumb.

"You win, Old Bones. But upon your head be the rainfall."

It was not I who felt compelled to charge off to the rescue.

It is possible, with great concentration, to shut him out—if he has other things on his minds. He always has to have the last word. There are times he has all the disadvantages of a wife, with none of the advantages.

"Amber. You feel up to telling me what you came to tell? All settled down now?"

Slauce started snarling. "Girl, you don't talk to this guy about nothing. You don't do nothing but march yourself straight home."

I scowled at the Dead Man and said, "You had to let him get his second wind."

Amber told Slauce, "Shove your elbow up your nose, Courter. You don't scare me anymore. In a couple of days you and Domina are going to be hanging out in the wind. Aren't you? Maybe you could bull-smoke your way around Karl, but not Karl *and* Amiranda. And I'm sure not going back there and give you guys a chance to explain to Mother about Karl and Amiranda and *me!*"

"What kind of crazy talk is that, girl? Your brother killed himself."

"Just like Amiranda ran away. Give me credit for knowing my brother. You're not going to sell me that. My mother isn't going to buy it, either. And I'm not going anywhere near any of you people. Not when two out of the three family heirs suddenly turned up murdered."

"Three out of four," I tossed in, just to see how high the water would splash. "Amiranda was pregnant. Three months. The child would have been male."

That was a surprise to both Amber and Slauce. It silenced them. But if it wakened any suspicions, they concealed them well.

I faced the Dead Man, indicated Slauce. "Shut him off, will you? I don't need him shoving his oar in while the lady is talking."

What lady?

Slauce went stiff as a corpse.

Timely revelation, Garrett. You have him rattled and reflective. But you may have cost yourself your credibility with the girl. She has begun to suspect that you have not been candid about your own motives.

Yeah.

said, "I think the best way would be for you to start right after the last time we talked."

Amber balked. "You aren't interested in anything but Ami."

"Oh?" I admitted an interest. "And I want whoever did this to her. I don't like people who waste attractive young women. But if you think I'm immune to the charms of a share of two hundred thousand marks gold, then you're a lot sillier than I think you are. Listen here. I'd be on this trail just as hot if that was you over there and Amiranda was standing where you are. I want the guy behind it. And I'll bet your mother will, too, once she gets here."

"There'll be hell to pay."

She is going to buy it, Garrett. You slick talker.

I gave the Dead Man the look he deserved. "Amber, right now all I have to work with is what you can tell me."

She stalled long enough to satisfy her ego, then got to it. "Courter saw you when you were leaving. He ran right to Domina. Naturally. And she flew into one of her rages. Only more so. I've seen her angry before but I never ever saw her lose control. She screamed and threatened and threw things and scared Karl so bad he told her everything we said. So it's good we didn't say anything about the gold. He would have told her about that, too. I didn't tell her anything. That made her mad all over again, so she had Courter give me a beating and lock me in my room. They didn't let me out till this morning."

She pirouetted, pranced over to Slauce, slapped him, and danced back. "There."

"They," it turned out, had been Karl, who had come to her while the house was asleep, unlocking her door. He had seemed severely troubled but had refused to explain except to say that he'd had all that he could take and was going away now and wouldn't be back.

"But that didn't mean he was going to kill himself."

I didn't believe he was the type, either. Not enough guts. "You'd better go over what he said. There might be some hint there. Try to recall his exact words and actions."

"I don't know how I could get his words more exact. Except that he asked me to go with him. I told him I wasn't miserable enough yet to give up and run without any prospects. But he was. Really. Something had shaken him badly. He was pale. He couldn't stand still. He was sweating."

"In other words, he was scared."

"Terrified."

"Like he had seen a ghost?"

"That's funny."

"What is?"

"That's exactly what I thought then. That he must have seen a ghost."

"Maybe he did. At least secondhand. Go on. He left?"

"As soon as he knew I wasn't going with him."

"Any hint where?"

"A safe place with an old friend is what he told me when I asked."

"Donni Pell?"

"Maybe. That's what I thought when he said it. The way he said it. Donni Pell or Ami. I just figured he knew where Ami went."

"Why Amiranda?"

"They grew up together. They were close. They always had their heads together. If she ran away, he had to know where she went. She wouldn't go without leaving him a message somehow. Even if he was kidnapped when she went."

The more I saw of them, the more the workings and relationships of the daPena family baffled me. "All right. It could have been Amiranda but it wasn't because she was dead. We have to assume it was Donni Pell. That might not be true but anything else seems unlikely. Given his nature, it would have been a woman. Correct? Who else did he know? No one you or I know about. I guess I'll have to go there and see."

This business was all legwork. Morley would approve of the exercise I was getting. "Go on with the story. Your brother decamped, headed for parts unknown, frightened. Then what?"

"Twenty minutes later, Courter came. They knew Karl was out. They wanted me to tell them where he went."

"They?"

"Courter. It wasn't really they till later. But Courter didn't come on his own. They sent him."

"I assume you gave him valuable advice on the placement of his elbow."

"Yes. So my father took his place. He was as pale and sweaty as Karl had been. And he had a wild look that scared me. Like he was so terrified he was capable of anything. He didn't get anywhere, either. He did a lot of yelling. My father yells a lot. I mostly just stayed out of his reach till Domina came in. She tried to keep me from hearing what she said, but I heard part of it. She'd heard from one of the staff that Karl had heard that Mother was in Leifmold. Meaning Mother could show up anytime because she could get to TunFaire almost as fast as the news that she was coming. Father really got excited then."

"And?"

Amber seemed ashamed. "I want you to know, I love my father. Even when he does irrational things."

I tried my raised-eyebrow trick. I hadn't been practicing lately. She wasn't impressed.

"He screamed at Domina to get Courter. They'd beat it out of me. She couldn't calm him down, so she went out, I guess to get Courter. Father came after me. And he actually did hit me. He never did that before. Not himself."

"And?"

"I picked up a shoe and bopped him over the head. He went away. And he didn't come back. A couple hours later I heard him and Domina having a screaming match all the way from her side of the house. But I couldn't tell what it was about. I thought about sneaking over and eavesdropping but I didn't. I was scared to go out of my room. Everybody was going crazy. And then a little while after that, I decided I had to get out of that house. Forever. No matter what. Even if you can't find the gold."

"Why?"

"Because one of the servants told me that Karl had committed suicide. When I heard that, I knew I had to get away. Far away, where nobody could find me. Or I might be dead, too. Only I didn't run fast enough, I guess. Because Courter caught up with me just before I got here. He even tried to come in and drag me back out when your man let me in."

I considered Courter, then the Dead Man. He would be monitoring Slauce's reactions as closely as he could.

The man is a villain for certain, Garrett, but he appears to have no guilty knowledge concerning the death of Karl Junior or his supposed kidnapping. Much of what he has heard here has been news to him. He appears to be slow of wit and it could be that he is considered too stupid to be trusted.

I faced Amber. "You're convinced your brother was incapable of taking his own life?"

"Yes. I told you that already."

"All right. That gives me a new line of attack. Where, when, and how did it happen?"

"I don't know."

"You don't know? You mean you just—"

"Don't you start yelling at me, too!" She lifted a foot, snatched off a shoe, and brandished it.

Three seconds later we were shaking with laughter.

I got hold of myself, gave Slauce a look, shifted it to the Dead Man.

He knows.

"Dean, take Miss daPena to the guest room and get her settled. While you're at it, you might as well fix yourself up for a few more nights. We're going to need you here."

"Yes sir." He sounded excited. At least he was in on this thing. "Miss? If you'll come with me?"

She went reluctantly.

"**I** think I have to revise my strategy," I said. "I was going to let Slauce have the works so he could go home and get things stirred up."

I assumed as much. I believe it is time you approached Mr. Dotes on a purely business basis, instead of favor for favor. You need more eyes.

"Right. Things are stirred up enough without me sticking my hand in. Can you make him forget what he's seen and heard here?"

I think so.

"Then let's see what he has to tell about Junior checking out."

The Dead Man released his hold on Slauce.

Friend Courter was vulnerable. When I asked, he answered, and didn't start toughening up for several minutes. He gave me an address and an approximate time of death only two hours after Karl had fled his home.

"How did he do it?" I asked, for Courter's sake going with the suicide fiction.

"He slashed his wrists."

That was the clincher. "Aw, come on! And you believed that? You knew the kid. If you'd said he'd hanged himself, I might have thought it was just barely possible. But even I knew him well enough to know he couldn't cut on himself. He was probably the kind of guy who couldn't shave because he was afraid he might see a speck of blood."

Do not press, Garrett. You will get him to thinking. For him that might prove to be a dangerous new experience.

He just wanted his own job made easier.

You go see Mr. Dotes now. By the time you return, Mr. Slauce will have forgotten this episode entirely. He will be a bit intoxicated. Take that into consideration when you are planning how you will remove him from the premises. And you might as well consider doing the other one while you are at it.

Right. Grumble. I left him to his fun.

Morley rented me five thugs. His discount to the trade left their price only semi-usurious. I assigned one man to keep an eye on my place just in case something happened that the Dead Man couldn't handle alone. The world is filled with unpredictable people.

One man got the job of keeping track of Courter Slauce. The remaining three got the unenviable task of trying to keep tabs on the denizens of the Stormwarden's house. I told them they should report to Morley. Dotes would have a better chance of tracking me down if there was something I needed to know.

Five men weren't enough to do the job the way it ought to be done, but this one was out of my own pocket. The only client I had was one who had retained me on a contingency basis, and while I was willing to grab off a chunk of that ransom, I had a pessimistic view of my chances.

I made a mental note to quiz Amber about what she had learned regarding Domina Dount's handling and delivery of all that gold.

Disposing of Bruno and Slauce was an easy half hour's work with a borrowed buggy. An unconscious Bruno got dumped into an alley where he'd soon waken hungry enough to go into the cannibal business.

Courter wasn't all the way out. He was just roaring drunk. I don't know how the Dead Man managed that. He never said. I just walked Slauce into a tavern, sat him down with a pitcher, then took the buggy back where it belonged.

Then it was time to go see what could be seen at the scene of Junior's suicide.

T he wooden tenements, three and four stories tall, leaned against one another like wounded soldiers after battle. But the war never ended down here. Time was the enemy never to be conquered and there were no reserves to help stay the tide.

It was night and the only light in the street fell from doors and windows open in hopes the day's heat would sneak away. That was a hope only slightly less vain than the hope that poverty would take to its heels. The street was full of serious-faced, gaunt children and the tenements were filled with quarreling adults. The corners, though, lacked their prides of narrow-eyed young men looking for a chance under the guise of cool indifference. No dares issued or taken.

They were all in the Cantard, burning youth's energy in futility and fear, soldiering.

The war had that one positive spinoff. When you wanted to talk about your crime, you had to go find senior citizens who remembered the good old days before the war.

I still had to watch my step—for reasons evoking no romance at all. There were as many dogs in the street as kids. And at any moment the sky might open and spit out a cloudburst of refuse.

There were sanitary laws, but who paid attention? There was no one to enforce them.

The place I sought was one more crippled soldier in the host, three stories that had seen their youth spent before the turn of the century. I planted myself across the way and considered it. Assumption: Junior had run to his friend Donni Pell when he felt the heat. Assumption: Donni Pell had been in on and had helped stage Junior's kidnapping.

The nature of the place where young Karl had died implied that there was something wrong with one or both assumptions. Having collected possibly the biggest ransom ever paid in TunFaire, why would she hole up in such a dump?

If he hadn't run to Donni, then who? No other name had come up. Junior didn't have friends.

Not even one, apparently. Death had sniffed out his hiding place in under two hours.

All the excitement was over, and had been for many hours. In that part of town even the most grotesque death was a wonder only until the blood dried. I began to be an object of interest myself, standing there doing nothing but look. I moved.

There are no locks or bolts on the street doors of those places. Such would only inconvenience the comings and goings of the masses packed inside. I went in, stepped over a sleeping drunk sprawled on the battered floor. The treads of the stair creaked and groaned as I went up. There was no point in sneaking.

Sneakery would have been useless anyway. Getting to the right room on the third floor took me past two others that had no doors. Families fell silent, stared as I passed.

The death room had a door, but not one that would close tightly. It skidded against the floor as I pushed.

It was the sort of place I had pictured—one room, eight-by-twelve, no furnishings, one window with a shutter but no glass. A bunch of blankets were thrown against a wall for a bed, and odds and ends were scattered around. One corner had walls and floor spattered with patches and brown spots. It had been messy. But those things always are. There is a lot of juice in the human fruit.

They must have fastened him down somehow. You don't carve on someone without them putting up a fuss. I kicked around the place but found no ropes or straps or anything that might have bound him. I guess even ogre breeds have sense enough to pick up after themselves sometimes.

Or did they?

Mixed in with the tangle of bedding was a familiar item, from Karl's description. It was a doeskin bag with a heavy, long drawstring. Just the thing to pop over a guy's head and choke him unconscious.

It was stained with dried vomit. I pictured some fastidious thug hurling it aside in disgust.

You might not need to tie a guy if you strangle him before you cut. He could bleed to death before he woke up.

"It's a half-mark silver a week, as is. You want furnishings, you bring your own."

I gave the woman in the doorway my innocent look. "What about the mess?"

"You want cleanup, that's a mark right now. You want fix-up, take care of it yourself."

"Come off the rent?"

She looked at me like I was crazy. "You pay up front, every week. You show me you're reliable, after a few months I might understand if you're one or two days late. Three days and out you go. Got that?"

She was a charmer in every respect. Had she not possessed the winning personality of a lizard, a guy might have been tempted to have her hair and clothes washed. She couldn't have been much past thirty, only the inside had gone completely to seed. But the rest wouldn't be far behind.

"You're staring like you think the place comes with entertainment." She tried a cautious smile from which a few teeth were missing. "That costs you extra, too."

I had a thought. An inspiration, perhaps. What do hookers do when they get too old or too slovenly to compete? Not all can become Lettie Farens. Maybe this was someone Donni had known before she had become a landlady.

"I'm not so much interested in the room as I am in the tenant." I palmed a gold piece, let her see a flash. Her eyes popped. Then her face closed down, became all suspicious frowns framed by wild, filthy hair.

"The tenant?"

"The tenant. The person who lived in the room. Also the person who paid for it, if they weren't the same."

Still the suspicious eyes. "Who wants to know?"

I looked at the coin. "Dister Greteke." Old Dister was a dead king, of which we in TunFaire are blessed with a lot. We could use a live one—if he'd do something worthwhile.

"A double?"

"Looks like one to me."

"It was a kid named Donny Pell. I don't know where he went. He paid his own rent." She reached.

"You're kidding. Donny Pell, eh? Did you meet him while you were still in the trade?" I put the coin on the windowsill, drifted away. She licked her lips, took one step. She wasn't stupid. She saw the trap taking shape. But she couldn't shake the greed, and maybe she thought she could bluff me. She took another step.

In moments she was at the window and I was at the door. "You going to tell me?"

"What do you need to know?"

"Donni Pell. But female. From Lettie Faren's place. Came here to hide out maybe a week ago. Right?"

She nodded. She had a little shame left.

"You knew her before?"

"I was there when she first came to the place. She was different from the other girls. Ambitious. But kind of decent then. If you know what I mean. Maybe she got too ambitious." The knuckles of her right hand whitened as she squeezed the coin. She'd been out of the trade awhile. It had been awhile since she'd seen that kind of money. Doubtless when it had been easy come she hadn't thought to put any aside. Her gaze strayed to the bloodstains. "She developed weird tastes in friends."

"Ogre breeds?"

That surprised her. "Yeah. How did you—"

"I know some things. Some things I don't. You know some things and you don't know what I don't know." I borrowed a trick from Morley Dotes by getting my knife out and going to work on my nails. "So why don't you just tell me everything you do know about her and the people who visited her here."

Her bluff was a feeble bolt and she knew it. But she tried. "I yell and the whole place will be in here in half a minute."

"I'll bet the fellow in the corner thought the same thing."

She looked at the bloodstain again. "Fair is fair. I was just seeing if you'd pay a little more. All right? What do you want to know?"

"I told you. Everything. Especially who else was here this morning and where she is now." To forestall the next round of delays I added, "I don't mean her any harm. I'm looking for some of her playmates. She's gotten herself caught in the middle of a big and deadly game."

Maybe very deadly for her. If there was to be a next victim in this mess, I'd put all my money on Donni Pell. If I had any chance, I wanted to find her before the villains eliminated the next link in their chain of vulnerability.

"I don't know where she went. I didn't know she was gone till somebody found the mess. That's the gods' honest truth, mister."

She sounded like she was telling the truth. I must have had a ferocious look in my eye. She was getting nervous. But with a hooker you never know. Their whole lives are lies and some of the falsehoods run so deep they don't know the difference.

"Look, mister . . ."

"Just keep talking, sweetheart. I'll let you know when I've gotten my money's worth."

"Only three people ever visited her here that I know about. The one who killed himself here this morning." If she wanted to keep up the pretense on that, it was all right by me. "That was the only time he ever came that I know of. Another one came twice. Both times he was all covered up in one of them hooded cloaks rich guys wear when they go out at night. I never saw his face. I never heard his name."

Inconvenient for me, that, but she was doing all right, considering. "How tall?"

"Shorter than you. I think. I never was very good judging how tall people are."

"How old?"

"I told you, he wore one of them cloaks."

"What about his voice?"

"I never heard him talk."

"When did he come here?" I was determined to get something.

"Last night was the first time. He stayed about two hours. I guess you can figure what they were doing. Then he came back this morning."

I was all over her then, trying to pin down the order of events. But she couldn't get straight who had come when. "I think the cloaked man was first. Maybe not. Maybe it was the one who killed himself. The other one came last, though, I'm pretty sure. Two of them was here at the same time, I think, but I don't know which two."

She wasn't very bright, this woman. Also, she had been very scared. Donni's third visitor, who, it developed, had visited almost every night, had spooked her.

She was sure, almost, that the cloaked man had been the first to leave. Maybe.

"Tell me about this third man. This regular visitor. This guy who scared you so bad. He sounds interesting."

He wasn't interesting to her. She didn't want to talk about him at all. He was bad mojo.

I took that as a good sign. She knew something here. With a little sweet talk ... "I'm badder mojo, lover. I'm here." A little deft work with the knife ...

"All right, Bruno. All right. You don't have to get mean. He can take care of you himself. The guys he ran with called him Gorgeous. If you ever saw him, you'd know why. He was meaner than a wolfman on weed."

"Ugly?" Part ogre, I thought. What else? There had to be an ogre in it somewhere.

"Ugly! So ugly you couldn't tell if he was a breed or not. He came with different guys different times, some of them breeds, some of them not. But always with this one breed he called Skredli."

My eyes must have lit up, and not entirely with joy. She backed away a step, threw up a hand, looked for some place to hide. "Easy, woman. Skredli? Now that's a name I've been wanting to hear. Are you sure?"

"Sure I'm sure."

"You told me only three men ever came here. But now you've got this Gorgeous visiting with a crowd."

"The ones who came with him never came inside. They were like body-guards or something. Except that Skredli guy did come inside this morning, I think, and maybe one other time. Yeah. That's right. I think he even come here one other time, too, by himself, and stayed with her a couple hours, I forgot about that. Ick." She shuddered. "Doing it with an ogre."

"I want this Skredli. Where do I find him?"

She shrugged. "I don't know. Ogre Town, I guess. But when you find him, you're going to find Gorgeous, too. And maybe the girl. Only she'll probably be dressed like a boy again. Using Donny Pell. Why don't you get out of here? Why don't you leave me the hell alone?"

"Do you know anything else?"

"No."

"Of course you do. Who came for the body? What were they going to do with it?"

"I guess they were his family. Or from his family. Fancy people off the Hill with their own private soldiers and no charity in them for poor people. They talked like they were going to have him cremated."

I grunted. That was the thing to do if you didn't want anybody getting too close a look at the stiff. Like, say, the woman who had given life to the flesh.

Or maybe I was *too* suspicious. This business can do that to you. You have to remember to keep it simple. You don't need to look for the great sinuous, complicated schemes reeking of subterfuge and malice when a little stupidity followed by desperate cover-up efforts will explain everything just as well. And you have to remember to keep an eye out for who stands to gain. That alone will flag your villain eight times out of ten.

That, more than any other facet of the affair, baffled me this time. Not the gold side, of course. However that worked out, the gold was its own explanation. But who could profit from the death of Amiranda Crest? How and why?

I stared at the woman. She wouldn't know. I doubted that she knew anything more worth digging out. "Step back into the corner, please. That's fine. Now sit yourself down."

She grew pale. Her hands, clasped around her knees, were bone white as she fought to keep them from shaking.

"You'll be all right," I promised. "I just want to know where you are while I go over this place again."

I found exactly what I expected to find. Zip. I took the doeskin bag and headed out.

As I passed through the doorway the woman called after me, "Mister, do you know anybody who wants to rent a room?"

found myself a syrupy shadow and installed myself across from the tenement. The street was empty of people now, and of the more honest cats and dogs. The yelling and scuffling inside the buildings had died down. The slum was gathering its strength for tomorrow's frays.

I waited. I waited some more. Then I waited. A band of pubescent marauders swept past, in search of trouble, but they didn't spot me. I waited.

After two hours I gave up. Either the woman had no intention of running to Gorgeous and Skredli or she had left the building another way. I suspected she felt no need to take warning.

I set myself for a long night. First, home to let the Dead Man know what I'd learned, then to Morley's place to find out what his people had reported and to learn what he knew about a thug named Gorgeous. Maybe more after that if anything interesting had turned up.

The interesting stuff started before I got to the house. Despite the hour there were a bunch of guys hanging around out front. I held up and watched awhile.

That is all they were doing. Hanging around. And not trying to hide the fact. I moved a little closer. I could then see that they wore livery. Closer still, I saw that the livery belonged to the Stormwarden Raver Styx.

Not being inclined to cooperate if they were waiting around to do evil when I showed, I slid away and approached the house from the rear. We had no company back there. I rapped and tapped till I got Dean's attention. He let me in.

"What have we got, Dean?"

"Company from the Hill."

"I suspected that. That's why I'm so good in this business. When I see fifteen guys hanging around in the street, I have a hunch that we've got company. What about our guest?"

"Upstairs. Buttoned up tight and keeping quiet."

"She knows?"

"I warned her."

"Good. Where is the company?"

"In your office. Waiting impatiently."

"She'll have to keep on waiting. I'm hungry and I want to let the old boy in on what I picked up. And I wouldn't mind guzzling about a gallon of beer before I face that harpy."

That made two chances I'd given him to ask how I'd guessed that my company was Domina Dount and twice that he'd ignored the bait. He has his little ways of getting even.

"Won't do no good to bother his nibs. He's gone to sleep."

"With an outsider in the house?"

"I suppose he trusts you to handle it." Dean's tone suggested he had a suspicion that the Dead Man's genius had lapsed, that maybe he'd rounded the last turn and was headed down that final stretch toward Loghyr heaven.

It looked like I now had two of them who couldn't keep straight who owned the house and who was the guest or employee. I wouldn't be surprised if Dean wasn't thinking about moving in. He'd reached the occasional nag-about-money stage.

"Be nice, Dean. Or I'll leave you standing at the altar and run off with Willa Dount."

He didn't find that amusing.

"I might as well be married the way things are going around here."

He slapped a plate in front of me like an old wife in a snit. But the food was up to par.

I permitted myself a satisfied smirk.

29

U p north along the edge of the thunder-lizard country there is a region called Hell's Reach. It's not wholly uninhabitable but nobody lives there by choice. Everywhere you turn there are hot geysers, steaming sulfur pits, and places where the raw earth lies there molten, quivering, occasionally humping up to belch out a big *ka-bloop!* of gas.

The lava pools sprang to mind the instant I saw Willa Dount. All her considerable will was bent toward restraining a hot fury. She had an almost red glow about her, but was determined to give it no vent.

"Good evening," I said. "Had I expected a caller, I wouldn't have stayed out so late." I settled myself and my mug. "I hope you haven't been inconvenienced too much." Before I'd left the kitchen Dean had reminded me about sugar, vinegar, and flies, and I'd taken his advice to heart.

It's not smart to go out of your way to make enemies of the Hill, anyway.

"It has been a wait, but my own fault," she replied. Amazing that she would admit the possibility of fault in anything she did. "But had I sent someone to make an appointment, I would have been delayed even longer—if you would have been willing to see me at all. I'm certain you would have refused to come to me again."

"Yes."

"I'm aware that you don't hold me in high regard, Mr. Garrett. Certainly your contacts with my charges have done nothing to elevate your opinion. Even so, that shouldn't interfere with a business relationship. In our contacts thus far you have remained, for the most part, professionally detached."

"Thank you. I try." I do. Sometimes.

"Indeed. And I need you in your professional capacity once more. Not just for show this time."

It was my turn to say, "Indeed?" But I fooled her. I showed her my talented eyebrow instead.

"I'm desperate, Mr. Garrett. My world is falling into ruin around me and I seem to be incapable of halting the decay. I have come to my last resort—no. That's getting ahead of myself."

I told my face it was supposed to look enrapt with anything she might say.

"I have spent my entire adult life in the Stormwarden's employ, Mr. Garrett. Beginning before her father died. It's seldom been pleasant. There have been no holidays. The rewards have been questionable, perhaps. By being privy to inside information, I've managed to amass a small personal fortune, perhaps ten thousand marks. And I've developed an image of myself as a virtual partner in the Stormwarden's enterprises, able to be trusted with anything and capable of carrying any task through to the desired conclusion. In that spirit I've done things I wouldn't admit to my confessor, but with pride that I could be trusted to get them done and trusted not to talk about them later. Do you understand?"

I nodded. No point slowing her down.

"So a few months ago she was called to the Cantard because the course of the war seemed to be swinging our way and it was time to put on all the pressure we could. She left me to manage the household, as she has done a dozen times, and especially charged me with riding herd on her family, all of whom had been showing an increasing tendency toward getting involved in scandals."

"The two Karls, you mean? They're the ones the rumor mill loved. I never heard of the daughter till the other day."

"She was blind, the Stormwarden. Those girls were the ones who were deserving. Though Amber had begun to show signs of getting wild, just for the attention."

I nodded as my contribution.

She took a deep breath. "Since she's been gone this time, it's been like I've been under a curse. Father and son were determined to circumvent me at every turn. Then that kidnapping business had to come. I had to deplete the family treasury severely, selling silver at a discount, to get that much gold together. It was a disaster, but for a cause the Stormwarden could respect once her temper cooled. I might even have survived Amiranda's having taken flight during the confusion. The girl was restless for some time before she took off. The Stormwarden herself had remarked that it was coming. But putting out two hundred thousand marks gold to ransom Karl, only to have him take his own life, that's insupportable."

Was I supposed to know about Junior or not? Instinct told me to play it cautious. "Did you say that Karl killed himself?"

"This morning. He slashed his wrists and bled to death in a hole of a room in Fishwife's Close."

"Why the hell would he do that?"

"I don't know, Mr. Garrett. And to be perfectly frank, at this point I can't much care. He destroyed me by doing it. Maybe that was his motive. He was a strange boy and he hated me. But Karl isn't the reason I came here. I'm doomed when the Stormwarden returns, which she will very shortly. However, my pride—badly mauled but not yet dead—insists I go on, trying to salvage what I can on her behalf. Amber fled the house this morning. This is where you come in."

I told my face to look interested.

"Amiranda and Amber are at large and therefore at risk. If I can salvage that much for the Stormwarden, I will. I'm going to try. I have gone into my own funds to do so. I want you to find those girls. If you can."

She plomped a sack down in front of me.

"One hundred marks gold, to retain you. I'll pay a fee of one thousand marks gold each if you can return either of those girls before the Stormwarden comes home."

"Your man Slauce can't handle—"

"Courter Slauce is an incompetent imbecile. This morning I sent him after Amber. He turned up just before I left to come here, too drunk to recall where he'd been or what he'd been doing. I console myself with the certainty that he'll starve to death after the Stormwarden chucks the lot of us into the street. Will you look for my missing girls, Mr. Garrett?"

"Give me a few minutes to think." I had to smooth out some dents in my ethics and reach an accommodation with my conscience. I considered myself to be working for three clients already: myself, Saucerhead, and Amber. Though Amber wasn't getting the first-class production. And nobody was paying me.

Willa Dount would be paying, though she wouldn't be getting her money's worth. Still, an experiment had occurred to me.

"Suppose I had a notion where I could find one of the girls right now?"

"Do you?"

"Take it as a supposition. How can I be certain I'd get my fee?"

She levered herself out of her chair, straining like a woman decades older. "I came prepared for that possibility." What might have been a smile tickled the corner of her mouth.

She started digging sacks out of her clothing. In a minute there was a line of ten before me, each a twin of the one offered me as a retainer. I checked the contents of one at random.

It was good.

Eleven hundred marks gold. More than I'd ever had a chance at before. With prospects for another thousand, which I could collect easily. Certainly a temptation to test the dark side of a man's soul.

We all look for the big hit—hope for it, talk about it—but I don't believe we *think* about it. Not seriously. Because when it's suddenly there, a lot of thinking has to be done.

Amiranda was dead. And what was Amber to me? Morley always says the supply of women is inexhaustible. And who would I have to explain to or make excuses to?

Just to myself. With maybe the Dead Man smirking over my shoulder.

Still, there was the possibility of a useful experiment.

I rose and collected the gold in one big bear hug. "Come with me."

Dean had turned down the lamps in the Dead Man's room. I don't know why he thinks that makes any difference. The Dead Man doesn't care about light one way or the other. When he wants to sleep, he'll sleep through sun, lightning, or earthquake. I hied me down and deposited the take beside his chair.

Domina Dount asked, "Are you going to deliver something or not, Mr. Garrett?"

"Turn around."

For a moment she was human. She let out a little squeak and raised her hands to her cheeks. But she asserted control, taking a full minute to get the parts into the desired order. Then she murmured, "Will the disasters never end?"

She faced me. "I presume you can explain?"

"Explain what?"

She took ten seconds, eyes closed.

I prodded. "You engaged me to find and deliver to you, if possible, Amber daPena and Amiranda Crest. I've done half the job already."

She stared at me and hated me through narrowed eyelids. Her voice remained neutral, though, as she remarked, "I had hoped that you would deliver them in better health. She *is* dead? Not in a trance or ensorcelled?"

"Yes. Amiranda has been in poor health for some time now."

"Your attempts at wit become tiresome, Garrett. I suppose I can assume that you weren't the agent of death. I want to know the who, what, when, where, why, and how."

So did I.

My experiment had flopped. Domina Dount wasn't about to be flustered into giving anything away. If there was anything in her that I didn't already have.

"Well?" she demanded.

Why not? I might still shake something loose. "The day you were supposed to make the ransom payoff, Amiranda hired a friend of mine as her bodyguard. That night he accompanied her into the countryside north of TunFaire. She took several travel cases with her. She went to a crossroad near Lichfield, where she stopped. My friend thought she expected to meet somebody there and that he was supposed to have been dismissed when that somebody showed."

"Who?"

"I don't know. He, she, or it never came. A band of ogre breeds did instead. My friend killed some of them but he couldn't drive them off or keep them from killing Amiranda. He couldn't even save himself, though the ogres thought he was dead enough to throw into the bushes with Amiranda and the other casualties. When they scattered to keep from being seen by travelers, my friend found the strength to pick Amiranda up and carry her three miles to someone he knew who, he hoped, could save her."

"To no avail."

"Of course. My friend isn't very smart. He'd failed. He was outraged and his pride was hurt. Somehow, he got back to TunFaire, as far as the Bledsoe infirmary, where I got his story in the deathwatch ward."

Willa Dount frowned, uncertain why I'd told her what I had. "You've left something out, haven't you?"

"Yes."

"Why?"

"Because you don't need to know. Because no one needs to know except my friend's friends—some of them are the kind of guys who eat ogres for breakfast—who figure there's some balancing due for what got done."

You couldn't crack Willa Dount with a hammer. She looked at me straight in the eye and said, "That's why you've been digging around and poking your nose in."

"Yes."

"The Stormwarden resents people who pry into her family's affairs."

"I'll bet she resents people killing her kids even more." Me and my big damned mouth! I'd blown a potful for free there. But she didn't seem to notice.

"Maybe. But those who stick their noses in often become victims of deteriorating health."

I chuckled. "I'll keep that in mind. I'm sure my friend's friends will, too. They might even be so disturbed they'll give the problem enough attention to handle it before she gets home."

I'd abandoned the tactic of experimentation for the strategy of increasing the pressure on Willa Dount. Not that I had her fixed for anything, but she knew things *I* wanted to know. Maybe she would tell me some to get the heat off.

"How about you tell me the how, where, and when of the ransom payment?"

Domina Dount smiled a thin smile. "No, Mr. Garrett." She thought she was covered. If she had any need.

I shrugged. "So be it. Do you need a way to transport the body? I could send my man—"

"I came in a coach. That will do. I'll send my men in to get it."

"No you won't. You have the coach brought. I'll carry it out."

She smiled again. "Very well."

As I looked away from the coach, Domina Dount told me, "You will try to deliver Amber in better condition, won't you?"

I took a count of five, letting my irritation with her confidence in the power of her gold cool out. I kept reminding myself that it was just business. "I'll do my damnedest."

She climbed into her coach smiling, sure she'd taken the round by getting to me more than I'd gotten to her. I wasn't so sure she was wrong.

I went inside to see what the Dead Man thought of her.

The fat dead son of a bitch had slept through the whole damned thing.

finished a long cold one and wiped my lips. "I feel like killing the keg, but the night has only just begun. Tell Miss daPena the Domina has gone, but if she has the least sense and regard for her life, she won't even peek out a window. We may have reached a stage where people are cleaning up loose ends, real and imagined. I'm going to see Mr. Dotes. I'll slide out the back in case somebody is watching. You lock up tight. Don't answer the door unless you look first and see that it's me."

Dean scowled, but he'd been around long enough to have seen tight times before. He got out a meat cleaver and his favorite butcher knife, both sharp enough to take your leg off without you noticing. "Go on," he said. "I'll manage."

I went out thinking that someday I'd come home and find the house littered with dismembered burglars. Dean was the sort who would handle an invasion neither calmly nor with the minimum necessary force. Bruno and Courter Slauce were lucky that he'd been surprised and unarmed.

I didn't realize that I'd collected a tail until I was three-quarters of the way to Morley's place. It wasn't that I hadn't checked for one; he was that good. He was so good, in fact, that half a minute after I'd made him he knew it and didn't walk into either of the setups I laid to get a look at him.

I might as well have had a signed confession.

There are only three guys in TunFaire that good. Morley Dotes and I are two of them and Morley had no reason to skulk around behind me.

The other guy's name is Pokey Pigotta and he might even be better than we are. I've heard him accused of being half ghost.

Pokey is in the same line as me. Had Domina Dount hired him to keep an eye on her hired hand?

That seemed unlikely.

Who, then?

By then Pokey would have realized that I'd read his signature. He'd start trying to outguess me.

I resisted my impulse to play that game and call for him to join me. Silliness. Pokey Pigotta had conservative views of what constituted his obligations to a client.

To hell with it, I figured. I headed for Morley's place.

I went in the front door and straight around the bar. The surprised night barman just gawked as I shoved through the door to the kitchen. The rutabaga butchers stopped work and stared. I strolled through like a royal prince assessing the provincials. "Very good, my man. Very good. You. Let's have a little more thought to portion control. That whatever-it-is is sliced too thick."

I made it to the storeroom before the peasants rose and lynched me. The storeroom led me directly to the back door, which I used. I did a quick sprint down the alley and up the side lane to the corner in time to watch the front door swing shut behind Pokey.

Good.

He had decided that since I wasn't going to play games, he wasn't going to, either. He'd just trudge after me, not bothering to sneak. And that might suit his client fine, since it would inhibit my more surreptitious ventures.

I watched the door close and grinned, recapturing a view of the customers as I trotted through. It couldn't have been choreographed more beautifully.

"Suckered you, Pokey," I murmured, and ran for the door.

He had scanned the lay and turned to leave. He was a tall guy, without much meat on him—all bones and angles and skin so pale you'd have thought the breed half of him was vampire. He tended to make strangers very nervous.

"Sucked you in this time, Pokey." I peeked over his shoulder.

Saucerhead Tharpe was up and coming, hiding his infirmities well. I had no idea what the hell he was doing there but I was glad to see him.

Pokey shrugged. "I blew one."

"What you up to, Pokey?"

"You say something, Garrett? I been having trouble with my ears."

Saucerhead arrived. "What's up, Garrett?" Every eye in the place was on our get-together.

"Me and Pokey was just headed up to see Morley. I finally got a lead on those fellows you had the run-in with the other day. You're welcome to sit in." I gestured. Pokey surrendered to the inevitable, comfortably certain that I wanted nothing from him badly enough to make an enemy. I would have seen it the same if our roles had been reversed.

I followed Pokey. Saucerhead followed me. All eyes followed us up the stairs. Morley, of course, was expecting us.

"So what do you want to do with him?" Morley asked.

"Since he won't want to say why he's dogging me or who's paying him, I don't know whether to let him tag along or not. So, better safe than sorry. He's got to go into storage."

"How long?"

"A day, maybe."

"Pokey?"

"Sitting or following, it all pays the same."

Morley thought for half a minute, then told one of his boys, "Blood, you want to politely collect Mr. Pigotta's effects and put them on the table here?"

Pokey endured it.

I knew how he felt. I'd been through it several times myself.

Morley stirred through the take, which included a lot of silver. He examined one piece. "Temple coinage."

I took one. Private mintage, all right. The same as the tenth mark I found on that farm.

"Tell you something?" Morley asked.

"Yeah. Who he isn't working for." Domina Dount never had anything but gold.

So who?

"Put him away," I told Morley. "There's things to talk about and decide and maybe do, and it's late already."

"Blood. The root cellar. Gently and politely. Consider him a guest under restraint."

"Yes, Mr. Dotes."

31

Morley removed his troops from the room. With just two witnesses Saucerhead relaxed and betrayed how uncomfortable he really was. I spent a minute or two telling him what a dope he was. He didn't argue. He didn't go home to bed, either.

Morley told me, "Only thing my boys have told me that you probably don't know is that Junior daPena's body got taken to the crematorium by the Dount woman on her way over to your place. I assume you know he did himself in?"

"I know. Only he didn't kill himself. He had a lot of help from his friends."

"You have that gleam in your eye, Garrett. Does that mean you know who did it?"

"Yep. And one of them was an ogre breed named Skredli, and it just happened that a Skredli was involved in Junior's so-called kidnapping—and most likely in the attack on Saucerhead and Amiranda. And this Skredli runs with a character named Gorgeous, who sounds like he's some double-ugly . . . What's up, Morley?"

"Gorgeous? You did say Gorgeous?"

"Yeah. You know him?"

"Not personally. I know of him."

"I don't like that look in *your* eye."

"Then look at the wall or something while you tell us about it."

While I talked, Saucerhead sat nodding to himself. I pretty much opened the bag and dumped it. Morley got out paper and pen and ink and started doodling.

When I closed the sack up, Morley said, "The Donni Pell trick is like the hub of a wheel. You have connections between her and everyone but the Dount woman. You can't tell about the Crest woman, but you can assume she knew who Donni was since she was good friends with Junior. This Donni is the key. Let's see if we can't lay hands on her."

I exchanged looks with Saucerhead. "The man is a genius, isn't he? Think he's figured out that she's the next one who'll come floating belly-up? If the hard boys are nervous enough to cut the son of Raver Styx . . ."

Morley said, "I think the next casualty will be a guy called Gorgeous. Though maybe I'm wrong." He still had that look.

"Why?" Saucerhead asked. Always direct, friend Waldo.

"Tell me about Gorgeous. I've never heard of him."

"You ought to keep up better, Garrett. He's important."

"I'm trying. If you'll get to it."

"Sure. He hasn't been around long. His real name is Conrad Staley. He came from HasefBro after the kingpin checked out, figuring it was a good time to cut himself a piece of the big city. He's human but he's so damned mean and ugly he ranks with ogres. He brought his own gang to start but I hear most have gone back since he's found local recruits. Keeping the old base secure. There was a hot feud for a while with Chodo Contague but they sorted it out. Gorgeous got Ogre Town. He pays a percentage to keep it in peace. Chodo doesn't want a war because he's having trouble keeping his own people in line."

Chodo Contague was the thug who had taken over as kingpin after the old kingpin's demise. He was more powerful than most of the lords of the Hill, though he lived in the shadows.

"Anything we do that involves Gorgeous, Chodo is going to have to approve." Morley was moving toward the door now. "It could mean war. You guys sit tight. If you need anything, tell them downstairs. I'll be back in a couple hours."

"Where the hell are you going?" I asked.

"To talk to Chodo." He was out.

"You wondering what I'm wondering, Garrett?"

"I'm not wondering, Saucerhead. I know."

Chodo Contague was boss of the TunFaire underworld in part because a certain Morley Dotes had presented the old kingpin with a coffin containing a hungry vampire. The old kingpin had opened the box thinking the thing inside had been killed before delivery. Saucerhead and I had been pallbearers in that shenanigan. Our buddy Morley hadn't bothered to tell us what was going down beforehand.

His reason for the oversight was sound. He had figured we wouldn't help if we knew.

The perceptive little bastard had been right.

I was going to collect favors on that scam for a long time.

"He's in debt again, Saucerhead. The bug races again. But I don't want to try Ogre Town alone, so let him play his game. I'm not going to sit around here waiting for him, though. If I have to kill a couple hours, I'll do it getting something useful done."

Saucerhead just looked at me, a big, tired guy who had been pushing himself too hard. I knew that if we ended up going after Gorgeous—as I would do, one way or another—Saucerhead would go along if he had to drag himself. "You might as well get some sleep. See you in a couple."

I got scowls downstairs but nobody stopped me.

I went to Playmate's and pounded around until he got out of bed. He never
stopped grumbling and cussing, but he got out the wagon and hitched
up a team. He even managed the obligatory refusals when I tried to pay
him, though he did end up accepting the money. As he always does. He
needs it, no matter how much he pretends.

The Larkin crematorium was one mile away. I pushed, though there was
no real need. Junior's body had been delivered late, if I'd heard Morley right,
so it wouldn't have been sent to the oven yet. That wasn't permitted at night.
Religious and secular law both forbid cremation during the hours of darkness. A soul freed during that time would be condemned to walk the night
forever.

There are only three crematoriums in TunFaire. I was sure Junior was at
the Larkin place because it was convenient for anyone coming to my home
from the Stormwarden's. And the night porter wasn't an honest man.

The world is cancerous with people possessed; some have to vent their
sicknesses on the dead and others have to pander to them.

I pulled the wagon into an alley near the crematorium and left the team
bound in a spell woven of the direst threats I could conjure. At least I got
their attention.

I did it the way I'd heard it was done, going to the side entrance, tapping
a code, and waiting while I was examined through some hidden peephole.

The door opened. I had to grit my teeth to keep from laughing or groaning. The night porter was a character straight out of graveyard spook stories,

a hunchback ratman so ugly I suspected his beauty would undershine that of the creature Gorgeous. Hopefully before the night was done I'd have the opportunity to compare.

If there was a password I didn't know it and he didn't care. I showed him a gold piece and he showed me the room where the bodies were laid out. Like the old joke, people had been dying to get in. Seven of the ten slabs were occupied by the anxiously waiting dead.

Ratman was a born salesman. He lifted a sheet. "This here's the best we got. And you're the only customer tonight." He snickered.

The girl was about fourteen. There was no obvious cause of death.

"She might even be a virgin."

It was one of those times when you want to break bones, but for business reasons you put your feelings on ice and smile, I stepped past him and lifted a sheet at the head of a corpse that looked the right size. Not my man.

Second time was the charm.

"This one. How much to take him with me?"

I've never been looked at like that before and hope never to be again. I saw he was going to argue, so I laid a ten-mark gold piece on an empty slab. I doubt he'd ever seen one before.

Greed touched those hideous features. But caution was just a step behind. "That one came off the Hill, mister. You don't want to mess with it."

"You're right. I don't want to mess with it. I want to buy it."

"But . . . why?"

"For a keepsake. I'm going to have the head shrunk and wear it for an earring."

"Mister, I told you, that one's off the Hill. People are going to come for the ashes."

"Give them ashes. How many of these are city projects?" TunFaire has a pork-barrel ordinance requiring unclaimed, found, and paupers' corpses to be distributed in rotation among the dozen mortuary businesses, paid for out of the public purse. It's a racket that accounts for the majority of each business's income. Most families just bury their dead in the nearest churchyard.

"Four. But I'd have to bring the boss in—"

"How much?" He wouldn't be doing his business without the silent approval of his employer. "Without being greedy. I could just take it and leave you in its place." It was a definite temptation.

The ratman gulped. "Twenty marks."

"There's ten. Ten more when I have it loaded. I'll be back in a minute."

He might have taken his chances and locked me out, but that was unlikely while ten more marks were afloat.

He gobbled some but I ignored him. Ten minutes later I had what was left of Junior daPena installed in the wagon. I faced the hunchback, gold in hand. "The same people will bring another one today. Unless they insist on watching the job, I want that one, too. It'll be female. The gods help you if it's touched. Do you understand?"

He gulped.

"Do you understand?"

"Yes sir. Yes sir." Cautiously, he reached for the gold.

I avoided his touch when I let him have it.

Dean answered on the second knock. He was dressed. "Haven't you been to bed?"

"Couldn't sleep. What is this? Are you collecting bodies now, Mr. Garrett?"

"Just a few that might be useful. I'm taking it into the Dead Man's room. Get the doors for me. If he wakes up and wants to know about it, tell him it was Junior daPena and I'm saving him for his mother."

Dean turned green but handled his part. The corpse settled, a little shaky. I returned to the kitchen and put away a couple quarts of beer before leaving.

"You're off again, Mr. Garrett?"

"The night's work isn't done."

"Won't be night all that much longer."

He was right. The light would soon make its presence known.

beat Morley back to his place, but barely in time to wake Saucerhead. Then Dotes came with his men—Blood, Sarge, and the Puddle. He also had two other guys in tow. I didn't know them personally and didn't care to get acquainted. Because I knew who they were: Crask and Sadler, Chodo Contague's first-string life takers. They had been born human. Since then they'd been embalmed and turned into zombies without the nuisance of dying first.

"What the hell are those guys doing here?" I snapped. It didn't help that they seemed equally pleased to see me and Saucerhead.

Morley was up to his old tricks.

"Calm down, Garrett. Unless you want to go after Gorgeous by your lonesome."

I bit my tongue.

Morley said, "This is the way it's got to be, Garrett. Gorgeous holes up in Ogre Town. He's got those people buffaloed down there. But they won't lift a finger if he suddenly turns up missing. Him and his number-one boy Skredli. You want him. Chodo wants him. Chodo will back your play as long as you're the face out front. But he wants first crack at them once they're rounded up. You give him a list of questions you want asked, he'll get the answers."

"Wonderful. Thoroughly wonderful, Morley." I was hot. So hot I didn't trust myself to say anything else. Morley met my gaze evenly, shrugged. I got the message but I didn't have to like it.

Saucerhead was steamed, too, but he covered it better. He rose, laced his fingers, and bent them back until the knuckles cracked. "You got to live with what you got to live with. Let's do it while they're still asleep." He headed for the door.

"Wait!" Morley said. "This isn't a stroll in the woods with your girlfriend." He stepped behind his desk and fiddled with something. Part of the wall opened, exposing the biggest damned collection of deadly instruments I've seen since I parted with the Marines.

Saucerhead looked at the arsenal and shook his head. It wasn't a shake of refusal, but of astonishment. He joined Morley's thugs in stocking up. Crask and Sadler had brought their own. I had, too, and thought I was adequately outfitted. Morley's scowl told me he saw it otherwise. I selected one knife long enough to be a baby sword and another prissy little thing of the sort ladies (who aren't) carry on their garters. Morley didn't stop scowling but didn't comment, either.

I preferred my head knocker for all but the most desperate situations. And for those I had what the witch had given me.

We trooped downstairs, Morley's boys in the lead, Chodo's headhunters behind. Speculative eyes observed our descent and pursuit of the pathway I'd used on Pokey earlier. But at that hour there were few customers left and most of those were beholden to Morley. There should be no rumors born soon or messages run.

The barman beckoned Morley as we passed. Dotes stopped to trade whispers. He caught up at the door to the alley. "That was the latest from the river. The Stormwarden's boat was spotted at dusk twenty miles down tying up for the night."

"Then she'll be here tomorrow afternoon."

"Late, I'd guess. The winds are unfavorable."

It was something to think about. I didn't have enough to ruminate already.

The alley was filled with the huge black hulk of a four-horse closed coach. And two gargantuan characters with shiny eyes and sparkly fangs grinned down from twenty feet. "Hi, guys."

They were grolls—half troll, half giant, green by daylight, all mean, and tougher than a herd of thunder lizards. I knew these two. They were two-thirds of triplets who had gone with me into the Cantard to bring out a woman who had inherited a bundle. Despite what we had been through together, I hadn't the slightest notion whether or not I dared trust them.

They had been cursed with unlikely names, Doris and Marsha.

"A little of what I call ally insurance," Morley told me. "You think I'm a raving moron for bringing Chodo in?"

"No. I think you think it'll get you out from under your debts. I hope you're right."

"You're a cynical and suspicious character, Garrett."

"It's people like you who make me that way."

Morley's troops were inside the coach and Saucerhead was clambering aboard. Crask and Sadler were up on the guard's and driver's seats, donning the traditional tall hats and dark cloaks. Each man had immediate access to a pair of powerful, ready crossbows.

Such items are necessary on TunFaire's night streets if you're rich enough to use a coach but not powerful enough to have its doors blazoned with the arms of someone like a stormwarden.

Most high-class folk travel with outriders. We made do with a pair of grolls toting their favorite toys, head-bashers twelve feet long and almost too heavy for a runt like me to lift.

Morley followed me into the coach, then leaned out and told Crask to go. The vehicle jerked into motion.

"I suppose you've made a plan?" I said.

"It's all scoped out. That was one of the reasons I brought Chodo in. His boys know Gorgeous's place. I've never seen it. And neither have you."

I grunted. The rest of the ride passed in silence.

34

Ogre Town was quieter than death at that hour. There seems to be a cultural imperative that sends them to bed very late and brings them out in the afternoon. We were going in soon after most ogres had sacked out. The streets weren't entirely deserted, but it made little difference. Those who were out were scavengers. They made a point of being blind to our presence.

Twelve hours earlier or later we might have been in trouble. The streets would have featured a more treacherous cast.

We swung into a passage between buildings just wide enough for the coach, then continued until we could open the doors. Crask told us to disembark. We tumbled out. He backed the coach into the passage again so we could gather in the shadows, off the street.

"That's the place." Morley indicated a four-story vertical rectangle a hundred yards down the street. "The whole thing belongs to Gorgeous. He had the buildings on either side demolished so nobody could get to him that way. We're going after him that way."

"Wonderful." Light still shone in a couple windows on the top two floors. "You're a genius."

The buildings in Ogre Town are fifty to a hundred years older than the tenements in Fishwife's Close. In many cases that showed. But they had built in brick and stone in those days and Gorgeous's citadel had been kept up. It didn't need to lean on neighbors to remain standing.

There was a ghost of a promise of dawn.

Morley said, "Doris and Marsha are going to climb the buildings on either side. They'll drop ropes. Me, Crask, Blood, and Sarge will go up top the nearer one. The rest up the other. After we get our wind . . ." He droned on with the plan.

"It sucks," I told him.

"You want to march in the front door and fight your way to the top?"

"No. Hell, if I didn't have questions to ask, I'd just go start a fire on the ground floor. Ought to go up that thing like smoke up a chimney."

"But you do want to ask questions. Ready? So let's go." Doris and Marsha were already gone, not bothering to wait out my protests.

We were halfway there when the man came out the front door. His hands were shoved in his pockets and he was looking down. He was human, not ogre. He walked fifty feet toward us before he realized he wasn't alone. He halted, looked at us, and his eyes bugged.

"Bruno," I hissed.

He whirled and headed for the building.

Sadler's crossbow twanged.

It was a damned good try for a snap shot. I think it clipped Bruno's left arm. He veered right and headed up the street, concentrating on speed.

"Let him go. I'll hunt him down later," I said. "He has some answers I need."

While I talked, Crask sped a bolt that split Bruno's spine three inches below his neck. Sadler reached him seconds later and dragged the twitching body into the nearest shadows.

"Thanks a bunch," I snarled.

Crask didn't bother turning that embalmed face my way.

Doris and Marsha reached the roofs of their respective structures. They anchored ropes and dropped them. Inside Gorgeous's place the lights were dying. Saucerhead and I stood at the foot of the rope. "You going to make it?" I asked.

"You worry about yourself, Garrett. Ain't nothing going to stop me now." He started climbing. I held the rope taut. Saucerhead went up like he was seventeen and had never been hurt in his life. Sadler followed with not one but two crossbows slung on his back, then the Puddle. Lucky Garrett got to do it with no one to tauten the rope.

When I reached the roof, I found that Marsha had already leaped to Gorgeous's roof. Saucerhead was tying off the rope the groll had tossed back. Sadler was leaning on the chimney that anchored both ropes, sight-

ing one crossbow on the top-floor window. Light still leaked through its
shutters.

I wondered if Marsha's rooftop landing had been heard below. I didn't
see how Gorgeous could help but be forewarned with nearly two tons of
groll prancing over his head.

Puddle joined Marsha. Saucerhead and I followed. I pretended the void
below was really just water a foot beneath my dangling toes.

The pretense didn't help.

Sadler stayed where he was. He untied the rope so Marsha could haul it
across and resumed his lethal posture.

Marsha bent one end of the rope into a harness for me. As I got into it I
wondered what was wrong with Gorgeous and his boys. Were they deaf? Or
just chuckling as they got a little surprise ready for us?

I was going to find out all too quickly.

There was enough light now to see Morley getting into a similar rig.
Doris hoisted him and dangled him over the side.

The universe twisted. An abyss appeared beneath me. I turned at the end
of the rope, glimpsing Sadler aiming too close for contentment.

Marsha swung me in against the brick, then over to peek through the
cracks in the shutter.

At first I saw nothing. No ambush evidence, no excitement, nobody. Just
an empty room. Then an ugly someone opened a door and shoved his face
into the room and said something I couldn't hear to someone I couldn't see.
The back of the other someone appeared momentarily as he followed the
ugly someone out the door. The set of his shoulders said he was aggravated.

I waved. Saucerhead tied the rope to something. They left me hanging.

Evidently the report from the far side was favorable, too. Marsha leaned
over the edge and let go a mighty bash with his club. A second later he lowered Saucerhead at the end of a mile of arm and flipped him through the
window. Saucerhead grabbed me and dragged me inside. Puddle came
through an instant later.

The room was uninhabited except for the insect life infesting the stack
of bunk beds. Saucerhead and Puddle headed for the door while I battled
ropes like a moth in a spiderweb. There was one hell of a racket going on
somewhere else.

A guy came charging through the doorway just as Saucerhead got there.
His nose and Saucerhead's fist collided. No contest. The ogre's eyes rolled
up. Saucerhead thumped him again as he went down, just for spite.

I got loose and charged after Saucerhead and Puddle, into a narrow hallway that dead-ended to our left. As we turned right a couple of breeds popped out of another bunk-room doorway. They were no more fortunate than their predecessor. Saucerhead was in one of those moods.

In the meantime, heaven put on its dancing shoes and began hoofing it on the roof. The grolls were pounding away with their clubs.

The racket elsewhere revealed itself as a lopsided battle between Morley's crew and Gorgeous and about ten breeds. Several more ogres were down, with quarrels in them, and as we came to the rescue yet another made the mistake of stepping in front of the window. He squealed like a throat-cut hog as he fell. The bolt had gotten the meat of his thigh. Poisoned? Probably.

Being a nice guy, I just whapped a couple of heads with my stick instead of stabbing backs with Puddle. Saucerhead threw ogres around the way us ordinary mortals might work through a pack of house cats. Holes appeared in the ceiling as the grolls kept pounding away, their blows so powerful they smashed through two-by-ten oak ceiling joists.

Our rear attack turned the tide. Suddenly, the numbers were ours.

Gorgeous made a run for the stairs. I flung a foot out and got enough of his ankle to unbalance him. His momentum pitched him into the door-frame.

The fight seemed over but it wasn't yet won. Ogres are tough and stubborn. A few were still upright.

Morley's boys left them to us and went to work finishing the ones who were down. I yelled a complaint that got ignored.

I'd gotten through the worst without a scratch. The others had a few dings and small cuts, except Sarge, who had collected a rib-deep slash across the chest and had taken himself out of the action to tend it.

"Not that one!" Saucerhead roared at Puddle. "You save that one for me." He slammed the last upright ogre into unconsciousness, then explained, "That's the one that was in charge when they killed the girl."

Panting, I asked, "You see any others that were there?"

"Just him." He dragged his ogre out of the mess.

Morley said, "That's the one called Skredli."

I'd suspected as much.

For several minutes there had been considerable racket downstairs. Now Gorgeous levered himself up and roared. Morley and I jumped on him, too late to shut him up.

The stairs drummed to stamping feet.

An ogre stampede arrived.

There must have been twenty in the first rush. They pushed us across the room, into the far wall. Grolls hammering heads from above scarcely slowed them.

And more kept coming.

Sarge couldn't defend himself adequately. Puddle went down. I thought Morley was a goner. It looked grim for the rest of us. Gorgeous shrieked hysterical, bloodthirsty orders.

It was time for something desperate.

dropped the witch's gift and stomped on it. The crystal shattered. I followed instructions and covered my eyes, taking several vicious blows as
a result. A thread of fire sliced the outside of my left upper arm.

Hell called the proceedings to disorder.

I opened my eyes. The mob bawled like cows in a panic, flailed wildly,
purposelessly. Some howled and clung to the floor. I danced away from the
nearer crazies and unlimbered my head knocker.

According to the witch, they were seeing three of everything and their
universe was revolving. But that didn't make them easy meat. There were so
many of them flailing around. . . .

I watched Gorgeous bang into the wall three times trying to get to the
stairs. I tried to reach him before he got away. My luck ran its usual taunting
course. I was two ogres short of getting him when he made it out. He went
tumbling downstairs, caterwauling in pain and fear.

I wanted that man bad, but not bad enough to abandon friends to fate.
I returned to my harvest.

I took a few whacks myself getting the mob done, but lay them low I did.
Morley, I saw, had survived after all. He leaned against a wall, pale as death.
Saucerhead stood with feet widespread, grinning a big goofy grin. The
grolls, who had caught just the edge of the spell, looked in through the ceiling and grinned, too. They had helped with the head knocking. Morley's
man Blood sat in a corner puking his guts up. Sarge and Puddle were somewhere under the mess.

We all needed patching up.

I stumbled to the window.

It was light out now. And there were sounds outside. People sounds. Ogre Town folks were awake and interested.

It was time to pick up our toys and get out.

"Shut your eyes, you dopes," I told everybody. "Get your hands on the wall and follow it around to the door to the stairwell. Wait for me there."

"What the hell did you have up your sleeve this time, Garrett?" Morley asked in a voice pitched an octave too high. He gagged as he fought to avoid upchucking from the vertigo.

"None of your damned business. Just be glad I had it, you tactical genius. Come on. Get over by the door while I find Puddle and Sarge and Skredli."

An ogre groaned. I gave him a tap on the noggin. There would be plenty of headaches later.

I found Skredli first, dragged him over, and gave him to Saucerhead. Sarge turned up next. "Morley, Sarge checked out. You want to take him home?"

"What for? Hurry up. I smell smoke."

So did I. I started digging for Puddle.

"Oh, hell," Morley said. "What would I tell my guys if I left somebody behind? They'd tell me I was no better than these ogres." He babbled to the grolls in their tongue. They jabbered back. He told me, "Shove Sarge up where Doris can get ahold of him. And hurry. They say there's a mob shaping up. Crask and Sadler have been shooting the boys down when they run out the front door."

I found Puddle. He was alive, and would make it with help. I got him to Morley. "I'm going down first. You guys come as fast as you can." I bounded down the stairs.

Noises rose to greet me. It sounded like somebody dragging himself. . . .

I overtook Gorgeous on the second-floor landing as he was getting ready to head down the last flight. But to catch him I had to jump the fire he had started halfway to the third floor.

He had a broken leg. He wasn't seeing more than double now, and nearly stuck me before I bopped him. I checked for other enemies. The only ones left upright were down at the front door, three or four just inside, arguing about how they were going to get out. That door was the only ground-floor exit. Anybody who used it ran into a crossbow bolt.

I hustled back to help the others past the fire. It was growing, but we managed. Only Morley got singed. I couldn't restrain a chuckle at his pathetic appearance. He's one of those guys who spends hours on his appearance.

The problem of the ogres below solved itself. I went after them behind a bloodthirsty shriek, brandishing my knives, and they flushed like a covey of quail, hitting the street.

Now we'd learn the value of Morley's ally insurance.

I stuck my head out.

No bolt greeted me.

I stepped out carefully, looked around, frowned. What had become of the mob? I saw no one but the flying ogres and the grolls, who had clambered down the outside of the building.

The coach came pounding out of its alley, swung in, and stopped. Crask growled, "Get them in here! There's soldiers coming."

Troops? No wonder the streets were empty.

We tumbled inside, piling on the coach floor. Crask and Sadler took off before we sorted ourselves out. The grolls loped ahead, scouting.

I got myself seated. "This is weird, Morley. They don't call out the troops for squabbles in Ogre Town."

The coach thundered through alleys that *had* to be too narrow, around corners that *had* to be too tight. Whatever faults the boys up top had, lack of guts was not among them.

Morley grunted in response to my remark.

"They only come out for riots. And there's maybe only eight or ten people who can deploy them."

Morley grunted again. "You figure it out, Garrett. Right now I don't give a damn." He was in pain.

If Bruno hadn't gone down . . . Bruno was off the Hill. Bruno had been visiting Gorgeous. It took a lord from the Hill to order out the army. Maybe Bruno worked for somebody who thought enough of Gorgeous to call out the troops to save him.

The whole affair began to tilt in my head. Maybe Bruno and a few facts I'd ignored needed reexamining. "I've got to find out who he worked for."

Nobody bothered to ask what I was muttering about.

A frightening notion had crept into my mind. Perhaps Junior daPena, his family, and his keeper, were innocent of bloodletting.

The coach careened onto a major street, scattering pedestrians, drawing curses from the other drivers. Around another corner. Then a slowdown to become just another vehicle in the morning flow. I never saw a soldier. Five minutes later we halted behind Morley's place. Sadler growled at us to get the hell out.

I was exhausted and hurt and about as tired as I could get of someone else taking control of what I had started.

"Easy, Garrett," Morley said. "Keep your mouth shut and get inside."

"Stuff it, Morley. I've had it."

"Do what I tell you. It'll improve your long-term health picture." He grabbed me and, with help from Saucerhead, got me through the back door. I was more amenable once I noted that our ally insurance had vanished.

Morley had Saucerhead help get his men inside. Sadler crawled into the coach to babysit Gorgeous and Skredli. The coach rolled.

Morley suggested, "Why don't you go upstairs and make a list of questions you want asked? I'll have a messenger run it. Then go home and sleep. You'll feel more reasonable afterward."

I supposed if Saucerhead could endure not getting first crack at Skredli, I could live without an immediate shot at Gorgeous. "All right." But I had a feeling I wasn't going to get a lot of rest.

On the way upstairs I glanced out a window toward Ogre Town. A pillar of smoke stood like a gravestone over a ferocious fire. Maybe most of our grim handiwork would be erased, thanks to Gorgeous.

The last thing I needed was to get labeled a tool of the kingpin.

I made my list, pointless exercise that it was. The tricky part was wording questions about two hundred thousand marks gold so that my stand-in would not realize what he was asking and gleefully begin interrogating in his own cause. I solved the problem by mostly avoiding it and entering a plea for direct access to the boys, and maybe even possession of that trifle Skredli.

That done, I went back downstairs, where the survivors were getting patched up and trying to eat breakfast. I was so far gone I didn't comment on the platter they brought me, I just gulped a quart of fruit juice and stuffed my face.

I asked, "Saucerhead, you got anything left? I've got something I want you to do." After I finished with him, I cornered Morley and talked him into turning the tables on Pokey Pigotta. If we let him go and shadowed him he might lead us to some interesting places—if he didn't lead us into deep trouble first.

mber and Dean were in the kitchen when I got home. I went in and collapsed into a chair. Saucerhead thought my example so outstanding he copied it. Dean and Amber stared at us.

"Was it a difficult night, Mr. Garrett?" Dean asked.

"You might say. If you care to understate."

"You look like hell," Amber said. "Whatever it was, I hope it was worth it."

"Maybe. We caught up with the people who killed your brother and Amiranda."

I watched her carefully. She responded the way I had hoped, with no sign of panic or guilt. "You got them? What did you do? Did you find out anything about the ransom?"

"We got them. You don't want to know anything more. I didn't find out anything about the money, but I didn't have a chance. I'm still working on it. How well could you manage if you had a thousand marks to start your new life?"

"Pretty damn good. My needs are simple. You're up to something, Garrett. Spill it."

Dean muttered, "Been around him too long already. Starting to talk like him."

"I love you, too, Dean. Amber, Domina offered me a thousand marks if I could find you and turn you over to her before your mother gets home. I've had word that she'll get here this afternoon. If you want the money, I'll take you home around noon and my friend here will stay with you till you're convinced you're safe."

She eyed me through narrowed lids. "What's your angle, Garrett?" The girl could think when she felt the urge.

"Willa Dount. She knows things she won't tell me. There aren't any sanctions I can threaten to pry them out of her. All I can do is find ways to put the heat on and hope she does something interesting."

"What about the ransom, Garrett? That's what we're supposed to be working on." Her eyes remained narrowed.

"I don't think there's much chance of getting it. Do you? Really? With your mother home?"

"Probably not. But you don't act like you're trying."

Saucerhead began working on a breakfast Dean had offered him. I gawked. He was putting it away like he hadn't eaten in weeks, despite having just eaten at Morley's. But rabbit food will do that.

"Domina offered you that money last night? And you didn't grab it?"

"No." Dean was pouring apple juice. I realized I was dry all the way down to my corns. "Give me about a gallon." Nothing like a good tense situation to sweat you out.

Saucerhead grunted agreement around a mouthful.

"It isn't the money, is it, Garrett?" demanded Amber.

Saucerhead tittered.

"What's with you, oaf?"

"She figured you out, Garrett." He chuckled. "You're right, little girl. With Garrett it's almost never the money."

"You want to talk, Waldo? How rich do you figure on getting in this?"

He gave the name a black look, then shrugged. "There's just some things you got to make right."

Amber knew we meant much more than we said. She scowled. "If you can be noble, so can I. I'll go home. But cut it close. All right?"

"All right."

"What will you do now?"

"Get some sleep. It's been awhile since I've had any."

"Sleep? How can you sleep in the middle of everything?"

"Easy. I lie down and close my eyes. If you want to stay busy and vent some nervous energy, remember everything you can about Karl's friend Donni Pell."

"Why?"

"Because she looks like the common denominator in every angle of what's been happening. Because I want to find her bad."

I had a notion adding Donni Pell might even explain the marvelous appearance of troops in Ogre Town.

My guess was that with Gorgeous and Skredli out of the equation, she stood a chance of surviving long enough to be found and questioned. I hoped she hadn't suffered a sudden and uncharacteristic seizure of smarts and wagged her manipulating tail out of town.

I drank apple juice until I was bloated, then rose. "That's it. I'm putting myself on the shelf. Wake me up at noon, Dean. I've got to go rob a crypt before I sell Miss daPena into fetters. Saucerhead, you can sack out in the room Dean uses."

Dean grumbled and muttered what sounded like threats to revive his interest in finding me a wife among his female kin. I ignored him. He wouldn't learn, and I was too tired to fight.

37

Dean didn't wake me as instructed. Amber pirated that chore with a half-hour head start. The brief rest hadn't been enough to restore my resistance. I fear I succumbed.

Amber wasn't a disappointment.

When I ventured into the kitchen, I realized Dean had found his missing scowl mask. It was as ferocious as ever. He has pretensions to gentility, though, so he said nothing. I devoured a few sausages and hit the street.

I listened to the talk around Playmate's place, where the old men hang out. They had a dozen theories about what had happened in Ogre Town. Some were as crazy as the truth, but none were correct.

Collecting Amiranda's corpse was cut and dried. I paid, they delivered, I drove it home, and Dean helped me lug it into the Dead Man's room.

Have you taken up a new hobby, Garrett?

He was awake. I'd thought I might have to start a fire to get his attention.

Or are you getting into a new line?

"Once in a while I like to have somebody around who doesn't get temperamental."

Dean tells me you have been having adventures.

"Yes. And if you'd stay awake and do a little work, I'd have a lot fewer." I brought him up to date.

At last you have begun to understand that several things are happening at once. I am proud of you, Garrett. You have begun to think. I wondered how long you would discount the repeated appearances of the Bruno person. Particularly in view of your first collected fact having been that the younger Karl left his house to investigate a pilferage problem that the Dount woman suggested might have another Hill family at its root.

"You figured there might be a connection, eh?"

Of course.

"But you didn't bother to mention it."

You have become too dependent upon me. You need to exercise your brain yourself.

"The reason you're here at all is so I don't have to strain my brain. We humans are born bone lazy. Remember? With innate ambition and energy levels only slightly above those of a dead Loghyr."

Do not make a special effort to irritate me, Garrett. You have done adequately with your collection of corpses and your parade of frenzied females. If you have a question you cannot handle yourself, spit it out. Otherwise, relocate yourself in some demesne where the mentality is sufficiently naive to appreciate your wit.

"All right, genius. Answer me this. Who killed Amiranda Crest? Is that something else you've been holding back, waiting for me to get my head bashed in while I tried to find out the hard way?"

I suppose you mean do I know who gave the order that resulted in Miss Crest's death at the hand of the ogre breed Skredli and his henchmen?

"To be precise."

We must be precise, Garrett. An intelligent mind is not ambiguous.

I could have talked about that for hours, but I resisted. "Do you know who's responsible?"

No.

"Do you know why?"

Chances are if we knew that, we would know who as well, Garrett. I can render at least three plausibilities immediately, though I will discount the pregnancy as motive till such time as you produce evidence that she told someone. She did not tell you except by the most ambiguous implication, and young women empty the darkest corners of their souls into your ears.

"You know, with two marks and all the help you've given me I could buy a barrel of beer."

Find Donni Pell. Bring her to me. Find out who Bruno's master was. Look for any connections with the daPena family. Look into the pilferage at the daPena warehouse. It might open new avenues. Now begone. I cannot endure your vexatious importunities any longer.

"Right. I'll just conjure the Pell woman out of thin air."

You will not learn anything sitting here drinking beer.

"You have a point, I admit. But before I fare forth to keep my date with destiny, how about you clue me in on how Glory Mooncalled manages his magic show. Or hasn't the hypothesis withstood the test of time?"

The hypothesis has stood quite well, Garrett. But not enough time has passed to set it in concrete. I should not risk contradiction by events, but I will present you with the key. Glory Mooncalled has not found the secret of prolonged invisibility. He has invented invisibility by treaty. When you cannot escape the seeing eye, you convince the eye that blindness is in its own best interest. Begone. Take your tart back to her family.

"You ready to go?" I asked Saucerhead. I didn't have to ask Amber because I knew she wasn't—either emotionally or intellectually. She was scared to death. But for the thousand marks she would give it a shot.

Saucerhead grunted and got to his feet slowly. His exertions of the night before were exacting their price. I hoped he hadn't drawn too heavily on his reserves. Even the most stubborn will has its final limit.

"Let's do it, Garrett," Amber said.

Bitter Gold Hearts · 373

●●●**38**

Courter Slauce himself was on the daPena gate. He looked grim, still showing the effects of his carouse. I supposed he was being punished. He stared at me with a mixture of anger and uncertainty. I said, "Tell Domina Dount I'm out here with the other package she ordered."

He eyed Amber and Saucerhead, frowned puzzledly, as if a memory ghost were slithering around somewhere behind his eyes, too elusive to catch.

"You can go on in to her office. She left standing orders to the gate."

"Uh-uh. Not that I don't trust her, but you know how it is. There's a payment due, and if she brings it down here, chances are a lot better that I'll actually get it."

That look again. I had a feeling the Dead Man hadn't done as good a job as he thought. Some of Slauce's memories might return.

"Have it your way." He called to somebody in the court, told them to get Willa Dount and why. When he turned to us again, he was frowning, straining after that fugitive memory.

I figured I could distract him and find out something at the same time. I described Bruno and asked if he knew the man.

Slauce was more cooperative than I expected. "The guy sounds vaguely familiar. But I can't pin a name on him. Why?"

"I thought he might be connected with that pilferage problem you people were having at your warehouse. I don't know. Just something I heard. I don't know who he is, either, except he's supposed to be from up here somewhere. He had a job like yours, they say."

Slauce shook his head, trying to clear the cobwebs. Amber and Saucerhead both stared at me, wondering what the hell I was up to.

Just stirring the pot, friends. With the Stormwarden on the horizon, looming like a grandmother tornado, anything was likely to panic somebody and break something loose.

But not from Courter Slauce. He just stood there with a dumb look, trying to get both oars in the water.

Domina Dount came stomping across the courtyard wearing that contrived and controlled face that had become so familiar. "Garrett comes through again," I told her.

She glared at Amber so fiercely the girl stepped behind Saucerhead. "It's about time."

"It took more doing than you think."

"Get in here, Amber. Go to your suite."

Amber didn't come out of hiding.

I said, "There's a fee due."

"Yes. Of course. You're a parasite, Garrett."

"Absolutely. But unlike the ruling-class sort of parasite, I relieve pain instead of creating it." I winked, grinned. "Is the honeymoon over?"

She almost smiled back. "In about a minute." She produced several fat doeskin bags. I let her plunk their weight into my folded arms, then turned.

Amber came out of hiding, took a sack, counted out Saucerhead's fee, whispered, "You take care of this, Garrett. I'll pick it up as soon as I get away from my mother."

I lent her only enough ear to follow what she said. I asked Domina Dount, "Just as a matter of personal curiosity, did you ever tie the knot on that warehouse trouble?"

"Warehouse trouble?"

"Back when you first called me out here, you told me the younger Karl disappeared after you sent him out to check on a pilferage problem. I just wondered if you'd put the wraps on that yet."

"I haven't had time to worry about it, Mr. Garrett."

Amber and Saucerhead pushed past us while we talked. The Domina realized that Saucerhead was going inside.

"Hey! You! Come back here. You can't go in there."

Saucerhead ignored her.

"Who the hell is he, Garrett? What is he doing?"

"He's Amber's bodyguard. DaPena youngsters have been dropping like flies. The reason she ran away was she was afraid she might be next. To get her to come back I had to fix her up with a bodyguard so mean and ugly and stubborn he'd take on the gods themselves. Also one who has a lot of friends willing to get revenge if anything happens to him."

"I don't like your tone, Garrett. You sound like you're accusing me."

"I'm accusing no one. Not yet. But somebody had Amiranda and Junior murdered. I'm just letting people know it's going to get gruesome if it's tried on Amber."

"Karl took his own life, Mr. Garrett."

"He was murdered, Domina. By a man named Gorgeous. I think at the instigation of a third party. I'm going to be talking to friend Gorgeous later. One of the questions I'm going to ask is who put him up to it. Thanks for this. Enjoy your day."

I left her looking flustered and maybe—hopefully—frightened.

The name of the game was Garrett opens his bag of little horrors and lets out some of what he knows, hoping that knowledge looks like a thick and deadly wall against which the onrushing Stormwarden might crush the guilty. Maybe somebody would panic.

As I moved away, looking around to see if any of Morley's boys were lurking, I heard footsteps behind me. I looked back.

Courter Slauce was hurrying my way, an odd expression on his fat face. All the color was gone. "Mr. Garrett. Wait up."

Had my bolts pinked something in the bushes already? He obviously had something on his mind.

"Courter! Where are you? Come here! Immediately!"

Domina Dount sounded like a fishwife. I couldn't see her, so I assumed she couldn't see me. Slauce threw up his hands in despair and trotted back home.

What had he wanted to tell me?

Morley was waiting at the house when I got there. He hadn't been waiting long.

39

"What's up, Morley?"

"Chodo wants to see you. Right away."

"Now I'm not happy. What brought this on?"

Morley shrugged. "I'm just relaying a message Crask left with me. I'll say this. He didn't look like he thought his boss was going to feed you to the fishes."

"That's very reassuring, Morley."

"Chodo is an honorable man, in his own way. He wouldn't chop somebody down without warning."

"Like Gorgeous?"

"Gorgeous had plenty of warnings. Anyway, he put himself on the bull's-eye. Then he stood there with his tongue out. He begged for it, Garrett."

"What do you think? Should I go?"

"Only if you don't want the kingpin pissed at you. A time might come when you'd want him to give you a little leeway."

"You're right. Let's go. Lock it up, Dean."

Dean grumbled, I told him it wouldn't last much longer.

Chodo had set himself up in a manor house in the suburbs. The place beggared the Stormwarden's in size and ostentation, a commentary on the wages of sin if you're slick.

Sadler was waiting at the gate, a commentary on the confidence Chodo had in the terror of his name, I suppose. He said nothing, just let us follow him across the professionally barbered grounds. Having that kind of eye, I couldn't help but study the security arrangements.

"Don't step off the path," Morley cautioned. "You're only safe inside the enchantment."

I then noticed that in addition to the expected and obvious armed guards and killer dogs, there were thunder lizards lazing in the bushes. They were not the tenement-tall monsters we think of, but little guys four or five feet tall, bipedal, all tail, teeth, and hind legs built for running. They were the reason for the enchantment on the path. Unlike the dogs, those things were too stupid to train. All they understood was eating and mating.

"Nice pets," I told Sadler. He didn't respond. Wonderful company, the kingpin's boys.

But the grimness ended at the front door.

Chodo knew how to do it up royal. I've been inside several places on the Hill. None could match Chodo's.

"Don't gawk, Garrett. It's impolite."

A platoon of nearly naked cuties were playing in and around a heated bath pool three times bigger than the ground area of my whole place. We passed through. I muttered, "Business must be good."

"Looks like." The man who had cautioned me not to gawk was looking back, the gleam in his eyes a conflagration. "Never saw them before." He walked into a pillar.

The part of the house where we met the kingpin was less luxurious. It was, in fact, your basic filthy, miserable dungeon—except it was located on the ground level. The kingpin himself was a pallid, doughy fat man in a wheelchair who didn't look like he could whip potatoes until you met his eyes. I had seen eyes like those only a few times, on some very old and hungry vampires. They were the eyes of Death.

"Mr. Garrett?"

The voice went with the eyes, deep and dank and cold, with hints of awful things crawling around its underside.

"Yes."

"I believe I owe you a considerable debt."

"Not at all. I—"

"In your fumbling and poking after whatever it is you're seeking, you presented me with an opportunity to rid myself of a vicious pest. I seized the chance, trampling your interests in my rush, a presumption you'll have found close to intolerable. But you've been gracious about it. You participated in the operation which delivered me despite having little hope you would get what you were after. So I believe I am in your debt."

Were it not for his voice from beyond the grave, I might have been amused by his pedantic manner. When I didn't respond, he continued. "Mr. Dotes didn't make much sense when he tried to explain what you're doing. If you can satisfy me that your interests don't conflict with mine, I'll do what I can to help you."

I wanted to demur, quietly, still preferring to avoid any chance of becoming identified with him. But Morley gouged me gently, and the fact was, he had two of the people I most wanted to question. I explained as concisely as I could, carefully sliding around the matter of two hundred thousand marks gold floating free.

Sadler continued. "One of Gorgeous's enterprises was the fencing of goods stolen from the warehouses along the waterfront, sir."

"Yes. Continue, Mr. Garrett."

"Basically, I need to question Gorgeous and Skredli so I can define their sector of the web of intrigue." Does that top you, you villainous slug? "I need to ask them who told them to kill Amiranda Crest and the younger Karl daPena."

"I knew Molahlu Crest when I was a young man. You might say I was one of his protégés." He crooked a finger. Sadler went to him, bent down. They whispered.

After Sadler backed off, Chodo asked, "The questions you want answered are the ones Raver Styx will ask with a great deal less delicacy?"

"No doubt."

"Then not only must I pay my debt to you, I must move to avert the attention of the mighty. But I have erred, and today I demonstrated my fallibility to myself in no uncertain fashion. I'm able to give you only the lesser part of what you want. I overestimated Mr. Staley's endurance and he's no longer with us. He couldn't take it."

I sighed. I should have expected the grave to slam another door in my face. "He wasn't in very good shape the last time I saw him."

"Perhaps his injuries were more extensive than they appeared. Whatever, I learned very little of value. But the other, the ogre breed, has survived and is amenable. The trouble is, he doesn't seem to know much."

"He wouldn't."

Morley gouged me. "Donni Pell, Garrett."

"What?"

Chodo raised a plump, almost white caterpillar of an eyebrow. He was as good at it as I was.

"You said the hooker was the key, Garrett. And you don't even know where to start looking."

"Who is Donni Pell?" Chodo asked.

"The she-spider in this web." I gave Morley a dirty look. "She used to work for Lettie Faren, but ran out on her the day Junior was snatched. She could be related to Lettie. Human, but supposedly with a thing for ogres." I ran through the whole thing, how every way I turned the name Donni Pell popped up. I finished, "She could be masquerading as a boy but using the same name."

Chodo grunted. He stared at the nails on one plump pink hand. "Mr. Sadler."

"Yes sir?"

"Find the whore. Deliver her to Mr. Garrett's residence."

"Yes sir." Sadler left us.

"If she's in the city, she'll be found, Mr. Garrett," Chodo told me. "Mr. Sadler and Mr. Crask are nothing if not efficient."

"I've noticed."

"I suppose it's time I took you to my ogrish houseguest. Come." He spun his wheelchair and rolled. Morley and I followed.

40

The first thought that entered my mind when I walked in on Skredli was *drowned sparrow*. He looked very small, very weak, very bedraggled, and like he'd never been dangerous to anything bigger than a bug. Curiously, I recognized him now. I hadn't during the excitement in Ogre Town or later in the coach. He was one of the gang who had waylaid me the afternoon of my date with Amiranda, while I was on my way to the chemist for some stink-pretty.

Skredli was seated on a rumpled cot. He glanced up but showed no real interest. Ogres tend toward fatalism.

Morley held the door for Chodo, then stepped aside. The kingpin backed his chair against the door.

I studied Skredli, wondering how to get to him. A man has to have hope before he's vulnerable. This one had no hope left. He was deader than the Dead Man, but his traitorous heart kept pumping and his battered flesh kept aching.

"The good times always come to an end, don't they, Skredli? And the better the times are, the bigger the fall when they end. Right?"

He didn't respond. I didn't expect him to.

"The chance for the good times doesn't have to be gone forever."

His right cheek twitched, once. Ogres and ogre breeds may be indifferent to the fates of their comrades, but they aren't indifferent to their own.

"Mr. Chodo has gotten what he wants from you. He doesn't have any outstanding grievance. Mine isn't with you at all. So there's no reason you shouldn't be let out of here if you give me what I need."

I didn't bother checking to see how Chodo took me putting words into his mouth. It didn't matter. He would do what he wanted no matter what I said or promised.

Skredli glanced up. He didn't believe me, but he wanted to.

"The whole scheme is in the dump, Skredli. And you're down at the bottom. No way to go but up or out. The choice is yours." I had asked Chodo only one question coming to the cell: did Skredli know Gorgeous was out of it? He did. "Your boss is gone. No reason to stay loyal to him or be afraid of him. Your fate is in your own hands."

Morley shifted his weight against the wall, gave me a look that said he thought I was laying it on too thick.

Skredli grunted. I had no way of telling what that meant. I took it as a go-ahead.

"I'm Garrett. We had a run-in once before."

One bob of the head.

I had him. For a moment, though, I feared it had been too easy. Then I reflected that it was the ogrish way. When you've got nothing you've got nothing to lose.

"You recall the circumstances?"

Grunt again.

"Who put you up to that?"

"Gorgeous." That in a dry-throated croak.

"Why? What for? I'd never had anything on either of you."

"Business. We had a thing going on in the daPena warehouse and they thought you were going to horn in and spoil it."

"Who is they?"

"Gorgeous."

"You said they. Gorgeous and who?"

He'd reached his next point of decision. He decided to tell a warped truth. "A guy named Donny something who set up the deal."

"You mean a hooker named Donni Pell who worked for Lettie Faren and had a thing for ogres. Don't do that again, Skredli."

His shoulders sagged.

I took a moment to reflect. There was a question of timing that deserved it. Skredli had been in town, leading that pack, after Junior was snatched. But then he'd been at that farm the afternoon before Junior walked away, and the next morning he'd led the crew that did in Amiranda.

I tabled that for the moment. "I'm interested in that warehouse scheme. All the petty little details."

I'd caught him on Donni Pell, so now he was determined to spin me a good tale. "That was one of Donni's ideas. She was always bringing us things she'd dreamed up from stuff her johns told her. Some of them we went with, and she got a cut. This one was real sweet. Raver Styx had left town and Donni had a foreman that would let us siphon off ten percent of everything that went through. We took it on a fifty-fifty split with Donni, on account of she was the one keeping the daPena side in line, but the foreman's cut and expenses had to come out of her half. We moved a lot of stuff. As much as we were doing from the rest of the waterfront, practically. But then Donni warned us that people were getting suspicious. Raver Styx's woman Dount sent the kid to nose around. Then there was you, starting to snoop just when we had decided to close the thing out by cleaning out the warehouse in one hit. So they had me try to discourage you."

Interesting. Not worried about me and my reputation for getting into kidnap cases? "When we hit the place in Ogre Town, we saw a guy leaving. A Bruno off the Hill. Who was he?"

"I never heard his name. A guy Donni knew. He worked for the guy who was taking the stuff from the warehouse. The guy was worried. He hired some other guy to keep track of you and you grabbed him, he thought. He wanted us to do something about you. There was a big panic about covering tracks because Raver Styx had been seen in Leifmold and could turn up anytime."

I turned to Morley. "Pokey?"

"Probably."

"What became of him?"

"I turned him loose. He went home and sat tight. He knew I was watching."

"Uhm. Skredli. Who did the Bruno work for?"

"I don't know. I don't even think Gorgeous knew. Donni or the Bruno delivered all the messages."

"A cautious man. And wisely so, considering who he was stealing from. But the goods had to be transferred somehow."

"We had our own warehouse, partly legit. The Bruno hired teamsters to pick up the stuff there."

There was an opportunity for some legwork if I decided I really wanted to know where the Stormwarden's goods had gone. I wondered if I ought to ask what goods a Stormwarden dealt in that were so attractive to thieves, but decided ignorance might prove beneficial at a later date. I needed whos and whys but not many whats.

"Let's talk about the younger Karl daPena. One night as he was going out the back door of Lettie Faren's place, somebody popped a bag over his head, choked him, and threw him into a carriage. And after that the story gets confusing."

Skredli had come around to where I wanted him. He was able to volunteer information without upsetting whatever minuscule conscience resides in an ogrish heart.

"That whole mess started out as a fake. The kid wanted to run out on his old lady and rip her off at the same time. He fixed it up with Donni to make it look like a snatch and he'd split the payoff with her and start traveling. Donni was going to split her half with us for making it look good. It wasn't the kind of thing Gorgeous usually got into, but it looked like money for nothing, so he sent for the old gang and we did it."

"Only it didn't come off that way. What happened?"

"I don't know. Honest. The same night after you and me go around in the street, Gorgeous calls me in and says there's a big change of plans. I seen Donni leaving, so I know where the change came from. Anyway, he told me I had to go out where the kid was hid out and turn it into the real thing. And when the payoff came through, we was supposed to be a whole lot better off than with the old plan. We was going to leave the kid twisting in the wind."

"Uhm." I thought a moment. "What about Donni's cut of the fatter pot?"

"We got that whole wad. All the kid's share."

Something told me Donni Pell had gotten her share somewhere else.

"So that's that? You just went out, got the money, and headed north?"

My tone warned him.

"No. You know that, don't you?"

"You had to kill a girl to get that extra chunk."

"Gorgeous said it had to be done. I didn't like it."

"Why?"

"I don't know. Look, no matter what you do, I'm going to tell you that a lot. Because I *don't* know. I wasn't his partner. Gorgeous told me to do things and I did them and he paid me good. And part of what he paid me for was not asking questions. You want to know who wanted something done and why, you got to find Donni Pell and ask her."

"What you say is probably true, but you have eyes and ears and a brain. You saw things and heard things and you thought about them. Why do you *think* the girl had to die?"

"Maybe she knew too much about something. She knew the kidnap was a fake because she was supposed to run off with the kid and the money.

Maybe she found out the fake turned real. Maybe she just did something to make Donni want to get her. Maybe it was just because she was set to take the frame for the kidnapping and Gorgeous didn't want her turning up saying it wasn't so. I know we was supposed to make her disappear forever. Only when we showed up to do it she had some son of a bitch with her and he turned out to be a goddamned one-man army. And by the time we got him down, there was traffic coming and we had to throw them in the bushes and make it look like nothing happened. When we got back, we found out that big ape wasn't dead at all. He'd grabbed the girl and took off through the woods. I never thought he'd get far, cut like he was. And he left us with a lot of cleaning up to—"

"That's enough of that. Tell me about the payoff. Where. When. How."

"On the Chamberton Old Coach Road four miles south of where it runs into the Vorkuta-Lichfield Road, just north of the bridge over Little Cedar Creek. Set for midnight the night before what we was just talking about, but the delivery was two hours late. I guess Gorgeous wasn't pissed because he never complained."

I didn't know the place. On the map the Chamberton Old Coach Road cuts up through woody hill country four miles west of the route I'd taken when I'd gone out to explore. "Why that spot?"

"The road runs straight for a mile either way from the bridge. There's never any traffic at night, but if there was, you'd spot it coming in plenty of time. And you can look off northeast and see the ridge the Lichfield road runs on. I was up there to watch in case there was any tricks. I was supposed to light one signal flare if everything was all right and two if it wasn't."

"Did you expect trouble?"

"No. We had them by the short hairs. But you don't take chances with those people."

"And the delivery was late?"

"Yeah. But I guess that was just because the damn fool woman didn't know what she was doing. Any idiot should know a covered wagon with a four-horse team won't make time like a buggy or carriage."

Oh? "You weren't there for the actual payoff, then?"

"No. But Gorgeous said it went down exactly the way it was supposed to."

"Which was?"

"The wagon came down and stopped in the road. Gorgeous and Donni had their coaches off to the side. Gorgeous and Donni had their drivers transfer the moneybags, half and half. The woman and her wagon headed on south. Donni stayed put for an hour, then headed south, too. Gorgeous came up where I was and gave me my cut and enough to pay off the boys so they could go home after the business in the morning. We didn't want them coming to TunFaire, getting drunk, and shooting their mouths off."

"They knew what was happening?"

"Not the payoff. But they were in on a killing."

"There was no concern about just following the woman?"

"She wasn't told what to do about going back till she turned over the ransom."

"I see." Not very bright, this Skredli. "She didn't have anything to say when she didn't get the kid after the payoff?"

"I don't know. Maybe she did. Gorgeous never said."

"I guess you came out pretty good on the deal personally, eh?"

"Yeah. Look at me. Living like a lord. Yeah. I got my usual ten percent of Gorgeous's fifty percent. A big hit to you, maybe, but I did better on the warehouse business, even if it took longer to come in."

"You stripped the warehouse, then?"

"Yeah. I didn't think it was smart, but Gorgeous said we already had such a big investment we might as well finish it off."

"Uhm." I began to pace, to think. We'd been at it a long time. He'd given me a lot to think about. We were almost there, but I needed that moment to reflect, to reorder my forces.

"Where is Donni Pell, Skredli?"

"I don't know."

"She was there when we came after you, wasn't she?"

He nodded.

"And she ran out behind us and went for help."

He shrugged.

"It's going to be interesting, finding out who called out the troops. That was a stupid mistake. Very stupid. Panic thinking. Raver Styx will have his hide. Where's Donni Pell?"

"How many times I got to tell you I don't know? If she's got the sense of a cockroach, she's done got her butt out of TunFaire."

"If she had that much sense, she would have headed out of town as soon as she had her share of the money. She seems to have a certain low cunning, an ability to manipulate men, and complete confidence in her invulnerability, but no brains. I'll take your word. You don't know where she is. But where might she run? Who would hide her?"

Skredli shrugged. "One of her johns, maybe."

I'd had that thought already. I suspected Skredli was mined out on the subject. And he was relaxed enough for the next stage.

"Why did the Stormwarden's kid have to be killed?"

"Huh? Killed? I heard he committed suicide."

"We're getting along fine, Skredli. I'm starting to feel kindly toward you. Don't blow your chance. I know you and Gorgeous and Donni and somebody were in and out of the room where he died. And I knew him well enough to know he couldn't kill himself that way—if he could ever find guts enough to kill himself at all. I figure you used the choke sack on him and Gorgeous cut him himself. I think Donni—but what I think doesn't matter. The thing I can't figure is why he went within a mile of that woman after what she did to him."

"You don't know Donni Pell."

"No. But I intend to get acquainted. Go ahead. Tell me about that morning."

"You aren't going to spread it around, are you? I don't need no Raver Styx breathing down my neck."

"None of us do. But you don't worry about Raver Styx. You worry about me. I'm the only chance you've got to walk out of here. You've got to make me happy."

He shrugged. He wasn't counting on me. But he did have new hopes that he hadn't had a while ago.

"All right. What started it was you parading around with that dead woman. Somebody seen you by Lettie Faren's place. They told Donni and Donni must have told everybody in town. She sent a messenger to us. Gorgeous had a fit, but he believed me when I said she had to be dead and you was just trying to stir something up.

"But you did get Donni stirred. Like you said, she ain't too smart. She thought she had her handle on the daPena kid. She sent him a message that told him where to find her, that she had to see him. The dope went there. I don't know what she thought she was going to get him to do. He wasn't having none of her finger-wrapping no more. He'd figured some of it out, and like a dummy she told him the girl was dead.

"That did it. He was going to hike out of there and blow the whole thing wide open. And he would have, too, only me and Gorgeous showed up. On account of Gorgeous was worried about Donni maybe getting too excited and doing something really stupid."

"It wasn't planned, then?"

"I gotta be careful with that. I don't think it was. I wasn't in on no planning, which I usually was because I was the guy who had to go out and do things. But it did have a funny feel. Like maybe Donni rigged it so it would come out the way it did."

"You keep contradicting yourself. Is Donni Pell stupid or not?"

"She's good at coming up with schemes and playing them out, long as she's got the reins in her hands. You catch her by surprise, she don't do so good. She thinks slow, she gets flustered, she does dumb things. So Gorgeous figured we better get over there and sit on her till she calmed down and whatever was bugging her blew away."

"And Karl was there."

"There and throwing a fit. He figured some of it out and he was going to tell the world. Donni even tried to buy him off, saying she'd give him his share after all. Dumb. After the way she screwed him over, and him just about sure what was going on. We didn't have no choice. He wouldn't back down. Even with me and Gorgeous there. It was our asses or his. I thought we made it look good."

"You did. You just didn't know he was so chicken nobody would believe he did it himself. Who was the other guy who was there?"

"What other guy?"

"A man in a hooded black cloak."

"I never saw one."

"Uhm." I paced. There were more questions I wanted to ask, but most had to do with the money. I didn't want Chodo getting interested in that. And Skredli had given me plenty to untangle, anyway. Probably close to enough. Donni Pell would put the cap on it. She would throw some light into the hearts of some shadows. She would cast the bones of doom for somebody.

"I played it straight for you," Skredli said. "Get me out of here."

"I'll have to talk Mr. Chodo into it," I replied. "What will you do?"

"Head north as fast as I can run. I don't want to be anywhere around when Raver Styx hits town. And there ain't nothing here for me anymore, anyway."

"You'd keep your mouth shut?"

"Are you kidding? Whose throat would the knife bite first?"

"Good point." I wagged a hand at Morley, indicating the door. He moved to open it. Chodo rolled out of his way. Morley stepped aside. Chodo and I followed.

"Where do you stand?" I asked the kingpin, indicating the door with a jerk of my head.

"I got rid of the bloodsucker bothering me. That's just a hired hand. You can have him."

"I don't know if I want him. Maybe he swung the knife but didn't give the order." We walked for a while. I said, "You know Saucerhead Tharpe?"

"I've heard the name. I know the reputation. I've never had the pleasure."

"Saucerhead Tharpe has a grievance against Skredli. It supersedes mine. I think he deserves first choice in deciding."

We traveled through that vast room where the naked ladies played. Again Morley had trouble steering. To Chodo they were furniture. He said, "Tell Tharpe to come out if he wants a piece." And, "If I don't hear by this time tomorrow, I turn him loose." And, at the front door, "Sometimes you let one go so word gets around how it goes for those who don't get out."

"Sure." Morley and I stepped outside and waited for an escort. We didn't speak until we were on the public road. Then I asked, "You think Chodo will let him go?"

"No."

"Me, neither."

"What now, Garrett?"

"I don't know about you. I'm going home to sleep. I had a late night last night."

"Sounds good to me. You let me know if anything comes of all this."

"How's your financial position these days, Morley?"

He gave me a dark look, but replied, "I'm doing all right."

"Yeah. I figured you would be. Listen, knothead. Stay away from the damned water-spider races. I'm not getting killed in one of your harebrained schemes for getting out from under."

"Hey, Garrett!"

"You've done it to me twice, Morley. This time maybe not as hairy as last time, but that crap down in Ogre Town was too damned close. You hear what I'm saying?"

He heard well enough to sulk.

needed a sixteen-hour nap, but I devoured a roast chicken with trimmings and downed a couple quarts of beer instead. I went into the Dead Man's den, being careful not to trample on the bodies, and tiptoed over to the shelves on the short north wall. Among the clutter I found a fine collection of maps. I dug out several and settled in my reserved chair.

I see you had a productive day.

He startled me. I hadn't known he was awake. But that's the sort of game he likes to play—sneak and scare. Near my heart I nurture a suspicion that malicious and capricious spirits are dead Loghyr disembodied.

I didn't answer immediately.

A productive day indeed. You are smugly certain you have a handle on everything and no longer need badger me to do your thinking for you.

Just to be contrary—though that's probably what he wanted—I gave him a blow-by-blow of everything that had happened since my last report. He seemed amused by my having chewed Morley out.

While I talked, I ran my right forefinger along lines on one of the maps, trying to visualize points of interest barely noticed in the real world.

Looking for a place someone unfamiliar with the territory might have felt safe squirreling a pile of gold when pressed for time?

"I'm thinking about going for a ride in the country tomorrow, maybe stopping to go swimming under a few bridges."

An interesting notion. Though you may never get to put it to the test.

"Why not?"

You still need me to explain to you the consequences of your actions? The Stormwarden Raver Styx was due home today. She should, in fact, have been home for some hours now. She should be howling at the moon. And who has had his nose deep into the thing, from several angles? Who is she going to drag in to answer questions right beside Domina Dount and the Baronet daPena?

I suppose that had been lounging around in the back of my mind, over-shadowed by the puzzle. And maybe by a touch of gold fever. "Dean!"

He looked a bit exasperated when he stuck his head in. "Yes sir?"

"Don't answer the door tonight. I'll do it. In fact, why don't you go on home and put yourself out of harm's way? You haven't left for days. Maybe a few of your nieces have roped some men."

Dean smiled. "You aren't closing me out now, sir. I'll stay."

"It's your funeral."

As if conjured by the conversation, someone began pounding on the door. I went and peeked through the peephole. I didn't recognize any of the crowd, but they wore Raver Styx's colors. I shut the peephole and went for another beer.

Her men? the Dead Man asked when I returned.

"Yes." I turned to the maps again.

You ignore her at your peril.

Yours, too, I thought. "I know what I'm doing."

You usually think you do. Occasionally you are correct.

I ignored him, too.

It wasn't ten minutes before someone else knocked. This time when I peeped I found Sadler on the stoop.

"Chodo said tell you what we come up with," he said when I opened the door, making no move to come inside. "We asked around, places. Somebody got word to her we were looking. She took off. Out of town. Nobody knows where she landed. We asked."

I'll bet they did.

"Chodo says tell you he still owes you the favor."

"Tell him I said thank you very much."

"I don't say much to civilians, Garrett. But you done all right down in Ogre Town. You maybe pulled us all out with your trick. So I'll tell you, don't waste that favor on nothing silly."

"Right."

He turned away and hiked. I shut the door and went back to the Dead Man.

Good advice, Garrett. A favor due from the kingpin is like a pound of gold squirreled away.

"I don't like it anyway. I just hope he stays alive long enough for me to collect." Kingpins have a habit of turning up dead almost as often as our kings do.

It was quiet for an hour. So quiet I dozed off in my chair, the maps sliding out of my lap. The Dead Man awakened me with a sudden strong touch. *Company again, Garrett.*

I heard the knocking as I tried to get the body parts moving in unison. When I peeked, I saw Morley on the stoop. He was alone. I opened up and he slipped inside. "I wake you?"

"Sort of. I thought you were going to crap out. What's up?"

"I just heard something I thought you should know. They found that guy Courter Slauce in an alley a couple streets from here. Somebody busted the back of his head in for him."

"What?" I tried to shake the groggies. "He's dead?"

"Like the proverbial wedge."

"Who did it?"

"How should I know?"

"This don't make sense. I have to get some tea or something. Wash the cobwebs out."

"For that you'll need the high water of the decade. Sometimes I think the only substance inside your head is the dust on the cobwebs."

"Ain't nothing will perk you up like a vote of confidence from your friends. Dean. Tea."

Dean had water on. He always does. He favors tea the way I favor beer. He brewed me a mug thick enough to slice. In the meantime, I asked Morley, "Did you keep anyone watching the Stormwarden's place?"

"For all the good it did. Till today."

"And?"

"There's no way to do a decent job when you spend eighty percent of your time dodging security patrols."

"They got nothing?"

"Zippo. Zilch. Zero. Armies could have marched in and out and they would have missed them."

"It was a long shot anyway. What about Pokey?"

"What about him? Why keep on him?"

"He might have trotted off to somebody interesting."

"You're grasping, Garrett. Pokey Pigotta? You're kidding."

"There's always a chance."

"There's a chance the world will end tomorrow. I'll give you fifty-to-one odds it does before Pokey Pigotta does something unprofessional."

"I don't want to hear bet or odds from you."

He gave me a narrow-eyed look. "I laid off you and your poisonous diet, Garrett. I laid off your self-destructive knight errantry. You lay off me. I'll go to hell in my own way."

"I don't care how you go to hell, Morley. That's your business. But every time you head out you throw a rope on me and try to drag me along."

"You feel that way about it, quit pulling me into your quests."

"I pay you to do a job. That's all I want done."

"Somebody ought to profit. If you're so damned lily pure, you're willing to get paid off in self-satisfaction for righting deadly wrongs—"

Dean interjected, "You kids want to whoop and holler and call each other names, why don't you take it out in the alley? Or at least get it out of my kitchen."

I was about to patiently explain again who owned that kitchen and who just worked there, when someone else came pounding on my door and hollering for me. "Saucerhead," I said, and headed that way. Morley followed me. I asked, "Who killed Slauce?"

"I told you I don't know. I heard he was dead. I came to tell you. I didn't go turn out his pockets to see if he left a note naming his killer."

I peeked through the peephole, just in case. I was in one of those moods.

Saucerhead, all right. And Amber. And several of the Stormwarden's men, including a couple who had been around before. I let Morley peek. "You want to be here for this?"

"No. I'm done. With you, with them, with the whole damned mess."

"Have it your way." I opened the door as Saucerhead wound up to start pounding again. Morley shoved out, grumbled a greeting. I said, "You two can come inside. The army stays where it is."

•••42

"What's a matter with Morley?" Saucerhead asked. He had a glazed look, but I suppose even a statue would be numb after an exposure to the Stormwarden Raver Styx.

"He tried to take a bite out of something that bit him back. Or maybe it was the other way around. What're you two up to, with your private army out there?"

"Mother wants you," Amber said. "You should have seen Mr. Tharpe stand up to Domina and Mother. He was magnificent."

"I've heard him called a lot of things but magnificent was never on the list."

"I didn't do nothing but stand there and pretend I was deaf except when they absolutely had to have me say something. Then I just sounded stupid and said they had to talk to her on account of I was working for her."

"And what was it all about?" I asked Amber.

"They wanted him out. They really got mad because he wouldn't go and I wouldn't tell him to go."

"It'll do them good. So your mother wants me to come running."

"Yes."

"Why did she send you?"

"Because she sent Courter and he didn't even come back. Then she sent Dawson and you wouldn't open the door."

Courter? She sent him to get me?

"Dean! Come here a minute." He came in. "Did anybody come to the door today? Before I told you I would answer it myself?"

"No. Just the boy who brought the letter."

"What letter?"

"I put it on your desk. I assumed you'd seen it."

"Excuse me for a minute." I went to the office. The letter was there, all right. I gave it a read. It was from my friend Tinnie. Out of sight, she had slipped out of mind.

"Anything important?" Saucerhead asked when I returned.

"Nah. Red's headed for TunFaire."

He looked at Amber sidelong, smirked. "That ought to put some life back in this town."

"Amber, does your mother think I'll just hike out there because she crooked her finger?"

"She's the Stormwarden Raver Styx, Garrett. She's used to getting what she wants."

"She isn't getting it this time. I'm tired and I've been playing with thugs so much lately another one isn't going to bother me none. Tell her if she wants to see me, she knows where to find me. During normal business hours. If she comes down now, I won't answer the door."

Amber said, "I'm not going to tell her anything, Garrett. I'm not going back. I forgot how bad it could get till she came storming in. As far as I'm concerned, she can take it out on Father and Domina from now on. She's seen the last of her unbeloved daughter. . . . You did mean it when you let me have that gold, didn't you?"

I was tempted to say no just to see how quick she could turn in her tracks, but forbore. "Yes."

"Then I'm going upstairs. You can go home, Mr. Tharpe."

"Just a minute, girl. You're going to declare your independence, you're going to declare your independence. You can stay tonight because it's too late to do it now but tomorrow you go shopping for a place of your own."

For a moment she was stunned. Then she looked hurt.

I tried to soften it. "This is a dangerous place and I'm in a dangerous line."

"And I have a dangerous family."

"That, too. When you relay my message to the troops out there, tell them to tell your mother that Courter didn't run away after all. Somebody lured him into an alley and smashed his head in. She can sleep on that."

Amber gawked. She opened and closed her mouth several times.

"You look like a goldfish."

"Really? Courter was murdered, too?"

"Yes."

"Why would anyone do that?"

"I assume because he was coming to see me."

"Damn them!"

As I hoped, the anger I'd aroused now became a white righteous fury. She stomped to the door.

I raised a hand, delaying Saucerhead. "Chodo had me out to his place today. He still has that character that killed Amiranda. He offered him to me. I told him you had more claim. He said if you're interested, get your butt out there because tomorrow he's going to turn him loose."

Saucerhead pursed his lips and touched himself a couple of places where he still hurt. He grunted.

"I'd also like you to come back tomorrow. I'm figuring on taking a trip and I want you to keep on keeping an eye on Amber."

He nodded. "Yeah. They ain't getting this one, Garrett."

"Fine. I'll see you when you get—"

Amber's yell sent us hustling out front, me unlimbering my skull buster. Saucerhead picked up a couple of the Stormwarden's men and cracked their heads together. I thumped two behind the ears. That left three and two of those had all they could handle with Amber. Saucerhead peeled them off while I held their leader at bay. "What the hell you trying to do, shithead?"

"Take her home."

"I'm not going to argue. I'm just going to tell you she said she don't want to go. She's old enough to make up her own mind. Pick up your buddies and leave."

He looked at me like he wanted to tell me what it meant to get into the Stormwarden's way, then just shrugged. Saucerhead let go of the two he had. The bunch began getting themselves together.

Amber started to say something. I told her to go inside. We would talk after the crowd thinned out. She went, and Raver Styx's thugs did the same, leaving me with a flock of promising black looks.

"You're starting to catch on, Garrett. Talk *after* you kick ass. They're more inclined to hear what you have to say."

That was Morley Dotes talking from a perch on the stoop next door. He got up and came down, stood with us watching the Stormwarden's boys stumble off. I said nothing, not knowing what might set him off. He offered me a folded piece of paper. I looked him in the eye for a moment. His expression remained bland.

There was nothing on that paper but a name: *Lyman Gameleon.*

"I've heard of him. Big bear on the Hill, and so forth. What's the significance?"

"Just thought I'd save you some trouble, Garrett. That's the man who sent the soldiers into Ogre Town. A man who, coincidentally, happens to be your Stormwarden's next-door neighbor—and bitterest enemy, politically and personally. Not to mention being her husband's older half brother."

"Hey! Very interesting. Thanks, Morley."

"No big deal, Garrett." He waved one hand as he marched away.

The tidbit was Morley's way of extending the olive branch.

Saucerhead said, "It's time I was going, too, Garrett. Take care of Miss daPena."

I considered his broad back as he went. Had he said more than he had said? With Saucerhead it's hard to tell if he's just being a dumb goof or a mild cynic.

I went inside and locked up. I looked around for Amber, didn't see her. "Amber?"

"In your office."

I went in. She had parked herself in my chair and seemed to be sulking.

"Cheer up. You were marvelous."

"You manipulated me."

"Of course I did. Would you have stood up to those thugs if you weren't mad?"

"Probably not."

I settled on a corner of the desk. "One piece of news that might perk you up. I think there's a small chance we can lay hands on some of the gold."

"You're stringing me along again, aren't you?"

"No. It's a long shot but a real chance. I didn't think there was one before. It depends on how distracted your mother is by the emotional side of what's happened. I think I know what happened to some of the gold, but finding it is going to be like scratching through the proverbial haystack. We'll need time."

"You mean it, don't you?"

"Yes. Though I admit I'm riding a hunch." Dean brought beer and wine. We thanked him. I told Amber, "I can't stay awake much longer. I'm going to turn in. I'll see you in the morning."

She flashed me a wicked smile.

I understood the smile soon enough.

I didn't latch my door. Who does, inside his own house? Amber took that as an invitation. Not only did I see her sooner than I expected; I got less sleep than I hoped. Repeated clamors at the front door, ignored by the entire household, also interrupted my rest.

staggered out when the smell of breakfast overpowered my laziness. As I descended the stairs another hurrah broke out at the front door. I slipped over and peered through the peephole. An ugly face, bloated and red, bobbed outside. A mouth filled with bad teeth gaped and bellowed.

I closed the peephole and went to breakfast.

I leaned back and patted my belly. "Dean, of all the several geniuses infesting this place, I think you're the most valuable. Where the hell did you find strawberries?"

"My niece May brought them. They've been in the cold well for three days."

Nieces again? At that rate of regression the Dead Man would soon be interested in Glory Mooncalled again. "I'd better see if his nibs is awake." Sooner or later that front door was going to have to open. "Amber, your mother is bound to come. You going to want to be scarce?"

"I can face her as long as I've got a place to run when it gets gruesome."

"You're all right, then. Dean, I'll take a mug of tea while I rattle Old Bones."

Dean scowled and grumbled, not at all inclined to let me take matters into my own hands. He prepared the tea with such care and deliberation I was ready to do without before he finished. Tea is tea. Making a religious ceremony of fixing it doesn't improve it a bit.

There are those who would consider me a barbarian—the same ones who aren't civilized enough to appreciate good beer.

The Dead Man was awake. He wasn't in a mood to be interrupted. He knew we'd have company soon and was working himself up for it. I believe he had visions of using the Stormwarden—who had been in the Cantard for months—as a chamois to buff up his Glory Mooncalled theory.

I followed Amber's example and went to my room to groom myself for the hours ahead.

That done, I settled at a window and watched the street. It wasn't quiet out there. The Stormwarden's men remained at their posts but weren't watching the house. Their carrying on had drawn a crowd.

The lords of the Hill can get away with a lot. They usually remain above the laws that keep the rest of us from preying on each other. But the invasion of a home without the prior approval of the judges is something people won't tolerate.

Had the Stormwarden's men tried to break in during the night, they might have gotten away with something—had the Dead Man allowed it. Now it was too late. If they tried, the crowd would tear them apart. Our overlords have to exercise a delicate touch when they violate the sanctity of the home.

I hoped the uptown boys didn't get stupid. I had worked myself into a tight enough place already.

They kept me there. And company, when it came, did so from an unexpected quarter. From the corner of my eye I caught a stir coming from downtown. What to my wondering eye should appear but Saucerhead Tharpe in convoy with Sadler and Crask. The bunch looked like they had breakfasted on bitterbark soup at Morley's place.

I sighed. "I knew things were shaping up too damned well."

I ran into Amber in the hallway. She asked, "Is she here?"

"Not yet. It's Saucerhead and a couple guys you don't even want to know by sight. And I'm not going to be able to find out what they want if you don't let me get to the stairs."

"Oh." She stepped aside. "Grouch."

"You're probably right. You might warn Dean so he can get something ready. They look like they'll need it."

I was three steps from the door when Saucerhead knocked. I glanced through the peephole and opened up. As my guests entered I gave the Stormwarden's red-faced boy a glare and said, "Don't even think about it." He got redder, but I didn't have to watch. I shut the door on him.

I seated them in the small front room next to my office. Dean appeared with tea and sweetcakes just as though they were expected. I said, "Well? What is it? How bad is it?"

Saucerhead glanced at the other two. They were willing to let him do the talking. I couldn't quite tell what the threesome were up to. There was no tension between them, just a commonality of undirected disgust. Tharpe said, "Skredli got away."

"Skredli? Got? Away? What did he do? Sprout wings and fly? Was he some kind of werebuzzard?" I'd never heard of such a beast, but nothing in this world surprises me anymore. If a man can turn into a wolf, why not an ogre into a buzzard? Both transformations seem singularly fitting. Perhaps even symbolic.

Prejudiced? Who? Me?

The gods forfend.

"No, he didn't fly, Garrett. He just took off running."

I started to express my incredulity, but it struck me that I might learn a little more a lot faster with my mouth shut. I admit I don't often have these epiphanies.

Saucerhead explained. "It was just getting light when I went out there. They took me up to the front porch and told me to wait. Then they went in and brought Skredli out. And all of a sudden, like that was all he was waiting for, he took off like a bat out of hell."

Crask said, "It was chilly up there last night. The lizards get sluggish when their blood cools down."

Sadler added, "Dogs won't run an ogre 'less they're specially trained. Anyway, Chodo's mutts are supposed to keep people from getting in, not from getting out."

And Saucerhead, "It happened so sudden, and he was gone so fast, nobody had time to do nothing but gawk."

No point in whining. It wasn't my problem, anyway. Or was it? "You didn't come down here just to let me in on that, did you?"

Saucerhead hit me with the news. "Chodo thinks you're going to stick on what you're after till you find Donni Pell. He figures that when you find her, you'll find Skredli again, too."

"That sounds plausible."

"He wants Sadler and Crask to be there when you find them."

"I see." I can't say I was disappointed. I foresaw any number of potentialities right down the path. Those three guys would be handy if the fur began to fly. "All right. I'm expecting heavyweight company sometime today. Raver Styx."

"We know the game and the stakes, Garrett."

"Indeed?" Had Amber been running her mouth? No. Saucerhead just *thought* he knew the stakes.

Which alerted me to the fact that there would be no gold hunting until Skredli and Donni Pell turned up. Unless I decided I didn't mind Chodo's thugs hanging around when I turned it up.

"Go about your routine," Sadler told me. "We'll stay out of your way."

Sure they would. As long as it wasn't in their interest to do otherwise.

44

We killed time playing cards. Dean was in and out, laying scowls on me. I knew what he was thinking: I ought to whip all these bodies into a rehabilitation frenzy and get some work done on the house. He doesn't understand that characters like Saucerhead, Sadler, and Crask get no thrill out of domestic triumphs.

Amber popped in once, decided she couldn't handle all the joviality, and retreated upstairs. The Dead Man remained alert in his quarters. My neck prickled each time his touch passed through the room. He would never admit he was nervous, though.

Amber came back awhile later. "She's coming, Garrett. I thought she'd at least send Domina once first." She hesitated for a split second. "I think I'll stay upstairs."

"I was sure you'd want to suggest she learn to pick her nose with her elbow."

"I'm not quite ready for that yet."

"And if she insists on seeing you?"

"Tell her I'm not here. Say I ran off somewhere."

"You know she won't believe that. She's a stormwarden. She'll know where you are."

Amber shrugged. "If I have to face her, I will. Otherwise, just leave me out of it."

"Whatever you say."

The future began hammering on the door. Dean looked in to see if I wanted him to answer. I nodded. He headed out at a reluctant shuffle. I rose and went after him. Amber scurried up the stairs. Saucerhead and the boys folded their hands and strolled into the hallway.

I was five feet behind Dean when he swung the door inward. The Dead Man's attention was so intense the air almost crackled. I had one hand in my pocket, gripping one of the potencies given me by Saucerhead's witch, knowing that if I employed it, Raver Styx would notice the spell about as much as she might notice the whine of a mosquito.

She had come to the door alone, though she'd been accompanied on the journey from the Hill. A coach and small army cluttered the street behind her. My neighbors had made themselves scarce.

She was a short woman, heavy and gnarly, like a dwarf. She'd never had anything like Amber's beauty, even at sixteen, when they all look good. Her face was grim and ugly. She had bright blue eyes that seemed to blaze in contrast with her tanned, leathery skin and graying hair. If she was angry, though, she concealed it very well. She seemed more relaxed than most people who come to my door.

Dean had frozen. I moved forward. "Do come in, Stormwarden. I've been expecting you."

She stepped past Dean, glancing at him as though she was puzzled by his rigidity. Could she be that naive?

"Close the door, Dean."

He finally moved.

I led the Stormwarden into the room where we'd been playing cards. The office was not large enough for the crowd. As I seated my guest, I asked, "Can Dean get you anything? Tea?"

"Brandy. Something of that sort. And not by the thimbleful. I want something to drink, not something to sniff at."

Her voice was gravelly and as deep as ever I'd heard from a woman. It had a timbre that made her sound like she was used to being one of the boys.

That was the way they talked about her. I had no direct knowledge. I'd never crossed paths with her before.

"Dean, bring a bottle from that bunch the Bahgell brothers sent me."

"Yes sir."

I considered Raver Styx. That I might have grateful clients of the Baghell caliber didn't impress her.

"Mr. Garrett . . . You are Mr. Garrett?" she asked.

"I am."

"These others?"

"Associates. They represent the interests of a former protégé of Molahlu Crest."

If that news amazed or dismayed her or in any other way impressed her, she didn't show it. She said, "Very well. I've studied you briefly. I understand you carry on your business your own way or you don't do business. You get results, so you can't be faulted for your ways."

I examined her again while Dean delivered her bottle and glass. I wasn't sure how to play her. She was disappointing my expectations. I'd been steeling myself for a storm of imperial rage. I said, "I did say I was expecting you, having been drawn into the periphery of your family's affairs. But I'm not quite certain why."

"Don't be ingenuous, Mr. Garrett. It's wasted effort. You've been nearer the heart than the periphery. Maybe nearer than you know. My first question of you would be why."

"Representing a client or clients, of course."

She waited a moment. When I didn't add anything, she asked, "Who?" Then, "No, strike that. You won't tell me if you think it's to your advantage to reserve it. Let me think a moment."

After she'd reflected a moment, she continued. "Disaster after disaster has trampled my family the past few weeks. My son kidnapped, to be redeemed for a ransom so huge the financial future of the family is in doubt. And my adopted daughter decided she had to fly the nest and for her trouble got herself slaughtered by bandits."

I wagged a cautionary finger at Saucerhead.

"My son, after being freed, killed himself. And my natural daughter, despite your efforts and those of Willa Dount, fled home not once but twice."

"Not to mention trivia like Courter Slauce getting himself killed on his way down to see me last night, or the fact that thieves have stripped the daPena warehouse."

Her face shaded with the faintest cloud of emotion, the first she'd shown. "Is that true?"

"Which?"

"About the warehouse."

"Yes."

"I hadn't heard."

"Maybe Domina has been too distracted to keep track of what's happening on the commercial side."

"Horsefeathers. Domina is feeding me disasters in tidbits in hopes I won't have her flayed and use her hide for bookbinding."

It was a sour, trite remark, not meant to be taken seriously. Witches and sorcerers had stood the accusation so long it had become a joke of the trade.

Having done my dance to show off, I waited, leaving the next play in her hand.

"I'd suspected you possessed knowledge not at my command, Mr. Garrett. Now you've told me as much, for whatever motives move you. All right. We both know I want the rest. You want something for yourself. Can we arrive at a peaceful middle ground?"

"Probably. I doubt if our goals are too far apart."

"Indeed? What do you want, then?"

"The man or woman who gave the order that got Amiranda Crest murdered."

I guess when you play for stakes as high as she had for so long, you learn to keep yourself controlled. That face would have made her a deadly card-player. "Go on, Mr. Garrett."

"I want the person no matter who it is. That's what I want."

She surveyed my companions. Sadler and Crask were blanks, but Saucerhead had leaned a little toward us. "It's obvious you know a great deal that I don't."

Saucerhead couldn't restrain himself. "Skredli and Donni Pell, Garrett. We get them, too."

The Stormwarden looked at me. I said, "My friend was there when Amiranda was murdered. He tried to save her and failed. He feels obligated to restore a balance. He also has a personal score to settle. Show her."

Saucerhead understood. He started stripping. The wounds he exposed still looked nasty. The deeper cuts wouldn't lose their purplish red color for months.

"I see," the Stormwarden said. "Would you care to tell me how it happened?"

Saucerhead put his shirt back on. I said nothing. Raver Styx muttered, "So that's the way it's going to be."

All the while I stared smoke and fire at Saucerhead. He had to mention Donni Pell in front of the wife! I'd wanted to reserve Donni Pell for the moment of maximum impact.

She hadn't reacted to the name at all.

"I suppose the thing to do is hire you, Mr. Garrett. Then you might be more responsive."

"Maybe. Maybe not. I do my job my own way. Between the hiring and the results I don't put up with meddling from my principal. I'm the specialist. If I can't be trusted to do the job without interference, I shouldn't be hired in the first place." I don't think my voice squeaked. I sure hoped it didn't. "What did you want to hire me for, anyway?"

She looked at me like I was a moron.

"I don't mind having multiple clients, but I don't take them on when their goals conflict."

She continued to stare. Serpents of temper had begun to stir beneath the surface of her calm. No more pushing permitted.

"Before we go on there's something I've got to show you, Stormwarden. I warn you up front, you're not going to like it. You're going to be upset. But you need to see it so you don't walk into anything with the web of illusion across your eyes."

The Dead Man brushed me with a touch of approval.

The Stormwarden rose, her face carefully composed. I said, "You ought to finish that glass and pour yourself another before we go."

"If it's that tough, I'll take the bottle along."

Just one of the guys. "Come on, then."

I crossed the hall to the Dead Man's room, stepped inside, stepped aside. The parade followed, the Stormwarden first. The boys lined up against the wall beside the door. Crask and Sadler stared at the Dead Man and went gray around the edges.

Seeing is believing.

"A dead Loghyr!" the Stormwarden enthused, sounding like she'd just spotted a cute fairy toddler peeking out of the bushes. "I didn't know there were any around anymore. What do you want for it?"

"You wouldn't want this one. He's a social parasite. My personal charity project. He does nothing but sleep and amuse himself by playing with bugs."

"Laziness is a Loghyr racial characteristic. But even the dead can be trained to harness when you use the right lash."

"You'll have to explain that to me sometime. I can't get any work out of him. What you need to see is over here. Dean! Get some decent damned lamps in here!" He was supposed to have done that already.

He came sidling in with the necessary and stammered apologies. He was shaking all over, and I didn't blame him. This was the moment that could explode.

She stood there staring at the bodies, not a hairline cracking her composure. She raised a hand, beckoned Dean, took the lamp, knelt. She studied Karl for a long time, taking him in inch by inch. Finished, she took a long pull on the brandy bottle, then did it all over again with Amiranda.

Amiranda didn't get a second's less attention. In fact, she got a moment more.

The Stormwarden grunted, then set her bottle aside and rested the tips of two fingers on Amiranda's belly. After a minute she muttered, "So!" and reclaimed the bottle. She drew another healthy draft.

She rose. "I owe you a debt of gratitude, Mr. Garrett." She returned the lamp to Dean. "Can we talk now? Seriously? The two of us?"

"Yes. Dean, take these guys into the kitchen and feed them. Bring me a mug and a pitcher. In the office."

"Yes sir. Gentlemen?"

They didn't protest. I guess Chodo had given them orders to cooperate.

settled behind my desk. The Stormwarden sat opposite me, devoting herself to her bottle and her inner landscape. Finally, she said, "Karl was
murdered."

"He was. By a man named Gorgeous and an ogre breed named Skredli.
Gorgeous is dead. Skredli is on the loose but we intend to find him. He also
led the gang that killed Amiranda. But he was just a hired hand. Someone
paid for the blood."

"You have a great deal to tell me."

"If I take you as a client."

She thought for a while. "Your task now is to find the person responsible
for Amiranda's murder. Correct?"

"Yes."

"I have a great deal of power, as you're aware. But I don't know how to
go about rooting out a killer. Suppose I hire you to find Karl's murderer?"

"That might work. Assuming we agree on precedence of claims if the
same hand directed the blades in both murders."

"There'll be no problem of precedence if you meet one condition."

"Which is?"

"You may take precedence for yourself, your friends, and your client—if
you'll permit me to be present when you handle your end of it. It won't matter what you do. Not even death will be an escape for whoever did that in
there."

I felt a surge of elation, wondered why, then realized that most of it came from the Dead Man. He knew something, or had something. "I think we can deal."

"I'll stay out of your way, Mr. Garrett. I'll give you whatever aid and assistance you require."

Dean brought the beer in. I poured my mug full, damned near drained it. The Stormwarden did likewise with a second mug Dean thoughtfully provided.

The Stormwarden said, "I expect you're out of pocket considerably for the bodies. You wouldn't have gotten them cheaply."

"That's true."

"Add that to what you need for a deposit against your expenses and fee."

"Let me make sure we understand one another. You're willing to take me on and turn me loose, without shoving your hand in, as long as you're there for the showdown?"

"Yes."

"And you'll lend me your authority along the way?"

"If that's necessary."

"It will be in a few cases."

"I have one goal only, Mr. Garrett. Laying my hands on the person or persons responsible for what happened to my children. Cost is no obstacle. Neither is the emperor himself. Do you understand me?" Those ice blue eyes were ablaze now. "You do what you have to do to deliver. I'll back you to the gates of hell itself."

"Pact?"

"You want a witch's oath, written in blood?"

"The sworn word of the Stormwarden Raver Styx will do."

She did the whole formal thing after allowing me to word the undertaking.

"Settled," I said. "We're on. I owe you a story." And I began telling it from the moment it intruded upon my life. I gave her the crop, reserving only my personal interactions with Amber and Amiranda. I don't think she was fooled.

I reserved a couple thoughts about the gold, too. I did have a client, after all.

It took several hours. She didn't interrupt. Dean kept the pitcher full and brought in food when he felt it was time.

She didn't immediately comment when I finished. I gave her a few minutes, then asked, "Am I still retained?"

She gave me a don't-be-stupid look. "Of course." She thought awhile longer. "It doesn't make sense."

"Not from where we stand now. It probably looked slick at the start. Before people started doing unto one another and things started going wrong. Before the terror set in."

"It doesn't make much sense from that perspective, either. Not to me."

"Don't go closing your mind now."

She came into the real world for the first time in hours, fixing me with a basilisk's stare. "What?"

"You're ignoring the centerpiece at this hell's feast. The shadow that falls upon it all. The Stormwarden Raver Styx."

"Explain yourself, Mr. Garrett."

"I will. By example. Suppose everyone involved was exactly who he or she is, but you, instead of being the dread Raver Styx, were the heiress to the Gallard wine fortune, that what's-her-name. Would anyone have done what they did if you were her and she'd gone out of town for six months? Would anyone have been tempted? Donni Pell and her gang, maybe, but they were motivated by greed going in. Who you were or weren't didn't matter till the double crosses and foul-ups started and asses had to be covered."

She didn't like it a bit, though I'd barely skimmed the edges. But that woman had to be the most hard-hearted damned realist ever to cross my trail. She swallowed her ego. "I see." She made Willa Dount look like a kitten.

She took time out for more reflection. Then, "What do you plan to do, Mr. Garrett?"

"I'd like to interview your husband and Willa Dount in circumstances where they can't evade questions or avoid answering them."

"It can be arranged. When?"

"The sooner the better. Today. Now. That old man with the black sword has been busy enough. Let's not give him time to sniff out anybody else." Old Death is supposed to be blind but I've noticed he never misses.

"That's probably wisest. How do you want to set it up?"

We talked about it for fifteen minutes. I said I'd play it by ear, making sure she understood I wanted to be given my head. Then she rose. "I'll have the bodies taken away now, Mr. Garrett."

"Out the back would be best. They're supposed to have been cremated already. Nobody outside this house knows they haven't been."

"I understand."

I followed her to the front door, where she paused before she allowed me to let her out. "Take very good care of my daughter, Mr. Garrett. She may be all that I have left."

"I intend to, Stormwarden."

We locked gazes for a moment. We understood one another.

It is a pitiful truth that people like Raver Styx cannot express their love in any way that their beloved will find meaningful.

46

The door shut. I leaned against it and let out a long, heartfelt sigh of relief. I shook for about a minute while the tension drained away. I wanted to let out a big old war whoop.

Saucerhead leaned out of the kitchen. "She finally go?"

"Finally."

He counted my arms and legs. "Guess you worked something out."

"Yeah. We'll see how it stays together."

"What's the game?"

"First thing is, some of her boys are going to come to the back door to pick up those bodies. You guys can hand them over. I'm going to set a fire under the Dead Man."

Saucerhead gave me a dirty look, grumbling about "them that puts on aristocratic airs," but he went and got Sadler and Crask. I waited while they removed the corpses.

There, now. That was not so bad after all, was it, Garrett?

"A snap. So why the hell are you sweating?"

That startled him. I could almost see him checking to see if, by some miracle, some of life's processes had resumed.

Point for Garrett.

"You had some kind of epiphany while I was talking to her. What was it?"

I realized that by taking a short trip upcountry you could probably put the cap on the affair. He was all set to do some crowing about his genius.

"You mean by going out to that farm and rounding up Donni Pell?"

You reasoned it out!

"You've been telling me I have to use my own head. Using yours is too much like work. All the kingpin's hounds and all the kingpin's men couldn't catch more than a few whiffs of old backtrails. She'd used up her friends here in town. Where else would she go?"

Very good. Though we do rely on the assumption that she has not taken the proceeds of her multifarious treacheries and gotten herself somewhere where she can become a new and possibly even respectable person.

"I don't think she has the sense or character to make the clean break. If she did, she would've gotten out days ago."

You are going to return to that farm?

"I'm still formulating strategy," I fibbed. "Meanwhile I'll go up to the daPena place for a chat with the Stormwarden's old man and Willa Dount—maybe even her staff if it looks like that'll do any good. And in the back of my head I'll be trying to decide if Skredli is smart enough to have scoped it out himself."

I had not thought of that.

"Because you don't think like a thug. I guarantee you, the first thing Skredli did after he decided it was safe to stop running was start looking for somebody to blame for the fix he's in. It would be easy for him to get all righteous about Donni. And look what a great target she makes. She's got no friends left. No protector or avenger. And she's got buckets of money that can be taken without any comebacks. And on top of that, she's a woman."

You pity her?

"Not much. She's the one who decided to play with the hard boys."

Saucerhead was in the doorway, waiting for me to stop talking. I beckoned him inside. "They off?"

"Gone."

"You know what I was saying?"

"I heard your side."

"You heard everything worth hearing." I got the maps I'd studied after my talk with Skredli and opened one. "You see this? That's the crossroads where you and the girl had your run-in with Skredli's gang. If you head west to about here, you come to two young mulberry trees hiding the end of an old road. About a half mile down that road is an abandoned farm. The place where they took Junior back when this mess was just a kidnapping. I think that's where we'll find Donni Pell."

"You want me to go drag her back here?"

"Oh, no. I want her right where she sits. I'm going to organize a family outing to convene out there. But when I get there, I want to know what I'm walking into."

"You want me to go scout it out, then."

"Can you handle it?"

"No problem. When?"

"Soon as you can. Don't come at the place down that road."

He snorted. "Give me *some* credit, Garrett."

"Meet me at the crossroads tomorrow. I'll try to be there as close to noon as I can. I'll have some stops to make along the way."

Tharpe jerked his head in the general direction of the kitchen. "What about those guys?"

"I don't care. Let them tag along if they want. Or they can stick with me. If they decide to go with you, make sure they don't start playing their own game. I've got to head up the Hill in a few minutes. Go find out what they want to do."

What are you planning, Garrett? The Dead Man sounded suspicious.

"I don't know. I'm making it up as I go along."

It feels like you're setting something up.

"I wish I was. There're tags and threads that're going to hang loose after this's over and they could cause problems."

For instance, a certain Garrett getting caught in a collision between a young woman used to getting what she wants and a somewhat older, no-nonsense redhead who feels she has a certain proprietary interest in the man?

"That one hadn't occurred to me. I was thinking more along the lines of the Stormwarden wanting to get me for my presumptions and disrespect after she no longer has any use for me. Amber won't have any interest in me if she gets her meat hooks in that ransom money."

Garrett, you are, for the most part, an unusually sound-thinking representative of your species. But where members of the opposite sex are concerned, you are often a fool.

"A congenital weakness. My father was subject to it, too. I'm working on it."

You will break your beer habit first, I am certain.

"Speaking of Amber, I should let her know what's going on."

One piece of advice, since you wish to avoid a prime position on the Stormwarden's get-even list.

"What's that?"

Try to restrain that part of you which insists on being sarcastic, abrasive, and confrontational.

"I'm working on that, too. I think I'll clear that up right after I get straightened out about women."

I went to the kitchen doorway and stuck my head in. Saucerhead said, "They decided to stick with me." His smirk said that was because they weren't interested in doing anything that would bring them to the attention of Raver Styx.

I winked and headed upstairs.

tapped on Amber's door. "You there?"

"It's not locked."

I went inside. She was seated on the edge of her bed, looking pale and tired. "Is she gone?"

I settled into the room's sole chair. "She left. We managed to work something out."

"How heavily did she outbid me?"

"I don't like your mother, Amber."

"What does that mean?"

"People I don't like never outbid people I do like. Though sometimes I'll let them think they can."

"Thanks." She didn't sound cheered.

"What's the matter?"

"It's almost over, isn't it?"

"I expect to put the noose around somebody's neck tomorrow."

"Do you know who?"

"Not for certain. Not yet."

"It's not going to make anybody happy, is it?"

"No. Murder never does. Not for long."

"Then I won't be seeing you. . . ."

I had an impulse to trot down and give the Dead Man a swift kick. He was listening in and snickering, probably. Why is the old blubber boat always right?

"Who knows? Look, I'm just about to go up to your mother's house to question your father and Domina Dount. How's your nerve? You want to go along and stand silent witness? Maybe pick up a change of clothes?"

"Do I smell bad, or something?"

"What?"

"Never mind. What's a silent witness?"

"Somebody who just stands there and makes people stick to the truth because they know the silent witness can contradict them."

"Oh." She frowned. "I don't know if I'm up to that. My own father. . . ."

"It'd be a chance to see Domina Dount pick her nose with her elbow."

She rose immediately. "All right."

"My god. What enthusiasm."

"I don't want to hurt my father, Garrett. And I know you'll back him into a corner where things will come out that my mother won't be able to forgive."

Something in her tone suggested she was ready to spill family secrets. "Maybe if I didn't ask certain questions, your mother wouldn't have to know. As long as the answers don't have any bearing on what—"

"I don't know!" There was agony in that, and a plea for help.

"Tell me."

"Ami . . . He *has* to the father of the baby she was carrying."

"I'm not surprised to hear that, Amber. I even suspect that your mother already entertains the possibility, too."

"I guess she would. But even if she did, she wouldn't understand it." Pure misery, Amber. This was gnawing her good.

"It isn't exactly incest."

"It could've been."

"What? How so?"

"Ami . . . She wasn't a willing partner."

"He raped her?" I couldn't believe Amiranda would have tolerated that from anybody.

"Yes. No. Not the way you're thinking. He didn't hold a knife at her throat. He just . . . *coerced* her, I guess. I don't know how he did it. She never told me about it. Only Karl. But Karl told me. It started when she was thirteen. When you're that young it's hard . . . It's hard to know what to do."

"Not you, too?"

"No. But . . . But he tried. Twice. When I was fourteen. Almost fifteen. It was hard, Garrett. Maybe a man wouldn't even understand. The first time I just ran away when I realized what he wanted. The second time he made sure I didn't have anywhere to run. I . . . He . . . He wouldn't let me alone till I said I was going to tell mother."

"And?"

"He went into a panic. A psychotic panic. That's why . . ."

"Did he threaten you? Physically?"

She nodded.

"I see." I settled back to ruminate. I understood her fears. This didn't do Karl Senior any good at all. I already had him down as murder suspect number one, but I was still a little nebulous on motive.

"They were both dumb, Ami and Father. They had to realize it would happen sooner or later. There's too much free-floating residual energy around any place used by someone like my mother not to interfere with the spells on a contraceptive amulet."

"If she could see it coming—"

"Don't start, Garrett. You don't know what it was like. You aren't a woman. You aren't a daughter. And you've never been in a squeeze anything like it."

"You're right. All right, here's what I'll do. I'll talk to him without your mother being there. If it's not germane, she won't have to know."

"She won't allow that."

"I'll insist. I'll also insist that you be there with us."

"Oh! Do I have to?"

"I want him in a corner so tight he's got to think his only way out is the truth. He can't lie with you standing there ready to blurt, 'Remember the time when you—' "

"I don't like it."

"Neither do I. But you have to use the tools at hand."

"He couldn't *do* something like you're thinking."

"Amiranda would've begun to show soon. Your mother is inquisitive. And when she asks, she gets answers. How would she have reacted—"

"I know what you're going to say, Garrett. He'd panic. He'd go crazy out of fear. But not that crazy."

"Maybe you're right. If we get him deep enough into that corner, maybe we'll find out for sure." It seemed a good idea to forget that the Stormwarden had discovered Amiranda's pregnancy on her own.

"Garrett. Do we have time . . . ?"

I shook my head slowly.

"It's a pity, really."

"I'm sorry."

As we started down the stairs, she said, "I'll bet you he doesn't even know she was pregnant. Ami wouldn't have told anybody but Karl."

I responded with a noncommittal grunt. He knew now, though I was willing to grant the possibility that he hadn't known then.

I paused to stick my head into the Dead Man's room. "We're going now."

Take care of yourself, Garrett. And mind your manners with your betters.

"The same to you, Chuckles. Want to tell me Glory Mooncalled's secret now? Just in case the worst happens? I'd hate to check out still mystified."

With you entering a Stormwarden's lair? No. We'll consider it after this is done and the break is complete.

He had a point.

I gave Dean some unnecessary instructions about locking up behind me. Then we left.

decided to make a brief detour to Lettie Faren's. Maybe it was wrong. There are times when ignorance *is* bliss.

The man on the door knew me and knew my presence was considered undesirable, but he made only a token effort to keep us out. Inside, Amber gawked and whispered that she wouldn't have believed it if she hadn't seen it.

I gawked myself, but not for the same reasons.

The place wasn't open for business. Never, to my knowledge, had the house been closed before. Alarmed, I pushed past a barman and a swamper who made halfhearted efforts to stop us. I slammed into the pest hole Lettie calls home.

It only took one look. "Stay out there," I instructed Amber.

The mound of ruin that was Lettie Faren tried to glare with eyes blackened and swollen, and failed. She couldn't strike the spark. What remained was a feeble mask for fear.

I asked, "Chodo's boys?"

She croaked an affirmative.

"You should've told me where to find Donni when you knew, before the hard boys decided they wanted her, too."

She just looked at me. Chances were she'd just looked at Chodo's boys, too. For a while. She was damned near as tough as she thought.

"I'm working for Raver Styx these days. That's a tight crack to get caught in, between the Stormwarden and the kingpin."

"I didn't have nothing to tell them and I don't got nothing to tell you, Garrett. Bring on the old witch if you want."

"The wicked flee when no man pursueth. I'll wish you a speedy recovery. Good-bye."

As we headed for the exit, Amber asked, "Why didn't you want me to go in there?"

I gave it to her straight. "I'm not the only one looking for Donni Pell. Those other guys beat her up trying to find out where Donni went."

"Bad?"

"Very. They aren't nice people. In fact, I'm about convinced that you're the only nice person anywhere in this mess."

She laughed nervously and said, "You don't know me very well yet." Then, conversationally, "You're not so bad yourself, Garrett."

Perhaps she didn't know me very well yet, either.

49

The man at the Stormwarden's gate was a stranger. He had a competent, professional look. "How was the vacation in the sunny Cantard?"

It bounced off. "Grim as usual, Mr. Garrett. The Stormwarden is expecting you and is waiting in her audience room. Miss daPena can show you the way."

"Yeah. Thanks. You guys going to do anything for Slauce?"

"Say what?"

"You going in on flowers or anything? I thought I'd kick in if I could. It never would've happened if he hadn't been coming to see me."

"We haven't decided what to do yet. We'll let you know. All right?"

"Sure. Thanks."

When we were out of earshot, Amber said, "See? I told you you weren't all bad."

"A cynical, manipulative gesture meant to incite a sympathetic attitude among the troops."

"Right, Garrett. Whatever you say."

Raver Styx sat alone in the gloom of an unlighted room about the size of the Dead Man's. Her eyes were closed. She was so still and unresponsive I suffered a chill. Had we lost yet another daPena?

No. Those supposedly terrible eyes opened and fixed on me. I saw nothing but a tired and beaten old lady. "Please have a seat, Mr. Garrett." Like a wolfman under a full moon, she began to change. "Amber, I believe you'd do better to isolate yourself here in the house, but if you feel more confident with Mr. Garrett and his associates, you have my blessing." She was becoming the Stormwarden Raver Styx—with a measure of concerned mother.

Amber was within reach and my feet were out of the Stormwarden's line of sight. I nudged her ankle. She started, figured it out, said, "Thank you, Mother. I'd feel better with Mr. Garrett, I think. For now."

That wasn't so hard. Often all we need to be civil with one another is the presence of a referee we don't want thinking us fools.

"As you wish. Where would you like to begin, Mr. Garrett?"

"With Domina Dount."

"Willa Dount, Mr. Garrett. Loss of her position and title is a foregone penalty. Let's not extend any false hopes."

"You're the boss. Whatever, I want to do her first. Then your husband. Then the staff—if that appears productive."

"Wouldn't it be a bit trifling?"

"Maybe. But a few trifles are all I need to fill the gaps in the picture I already have."

"I'm tempted to invoke penalties on the lot and let the gods distinguish between the wicked and the merely incompetent."

Sometimes I felt that way about our ruling class. I observed the Dead Man's advice, though, and kept my opinion to myself. "I know what you mean."

"How do you want to work it? In my presence? In Amber's?"

"In Willa Dount's case, with you present and Amber absent. To begin. I've already told Amber how long to stay away. After she comes in, I want you to find a reason to leave. Having dealt with Willa Dount, I doubt the footwork will do any good, but I want to try."

"Very well."

"I'll want to see all the documents she has. Especially the letters from the kidnappers. Have you seen those?"

"Yes, I have."

"Did you recognize the hand?"

"No. It seemed feminine."

"I thought so, too. So precise, what I saw. I feared the one-in-a-thousand chance that Amiranda had written them."

"Amiranda had the penmanship of a drunken troll. There was no reading it, but no mistaking or disguising it, either."

"Good. Now, with your husband I'd prefer to begin with you out of the

room. As for the staff, I'll ask you and Amber person by person. If the intimidation factor inherent in your presence is counterproductive—"

"I understand. Let's get to it."

"Where is Willa Dount now?"

"In her office, doing the job that will be hers for a few more hours."

"Would you get her, Amber? Tell her she needs to bring the documents."

"Yes, master." She gave me a wink that her mother caught.

"I'd appreciate it if you'd hold off acting against Willa Dount or anyone
else for another day, Stormwarden. Tomorrow I want to take everyone on a
walk-through of what happened the night of the ransom payoff and the
morning of Amiranda's death."

"Is that necessary?"

"Yes. Absolutely. Afterward there'll be no lingering doubts."

She didn't press for details, a courtesy I appreciated. Maybe she wasn't
such a bad old gal after all.

We waited in silence.

50

Willa Dount marched in with a stack of papers. "You sent for me, madam?" She didn't seem surprised to see me—and shouldn't have since she had her agents among the staff.

"I've hired Mr. Garrett to hunt down the person or people responsible for the deaths of Amiranda, Karl, and Courter Slauce. He wants to ask you questions, Willa. Answer completely and truthfully."

I raised the eyebrow. Slauce, too? Surprise, surprise. But certainly a point for her.

"Give those papers to Mr. Garrett."

She did so with ill grace. "You're a vulture circling this family, aren't you? You won't rest till you've picked its bones."

"If you take a quick count of the number of noses on your face, you'll come up with more than the number of times I've approached the daPena family soliciting employment."

"Your wit hasn't suffered any improvement."

"Willa. Sit down and be quiet. Restrain your prejudices and speak only when you're spoken to."

"Yes, madam."

Did the whip crack there, or did it crack?

Willa Dount planted herself in a chair, face blank and cool.

If she was going to perch I was going to prowl. I rose, began moving, shuffling the papers. The kidnappers had gone to great lengths to make sure Domina Dount understood exactly what she was supposed to do. I slipped a finger behind the letters I'd met already, looked Willa Dount in the eye, and asked, "When did you first suspect that Karl's kidnapping was contrived?"

"When Amiranda disappeared. She'd been odd for weeks, and had her head together with Karl for days before he vanished."

Lie number one, straight out of the chute? Willa Dount should have been on the road to her payoff appointment before Amiranda made her break. Unless . . .

Unless she'd known beforehand what Amiranda planned.

"When did you begin to suspect the game had become real?"

"When I reached the place where I was supposed to hand the gold over. Those people weren't playing. They were deadly real. I'm afraid I almost lost my composure. I've never been that afraid."

"Describe the people you met there."

She frowned.

I told her, "I've asked you before about the payoff. You wouldn't talk. It was your right at the time. But not now. So tell me about those people, and about that night." I thumbed the first letter I hadn't yet read.

"There were two closed coaches and at least four people. Two coachmen of mixed parentage, probably ogre and human. The ugliest man I've ever seen. And a fairly attractive young woman. The ugly man was in charge."

"You said at least four. What does that mean? Was there somebody else?"

"There might have been someone inside the woman's coach. Twice I thought I saw movement in there, but they made me stay on the wagon. I wasn't close enough to be sure."

"Uhm." I picked a spot near a good light and adjusted a chair. "From the beginning of that night. Every trivial detail."

She began. And soon I was hearing what I expected, a tale with no significant deviations from the one Skredli had told me.

I lent her both ears and one eye while I skimmed the letters. Then I went over a few again. Then again. And finally I thought I saw what I'd half expected to see, though I'm no expert on forgery.

Willa Dount reached her departure from the bridge over Cedar Creek. I didn't figure anything interesting happened after that. "Hold it there."

She stopped dead. And dead is the way I'd describe the voice she'd been using. She'd been under so much strain for so long she had very little fire left.

"That payoff setup was as queer as a nine-foot pixie. No swap on the spot—though I admit there wasn't a lot you could do once you got there. You

couldn't run away. But they let you see them. And then they let you go without killing you. Knowing who you worked for. At a time when at least one
of them knew there'd be a murder within a few hours."

"I can't explain that, Mr. Garrett. Death is all I expected when I realized
that Karl wasn't there."

Unless you took out some kind of insurance, I thought. Like maybe not
delivering the whole ransom, and, maybe, refusing to let the balance go
until you and Karl were safe. Maybe even not knowing where the rest was,
or saying you didn't, so they wouldn't try anything rough. There was something or you wouldn't be here now.

I thought it but didn't say it.

"Did you hear any names mentioned? Did you get a good look at any of
them?"

"No names. There was moonlight. I saw all four well enough to recognize again, though the woman and the ugly man stayed back. I have excellent night vision. Maybe they didn't realize how clearly I saw them."

"Maybe. It probably doesn't matter now, anyway. They're all dead but the
woman."

She just looked at me. You couldn't crack her with a sledgehammer.

I had everything I wanted to get with the Stormwarden watching. I was
wondering how I could stall just as Amber let herself in.

Raver Styx made no pretenses and no excuses. She stood and left.

Amber whispered, "I didn't find anything in her quarters. She doesn't
keep a journal or—"

"You don't have to talk behind my back in front of me, Amber. Spit it
out."

I nodded.

"The accounts didn't look jiggered. The silver was sold for anywhere
from seven to fifteen percent below market. I'm not sure, but I'd guess that
would be reasonable in the circumstances. Whatever, the price of silver has
fallen enough that now the buyers are the losers."

That was my Amber, keeping up with the metals market despite everything.

"Who did the buying?"

She handed me a list.

"Interesting. The top name here, Lyman Gameleon, is down for a hundred twenty thousand at the maximum discount. Gameleon is one of our
big-three suspects."

Even that didn't rock Willa Dount. She said only, "It was an emergency and I went where I had to go to get enough gold. The Stormwarden has examined the accounts of these transactions and expressed no disapproval."

A thought. Maybe even an inspiration. "Do you recall the dates and times of the transactions, Amber?" She had not noted those.

"No. Should I go get them?"

Willa Dount said, "That won't be necessary. I remember." She rattled off every deal as though she was reading from the record.

The timing made it conceivable that the deals themselves had initiated the chain of complications. Or, at least, could have led to intensive recomplication.

"Did Gameleon know what the gold was for?"

"Lord Gameleon, Garrett," Domina scolded.

"Look, I don't care if you call him Pinky Porker. Just answer the question."

"Yes. He had to be told before he'd deal."

I'd already established, to my own satisfaction, a link between Gameleon and Donni Pell. "Was that wise?"

"In retrospect, probably not. But at the time Lord Gameleon was a last resort."

"Hardly. But let's not fight about it. That's it for tonight."

"Tonight?"

"I'll need you again tomorrow. Early. We're all going to walk this through."

She gave me a puzzled look as she rose. What chicanery was I planning?

"Find the Baronet and send him in," I said.

I'd grown impatient and irritable by the time the door opened. And that opening didn't make anything better.

Willa Dount and Raver Styx came in, the Stormwarden looking like one of the tempests she brewed. "Will you want to question the staff, Mr. Garrett?"

"Where's your husband?"

"I don't doubt the answer to that question would be quite interesting. He left the house shortly after you arrived. When last seen he was entering the house of Lord Gameleon, his half brother, who lives across the street. Lord Gameleon admits that he was there earlier but denies that he is now. About the staff?"

There was no juice left. My candle had begun to gutter. "The hell with them. I can tie the knot on it without them. I'm going home to get some sleep. Meet me at my place at eight, ready for a trek upcountry. Don't let anybody else wander off. Make a production of leaving so anyone interested will know something is up."

"As you will, Mr. Garrett. That will be all for tonight, then, Willa."

I asked, "Amber, are you coming or staying?"

Staring at the floor, she replied, "I'll go with you. But I need to get some things first."

I guess that was as close as she could come to telling her mother to pick her nose with her elbow. The Stormwarden developed a severe tic in her left cheek but she said nothing. She understood battles lost as well as battles won.

The first thing I did when we got to the house was write a letter to Morley Dotes. I had one of the neighbor kids deliver it. Then I brought the Dead Man up to date and feigned an effort to pry a few secrets out of him just to keep him feeling wanted. I joined Amber in the kitchen, where we shared one of Dean's finer productions. Then I stashed myself away for the night.

My dreams, which I usually don't recall, weren't the kind I'll treasure forever.

51

Dean rousted me out in plenty of time to get ready. We breakfasted well and packed our field rations. I took a look at my arsenal and picked a couple of lethal engines suitable for a lady. I made Amber practice with them until her mother's cavalcade arrived.

A thoughtful woman, the Stormwarden. She had somehow ascertained that I didn't have transportation of my own. She rolled up with a coach, a carriage, and a spare horse. She was in the coach. Willa Dount was driving the carriage. Amber stepped up on the seat beside her. What a lighthearted and friendly drive that would be.

I went around the front of the horse and looked him in the eye. He looked back. I saw none of the tribe's usual malice. He obviously hadn't heard of me.

The Stormwarden had shown some sense in another direction. I had expected to have to nag her into sending her army home, but she'd brought only the two men atop her coach. I couldn't squawk about them.

I suppose when you're a stormwarden, you need guards only for show.

"You lead the way," I told Domina Dount. Her face was old stone as she nodded and started her team. Amber settled facing backward when she saw that I would ride rear guard, though most of the time the Stormwarden's coach obscured our views of one another.

Willa Dount set a brisk pace, occasionally slowing so her boss could catch up. I stayed fifty yards behind the coach. In the city I watched the citizenry watch it. In the country I watched farmers. And as we moved upcountry I kept mentally reviewing my maps.

I didn't see a single place that looked suitable for what I suspected had happened.

I thought about moving up beside Willa Dount. She might have given something away.

Sure. Like stones flinch.

But I had a reason for lying back.

Morley overtook me two-thirds of the way to the deadly crossroads. At that point the road passed among trees and travelers couldn't be watched from afar. He dared rein in and talk.

"They're back there," he told me. "Gameleon and six men. They won't be easy."

"They trying to catch up?"

"No."

"Good. We'll put everybody in the sack at once."

"You're crazy, Garrett. Seven of them and no telling what's up ahead, and you're talking like you've got them by the short hairs?"

"All they've got is numbers. I've got a stormwarden. Hustle on up and tell Saucerhead."

Morley resumed his lone-rider act in a hurry.

It was coming together beautifully. I just hoped I wouldn't be in the middle when it crunched.

I wasn't the most pleased of men when we reached the crossroads. I hadn't spotted one place that fulfilled the criteria for my concept of what had become of most of the ransom gold—though I'd seen a few side roads and whatnot that would later bear further examination. If there was a later. If Amber wasn't more defeatist than I was becoming.

I made the mistake, for a short time, of thinking I saw a chance for the big hit. You don't want to fall into that trap. It can shatter your perspective. It can narrow your focus until the rest of the world slides out of touch.

"Hold up!" I yelled at Willa Dount. She had turned west without pausing. My fault. I hadn't told her we would be stopping.

We got out of traffic's way. I dismounted. Where was Saucerhead? I'd expected him to be waiting.

He stepped out of the woods on the south side of the road. From the corner of my eye I noted Willa Dount's surprise. I joined him. "What have we got?"

"You were right. She's down there."

"Alone?"

"Nope. Company, and plenty of it. One guy by himself showed up about midnight last night. Then a mob of ogre breeds got there just before I left."

"Skredli?"

He nodded.

"How many?"

"Fifteen."

"Crask and Sadler behaving?"

"They aren't stupid, Garrett. They know their limitations."

"I suppose. I'd better tell the Stormwarden. You scout out a workable approach?"

"Sure. What about those guys behind you?"

"They can take care of themselves." I waited while a string of goat carts trundled past, trotted to the Stormwarden's coach, and invited myself inside.

"Why have we stopped, Mr. Garrett?"

I explained. "I didn't expect it to turn into so large a party. Otherwise, everything's come together. Any suggestions?"

"The man who arrived last night. My husband?"

"Probably. My friend wouldn't know him by sight."

"Does Lord Gameleon know where he's going?"

"I don't know."

"He may need someone to follow."

"We can't sneak up on anybody going straight in."

"I realize that, Mr. Garrett."

"I've got a little help but not enough to handle four-to-one odds."

"You have me."

What was that worth? I didn't ask. "All right. My friend and I will sneak up through the woods. You be careful."

"Take Amber. And *you* be careful, Mr. Garrett. I have to salvage something from this disaster."

"She'll be all right." I left the coach. "Amber. You come with me."

The Stormwarden left the coach on the other side. She said something to the men on top. The driver nodded. The other descended. He and Raver Styx boarded the carriage. It rolled away as Amber joined Saucerhead and me.

"What are we doing?" she asked.

"Going for a walk in the woods." I tied my mount's reins to the coach. We ducked into the trees.

Just in time. Lord Gameleon and his boys trotted past. They weren't in livery and made a big deal of ignoring the coach.

When they were gone, Saucerhead asked, "She's going straight in?"

"I guess. We'll have to hurry. Where's Morley? With Crask and Sadler?"

"Right. Follow me. Miss daPena?"

"Just lead, Mr. Tharpe. I'll keep up."

52

Our timing was perfect.

We were near the edge of the clearing when Morley appeared out of nowhere. "Not bad for a city boy," I told him. Crask and Sadler popped up as suddenly. If we'd been unfriendly, we would have been in big trouble. "Anything happening over there?"

"Lot of screaming."

"What?"

"Started right after I got here. Somebody's asking some questions. Somebody else isn't giving the answers they want to hear."

I wasn't surprised.

Crask said, "Something's happening."

I joined him. From where he stood the farmhouse could be seen plainly. Ogre breeds boiled out, raced across the weedy field toward the gap where the road left the woods. "Their lookout must have spotted the Stormwarden."

Someone grunted.

"They been doing any patrols? Or just watching the road?"

"Watching the road," Sadler said. "They're ogres."

"Stupid. The Stormwarden may have overestimated herself. They might kill first and ask questions later."

"They're distracted now," Saucerhead said. "Be a good time to move up. If we keep low along the downhill side of that swale there, we can get pretty close. Maybe up to the foundation stones where the barn used to be."

I recalled a deer trail through the high grass that followed the route Saucerhead recommended. I looked but I couldn't see the stones. "You've been over there?"

"Yeah. I had to look in and make sure."

"Let's go."

Saucerhead went first, then Crask, then Morley. I told Amber to keep down and sent her next. I followed her. Sadler brought up the rear.

We were halfway across when the brouhaha broke out in the woods. We stopped. I said, "That doesn't sound like ogres running into surprise sorcery."

"No."

"Let's move."

As we crouched among the stones, thirty yards from the rear of the house, Skredli's gang emerged from the woods uphill. They had five or six prisoners.

"Gameleon," I said. "What happened to the Stormwarden?"

"There are twelve breeds up there, Garrett," Morley said. "In a minute they won't be able to spot us behind the house. Why don't we make our move? Be waiting for them inside when they get there?"

I didn't like it. But the odds weren't going to get any better. I checked the others. They all nodded. "Amber, stay put. I'll holler when it's safe."

She had developed a case of deafness. When we moved toward the back door, she moved with us. I cursed under my breath but there was nothing I could do short of bopping her and laying her out.

We reached the house unnoticed. Morley volunteered to lead. Nobody argued. He was the best.

We moved.

Inside there were three ogres, one woman, and Karl daPena, Senior. Morley creamed two of the ogres before they knew they were in trouble. The third tried to yell and only got out a bark before Crask stuck a knife through his throat.

Sadler finished the other two.

Amber dumped her breakfast.

"I told you to stay out." I ground my teeth and examined our prizes. Neither seemed particularly pleased to see us.

"Frying pan into the fire, eh, Baronet?"

Both were strapped into chairs. DaPena was gagged. The woman wasn't, but she was yelled out. Both had been tortured, and with little finesse.

"You must be the marvelous Donni Pell. I've been anxious to meet you. Right now you don't look like something that men would kill for."

"Cut the sweet talk, Garrett," Morley said. "They're coming."

I peeked. "That clown Skredli must have raised an army."

"We can take them. They have to keep hold of their prisoners."

"I like a man with a positive attitude. Why don't I slide out the back way and you holler when you've got them?"

"You going to mouth your way through the gates of hell or are you going to decide what to do?"

"Crask, Sadler, you guys get out of sight down that hall. Saucerhead, wait behind the door. Let four or five get in, then slam it and bolt it. Morley and I will jump out from the kitchen. We ought to polish off the bunch before the rest bust in. Amber, you get out back."

This time she did what I told her. Nothing like a good scare.

"And you call me a tactical genius," Morley grumbled. But he ducked into the kitchen without offering a suggestion of his own.

Even tactical geniuses stumble. When Saucerhead went to slam the door, Skredli and two other breeds were on the transom. He had the strength to bounce two of them back into the yard, but the third got caught between the edge of the door and the frame. He did a lot of yelling and flailing while Saucerhead grunted and strained, trying to shut the door right through him. And Tharpe did manage to hang on while we thumped the five he'd let in.

Morley chuckled. "Seven to go. Let them in, Saucerhead."

Tharpe jumped back. Skredli and the guys stomped in.

We did expect them to have their cutlery out, ready for carving. We didn't expect Gameleon's Brunos to help them. They did. "We been suckered, Garrett," Saucerhead said as he stumbled back past me.

Long knife in one hand and head thumper in the other, fending off two ogres and a man, I fell past a window and shot a quick look to see if help was coming.

No stormwarden.

Had the gang dealt with her already? Had they caught her in a pincer up in the woods?

I kicked one guy in the groin but not good enough to slow him much. The three pushed me toward the kitchen, keeping me too busy staying alive to keep track of what was happening to everybody else. Win or lose, Skredli and his bunch would get hurt. They were up against the best TunFaire offered.

Small consolation.

I got in a solid thump to an ogre's head as I backed through the kitchen doorway. He reeled, stalling his companions. I whirled and dove through a window.

I did not land well. The breath went out of me and didn't want to come back. But I got my feet under me in time to lay a whack on the skull of a guy trying to climb after me. It was no head breaker, but it discouraged him.

I limped to the front door, wound up and flung one of the witch's crystals. Then I held up a wall while my breath caught up with me and the crystal did its deed.

The uproar inside died.

When I went in, everybody was folded up puking. I shambled around thumping heads. When I had the bad guys down I scrounged what I could and tied them up. I got done just before the spell wore off.

Sitting against a wall, Morley glared and croaked, "Thanks a bloody bunch, Garrett. I'm ruined."

"Ingrate. You're alive."

I don't dare describe the looks the ingrates Crask and Sadler gave me. It was a good thing they had stomachs and a few wounds to patch.

I heard sounds outside. I went to the door.

The Stormwarden was coming. Finally.

She left the carriage and strode toward me. I stepped out of her way. She entered, scanned the battleground, sniffed, looked at me suspiciously. I said, "We're all here now. I'll get things sorted out and we'll start."

"All right." She marched over to the Baronet. His chair had overturned during the struggle. She stared down at him briefly, then turned to Donni Pell. "Is this the infamous whore, Mr. Garrett?"

"I didn't ask yet. I think so."

"She doesn't look like much, does she?"

"With females you never know. She might be a whole different act cleaned up and set down where she thought she could work her magic."

That got me the darkest look she'd given yet.

Meanwhile, Domina Dount just stood in the doorway, for the first time in our acquaintance, at a loss.

"Saucerhead. Why don't you get Amber?"

He gave me a look as loving as the Stormwarden's, but nodded and went out back. I said, "Stormwarden, I don't know if it's within your expertise, but if you can, we'd all appreciate a little healing magic here."

"Everyone who faces the Warlords of Venageta must learn elementary field medicinal spells, Mr. Garrett."

"Maybe everyone of a certain class." Amber came in. Her face went gray.

I thought she was going to upchuck again. "It gets rough sometimes, Amber. Gut it out. You all right, Saucerhead?"

"I'll live, Garrett. Why the hell don't you ever warn anybody when you're going to pull something out of your sleeve?" He winced and clapped one hand to his stomach.

I didn't bother explaining that if I'd warned him I'd have warned the bad guys, too.

We dumped the ogres and Brunos in the weeds, live or dead. The farmhouse was still as crowded as a rabbit warren. We found seats for everybody. Only Amber and I remained standing. She leaned against the doorframe, too nervous to sit. Though the Stormwarden's perch was no better than anyone else's, her manner turned it into a throne.

She said, "Proceed, Mr. Garrett."

"Let's start with my old buddy Skredli. Skredli, tell the nice people the story you told me at Chodo's place. Keep in mind that the lady there can make you hurt a lot worse than Chodo ever did."

Skredli got fatalistic again. He told his story. The same story.

Donni Pell was the villain of his piece. She was a wonder to watch as she tried working on him so he would cast her in a better light.

Gameleon and daPena were worth watching, too. And Domina Dount, for that matter, as she learned that some things she'd heard but not gut-believed were true.

When Skredli finished, I looked at Gameleon. "You think you can talk your way out of here?"

"I'll have your head."

Morley asked, "You want me to knock him around a little to improve his attitude, Garrett? I always wanted to see if blue-blood bones sound different when they break."

"I don't think we'll need to."

"Let me twist his arm a little. How about you, Saucerhead? We could hang him up by the ankles and break him like a wishbone."

I snapped, "Knock it off!"

Raver Styx lifted her left hand and extended it toward Gameleon, palm forward, fingers spread. Her face was bland. But lavender sparks danced between her fingers.

Gameleon yelled, "No!" Then he screamed a long, chilly one. I wouldn't believe anybody had that much breath in him. He went slack.

"So much for him. For now. Baronet? How about you? Want to sing your song?"

Hell no, he didn't. His old lady was sitting right there. She'd have his nuchos on a platter.

She said, "Karl, whatever you're thinking, the alternative will be worse." She raised her left hand again. A few sparks flew. He flinched, whimpered. She dropped her hand into her lap, smiled a cruel smile. "I'd do it, too, you know." And she would. I was convinced.

There were some bleak faces in that place.

I looked at Gameleon, at daPena, at Domina Dount, at Amber, who sincerely regretted having come. Poor old Skredli was damning himself for not running instead of trying to make a last score.

Donni Pell . . . Well, I concentrated on the spider woman for the first time. I had avoided that because even I, a bit, was subject to whatever made her so dangerous.

She didn't look dangerous. She was a small woman, fair, well into her twenties, but with one of those marvelous faces and complexions that make some small, fair women look adolescent for years beyond their time. She was pretty without being beautiful. Even ragged, filthy, and abused, she had a certain something that touched both the father and the lech in a man, a something that made a man want to protect and possess.

I don't play with little girls, but I know the feeling a man can get looking at a ripening fifteen-year-old.

In my time I have encountered several Donni Pells. They are conscious of what they do to men—manipulate it like hell. The sensual frenzy is balanced by manipulating the fatherly urge as well. Usually they come across as being empty between the ears, too. In desperate need of protection.

Donni Pell, I suppose, was an artist, having turned an essentially patriarchal society's stereotype of a woman's role into a bludgeon with which she worked her will upon the male race. She was still trying to do it, bound and gagged.

Under it all she was tough. As hard and heartless as a Morley Dotes, who might qualify as the male counterpart of a Donni Pell. Skredli and his boys hadn't broken through.

The Stormwarden said, "Will you get on with it, Mr. Garrett?"

"I'm trying to decide where to poke the hornet's nest. Right now these people have no incentives."

"How about staying alive?" She rose and joined me. "Somebody here had Amiranda killed. Somebody here had my son killed. Somebody here is going to pay for that. Maybe a lot of somebodies if the innocent don't convince me of their lack of guilt. How's that for motivation, Mr. Garrett?"

"Excellent. If you can convince a couple men who figure their place in the world entitles them to immunity from justice."

"Justice has nothing to do with it. Stark, bloody, screaming, agonizing vengeance is what I'm talking about. I'm not concerned about political repercussions. I no longer care if I get pulled down."

Her intensity convinced me. I looked at her husband and Gameleon. DaPena was convinced, too. But Gameleon was holding his own.

Softly, I said, "Courter Slauce."

Equally softly, the Stormwarden replied, "I haven't forgotten him. Continue."

I scanned them all again—then turned on Domina Dount. "You feel like modifying anything you've said before?"

She looked blankly at me.

"I don't think you're directly repsonsible for any deaths, Domina. But you helped turn a scam into something deadly."

She shivered. Willa Dount *shivered*! She was ready to break. The blood had reached her when she'd had to see it firsthand. Amber sensed it, too. Despite the state of her nerves, she glared at me. I winked.

"Nobody wants to kick in?"

Nobody volunteered to save himself.

"All right. I'll reconstruct. Correct me if I get it wrong, or if you want somebody else to get the shaft."

"Mr. Garrett."

"Right, Stormwarden. So. It started a long time ago, in a house on the Hill, when a woman who shouldn't have had children did so."

"Mr. Garrett!"

"My contract is for a job done without interference, Stormwarden. I was going to walk lightly. But since you're impatient, I'll just spit it out. You made life such hell for them that your whole family was ready to do anything to get away. Nobody worked up the guts to try till you went to the Cantard, though. It's unlikely anybody would have then if your husband hadn't, in the course of continued unwanted attentions, gotten Amiranda pregnant."

Amber glared daggers. Domina Dount squeaked. The Stormwarden glared, too, but only because I was making public something she already suspected. The Baronet fainted.

"As soon as she knew, Amiranda went to the only friend she had, your son. They cooked up a scheme to save her from shame and get them both away from a house they loathed. Junior would get kidnapped. They would use the ransom to start a new life.

"But they couldn't work it out by themselves. They wanted it to look so real the Stormwarden Raver Styx would believe that her son had been done in by dishonorable villains. Why? Because whatever else they felt, the da-Pena brats loved their father and didn't want him crucified. They wanted to cover for him."

"Mr. Garrett—"

"I'm going to do it my way, Stormwarden." I faced Donni Pell. "They couldn't pull it off without help. So Junior went to his girlfriend. She said she'd arrange everything. And things started going wrong right away, because Donni Pell can't do anything straight.

"She told the guys she hired what was happening, figuring she could work it for a profit. She told the Baronet, figuring she could get something out of him. She told Lord Gameleon, maybe. Or maybe he got it from another direction. There are several ways he could have known.

"Donni planned to do the stunt using ogres who were stealing from the daPena warehouse and selling to Gameleon. That was a big screwup. Domina Dount already had Junior investigating shortages at the warehouse." I spoke directly to Donni. "And you knew it.

"Meanwhile, Karl Senior let Domina Dount in on the news."

Willa Dount registered an inarticulate protest.

"Karl got grabbed on schedule and taken here, where Donni grew up. Then Willa Dount, to keep it looking good at her end, asked me to put my stamp of approval on what she was doing to get him back. The kidnappers thought I'd been hired to poke into the warehouse business. They tried to convince me to keep out.

"Now it gets confusing as to who did what to who and why. None of the principals understood what they were doing because they were all being pulled in several directions. Everybody at the Stormwarden's house thought they had a chance for a big hit and a break with Raver Styx. Everybody outside saw the big hit. But the pregnancy and warehouse might come out if the kidnapping was investigated. Junior had to be sent home and kept quiet so the trails could get stale before the Stormwarden got back. But then I was suddenly in the middle of the thing. Nobody knew what I was doing, and I wouldn't go away.

"So. The ransom demand was made. The delivery was set. Domina raised the money. And Amiranda, who sensed that it wasn't going according to plan, headed for her rendezvous with Junior.

"But Donni had gotten other folks involved. And they fancied a hunk of ransom. The hell with the kid. What could he do? Go cry to his mother?

"But Karl Senior, who figured to get half of Donni's half of the ransom, warned her that Ami was tough enough to blow the whole thing." I glared at the Baronet. He was awake now, and bone white. "So Donni arranged for Ami to do what she had planned: disappear forever. I guess Junior was supposed to think it was Ami who left him without his share."

Donni Pell made noise and shook her head. The Stormwarden stared at her with the intensity of a snake sizing up supper.

I didn't know if I had that part right. Amiranda's death, otherwise, benefited no one but the Baronet. But I couldn't figure him for the order. He wouldn't have done it for his piddling share of the ransom. Or maybe he never got it, because he hadn't made tracks when he should have had cash in hand.

I glared into Donni's eyes. "You going to tell us who wanted the girl killed? Or are you just going to tell us it wasn't you?"

She had a very dry throat. I don't think anybody heard her but me. "It was the kid. He said—"

I don't bash women often. When I backhanded her I told myself it was because she wasn't one. Not in the lady sense.

With her talent she might have sold the idea to somebody. But I'd been back and forth with it from the beginning, and if there was one thing I'd learned from it all, it was that the son wasn't guilty of that one. His big crime was stupidity compounded by gutlessness.

"Better come up with a more likely sacrifice, kid. Or you're it."

The trouble with Donni Pell was that she had no handles. She knew exactly where she stood and exactly what her chances were. She was the only person alive who really knew what had happened. I could guess, and spout, and maybe come close, but I couldn't get more than seventy-five percent.

The Stormwarden said, "Mr. Garrett, I'm willing to be patient in the extreme, but this approach isn't unmasking anything. With what you've already given me I've reached several conclusions. One: that my brother-in-law, Lord Gameleon, for reasons he considered adequate, had my son killed. In his instance my only interest is to determine the extent to which my husband had knowledge of that and was involved in the effort to financially weaken me by siphoning my sources of income."

She wasn't stupid. And just because she wasn't in the trade didn't mean she had to be blind. "All right. I would've gotten to that eventually. I was hoping friend Donni would nail it down when the flood started."

"There won't be a flood with her, Mr. Garrett. You know that. The woman has the soul of a . . . a . . ."

At a loss for words? I would have suggested "Stormwarden" to fill her metaphor, but she was already unhappy with me. It was no time to press my luck.

She said, "I'm also certain that my husband killed Courter Slauce. That much detecting I could manage myself. He was away from the house when it happened. He left on Slauce's heels, in a panic according to the men on the gate."

The Baronet tried to protest. Nobody listened. I asked, "Why?"

"Slauce knew something. Karl was frightened enough to murder him to keep him from telling you. Courter would have been easy for him. Comparatively. Karl hated the man, and Slauce wouldn't have felt he was in any danger from such a coward. That leaves Amiranda."

54

Who *did* kill Amiranda Crest?

It was the question of the case. I'd begun to suspect we'd never get an answer. Only one person knew—maybe—and he or she wasn't talking.

"I have a suggestion, Mr. Garrett," the Stormwarden said in a tone that made it clear it was a command. "You take your friends, and the ogre, and Amber, and go back to TunFaire. I'll finish here. When you've settled your accounts, bring the ogre to my home."

From the corner of my eye I caught Morley making a little jabbing motion with his thumb. He thought it was time to go and he was probably right. I said, "You were going to work on our wounds."

"Yes." No sooner said than done. Crask and Sadler were awed. With Saucerhead's help they grabbed Skredli and dragged him out the front door. He hollered and carried on like he thought the Stormwarden was going to save him.

"Into the carriage," I told them.

Morley raised an eyebrow and jerked his head toward the house.

"Her problem. You, get down," I told the man who had driven down the Stormwarden and Willa Dount. "Amber. Get up on the seat. No. Don't argue. Just do it. Shut him up, Saucerhead." The Stormwarden's man backed away from us, looking at me like he was looking death in the eye. He went around the side of the house instead of going inside. "Sadler, you drive. Crask, keep the ogre under control."

They gave me dark looks. I didn't care. I wanted words with Morley and Saucerhead as we walked up the slope.

"Roll."

They rolled. We trudged along behind. I looked back once. The Stormwarden's man was headed across the clearing. Evidently he understood what was going on and wanted to be far away.

Morley spoke first. "I don't like the way she took over all of a sudden, Garrett."

And Saucerhead. "You don't ever want to go to her place again."

"She'd hand me my head. I know." We walked until we reached the woods. I told Sadler to stop. "You guys understand what was happening down there? What the old bitch was thinking?"

Crask knew. "She's going to rub them. Then she's going to arrange something for us because she don't want nobody around who knows she did it to guys like her old man and Gameleon."

I looked up at Amber. She wanted to argue, but she shivered. After a moment, she said, "I think I saw the change come over her before you did, Garrett. What are you going to do?"

"If we took a vote, none of us would go for letting her do what she wants."

Morley said, "Kill them all and let the gods sort them out."

Saucerhead said, "It isn't like they're innocent. Except maybe the Dount woman."

"Amber. Where will Willa Dount stand?"

"I don't know. She's been into things like this with Mother before. Mother would trust her to keep her mouth shut. But Mother seemed a little crazy. She might include Willa with the others. She had to be guilty of something, even if she didn't kill anybody."

"Yeah. She was guilty of a lot. But not the killings. I don't think."

Friend Skredli flopped in the back of the carriage.

A scream came from the farmhouse. "Gameleon," Morley said. "I figured she'd start with him."

"She'll stay with him for a long time. Amber. Do you see the position we're in?"

She didn't want to.

"Your mother plans to kill those people, then kill us so we can't accuse her," I reiterated. "Right?"

Weakly, "Yes. I think so."

"What options does that leave us?"

She shrugged.

I let her stew it awhile. "You think she thinks we're dumb enough not to see that?"

Nobody thought that.

Skredli thumped around again. Nobody paid any attention.

"Does she think we'll go back to town and try to insure ourselves? Or does she figure we'll do something about it now?"

"How well does she know us?" Morley asked.

"I don't know. She told me she checked me out when she hired me."

"She expects us to move now, Garrett."

Saucerhead said, "She'll never be more vulnerable."

Amber snapped, "Wait a damned minute!"

"Sweetheart, you said yourself—"

"I know. But you can't—"

"You think we should let her hunt us down instead?"

"You could get out of TunFaire. You could—"

"So could she. But she won't. And neither will we. TunFaire is home. Crask. Sadler. What do you think?"

They huddled and muttered for half a minute. Crask elected himself spokesman. "You're right. We're in it with you for whatever you have to do. If it looks practical."

Gameleon had stopped yelling. He'd probably passed out. After a pause, the Baronet took up the song. I moved downhill a little, to where I could see the farmhouse. "I wish I knew more about her skills. Can she tell we're up here? Does she know exactly where we are?" I looked at Amber.

"Don't expect me to help you, Garrett. Even if she does plan murder."

I surveyed the others. They were waiting on me. "I have a suggestion. You take the carriage and go home. Or to my house, if you want. Then you won't be involved. You won't know anything."

"I'll know who came home."

"But that's all you'll know. Get along now. Saucerhead, drag the ogre out before she leaves. You can drive the damned thing, can't you, Amber?"

"I'm not completely helpless, Garrett."

"Scoot, then."

She scooted.

The Baronet had stopped yelling. Donni Pell was tuning up. I said, "We've got to assume she knows we're here. It makes no sense to bet the other way."

Crask asked, "So how you figure to get to her?"

"Something will come to one of us."

Morley gave me a hard look. It said he knew I had something in mind already. I did, but the seed hadn't yet sprouted.

"It's going to be dark soon," Saucerhead predicted. "That what you're waiting for?"

"Maybe. Let's have a chat with friend Skredli."

We set him up against a tree. The others stood behind me, baffled, as I squatted. "Here we are again, Skredli. Me with an idea how you can get out of this with your butt still attached."

He didn't believe there was any such idea. I wouldn't have in his place.

"I'm going to give you a chance to bail me out of a jam. You do it, the worst off you can be is with a head start from here to the farmhouse. I hear you can pick them up and put them down when you want."

A flicker of interest betrayed itself. "Untie him while I explain," I said. "He'll need to get loosened up."

Saucerhead did the honors, not gently.

"Here it is, Skredli. You go down in the field and get your buddies loose. Then you hit the Stormwarden. Take her out. Then give a holler and light out. I have business in that house so I won't be after you. No promises about Saucerhead, but you'll have your head start."

He looked at me hard.

"What do you say?" I asked stonily.

"I don't like it."

"How does it stack up against your current chances?"

I never knew an ogre with a sense of humor. Skredli stunned me when he said, "You talked me into it, you smooth-talking son of a bitch."

"Good. Get up. Work the kinks out." I took one of the witch's crystals from my pocket. This one didn't need to be stomped for activation. "This little treasure here," I said. "It's from the same source as the spell that had everybody puking awhile ago. And that had everybody spinning when we raided your place in Ogre Town. Just so you know it's the real thing, Skredli." I shoved it into his pocket, said the proper word. "If you try to take it out, or if you do anything that makes me want to repeat that word, it'll blow up. It'll tear you in half."

"Hey! We made a goddamn deal!"

"It stands. I'm just trying to make sure your side does. The spell isn't good for more than an hour, and the crystal won't activate if you're too far away for it to hear me yell. I figure the farmhouse is barely in yelling distance. You follow me?"

"Yeah. You human bastards never let up, do you? Never give a guy a break."

"That's the way you want to look at it, Skredli, that's all right with me. Long as you whack the witch."

Skredli drained a long, put-upon sigh from his long-suffering body. "When?"

"As soon as it's dark." Minutes away. I could distinguish the farmhouse only by looking to one side of it.

Five minutes later I told Skredli, "Anytime you feel like getting started."

"How about next New Year's?" He started down the slope.

55

S kredli apparently had an honest streak. If somebody had tried that stunt on me, I would have tested the trick somehow. Unless they were better talkers than I.

"You guys gather around close," I said, after I'd given the breed fifteen minutes to get started. "I've got two tricks left. This one is the best." I took out a crystal bigger than the others the witch had given me. It gave off the minutest amount of soft orange light. I suspect it had stretched her limits to create it—if it did what she claimed it would.

"When I break this, we'll be invisible to the second sight, or whatever you call it, for about ten minutes. We'll still be visible to regular eyes. Once I crack it, don't waste any time."

"You fibbed to Skredli, you bad boy," Saucerhead said.

"Sideways. Sort of. Maybe. If he runs after he makes his diversion, I won't chase him."

"What about me?"

"I warned him. You do what you want when we have the Stormwarden wrapped up."

He grinned big enough to see in the dark.

"Everybody got it?"

They said they did. Morley asked, "What else have you got?"

"What?"

"You said you had a couple of things. I know you, Garrett. What are they?"

"Just one more. A crystal from the same family I used before. This one causes violent muscle cramps."

"Please yell or something this time, Garrett."

"All right. Here goes."

I broke the glowing crystal.

Skredli found half a dozen guys to back him and made his move when we were a hundred fifty yards from the farmhouse. It wasn't a happy move for the most. The attack was over before we were two-thirds of the way to the house. Worms of blue light snapped and snarled around the place. Men yelled. A couple staggered away ablaze. But nothing reached us.

I watched Skredli brush off a patch of fire and head for the woods beyond the house. Saucerhead saw him, too. He growled but stuck.

The Stormwarden stepped out the front door. We dropped down in the grass. There was enough light cast by burning men to show her grinning. She turned back into the darkened house.

I flung my last crystal. I hit the dirt.

Tinkle. And a long scream.

I charged. The others damn near stomped on my heels. They knew as well as I that we had to get her wrapped up in the few seconds when the pain distracted her too much to protect herself.

She was fighting it when we arrived. I tried to clap a hand over her mouth. She ducked me. Morley let her have a fist in the temple that loosened her up, then Crask and Sadler pinned her to the floor. I got back around and clamped my hand over her mouth. "Get the damned light going, Saucerhead."

The woman couldn't remain still. The spasms racking her were as violent as convulsions.

A lamp came to life. But Morley had lighted it. Saucerhead was nowhere to be seen.

Morley set the lamp down and brought a rag that I stuffed into the Stormwarden's mouth. In seconds he returned with rope. We bound her. Her spasms began to ease. "Where did you come up with rope all of a sudden?"

"They didn't need it anymore."

I looked. He was right. Gameleon and the Baronet had checked out. Donni Pell was alive but that was about all. Domina Dount was unbound but standing in a corner, her face a mask of horror, eyes wide but unseeing, skin as pale and cold as a human's can get. I don't think she knew we were there. "Not a very nice lady at all," I said. I sort of wished Amber could be there to see what had happened to her father.

There wasn't a lot left of him or his half brother. I understood why he'd been scared enough to murder Courter Slauce. Had he foreseen this, I could see him being scared enough to ice Amiranda.

Even Sadler and Crask were impressed. And they weren't the types one impresses with human messes.

The Stormwarden was recovering. Her eyes were open, hard, unfriendly. "What now?" Sadler asked.

Our next move was obvious. There was only one way to save our butts: do unto others first. But that was a hell of a giant step, even after we'd started taking it. I've got no use for our masters from the Hill, and the others had none either, but we'd been conditioned to think them immune to our ire.

A wish came true.

A sound. I thought it was Saucerhead. But Sadler and Crask, nearer the door, whipped out blades and got set for trouble.

Amber walked in. And right behind her was Saucerhead's witch.

I gawked.

Shaggoth stuck his head in the door while Morley muttered something elvish, sniffed disgustedly, and withdrew into the night.

Morley finally managed, "What the hell was that?"

"A troll."

Amber didn't react physically this time. She looked at her father's remains. She looked at her mother. She looked at Gameleon and Donni Pell. She looked at her mother again. She looked at Willa Dount, then she looked at me. Her lips were tight and white. She shook her head, took Willa Dount into her arms and began making soothing sounds.

"What now?" Sadler asked again.

I looked at the witch. "Your stuff came in handy."

"I guessed it might." She looked like *she* might lose her most recent meal.

"What're you doing here?"

"Shaggoth came upon this child on the road, in hysterics. He brought her to me. I wheedled some of her story out of her and guessed some more and thought you might be in trouble. We've been on the hill behind you for the past hour."

"Ran into Amber just by chance, eh?"

She smiled. "We like to keep track." She glanced around. "Your associate has asked twice what you want to do now."

"It isn't a matter of what I want to do. It's what I have to do to stay healthy. I was planning to dump them down the well and fill it. By the time anyone digs them up they won't be identifiable."

"You tend to think as grimly as those you oppose today, Garrett. You're the knight in the nighted land, remember? A rage for justice? That's what you brought with you when you visited me. Not kill or be killed."

"Show me the way. My head's locked in. It's gotten too bloody and too brutal."

"Amber. Come here."

Amber left Willa Dount, who had begun to show some color. "Yes?"

"Explain to Garrett what we discussed while we waited on the hillside."

"Discussed? You told me . . . Garrett, all we have to do now is get some people from the High Council to come and see what's happened. Nobody else has to get killed. We can just sit tight and keep things the way they are. Answer questions honestly. My mother has overstepped her rights. They'll take appropriate steps. Including making certain Mother never hurts anybody again. You and your friends included."

I thought about it. I thought about it some more. Maybe they were too damned idealistic. But if the right bunch came out, some of the Stormwarden's enemies, we might come up smelling like roses. They could tie it in a knot and make a good show, get what they wanted, and come out looking like champions of justice themselves. "It's worth a think. Let's take a walk." I grabbed her hand and went outside.

"What is it?" she asked.

"The gold?"

"It's gone. Isn't it? Anyway, if it turns out the way the witch said, it won't matter. I'll get everything that belonged to my mother and father and *she* won't be there to—"

"The gold isn't gone. Not most of it. Willa Dount hid it somewhere. Skredli's bunch weren't after two hundred thousand. They asked for twenty thousand. Domina forged an extra cipher into all those letters."

"Oh. I see. You want your half."

"Not really. I never counted on getting it. I just want you to keep it in mind if you bring in a tribunal. They get a sniff of that, they could get itchy to grab."

"It's all right with you? To do it this way?"

"It's fine with me. It's you I'm asking about."

"She said it would be."

"The witch?"

"Yes. She knows you better than I do, I guess."

"Let's go inside." We went. I told Crask and Sadler, "You guys got any reason to hang around?"

Crask was leaning against a wall, watching the witch. He said, "Yeah." He pointed. "Her." He meant Donni Pell. "Chodo wants her. When you're done with her. If she's still breathing."

"What for?"

"An ornament. Like the broads that hang around the pool. He thinks she'd be interesting, all he's heard."

"I see." I liked an aspect of the idea. I examined my conscience. Better than killing her. Maybe. "It's all right with me. Take her now."

The witch gave me an unreadable look. Then she stepped over and did something to Donni Pell. The girl began breathing easier.

Saucerhead came strolling in. He saw the witch and looked sheepish immediately. I got the distinct impression the world would be plagued by an ogre breed named Skredli no more.

Morley said nothing. In fact, he did one of the fanciest fades ever. I paid no attention while Crask and Sadler started out with Donni Pell on a crude stretcher. And when I looked, Morley was nowhere in sight.

56

The investigators came in a body of eight. They were painfully thorough, yet there was never any doubt of their ruling. The final decision found Lord Gameleon, Baronet daPena, and the Stormwarden Raver Styx all guilty of murder. Amiranda's death they ascribed to person or persons unknown.

On the Hill they don't hang each other. Raver Styx was sentenced to be stripped of her property and sorcerous powers and ejected from the Hill, to make her way alone in the world. Except she didn't exactly go alone. Willa Dount vanished, and the last I heard Raver Styx was trying to hunt her down. One hundred eighty thousand marks gold!

I wonder if Raver Styx will have any luck. I never managed to locate Willa Dount or the gold, despite months of searching whenever I had free time.

I did figure out that she had kept it with her all the time. She hadn't been late to the payoff meet because she'd stopped on the way, but, as Skredli had thought, she'd miscalculated the speed a heavily loaded wagon could make. The cut she'd forged for herself had been concealed under a false bottom. I found the very wagon and the man who had modified it for her. Whatever she did with the gold, she did it after the payoff.

I did all right, though. I found ways to recover most of the rest, and Amber made sure I got ten percent.

I've had no direct contact with Amber since we got back to TunFaire. She's been too busy muscling into her mother's place in the scheme of the Hill to visit me. I haven't dared go there.

• • •

I looked like I'd spent six weeks in the wild islands when I got home. Dean took one look and rolled up his nose. He said, "I'll put some water on to heat, Mr. Garrett."

I heard a woman say something in the kitchen. I was not up to coping with one of his nieces. "What have I told you about . . ."

Tinnie stepped into the hallway, an angry red-haired vision. "I'm going to give you one chance to explain, Garrett," she said, and went back into the kitchen.

"What the hell is that?"

"She saw you coming out of Lettie Faren's place with a woman the afternoon she got back to town." Dean looked smug.

"And you, knowing who I was with and why, didn't bother to explain because you figured it would serve me right to get on her shit list. Eh?"

He refused to look abashed. The rat.

Tinnie took my word. More or less. After I explained everything six times and showed her that, yes, I'd even made money on this one. But it took some doing, and some of the money had to be spent in fancy eating places and whatnot, before she decided to forgive me for whatever it was she imagined I might have done.

She finally relented when I started muttering about marrying one of Dean's nieces. She wanted to save me from a fate worse than death.

A week had passed when Crask came to the door. I wasn't in a good mood. Dean and the Dead Man and Tinnie were all riding me for one reason or another. Saucerhead was avoiding me because of what he'd gone through during the investigation. Morley's boys wouldn't let me get anywhere near his place. Every time I left the house, Pokey Pigotta followed me. For no special reason, just because he wanted to hone his skills to the point where he could do it without me getting wise. I wasn't in a good mood.

"Yeah?" I saved my nastiest tone. I'm not so stupid I'd lay that on one of Chodo Contague's head breakers. The next one that came around might not be somebody I recognized—and he might play a few drumrolls on my skull with pieces of lead pipe.

"Chodo wants to see you."

Wonderful. I didn't want to see Chodo. Not unless I got into a pinch so bad it was time to collect my favor. "Social?"

Crask smiled. "You could say that."

I didn't like it. I hadn't seen Crask smile since he'd turned up in my life.

He said, "He has a gift for you."

Oh boy. A gift from the kingpin. The way those boys operate, that could mean anything. With my imagination it couldn't mean anything good. But what could I do? I'd been summoned. I have enough enemies without adding the kingpin just to snub him. "Let me tell my man. So he can lock up."

I told Dean. I glanced in on the Dead Man. The fat son was still asleep. He'd dozed off while we were out at the damned farm. He still hadn't told me how Glory Mooncalled was working his military magic.

I had a surprise for him.

57

Chodo could put on a show. Crask took me out there in a coach as fancy as anything off the Hill. Maybe the same one we had used going into Ogre Town.

The kingpin met me by his pool. He was in his wheelchair, but they had just dragged him out of the water. The girls finished setting him up and bounced off, giggling. What a good life they had. Until their knockers started to sag.

One cutie stayed.

I didn't recognize her at first. When I did, I was startled.

This wasn't the Donni Pell I'd known so briefly. Not the Donni who had been so tough on that farm. This Donni had been broken down and rebuilt. She looked as eager to please as a puppy.

Chodo noticed my surprise. He looked me in the eye and smiled. His smile was like Crask's. That was like looking Death in the face and having him grin. "A gift, Mr. Garrett. Not to be considered for the favor I owe. Just a token of my esteem. She's quite tame now. Quite pliable. I have no more use for her. I thought you might. Take her."

What could I do? He was who he was. I said thank you and told Donni Pell to get dressed. Then I let Crask take us back to my place.

What the hell was I going to do with her?

What had he done to her? She wasn't really Donni Pell anymore.

She spoke only when spoken to.

I took her into the Dead Man's room, sat her down, woke him up.

Garrett, you pustule on the nose of... Heavens! Not another one. You have had that redhaired trollop in and out for—

"How would you know? You've been snoring."

You truly believe I can sleep through—

"Can it, Chuckles. This one is the famous Donni Pell. A few weeks with the kingpin has given her a whole new attitude."

Yes. He seemed mildly distressed. Maybe even pitying, though the gods knew the woman didn't deserve that.

"I think she'll give me answers if I ask questions."

She will. Yes. Does that mean you have not unraveled the last few for yourself?

"Sort of." It meant I'd been trying to put the mess out of mind. With a little help from Tinnie, it had begun to recede. "You going to claim you figured out who killed Amiranda?"

Yes. And why. You never cease to amaze me, Garrett. It is quite obvious, actually.

"Illuminate me."

Illuminate yourself. You have all the information. Or ask that tortured child.

He meant tormented. Only "tormented" really described Donni Pell.

I tried, running it right through from the beginning. I didn't get it. Maybe I was just lazy because the answer was there for the asking. "Donni, who killed Amiranda Crest?"

"The Domina Willa Dount, Mr. Garrett."

"What? No!" But . . . Wait. "Why?"

"Because Amiranda helped Karl make up the ransom notes I wrote out and sent. Because Amiranda knew we were going to ask for twenty thousand marks gold, and when she saw the notes, they said two hundred thousand. Because as soon as she met Karl she was going to find out that it wasn't because he'd gotten greedy or I'd made a mistake."

Right. And I had to believe the Dead Man had come to that conclusion. Because I'd given him the details of my interview with Willa Dount with the Stormwarden standing by, when I'd gotten an indication that the Domina'd had prior knowledge that Amiranda was going to run. . . .

But I'd had my mind made up another way. Damn me.

I'd had her and I'd let her get away. She'd pulled it off. She had all that gold now.

I'd closed my mind and she was home free. Nothing to worry about the rest of her life—except staying a step ahead of Raver Styx.

I felt like a moron. The Dead Man was greatly amused at my expense.

He was even more amused because now I was stuck with Donni Pell. I had no idea what the hell to do with her. I couldn't keep her. I couldn't kick her out in the street in her condition. I sure as hell wasn't going to give her back to Lettie Faren. . . .

"All right, Old Bones. Before you doze off, you tell me how Glory Moon-called is getting away with all these amazing triumphs because he's worked some kind of deal with the centaur tribes."

I can figure some things out, given a few hints. I grinned. I'd stolen his big thunder.

Both sides in the Cantard use centaur auxiliaries for almost all their scouting. They are almost entirely dependent upon them. If the centaurs decided not to see something, the warlords would be blind. I wondered *what* the deal was, and if maybe someday it might not embarrass Karenta as much as it was embarrassing the Venageti right now.

It can't be too long before the Venageti War Council gets a handle on it. Even when you have your mind made up, you can't stay blind to reality forever.

I left the Dead Man fuming and took Donni Pell to the kitchen so Dean could feed her.

If Garrett is a sucker for a damsel in distress, Old Dean is a sucker for one who is hurting. He never did tell me where, but he got her a good position as housekeeper and companion to an older, handicapped woman. They were supposedly very good for each other.

Sometimes I think about changing my line of work. Nobody emerged happy from this one except the worst villain of the piece.

Maybe I should just thank the gods that I got out of it alive with a few friends—and a profit.

That's why you do a job, isn't it? To survive?

•••Cold Copper Tears

●●●1

Maybe it was time. I was restless. We were getting on toward the dog days, when my body gets terminally lazy but my nerves shriek that it's time to do something—a cruel combination. So far sloth was ahead by a nose.

I'm Garrett—low thirties, six feet two, two hundred pounds, ginger hair, ex-Marine—all-around fun guy. For a price I'll find things or get the boogeys off your back. I'm no genius. I get the job done by being too stubborn to quit. My favorite sport is female and my favorite food is beer. I work out of the house I own on Macunado Street, halfway between the Hill and waterfront in TunFaire's midtown.

I was sharing a liquid lunch with my friend Playmate, talking religion, when a visitor wakened my sporting nature.

She was blond and tall with skin like the finest satin I'd ever seen. She wore a hint of unusual scent and a smile that said she saw through everything and Garrett was one big piece of crystal. She looked scared but she wasn't spooked.

"I think I'm in love," I told Playmate as old Dean showed her into my coffin of an office.

"Third time this week." He drained his mug. "Don't mention it to Tinnie." He stood up. And stood up. And stood up. He's nine feet tall. "Some of us got to work." He waltzed with Dean and the blonde, trying to get to the hall.

"Later." We'd had a good time snickering about the scandals sweeping

TunFaire's religion industry. Playmate had considered a flyer in that racket once but I had managed to collect a debt owed him, and the cash had kept him alive in the stable business.

I looked at the blonde. She looked at me. I liked what I saw. She had mixed feelings. The horses don't shy when I pass, but over the years I've been pounded around enough for my face to develop a certain amount of character.

She kept smiling that secret smile. It made me want to look over my shoulder to see what was gaining on me.

Dean avoided my eye and did a fast fade, pretending he had to make sure Playmate didn't forget to close the front door behind him. Dean wasn't supposed to let anybody in. They might want me to work. The blonde must have charmed his socks off.

"I'm Garrett. Sit." She wouldn't have to work to charm the wardrobe off me. She had that something that goes beyond beauty, beyond style—an aura, a presence. She was the kind of woman who leaves eunuchs weeping and priests cursing their vows.

She planted herself in Playmate's chair but didn't offer a name. The impact was wearing off. I began to see the chill behind the gorgeous mask. I wondered if anybody was home.

"Tea? Brandy? Miss? . . . Or Dean might find a spot of TunFaire Gold if we sweet-talk him."

"You don't remember me, do you?"

"No. Should I?"

The man who could forget her was already dead. But I left the remark unspoken. A chill had dropped over me, and the chill had no sense of humor.

"It's been a while, Garrett. Last time I saw you I was nine and you were going off to the Marines."

My memory for nines isn't what it is for twenties. No bells rang, though that was more years ago than I want to remember; I've tried to forget the five in the Marines ever since.

"We lived next door, third floor. I had a crush on you. You hardly noticed me. I'd have died if you did."

"Sorry."

She shrugged. "My name is Jill Craight."

She looked like a Jill, complete with amber eyes that ought to smolder but looked out of arctic wastes instead. But she wasn't any Jill I ever knew, nine years old or not.

Any other Jill, and I would have come back with a suggestion about making up for lost time. But the cold over there was getting to me. My restraint will get me a pat on the head next time I go to confession. If I ever go. Last time was when *I* was about nine. "You got over me while I was gone. I didn't see you on the pier when I came home."

I'd made up my mind about her. She had stoked the fire to get past Dean, but it was out now. She was a user. It was time she stopped decorating that chair and distracting its owner from his lunch. "You didn't just drop by to talk about the old days on Peach Street."

"Pyme Street," she corrected. "I may be in trouble. I may need help."

"People who come here usually do." Something told me not to shove her out the door yet. I looked her over again. That was no chore.

She wasn't a flashy dresser. Her clothes were conservative but costly, tailored with an eye to wear. That implied money but didn't guarantee it. In my part of town some people wear their whole estate. "Tell me about it."

"Our place burned when I was twelve." That should have rung a bell, but didn't till later. "My parents were killed. I tried staying with an uncle. We didn't get along. I ran away. The streets aren't kind to a girl without a family."

They aren't. That would be when the iceberg formed. Nothing would touch her, or get close to her, or hurt her, ever again. But what did yesterday have to do with why she was here today?

People come to me because they feel disaster breathing down their necks. Maybe just getting through the door makes them feel safe. Maybe they don't want to go back out again. Whatever the reason, they stall, talking about anything but what's bothering them. "I imagine."

"I was lucky. I had looks and half a brain. I used them to make connections. Things worked out. These days I'm an actress."

That could mean anything or nothing, a catchall behind which women pursue uncomfortable ways of keeping body and soul together.

I grunted encouragement. Garrett is nothing if not encouraging.

Dean peeked in to make sure I hadn't gone rabid. I tapped my mug. "More lunch." It looked like a long siege.

"I've made some important friends, Mr. Garrett. They like me because I know how to listen and I know how to keep my mouth shut."

I had a notion she was the kind of actress who gives the same service as a street girl but gets paid better because she smiles and sighs while she's working.

We do what we have to do. I know some good people in that line. Not many, but some. There aren't that many good people in any line.

Dean brought my beer and a whistle-wetter for my guest. He'd been eavesdropping and had begun to suspect he'd made a mistake. She turned on the heat when she thanked him. He went out glowing. I took a drink and said, "So what are we sneaking up on here?"

The glaciers re-formed behind her eyes. "One of my friends left me with something for safekeeping. It was a small casket." She made hand gestures indicating a box a foot deep, as wide, and eighteen inches long. "I have no idea what's in it. I don't want to know. Now he's disappeared. And since I've had that casket there have been three attempts to break into my apartment." Bam. Like a candle snuffed, she stopped. She had said something she shouldn't have. She had to think before she went on.

I smelled a herd of rats. "Got any idea what you want?"

"Someone is watching me. I want it stopped. I don't have to put up with that kind of thing anymore." There was some passion there, some heat, but all for some other guy.

"Then you think it could happen again. You think somebody's after that casket? Or could they be after you?"

What she thought was that she shouldn't have mentioned the casket. She ran it around inside her head before she said, "Either one."

"And you want me to stop it?"

She gave me a regal nod. The snow queen was back in charge. "Do you know what it's like to come home and find out that someone's been tearing through your stuff?"

A minute ago they were just trying to get in.

"A little like you've been raped, only it doesn't hurt as much when you sit down," I replied. "Give me a retainer. Tell me where you live. I'll see what I can do."

She handed me a small coin purse while she told me how to find her place. It was only six blocks away. I looked in the purse. I don't think my eyes bugged, but she had that little smile on again when I looked up.

She'd decided she could run me around like a trained mutt.

She got up. "Thank you." She headed for the front door. I got up and stumbled over myself trying to get there to see her out, but Dean had been lying in ambush to make sure he got the honors. I left him to them.

Dean shut the door. He faced it for a moment before he turned to face me, wearing a foolish look.

I asked, "You fall in love? At your age?" He knew I wasn't looking for clients. He was supposed to discourage them at the door. And this sweet ice with the tall tales and long legs and nonsense problem and sack of gold that was ten times what a retainer ought to be looked like a client I especially didn't want. "That one is trouble on the hoof."

"I'm sorry, Mr. Garrett." He gave me feeble excuses that only proved a man is never too old.

"Dean, go to Mr. Pigotta's. Tell him he's invited to supper. You'll be fixing his favorites if he gets balky." Pokey Pigotta never turned down a free meal in his life. I gave Dean my best glower, which struck him like rain off a turtle.

You just can't get good help.

I retired to my desk to think.

Life was good.

I'd had a couple of rough ones recently and I'd not only gotten out alive, but also managed to turn a fat profit. I didn't owe anybody. I didn't need to work. I've always thought it sensible not to work if you're not hungry. You don't see wild animals working when they're not hungry, so why not just fiddle around and put away a few beers and worry about getting ready for winter when winter comes?

My trouble was that word was out that Garrett could handle the tough ones. Lately every fool with an imaginary twitch has been knocking on my door. And when they look like Jill Craight and know how to turn on the heat, they have no trouble getting past my first line of defense. My second line is more feeble than my first. That's me. And I'm a born sucker.

I've been poor and I've been poorer, and the practical side of me has learned one truth: money runs out. No matter how well I did yesterday, the money will run out tomorrow.

What do you do when you don't want to work and you don't want to go hungry? When you were born you didn't have the sense to pick rich parents.

Some guys become priests.

Me, I'm trying to get into subcontracting, the wave of the future.

When they get past Dean and they fish me with their tales of woe, I figure I ought to be able to give the work to somebody else and scrape twenty percent off the top. That should keep the wolf away for a while, save me exercise, and put some money in the hands of my friends.

For tail and trace jobs I could call on Pokey Pigotta. He's good at that. For bodyguard stuff there was Saucerhead Tharpe, half the size of a mammoth and twice as stubborn. If something hairy turned up I could yell for Morley Dotes. Morley is a bonebreaker and life-taker.

This Craight thing smelled. Damn it, it reeked! Why give me that business about being a neighbor when she was a kid? Why drop it at the first sign I doubted her? Why back off so fast on the high heat and shift to the ice maiden?

There was one answer I didn't like at all.

She might be a psycho.

People who get into a fix where they think I'm their only out are unpredictable. And weird. But when you've been at the game awhile you think you get a feel for types.

Jill Craight didn't fit.

For a second I wondered if that wasn't because she *was* an actress who had done her homework and had decided to grab my curiosities with both hands. I can be had that way sometimes.

The clever, cutesy ones are the worst.

I could go two ways here: lie back and forget Jill Craight until I give her to Pokey, or walk across the hall and consult my live-in charity case.

That woman had given me the jimjams. I was restless. The Dead Man it was, then. After all, he's a self-proclaimed genius.

They call him the Dead Man. He's dead, but he's not a man. He's a Loghyr, and somebody stuck him with a knife about four hundred years ago. He weighs almost five hundred pounds, and his four-century fast hasn't helped him lose an ounce.

Loghyr flesh dies as easily as yours or mine, but the Loghyr spirit is more reluctant. It can hang around for a thousand years, hoping for a cure, getting more ill-tempered by the minute. If Loghyr flesh corrupts it may do so faster than granite, but not much.

My dead Loghyr's hobby is sleeping. He's so dedicated he'll do nothing else for months.

He's supposed to earn his keep by applying his genius to my cases. He does, sometimes, but he has a deeper philosophical aversion to gainful employment than I do. He'll bust his butt to shirk the smallest chore. Sometimes I wonder why I bother.

He was asleep when I dropped in—much to my chagrin, but little to my surprise. He'd been at it for three weeks, taking up the biggest room in the house.

"Hey, Old Bones! Wake up! I need the benefit of your lightning intelligence." The best way to get anything out of him is to appeal to his vanity. But the first task is waking him, and the second is getting him to pay attention.

He wasn't having any today.

"That's all right," I told the mountain of cheesy flesh. "I love you despite yourself."

The place was a mess. Dean hates cleaning the Dead Man's room, and I hadn't kept after him so he'd let it slide.

If I didn't watch it the bugs and mice got in. They liked to snack on the Dead Man. He could handle them when he was awake, but he wouldn't stay awake anymore.

He was ugly enough on his own, without getting eaten.

I puttered around, sweeping and dusting and stomping, singing a medley of bawdy hymns I learned in the Marines. He didn't wake up, the stubborn hunk of lard.

If he wasn't going to play, neither was I. I packed it up. I reloaded my mug with beer and went out to the stoop to watch the endless and ever-changing panorama of TunFaire life.

Macunado Street was busy. People and dwarfs and elves hurried to arcane destinations, to clandestine rendezvous. A troll couple strolled past, kids so infatuated they had eyes for nothing but one another's warts and carbuncles: Ogres and leprechauns hastened to assignations. More dwarfs scurried by, dependably industrious. A fairy messenger more beautiful than my recent visitor cussed like a sailor as she battled a stubborn head wind. A brownie youth gang, chukos, way off their turf, played whistle past the graveyard, probably praying the local Travelers would not come out. A giant, obviously an up-country rube, gawked at everything. He had fantastic peripheral vision. He almost batted the head off a pixie who tried to pick his pocket.

I saw half-breeds of every sort. TunFaire is a cosmopolitan, sometimes tolerant, always venturesome city. For those with that turn of mind, it's interesting to speculate on the mechanics of how some of their parents managed to conceive them. If you're of a scientific mind and want to take your data from direct observation, you can visit the Tenderloin. They'll show you anything down there as long as you come across with the money.

My street was always a carnival, like TunFaire itself. But it's all darkness grinning behind a party mask.

TunFaire and I have a ferocious love-hate relationship that comes of us both being too damned stubborn to change.

When they built Pokey Pigotta they used only leftover angles and extralong parts, then forgot to give him a coat of paint. He was so pallid that, after dark, people sometimes took him for one of the undead. He had no meat on him and his gangly limbs were everywhere, but he was tough and smart and one of the best at what he did. And he had an appetite like a whale-shark. Whenever we have him over he eats everything but the woodwork. Maybe it's the only time he gets to eat real cooking.

Dean is good for that. Sometimes I claim it's the only reason I keep him on. Sometimes I believe what I say.

We hadn't had a strange face in for a while, which spurred Dean to one of his better efforts. That and the fact that Pokey can lay it on with a shovel when he wants and Dean is addicted to everybody's flattery but mine.

Pokey leaned back and patted his stomach, drenched Dean with a bucket of bullhooly, belched, and looked at me. "So let's have it, Garrett."

I lifted an eyebrow. It's one of my best tricks. I'm working on my ear-wiggling. I know the ladies will love that.

"You took on a client you want to farm out," Pokey went on without waiting. "Good-looking woman with style, I'd guess, or she wouldn't have gotten past Dean. And if she had, you wouldn't have listened to her."

Had he been listening at the keyhole? "Regular deductive genius, isn't he, Dean?"

"If you say so, sir."

"I don't. He was probably hanging around trying to beg crumbs from our castoffs." I told Pokey the story. All I left out was the size of the retainer. He didn't need to know that.

"Sounds like she's running a game," Pokey agreed. "You said Jill Craight?"

"That's the name she gave. You know it?"

"Seems like I should. Can't put a finger on why." He used his pinkie to scratch the inside of his ear. "Couldn't have been important."

Dean produced a peach cobbler, something he'd never do without company present. It was hot. He buried it in whipped cream. Then he served tea. Pokey went to work like he wanted to store up fat for the next ice age.

Afterward we leaned back, and Pokey lighted one of those savage little black stink sticks he favors, then went to catching me up on the news. I hadn't been out of the house for days. Dean hadn't kept me posted. He hoped silence would drive me out. He never says so but he worries when I'm not working.

"The big news is Glory Mooncalled did it again."

"What now?" Glory Mooncalled and the war in the Cantard are special interests around my house. When he's awake the Dead Man makes a hobby of trying to predict the unpredictable, the mercenary Mooncalled.

"He ambushed Firelord Sedge at Rapistan Sands. Ever heard of it?"

"No." That was no surprise. Glory Mooncalled was operating farther into the Venageti Cantard than any Karentine before him. "He took Sedge out?" It was a safe guess; his ambushes had yet to fail.

"Thoroughly. How many left on his list?"

"Not many. Maybe three." Mooncalled had begun his war on the Venageti side. The Venageti War Council had managed to tick him off so bad he'd come over to Karenta vowing to collect their heads. He'd been picking them off ever since.

He's become a folk hero for us ordinary slobs and a big pain in the patoot for the ruling class, though he's winning their war. His easy victories have shown them to be the incompetents we've always known they are.

Pokey said, "What happens when he's done and all of a sudden we don't have a war for the first time since before any of us were born?"

The Dead Man had an answer. I didn't think it would go over with Pokey. I changed the subject. "What's the latest on the temple scandals?" Playmate had tried to give me the scoop but his heart hadn't been in it. The scandals weren't the circus for him they were for me. His religious side was embarrassed by the antics of our self-anointed spiritual shepherds.

"Nothing new. Plenty of finger-pointing. Lot of 'I was framed.' On the retail level it's still at the swinging-drunks-in-the-tavern stage."

For now. It would turn grim if Prester Legate Warden Agire and his Terrell Relics didn't turn up.

Agire was one of the top ten priests of the squabbling family of sects we lump together as Orthodox. His title Prester indicated his standing in the hierarchy, at about the level of a duke. Legate was an imperial appointment, supposedly plenipotentiary, in reality powerless. The imperial court persists and postures at Costain but has had no power for two hundred years. It survives as a useful political fiction. Warden is the title that matters. It means he's the one man in the world entrusted with guardianship of the Terrell Relics.

Agire and the Relics had disappeared.

I don't know what the Relics are. Maybe nobody but the Warden does anymore. He's the only one who ever sees them. Whatever, they're holy and precious not only to the Orthodox factions but to the Church, the Eremitics, the Scottites, the Canonics, the Cynics, the Ascetics, the Renunciates, and several Hanite creeds for whom Terrell is only a minor prophet or even an emissary of the archenemy. The bottom line is that they're important to almost all the thousand and one cults with followings in TunFaire.

Agire and the Relics had vanished. Everyone assumed the worst. But something was wrong. Nobody claimed responsibility. Nobody crowed over having gotten hold of the Relics. That baffled everybody. Possession of the Relics is a clear claim for the favor of the gods.

In the meantime, the whispering war of revelation had intensified. Priests of various rites had begun whittling away at rivals by betraying their venalities, corruptions, and sins. It had begun as border-incident stuff, little priests excoriating one another for drunkenness, for selling indulgences, for letting their hands roam during the confessional.

The fun had spread like fire in a tenement block. Now a day was incomplete without its disclosure about this or that bishop or prester or whatnot having fathered a child on his sister, having poisoned his predecessor, or having embezzled a fortune to buy his male mistress a forty-eight-room cabin in the country.

Most of the stories were true. There was so much real dirt, fabrication wasn't necessary—which satisfied my cynical side right down to its bunions. Reputations were getting reaped in windrows, and it couldn't happen to a nicer bunch of guys.

Pokey was bored by the whole business. If he had a weakness it was his narrowness. His work was his life. He could talk technique or case histories forever. Otherwise, only food held his attention.

I wondered what he did with his money. He lived in a scruffy one-room walk-up although he worked all the time, sometimes on several projects at once. When clients didn't find him, he went looking. He even went after things—deadly things—just to satisfy his own curiosity.

Whatever, he didn't feel like yakking up old news. His belly was full. I'd tantalized him with a wicked aroma. He wanted to get hunting.

I helped him puff Dean's ego, then walked him to the door. I sat down on the stoop to watch him go out of sight.

4

T he descending sun played arsonist among high, distant clouds. There was a light breeze. The temperature was perfect. It was a time to just lean back and feel content. Not many of those times fell my way.

I yelled for beer, then settled in to watch Nature redecorate the ceiling of the world. I didn't pay attention to the street. The little man was there on the stoop, making himself at home, passing me the big copper bucket of beer he'd brought, before I noticed him.

Up to no good? What else? But the beer was Weider's best lager. I don't get it that often.

He was a teeny dink, all wrinkled and gray, with a cant to his eyes and a yellow of tooth that suggested a big dollop of nonhuman blood. I didn't know him. That was all right. There are a lot of people I don't know, but I wondered if he was one of the ones I wanted to keep on not knowing.

"Thanks. Good beer."

"Mr. Weider said you'd appreciate it."

I'd done a job for Weider, rooting out an in-house theft ring without getting his guilty children too dirty. To discourage a relapse the old man kept me on retainer. I wander around the brewery when I have nothing better to do. I make people nervous there. Considering what he'd been losing, I'm cheap insurance. The retainer isn't much.

"He tell you to see me?"

The dink took the bucket back, sipped like an expert. "I'm unfamiliar with many facets of the secular world, Mr. Garrett. Mr. Weider is face-to-face with it every day. He said you were the man I need. Provided, as he put it, I can pry you off your dead ass."

That sounded like Weider. "He's more achievement oriented than I am." And how. He started out with nothing; now he's TunFaire's biggest brewer and has fingers in twenty other pies.

"So I gather."

We passed the bucket back and forth.

He said, "I looked you over. You seem perfect for my needs. But the factors that make you right make it hard to recruit you. I have no way to appeal to you."

It was a mellow evening. I was too lazy to move. I had nothing else on my mind but a couple of oddballs down the way who were dead ringers for a couple of oddballs who were hanging around last time I came out. "You bought the beer, friend. Speak your piece."

"I'd expected that courtesy. Trouble is, once I tell you, the cat will be out of the bag."

"I don't gossip about business. That's bad for business."

"Mr. Weider did praise your discretion."

"He's got reason."

We went back and forth with the beer. The sun ambled on. The little guy held a conference with himself to see if his trouble was really that bad.

It was worse, probably. Usually they're going down for the third time when they ask for help—and then they want to sneak up on it like a virgin.

"My name is Magnus Peridont."

I didn't wilt. I didn't gasp or faint. He was disappointed. I said, "Magnus? Nobody in real life is named Magnus. That's a handle they stick on some guy who's been dead so long everybody's forgotten what a horse's ass he was."

"You've never heard of me?"

It was one of those names you ought to know. It had turned up on a loo wall somewhere, or something. "Doesn't ring any bells."

"My father thought I was destined for greatness. I'm sure I was a disappointment. I'm also known as Magister Peridont and Peridontu, Altodeoria Princeps."

"I hear a distant campanile." A Magister is that rarest of all fabulous beasts, a sorcerer sanctioned by the Church. The other title was a relic of antiquity. It meant something like he was a Prince of the City of God. There was a bunk in heaven with his name on it, guaranteed. The bosses of the Church had made him a saint before he croaked.

A thousand years ago that would have made him a dyed-in-the-wool, hair-shirt-wearing, pillar-sitting holy man. These days it probably meant he scared the crap out of everybody and they wanted to buy him off with baubles.

I asked, "Would Grand Inquisitor and Malevechea fit in there somewhere?"

"I have been called those things."

"I'm getting a fix on you." *That* Peridont was one scary son of a bitch. Luckily, we live in a world where the Church is always one gasp short of being a dead issue. It claims maybe ten percent of Karenta's human population and none of the nonhuman. It says only humans have souls and other races are just clever animals capable of aping human speech and manners. That makes the Church real popular with the clever animals.

"You're dismayed," he said.

"Not exactly. Say I have philosophical problems with some of the Church's tenets." Elvish civilization antedates ours by millennia. "I didn't know Mr. Weider was a member."

"Not in good standing. Call him lapsed. He was born to the faith. He spoke to me as a favor to his wife. She's one of our lay sisters."

I remembered her, a fat old woman with a mustache, always in black, with a face like she had a mouth full of lemons. "I see."

Now that I knew who he was, we were on equal ground. Now he needed leading around to the point. "You're out of uniform."

"I'm not making an official representation."

"Under the table? Or personal?"

"Some of both. With permission."

Permission? Him? I waited.

"My reputation is greatly exaggerated, Mr. Garrett. I've encouraged that for its psychological impact."

I grunted and waited. He didn't look old enough to have done all the evil laid at his doorstep.

He said, "Are you aware of the tribulations besetting our Orthodox cousins?"

"I haven't been so entertained since my mother took me to the circus."

"You've put a finger on the crux, Mr. Garrett. The mess has become a popular entertainment. There are no heretics more deserving of Hano's justice than the Orthodox. But no one views these events as a scourging. And that fills me with dread."

"Uhm?"

"Already the rabble have begun to step forward with revelations just to keep the pot boiling. I fear the day when the Orthodox vein plays out and they seek new lodes."

Ah. "You think the church might be next?" That wouldn't break my heart.

"Possibly. Despite my vigilance, some will stumble into sin. But no, my concern isn't for the Church, it's for Faith itself. Every revelation slashes Belief with a brutal razor. Already some who never questioned have begun to wonder if all religion isn't just a shell game perpetrated by societies of con men who milk the gullible."

He looked me in the eye and smiled, then passed the beer. That could have been a quote. And he knew it. He had done his homework.

"You have my attention." I suddenly knew how Pokey felt when he took a job just to satisfy his own curiosity.

He smiled again. "I'm convinced there's more here than a scandal gone brushfire. This is being orchestrated. There's a malign force bent on savaging Faith. I think a rock needs to be lifted and that social scorpion revealed."

"Interesting and interestinger. I'm surprised by your secular way of stating it."

He smiled again. The Grand Inquisitor was a happy runt. "The diabolical provenance of the attack is beyond question. What interests me are the identities, resources, goals, and whatnot of the Adversary's mundane adjuncts. All that can be defined in secular terms, like a street robbery."

And a robbery could, no doubt, be defined in sectarian cant.

The runt seemed awfully reasonable for a supposed raving fanatic. I guess the first talent a priest develops is acting ability. "So you want to hire me to root out the jokers putting the wood to the Orthodox priesthoods."

"Not exactly. Though I have hopes that their unmasking will be a by-product."

"You just zigged when I zagged."

"Subtlety and credibility, Mr. Garrett. If I hire you to find conspirators and you unearth them, even I couldn't be completely sure you hadn't cooked the evidence. On the other hand, if I hire a known skeptic to search for Warden Agire and the Terrell Relics and in the course of the hunt he kicks some villains out of the weeds. . . ."

I took a long drink of his beer. "I admire your thinking."

"You'll take it on, then?"

"No. I can't see getting in a mess just for money. But you know how to pique a guy's curiosity. And you know how to scheme a scheme."

"I'm prepared to pay well. With an outstanding bonus for recovery of the Relics."

"I'll bet."

The Great Schism between Orthodoxy and its main offshoot happened a thousand years ago. The Ecumenical Council of Pyme tried to patch things up. The marriage didn't last. The Orthodox snatched the Relics in the settlement. The Church has been trying to snatch them back ever since.

"I won't press you, Mr. Garrett. You were the best man for the job, but for that reason the least likely to take it. I have other options. Thank you for your time. Have a nice evening. Should you have a change of heart, contact me at the Chattaree." He and his bucket marched off into the dusk.

I was impressed with the little guy. He could be a gentleman when he wanted. You don't see that much in people accustomed to power. And he was one of the most feared men in TunFaire, within his sphere. A holy terror.

5

Dean stepped outside. "I've finished up, Mr. Garrett. I'll be going home if there's nothing else."

He always talks like that when he wants something. Right now he hoped I'd have that something else. He lives with a platoon of spinster nieces who make him crazy.

One of the legacies of the war in the Cantard is a surplus of women. For decades Karenta's youth have gone south to capture the silver mines and for decades half of them haven't come back. It makes it nice for us unattached survivor types, but hell on parents with daughters to support.

"I was sitting here thinking it would be a nice evening for a walk."

"That it would be, Mr. Garrett." When the Dead Man is sleeping somebody always stays in to bolt the door and wait for whoever is out. When the Dead Man is awake we have no security problems.

"You think it's too early to see Tinnie?" Tinnie Tate and I have a tempestuous friendship. She's the one they had in mind when they set the specs for redhead stereotypes, only they toned them down because nobody would believe the truth.

You might call Tinnie changeable. One week I can't run her off with a stick, the next I'm tops on her hate list. I haven't figured out the whys and wherefores.

I was listed this week. Past the peak and dropping but still in the top ten.

"It's too early."

I thought so, too.

Dean is in a bind where Tinnie is concerned. He likes her. She's beautiful, smart, quick, more square with the world than I'll ever be. He thinks she's good for me. (I don't dare risk his opinion on the flip-flop issue.) But he has all those nieces in desperate need of husbands and half a dozen have standards low enough to covet a prince like me, squeaky armor and all.

"I could go see how the girls are."

He brightened, checked to see if I was teasing, and was set to call my bluff when he realized that would put me there while he was here, unable to defend their supposed virtues. He imagined me in there like a bull shoulder-deep in clover, like they couldn't possibly have sense enough to look out for themselves. "I wouldn't recommend that, Mr. Garrett. They've been especially troublesome lately."

It was all a matter of perspective. They hadn't troubled me. When I first took Dean on, they did. They kept me up to my ears in cookery, trying to fatten me up for the kill.

"Perhaps I should just go, Mr. Garrett. Perhaps you should wait another day or two, then go apologize to Miss Tate."

"I got no philosophical problem with apologizing, Dean, but I like to know why I'm doing it."

He chuckled, pulled on the mantle of worldly-wise old warrior passing his wisdom along. "Apologize for being a man. That always works."

He had a point. Except I have a flair for getting sarcastic.

"I'll just stroll over to Morley's, quaff me a few celery tonics."

Dean pruned up. His opinion of Morley Dotes is so low it has to look up at snakes' bellies.

We all have rogues in our circles, maybe just so we can tell ourselves, "What a good boy am I."

Actually, I like Morley. Despite himself. He takes some getting used to but he's all right, in his way. I just keep reminding myself that he's part dark elf and has different values. Sometimes, very different values. Always malleable values. Everything is situational for Morley.

"I won't be out long," I promised. "I just need to work off some restlessness."

Dean grinned. He figured I was getting bored with loafing and we'd see some excitement pretty soon.

I hoped not.

t isn't a long walk to Morley's place, but it is a walk over the border into another world. The neighborhood hasn't acquired a name like so many others, but it is a distinct region. Maybe call it the Safety Zone. Members of all species mix there without much friction—though humans have to put in overtime to be acceptable.

There was a little light still in the air. The clouds out west hadn't quite burned out. It wasn't yet time for the predators to hit the streets. I was no more than normally wary.

But when the kid stepped into my path I knew I had trouble. Big trouble. It was something about the way he moved.

I didn't think. I reacted.

I gave him a high kick he wasn't expecting. My toe snapped in under his chin. I felt a bone break. He squealed and ran backward, arms flapping as he tried to keep his balance. A hitching post jumped in his way and gored him from behind. He spun around and went down, losing his knife as he fell.

I slid toward the nearest building.

Another came at me from what had been behind. He was an odd one, kid-sized but clad in a cast-off army work uniform. He was an albino. He had a nasty big knife. He stopped eight feet away, awaiting reinforcements.

There were at least three more, two across the street and one back up the way, standing lookout.

I took off my belt and snapped it at the albino's eyes. That didn't scare him but did give me time to frisk the building.

The buildings around there were a week short of falling down. I had no trouble finding a loose, broken brick. I pulled it out and let fly. I guessed right and he ducked into it. I got him square in the forehead, then jumped him while his knees were watery, took his knife, grabbed him by the hair, and flung him toward the two coming across the street. They dodged. He sprawled.

I screeched like a banshee. That stopped the two. I feinted left, right, came back to fake a cut at the knife hand of the guy with the blade I'd taken, then snapped my belt at his eyes. He saved himself by jumping back.

He fell over the albino. I shrieked again and flung myself through the air. It never hurts to have them think you're crazy. I landed with both knees on the guy's chest, heard ribs crack. He squealed. I bounced away as the other came at me.

He stopped when he saw I was ready. I sidestepped and kicked the albino in the head. That's me, Fairplay Garrett. At least I was going to get out alive. I looked around. Broken Jaw had taken a hike, leaving his knife. The lookout had opted for discretion.

"Just you and me now, Shorty." He was no kid. None of them were, really. I should have seen it sooner. Kids that size aren't out roaming the streets of TunFaire, they're in the army. They keep taking them younger and younger.

They were dark-elf breeds, half elf, half human, outcasts from both tribes. The mix is volatile: amoral, asocial, unpredictable, sometimes crazy. Bad.

Like Morley, who'd managed to live long enough to learn to fake it.

My short friend wasn't impressed by the fact that he was alone against somebody bigger. That's another problem with darko breeds. Some don't have sense enough to be scared.

I went back for my brick.

He shifted stance, held his knife like it was a two-handed sword. I teased him with the belt and tried to guess what he'd do when I let the brick fly. He was deciding to come at me when I did.

I went around and head-kicked the others to make sure they stayed down.

That got Shorty pissed. He came. I threw the brick. He dodged. But I hadn't gone for the head or body. I'd gone for the foot I'd hoped he'd push off from. The part of him that would be last to move.

I got his toes. He yelped. I went in after him, belt, knife, and feet.

He held me off.

Hell, we could dance all night. I'd done what I needed to do. How fast could he chase me on a bad foot?

I looked at the two guys down and heard my Marine sergeants: "You don't leave a live enemy behind you."

No doubt cutting their throats would have been a boon to civilization. But that wasn't my style.

I collected dropped knives.

Shorty figured I was going to pull out. "Next time you're dead."

"Better not be a next time, chuko. Because I don't give second chances."

He laughed.

One of us was crazy.

I went away with a chill between my shoulders. What the hell was all that? They hadn't been out to rob me. They'd been out to bust me up. Or kill me.

Why? I didn't know them.

There are people who don't have much use for me, but I couldn't think of any who would go that far. Not all of a sudden, now. It was lightning out of a clear blue sky.

●●●7

I t never fails. When I step through the doorway into Morley's place, the joint goes dead and everybody stares. They ought to be used to me by now. But I have this reputation for thinking I'm on the side of the angels and a lot of those guys are anything but.

I saw Saucerhead Tharpe at his usual table, so I headed that way. He was alone and had a spare chair.

Before the noise level rose, a voice said, "I'll be damned! Garrett!" Whip crack with the name.

What do you know? Morley himself was working the bar, helping dispense the carrot, celery, and turnip juice. I'd never seen that before. I wondered if he watered their drinks after they'd had three or four.

Dotes jerked his head toward the stairs. I said, "How you doing?" to Saucerhead and sailed on by. He grunted and went on massacring a salad big enough to founder three ponies. But he was the size of three ponies and their mothers, too.

Morley hit the stairs behind me. "Office?" I asked.

"Yes."

I went up and in. "Things have changed." It looked less like the waiting room in a bordello, maybe because the inevitable lovely was absent. Morley, relaxing at home, always had something handy.

"I'm trying to change myself by changing my environment." That was Morley sounding like Morley the vegetarian crackpot and devotee of obscure gurus. "What the hell are you up to, Garrett?" That was Morley the thug.

"Hey! How come the ice? I get antsy and walk down here to maybe tip a rhubarb brew with Saucerhead and I—"

"Right. You just decide to show up looking like the losing mutt at a dog-fight." He shoved me in front of a mirror.

The left side of my face was pancaked with blood. "Hell! I thought I ducked." The short guy had gotten me while we were dancing, somehow. I still didn't feel the cut. Some sharp knife.

"What happened?"

"Some of your crazy cousins jumped me. Chukos." I showed him the three knives. They were identical, with eight-inch blades and yellowed ivory grips into which small black stylized bats had been inset.

"Custom," he said.

"Custom," I agreed.

He picked up the speaking tube connecting with his barmen. "Send me Puddle and Slade. And invite Tharpe if he's interested." He smothered the tube, looked at me. "What are you into now, Garrett?"

"Nothing. I'm on vacation. Why? You looking for another chance to kite me and get out from under your gambling debts?" I realized it was the wrong thing to say before I finished saying it. Morley was worried. When Morley Dotes worries about me it's time to shut my yap and listen.

"Maybe I deserve that." His cohorts Puddle and Slade came in. Puddle I'd met before. He was a big, sloppy fat guy with flesh sagging in gross rolls. He was as strong as a mammoth, smart as a rock, cruel as a cat, quick as a cobra, and completely loyal to Morley. Slade was new. He could have been Morley's brother. Short by human standards, he had the same slim, darkly handsome looks, was graceful in motion, and was totally self-confident. He, like Morley, was a flashy dresser, though Morley had toned it down consid-erably tonight.

Morley said, "I've managed not to put a bet down for a month, Garrett. With my willpower and a little help from my friends."

Morley had a bad problem with gambling. Twice he's used me to get out from under debts of lethal scale, which has been a cause of friction.

Morley's vegetarian bar and restaurant and thug hangout is more hobby and cover than career. What he really does is bust kneecaps and break heads, freelance. Which is why he has his Puddles and Slades around.

Saucerhead came in. He nodded to everybody and dropped into a chair. It creaked. He didn't say anything. He doesn't talk much.

Saucerhead's line splits the difference between mine and Morley's. He'll pound somebody for a fee but he won't kill for money. He does mostly bodyguard and escort work. If he's really short he'll do collections. But never assassinations.

"Right, then," Morley said, with the players in place. "Garrett, you've saved me a trip. I was going to drop by your place after we closed."

"Why?" They looked at me like I was a freak-show exhibit instead of a broken-down, self-employed ex-Marine.

"You sure you don't have something going?"

"Nothing. Come on. What gives?"

"Sadler dropped by. He had a message for the trade from the kingpin." The kingpin is Chodo Contague, emperor of TunFaire's underworld. He is a very bad man. Sadler is one of his lieutenants and a worse man. "Someone wants your head, Garrett. The kingpin is putting out word that whoever tries for it will answer to him."

"Come on, Morley."

"Sure. He's as drifty as a fairy girl on weed. He's obsessed with honor and favors and debts and balances. He thinks he owes you big and he's by damned going to keep you alive to collect. If I was you I'd never do it, so I'd always have him behind me like my own pet banshee."

I didn't want a guardian angel. "That's only good for as long as he stays alive." Kingpins have a way of dying almost as frequently as Karenta's kings.

"Gives you a vested interest in his health, don't it?"

"One hand washes the other," Saucerhead rumbled. "You really don't got nothing shaking?"

"Nothing. Zero. Zip. I've only had two prospects in the last ten days. I turned them both down. I'm not working. I don't want to work. It's too much like work. I'm perfectly happy just sitting around watching everybody else work."

Morley and Saucerhead made faces. Morley worked as much as he could because he thought it was good for him. Saucerhead worked all the time because he had to feed his huge body.

Morley asked, "What about those prospects?"

"Good-looking blonde this afternoon. Probably a class hooker. Had somebody harassing her and wanted it stopped. I gave it to Pokey Pigotta. Just before I came down here, an old guy who wanted me to find something he thought was lost. Now he's looking for somebody else."

Morley frowned. He looked at the others and found no inspiration there. He picked up the three chuko knives, handed one to Puddle, one to Slade, and tossed the other to Saucerhead, who said, "Chuko knife."

Morley said, "Garrett had an encounter on his way down here. We don't usually see gangs in the neighborhood. They know better. Tell us about it, Garrett."

My feelings were hurt. Nobody was impressed by the fact that I'd taken away three knives.

I told it all.

Saucerhead said, "I gotta remember that brick-on-the-toes trick."

Morley looked at Puddle. Puddle said, "Snowball."

Morley nodded. "That's the albino, Garrett. A total crazy. Boss of a gang called the Vampires. He halfway thinks he's a vampire. The one you left standing sounds like Doc, the brains of the gang. He's crazier than Snowball. Won't back down from anything. And him a bleeder. I hope you had sense enough to finish it while you could."

He looked at me and knew I hadn't.

"They're crazies, Garrett. A big gang. As long as Snowball is alive they'll keep coming. You embarrassed him." He got out pen, ink, paper, and started writing. "Puddle. Take two men and see if there's still anyone around out there."

"Sure, boss." A real genius, Puddle. I wondered who tied his shoes.

Morley scribbled. "The Vampires were way off their turf, Garrett. They come from North Reservoir Hill. Priam Street. West Bacon. Around there."

I understood. They hadn't come south on a lark. I hadn't been a target of opportunity.

I got that chill between my shoulders again.

Morley sanded what he'd written, folded it, dashed something on the outside, then handed it to Slade. Slade looked at it, nodded, and walked out. Morley said, "If I was you, Garrett, I'd go home and bar my doors and sit tight with the Dead Man."

"Probably a good idea."

We both knew I wouldn't. What if word got around that Garrett could be pushed?

Morley said, "I don't keep up with street gangs. There're too many of them. But the Vampires have been making a name. Getting ambitious. Snowball wants to be top chuko, captain of captains . . . Excuse me."

His speaking tube was making noises. He picked it up. "I'm listening." He held it to his ear. Then, "Send him up." He looked at me. "You leave a broad trail. Pokey Pigotta is here looking for you."

Pokey wandered in looking like a living skeleton. Morley said, "Plant yourself, Pokey," and gave him that look he gives when he's planning a new diet for someone. Part of Morley believes there's no problem that can't be solved by upping your intake of green leafies and fiber. He was certain we could achieve peace in our time if we could just get everybody to stop eating red meat.

I asked, "You looking for me?"

"Yes. I have to give you your money back. I can't do the job."

Pokey refusing work? "How come?"

"Got a better offer to do something that's more interesting, and I can't handle both jobs. You want to farm it out to Saucerhead? I'll give you what I got. For nothing."

"You're a prince. You doing anything, Saucerhead?" He wasn't the best man for the job but what could I do? Pokey had set me up.

"Give me the skinny," Saucerhead said. "I ain't buying no pig in a poke." He was suspicious because Pokey wanted out.

I gave him what I'd given Pokey, word for word.

Pokey gave me my retainer, said, "I cased the area but didn't make contact with the principal. The building is being watched, front and rear, by nonprofessionals. I assume the principal is their target, though the building contains nine other apartments. There's a caretaker who lives in the basement. The tenants are all single women. The watchers left when it got dark. They went to the Blue Bottle, where they share a third-floor room as Smith and Smith. Once it was apparent they were off duty and were not going to be replaced, I went home. I found my new client waiting."

Pokey described Smith and Smith, who sounded like your basic nondescript working stiffs.

"I can handle it, Garrett," Saucerhead said. "If you don't want to keep it for yourself."

I handed him the retainer. "Take care of the woman."

Pokey said, "That takes care of my business. I'd better go. I want to get an early start."

Morley grunted a farewell. He *was* changing. He ached to give Pokey some wholesome dietary advice, for his own good, but he bit his tongue.

What the hell? The world wouldn't be half as interesting if Morley changed that much.

When just the two of us were left, he looked at me. "You're *really* not into anything?"

"Promise. Cross my heart."

"I never saw anyone like you, Garrett. I don't know anybody else who could have chukos come all the way from the North End to whack him for taking a walk."

That bothered me, too. It looked like I'd have to go to work whether I liked it or not. And it would be a double not. I make a lousy client. "Maybe they heard where I was headed."

"What?"

"They might have gotten carried away by compassion for my stomach."

"Stuff it, Garrett. I don't need the aggravation."

"Testy, eh? Maybe cold turkey on everything isn't the way to go."

"Maybe not."

Puddle lurched in before we got going good. "Nothing but blood spots, Morley."

"Didn't think there would be. Thanks for going." Morley looked at me. "When are you going to learn? Now Snowball has his ego tied up in it."

"Maybe if I'd known who he was and his reputation—"

"Crap! That hasn't got anything to do with giving him a second chance. You going to ask for references? Even Snowball probably has a mother who loves him. That won't keep him from setting your balls on fire if he gets the chance. I'm amazed that you've stayed alive as long as you have."

He had a point. The world sure as hell doesn't care about one man's moral parameters. But I have to live with myself, too. "Might be because I have friends who look out for me. Come on downstairs. My treat."

"I'll pass. Buy yourself one. Carrot juice. Carrots are good for your eyes. You could stand to be a little more clear-sighted. Eat some fish, too. It's supposed to be brain food."

●●●9

got a drink, but I did it after I got home, after I sent Dean off and got the place locked up. I drew a pitcher off the keg in the cold well, took it to the office, put my feet up, and tried to brainstorm.

I had a tempest in a beer mug.

I came up with no angles at all.

I considered a connection with Jill Craight's visit. I considered one with the holy terror. If the connection was there, nothing betrayed it.

In any case, Snowball's bunch would have started from the North End before Peridont reached my place.

I reflected on old cases, trying to recall individuals who might be vindictive enough to want me smoked. There could be some out there, but I couldn't come up with any names.

What if Snowball had simply picked the wrong target? Suppose he was after somebody else?

Pure reason liked that hypothesis. Intuition screamed, "Bullshit!"

Somebody wanted me dead. And I didn't have a notion why, let alone who.

Maybe the Dead Man could spot a fact I'd overlooked. I wandered across the hall. No good. He was out of it. I worked off some nervous energy cleaning, then went back to the office to settle down and think it all through again.

I was still there when Dean pounded on the door in the morning. I was so stiff it was a task getting down the hall to the door. Morley wasn't all wrong when he talked about me abusing myself. I'm not seventeen anymore. The body won't stay in tune by itself. I pinched a few pounds of muscle that had drifted south. I needed to get more selective about my loafing.

I would start exercising first thing tomorrow. I didn't feel up to it today. My schedule was full, anyway.

I went upstairs and napped in a real bed while Dean started in the kitchen. He woke me when he had breakfast ready.

"You sure you're all right?" he asked when he brought my hotcakes. I hadn't told him much. "You look like hell."

"Thanks. You're one of Nature's great beauties yourself." I knew what he meant. But I have to ride him or he thinks I don't appreciate him. "You should've seen the other guys."

"I expect it's just as well I didn't." Someone rapped at the door. "I'll get it."

I grunted around a mouthful of hotcakes smothered in blueberry preserves.

Our visitor was Jill Craight. Dean brought her into the kitchen. Remarkable. She really had him whammied.

She didn't have as much impact this morning. She hadn't fixed herself up for it. She looked like she'd had a bad night. And she was spoiling for a fight.

"Good morning, Miss Craight. Won't you join me?"

She sat. She took tea when Dean offered it but declined anything more substantial. She had fire in her eyes. Too bad it wasn't for me. "I had a visit from a man named Waldo Tharpe."

"Saucerhead? Good man. Though sometimes his manners lack polish."

"His manners were adequate. He told me he was supposed to find out who was giving me trouble. He told me you sent him."

"I did. Anybody ever tell you you're beautiful when you're mad?"

"Men tell me I'm beautiful whatever my mood. It's bullshit. Why did you send that man? I hired you."

"You brought me a situation you didn't like. I sent somebody to take care of it. Where's your problem?"

"I hired you."

"And only I will do?"

She nodded.

"That's great for the ego, but—"

"I didn't pay for some second-rate unknown."

"Interesting. Considering Saucerhead is probably better known than I am." I looked her hard in the eye for a dozen seconds, until she shifted her attention to Dean. "I wonder what your real game is," I said softly.

She jerked her attention back to me.

"First you tried to con me. Then you gave me way too much money. If you wanted to buy a man to impress somebody, anybody who knows me will know Saucerhead. And be more intimidated by him. I'm a pussycat. Finally, and dearest to my heart, not five hours after you saw me, somebody tried to kill me."

Her eyes got big. I had to remind myself she'd said she was an actress.

"It was a cold-blooded ambush, Jill. Five men, plus whoever did the watching and running messages. A major effort."

Her eyes got bigger.

"You know an albino half-breed chuko called Snowball?"

She shook her head. It was a very impressive head. She was beautiful when she was frightened.

"How about a street gang called the Vampires?"

She shook her pretty head.

I had obviously recovered from my unpleasant night, because I was starting to pant. I slapped myself down. "What *do* you know? Anything? How about why you want to play me for a sucker. Or has that slipped your mind, too?"

She got mad again. But she swallowed her anger. She'd decided to clam.

I got up. "Come with me." Sometimes a good surprise loosens them up.

I took her into the Dead Man's room. Her response was cliché. "Yuk! That's gross!" But that was it.

I fished her retainer out from under the Dead Man's chair, which is the safest place in TunFaire. "I'll hang on to some of this, for Saucerhead's time and my aggravation." I took a couple coins in a gesture mainly symbolic, and handed the rest to her.

She eyed that purse like it was a snake. "What are you doing?"

"You're unhappy. I'm giving your money back and getting out of your life."

"But . . ." She went into a huddle with herself. While the committee was in conference I sneered at the Dead Man. Brought one right in here with you, Chuckles.

I was trying to get two birds with one big hunk of alum.

There's no prod more effective than bringing a woman into the house. The prettier the gal the more heated the reaction. Jill Craight could set the house afire. If he was sandbagging he wouldn't be able to keep it up.

Damn him. He didn't do a thing. And I'd been halfway sure he was hiding out from the rent collector.

"Mr. Garrett?"

"Yeah?"

"I'm scared. I made a promise. I can't tell you any more till I know who I have to be afraid of. Take this back. I want you. But if you can't do the job I'll take what I can get."

She *was* scared. If she'd been five feet tall and baby-faced, my protective instincts would have been inflamed. But she was damned near tall enough to look me in the eye and had no knack for playing helpless. You looked at her and you wanted to get into mischief with her, but you didn't have much inclination to take care of her. You knew she could take care of herself.

"If it wasn't for last night I'd give in about now, Jill. But somebody tried to whack me. Finding out who and why and talking him out of trying again is going to occupy my time. So Saucerhead is what you get."

"If I must, I must."

"You must." I put her retainer back under the Dead Man. "Now that we're done yelling at each other and we're all friends again, why don't you come by for dinner? Dean's culinary skills don't get much exercise."

She opened her mouth to turn me down, but inclination ran head-on into her instinct for self-preservation.

She didn't have to be nice to me. That wasn't a condition here. But I'm not so nice a guy I wouldn't let her find that out for herself. "It would have to be late," she said. "I do have to work."

"Pick your time. Tell Dean. Give him an idea what you'd like. It'll be better than anything you've had for a while."

She smiled. "All right." I think that was the first genuine smile she'd shown me. She marched off to the kitchen.

I paused, leaned against the doorframe, and sneered at the Dead Man. I had my ulterior motives for wining and dining Jill Craight—beyond those I'd been born with. She still might stir old Chuckles up. I'm also a great believer in synchronicity.

It was a lead-pipe cinch that, because I'd made a date, Tinnie would suffer a miraculous remission from the sulks. Somebody from the Tate place would come to let me know before Jill went home.

Jill came back. "Dean is a nice man."

Was the implication that I was not? "Tricky, too. You got to watch him. Especially if you're not married. A great ambassador for the institution of marriage, Dean is."

"But he's not married himself."

A quick vixen, friend Jill. How much had she pried out of him? "Not married and never has been. But that doesn't slow him down. Come on. I'll walk you home."

"You sure you can spare the time?"

"It's on my way," I lied. I figured I could use a chat with Saucerhead.

●●● **10**

T harpe fell in on Jill's far side before we'd walked a hundred yards. She was startled. I chuckled. "Get used to it."

That didn't excite her. It was one more hint that things were going on that she didn't want known.

I still had her pegged for a working girl, if a class model of same.

"Anything interesting going on?" I asked Saucerhead.

"Nope."

"Smith and Smith watching the place again?"

"Yeah. Pokey was right. They're amateurs. They look like a couple of farmers. Want me to grab one and tie him in knots till he talks?"

"Not yet. Just keep an eye on them. See who they report to."

Saucerhead grunted. "There's somebody watching your place, too. I spotted them while I was waiting."

I wasn't surprised. "Chukos?"

He shrugged. "Could be. They was young. But they wasn't showing colors."

"They wouldn't be if they were Vampires." I live in Travelers' territory, just inside their frontier with the Sisters of Doom.

We walked on. As we approached Jill's place I tried to talk us inside for a look around. She wouldn't have it. In fact, she didn't want to be seen with us in her own neighborhood. She probably thought we'd lower property values.

Saucerhead and I wandered around so I could get a look at Smith and

Smith. They did look like farmers. They certainly didn't look dangerous, but I didn't spend much time worrying about them. That was Saucerhead's job.

I jogged a block out of my way going home, stopping at a tenement so decayed derelicts shunned it. I went around the side, down to a cellar door. Standing a foot deep in trash, I knocked. The door almost collapsed.

It opened an inch. An eye looked at me from brisket level. "Garrett," I said. "I want to talk to Maya." I flashed a piece of silver. The door shut.

Now a little game, a stall just to show me who ran things here.

The door opened. A girl of thirteen wearing nothing but a potato sack—probably stolen with the potatoes still inside—and a lot of dirt stood there. The sack was so frayed one ripening rosebud peeked out. She caught my glance and sneered.

"Love your hair, kid." It might have been blond. Who could tell? It hadn't been washed in recent generations.

From inside I heard, "Cut the comedy, Garrett. You want to talk to me get your butt in here."

I stepped into the citadel of the Sisters of Doom, TunFaire's only all-human, all-female street gang.

There were five girls there, the oldest sneaking up on eighteen. Four of the five shared the urchin's hairdresser and tailor. Maya wore real clothing and was better groomed, but not much. She was eighteen going on forty, war-chief of a gang claiming two hundred "soldiers." She was so emotionally sliced up you never knew which way she would jump.

Most of the Sisters were emotional casualties. They'd all suffered severe abuse, and a murmur of defiance had driven them into the Doom's never-never land. That hung, precariously and eternally, at right angles to reality, between childhood as it should have been and the adulthood of the untormented. They'd never recover from their wounds. Most of the girls would die of them. But the Doom gave them a fortress into which they could retreat and from which they could strike back, which left them better off than the tortured thousands who went through the hell without support.

Maya had suffered more than most. I met her when she was nine, when her stepfather offered to share her if I'd buy him some wine. I'd declined to the crackle of his breaking bones.

She was a lot better now. She was normal most of the time. She could talk to me. Sometimes she came to the house to cadge a meal. She liked Dean. Old Dean was every girl's ideal uncle.

"Well, Garrett? What the hell you want?" She had an audience. "Let's see the color of your money."

I tossed her a coin. "Faith offering," I told her. "I want to swap information."

"Come ahead. I'll tell you to go to hell when you get on my nerves."

If she took a fit, I could go out looking like chopped meat. Those girls could be vicious. Castration was a favorite sport.

"You know the Vampires? Run by an albino darko called Snowball and a crazy bleeder named Doc? North End."

"I've heard of them. They're all crazy, not just Doc. I don't know them. Word is, Doc and Snowball are getting ambitious, trying to rent muscle and recruit soldiers from other gangs."

"Somebody might take exception."

"I know. Snowball and Doc are too old for the street but not old enough to know they can't trespass."

It's a classic cycle. And sometimes the young ones pull it off. About once a century.

Today's kingpin was a street kid. But that organization recruited him from a gang and promoted him from within.

"The Doom have any relationship with the Vampires?" The girls prefer being called the Doom. They think it has a nicer ring than the Sisters or the Sisterhood.

"All take and no give, Garrett. I don't like that."

"If you're running with the Vampires I don't have anything to give you." She gave me the fish eye.

"Snowball and Doc tried to take me out," I said.

"What the hell were you doing in the North End?"

"I wasn't, sweetie. I was on Warhawks' turf. Warhawks have a treaty with the Vampires?"

"No need. No contact. Same with the Doom." She shifted. "You're sneaking up on something, Garrett. Get to the point."

"There are a couple guys watching my house. I'd guess chukos. Probably Vampires, considering last night."

She thought about that. "A genuine hit? You're sure?"

"I'm sure, Maya."

"Your place is on Travelers' ground."

"You're starting to get it. Trouble is, I don't have any friends with the Travelers since Mick and Slick got caught in the sweep."

The relationships between the races have become terribly complex, them being all mixed together but each owning its own princes and chiefs and quirky root cultures. TunFaire is a human city. Human law prevails in all civil matters. A plethora of treaties have established that entering a city voluntarily constitutes acceptance of the prevailing law. In TunFaire a crime in human law remains a crime when committed by anyone else, even when the behavior is acceptable among the perpetrator's people.

Treaties deny Karenta the power to conscript persons of nonhuman blood, nonhuman being defined as anybody of quarter blood or more who wants to revoke his human rights and privileges forever. Lately, though, the press gangs had been grabbing anybody who couldn't produce a parent or grandparent on the spot. That's what happened to the captains of the Travelers, though they were breeds.

Maya said, "So you want a couple of chukos off your back."

"No. I want you to know they're there. If they bother me I'll just knock their heads together."

She looked at me hard.

Maya has a byzantine mind. Whatever she does she has a motive behind her surface motive. She isn't yet wise enough to know that not everyone thinks that way.

"There're a couple of farmer types staying at the Blue Bottle, using the names Smith and Smith. If somebody was to run a Murphy on them and it was to turn out that they had documents, I'd be interested in buying them." That was spur of the moment but would satisfy Maya's need for a hidden motive.

It couldn't be that I just wanted to see how she was doing. That would mean somebody cared. She couldn't handle that.

I paused at the door. "Dean says he's whomping up something special for supper. And a lot of it." Then I got out.

I hit the street and stopped to count my limbs. They were all there, but they were shaky. Maybe they have more sense than my head does. They know every time I go in there I run the chance of becoming fish bait.

ean was waiting to open the door. He looked rattled. "What happened?"

"That man Crask came."

Oh. Crask was a professional killer. "What did he want? What did he say?"

"He didn't say anything. He doesn't have to."

He doesn't. Crask radiates menace like a skunk radiates a bad smell.

"He brought this."

Dean gave me a piece of heavy paper folded into an envelope. It was a quarter-inch thick. I bounced it on my hand. "Something metal. Draw me a pitcher." As he headed for the kitchen I told him, "Maya might turn up tonight. See that she eats something and slip her a bar of soap. Don't let her steal anything you're going to miss."

I went into the office, sat, placed Crask's envelope on the desk, my name facing me, and left it alone until Dean brought that golden draft from the fountain of youth. He poured me a mug. I drained it.

He poured again and said, "You're going to get more than you bargained for if you keep trying to do something for those kids."

"They need a friend in the grown-up world, Dean. They need to see there's somebody decent out there, that the world isn't all shadow-eat-shadow and the prizes go to the guys who're the hardest and nastiest."

He faked surprise. "It isn't that way?"

"Not yet. Not completely. A few of us are trying to fight a rearguard action by doing a good deed here and there."

He gave me one of his rare sincere smiles and headed for the kitchen.

Maya would eat better than Jill and I if she bothered to show.

Dean approved of my efforts. He just wanted to remind me that my most likely reward would be a broken head and a broken heart.

I wasn't going to get into heaven or hell letting Crask's present lie there. I broke the kingpin's wax seal.

Someone had wrapped two pieces of card stock tied together with string. I cut the string. Inside I found a tuft of colorless hair and four coins. The coins were glued to one card. One coin was gold, one was copper, and two were silver. They were of identical size, about half an inch in diameter, and looked alike except for the metal. Three were shiny new. One of the silver pieces was so worn its designs were barely perceptible. All four were temple coinage.

Old-style characters, a language not Karentine, a date not Royal, apparent religious symbology, lack of the King's bust on the obverse, were all giveaways. Crown coinage always shows the King and brags on him. Commercial coinage shouts the wonders of the coiner's goods or services.

Karentine law lets anyone coin money. Every other kingdom makes minting a state monopoly because seigniorage—the difference between the intrinsic metal value of a coin and its monetary value—is a profit that accrues to the state. The Karentine Crown, though, gets its cuts. It requires private minters to buy their planchets, or blanks, from the Royal Mint, costs payable in fine metal of a weight equal to that of the alloy planchets. There's more state profit in not having to make dies and pay workmen to do the striking.

The system works most of the time and when it doesn't, people get roasted alive, even if they're Princes of the Church or officials of the Mint who are cousins of the King. The foundation of Karentine prosperity is the reliability of Karenta's coinage. Karenta is corrupt to the bone but will permit no tampering with the instrument of corruption.

I gave the gold piece the most attention. I'd never seen private gold. It was too expensive just to puff an organizational ego.

I picked up the top piece of card stock and read the terse note, "See the man," followed by a fish symbol, a bear symbol, and a street name that constituted an address. Few people can read so they figure out where they are by reference to commonly understood symbols.

Crask wanted me to see somebody. This provocative little package was supposed to provide useful hints.

If Crask was dishing out hints, that meant Chodo Contague was serving up suggestions. Crask didn't take a deep breath without Chodo telling him. I decided to check it out. There was no point getting Chodo miffed.

The address would be way up north. Of course. I needed a long hike.

I didn't have anything going until Jill arrived. And I'd been telling myself I needed exercise.

North End, eh?

I went upstairs and rummaged through my tool locker, selected brass knucks, a couple of knives, and my favorite eighteen-inch, lead-weighted head knocker. I tucked everything out of sight, then went down and told Dean I'd be out for a few hours.

12

Most of us are in worse physical shape than we like to think, let alone admit. I'm used to that being more the other guy's problem than mine. But by the time I covered the six miles to the North End, I felt it in my calves and the fronts of my thighs. This was the body that had carried me through weeks of full-pack marches when I was a Marine?

It wasn't. This body was older and it had been beaten up and banged around more than its share since.

The neighborhood was elfin and elfin-breed, which means it was tidy and orderly in an obsessive fashion. This was a neighborhood where elvish wives whitened stonework with acids and reddened brickwork with dyes once a week. When it rained the gutters ran with color. Here the men tended trees as though they were minor deities and trimmed their tiny patches of lawn with scissors, one blade of grass at a time. You had to wonder if their private lives were as ordered and passionless and sterile.

How had this environment, with its rigid rectitude, produced Snowball and the Vampires?

I turned into Black Cross Lane, a narrow two-blocker in the shadow of Reservoir Hill. I looked for the fish and bear and stray Vampires.

It was quiet. Way too quiet. Elvish women should have been out sweeping the streets or walks or doing something to stave off the entropy devouring the rest of the city. Worse, the silence smelled like an old one, in place because something unimaginably awful had happened and the street remained paralyzed by shock. My advent had not caused it. Even in this neighborhood there would have been folks getting out of the way if I was headed into an ambush.

I have such comforting thoughts.

I found the place, a four-story gray tenement in fine repair. The front door stood open. I went up the stoop. The silence within was deeper than that which haunted the street.

This was the heart of it, the headwater from which the treacle of dread flowed.

What was I supposed to do?

Do what I do, I guessed. Snoop.

I stepped inside figuring I'd work my way to the top floor. I didn't need to. The first apartment door stood open a crack. I knocked. Nobody answered but I heard a thud inside. I gave the door a push. "Yo! Anybody home?"

Frantic thumping sounded from another room. I proceeded with extreme caution. Others had been there before me. The room had been stripped by locusts.

There was a smell in the air, faint yet, but one you never mistake. I knew what I'd find in the next room.

It was worse than I thought it could be.

There were five of them, expertly tied into wooden chairs. One had tipped himself over. He was doing the thumping, trying to attract attention. The others would attract nothing but flies ever again.

Someone had placed a loop of copper wire, attached to a stick, around each of their necks, then had twisted the loops tight. The killers had taken their time.

I recognized everybody—Snowball, Doc, the other two who had tried to whack me. The live one was the kid who had stood lookout. They were efficient that way, Crask and Sadler.

It was a little gift for Garrett from Chodo Contague, an interest installment on his debt. The vig, against the day I called in the nut.

What do you think at a moment like that, surrounded by people snuffed as casually as you would stomp a roach, without anger, malice, or remorse? It's scary because it's death without fire behind it, as impersonal as accidental drowning.

Squish! Game's over.

The wire loop is Sadler's signature.

I could see Slade giving Sadler the message Morley had written. I could see Sadler telling Chodo. I could see Chodo getting so worked up he might adjust the blanket covering his lap. "So take care of it," Chodo might say, like he'd say, "Throw out that fish that's starting to smell." And Sadler would take care of it. And Crask would bring me a few coins and a lock of a dead man's hair.

That was death in the big city.

Did Doc and Snowball and the others have anyone to mourn them?

I was getting nowhere standing around feeling sorry for guys who'd had it coming. Crask wouldn't have made a trip across town if he hadn't thought I'd find something interesting here.

I guessed I'd get it from the one they'd left alive.

I sat him up facing the wall. I hadn't let him see me yet. I walked around and leaned against the wall, looked him in the eye.

He remembered me.

I said, "Been your lucky day so far, hasn't it?" He'd survived Crask and Sadler and those opportunists who had taken everything that wasn't nailed down. I waited until his eyes told me he knew his luck had run out. Then I abandoned him.

I scrounged around until I found a water jug in a second-floor apartment. The locusts hadn't gone that high, fearing they'd get cut off. I checked the street before going back to my man. It was still quiet out there.

I showed the chuko the jug. "Water. Thought you might be dry."

He wasted a little moisture on tears.

I cut his gag off, gave him a sip, then backed off to prop up the wall. "I think you have things to tell me. Tell me right, tell me straight, tell me everything, maybe I'll let you go. They make sure you heard everything during the interviews?" Clever euphemism, Garrett.

He nodded. He was about as terrified as he could get.

"Start at the beginning."

His idea of the beginning antedated mine. He started with Snowball taking over the building by dumping his human mother in the street. She had inherited it from his father, whose family had owned it since the first elvish migrated to TunFaire. The entire neighborhood had been elvish for generations, which was why it was in such good shape.

"I'm more interested in the part of history where the Vampires got interested in me."

"Can I have another drink?"

"As soon as you've earned it."

He sighed. "A man came yesterday morning. A priest. Said his name was Brother Jercé. He wanted Snow to do some work. He was a front guy, like, you know? He wouldn't say who sent him. But he brought enough money so Snow's eyes bugged and he said the Vampires would do whatever he wanted. Even when Doc tried to talk him out of it. He never went against Doc's advice before. And look what that got him."

"Yeah, look." I knew what it got him. I wanted to know what he did to get it.

The priest wanted the Vampires to keep tabs on me and a priest called Magister Peridont. If Peridont came to see me, the Vampires were supposed to make me disappear. Permanently. For which they would get a fat bonus.

Snowball took it because it made him feel big-time. He didn't care that much about the money. He wanted to be more than a prince of the streets.

"Doc kept trying to tell him that takes time. That you can't go making a name without the big organization noticing you. But Snow wouldn't back down even after word hit the streets that the kingpin was saying lay off a guy named Garrett. He was so crazy he wasn't scared of nothing. Hell. None of us was scared enough."

He had that right. They were too young. You have to put a little age on before you really understand when to be afraid. I gave him a small drink. "Better? Good. Tell me about the priest. Brother Jercé. What religion was he?"

"I don't know. He didn't say. And you know how priests are. They all dress the same in those brown things."

He had that right, too. You had to get close and know what to look for to tell Orthodox from Church from Redemptionist from several dozen so-called heretical splinter cults. Not to mention that Brother Jercé's whole show could have been cover.

I asked myself if any man could have been dumb enough—or confident enough—to have given these punks his right name and have paid them in the private coin of his own temple. Maybe it was just my dim opinion of priests, but I decided it was possible. Especially if Brother Jercé was new to all this. After all, how often does a job get botched up as thoroughly as the Vampires had done? I should have been dead and nobody the wiser.

I asked many more questions. I didn't get anything useful until I took out the coins Crask brought me. "Was all the payoff money like this?"

"The money I seen was. Temple stuff. Even gold. But Snow didn't make a show. I bet he lied about how much he got paid."

No doubt. I hit him with the big question. "*Why* did this priest want me hit?"

"I don't know, man."

"Nobody asked?"

"Nobody cared. What difference did it make?"

Apparently no difference if smoking somebody is just business. "I guess that's it, then, kid." I took out a knife.

"No, man! Don't! I gave it to you straight! Come on!"

He thought I was going to kill him.

Morley would say he had the right idea. Morley would tell me the guy would haunt me if I didn't, and that damned Morley is right more often than not. But you have to do what you think is right.

I wondered if surviving this mess would scare the kid off the road to hell. Probably not. The type can't see danger until it's gnawing their legs.

I moved toward him. He started crying. I swear, if he'd called for his mother . . . I cut the cord holding his right arm and walked out. It would be up to him whether he got loose or stayed and died.

I stepped out into another gorgeous evening.

I marveled at my surroundings. Once I got out of Black Cross Lane I saw elvish women sweeping and washing their stoops and walks and the streets in front of their buildings. I saw their menfolk manicuring greenery. It was the evening ritual.

The elvish do have their dark underside. They have little tolerance for breed offspring. Poor kids.

13

I t was thoroughly dark before I got home. I spotted several shooting stars, supposed by some diviners to be good omens and by others the opposite. One gaudy show-off broke up into lesser streaks.

Dean let me in. "Damn, that smells good," I said.

"It will be," he promised. He smiled. "I'll bring you a beer. Did you learn anything useful?"

"I don't know." What was this? He wasn't himself. "What are you up to?" He gave me his kicked-puppy look. I think he practices it. "Nothing."

"What happened while I was gone?"

"Nothing. Except Maya came. In fact, she just left. When you knocked."

I grunted. She had obviously been working on Dean. "You'd better count the silver."

"Mr. Garrett!"

"Right. Any sign of Miss Craight?" Walking home I'd decided she wouldn't show. What was in it for her? I was pretty sure she was a gal who didn't take a deep breath without calculating her return on investment. Such a shame; all that beauty wasted.

"Not yet. She did say it would be a late dinner."

How late was late? "I'm going to freshen up." I went upstairs. A wash would help clean the body, but it couldn't do anything for the stains on my soul.

Jill was there when I came back down. She had charmed old Dean again. He was letting her set the table. Unprecedented.

They were gossiping like old friends.

I said, "I hope that's not me you're ripping."

Jill turned. "Hi, Garrett. Nope. You aren't that lucky." She smiled. There wasn't any more heat in it than in a forest fire.

"Had a good day?"

"The best. Business was marvelous. And I talked to my friend. He apologized for the trouble he'd caused me. He hadn't expected it. He's taken care of it. I won't be bothered again."

"That's nice." I checked her over. I tried not to be too obvious. She could set dead men panting. Her fear had gone. "I'm glad for you. But poor Saucerhead will be brokenhearted."

Dean gave me a disappointed scowl. Couldn't I get my mind off *that* for five minutes?

Are you kidding? I'm not dead yet. But I took his hint. It wouldn't be worth the trouble, anyway, just to get turned down. Sour grapes.

She got along with him better than she did with me. For us it was one of those things where nobody could think of anything to say.

Garrett tongue-tied around a gorgeous blonde? That did wonders for my self-esteem. But Dean's ducks were so good they made up for the lack of crisp repartee.

The main trouble was that Jill Craight wasn't about to tell me anything about Jill Craight. Not about her now, not about her then. She was slick, changing the subject or just sliding away from it so smoothly I didn't realize what she was doing until she'd done it several times.

Giving up on her left me only one area of expertise where I could talk extensively: Garrett. And a little bit of Garrett goes a long way.

I guess the high point was the wine she'd brought. It was an import. It was almost good.

To me wine is just so much spoiled fruit juice. It all tastes the same, with rare exceptions. This was the rarest. It was as good as the famous TunFaire Gold, which meant I drank most of my gobletful without sneaking off to wash the taste out of my mouth with a slug of beer.

The ice maiden was on holiday, but this thing wasn't going anywhere. I figured as soon as dessert was over we ought to put it out of its misery.

Jill was more a lady than I thought. She got us through the difficulties. We helped Dean clear the dead soldiers, then I walked her home.

We'd gone less than a block when I missed something you can't miss if he's in the neighborhood. "What's happened to Saucerhead?" It wasn't like him to wander off.

"I let him go. I don't need him now. My friend straightened things out."

"I see." Especially why she was willing to let me walk her home.

I didn't say much after that. I watched for shooting stars but the gods had closed the show. We said good night outside her apartment building, a refurbished tenement. Jill did not ask me in for a nightcap and I made no attempt to fish an invite. She gave me a sisterly peck on the cheek. "Thanks, Garrett." She marched inside. She never looked back.

I considered the newly risen moon with misdirected animosity. I muttered, "Sometimes you have nothing at all in common." Not even a language where the words mean the same things.

I turned toward home and almost fell over Maya.

14

She'd come out of nowhere. I hadn't heard a sound. She laughed.

"What were you doing with that woman, Garrett?" She sounded like Tinnie asking the same question. What was this?

"We had dinner. You object?"

"I might. You never took me to dinner."

I grinned. "I didn't take her, either. She came to the house." I'd call her bluff. "You want me to take you someplace classy? The Iron Liar? You got it. But get yourself a bath, comb your hair, put on something a little more formal." I chuckled. I could just picture the Liar if Maya walked in. They'd scatter like roaches in sudden light.

"You're making fun of me."

"No. Maybe going at it the long way around, telling you to think about growing up." I hoped she wouldn't be one chuko who fought that.

She sat down on somebody's steps. The moonlight was in her face. She was pretty under the grime. She could even be a heart stopper if she wanted to be. First she'd have to come to terms with her past and decide she wanted to attack the future. If she kept drifting she'd be another burned-out whore living off garbage in fifteen years, brutalized by anyone who wanted to bother, protected by no one.

I sat down beside her. She seemed to want to talk. I didn't say anything. I'd said enough to make her defensive.

"Nobody watching your place anymore, Garrett. Vampires or anybody else."

"Probably pulled out when they heard about Snowball and Doc."

"Uhm?"

"The kingpin had them put to sleep."

She didn't say anything while that sank in. Then, "Why?"

"Chodo doesn't like people who don't listen. He put it out to lay off me and they didn't."

"Why would he look out for you?"

"He thinks he owes me."

"You get to meet a lot of people, don't you?"

"Sometimes. Usually they turn out to be the kind I wish I didn't know. There are some bad people in this world."

She was quiet for a while. She had something on her mind. "I met some of those today, Garrett."

"Oh?"

"Those guys you said to run a Murphy on. I used Clea because she can get a statue excited. They almost killed her." She got graphic with her account of the torture of a thirteen-year-old.

"I'm sorry, Maya. I had no idea they were . . . What can I do?"

"Nothing. We take care of our own."

I had a bad feeling. "And the two Smiths?" The Doom wouldn't have been kind.

She mulled over how much to admit. "We were going to cut them, Garrett." That was a mark of the Doom. "Only somebody already did it."

"What?"

"Both of them. Somebody took all their business off. They'll have to squat like women."

This was getting weird. They don't make eunuchs anymore, even as a criminal punishment.

"So we just broke their legs."

"Remind me not to get on the bad side of the Doom. Did you find out anything?"

"Garrett, if those guys weren't walking around they wouldn't exist. They didn't have anything but their clothes. You should see the woman at the Blue Bottle. A cow."

"Weirder and weirder, Maya. What do you think?"

"I don't, Garrett. You do that."

"Eh?"

"You said do a Murphy on two guys watching that place. Tonight you go strolling over there with Tawny Dawn Gill, she gives you a peck on the cheek, I figure you're working for her and you know what's doing."

"I didn't even know that name. She told me it was Jill Craight. You know her?"

"She was in the Doom when they took me in. Never told the truth when a lie would do. Had a different name every week. Toni Baccarat. Willi Gold. Brandy Diamond. Cinnamon Steele. Hester Podegill. That's the only one that sounded dumb enough to be real. She lied all the time about who her family was and the famous people she knew and all the stuff she'd done. She mostly hung out with the younger girls because everybody else had her figured out and wouldn't listen to her shit."

"Hold on. Hester Podegill?"

"Yeah. One of her thousand and one names." She looked at me oddly.

There were Podegills off in a back room of my mind. Neighbors in the old days. Bunch of daughters. A couple of them turned up pregnant at thirteen. I began to recall the talk and the way people had shunned the parents . . . Third floor, that's where they'd lived. And the little one, a blonde named Hester, would have been about ten when I left for the Marines.

But the Podegills were dead.

The only letter my brother wrote in his life he wrote to tell me how the Podegills died in a fire. The tragedy really broke him up. He'd had it bad for one of the girls.

That letter had taken two years to catch up to me. By the time it did my brother had been in the Cantard a year himself. He's still down there. Like a lot of others, he won't be coming home.

Maya asked, "That name mean something to you, Garrett?"

"It reminded me of my brother. I haven't thought about him for a long time."

"I didn't know you had one."

"I don't now. He was killed at Flat Hat Mesa. Ask me sometime and I'll show you the medal they gave my mother. She put it in a box with the ones for her father, her two brothers, and my father. My father got it when I was four and Mikey was two. I used to be able to remember Dad's face if I tried hard. I can't anymore."

She was quiet for a few seconds. "I never thought about you having a family. Where's your mom now?"

"Gone. After they gave her Mikey's medal she just gave up. Nothing to live for anymore."

"But you—"

"There's another medal in that box. It has my name on it. The Marines delivered it four days before the Army delivered Mikey's."

"Why? You weren't dead."

"They thought I was. My outfit was on an island the Venageti invaded. They claimed they killed us all. Actually, we were out in a swamp, living on cattails and bugs and crocodile eggs while we picked them off. Mom was gone before the news got back after Karenta recaptured the island."

"That's sad. I'm sorry. It isn't fair."

"Life isn't fair, Maya. I've learned to live with it. Mostly, I don't think about it. I don't let it shape me or drive me."

She grunted. I was getting preachy and she was getting ready to respond the way kids always do. We'd been sitting there no more than ten minutes but it seemed a lot longer.

"Somebody's coming," she said coldly.

S omebody was Jill Craight looking like she'd seen a zombie and his seven
brothers. She would have run past us if I hadn't said, "Jill?"

She squeaked and jumped. Then she recognized me. "Garrett. I was
coming to see you. I didn't know where else to turn." Her voice squeaked.
She looked at Maya but didn't recognize her.

"What's the trouble?"

Jill gulped air. "There's . . . There are dead men in my apartment. Three
of them. What should I do?"

I got up. "Let's go look."

Maya bounced up and invited herself along. Jill was too rattled to care.
I figured she'd be safer tagging along than wandering around alone.

Near the door to Jill's building I spied something I'd missed when the
light was poorer—blood. The women didn't notice.

I found more spots inside, small, nothing to grab the attention if you weren't
looking. I noted that the building was in better shape than its contemporaries.

Lamps on the landings lighted the stairs. I caught sounds of life as we
stole to the second-floor landing, first a woman's laughter sudden as the
shattering of a glass, then sounds of a woman either having one heck of a
good time or fighting a bad bellyache.

There were four doors down the second-floor hall from which the sounds
came. There had been four on the first. The apartments couldn't be big,
sound not much retarded. How come the place wasn't an overturned anthill
if three guys had gotten killed?

Because Jill lived higher on the hog. Her floor was class, only two larger apartments. "Who lives across the way?"

Jill pushed her door open. "Nobody right now. It's empty."

"Wait." I wanted to go in first just to be sure. I checked the door. The lock was designed to keep the honest folks out. Anyone with a little know-how could get past it.

So somebody with no knowledge had used a wrecking bar for a key. And nobody had heard that?

People do tend to mind their own business.

The room appeared untouched. It was a lot classier than a Jill Craight could afford. I'd seen less luxury in places on the Hill.

Jill Craight had a sugar daddy. Or she had something heavy on somebody with a lot to lose, which could be an explanation for somebody watching and trying to get in. Maybe she had a piece of deadly physical evidence.

A trail of blood led to a door standing two inches ajar. It opened on a room eight feet by eight, jammed with stuff. That's all you could call it. Stuff. Jill was a pack rat.

Sprawled amid the plunder was a body, blond, middle twenties, still marked by that weathered look you pick up in the Cantard. He might have been handsome. Now he just looked surprised and uncomfortable. And very dead.

"Know who he was?" I asked.

Jill said, "No." Maya shook her head. I frowned. Maya let go of the silver doohickey she was about to pocket.

"I'd guess he walked in on somebody who was digging through your stuff and both of them were surprised." I stepped over the dead man to a door.

The room beyond was where Jill slept and maybe paid her rent. It had that look.

There were two more stiffs in there, and blood all over, like somebody lugged in buckets and threw it around. It looked like several men had chased the guy from the walk-in while more had headed him off at the bedroom door, which opened on a hallway. Both bodies were near the door.

Maybe if you're a Crask, or Sadler, or even Morley Dotes, you get so the red messes don't touch you. It took me a minute to get my brain moving, judging the splash patterns and the way things were kicked around. I went over to eyeball the dead men.

I don't know how long it was. A while. Jill touched my arm. "Garret? Are you all right?" There wasn't any ice in her eyes. For a moment the woman behind the masks looked out, humanly concerned.

"I'm all right." As all right as I could be looking at a guy I'd had over to supper less than thirty hours ago.

What the hell was Pokey doing in Jill's apartment in the first place, let alone getting himself killed there? He'd given the job to Saucerhead and Jill had fired Tharpe before he'd gotten started.

I went to the bed, picked a clean spot, and sat down. I had some thinking to do.

Pokey had been less of a close friend than a professional acquaintance I respected. And he hadn't been working for me when he'd gotten it. I didn't owe him. But something got me on a level where there isn't any common sense.

I wanted whoever had done it.

Maya spoke for the first time. "Garrett," was all she said but her tone told me it was important.

She was in the walk-in, squatting by the dead man. I joined her. Jill stayed in the doorway, paying attention to Maya for the first time. She did not look happy.

"What?"

"Pull his pants down."

"Say what?"

"Just do it, Garrett."

Maya was too serious to answer with a wisecrack. I did it, turning a pretty shade of pink. "Hunh?"

He'd been surgically and thoroughly desexed. He'd healed but the scar tissue was still a virulent purple. It had been done since his return from the Cantard.

I scrunched up like I had spiders stomping on my naked skin.

Jill said, "That's sick."

I agreed. I agreed just a whole hell of a lot. That mess of scars gave me the heebie-jeebies.

I didn't want to, but I went and checked the other one.

He was older. His scars had lost their color long ago.

I went back to my place on the bed. After a while, I told Jill, "You can't stay here. Somebody will come to clean up."

"You think I could stay here with this? Are you crazy?"

"You got anywhere to go?"

"No."

I sighed. It figured. "What about your friend?"

"I don't know how to get ahold of him. He finds me."

Of course he would. Nobody's husband wanted his mistress turning up on his doorstep. Had he given her his real name? "Put together what you'll need for a few days." Now I had to make a choice. I wanted to track the guys who had gotten away. They'd left a bloody trail. But somebody ought to walk Jill over to my place.

I glanced at Maya, looking bad in her colors. She said, "No way, Garrett. I'm sticking with you."

Hell, it was bad enough having the ones my own age read my mind. Now kids were going to start, too?

Jill said, "I can make it from here to your place, Garrett."

I didn't argue. She wasn't high on my list of favorite people. "You have a lantern around here?"

She told me where to find one.

t was quiet out, but it wasn't trouble quiet. There just wasn't anybody around.

It was after midnight but that doesn't make much difference most places. The day people go to bed, then the goblins and kobolds and ratmen and whatnot come out to do the night work. I guess it just wasn't their kind of neighborhood.

I opened the lantern's shutter and looked for blood spots. They got harder to see as they dried.

Maya asked, "How come all the lights in her place, Garrett? She must have had twenty lamps burning."

"You got me." It had been bright in there. I hadn't paid attention, though. "Guess they wanted to see what they were doing."

"She done pretty good since she left the Doom."

"If you say so." Was she going to chatter at me all night?

"You don't think so?"

"Is that your goal in life? To have some guy keep you in an apartment full of dead men? Those guys came with whatever is going on in her life."

She had to think about that. I finally got some quiet.

It didn't last. "You notice she had real glass windows in that fancy sitting room?"

"Yeah." That I'd noticed. Real glass is expensive. I know. I've had to re-place a few panes. Those had impressed me.

"The other apartment had them, too."

"Yeah. So?"

"So somebody was watching us from there when we left."

"Oh?" Interesting. "What did he look like?"

"I couldn't even tell if it was a he. All I saw was a face. It was only there for a second. Plain luck I saw it."

I grunted, not giving her my complete attention. The trail was getting harder to follow, like maybe the guy doing the bleeding had had most of the juice squeezed out. The going was getting slower.

The trail led into an alley so narrow a horseman would lose his knees if he tried to get through. It was not an inviting place. I shone the light in but couldn't see anything.

"You're not going in there, are you?"

"Sure I am." I fished out my brass knuckles. I hadn't brought my favorite head knocker. It hadn't seemed appropriate dress for a dinner date.

"Is that smart?"

"No. Smart would be to throw you in first and see what eats you." Either Maya had begun to wear or I was getting crabby. "How come you're following me around, anyway?"

"So I can learn the trade. So I can find out what kind of man you are. You put on a good show but nobody is that decent. There's something weird about you. I want to find out what it is."

Maya was wearing real thin. Weird! No woman had called me that before. "Why's that?"

"I'm thinking about marrying you."

"Hoo!" I went into that alley without throwing rocks first. There was nothing in there that scared me now.

I found the dead guy ten paces into the darkness. Somebody had set him down with his back against a building, had made him comfortable, then had gone on, presumably to get help. He'd bled to death there.

I squatted, checked him out. Maya held the lantern.

He was still dead. He didn't have anything to tell me. I figured he was even less happy about the situation than I was. But he wasn't complaining.

I took the lantern and moved on.

There was more blood, but not much.

Poke had put him up a hell of a fight.

The trail petered out in the next street. I gave it my best look but couldn't take it any farther.

Maya asked, "What're you going to do now?"

"Hire a specialist." I started walking. She caught up. I asked, "Doesn't any of this bother you?" She'd stayed cooler than Jill Craight.

"I've been on the street five years, Garrett. Only things that bother me are the ones people try to do to me."

She wasn't that tough, but she was getting there. And that was a shame.

Sometimes it seems Morley's place never closes. It does, but only during those hours of the dawn and morning when only the most twisted are up and about. Noon to first light the place serves its strange clientele.

It had thinned out, but forty pairs of eyes watched us from the entrance to the serving counter, eyes more puzzled than hostile.

Wedge was behind the counter. Of all Morley's henchmen he's the most courteous. "Evening, Garrett." He nodded to Maya. "Miss." Just as though she didn't look like death on a stick and smell like it, too.

"Morley still up?"

"He's got company." The way he said it told me the company wasn't business.

"That resolution didn't last long."

Wedge flashed me a smile. "Were you in the pool?"

"No." They would, that bunch.

Wedge went to the speaking tube, talked and listened, talked and listened, then came back. "He'll be a while. Said have dinner while you wait. On the house."

Ugh.

Maya said, "That sounds great," before I could turn him down. "I could eat a horse."

I grumbled, "You won't eat one here. Horseweed, horse fennel, horseradish, horse clover, yeah, but . . ."

Wedge yelled into the back for two specials, then leaned on the counter. "What you need, Garrett? Maybe I can save you some time."

I glanced at Maya. She smiled. She knew damned well Wedge was being nice because I had a woman along.

How do they get that way so young?

"I need a stalker, Wedge. A good one. I'm trying to track a guy."

"Cold trail?"

"Not very. And he was bleeding. But it's getting colder."

"Back in a few. I know what you need." He went into the kitchen. Another human-elf breed took his place. He was younger. He plunked a couple of platters on the counter, tossed up some utensils, looked at Maya like he wondered if it was catching, and went to the end of the counter to take somebody's order.

"That one's no prince," Maya told me. "But the old guy was all right." She eyed her platter.

The special looked like fried grass on a bed of blanched maggots covered in slime sauce filled with toadstool chunks and tiny bits of black fur. I muttered, "No wonder vegetarians are so nasty."

Maya assaulted her meal. When she stopped to catch her breath she said, "This ain't bad, Garrett."

I'd begun nibbling the mushrooms out of mine. She was right. But I wasn't going to admit it out loud, in front of witnesses. I muttered, "Wedge is no prince, either. He takes people out on the river, ties rocks to their feet, dumps them in, and tells them he'll race them back to shore. Tells them he'll turn them loose if they beat him. I hear some of them paddle like hell all the way to the bottom."

She checked to see if I was joking. She saw I wasn't. Well, maybe I'd exaggerated a little, but Wedge wasn't nice people. Morley Dotes didn't have nice people working for him.

She was reading my mind again. "Aren't there any decent people anymore?"

"Sure. We just don't run into many."

"Name two," she challenged.

"Dean. Friend of mine named Tinnie Tate. Her uncle Willard. Friend of mine called Playmate."

"All right."

"Not to mention I have a fair opinion of myself."

"You would. I said all right, Garrett. Forget I asked. You going to finish that? I'll take it."

I pushed my platter over. Where was she putting it?

Wedge came back with the sleaziest ratman I'd ever seen. He had a lot of the old blood: long whiskers, a long snoot, patches of fur, a four-foot tail. He'd be a descendant of one of the less successful experimental strains of two centuries back, when the life magics were the rage and anybody who could diddle up a spell was trying to create new forms. None of those sorcerers are remembered today but their creations are with us still. They'd been inordinately fond of messing with rats.

I pride myself on my open mind and freedom from prejudice, but I've always found room to exclude ratpeople. I can't help it. I don't like them and none of them have done anything to improve my opinion.

Wedge told me, "This is Shote, Garrett. As good a stalker as you'll find. And he's available."

I nodded to Shote and tried to shelve the prejudice. "Wedge tell you what I need?"

Shote nodded. "Forrow sssomebody whosss breeding."

I grinned. None of those guys were going to do any breeding. "Basically, I've got a solid starting point. Shouldn't be hard."

"Two marks frat fee, I take you to the end of the track. Arr I do is track. No fighting. No portering. No nothing erse."

"That's fine with me." I dug out two marks silver.

Morley arrived. He leaned on the counter beside me. He looked at Maya. "Picking them a little young, aren't you?"

"This is Maya, my self-appointed assistant and understudy. Maya, the famous Morley Dotes."

"Charmed." She eyed him. "He a friend of yours, Garrett?" She'd know the name.

"Sometimes."

"You going to invite him to the wedding?"

She had set me up and cut me off at the knees.

Morley had to ask. "What wedding?"

"Him and me," Maya said. "I decided I'm going to marry him."

Morley grinned. "I'll be there. Wouldn't miss it for a barge loaded with gold." I've seen toads with straighter faces than he had on.

I bet they heard my teeth grind all the way to the waterfront.

"Maya Garrett?" Morley said. "It does have a ring." He looked at the ratman. "Shote. How you doing? I thought you didn't have anything going, Garrett." He was having a hell of a time keeping from laughing.

"I didn't. Now I do. Somebody offed Pokey Pigotta. I want to ask them why."

That took the grin off his clock. "You taking it personal?" He thinks I take everything personal.

"I don't know. Pokey was all right, but he wasn't really a friend. I just want to know why he turned up dead where he did."

Morley waited for me to tell him where and when. I disappointed him. I asked Shote, "Are you ready? Let's go."

Maya downed the rest of my celery drink and pushed away from the counter. She grinned at me.

Morley asked, "Mind if I tag along?"

"Not at all." He'd be useful if we walked into something.

expected the dead man's friends would have collected him, but when we reached that death-trap alley, there he was, taking it easy, like a drunk sleeping it off.

"They left this one where he croaked," I said. "At least one more was bleeding when they left."

The ratman grunted and started sniffing around.

"Morley, I want to show you something." I had Maya hold the lantern while I pantsed the dead guy.

"What are you, some kind of pervert?" Morley asked.

"Just take a look. Ever seen anything like this?"

Morley looked for a long time. Then he shuddered and shook his head. "No. I've never seen anything like that. That's sick. Crazy sick. How did you know? What have you gotten yourself into?"

"This is the fifth one today. All cut bald." I didn't go into detail.

Morley said, "Why would anybody let somebody do that?"

"There are a lot of crazies in this world, old buddy."

"I didn't think there was anybody that crazy."

"That's because you think with yours."

"Ha! The pot calling the kettle black."

"If you're ready?" The ratman sounded offended.

"Whenever you are," I told him.

"One man went on from here. He was wounded, as you surmised." Put me in my place. He led off, dropping to all fours so his legs folded up like a grasshopper's hind legs. That hurt just to see but didn't bother him. He snuffled and muttered and scooted along, growling at Maya to douse the damned light.

The trail turned south, headed across town a mile, a mile and a half into a better part of the city, not wealthy like the Hill and the neighborhoods clinging to its skirts, but definitely middle-class.

I began to get the feeling I'd missed something important. I suspected I knew something I didn't know I knew. I tried going over everything.

I should know better than to force it. That never works. Thinking just confuses me.

The stalk turned out to be a giant anticlimax. We caught our quarry in another alleyway. "Dead as a wedge," Shote announced. "Been gone a couple of hours."

"He was alone?" Morley asked.

"Did I tell you he was alone? I told you he was alone. He was alone."

"Touchy, touchy."

Maya searched the body. I hadn't done that with the others, except cursorily. I expect it would have been a waste of time. Maya didn't find anything.

Morley said, "I didn't know old Pokey had it in him. He was always a talker. He could bullshit his way out of anything."

"I don't think he had time to talk."

Maya asked, "What do we do now, Garrett?"

"I don't know." My inclination was to go home and sleep. We'd hit a dead end here. "We could keep going the way we were headed, see if we run into anything that bites."

Morley said, "There's nothing ahead but the Dead Zone, the Dream Quarter, and the Slough of Despond." Those were vulgar names for the diplomatic community, the area where TunFaire's religions maintain their principal temples, and the tight island where the city maintains two workhouses and a jail, a madhouse, and a branch of the Bledsoe charity hospital. The Slough is surrounded by a high curtain wall, not to keep anyone in or out but to mask the interior so as not to offend the eyes of passersby headed for the Dead Zone or the Dream Quarter.

There was a lot more to the South End, including industry, fairgrounds, shipyards, acres and acres of graveyards, and most of the Karentine Army's city facilities. But I thought I caught what Morley meant.

There was a chance our dead madmen had originated in one of those three areas. I'd be hard put to decide which was the craziest.

I said, "Whoever sent those guys might be wondering what happened to them. I'm going back where Pokey got it and see if anybody turns up."

Maya thought that was a good idea. Morley shrugged. "I've had a long day. I'm going to get some sleep. I'd be interested in hearing if you find something, Garrett. Want to head back, Shote?"

The ratman grunted.

I had a thought. That happens. So do lunar eclipses. "Wait up. I want you to look at something. Everybody." I took out my coin card. "Shine the light on this, Maya."

"Temple coinage," Morley said. "Can't tell what temple."

Maya and Shote couldn't tell me anything, either.

Morley asked, "It have anything to do with this?"

"No. These have to do with who sicced Snowball on me. Whoever hired him paid him in these."

Morley pruned his lips. "Check the Royal Assay. They're supposed to keep samples of private coinages."

That was a good idea. I wished I'd thought of it. I thanked him and said good night.

•••**19**

Maya and I had a quiet walk back. Maybe she was as worn out as I was. I didn't try to make conversation.

I tried to stay alert. It was late for chukos but I was crossing town with the warchief of the Doom, showing her colors, asking for trouble if she was spotted.

Trouble didn't find us. We saw mostly ratpeople sweeping streets, clearing trash, scrounging, stealing whatever wasn't nailed down. I have to admit they contribute, mainly by doing work no one else wants. They are industrious.

I went back to the steps where Maya and I had been sitting when Jill brought the bad news. The moon had moved along. The place was no longer in the light. Jill's building was. I watched.

Maya helped. She seemed disinclined to head for her lair. After a while, she said, "The Vampires were really trying to kill you?"

"Sure seemed like it." I shrugged. "Doesn't matter now."

"Huh? That Snowball is crazy. He'll try again."

Was she kidding? "No he won't. He really is dead, Maya."

The look she gave me.

After that we didn't talk much.

I ran out of patience. Weariness will do that. "I'm going over there. See what happened while we were roaming."

Maya followed me. She moved like she was worn out. At eighteen? After only these few hours? Hell, I was the old-timer here.

We had no trouble getting in the street door, same as before. That implied the place had heavyweight protection, something to check on, though it would lead back to Chodo if the women were what I thought. If the place was his and he found out who sent those men, somebody was in for hard times. Chodo's enforcers go after their jobs with the gusto and arrogance of tax collectors. They don't stop coming and they don't leave you anywhere to hide.

The place was quiet. The keepers had gone home to less winsome company. The kept were asleep, visions of presents prancing in their pretty heads.

We went up slowly, carefully. Earlier there had been lamps to light the way, but now they were dark. I figured the caretaker had extinguished them but I wasn't going to dance into an ambush because it seemed unlikely.

We reached Jill's door. I listened. Nothing. I pushed the door. It swung inward, as it should, quietly. I stuck my head inside.

All but two lamps had burned out, and those wouldn't be with us long. I saw no evidence that we weren't alone. "See if you can find some oil." While she looked I checked the corpses. They hadn't walked away.

I came back to find Maya filling lamps. "Long as we're here I'm going to toss the place. Those guys were looking for something and they didn't find it."

"How do you figure?" She got a couple of refills burning.

"They didn't have anything when we found them. And we accounted for all of them. So whatever it was it's here or wasn't here to begin with." I thought. I hoped.

"Oh."

"I'll do this room first so we can get the lights out. Keep an eye on the street. Anyone comes, holler."

I ripped the room apart. Jill would be pissed if she found out. I wouldn't tell her. Let her think the bad boys did it.

I demolished furnishings. I looked for secret hiding places. I didn't find doodly squat. And Maya didn't see anything in the street.

"Darken the room so nobody will see the lights and wonder. Stay back a few feet so the moonlight doesn't hit your face." I recalled the face she'd seen in the window of a supposedly empty apartment. Maybe we'd take a look in there, too.

"All right."

"Getting tired?" She sounded it.

"Yes."

"I'll hurry."

"If you're going to do it, do it right. I'll stay awake."

I hoped so. I didn't need a surprise like the one Pokey got.

I did the walk-in next. All I found out was that Jill couldn't get rid of anything. There are two kinds—sentimentalists who keep everything for what it meant, and the ex-poor, who keep everything as a hedge against revenant poverty. I pegged Jill for the latter.

I hit the kitchen next. All I learned there was that Jill didn't eat at home. In fact, as I went along, despite the heap of stuff in the walk-in, I began to suspect that Jill didn't really *live* there, but just kept stuff there and met someone there.

I stalled doing the bedroom until I'd drawn blanks everywhere else. I didn't want to keep climbing over Pokey, reminded that life is chancy for guys like us. It might be enough to rattle me into getting a job.

I didn't like it but I went at it, doing a fast round first, in case something turned up the easy way.

It didn't. I hadn't counted on it, anyway. The only thing that comes easy is trouble.

I went after it the hard way.

Still nothing.

Well, Jill hadn't struck me as stupid. She'd had plenty of storm warnings.

I wondered if she'd carried whatever it was over to my place. I hadn't watched her pack. Sure she had, if it had been here and was portable.

Had I just wasted a couple of hours I could have spent sleeping?

I made only one find of more than passing interest.

A small chest of drawers stood beside the bed. It was an expensive piece. The top drawer was just two inches deep. Jill had used it to dump small change. There had to be a pound of copper in there. Junk money to her, probably, though there were characters on the street who would take her head off for less.

I sat on the bed, pulled the drawer into my lap, and stirred its contents. The coins weren't all copper. Maybe one in twenty was a silver tenth mark.

The mix was eclectic, new and old, royal and private, as you'd expect of general change. Should I let Maya know the rainbow ended here?

Whoa! A perfect, mint-condition brother of the copper coin on the card in my pocket. A gem of the minter's art. I fished it out.

It meant nothing, of course. . . .

"Garrett!" Maya called.

I shoved the drawer into the chest and headed for the front room. "What you got?"

"Take a look."

I looked. Six men moved around the street below, furtive, studiously ignoring the building while they talked.

Maya asked, "How do we get out?"

"We don't. Keep watching. I'll be across the hall. Let me know when they come inside." I got a lamp, scurried across the hall, knelt, and got to work with a skinny knife.

I had the door open when Maya arrived. "Four are coming in."

I doused the lamp and moved forward into darkness, assuming the layout to reflect that of Jill's apartment, going slowly so I wouldn't get bushwhacked by rogue furniture.

I'd gone about eight feet when somebody knocked me ass over appetite. I never saw him, just heard his feet and Maya's squeak as he pushed past her. I fought off a man-eating chair with fourteen arms and legs. "Close the door. Quietly."

She did. "What do we do now?"

"Sit tight and hope they don't break in here. You carrying?"

"My knife."

They always have that. For chukos the knife is who they are. Without it they're just civilians.

"You get a look at that guy?"

"Not really. He was bald. He was carrying something. A corner of it hit me in the tit. I thought I'd scream."

"Don't talk like that."

"What'd I say?"

"You know . . . Ssh!" They were in the hall. They were trying to be quiet but had invaded unfamiliar territory in the dark.

Maya whispered, "He had a funny nose, too."

"Funny how?"

"Big and bent. Like it was broken or something."

"Sshh."

We waited. After a while I sent Maya to watch from the window, in case they left without us hearing them. I got into ambush near the door in case they decided to drop in. I wondered what had become of the guy who had run out. If he'd been one of them we'd have had company by now. And if he'd run into them there would have been some kind of uproar.

It was a long wait. The sky had begun to show some color when Maya said, "They're leaving."

I went and watched. The two biggest men each carried one of the lighter corpses. The other two carried the heavier corpse. The whole bunch got out of there fast.

I figured the smart thing would be to follow their example. So of course I took my dead lamp across the hall to see if I couldn't get it lit.

I was so long Maya was in a panic when I got back. "They cleaned the place up so it looks like nothing happened."

"Why would they do that?"

"You tell me and we'll both know."

"You going to follow those guys?"

"No."

"But—"

"There are six of them and one of me and they're going to be looking for trouble. They're real nervous right now, I guarantee you. I've been there. If they've got the sense the gods gave a duck they'll get rid of those bodies fast, then scatter. And anyway, I'm so tired I couldn't not walk into something. The best thing we can do is get some sleep."

"You're just going to drop it?" There was a peculiar edge to her voice.

"What's it matter to you?"

"How am I going to learn?"

"You don't have an audience here, Maya." That proved how tired I was.

She took it like a slap in the face. She didn't have anything to say after that.

I glanced around a minute later. Maya wasn't with me anymore.

I suffered a twinge of self-disgust. I hadn't needed to stomp all over her. She'd had enough of that from the rest of the world.

slept past noon. When I stumbled into the kitchen I found Jill Craight with Dean, the two of them chattering like old girlfriends who'd been out of touch for years.

Jill asked brightly, "What did you find out last night?"

Dean looked expectant. I hadn't told him anything when he'd let me in. I'd growled and snorted and stamped hooves some and gone to bed. Anything he knew he'd gotten from Jill.

"A whole bunch of nothing," I grumbled. I plopped into a chair. It barked back at me. "That damned Pokey put up too damned good a fight. Both guys that got out croaked before they got wherever they were headed."

Dean filled my teacup. "Mr. Garrett is a little ragged before he's had breakfast."

I folded my lips back in a snarl.

"Don't work so hard at it, Garrett," Jill said. "I know you're a wolf."

"Ouch."

She laughed. That surprised me. Snow queens can't have a sense of humor. That's in the rule book somewhere.

She said, "So they're all dead. That mean it's over?"

"No. They didn't find what they were after. But you deal with that however you want. It's your problem."

Dean brought me a platter piled with rewarmed biscuits, a pot of honey, butter, apple juice, and more tea. Just a morning snack for the boss. But the boss's houseguest had eaten better than the king had this morning.

Jill looked at me. "You said Pokey did too well. Who is Pokey?"

I had stepped right in that time. I would have to be more careful not to put that foot in my mouth. "Pokey Pigotta. The skinny dead man in your apartment. He was in the same business as me, more or less. You paid him, he found things out, took care of things for you. He was the best at what he did, but his luck ran out."

"You knew him?"

"There aren't a lot of us in this racket. We know each other."

Dean looked at me weird. He didn't give me away.

She thought a bit. "You couldn't guess who might have sent him, could you?"

I did have a notion and planned to check it out. "No."

"Looks like I'll have to try to hire you again. I can't live like this."

"You ever tried running through the woods in the dark?"

"No. Why?"

"You do, you keep smashing your face against things you can't see. Running in the dark can shorten your life. I don't run in the dark."

She got the message. There was no way I'd work for her if she wouldn't tell me what was going on. "I have a prior commitment, anyway."

"What's that?"

"Somebody tried to kill me. I want to find out who."

She didn't try to con me out of that.

I told her, "Get Saucerhead Tharpe. He's no investigative genius but he'll keep you safe. You thought about what might've happened if you'd been home when those guys dropped in?"

I could see that she had. She was worried.

"Get ahold of Saucerhead." I got up. I told her how to find Tharpe. "Dean, on the off chance Maya turns up, tell her I apologize for running my mouth. For a minute I forgot she wasn't a civilian."

Dean's face pruned up and I knew he was going to say something I didn't want to hear. "Mr. Garrett?" There it was. Hard proof. Bad news, bad news. "Miss Tate was here this morning."

"Yes?"

He wilted. "I . . . Uh . . ."

"What did she say?"

"Well, I . . . Uh . . . Actually, Jill . . . Miss Craight answered the door. Miss Tate left before I could explain."

That was my gal Tinnie. She kept her gorgeous figure through vigorous exercise jumping to conclusions.

"Thanks." I wasted a raised eyebrow on him. "I'm going out." I did. I stood on the front stoop and wondered what else could go wrong.

I figured I had two choices. I could go to the Royal Assay Office to check the provenance of the temple coinage or I could go to the Dream Quarter after Magister Peridont and the answer to a question that had nagged me since I'd found Pokey.

Or I could find Tinnie. But right now hunting thunder lizards held more appeal.

The Assay Office seemed of more immediate interest, yet . . . I took out the coin I'd swiped from Jill's drawer. I flipped it. Well. The Grand Inquisitor it was.

I started walking. Though I shuffled along and might have looked preoccupied, I was reasonably alert. I noticed, for example, that the sky was overcast and a chill breeze was as busy as a litter of kittens tumbling leaves and trash. There wasn't much else to notice as far as I could see.

21

Chattaree, the Church's citadel-cum-cathedral, sits at the hub of the Dream Quarter. I looked it over from across the avenue. How many millions of marks did it take to erect that limestone monstrosity? How many more to keep it up?

In a city where you see uglies as a matter of course, artisans had had to stretch to make Chattaree hideous. Ten thousand fabulous beasties snarl and roar from the cathedral's exterior—supposedly to keep Sin at bay. The Church has that neatly personified in a platoon of nasty minor demons. Maybe the uglies work. They gave me the creeps as I started across to the cathedral steps.

There are forty of those. Each has a name and they surround the cathedral completely. It looks like somebody started to build a pyramid and suffered a change of heart a third of the way through the project. The cathedral itself starts thirty feet above street level, all soaring spires covered with curlicues and ugly boys. The steps are uneven in width and height to make running difficult for unfriendly people in a hurry to drop in. There was a time when rivalries between sects were less restrained.

The dungeons where Magister Peridont reputedly had his fun were supposed to exist as catacombs wormholed into the foundations beneath the steps.

Halfway up I met an old priest. He smiled and nodded benevolently, one of those guys who are what priests are supposed to be, and as a consequence, remain at the foot of the episcopal ladder throughout their lives.

"Excuse me, Father," I said. "Can you tell me how to find Magister Peridont?"

He seemed disappointed. He studied me and saw I wasn't one of the faithful. That left him perplexed. "Are you sure, my son?"

"I'm sure. He invited me over, but I've never been here before. I don't know my way around."

He looked at me funny again. I guess people don't come prancing in looking for Malevechea every day. He gave me a lot of near-gibberish Church cant. Boiled down, it told me I should ask the guy on guard duty inside the cathedral door.

"Thanks, Father."

"For nothing, my son. Have a pleasant day."

I clambered to door level and surveyed the Dream Quarter. The Church's nearest neighbor was also its most bitter competitor. The sprawling grounds of the Orthodox basilica and bastion began a hundred yards to the west. Its domes and towers looked somber behind surrounding trees. People came and went at the minority temple but nothing moved over there. It was as silent as a place under siege. I guess the scandals were bad for business.

I stepped in out of the gloom, found the guard and woke him up. He didn't like that. He liked it even less when I told him what I wanted.

"What do you want him for?"

"About twenty minutes."

He didn't get it, which was why he had a guard's job. He wasn't smart enough for anything else. He wasn't your everyday parish priest. He was a no-neck kind of guy who probably should have been a wrestler. His frown threatened to fold a mountain range in the center of his forehead. He deduced that I was poking fun and didn't like it.

I told him, "Me and the Magister are old war buddies. Tell him Garrett is here."

A second mountain range rose atop the first. An old buddy of Malevechea? He knew he'd better be careful until he got the go-ahead to stomp me. "I'll tell him you're here. You keep an eye out. Don't let nobody carry nothing off." He looked at me like he wondered if maybe I might plunder the altars.

It was not a bad idea if you could get away with it. You'd need a train of wagons to haul the goodies away.

He was gone awhile. I hung around beaming at passersby. The regulars did a double take and frowned, but went about their business when I told them, "New on the job. Don't mind me." A dumb smile helped.

The guard came back looking perplexed. His world was tilting. He'd expected Peridont to tell him to bounce me down all forty steps. "You're supposed to come with me."

I followed him, surprised that it had been so simple. I trod warily. When it's easy you don't go barefoot because there's always a snake in the grass.

I didn't see any prisoners. I didn't hear any wails of despair. But the ways we followed were narrow and dark and damp and rat-haunted and sure would have made nice dungeons. Hell, I was disappointed.

No-Neck brought me to a cadaverous, bald, hook-nosed character about fifty years old. "This is the guy. Garrett."

Hawknose gave me the fish eye. "Very well. I'll take charge. Return to your post." His voice was a heavy, breathy rasp, like somebody had smashed his voice box for him. It's hard to describe how creepy it was, but it gave me the feeling he was the guy who had all the fun tightening the thumbscrews.

He gave me the evil eye. "Why do you want to see the Magister?"

"Why do you want to know?"

That caught him off balance, like what I wanted *really* wasn't any of his business.

He looked away, got himself under control, grabbed papers off his escritoire. "Come with me, please."

He led me through a maze of passages. I tried to picture him as the guy who'd run over me and Maya last night. He had no hair and a weird nose but was about a foot too tall. He tapped on a door. "Sampson, Magister. I've brought the man Garrett."

"Show him in."

He did. Behind the door lay a chamber twenty feet by twenty and cheerful for a place that was buried. Magister Peridont didn't have ascetic tastes, either. "Doing all right for yourself, I see."

Hawknose pursed his lips, handed over his papers, bowed toward Peridont, and hurried out, closing up behind me.

I waited. Peridont didn't say anything. I told him, "That Sampson is a creep."

Peridont put the papers on a table twelve feet long and four wide. They vanished in the litter already there. "Sampson has social disabilities. But he makes up for that. So. You've reconsidered?"

"Possibly. I'll need some information before I make up my mind. It may have become personal."

That puzzled him. He studied me. I was doing a boggle on everybody today. It's all in knowing how, I guess. "Let's have the questions, then. I want you on the team."

I never trust guys who want to be my pal. They always want something I don't want to give.

I showed him the coins. "You recognize these?"

He placed the card on his table, put on bifocals as he sat down. He stared for half a minute and took his cheaters off. "No, I don't. Sorry. Do these have a bearing on our business?"

"Not that I know of. I thought you might know who put them out. They're temple coinage."

"Sorry. That's strange, isn't it? I should." He perched those bifocals on the tip of his nose and eyed the coins again. He handed me the card. "Curious."

I'd tried. "More to the point. Did you hire somebody else when I turned you down?"

He poked at that question before he admitted he had.

"It wouldn't have been Pokey Pigotta, would it? Wesley Pigotta?"

He wouldn't answer that one.

"It's a small field. I know everybody. They know me. Pokey would have suited your requirements. And he took on a new client right after I turned you down."

"Is this important?"

"If you did hire Pokey, you're short a hired hand. He got himself killed last night."

His start and pallor answered my question.

"So. A big setback?"

"Yes. Tell me about it. When, where, how, who. And why you know about it."

"When: last night after dark sometime. Where: an apartment on Shindlow Street. I can't tell you who. Four men were involved. None survived. I know about it because the person who found the bodies asked me what to do about them."

He grunted, thought. I waited. He asked, "That's why you came? Pigotta's death?"

"Yes." That was partly true.

"He was a friend?"

"An acquaintance. We respected each other but kept our distance. We knew we might butt heads someday."

"I don't quite see your interest."

"Somebody tried to kill me, too. Me and Pokey both doesn't read coincidence to me. I talk to you and somebody tries to off me. You hire Pokey, he gets it. I wonder why but even more I wonder who. I want to cool him down. If that helps you, so be it."

"Excellent. By all means, if the people responsible for Pigotta's death tried to kill you, too."

"So who did it?"

"I don't follow you, Mr. Garrett."

"Come on. If somebody wants in your way bad enough to kill anybody you talk to, you ought to know who. There can't be so many you can't pick somebody out of the crowd."

"Unfortunately, I can't. When I tried to hire you I told you I think there's a concerted effort to discredit Faith, but I don't have one iota of evidence that points in any particular direction."

I gave him my eyebrow trick in its sarcastic mode. He wasn't impressed. I'll have to learn to wiggle my ears. "If you want me to find somebody or something—like the Warden and his Relics—you'll have to give me somewhere to start. I can't just yell 'Where the hell are you?' Finding somebody is like picking apart an old sweater. You just keep pulling loose threads till everything comes apart. But you have to have the loose threads. What did you give Pokey? Why was he where he was when he got killed?"

Peridont got up. He prowled. He lived on another plane. He was deaf to anything he didn't want to hear. Or was he? "I'm disturbed, Mr. Garrett. Being outside this you miss the more troublesome implications. And they, I regret, tie my hands and seal my lips. For the moment."

"Oh?" I gave my talented eyebrow one last chance.

He missed it again. "I want your help, Mr. Garrett. Very much. But what you've told me puts matters into a new perspective. Contrary to popular imagining I'm not a law unto myself. I'm one tree in a forest of hierarchy."

"A tall tree."

He smiled. "Yes. A tall one. But only one. I'll have to consult my peers and ask for a policy decision. Bear with me a few hours. If they want to pursue this I'll give you the information at my disposal. Whatever the decision, I'll be in touch. I'll see you're compensated for what you've already done."

How very thoughtful of him. How did such a nice guy get such a nasty reputation?

He was being nice because he wanted something he couldn't get by tossing me into a cell and pulling my nails. I said, "I have to get moving on my own hunt."

"I'll get in touch at your home. Before you go—"

I interrupted. "The name Jill Craight mean anything to you?"

"No. Should it?"

"I don't know. Pokey died in an apartment occupied by a Jill Craight."

"I see. Would you hold on a minute?" He opened a cabinet. "I don't want to lose another man. I want you to take something as a hedge against the kind of surprises that got Pigotta." He pawed around among several hundred small bottles and vials, selected three.

He placed those on the table, three colorful soldiers all in a row: royal blue, ruby, and emerald. Each bottle was two inches tall. Each had a cork stopper. He said, "The ultimate product of my art. Use the blue where maximum confusion would benefit you. Use the green where death is your only other out. Break the bottles or just unstop them. That doesn't matter."

He took a deep breath, lifted the red bottle carefully. "This is the heavyweight. Be careful. It's deadly. Throw it against a hard surface at least fifty feet away. You don't want to be any closer. Run if you have the chance. Got that?"

I nodded.

"Be careful. Twenty years from now I want to tip one with you and reminisce about the bad old days."

"Careful is my middle name, Magister." I put the bottles away gingerly, where I could grab them in a hurry. Garrett never argues with a gift horse. I can always deal it to the glue works.

I sneaked a peek at his cabinet. What could those other bottles do? They came in every color. "Thanks. I can find my way out." I shot my final question as I neared the door. "You ever hear of a cult that cuts its members? Takes all their equipment, not just their testicles?"

He blanched. I mean, he really turned white. For a second I thought his hair would change. But he showed no other reaction. He lied, "No. That's grisly. Is it important?"

Lie to me, I'll lie to you. "No. It came up in a bull session the other night. The weather was pretty drunk out. Somebody heard something like that from somebody who heard something about it from somebody else. You know how that goes. You can't trace the source."

"Yes. Good day, Mr. Garrett." Suddenly he wanted me out of there.

"Good day, Magister."

I closed the door behind me. Smiling Sampson was right there to make sure I had no trouble finding the street.

A drizzle had started. The breeze had freshened. I put my head down and walked into it, grumbling. I wouldn't be out in this if the world would learn to leave me alone. How thoughtless of it.

Head down with not much going on inside—some would say that's the normal state of my bean—I trudged toward that small district beyond the Hill where both city and Crown maintain their civil offices. I hoped the Royal Assay people could tell me what Peridont wouldn't.

He had recognized the coins.

I didn't believe much of what he'd told me—though some of it might have been true. I disbelieved only selectively. I took nothing at face. Everywhere I turned religion popped up, and that's a game of masks and deceits and illusions if ever there was one.

My course took me within a block of the Blue Bottle, where curiosities Smith and Smith had holed up. Wouldn't hurt to stop by, see what Maya had missed.

The place didn't look promising. There'd been no upkeep done in my lifetime. But it was a cut above places where all you got for your copper was a place on a rope that would support you while you slept standing up.

It was the sort of place frequented by the poor and the lowest-order bad boys. The people who operated it wouldn't be eager to talk. I'd have to use my wits to get anything.

Not always the best hope with me.

The interior delivered the promise of the outside. I stepped into a dingy common room inhabited only by a flock of three winebirds hard at their trade. Some invisible force had pushed them to the extremities of the room. One was educating himself in a continuous muttered monotone. I couldn't make out one word in five but he seemed to be engaged in a furious debate on social issues. His opponent wasn't apparent and seemed to have a hard time making himself heard.

I didn't see anybody who looked like a proprietor. Nobody responded to the bell over the door. "Yo! Anybody home?"

That didn't bring any customer-conscious landlord charging in from his toils in the kitchen. But one of the silent drunks detached himself from his chair and reeled toward me. "Wha'cha need? Room?"

"Looking for a couple of my pals, Smith and Smith, supposed to be staying here."

He leaned against the serving counter, bathed me in fumes and knotted his face into a ruddy prune. "Uh. Oh. Third floor. Door at the end." He didn't work up much disappointment over the fact that I wasn't going to put money in his pocket.

"Thanks, pal." I gave him a couple of coppers. "Have one on me."

He looked at the coins like he couldn't figure out what they were. While he pondered the mystery I went upstairs. Carefully. The way those steps creaked and sagged it was only a matter of hours until one collapsed.

I wasn't disappointed by the third floor, either. It was more like a half story—five rooms under the eaves, two to either side of a claustrophobically narrow hall and one at the end. Two of the side rooms didn't have a hanging to ensure privacy. One still had a door that hung on one hinge, immobile. My destination was a door that wouldn't close because of a warp in the floor.

The Smiths weren't home. Surprise, surprise. I hadn't expected them to be after their encounter with the Doom. I pushed inside.

Whatever plot or conspiracy or outfit the Smiths were with, it was miserly. They'd slept on blankets on the floor. And they hadn't had a change of clothing to leave behind.

I started going over the room anyway. You never know when something minute will make everything fall together.

I was on my knees looking into the canyons between floorboards when the hallway floor creaked. I looked over my shoulder.

The woman looked like the Dead Man's wife. There was enough of her to make four women with some to spare. How had she gotten that close without raising a roar? How had the stairway survived? Why was the building standing? It was top-heavy enough to tip over.

"What the hell you doing, boy?"

She was spoiling for a fight and there wouldn't be any getting around it. "Why do you ask?"

"Because I want to know, shithead."

So it don't always work.

She was carrying a club, a real man-sized head buster. I pitied the guy who got hit when she got her weight behind it.

It looked like I might get a chance to practice my self-pity if I didn't use those wits I'd been daydreaming about. "Who the hell are you? What the hell are you doing sticking your face in my room?"

When you don't have space to dazzle them with your footwork you try baffling them with bullshit.

"*Your* room? What the hell you yelling, boy? This room belongs to two guys named Smith."

"The guy I paid said take this room. I did what he told me. You got a problem with that you take it up with the management."

She glared at me. "That goddamned Blake up to his old tricks, eh?" Then she yelled, "I *am* the management, shithead! You been conned by a wino. Now get your ass out of here. And don't come whining to me for your money back."

What a dreamboat.

She turned around and stomped away. I held on to the floor. If the building went I could ride it down. She kept grumbling. "I'm going to kill that sonofabitch this time."

What a sweetheart. It was a good thing she didn't get physical, because I don't think I could have taken her.

I did some more quick looking, but when the yelling started downstairs I figured it was time I made my getaway.

Then I spotted something.

It was a copper coin all the way down in a crack. I whipped out a knife and started digging.

There was no reason to believe the coin had been lost by the Smiths. It could have been there for a hundred years.

It could have been. But I never believed that for a second.

Maybe I wished hard enough. That scrungy little hunk of copper was the brother of those I'd collected already.

Click. Click. Click. Pieces started falling together. Everything was part of the same puzzle, except, improbably, Magister Peridont. Improbably because he'd lied. He knew something about what was going on even if he wasn't involved himself.

It was time to go.

●●●**23**

Big Momma was in full cry when I hit the bottom of the stairs. She was after the drunk I'd tipped. He dodged her with the nimbleness of long practice. She took a mighty swing as I arrived, but missed him. Her club smashed a bite out of a table. She yowled and cursed the day she'd married him.

The muttering drunk paid no attention. Maybe he was a regular and had seen it all before. The other drunk had disappeared. I thought he'd set a good example.

I slid toward the door.

Big Momma spotted me. She whooped. "You sonofabitch! You lying sonofabitch!" She headed my way like a galleon under full sail.

I'm not a fool every time. I got the hell out of there. The drunken husband must have zigged when he should have zagged. He came flying through the doorway, ass over appetite, and lay panting and puking in the drizzle. The woman did some yelling but didn't come out for the kill. When she quieted down I went to see how the guy was.

He had scrapes and a bloody nose and needed throwing into a river but he'd survive. "Come on." I offered him a hand up.

He took it, got up, teetered, looked at me with eyes that wouldn't focus. "You really done it to me, man."

"Yeah. Sorry about that. I didn't know your personal situation was so bad."

He shrugged. "Once she calms down she'll beg me to come back. A lot of women don't got any husband at all."

"That's true."

"And I don't cheat on her or beat her."

Somehow I couldn't picture him as a wife-beater. Not with that wife.

He asked, "What the hell were you trying to do, anyway?"

"Find out something about those guys Smith and Smith. Some friends of theirs killed a buddy of mine. Come on. Let's go somewhere out of the wet."

"Why should I believe anything you tell me after the stories you told already?" His speech wasn't that clear but that's what he wanted to say.

He was unhappy with me but that didn't keep him from tagging along. He muttered, "I need to get cleaned up."

So he wasn't all the way gone to wine. Yet. There's a point beyond which they just don't care.

I led him to a place a couple blocks away, as seedy as his own. It was a little more densely populated—five guys had gotten there ahead of us—but the ambience was the same: gloom laden with despair.

The operator was more businesslike. A frail ancient slattern, she was on us before we got through the doorway. She made faces at my newfound friend.

"We need something to eat," I told her. "Beer for me and tea for my buddy. You got someplace he can clean himself up?" A flash of silver stilled her protests.

"Follow me," she told him. To me, "Take that table there."

"Sure. Thanks." I let them get out of the room before I went to the door for a peek outside. I hadn't imagined anything. Mumbles had followed us. He was doing his routine against a wall down the street. I suppose he was talking about the weather.

If he'd taken a notion to keep an eye on me he wouldn't be going anywhere. I could handle him when I wanted. I planted myself at the appointed table and waited for my beer. The prospect of the kind of food such places served depressed me.

My pal didn't look much better when he came back but he did smell sweeter. That was improvement enough for me. "You look better," I lied.

"Bullshit." He dropped into a chair, slouched way down. The old woman brought beer and tea. He gripped his mug with both hands and looked at me. "So what do you want, pal?"

"I want to know about Smith and Smith."

"Not much to tell. Them wasn't their real names."

"No! Do tell. How long did they stay there?"

"They first come two weeks ago. Some old guy come with them. Paid for them to stay, room and board, for a month. He was a cold fish. Eyes like a basilisk. They wasn't none of them from TunFaire."

That got my attention. "How do you figure?"

"Their accents, man. More like KroenStat or CyderBen, somewhere out there, only not quite. Wasn't one I ever heard before. But it was like some. You get what I'm saying?"

"Yeah." I got it. Sometimes I catch on real fast. "That man who came with them. Did he have a name? What was he like?"

"I told you what he was like. Cold, man. Like a lifetaker. He didn't exactly encourage you to ask questions. One of the Smiths called him Brother Jersey."

"Jercé?"

"Yeah. That's it."

Well, well. The very boy who hired Snowball and Doc. That coin from up there maybe didn't prove anything but this did. "Any idea how I could find him? He's got to be the guy who had my friend killed."

"Nope. He said he'd come around again if Smith and Smith had to stay more than a month."

"What about them? Anything on them?"

"You kidding? They never said three words. Didn't socialize. Ate in their room. Mostly they was out."

I nibbled at him this way and that while we ate a chicken and dumpling mess that wasn't half bad. I couldn't get anything else until I showed him my coin collection.

He barely glanced at them. "Sure. That's the kind that Brother Jersey used to pay the rent. I noticed on account of most all of them was new. You don't see a bunch of new all together at once."

You don't. It was a dumb move, calling attention that way. Except Jercé probably figured Smith and Smith would never get made.

"Thanks." I paid up.

"Been a help?"

"Some." I gave him a silver tenth mark for his trouble. "Don't spend it all in one place."

He ordered wine before I got to the door.

I went out thinking I had to bone up on my geography. KroenStat and CyderBen are out west and west-northwest, good Karentine cities but a far piece overland. I'd never been out that way. I didn't know much about the region.

I also thought about asking Jill Craight a few more questions. She was in the center of the action. She knew a lot more than she'd admitted.

Mumbles was on the job. I'd make it easy for him to stick if he wanted—if he wasn't following my drunken buddy or wasn't there by absurd coincidence. I didn't care if I was followed.

●●●24

I was followed.

The drizzle tapered off to nothing most of my walk. But as I neared the Royal Assay Office the sky opened up. I ducked inside grinning, leaving Mumbles to deal with it.

Considering the size of Karenta as a kingdom and considering Tun-Faire's significance as largest city and chief commercial center, the Assay Office was a shabby little disappointment. It was about nine feet wide, with no windows. A service counter stood athwart it six feet inside. There was no one behind that. The walls were hidden behind glass plates fronting cases that contained samples of coins both current and obsolete. Two antique chairs and a lot of dust completed the decor.

No one came out though a bell had rung as I entered.

I studied the specimens.

After a while somebody decided I wouldn't go away.

The guy who came out was a scarecrow, in his seventies or eighties, as tall as me but weighing half as much. He was thoroughly put out by my insistence on being served. He wheezed, "We close in half an hour."

"I shouldn't need ten minutes. I need information on an unfamiliar coinage."

"What? What do you think this is?"

"The Royal Assay Office. The place you go when you wonder if somebody is slipping you bad money." I figured I could develop a dislike for that old man fast. I restrained myself. You can't get a lot of leverage on minions of the state. I showed him my card. "These look like temple coinage but I don't recognize them. Nobody I know does, either. And I can't find them in the samples here."

He'd been primed to give me a hard time but the gold coin caught his eye. "Temple emission, eh? Gold?" He took the card, gave the coins a once-over. "Temple, all right. And I've never seen anything like them. And I been here sixty years." He came around the counter and eyeballed the coins on one section of wall, shook his head, snorted, and muttered, "I know better than to think I'd forget." He hobbled around the counter again to get a scale and some weights, then took the gold coin off the card and weighed it. He grunted, took it off the scale, gouged it to make sure it was gold all the way through. Then he fiddled with a couple other tests I figured were meant to check the alloy.

I studied the specimens quietly, careful not to attract attention. Nowhere did I spy a design akin to the eight-legged fabulous beasties on those coins. Real creepies, they looked like.

"The coins appear to be genuine," the old man said. He shook his head. "It's been a while since I was stumped. Are there many circulating?"

"Those are all I've seen but I hear there's a lot more." I recalled my drunk's remark about accents. "Could they be from out of town?"

He examined the gold piece's edge. "This has a TunFaire reeding pattern." He thought a moment. "But if they're old, say from a treasure, that wouldn't mean anything. Reeding patterns and city marks weren't standardized until a hundred fifty years ago."

Hell, practically the night before last. But I didn't say that out loud. The old boy was caught up in the mystery. He'd already worked past his half hour. I decided not to break his concentration.

"There'll be something in the records in back."

I bet on his professional curiosity and followed him. He didn't object though I'm sure I broke all kinds of rules by passing the counter.

He said, "You'd think the specimens out there would be enough to cover every inquiry, wouldn't you? But at least once a week I get somebody who has coins that aren't on display. Usually it's just new coinage from out of town and I haven't gotten my specimens mounted. For the rest we have records which cover every emission since the empire adopted the Karentine mark."

Hostility certainly fades when you get somebody cranked up on their favorite thing.

"I've been at this so long that most of the time I can take one look and tell you what you need to know. Hell. It's been five years since I had to look anything up."

So, he was excited by the challenge. I'd brought novelty into his life.

The room we entered was twenty feet deep. Both side walls, to brisket level, boasted cabinets containing drawers three-quarters of an inch high. They contained older and less common specimens, I presumed. Above the cabinets, to the ten-foot ceiling, were bookshelves filled with the biggest books I've ever seen. Each was eighteen inches tall and six inches thick, bound in brown leather, with embossed gold lettering.

The back wall, except for a doorway into another room, was covered with shelves bearing the tools and chemicals an assayer needed. I hadn't realized there was so much to the business.

A narrow table and reading stand occupied the middle of the room.

The old man said, "I suppose we should start with the simple and work toward the obscure." He hauled out a book entitled *Karentine Mark Standard Coinages: Common Reeding Patterns: TunFaire Types I, II, III.*

I said, "I'm impressed. I didn't realize there was so much to know."

"The Karentine mark has a five-hundred-year history, as commercial league coinage, as city standard, then as the imperial standard, and now as the Royal. From the beginning it's been permissible for anyone to mint his own coins because it began as a private standard meant to guarantee value."

"Why not start with my coins?"

"Because they don't tell us much." He snagged a shiny new five-mark silver piece. "Just in. One of one thousand struck to commemorate Karentine victories during the summer campaign. The obverse. We have a bust of the King. We have a date below. We have an inscription across the top which gives us the King's name and titles. At the toe of the bust we have a mark which tells us who designed and executed the engraving for the die, in this case Claddio Winsch. Here, behind the bust, we have a bunch of grapes, which is the TunFaire city mark."

He placed my gold coin beside the five-mark piece. "Instead of a bust we have squiggles that might be a spider or octopus. We have a date, but this is temple coinage so we don't know its referent. There are no designer's or engraver's marks. The city mark looks like a fish and probably isn't a city mark at all but an identifier for the temple where the coin was struck. The top inscription isn't Karentine, it's Faharhan. It reads, 'And He Shall Reign Triumphant.' "

"Who?"

He shrugged. "It doesn't say. Temple coinage is meant for use by the faithful. They already know who." He stood the coins on edge. "TunFaire Type Three reeding on the five-mark piece. Used by the Royal Mint since the turn of the century. Type One on the gold. All Type One means is that the reeding device was manufactured before marking standards were fixed. Minting equipment is expensive. The standardization law lets coiners use their equipment until it wears out. Some of the old stuff is still around."

I was intrigued but also beginning to feel out of my depth. "Why city identification by marks and reeding both?"

"Because the same dies are used to strike copper, silver, and gold but copper coins and small fractional silver aren't reeded. Only the more valuable coins get clipped, shaved, or filed."

I got that part. The little lines on the edge of coins are added so alterations will be obvious. Without them the smart guys can take a little weight off every coin they touch, then sell the accumulated scrap.

The human capacity for mischief is boundless. I once knew a guy with a touch so fine he could drill into the edge of a gold coin, hollow out a quarter of it, fill the hollow with lead, then plug the drill hole undetectably.

They executed him for a rape he didn't commit. I guess you'd call that karma.

The old man turned the coins facedown and went on about the markings on their reverses. They told us nothing about the provenance of my coins, either.

"Do you read?" he asked.

"Yes." Most people don't.

"Good. Those books over there all have to do with temple coinage. Use your own judgment. See if you can luck onto something. We'll start from the ends and see what we can uncover."

"All right." I took down a book on Orthodox emissions just to see how it was organized.

The top of each page had an illustration of both sides of a coin from a rubbing of the original, lovingly and delicately inked. Below was everything anyone could possibly want to know about the coin: number of dies in the designs, the date each went into service, the date each was taken out and destroyed, dates of repairs and reengravings on each, quantities of each kind of coin struck. There was even a statement about whether there were known counterfeits.

I had a plethora of information available to me for which I could see little practical use. But the purpose of the Assay operation is partly symbolic. It is the visible avatar of Karenta's commitment to sound, reliable money, a commitment which has persisted since before the establishment of a Karentine state. Our philosophical forebears were merchants. Our coinage is the most trusted in our end of the world, despite the absurdities of its production.

I spent an hour dipping into books and finding nothing useful. The old man, who knew what he was doing, moved from the general to the particular, one reference after another, narrowing the hunt by process of elimination. He came to the wall I was working, scanned titles, brought a ladder from a corner, went up, and brushed a century's worth of dust off the spines of some books on the top shelf. He brought one down, placed it on his worktable, flipped pages.

"And here we are." He grinned, revealing bad teeth.

And there we were, yes. There were only two examples listed, one of which matched the coins I had except for the date. "Check the date," I said.

It had to be important. Because according to the book these coins had last been struck a hundred seventy-seven years ago. And if you added one hundred seventy-six to the date pictured you got the date on the gold piece I'd brought in.

"Curious." The old man compared coin to picture while I tried to read around his hands.

My type of coin had been minted in TunFaire for only a few years. The other, older type had been minted in Carathca . . . Ah! Carathca! The stuff of legend. Dark legend. Carathca, the last nonhuman city destroyed in these parts, and the only one to have been brought low since the Karentine kings had displaced the emperors.

Those old kings must have had good reason to reduce Carathca but I couldn't recall what it was, only that it had been a bitter struggle.

Here was one more good reason to waken the Dead Man. He remembered those days. For the rest of us they're an echo, the substance of stories poorly recalled and seldom understood.

The old man grunted, turned away from the table, pulled down another book. When he moved away I got my first clear look at the name of the outfit that had produced the coins. The Temple of Hammon.

Never heard of it.

The TunFaire branch was down as a charitable order. There was no other information except the location of the order's temple. Nothing else was of interest to the Assay Office.

I hadn't found the gold at the end of the rainbow but it had given me leads enough to keep me busy—particularly if I could smoke the Dead Man out.

I said, "I want to thank you for your trouble. How about I treat you to supper? You have time?"

Frowning, he looked up. "No. No. That's not necessary. Just doing my job. Glad you came in. There aren't many challenges anymore."

"But?" His tone and stance told me he was going to hit me with something I wouldn't like.

"There's an edict on the books concerning this emission. Still in force. It was ordered pulled from circulation and melted down. Brian the Third. Not to mention that there's no license been given to produce the ones you brought in."

"Are you sneaking up on telling me I can't keep my money?"

"It's the law." He wouldn't meet my eye.

Right. "Me and the law will go round and round, then."

"I'll provide you with a promissory note you can redeem—"

"How young do I look?"

"What?"

"I wondered if I look young enough to be dumb enough to accept a promissory note from a Crown agent."

"Sir!"

"You pay out good money when somebody brings you scrap or bullion. You can come up with coins to replace those four."

He scowled, caught on his own hook.

"Or I can take them and walk out and you won't have anything left to show anybody." I had a feeling they'd constitute a professional coup when he showed them to his superiors.

He weighed everything, grunted irritably, then stamped off through the rear door. He came back with one gold mark, two silver marks, and a copper, all new and of the Royal mintage. I told him, "Thank you."

"Did you notice," he asked as I turned to go, "that the worn specimen is an original?"

I paused. He was right. I hadn't noticed. I grunted and headed out, wondering if that, too, had been part of the message I was supposed to get.

I didn't want to go anywhere near the kingpin but I was starting to suspect I'd have to. He might know what was going on.

25

I t had turned dark. The rains had gone. My pal Mumbles hadn't. He was right where I'd left him, soggy, and shivering in the breeze. It was cold. A freeze before dawn wouldn't be a surprise.

I passed within two feet of him. "Miserable weather, isn't it?" I wish there'd been more light, the better to appreciate his panic.

He decided I was just being friendly, that I hadn't made him. He gave me a head start, then tagged along. He wasn't very good.

I wondered what to do with him. I couldn't see him as a threat. And he couldn't report on me while he was on my trail—if he wasn't just a drunk who liked to follow people.

I thought about going back to the Blue Bottle to check him out but couldn't bring myself to go nose to nose with Big Momma again. I thought about giving him the shake, then reversing our roles. But I was tired and cold and hungry and fed up with walking around alone in a city where some strange people were taking too much interest in me. I needed to go somewhere where I could get warm, get fed, and not have to worry about watching my back.

Home and Morley's place recommended themselves. The food would be better at home. But at Morley's I could work while I loafed. If I played it right I could get my job on Mumbles done for me. The disadvantage was the food.

It was the same old story. The crowd—down a little because of the weather—went silent and stared when I stepped inside. But there was a difference. I got the feeling that this time I wasn't just a wolf from another pack nosing around, I was one of the sheep.

Saucerhead was at his usual table. I invited myself to join him and nodded politely to the cutie with him. He has a way of attracting tiny women who become fervently devoted.

"I take it Jill Craight didn't get in touch."

He wasn't pleased by my intrusion. The story of my life. "Was she supposed to?"

"I recommended it." I had the feeling he was surprised to see me. "She needs protection."

"She didn't."

"Too bad. Excuse me. Morley beckons." I nodded to his lady friend and headed for Dotes, who had come to the foot of the stairs.

Morley looked surprised to see me, too. And he was troubled, which wasn't a good sign. About the only time Morley worries is when he has his ass in a sling. He hissed, "Get your butt upstairs quick."

I went past him. He backed up the stair behind me. Strange.

He slammed his office door and barred it. "You trying to start a riot, coming around here?"

"I thought some supper would be nice."

"Don't be flip."

"I'm not. What gives?"

He gave me the fish eye. "You don't know?"

"No. I don't. I've been busy chasing a two-hundred-year-old phantom charity. Here's your chance. What gives?"

"It's a marvel you survive. It really is." He shook his head.

"Come on. Stop trying to show how cute you are. Tell me what's got your piles aching."

"There's a bounty out on you, Garrett. A thousand marks in gold for the man who hands over your head."

I gave him a hard look. He has the dark-elfin sense of humor.

He meant it.

"You walk into this place, Garrett, you jump into a snakepit where the only two cobras that won't eat you are me and Tharpe."

And I wasn't so sure about Morley Dotes. A thousand in gold can put a hell of a strain on a friendship. That's more than most people can imagine.

"Who?" I asked.

"He calls himself Brother Jercé. Staying at the Rose and Dolphin in the North End, where he'll take delivery anytime."

"That's dumb. Suppose I just waltzed in to take him out first?"

"Want to try? Think about it."

There'd be a platoon of smart boys hanging around figuring I might try that.

"I see what you mean. That old boy must be worried I'll get next to him somehow."

"You still not working on something that's going to get you killed anyway?"

"I'm working now. For myself. Trying to find out who wants to kill me. And why."

"Now you know who." He chuckled.

"Highly amusing, Morley." I dragged one of my copper temple coins out. I hadn't shown them all at the Assay Office. I sketched what I'd learned. Then, "Carathca was a dark-elfin city. Know anything about it? This thing seems to go back there."

"Why should I know anything more about Carathca than you do about FellDorhst? That's ancient times, Garrett. Nobody cares. This thing keeps yelling religion. Find your answers in the Dream Quarter." He studied the coin. "Doesn't say anything to me. Maybe you ought to have a skull session with the Dead Man."

"I'd love to. If I could get him to take a twenty-minute break from his crusade against consciousness."

Someone pounded on the door. Morley looked startled, then concerned. He indicated a corner. "What is it?"

"Puddle, boss."

Morley opened a large cabinet. It was the household arsenal, containing weapons enough to arm a Marine platoon. He tossed me a small crossbow and quarrels, selected a javelin for himself. "Who's with you, Puddle?"

"Just me, boss." Puddle sounded confused. But life itself confuses Puddle.

Morley lifted the bar and jumped back. "Come ahead."

Puddle came in, looked at the waiting death, asked, "What'd I do, boss?"

"Nothing, Puddle. You did fine. Close the door and bar it, then fix yourself a drink." Morley replaced the weapons, closed the cabinet, and settled into his chair. "So what do you have for me, Puddle?"

Puddle gave me the fish eye, but decided it was all right to talk in front of me. "Word just came that Chodo put a two-thousand-mark bounty on that guy who put the thousand on Garrett."

Morley laughed.

Great. "It isn't funny." Here was a chance for the daring to make a truly outrageous hit by selling my head to Brother Jercé, then taking his and selling it to Chodo.

Morley laughed again, said, "It is funny. The auction is on. And this Brother Jercé would have to be awful naive to think he could outbid the kingpin."

TunFaire is full of people who want to do favors for Chodo.

Puddle said, "Chodo says he'll give two hundred a head for anybody who even talks about laying a hand on Garrett. Three if you bring him in alive so he can feed him to his lizards."

My guardian angel. Instead of using guard dogs he has a horde of carnivorous thunder lizards that will attack anything that moves. He favors them because they dispose of bodies, bones and all.

"What a turnaround!" Morley crowed. "Suddenly you've got everybody in TunFaire looking out for you."

Wrong. "Suddenly I've got everyone watching me. Period. And getting underfoot, maybe, while they wait for somebody to take a crack at me so they can snag him and collect on him."

He saw it. "Yeah. Maybe you'd be better off if everybody thought you were dead."

"What I should do, if I had any sense, is say the hell with it all and go see old man Weider about a full-time job at the brewery." I got myself a drink uninvited. Morley doesn't indulge but he keeps a stock for guests. I thought. Then I told Morley about Mumbles and how I'd like to know a little more about him, only I'd had about all I could take for one day and just wanted to go home and get some sleep.

Morley said, "I'll put a tag on him, see where he goes." He seemed a little remote since Puddle's advent, which is how he gets when he's thinking about pulling something slick. I didn't see how he could make things worse so I didn't really care.

"It should be safe now. I'm heading out." I no longer wanted what I'd gone there to find. The quiet and loneliness of home had more appeal.

"I understand," Morley said. "Keep Dean over and have him wait up. I'll get word to you. Puddle, send me Slade."

"Thanks, Morley."

Things had changed downstairs. Word was out. I didn't like the way they looked at me now any more than I'd liked their looks before.

I went out into the night and stood a few minutes in the cold letting my eyes adjust. Then I headed for home. As I passed Mumbles I said, "There you are again. Have a nice evening."

26

I strolled onto Macunado Street daydreaming about a pound of rare steak, a gallon of cold beer, a snuggly warm bed, and a respite from mystery. I should have remembered my luck doesn't run that way.

The pill-brain microdeity whose mission is to mess with my life was on the job.

There was a crowd in front of the house. Floating in the air around it were a half dozen bright globules of fire. What the hell?

I was running slow in the gray matter. It took me a minute to realize what had happened.

Some fans of mine had decided to firebomb my house. The Dead Man had sensed the danger and wakened, catching the bombs on the fly and juggling them now, to the consternation of bombers and witnesses.

I pushed through. The bombers were still there, rigid as statues, faces contorted into shapes as ugly as the gargoyles on Chattaree. They were alive and aware and as frightened as men can be. I stepped in front of one. "How you doing? Not so good, eh? Don't worry. It'll turn out all right."

The bombs began to sputter. "I have to go inside. Wait right here. We'll chat when I get back." I knew he'd be thrilled.

Dean opened the door a crack. "Mr. Garrett!"

Yeah. Right. I shouldn't be playing with these guys. "See you in a couple." I trotted up the steps. Dean let me in, slammed the door, secured all the bolts.

"What's going on, Mr. Garrett?"

"I kind of hoped you'd tell me."

He looked at me like I was off my nut. He probably wasn't far wrong. "So let's see what Chuckles has to tell us." I wouldn't need to bust my butt and theirs if I could get the Dead Man to read their minds. It would save everyone a lot of trouble—except for him.

I went into the room. Dean waited outside. He won't go in unless he has what *he* considers a compelling reason. "I'll keep an eye on those brigands, Mr. Garrett."

"You do that." I faced the Dead Man. "So, Old Bones. You will wake up to save your own skin. Now I know how to get your attention. Light a fire under you."

Garrett, you plague upon my final hours, what have you brought down upon my house this time?

"Nothing." It was going to be one of those discussions.

Then why are those maniacs pitching bombs at me?

"Those boys outside? Hell. They don't even know about you. They're just having fun trying to burn *my* house."

Garrett!

"I don't have the slightest idea. You want to know, poke around in their brains."

I have. And I have found a fog. They did it because they were told to do it. They believe they need no other reason than the will of the Master. They were joyful because they had been entrusted with a task that would please him.

"Now we're cooking. The Master? Who is he? Where do I find him?"

I can answer neither question. It may not be possible. I do not exaggerate when I tell you it is their express and certain belief that the Master they serve has neither form nor substance and manifests himself only where and when he chooses, in any of a hundred forms.

"He's like a ghost or spirit or something?" I wasn't going to say the word god.

He is a bad dream that has been dreamed by so many so intensely that he has gained a life of his own. He exists because will and belief compel him to exist.

"Woo-oo! We're getting weird here."

Why did you stir these madmen up, Garrett?

"I didn't stir anybody, Chuckles. They stirred me. Out of the blue, for no reason, somebody has been trying to send me off. Crazy stuff has been happening all over. Especially in the Dream Quarter. Maybe I ought to catch you up on the news."

I am supremely uninterested in your squalid little slitherings through the muck and stench of this cesspit city, Garrett. Save it to impress the tarts you drag under my nose to harass me.

So, he was crabbed about Jill. He doesn't like women much. Having one in the house will set him off every time.

Tough.

"So we're going to go straight from the snooze stage to the sulks, eh? Saves us time on courtesy and catching up on the latest adventures of Glory Mooncalled. We'll just wake up and act like a cranky three-year-old."

Don't vex me, Garrett.

"The gods forfend! Me be vexatious? With my angelic disposition?" I didn't like this.

We go at it tooth and claw but it's always a game. There was a dark undercurrent of hostility this time. This wasn't play. I wondered if he was moving into some new and darker phase of being dead. Nobody knows much about dead Loghyrs, or even much about live ones for that matter since both kinds are so damned rare.

You have had the benefit of my wisdom and instruction long enough to stand on your own legs now, Garrett. There is no justification for your incessant pestering.

"There isn't any for your freeloading, either, but you do it." My temper was shorter than I'd thought. "The Stormwarden Raver Styx wanted to buy you a while back. She made a damned good offer. Maybe I shouldn't have been so damned sentimental."

I stepped out then, before the foolishness got out of hand. I looked for Dean.

He was watching the street.

The firebombs had burned out. With no entertainment to be had the crowd had dispersed. But the bombers were still there, rigid as lawn ornaments. "Help me carry one of those guys in so I can ask him what he was doing." I opened the door.

"Are you sure that's wise?" No Mr. Garrett anymore. He'd stopped being scared.

"No. I'm never sure of anything. Come on . . . Damn his infantile soul. Look at that."

The Dead Man had turned them loose. The bombers were running like frightened mice.

Even in my anger I didn't really think he'd let go out of spite. He's long on argument but he's also long on sense. My guess was he'd hoped I could track them to their hideout. Which meant he hadn't taken a close enough look at me.

I couldn't fault the reasoning but I couldn't carry it off, either. I didn't have any energy left. Too much activity, not enough rest.

I shrugged. "The hell with them. I'll settle up with them pretty soon, anyway." Garrett whistling in the dark. "Ask Miss Craight to come to my office. Then bring me a pitcher of beer. Then cook supper. Bring it when it's ready. She knows what's going on. It's time to squeeze a little blood out of that stone. Why the hell do you keep shaking your head?"

"Jill left shortly after you did. She said to tell you she was sorry for the trouble she'd caused you. She hoped your retainer would make up for it. Before you ask, yes, she sounded like she wouldn't be back. She left a note. I put it on your desk."

"Beer and dinner, then, and I'll question the note." Nothing was going to stay still long enough for me to grab it.

I went to the office, planted myself, put my feet up, and waited until I had beer before I opened Jill's note.

Garrett:
I really did have a crush on you. But things happened and that little girl's heart petrified. She is only a bittersweet memory, cold copper tears. But thank you for caring.

Hester P.

I leaned back, closed my eyes, and considered the snow queen.

The little girl wasn't dead yet. She was hiding, way back somewhere, afraid of the dark, letting Jill Craight take care of the business of staying alive. The little girl wrote that note. Jill Craight wouldn't have been able. I don't think she'd have thought of it.

With a few beers inside, then a decent supper stacked in on top, Garrett turns halfway human. I asked Dean to stay late again. Over more beer I told him the whole story, not because he needed to know but because I knew the Dead Man would be listening. If he wouldn't take my news direct he'd get it this way.

I'd try to talk to him in the morning, when I was rested and feeling civil and he'd had a chance to contemplate his sins.

I set a record falling asleep.

didn't set any record staying asleep, though I did get in four hours of industrial-weight log-sawing before Dean interceded. "Hunh? Wha'zat? Go way." Other highly intellectual remarks followed. I don't wake easily.

"Mr. Dotes is here," Dean told me. "You'd better see him. It's important."

"It's always important. Whoever it is or whatever it is, it's always more important than whatever I want to do."

"If that's the way you feel, sir. Pleasant dreams."

Of course it was important if Morley had bestirred himself enough to come over personally. But that didn't touch off any fires of enthusiasm.

It just isn't good to ask me to do more than one thing at a time. And right then sleeping was the skill I was honing.

Dean came back after only a flirtation with retreat. "Get up, you lazy slob!"

He knows how to get me started—just get me mad enough to want to brain him.

His technique is somewhat like the way I get the Dead Man started.

Rather than endure his harassment I got me up and halfway dressed and headed downstairs.

Dean had Morley settled in the kitchen, where he was drinking tea and commiserating with the old man over the trouble he was having getting his gaggle of nieces decently—or even indecently—married and out of his house. Dean nattered on about how they were driving him crazy. I think he has some notion that someday I'll feel guilty enough to take one of them off his hands.

I suggested, "Why not sell them?"

"What?"

"They've got some good years on them yet. And they're all good cooks. I know a guy might give fifty marks apiece. He sells brides to the guys who hunt and trap up in thunder-lizard country."

"Your sense of humor leaves something to be desired, Mr. Garrett." He used his admonitory "Mister."

"You're right. I'm not at my best lately. Not getting enough rest, I think."

"You can relax now," Morley told me. "Your nemesis, Jercé, got excited and lost his head a while ago."

The way he made a joke of it I suspected he'd had something to do with that.

It *is* his line and he's the best there is. And two thousand is enough to get his attention.

Maybe I should have been grateful. But grateful doesn't come easy for most people and my mood was too black to make me the rare exception. I kept it bottled up. I kept most of my sour in there with it, too, though. I didn't need to hand out more excuses for folks to get ticked off at Garrett. So I just hinted. "I wonder what he could have told me."

Morley scowled. "What difference does that make? He's a closeout. You can get on with your life without watching over your shoulder."

"Want to bet?"

He gave me an ugly look.

"Sorry. Bad choice of words. What I mean is, he wasn't the source. He was an agent of the source. Unless his getting killed is enough to scare them off, we'll both hear from them again. I don't have the faintest idea what they're up to, but they're serious about it and they're not worried about the costs or consequences."

Morley wanted to disagree but had no facts. He was wishful thinking and he knew it.

I asked, "What became of the guy who was following me?"

"I put Puddle, Wedge, and Slade on him. They followed him following you here. He tried to talk to some men who were part of the excitement. They decided to each take one and see what happened."

I know my Morley Dotes. He was stretching it out because he didn't want to get to the bad news. "So what happened?"

"Puddle and Wedge lost their men. Slade hasn't reported back yet."

So the big news was that there was no news. "Odd. Those guys strike me as amateurs."

Morley shrugged. "Even an amateur is hard to stay with one-on-one."

True. A decent tail job needs at least four men.

Somebody pounded on the front door. I told Dean, "I'd better," and wondered what it was now. I'd just started wondering how I could ease Morley out and now somebody else wanted in. Jill, I figured, after some thinking about being a walking target.

I peeked before I opened up.

There were no gorgeous blondes on Garrett's stoop this time, panting for protection. This was an ugly, little old Magister who was very unhappy.

I opened up and checked to make sure nobody would come speeding in behind him. "Come in. I'd given up on you." Actually, I'd forgotten he'd said he'd be coming.

He pushed inside. "Those morons! Those shortsighted fools! They force me—me!—to sneak out in the dark, like a thief, because they're too scared to let me out on my own."

What the hell? At least he wasn't mad at me. I guided him into my office, planted him in the good chair, got some lights burning, and asked, "Can I get you something to drink?"

"Brandy. In a jar. I haven't gotten blotted since I was in the seminary. If ever there was an appropriate time, it's now."

"I'll find something." I hustled into the kitchen. Dean and Morley had heard enough to keep them quiet. Dean had drawn my pitcher and was digging for a bottle of brandy. Morley tried to look like he'd explode if I didn't whisper a name. I didn't. He stayed in one piece. I grabbed everything and headed for my office.

We got comfortable. Peridont poured himself some brandy, sipped, looked surprised. "Not bad."

"I thought you'd appreciate it." I wet my whistle. "I gather things aren't going well."

"To understate. My brothers in God are cowards. I presented my information and suspicions and instead of responding vigorously, with the full power of the Church, they've chosen to turn their backs and hope the whole thing fades. They've withdrawn permission for me to employ you. They've enjoined me from telling you anything. They've done their damnedest to sew me up, to tie my hands, to shut my mouth, knowing I can't possibly disregard canon law after having spent a career enforcing it."

"In other words you came over to tell me to forget it instead of to point me in the right direction."

He smiled. The nasty man of legend shone through. "Not quite. They overlooked a possibility. They didn't rape away my rights as a private person."

I tried my eyebrow trick. This time it worked.

"Mr. Garrett, they failed to overrule my right to, say, employ an investigator to look into the death of Wesley Pigotta. I give you that as your express brief. Whatever else you stir up, well, that's beyond my control."

I smiled back. "You think as sneaky as a lawyer. I like that. In this case." I put the smile away. "How blind do I have to fly?"

"Almost completely. They sewed me up on that. You already know enough to realize you have to be careful. You're well grounded in the basic information. You'll have to develop from that. Once you flush the villains we can put our heads together again. My brethren might be moved by an opportunity for a quick resolution."

I don't like that kind of game. But I smiled and pretended. I wanted to stay on good terms with him. He could be helpful even while playing mental chess to get around telling me anything. "All right. I'll play along." That had been my intention no matter what he wanted. "Is there anything you *can* give me?"

He took a long pull of brandy. He was serious about getting ripped. He grinned and tossed a bag of money my way. A big bag. "My own money. Not Church money." He sobered a little. "The only thing I can tell you is that the woman who occupied the apartment where Pigotta died was my mistress. I knew her as Donna Soldat. I think that was a false name. She was a difficult woman. Though I kept her in style she had other lovers. One of those men may have been why Pigotta went there that night."

I asked him some standard questions about his relationship with Jill and got some ordinary, sleazy answers. They embarrassed the hell out of him.

"I'm sure this is all more amusing than sordid to you, Mr. Garrett. I'm sure you see worse every day."

Right.

"For me it was a traumatic surrender to my sinful side." He took a long pull of brandy. He was drinking straight from the bottle now. "I've always suffered from a weakness for female flesh."

"Don't we all."

He scowled. "That wasn't a problem when I was younger. If I visited a prostitute and she found me out, she'd laugh. Priests are their best customers. But if I were found out now I could be destroyed."

I understood. It was not that it would make him a better or worse person, but it would be a tool that could be used to bludgeon him.

"I wrestle the demon within but in the end I always lose, so discreet women are a must. Donna was a godsend. Whatever her faults, she kept her mouth shut."

She did that. "Did she know who you were?"

"Yes."

"That's a lot of power to hand a working girl."

"It was accidental. And she never abused it."

Maybe. "How did you meet her?"

"She was an actress. Working in a playhouse on Old Shipway. I saw her. I wanted her. She led me on a long chase but persistence paid off."

For both of them. But I didn't say that.

"I moved her into that place barely three months ago. It was less dangerous to visit her there. Those were three happy months, Mr. Garrett. And now all this."

He finished the brandy. He looked the sort to become a maudlin drunk. I didn't need that. I had no time to feel sorry for anybody but me. It was time to start easing him toward the door. "How should I get in touch?"

"Don't try. I'll find a way to see you." Suddenly, he was as ready to leave as I was to have him go. The beer had me too sleepy to concentrate. He started toward the door. "Good luck, Mr. Garrett. And thank you for a fine brandy, though I cheapened it by swilling it like bottom-grade wine."

I got him out the front door, locked up, and hurried back to see how many marks could be stuffed into a bag a little bigger than my clenched fist.

Morley invited himself in as I got started. "What was that, Garrett? He was weird."

"A client who prefers to remain anonymous."

He didn't like that. Like everybody else, he thought I should make an exception and trust his discretion.

"I don't want to seem impolite, Morley. But I haven't been getting much sleep."

"I can take a hint, Garrett. Let me say good night to the old man."

"Go ahead."

A minute later, as I took the money to the Dead Man's room, I overheard him giving Dean advice about how to adjust my diet so I wouldn't be tired and cranky all the time.

Good old Morley, looking out for my well-being behind my back. If Dean started trying to feed me salads and bean curd, I'd strangle them both.

28

I closed the door behind Dotes, bolted up, leaned against the doorframe, and sighed. Now back to my dreams of blond sugarplums. I'd stay with them awhile. No need to be a fanatic about getting an early start.

Then I recalled that I hadn't tried to straighten things out with Tinnie. The longer I let that slide, the more difficult it would be. And I really needed to find Maya and apologize to her.

There are only so many hours.

The street was so quiet I heard the hollow, echoing clop-clop of a horse approaching, the metallic rattle of iron rims on cobblestones. I listened. There isn't much vehicular traffic after dark. It advertised the fact that here was somebody worth robbing.

The sound died.

My heart sank, though there was no obvious reason it should.

I went to the kitchen to see if Dean could use some help. Maybe I'm a little psychic and sensed there was no point in trudging upstairs.

Someone pounded on the door. The knock had a ring of determination, as though whoever was there had no intention of going away.

I employed my best put-upon sigh and went to see what it was.

It was the kingpin's man Crask, looking uglier and meaner than ever because he was trying to be friendly and courteous. "Chodo says he'd consider it a big favor if you'd come out to the house right away, Mr. Garrett. He said to give you his assurance that it's important and that you'll be compensated for your trouble."

I was getting compensated by everybody in sight without having the slightest notion what was going on. I'd get rich if the mess never sorted itself out.

And the Dead Man thought I couldn't survive without him.

I didn't turn Crask down. Sooner or later I'd end up butting heads with his boss, but when that happened it would be over something more substantial than lost sleep.

"Let me finish getting dressed," I said. Damn, Crask gave me the creeps. I never met anybody who reeks of menace the way he does, except his sidekick Sadler, who has a soul struck from the same cold mold.

Five minutes later I clambered into Chodo Contague's personal coach. Chodo wasn't aboard. Morley Dotes was. I wasn't surprised. He looked as sour as I felt.

Not much was said during the trip. Crask is no conversationalist. His presence tends to put the damper on a party.

Chodo's estate is a few miles north of TunFaire's northernmost gate, in a manor that would do any duke proud. The grounds are extensive, manicured, and surrounded by a wall meant more to keep in than to keep out. Several hundred thunder lizards cruise the grounds and provide protection more certain than any moat or castle wall. I've heard that Chodo has survived assassination attempts he knows nothing about because his guardians ate everything but the assassins' names.

I looked out the window. "Chodo's pets seem frisky tonight." It was cold out. The colder it gets the more sluggish thunder lizards become.

"He had them warmed up," Crask said. "He thought there might be trouble."

"That why we're here?"

"Maybe."

There must be two guys living inside Crask's skin. One is the stiffly formal butler character that Chodo turns loose on diplomatic errands, and the other is the Crask who grew up on the waterfront, whose hobby is biting the heads off cobras. I hope I never have to deal with that Crask, though I expect it's inevitable. He's a completely casual and remorseless killer and he's smart. If he got the word to get me, he'd have me before I knew he was coming.

The coach stopped at the foot of steps leading to Chodo's front door. There was light enough to read by, lanterns by the dozen burning, like Chodo was throwing a party and we were the first to arrive. Crask said,

"Don't get out." Like Morley or I might be dumb enough to step outside and pet the monsters snuffling around the coach. He got out and went up the steps. The beasts didn't bother him.

Morley employs profanity sparingly so when he spat, "Shit!" I knew he was rattled. I looked around.

A thunder lizard with a head the size of a five-gallon bucket and breath that would gag a maggot was peeking in on Morley's side. It had about a thousand teeth, every one like a four-inch knife. When it stood back up to claw at the door with its silly little hands, it stood about twelve feet tall. Its scales were a lovely shade of putrescent gray-green. The coach driver whacked it across the snout with the haft of his whip. It made a noise like twenty jackasses singing and stomped away.

Morley said, "Reminds me of a woman I knew once. Only this one had better breath."

"I always knew you'd plook anything that moved. What did you do with her tail?"

"You got room to talk, don't you? I've seen the woolly mammoths you go around with."

"They still have their own teeth."

"I noticed the other night. Snappy dresser, too, with an amazing concept of what constitutes good grooming. You going to dump her when she loses her baby teeth?"

I was saved having to defend Maya by Crask's return. He got into the coach. He handed us each a stone pendant on an iron chain. "Wear these while you're here. They'll keep the lizards off. Come on."

I put my gizmo on and got out behind him. A shoulder-high lizard muzzled me but didn't nibble. I managed to keep from drizzling down my leg.

The inside of Chodo's place is plush. The King himself should live so good. It was quieter than the last time I'd visited, though there were more hoods around. Last time the place had been overrun with naked women, part of the decor. There were no girls tonight.

Chodo awaited us beside the indoor lake of a pool where the cuties liked to congregate. I resisted an urge to chide him for disappointing me.

Chodo was a hairless, colorless, ugly lump confined to a wheelchair. People wonder how a cripple can be so feared. They haven't gotten close enough to look into Chodo's eyes. What Crask and Sadler have, Chodo has squared. And he has them to be his hands and legs. In some ways they have no independent existence. But they seem content.

Sadler was there behind Chodo's chair. So were several lesser lieutenants I didn't know by name. I stopped six feet from the old man, didn't offer to shake. He doesn't like to be touched.

"Mr. Garrett. Thank you for responding so promptly." His voice wasn't much more than a raspy wheeze.

"Crask said it was important. He implied some urgency."

Chodo smiled thinly. He knew the smell of crap. We understood one another, which was maybe more to his advantage than to mine.

"There's something strange afoot, Mr. Garrett." So much for the amenities. "Because of that, because I've striven to keep you alive, I've been drawn into it and have, perhaps, fallen deeper into your debt."

I opened my mouth to deny that. He lifted one white hand an inch off the drab brown blanket covering his lap. For Chodo that was an impassioned gesture. I kept silent.

"Earlier today I learned that the people chasing you had the temerity to invade a building owned by the organization. They killed a man there. I find this intolerable."

I didn't look at Morley, though he had to be Chodo's source. And he'd had the nerve to get indignant when I wouldn't give him Peridont's name.

"Still, I might have overlooked that, crediting it to youthful high spirits, had they not, tonight, offended me again in an inexcusable manner."

Now I saw it. He was hot. He was so angry smoke should have been pouring out his ears.

"Sadler. Tell Mr. Garrett." The old man wanted to gather his energy.

Sadler had a voice like winter. "Shortly after sunset three men, representing someone they called the Master, came to the gate. Their manners were so offensive that Chodo asked to see them himself."

The kingpin's indignation bubbled over. "In fine, Mr. Garrett, this Master has *ordered* me to stop interfering in his business. He *threatened* me."

I call that a stupid move. Not even the King dares make a direct threat against the prince of the underworld. Whatever else he lacks, Chodo has an ego. It wouldn't let something like that slide. I pitied the guys who brought the message. They would've paid the first installment on the tribute Chodo was going to extract.

Sadler smiled thinly, divining my thoughts. "One survived to carry the heads of the others back to the fool who sent them."

I said, "These people are raving amateurs. They don't bother finding out what they're jumping into before they leap."

Chodo growled. "Nevertheless, their confidence may not be misplaced.

They don't mind wasting men. Maybe they have them to throw away." He paused to gather his strength again, signing that we were to wait.

Finally, he said, "I suggest we join forces, Mr. Garrett, to the extent that we have a common interest." He was a realist, that old thug. He knew I had no love for him or his. "You haven't the resources to battle an organization. It would take you an age to do the footwork. I have those kinds of resources. On the other hand, you have your network of friends and contacts, your knowledge in hand, your access in places where my men have no entrée." He ran out of energy again.

I surprised myself. "I wouldn't mind that. But I don't have much to kick in. I don't have any idea what's going on. I *think* that way back in the shadows there's a nasty dragon waking up, that has religious overtones, and the guys involved don't have any qualms."

"Why don't we pool what we know?" Sadler said. I'm sure Chodo fed him that line before I got there. He started talking.

He gave me everything they had, which wasn't diddly. For them the thing had been a triviality until Chodo got his feelings bruised. There had been no special significance to the coins he'd sent me, for instance, except he'd thought they'd point me toward the temple that had put them out.

"They did," I said. "Only the outfit is supposed to have been out of business for two hundred years. Banned by Brian the Third." I told the story. In for a copper, in for a mark in gold. I gave them everything but the name of my connection inside the Church, and they got that soon enough.

Chodo said, "This would be a good moment for refreshments."

One of his lesser lieutenants took off. He was back in two minutes pushing a cart loaded with goodies. In the silence, while Chodo ruminated, we became aware of a nasty thunderstorm approaching from downriver.

There was beer for me. I went after it determined to make the trip worth the trouble. It had to be getting on toward dawn. By the time I got home it would be so late there would be no point hitting the sack.

Chodo said, "This churchman knows things. Maybe I should press him."

"That might not be wise." I named the name.

"Malevechea himself?" Chodo asked. He was impressed. There are powers whose indignation he won't risk needlessly.

"The very one." The kingpin's organization is powerful and deadly, but the Church is bigger and has heaven on its side and might not have much trouble recruiting the support of the state.

Thunder crashed as though to make a point.

"The woman will be the key, then. Mr. Garrett, I'll deal with the Master.

I'll haunt him and hunt him and hold his attention. I'll become his worst nightmare. You find that woman." Because I was the only one who knew what to look for, I presumed.

Life must be simple when you have no conscience and enough power to just say you want something and have people bust their butts to get it for you.

Morley spoke for the first time. "The gods must be holding a barn dance." The thunder had gotten unruly.

Chodo made a sign. Sadler took two sacks from beneath the kingpin's chair. He tossed me one and handed a bigger one to Morley. Morley's two thousand, I supposed. Sadler said, "You've been avoiding the waterbug races, I hear."

A thug came in and whispered to Crask. He looked excited.

Morley told Sadler, "I've been trying."

Sadler looked at the sack and smiled, confident Dotes couldn't resist betting now, confident that money would find its way home.

Crask said, "Sadler, problems. Out front." He took off. Everybody but Chodo and a bodyguard went with him.

Chodo said, "I'll keep in touch, Mr. Garrett. Let me know when you find the woman. Crask will take you home once he's dealt with whatever is brewing out there."

I nodded, turned away, dismissed.

He had such confidence in Sadler and Crask. But confidence was one of the attributes that took him to the pinnacle of TunFaire's underworld.

Morley didn't move. He'd received some sign that Chodo wanted to talk privately.

I headed to the front door, bemused; I'd made an alliance with the man I disliked most in this world.

I hoped I wouldn't regret it.

stepped out of Chodo's house into weirdness like nothing I'd ever seen.

Crask, Sadler, a dozen goons, and a herd of thunder lizards had gathered out front. They gawked at the heavens.

The storm kicking up the racket didn't cover more than a few acres of sky. And it was headed straight for Chodo's place. I'd never seen a storm so close to the ground.

Lights bobbed inside that thunderhead, three the color of candle flames, the fourth a malignant red. When the cloud arrived, the yellow lights dropped toward the crowd on the lawn. When they got closer I saw that they were three guys walking on air, all of them in old-time armor.

The mind works funny. I didn't boggle over them walking on air; I wondered what museum they'd robbed to get their iron suits.

A couple of thugs headed for the house. Their eyes were huge when they stampeded past me. Crask and Sadler decided their move made practical sense and ordered everybody inside. They weren't equipped to face men in armor, let alone guys who pranced on moonbeams.

They pushed by without a word. Inside, Crask and Sadler started yelling about crossbows and pikes and whatnot. If they had the weapons they'd know how to use them. They'd served their five in the Cantard, too.

Nobody invited me to the party.

My feelings weren't hurt.

The first floating guy touched down. The light around him faded. He took a step toward me, raising a hand.

The thunder lizards hit him. They took him apart in two blinks of an eye. Lucky for him he was wearing plate. Without armor they would've killed him quick.

The other two changed their minds about coming down. I don't know what they'd thought they were headed into, but they weren't here to become monster snacks. They hung there trying to decide what to do. The lizards started snapping at their heels. The guys decided to go up a little.

They started whipping lightning bolts around. The thunder lizards were too dumb to hightail it but Garrett knows when he's overmatched.

As I turned away I noticed the red light was missing from the thunderhead.

I got a bad feeling.

Crask, Sadler, and the boys went racing outside, carrying enough deadly equipment to mount a siege. I hadn't seen any of the big wizardries during my war, but I'd seen enough little ones to realize those flying guys could be in trouble.

They couldn't do three things at once. If they protected themselves from missiles and kept flailing around with thunderbolts, they were going to have to come down. Bingo. Instant monster munchies.

It was not my worry. I was headed for the pool.

The whole manor shook.

I hit the doorway and skidded to a halt.

Something was tearing its way into the pool room through the roof, going at it like the place was made of paper. A big, shiny, ugly, purplish black face like that of a fangy gorilla glared through the hole. Then it started ripping the hole bigger.

Damn, it was huge!

Chodo's bodyguard headed for it. I don't know what he thought he was going to do. Maybe he just wanted to show the boss how brave he was.

I arrived beside Morley and Chodo. "Might be smart to get him out of here. That thing don't look sociable."

It dropped through the hole, and landed at the far end of the pool, fifty feet away. It was twelve feet tall, had six arms, and might have been the thing on those temple coins. It wavered as though I was seeing it through an intense heat shimmer. Or as though it didn't know if it wanted to be a six-armed gorilla or something even uglier.

Chodo's bodyguard stopped charging. I guess he had suffered a fit of sense.

Morley said, "I think you're right."

The thing jumped Chodo's man before he could turn around. Their struggle was a one-second contest. Pieces of thug flew. The ape thing munched on a leg and eyed the rest of us.

Chodo cursed. Morley got his chair moving. I dipped a hand into a pocket. This seemed like the time.

The thing roared and charged. I let fly with the ruby bottle Peridont had given me. It splattered on the monster's chest. I spun to race Morley and the kingpin.

The monster skidded to a halt, scratched itself, and woofed puzzledly before it let out a howl. I reached the doorway and turned.

Flesh dribbled down the thing's chest like wax on a candle. And it was evaporating, shedding a red mist. It screamed and clawed itself and threw gelatinous gobbets of itself that splattered on the marble floor, evaporated, left pitted stains. It went into convulsions, tumbled into the pool, thrashed the water into a scarlet lather.

Morley said, "I'd hate to be the one who has to clean that up."

Chodo croaked, "Now it's a life I owe you, Mr. Garrett."

And Morley said, "Garrett, I grow ever more fearful that someday I'll be with you and you won't have a trick up your sleeve."

"Me, too, Morley. Me, too."

"What the hell was that thing?"

"Tell me and we'll both know."

"Never mind," Chodo growled. "Talk later. Take me to the front door."

He was right. We weren't out of anything yet. There was a brawl out front.

We arrived as it broke up. Most of the thunder lizards and half the thugs were out of action. But the effort put out by the airborne guys cost them, too. An athletic lizard caught one with a flying leap and dragged him down. The other, with about twenty missiles stuck in his armor, shot off like a comet going the wrong way.

Crask and Sadler noticed their boss. They came over as fast as they could limp.

Chodo told them, "Gentlemen, I'm angry." He didn't sound it. He's one of those guys who is at his nastiest when he seems his coolest. "There will be no more surprises."

The house and grounds shuddered. A scarlet fog belched through the spine of the house and dispersed in the breeze.

A diminished thunderhead went off with the last skywalker. And the sun peeked over the horizon, checking to see if it was safe to come out.

Chodo told his boys, "Find those people. Kill them." What a sweetheart. He looked at me and Morley. "Have someone drive these men home." He seemed blind to the fact that Crask and Sadler had been knocked around like shuttlecocks. "Here come Cage and Fletcher. Get their reports. Then move."

Two thugs were coming up the drive, their chins dragging on the ground.

30

I dropped out of the coach in front of my place and thought I'd keep dropping. "Getting too old for this," I muttered. This thing had become too deadly. I barely had time for a cleanup and maybe an hour nap before I started tracking Jill down.

If I could decide where to start.

I was sure she hadn't gone back to her apartment, though I'd check. She'd have more savvy.

Dean let me in. He fed me. I told him what had happened so my useless boarder could listen in. Dean was properly appalled, though he thought I'd exaggerated an incident into a whopper. Afterward I went upstairs, stretched out, and continued to worry the problem I'd badgered all the way home.

Was I becoming identified with the kingpin?

People were getting killed and people were trying to kill me and all I could think about was the chance that my reputation for independence might be sullied.

That rat Dean let me snore for four hours. I yelled at him. He just smiled. I didn't yell too much. Chances are his reasoning was sounder than mine. Rested I was less likely to do something stupidly fatal.

I jumped up, did a quick change and cleanup, a quicker meal, and hit the street. My first stop was Jill's apartment. I had no problem getting inside. At first glance nothing had changed. But I felt a change. I looked around until I caught it.

The coin drawer was empty. Anybody could have gotten to that. But a battered old rag doll had disappeared, too. I was willing to bet nobody but Hester Podegill would bother taking that.

So she'd risked coming back, if only for a moment. Just to grab a doll and some change? I didn't think so, not the ice maiden. It felt like a by-product of a more desperate mission. So I tossed the place again. And I didn't find another thing added or taken away.

I wasn't pleased as I slipped out. There should have been something . . .

I eyeballed the doorway across the hall.

Why not look?

The door swung quietly as I pushed it inward. Nobody stampeded over me. I went inside. And there it was, lying in plain sight on a small writing table.

Darling:
　　The key is safe. I have to disappear. They are getting desperate. Be careful. Love.

Marigold

Marigold? The handwriting matched that in a note written to me by one Hester Podegill. Did she have a different name for every person she knew? That would make her hard to find. No one would know who I was talking about.

She was an actress. Suppose she *became* a different person each time she donned a different name? She'd really be hard to find then.

I had to get to know who Jill had been before I looked for the Jill who existed now. That was a technique Pokey had used when he was after some-one who was voluntarily missing. He talked to relatives, friends, enemies, neighbors, acquaintances, seducing them into talking however he had to, until he knew the missing person better than anyone else alive—until he was able to think like his quarry.

But that took time, and time was at a premium.

My best bet was Maya and the Doom. They were handy. And I owed Maya that apology.

I hit the street, troubled by a vague certainty that I'd overlooked some-thing critical. But what? Nothing came. I moved slowly, checked my sur-roundings. Yep. The boys were out there.

They'd picked me up as I'd left my place. I'd spotted three of them com-ing over. They weren't getting close. They didn't seem inclined to get in the way. Nor did they work real hard at staying out of sight. I couldn't get a close look but they didn't have the lean, impoverished look I'd seen in my recent enemies.

If they were going to keep their distance I'd worry about them when the time came.

I was a block from the Doom's lair when I realized those guys weren't the only folks stalking me. The Sisters of Doom were on me, too.

People don't pay enough attention to kids, especially youngish girls not showing colors. I didn't get it until I realized I'd seen the same faces several times. Then I paid enough attention to pick out a couple I'd seen before.

Now what?

They closed in as I neared their hideout. I must have hurt Maya's feelings more than I'd thought.

She always was touchy and unpredictable.

If there was a confrontation it would come off better in the open, where I'd have some choice about which way I'd run.

I sat down on a tenement stoop.

That threw them, which was the plan. I expected them to get Maya and she'd come explain what a horse's ass I am.

It didn't work that way.

After a few minutes the girls understood that I was calling. They moved in. Some electric sense of trouble flooded the street. Everybody who wasn't part of it disappeared, though nobody ran and nobody hollered. The girls edged toward me with the group confidence of pack animals. I slid a hand into a pocket and toyed with one of Peridont's gifts.

I picked a sixteen-year-old I recognized, looked her in the eye and said, "Maya is overreacting, Tey. Tell her to get her tail out here and talk before somebody gets hurt."

The girls looked at each other, confused. But the one I'd spoken to didn't let an antique baffle her with bullshit. "Where is she, Garrett? What did you do with her?"

The gang was in close now, feeling nastier. And those guys that I'd noticed before were moving in behind the girls. There were five of them and I knew two, Saucerhead Tharpe and a slugger named Coltrain.

I got it.

Chodo was sure he'd need Jill's knowledge before he could settle with the Master. He was just as sure that I'd be the guy to find her. So he'd gotten Morley to lay on a loose cover to make sure I stayed healthy and to keep him posted.

Morley is a friend, sort of. He's a lot better friend when you keep an eye on him. He works these deals with his conscience.

I watched those five drift in behind the girls. I chuckled.

"You think it's funny, Garrett? You want to find out what we do with comedians? You want to see if you can laugh with your balls down your throat? What did you do with Maya?"

"I didn't do anything with her, Tey. I haven't seen her. That's why I came here. I want to talk to her."

"Don't feed us a ration of shit, Garrett. The last time anybody saw Maya she was hanging out with you, with moon eyes as big as a cow."

One of the little ones noticed my guardian angels. "Tey. We got company." The girls all looked around. The level of hostility dropped dramatically. Five guys like those five guys are enough to dampen anybody's belligerence.

"So," I said, grinning. "Tey. Why don't you sit down and we'll talk like civilized people." I patted the step.

Tey looked around. So did her friends. Those guys didn't look like their consciences would bother them much if they stomped a bunch of girls. They looked like they ate kids for snacks.

Tey was one of Maya's lieutenants. She fancied herself Maya's successor. She was a nasty little thing, uglier than a boiled turnip, with manners that made Maya seem genteel. But she had brains. She understood talk as an alternative to more popular methods of resolving disputes. She sat. I said, "I get the impression you guys have misplaced Maya."

"She never came home. Things she said made it sound like she had plans."

"She was with me," I admitted. "We wandered around trying to get a lead on some guys who killed a buddy of mine." I outlined our evening. The mob listened like they wanted to catch me in a lie.

Tey said, "You don't know Maya the way you think. You've got to take her seriously. She don't say it unless she means it. You know what she's done, don't you?"

"She tried to follow those guys so she could show me what she could do on her own," I said.

"Yeah. She gets dumb stubborn sometimes. What're we going to do?"

"I'll find her, Tey."

"She belongs to the Doom, Garrett."

"These guys play rough. This isn't a turf rumble, bang a few heads and it's over. These guys tried to hit Chodo Contague. They used sorcery."

She didn't bat an eye. "Sorcerer bleeds same as anybody else."

I looked at her hard. She wasn't whistling in the dark.

"You recall a blond gal used to belong to the Doom, used a lot of made-up names, told a lot of lies about herself to make herself look important?"

"Hester Podegill?"

"That's one name she's used. She may be a little crazy."

"More than a little, Garrett. Sure, I remember her. Hester was her real name. She *wanted* to be crazy. She said when you're crazy the truth is whatever you want it to be. She wanted what she remembered not to be true."

I gave her the hard eye again. "You were close?"

"I was her only friend because I was the only one who listened. I was the only one who understood. I was the only one who knew what she had to forget."

Sometimes you cross the river so fast you don't get your toes wet getting to the other side. I flashed on all those lamps in Jill's apartment. "She started the fire that killed her family."

Tey nodded. "She dumped a gallon of oil on her stepfather when he was passed out drunk. She didn't think what the fire could do. She just wanted to hurt him."

If I'd killed my whole family I'd want to be somebody else, too. I'd want to be crazy. I might even want to be dead like them.

"What about her?" Tey asked.

"She's the key in the mess Maya and I were snooping around." I gave her more background. "She might be able to tell us something." I spoke softly, not wanting word to get around that Garret wasn't the only one who might get a line on Jill Craight. For my sake and the Doom's.

Like I said, Tey had a brain. I'd told her enough for her to put a lot more together. "You're a snake, Garrett. A slick-talking snake. We're going to turn you loose. But next time you see me I just might be Maya's maid of honor."

I didn't handle that well. She laughed at me. It wasn't a pleasant laugh. She said, "I have some ideas where to look for Hester. I'll let you know."

I wanted to argue but it was too late. My convoy had decided I was safe and had faded. If I pressed I'd get the hostility perking again. So I sat quietly while the girls went off to do the hunting themselves.

I could think of nothing better to do so I went home, where Dean told me there had been no message and no visitors. I told him Maya might be in trouble. That upset him. He blamed me without saying a word. I asked if the

Dead Man's temper had improved. He told me the old sack of lard had gone back to sleep.

"Fine. If that's the way he wants it, we'll just leave him out of our lives. We won't even bother him with the latest about Glory Mooncalled."

I was bitter. I blamed me for Maya's predicament, too. I had to take something out on somebody. The Dead Man could handle it.

took a bath, changed again, ate, then, for lack of any brilliant plan, walked up to the Tate family compound and had a big row with Tinnie. Then we made up.

Making up was so much fun we decided to do it twice.

It was getting dark by the time we finished making up for the third time and I started having trouble keeping my mind off business, so we had another little row to give us an excuse to make up again later. Then I headed out.

On the way I bumped into Tinnie's uncle Willard and he kind of obliquely wondered when Tinnie and I would be setting the date. He had the same problem Dean had.

It was going to start with him, too?

How come there are so many people trying to get other people hitched? Maybe if they backed off and didn't keep reminding a guy, he might drift into it before he sensed his danger.

Why was I so sour?

Because it had been such a nice afternoon. Because while I was playing, the bad guys were hard at work. Because a troubled kid that I liked was in it up to her ears and I hadn't lifted a finger to do anything about it.

"Oh, boy. Here we go again." I knew the signs. Out comes the squeaky old armor and the rusty old sword. Garrett was going to get all noble.

At least this time somebody would pay me for my trouble—though I wouldn't exactly be doing what they were paying me to do.

But I never quite do what they want done. I do what I think needs doing. That is why not all of my former clients give me favorable references.

Not having any better idea what to do, I headed for the Old Shipway theater district. Who knew? I might stumble onto something blond.

My convoy went with me. The faces changed periodically but there were never fewer than four men hovering around. It's nice to know you're loved.

I wondered why the Master's gang hadn't tried to pick me up again. Those I'd seen already had been too unskilled to notice I was traveling with protection.

I talked to everybody I knew in theater. They knew gorgeous blondes by the cartload, but none they could connect with any of the names I could tie to Jill. Since there was nothing about her that wasn't shared by a platoon of others, my sources couldn't help much. They were reduced to showing me the crop of blondes (some of them *very*) available, all of them squeezably lovely, and none of them Jill Craight.

Some of those lovelies were pleased to speculate on other lovelies not present, usually in less than flattering language, but that didn't help. Some just purred and begged to be petted.

It's a hard life.

Had I been in another mood it might have been a marvelous little treasure hunt. I made a mental note to cook a similar story someday and come wander through wonderland again, taking time to smell the flowers.

Where did they all come from? Where were they on my better days?

Sometime toward the end what was old news to everybody else caught up with me when I overheard a conversation among City Watch officers and their wives.

What the Watch is most famous for is its invisibility. TunFaire has one thousand men employed in the interest of public safety, but over the past century the Watch has become a place to hide freeloading nephews and other embarrassing relatives without recourse to the familial purse. These days ninety percent of those guys do their damnedest to stay out of harm's way and not interfere with the disorderly progress of life. When they do try something, it's invariably the wrong thing and they screw it up anyway.

The officers get to wear pretty uniforms and they like to show them off. The theater is a good place.

This bunch was grumbling about a crime so monstrous that popular outrage might get their butts kicked until they had to go out into the streets and *do* something. The consensus among the wives was that the Army ought to evict all the lower classes and nonhumans.

I wondered who they thought would cook for them and garden and do their laundry and make their cute little shoes and lovely gowns.

"What the hell was that all about?" I asked the guy who was squiring me from blonde to blonde at the Stratos.

"You haven't heard?"

"Not yet."

"Biggest mass murder in years, Garrett. A real massacre. It's all over town. You had your head under a rock?"

"A sheet. Cut the editorializing. What happened?"

"In broad daylight this afternoon a bunch of gangsters busted into a Wharf Street flophouse down in the South End and killed everybody. Smallest number I've heard is twenty-two dead and half a dozen dragged away as prisoners. They're saying Chodo Contague did it. Looks like we're in for a gang war."

I muttered, "When Chodo gets mad you don't have any trouble understanding his message." I wondered what Crask and Sadler were getting out of their prisoners. I'd hate to think they were ahead of me because they were less restrained in their methods.

What could I do? The one angle I had was Jill Craight. And that was turning up a big dead end.

Hell. Might as well go home, get in eight hours, and make an early start in the morning.

●●●32

As Dean let me in he whispered, "There's a young woman here who wants to talk to you about Maya." His wrinkled nose told me what he thought of the visitor. And gave me a good idea who she was.

"Tey Koto?"

"She didn't offer a name."

Tey had gotten into the beer while Dean was away. "You got it whipped, you know that, Garrett?" She tried to pour beer down like she'd been drinking for twenty years, got some down the wrong pipe. She coughed foam all over the kitchen. Dean wasn't pleased. I pounded her on the back.

And as though he'd been waiting for me to get home, someone started pounding on the front door.

"Damn it! Now what?" I stomped up the hall, took a peek. It wasn't anybody I knew. He did have the rangy, weathered, impoverished look I associated with the Master's gang. So Chodo hadn't gotten them all.

I gave a look around to make sure he wasn't part of a tribe, then eyeballed him to get an estimate of what he might do himself. He kept pounding away.

"Guess I'd better talk to you before Saucerhead eats you up." Having a flight of guardian angels occasionally gets in the way.

I yanked the door open, grabbed him by the jacket, jerked him inside, and slammed him against the wall. He was astonished. "What?" I demanded.

He gobbled air and stammered.

I slammed him against the wall a couple more times. "Talk to me."

"The Master . . . The Master . . ." He had a set speech to make. My welcome had put him off his pace. He'd lost his lines.

Slam! "I can't play all night, low grade. You got something to say, spit it out. I'm ticked off at you guys already. Try my patience and I'll hurt you."

In a semi-coherent babble he let me know that the Master felt the same about me and was going to allow me one chance to get out of his way and start minding my own business. Or else.

"Or else he'll put a bug down my shirt? Come on. The creep has more nerve than brains. He's dead meat. He's got about as long as it takes Chodo Contague to find him. If you and your buddies have the sense of a goose you'll dump him and run back where you came from." I started muscling him out the door. "Tell your harebrained boss he *is* my business and I intend to mind it real close."

"Wait!"

The "or else" came. It wasn't the personal threat I expected. I've been threatened plenty so I don't pay much attention anymore. But this guy told me, "The Master said to tell you he has your friend Maya Stump and it will be she who pays if—"

Wham! Back against the wall. "And I have you, old buddy."

"I am nothing. I am a finger on his hand. Cut me off and another will grow in my place."

"You really believe that crap?" He did. What our commanders in the Cantard wouldn't give for a few thousand guys who didn't mind being expendable. "Tey! Come in here."

She came. She'd been eavesdropping, anyway. "What?"

"This guy says his boss has got Maya and they're going to do nasty things to her. He doesn't care what we do to him."

She sneered. "He'd care before *I* got through with him." Oh, the easy cruelty of the young.

"He would. But his boss wouldn't have sent him if he knew anything. So I think I'll just bruise him a little and throw him out with the trash."

Like I said, she was a smart kid. She figured out what to do. "Well, if I can't have him, the hell with you." She pranced back to the kitchen. And out the back door to talk to the Sisters she would've left around the neighborhood.

I banged the guy off the wall again. "You tell your boss if he messes with Maya he better pray Chodo finds him first. All Chodo wants to do is kill him.

"There. We've threatened each other and pounded our chests and acted like jerks. Get out before I lose my temper."

He looked at me like he thought it was a trick. Then he edged toward the door. When he was almost there I jumped at him. He yelped and took off.

I settled on the stoop and watched him go.

All that bullying hadn't accomplished a thing. I hadn't gotten any pleasure out of it. It didn't make me feel good now. I couldn't even convince myself there had been purpose in it.

33

Tey came out of the dark. I asked, "You got somebody tailing him?"

"Yeah."

"So that's taken care of. Why did you come? Dean said it was about Maya."

"Yeah. I think we've got a lead."

I gave her my raised eyebrow. It went to waste in that light, so I said, "How's that?"

"You hear about that mess on Wharf Street? Where Chodo's boys offed a whole mob? That sounded like some of what you told me about. We went down there and talked to kids who live there. Some of them saw the whole thing. Chodo's guys didn't kill everybody. A bunch got away out the back. They dragged a couple people with them. One of them sounded like Maya."

Well, well. "Very interesting. Where did they go?"

"We couldn't find out. They jumped into boats and headed down the river. But they didn't go far. The kids told us what the boats looked like. We found one of them a half mile away. And we know they didn't leave TunFaire because that one just came here to threaten you."

I sure as hell didn't feel like taking a walk but I said, "Suppose we go nose around?"

I told Dean what I'd be doing. I expected some backchat, because he'd had to stay away from home a lot. But he didn't say a word. I bet he would've said a few if I hadn't been looking for Maya.

●　●　●

It was several miles to the Wharf Street massacre site. Tey's boats had gone south from there, a goodly hike. After a while we started talking, mostly Tey making herself shine bright in the Doom. I asked her about Maya. She wouldn't tell me anything I didn't already know. From time to time a messenger came to tell her about the man being followed. He was headed the same direction we were. Tey told the messengers our anticipated route so she could be found again.

My angels were out there, too, shadowing me.

We had a parade going.

"I tried looking for Hester tonight," I said at one point. "I looked at every blonde who works Old Shipway. None of them were her."

Tey laughed. "Old Shipway? You're precious, Garrett."

"Eh?" *Precious?*

"You *believed* that actress stuff?"

Well, yes, I'd bought it after Peridont validated it.

"Garrett, the only acting she ever did was the kind where the other actors are donkeys or guys that should have been born donkeys or ogres or trolls. You know what I mean?"

I grunted. I knew. I was disgusted, not so much because of what Jill might be doing as because of a failure of my vaunted eyesight. I'd let myself see only what I'd expected to see. I'd swallowed it whole when Peridont had fed me a whopper about the provenance of his mistress. I'd forgotten the first rule: everybody lies about sex, and the client *always* lies about it.

I felt pretty dumb.

Tey said, "She's back in the Tenderloin. I had a couple kids go down there. They saw her but she disappeared before they got close enough to find out anything."

I wondered if I ought to buy that. Jill had come up with the Doom. They didn't have much reason to turn her up for me.

This was an odd one, all intangibles. In a case where a pot of money is the stake, you know where the axis is. You watch the money and soon enough everything becomes clear—even when some of the players aren't motivated primarily by greed. For them the pot becomes an excuse, a lever.

So far I hadn't caught a whiff of a pot, excepting maybe the Relics Peridont had mentioned the first time we talked, or whatever it was the boys had been so sure they could steal from Jill. That seemed to have been forgotten in the fussing and feuding since.

I'm a guy who doesn't understand intangible stakes. I know some would argue that I have a set of values I take pretty seriously, but if I can't eat it or spend it or make it go purr in the night, I don't know what to do with it. It's a weakness, a blind spot. Sometimes I forget there are guys willing to get killed over ideas. I just go bulling ahead looking for the pot of gold.

We got onto Wharf Street. The guy who had dropped by my place was still ahead of us. My angels were out there in the dark, probably cussing me for my thoughtlessness in running them all over the city. Didn't I ever sleep?

Guys, I was cussing me, too. For the exact same reason.

"There's the place where it happened."

Wharf Street, the waterfront, the whole commercial and industrial strip down there facing the river, is a whole lot like me. It never goes to sleep. When the day people move out, the night workers come in and the economy keeps rolling along.

Forty or fifty goblins and ogres and whatnot were standing around gossiping while a group of city ratmen got set to load the bodies on wagons for delivery to crematoria. Moving with its customary lightning efficiency, the city was just now getting around to cleaning up.

The operation was proceeding in the usual fire-drill state of confusion.

The ratmen moved at a velocity barely perceptible. I said, "I'm going to go nose around."

"Won't they stop you?"

"Maybe. But any human who turns up this time of night looking officious they'll figure belongs."

I was right. I got some dark looks but they were the kind reserved for bosses in general, for being bosses. Nobody said a word.

I didn't expect to find much and I was right again. The scavengers and sightseers and souvenir hunters had picked the bones clean. They'd even stripped the stiffs. The ratmen were bitching because there wasn't anything left.

If they want the cream, they ought to get there in time to skim it.

I did notice one thing right off. Those sopranos had taken over the whole building and had been there long enough to turn it into a weird residential temple. One wall in every room had been replastered and painted with murals depicting creatures with eight limbs, no two the same. I saw a spider, a crab, an especially ugly octopus, and a lot of things that don't come with eight limbs, including a ringer for the thing that had visited Chodo. One double-ugly was human except that it had a skull for a face and something disgusting in every hand. Above him was the same motto as on the temple coins, "He Shall Reign Triumphant."

I said, "I don't think I'd like that."

"Ugly mother, ain't he?" a ratman remarked.

"He is. Any idea who he's supposed to be?"

"You got me, chief. Looks like something somebody dreamed up while he was doing weed to get him through a withdrawal fit."

"Yeah. Not your average boy next door."

There wasn't anything else. I hit the street. We headed south. I didn't have much to say. I was thinking that if I ever stopped chasing around long enough I'd have to spend some time researching these guys and their devil god.

We walked another mile. I started mumbling about only now realizing how damned big TunFaire is. One of the Sisters told us the guy we were following had gone into a warehouse half a mile ahead, fifty yards from where the one getaway boat had been abandoned.

The girls had the place scouted when we got there. There were two doors, front and back, and no windows at ground level, just some high up to let out the heat during the summer. The main door was big enough to roll wagons in and out. The girls had the back covered. They had no idea who or what was inside. They didn't want to find out.

I looked at the place. What did I have here? An army of kids, nasty but not real fighters. My angels, who had no interest in launching a raid. And a big unknown.

"I'm going in there," I said.

"You're crazy, Garrett." Tey shook her head slowly.

"Sometimes you have to make things happen."

34

The man-sized door in the wagon door wasn't locked. I stepped inside. The place was as dark as a tax man's heart. I listened. I heard nothing but what might have been mice scurrying, then what sounded like a door slamming at the far end of the place.

I eased forward, sliding my feet, feeling the air with my left hand. Far away, I glimpsed a flicker of light above head level. I kept moving cautiously, wishing I had owl's eyes.

I didn't get that wish but I did get light.

A bunch of guys jumped out of nowhere, opening the shutters of lanterns they'd kept well hidden. I counted nine. A tenth, from behind the others, said, "Mr. Garrett. We'd begun to fear you hadn't taken the bait."

"Sorry I'm late. Had trouble with tardiness all my life."

Weapons appeared. My sense of humor wasn't going to play with this crowd.

"If I'd known it was that kind of party I'd have dressed."

I had no idea how I'd be affected myself, but I let loose with my green bottle.

I reacted the same as everyone else. In three seconds I not only didn't know where I was or why I was there, but I wasn't too sure who I was. I couldn't move in a straight line. I tried—and hung a left and walked into a stack of crates. They were empty. I kept going. The whole pile came down on top of me.

That was one to brag to the grandkids about.

I tried to fight the crates, but they were too quick. So I just gave up and let them have their way with me. I would have taken a nap except a bunch of people kept yelling at some guy called Garrett and I couldn't get to sleep for all the racket.

Somebody dug me out of the pile. Two of my angels stood me up while another popped me in the face. That didn't help a whole lot.

The other two started tying guys up. There were girls all over the place, looking for something portable and valuable. I got my tongue untangled. "Maya."

Kids started running around yelling, "Maya!"

Guys yakked about getting hold of some guy named Chodo, they could sell him their prisoners for a fortune. I seemed to remember them as angels. They didn't sound very angelic.

My head began to clear. "I'm all right now, guys. You don't need to hold me up."

Wedge snapped, "What the hell kind of stunt was that, Garrett? Walking into a trap you knew was there."

"Had to make something happen." I wasn't going to admit the ambush had been a surprise to me, too. Anyway, I figured it would not be smart to brag that I'd wanted to make them come in the warehouse after me. They might not appreciate that.

They grumbled and let me go. I picked up a lantern and tottered back into the warehouse, following shouting girls.

Maya was in a loft office all the way back, above another double-ugly homemade temple. She was tied up enough for four kids. She looked a little shopworn, with bruises and abrasions that said she hadn't been a cooperative prisoner.

I didn't find her. The girls got there first. They were slicing her out of her cocoon when I arrived. But I got the credit. "Garrett! I knew you'd come."

"Had to, Maya. When somebody does something to a guy's partner, a guy is supposed to do something about it."

She squealed and stumbled at me.

Some females can't tell a wisecrack from a marriage proposal. "I don't want to hurt your feelings, kid, but maybe you ought to stand downwind till we get you next to some soap and water."

"We can throw her in the river, Garrett," Tey suggested.

Maya glared green death. Tey glared back. There was no love lost between those two. I asked, "How many got away?"

"None." Tey snapped it. "They were all waiting for you except one. They have him out back."

"Good. Can you walk, Maya? We can't hang around. These guys have friends who'll check up on them. Not to mention the Doom is way off its turf."

"You're not going to ask those guys questions?"

"If I was to set an ambush I wouldn't use guys that could tell anybody if they blew it. And these guys are making a career of screwing up. You think any of them can tell me anything you didn't pick up while you were their guest?"

She admitted it was unlikely. "They were a bunch of farmers before they came to TunFaire. They don't know spit from dog doo. They're just trying to do what their wacko god wants." But she wanted to get back at somebody.

"Kick somebody in the ribs on the way. Come on. We've got to go. Thank Tey for helping find you. She didn't have to."

Maya did, but not very graciously. She must have felt threatened. When you're a chuko, you have to prove yourself every day.

There wasn't anyone for her to kick. Wedge had decided reinforcements were likely to arrive so he and his buddies had made sure they'd collect whatever bounties Chodo had put on those guys.

Maya looked bad when we hit the street. I said, "I told you Wedge wasn't nice people."

"Yeah." After we walked awhile, she said, "Men like that Wedge, they're a whole different kind of bad, aren't they? People like my stepfather . . . He was cruel, but I don't think he could've killed a dog. That Wedge did it like it was nothing."

Chukos put a lot of value on being tough. And a lot of them are hard, nasty little critters—especially in front of an audience. Some are dead losses at thirteen. But some still have the kid in there somewhere behind the defenses, and that kid wants to believe there's some point to living. Maya still contained that hidden child. And it wanted some reassurance.

"Who do you think does the most real harm?" I asked, thinking maybe anybody else was better qualified for this. "The emotional cripple who tries to cripple people who can't protect themselves? Or the emotionally dead killer like Wedge who basically doesn't bother anybody but them that asked for it?"

That wasn't saying what I wanted to say the best way. Maybe there were big holes in it, but there was plenty of truth, too. The hurt a creep like her old man did lasts a lifetime. It gets passed on to the next generation. Wedge's kind of hurt is flashy but it doesn't last. And it doesn't eat up kids who can't fight back.

I didn't like Wedge. I didn't like what he was. He probably didn't have much use for me but I'd bet he'd agree.

Anyway, I knew what I was saying. And Maya seemed to get the message. "Garrett . . ."

"Never mind. We'll talk when we get home. The bad time is over."

Sure it was. You smooth talker, Garrett. Now try to convince yourself.

Dean fussed over Maya like he was her mother. I didn't get a chance to talk to her. The sun was coming up, so I said to hell with it and went to bed.

35

My own body turned traitor. I woke up at noon and couldn't get back to sleep. I should have been smug, the hero who had gone out to save the damsel and had succeeded, but I didn't feel smug or heroic. I felt confused, angry, put upon, frustrated. Most of all I felt out of control.

I'm not used to getting knocked around without at least some idea of what's happening and why. In this one I was starting to suspect that maybe nobody knew and everybody was too busy bobbing and weaving to figure out why we were in the ring.

Well, hell! I'm a thug for hire. I get paid. Do I have to think, too?

I want to know, for my own peace of mind. I'm no Morley Dotes, for whom the money is the only morality.

I went downstairs to stoke the body's fires.

Dean had heard me knocking around and had gotten a meal started. Hot tea was on the table. Rewarmed muffins landed beside it as I entered the kitchen. There was butter and blueberry preserves and apple juice, and sausages were popping in the pan while eggs boiled.

The place was crowded. "You having a party?" Two women were there with Dean.

He gave me one of his looks.

I recognized one of his more determined nieces, Bess, but the other woman, whose hair Bess was plaiting . . . "Maya?"

"Do I look too awful?"

No. "Stand up. Turn around. Let me look at you." She didn't look awful at all. They'd drum her out of the Doom if they saw her like this. "I just ran out of excuses for not taking you out. Except for maybe there'd be riots." She looked good. I'd guessed that. But I hadn't guessed just how good.

Bess said, "Down, boy."

Dean said, "Mr. Garrett!" He used his protective father tone.

"Phoo! I don't mess with children."

"I'm not a child," Maya protested. And when you thought about it, she wasn't. "I'm eighteen. If it wasn't for the war I'd be married and have a couple of kids."

It was true. In prewar times they'd married them off at thirteen or fourteen and had given up hope of getting rid of them by the time they were fifteen.

"She's got a point," I told Dean.

"You want these eggs the way you like them?"

How typical of him to drag in extraneous issues. "You won't hear another word from me."

"Grown men," Maya told Bess, who nodded in contempt. That nearly sent Dean off on one of those tirades that bust out of him every time one of his nieces opens her mouth.

It occurred to me that Bess was barely three months older than Maya. Dean had no trouble picturing Bess married to me.

People seldom see any need to be consistent.

The key word there, though—of course—is "married."

I said, "Let's forget it. Maya. Tell me what you learned while those people had you." I went to work eating.

Maya sat down. Bess started on her hair again. "There isn't much to tell. They didn't try to entertain or convert me."

"You always pick up more than you think, Maya. Try."

She said, "All right. I got the bright idea I could show you something if I followed those guys. All I showed you was a fat chance to tell me you told me so."

"I told you so."

"Smart-ass. They grabbed me and dragged me off and kept me in a place they used for a temple. A weird, grungy place they'd made over by painting the walls with ugly pictures."

"I saw it."

"I sat through their religious services. Three times a day I sat through them. Those guys don't do anything but work and eat and pray for the end of the world, I think. Mostly they didn't use Karentine in their services."

"They sound like a fun bunch."

Maya snatched a buttered muffin off my plate and smiled brightly. She was moving right in. "Get used to it, Garrett. Yeah. They were fun. Like an abscessed tooth."

I chewed sausage and waited.

"They're really negative, Garrett. In the Doom I know people who are negative, but those guys could give lessons. I mean it. They were praying for the end of the world."

"You're telling me things I didn't know. Keep going."

That was praise enough to light her up. It takes so little sometimes. I had a feeling she'd turn out all right, given encouragement. "Tell me more."

She said, "They call themselves the Sons of Hammon. I think Hammon must have been some kind of prophet, about the same time as Terrell."

Dean said, "He was one of Terrell's original six Companions. And the first to desert him. A bitter parting over a woman."

I looked at him in surprise.

He continued. "Later dogma says Hammon betrayed Terrell's hiding place to the Emperor Cedric—if you find him mentioned at all. But in the Apocrypha, written that same century and kept intact in secret since, it's the other way around and Hammon died two years before Terrell was turned in by his own wife. Known to us as Saint Medwa."

"What?" I gave the old man the long look now. He'd never shown much interest in religion or its special folklore. "What is this? Where'd you get all this? When did you become an expert? I've never heard of this Hammon character and my mother dragged me to church until I was ten."

"Council of Ai, Mr. Garrett. Five Twenty-one, Imperial Age. Two hundred years before the Great Schism. All the bishops and presters and preators attended, along with a host of imperial delegates. In those days every diocese spawned its own heresy. And every heretic was a fanatic. The emperor wanted to end a century of fighting. In Five Eighteen in Costain, in one day of rioting, forty-eight thousand had been killed. The emperor was a confirmed Terrillite and he had the swords. He ordered the Council to expunge the memory of Hammon, so the proto-Church and Orthodox sects wrote him out of their histories. I know because my father taught me. He was a Cynic seminarian for three years and a lay deacon all his life."

You never know everything about somebody, do you?

You can't argue with an expert. Besides, the "facts" I'd been taught had never made sense. The histories of Terrell's time, outside the religious community, didn't jibe with what the priests wanted us to believe.

We had been told that Terrell had been martyred for his witnessing to the masses. But the way the secular histories go, the religion business was wide open in those days. Every street corner in the cities and every hamlet in the country had its prophet. They could rave all they wanted. Moreover, Terrell had been a prophet of Hano, who had had more followers then than he does now.

"Then why did Cedric kill him?"

"Because he started in on the imperial household and establishment. He got political. And he didn't have sense enough to shut his mouth when they told him to stick to putting words into the mouth of Hano, who can look out for himself."

I always figured that. Why would Hano need henchmen down here to knock the heads of unbelievers when he's the Great Head Knocker himself? "So who are these Sons of Hammon?"

"I don't know. I've never heard of them."

Maya said, "They're devil-worshipers, Garrett. They won't even speak their god's name. They just call him the Devastator and beg him to bring on the end of the world."

"Crazies."

"He answers them, Garrett." She started shaking. "That was the bad part. I heard him. Inside my head. He promises them the end of the world before the turn of the century if they carry out his commands faithfully. Many will die in the struggle but the martyrs will be rewarded. They will be drawn to his bosom in peace and ecstasy forever."

I exchanged looks with Dean. Maya's eyes had glazed and she was babbling like something had taken possession of her. "Hey! Maya! Come back." I clapped my hands in front of her nose.

She jumped and looked bewildered. "Sorry. I got carried away, didn't I? But it got pretty intense when those guys got a service going and their god talked to them. Hell. It was really bad the night before last. He showed up in person."

"Yes?" Did I want to know about this? "A thing like an ape, six arms, twelve feet tall?"

"That was the shape he assumed. Uglier than a barrel of horned toads. How did you know?"

"I met him. Out at Chodo's. He didn't make good company. But he seemed kind of puny for a god."

"That wasn't really the god, Garrett. I'm not sure what they meant but the thing was something like what the real god dreamed. Only he had control of the dream, like you do sometimes. You know?"

The more she talked the more nervous she got. I wondered if they'd done something to her that she either wouldn't talk about or couldn't remember. "Is this upsetting you?"

"Some. Things like that don't happen to people like me."

"Maya, things like that don't happen to people like me, either. Or anybody else. I've had some weird cases but I've never gone up against a god. Nobody these days has to deal with gods who really show up."

I glanced around. Dean was troubled. Maya was troubled. Even Bess, who didn't have a notion what we were talking about, bless her vacant head, was worried. I thought back on what I'd said.

A god who really shows up.

That's nightmare stuff. Who expects the gods to take an active role these days? Not even guys like Peridont. The gods haven't busybodied since antiquity.

What Maya had to tell was interesting, but useful only in a cautionary sense. I still had to get my hands on Jill Craight and maybe squeeze her. Something had started all this excitement bubbling.

I recalled the note Jill had left in that apartment. I had made maybe the biggest screwup of a career checkered with goofs.

I should have sat on that sucker for as long as it took. Somebody was going to come and get it—somebody who might be at the root of this whole damned business.

Maybe I hadn't needed Jill at all. If only I had waited there until he came . . . But then I wouldn't have gotten Maya loose . . .

Maybe it wasn't too late. "I have to go out."

t was too late. The note was gone. I cussed my blindness. I tore that apartment to shreds looking for something, anything, and found exactly what I deserved to find. Nothing.

So it would be the hard way after all, hunt Jill Craight until something shook loose.

I hoped I wouldn't be hearing from the Sons of Hammon for a while. The way they'd taken it on the chin, I couldn't see them doing anything but backing off to regroup. I just hoped the bastards were as confused as the rest of us.

I got out of there and headed to the area where Tey Koto claimed Jill was likely to be found.

There are pimples and pockets of Hell and Purgatory all over TunFaire. People wouldn't want their daughters hanging out there. The kingpin probably has a finger in all of them. The worst, the biggest, where Chodo's presence is heavier than that of a king, is the Tenderloin, sometimes called the Street of the Damned. If you want it, someone there will sell it. And the kingpin will get his cut.

It's Hell on earth for those who survive that way, used and abused and discarded the instant they lose their marketability. For those who haven't been to the underside and haven't lived with the ticks on society's underbelly, it's difficult to believe people will use each other so badly.

Believe me, there are people out there who'll destroy a hundred lives for pocket change and never know a moment's remorse. Who wouldn't, in fact, understand if you told them they'd done something wrong by addicting a twelve-year-old so she'd cooperate as a thirty-a-day flat-backer.

They understand "against the laws of Man" but not "against the law of humanity." Right is whatever you make it, for as long as you can make it last.

They're out there. And they're the real bogeymen.

And through those mean streets walks a lonely man, a solitary knight-errant, the last honorable man, bent but not broken by the lowering storm . . .

Boy! Pile it on like that and I might have a future as a street-corner prophet—complete with all the kicks in the teeth that implies.

People don't want to be told to do right. They don't really *want* to do right. They want to do whatever they want—and whine that it's not fair, it's not their fault, when it comes time to pay the piper.

There are times when I don't care much for my brothers and sisters, when I'd gladly see half of them buried alive.

I don't go into my high holy mode too often, but a trip to the Tenderloin gets me every time.

So much that goes on there is unnecessary. In many cases neither the exploiters nor the exploited need to be doing what they do to survive. Tun-Faire is a prosperous city. Because of the war with the Venageti and Karenta's successes in it, there's work for anyone who wants it. And honest jobs go begging until nonhuman migrants come to the city to fill them.

A century ago nonhumans were curiosities, seldom seen, more the stuff of legend than real. Now they make up half the population and the bloods are becoming inextricably mixed. For real excitement wait until the war is over and the armies disband and all the war-related jobs dry up.

I'll step down off my box with the observation that, hell though the Tenderloin is, and as vile, vicious, or degraded as its habitués may be, most have some choice about being there.

"Garrett."

I think I jumped about four feet high because my sense of survival had gone into hibernation. I came down so ready for trouble I had the shakes. "Maya! What the hell are you doing here?"

"Waiting for you. I figured you'd come this way."

Was the little witch turning into a mind reader? "You didn't say why." I knew why, though.

"We're partners, remember? We're looking for somebody. And there's some places a man isn't going to get into no matter what he tries."

"You get hiking right back home. I'm going into the Tenderloin. That's no place for—"

"Garrett, shut your mouth and look at me. Am I nine years old and fresh out of a convent?"

She was right. But that didn't make me like it, or incline me to change my mind. It's weird how the symptoms of fatherhood had set in. But damn it, Maya out of her sleazeball duds and chuko colors wasn't anybody's little girl. She was a woman and it was obvious.

And that was maybe two-thirds of my problem. "All right. You want to stick your neck out, come on."

She joined me, wearing a smug smile filled with good teeth.

I said, "You snuck up on me, you know. You grew up. I can't help remembering the filthy brat I found beat to hell all those years ago."

She grinned and slipped her arm through mine. "I didn't sneak, Garrett. I took my time and did it right. I knew you'd wait for me."

Whoa! Who was talking shit to who here?

Maya laughed. "If we're going to do it, let's go."

••• 37

To understand the Tenderloin—to even picture it if you've never been there—you have to get in touch with the seamiest side of yourself. Pick a fantasy, one you wouldn't tell anyone about. One that makes you uncomfortable or embarrassed when you think about it. In the Tenderloin there's somebody who'll do it with you, for you, or to you, or somebody who'll let you watch if that's your need.

Let your imagination run away. You can't think of anything somebody hasn't thought and done already. Hell, somebody's thought of something even more disgusting. And it's all available there in Wonderland. And not just sex, though that's the first thing that jumps to mind.

At that time of day, late afternoon, most of the Tenderloin was just waking up. The district worked around the clock, but the majority of its patrons were like insects who shun the light. The district wouldn't get white-hot until after sunset.

I asked Maya, "You been down here before?"

"Never with a gentleman." She laughed.

I tried to scowl but her constant good humor was catching. I smiled.

"Sure," she said. "One of our favorite games. Come down here and watch the freaks. Maybe roll a drunk or kick the shit out of a pimp. We got up to lots of stuff. Most of the people who come here don't dare complain."

"You know how dangerous that is?" The people of the Tenderloin are solicitous of their customers.

She gave me the look the young save for old farts who say dumb things. "What did we have to lose?"

Only their lives. But kids are immortal and invulnerable. Just ask them.

It wasn't yet dark but we had plenty of company on the outer fringe, where the offerings are relatively tame. Gentlemen were window-shopping, barkers were barking, my angels were lurking, and a dozen prepubescent boys were trying to mooch copper. When I turned one down he took a big pinch of Maya's bottom and ran off. I roared in outrage, as I was supposed to do, and took a step after the brat, then the humor hit me. "You're on the other side now, sweetheart. You're one of the grown-ups."

"It hurts, Garrett."

I laughed.

"You bastard! Why don't you kiss it better?"

There in the tamer parts the houses display their wares in big bay windows. I couldn't help admiring what I saw.

"You're drooling, you old goat."

I probably was but I denied it.

"What's she got that I don't?" she demanded half a minute later. And I couldn't answer that one. The delicacy in question was younger than she and no prettier, but provocative as hell.

I needed blinders. My weakness was getting me into deep shit.

"There she is."

"Huh? Who? Where?"

Maya gave me a nasty look. "What do you mean, who? Who the hell are we looking for?"

"Take it easy. Where did you see her?" Grow up a little, Garrett. You got somebody's feelings to consider.

"Right up ahead. About a block."

Her eyes were better than mine if she could pick somebody out of the crowd at that distance.

I caught a glimpse of blond hair in a familiar style. "Come on!"

We hurried. I tried to keep that hair in sight. It vanished, reappeared, vanished, reappeared. We gained ground. The hair disappeared in the swirl near the entrance to a "theater" just opening for the first show. And it didn't reappear.

I was as sure as Maya that we'd spotted Jill.

I tried asking questions of the theater's barker. He was a lean whippet of a man, hide tanned from exposure to the weather. He didn't look like a nice guy. He looked at me and saw something he didn't like, either. The promise of five marks silver got me a look of contempt. This guy not only didn't know anything about any blonde, he'd forgotten how to talk.

Maya pulled me away before I tried to squeeze something out of him. One must be careful putting the arm on the help in the Tenderloin. They hang together like grapes, them against the world. "Next time how about I do the talking?" she said. "Even these jaded apes will listen to me."

They would, just to spite me. "All right. Let's go across the street and sit and give this a think." The Tenderloin does boast a few amenities absent from the rest of the city, like street-side loos and public benches. Anywhere else benches would get busted up for firewood and loos kicked down for the hell of it. Here the busters themselves would get broken up for kindling before they got done with their fun.

The organization has no patience with people who cost it money.

We went across. We sat. I considered the area and my options while Maya turned away offers by explaining that she was engaged. "Although," she told one would-be swain, "I might be able to shake this old guy later."

"Maya!"

"What do you care, Garrett? You're not interested. He looked like he might know how to have a good time."

Damn them all! I swear, before they let them go into puberty, they make them sign a contract in blood saying they'll cause us all the aggravation they can. "Give me a break, Maya. At least give me a chance to get used to the idea of you being a woman."

That put a smug look on her face. She chalked up six points for Maya on her secret scoreboard.

The majority of nearby businesses catered to spectators rather than participants. My stomach did a little growl and knot at the thought of Jill Craight starring in one of those shows.

Nothing is impossible, of course. I just didn't like it.

I didn't have much trouble believing it. The woman obviously had mental problems. I could see her making the kinds of connections that would convince her she was fit for nothing else. The human mind does weird things.

What amazes me is that we manage to cope as well as we do, that the race not only survives but manages to make the occasional stumbling advance. Maybe there is a force greater than ourselves, an engine driving us toward greatness.

It would be comforting to know my species is destined for something that will outshine its past and present. The Church, the Orthodox sects, all the Hanite cults and factions and denominations, offer that hope, but they've surrounded it with so much bullshit and in so many cases have given in to worldly temptations which act against the hope, that they've forfeited any right to guide us toward the brighter day.

Maya snuggled a little closer, as though the evening breeze had begun to bite. "What're you brooding about, Garrett?"

"The Sons of Hammon as a committed entropic force, convinced that our proper destiny is oblivion."

She leaned back and looked me in the eye. "You trying to shit me? Or are you just talking dirty?"

"No." I started to explain. After a minute she snuggled up again, got hold of my hands, and rested her cheek on my shoulder. She grunted in the right places to show she was listening. I'm sure we made a touching picture.

After a bit I said, "We got to get our minds back on business." I had to anyway. The little witch was getting to me. "You know anything about this area?"

"There's a lot of freaks."

I didn't need to be told that. I have pretty fair eyesight.

Six of the nearer buildings hosted live shows. Several more were havens for those who provided special services. A few seemed to be genuine residential hotels. And there was one place I couldn't pin down at all.

It had no barker. It had no sign. It had no heavy traffic, but in the time we'd been sitting, five men and a woman had entered the place. Four had come out. Only one had shown the furtiveness which characterizes a move toward an act considered perverse. Those who had come out had looked pleased and relaxed, relieved, but not in the way the sexually sated do.

"What about that place?" I pointed. "Know it?"

"No."

Curiosity had ahold of me. A lamplighter was working his way toward us, pushing his cartload of scented oils from post to post, topping things up and lighting the parti-colored lights that lend Tenderloin evenings a sleazy mask of carnival. When he stopped at the lamppost at the end of the bench I opened my mouth to ask about the place that intrigued me.

Maya elbowed me in the ribs. "My turn, remember?"

She got up.

It must be something they get in their mother's milk. I've never seen a woman yet who couldn't turn on the heat when she wanted. She whispered. The lamplighter's eyes took fire without help from his match. He nodded. She touched him over the heart and let her fingertips slide over a half foot of his jacket. He grinned and looked at the place that caught my eye. Then he saw the deaf barker looking daggers his way.

He ran out of words before he spoke. He turned stupider than an ox. I told Maya, "I'm getting irritated. Let's go."

I got up, took her hand, headed for the entrance to the curious place.

The barker saw my intent and abandoned his post. He hustled up the street, planted himself in my path. I told him, "Friend, you're getting on my nerves. In about two seconds I'm going to break your leg."

He grinned like he hoped I'd try. Maya said, "Garrett, be careful."

I looked around. Half a dozen natives were closing in. They looked like they'd been deprived of the pleasure of stomping somebody for a long time. But my angels were moving in behind them, and Saucerhead was leading the pack. He could handle this bunch by himself. I told the barker, "Move it or lose it, Bruno."

"You asked for it. Take him."

Saucerhead smacked a couple of heads together. Wedge cracked a couple more with a club. The barker's eyes got big. I asked, "You ready to move?"

Saucerhead said, "Garrett, you got to quit this crap. You're going to start a riot."

The barker's eyes popped. He had a nasty suspicion. "You the Garrett that works for Chodo?" He stepped out of the way. "Why didn't you say so?"

Saucerhead rumbled. "Yeah, Garrett. Why didn't you say so?"

"Because I don't care what Chodo claims, I *don't* work for him. I work for me." I had to keep that point clear for my own peace of mind.

The barker said, "You understand, I didn't know you was working for Chodo. We get all kinds down here. I wouldn't of give you no shit if you'd told me."

It was going to be a long fight, shaking loose from that tie. "Look, all I want to do is go in there and see what goes on."

The barker said, "You was asking about some blond bitch. What you want to know? If I can help . . ."

And Saucerhead, at the same time, said, "I come down here to tell you Morley needs to see you. Says he got some news for you."

"Good for Morley. If you'll all excuse me?" I pushed past the barker and headed inside. Maya stuck close and kept her mouth shut. Good for her, too.

The door to the place was unlocked. Maybe it couldn't be locked. It sagged in its frame. Inside there was a scrawny old guy in a rickety chair shoving sticks into a stove. It was hot enough to broil steaks but he was grumbling about the cold. He was one giant liver spot. "Drop it on the counter," he said, not bothering to look up.

"What?"

He looked, then. At me, then at Maya. His brushy white eyebrows wormed around. "You together?"

"Yes."

"Well, whatever. Have to charge you. Six marks silver. First time? Take any box where the curtain is open. You don't like what you get, you can move once on the house. You still ain't satisfied, it's another mark every move until you light."

I put the money down. He went back to feeding the fire. Maya gave me a puzzled look. I shrugged and stepped up to a curtained doorway.

It opened to reveal a long hallway. A half dozen curtained alcoves opened to either side. Four had their curtains drawn. We walked down the hall and back. I heard soft voices behind the drawn curtains. Where the curtains were open there was nothing but a chair and a table pushed against a wall of glass. There was nothing behind the glass but darkness.

"What is this place, Garrett?"

"I guess if you have to ask you don't belong here." I led her into the nearest open room and drew the curtain. The place was five feet deep by six wide and very dark with the curtain closed. I felt for what looked like a pull cord and gave it a tug. Bells tinkled somewhere overhead, muted. A light appeared high on the other side of the glass.

A well-dressed and impossibly beautiful woman came down a spiral staircase into an eight-by-twelve room that might have been a lady's bedroom transported from the Hill. It was a set, obviously, but just as obviously perfect in every detail.

"Garrett," Maya whispered, "that woman isn't human. She's pure high elf."

I saw it but I didn't believe it. Who ever heard of an elvish whore? But Maya had it right. She was elvish, and so damned beautiful she hurt my eyes.

She began to undress as though unaware that she was being observed, pulled a chair up to a table facing the glass from the far side, then sat in her underthings. She began removing makeup slowly. The glass must be a mirror on her side.

Maya pinched me. "Stop panting. You'll fog the glass."

The elvish woman heard something. She cocked her head quizzically. She asked, "Is someone there?"

That was a voice men could kill for. I didn't know her from dog food. I like to think I'm as hard-nosed a cynic as they make, but I had no problem imagining that silver-bells whisper on my pillow, sending me whooping through the teeth of Hell.

She stood up and slipped out of another layer of clothing.

Maya said, "I'm not going to ask what this one has that I don't." She sounded awed.

I was petrified.

"Is someone there?" she asked again.

I reached out and touched the glass. A sound-permeable glass that could be seen through from one side only? Someone had invested heavily in some very specialized designer sorcery. And I could see the touch of genius in it. This mundane bit of voyeurism and pretense was a hundred times as erotic as any crude stage coupling of women with one another, nonhumans, apes, or zebras. And the main reason was the natural talent of the woman behind the glass. She turned every move into something ripped out of a blazing fantasy.

She touched the glass where my fingertips rested. "That's all right. You don't have to talk if you don't want." It felt like my fingers were pressed to a grille.

I wanted. I wanted desperately. I was in love. And I was as tongue-tied as a twelve-year-old with designs on someone Maya's age.

I yanked my hand away.

I didn't know what to do.

Maya stepped in. "Who are you?"

"I'm whoever you want me to be." She registered no surprise at a woman's voice. "I'll be whatever you want. I'm your fantasy."

Yes. Oh, yes.

She started on the last layer of clothing.

I turned around. I couldn't handle it, not with Maya there.

I wondered if there was some drug in the air, or maybe a subtle sorcery that enhanced the normal magic of a beautiful woman disrobing.

I *knew* what kind of acting Jill did. She'd be a natural here. She had the looks, she had the style, and she had the heat when she wanted. Put her in one of those rooms, and she could be bewitching.

I rested my hand on Maya's shoulder, whispered, "I'm going to check the other boxes."

She nodded.

When I stepped out only two sets of curtains were drawn. A man was just leaving. I went up and down the hall quickly. Four of the empties had signs up indicating there would be no response if you rang. I guessed the place was a twenty-four-hour operation and only one woman used a setup. Most would be on duty now because the Tenderloin was headed into its busy hours.

I rang a bell and conjured a redhead who reminded me of Tinnie but wasn't Jill Craight. I got out before she worked a spell on me.

The old man was in the hall. He looked at me quizzically. I dropped coins into his hand. "I'm going to take the tour."

"Suit yourself." An old veteran of the Tenderloin. No surprises. None of his business what I did as long as I paid.

Each woman was as marvelous as the last but none were Jill. I even waited out the occupants of the two busy boxes. One of the ladies wasn't Jill and the other put out her sign and refused to answer her bell.

Twelve possibilities whittled down to five. I considered working on the old man, discarded the idea. Unless I wanted to sit on him he'd warn Jill that somebody was asking questions. I knew where to look now. All I needed to do was come back until I'd seen them all.

I went back to box one. Maya and the elvish woman were chattering like sisters. The woman had her clothes on. Just as well. There are limits to what a man can take.

Maya glanced back to make sure it was me. "I'm almost done. Time's up anyway."

They exchanged a few pleasantries in a way that made me suspect I'd interrupted some girl talk. Maya got up and leaned close, whispered, "You have to leave a tip. That's the way they make their money. The old man keeps what he takes."

Except for the kingpin's cut, of course. Which would come out of the tips, too.

"Where?"

Maya showed me a slot in the tabletop which was the only way to pass objects from one side of the glass to the other. I filled it with a generous sprinkle of silver. I wasn't out much. It had come from the kingpin to begin and some of it might have gone to him from here.

Maya squeezed my arm. She was pleased with me. I figured the woman had run a good game on her. I led her out of there.

A man was coming in the front door as I parted the hall curtains for Maya. I caught only a glimpse of a little dink with a shiny head and an epic schnoz. He froze. Maya froze. I walked into her. We tangled. When we untangled he was gone. "What the hell?"

"That was him, Garrett. He recognized me."

"That was who?"

"The guy that was in that apartment. The one that ran me over."

The old man fed his fire. He saw nothing. He heard nothing.

That runt had some eye if he'd recognized *this* Maya as the filthy girl who'd been in that apartment.

I plunged into the street and saw a lot of what the old man saw inside. The dink was a magician. Or maybe he was just so short he couldn't be spotted in the crowd.

It's carnival every night down there. I have to admit it's not all whoring and sleaze. There are tamer entertainments. Hell, two doors from where I stood there was a bingo hall with the vanguard of its regiment of old ladies just arriving. But sleaze is the axis of the Tenderloin and the misery there outweighs the innocuous entertainments.

I asked my angels if they'd seen the little guy. They didn't know what I was talking about. I asked the barker. He hadn't seen a thing and was too busy to chat. Irked, I told him, "I'll be back tomorrow. We'll talk when you're not so pressed."

"Yeah. Sure. Nobody's going to say I don't cooperate with the organization."

Exasperated, I collected Maya and headed home.

39

We didn't say much for a while. Then I recalled something and changed course abruptly.

"What're you doing now?"

"Almost forgot I have to see Morley."

"Oh. Mr. Charm."

"He gets a look at you tonight you might have to fight him off with a stick."

She gave me a look. "Thanks for the compliment. I think."

Half a block later she told me, "I was going to seduce you tonight. But now I can't."

"Hunh?" Investigators are fast on their feet and quick with a comeback.

"If I did, it wouldn't be me you were with. You'd be thinking about her."

"Who her?" Look at that footwork. The boy is so fast you can't see him move.

"Polly. The elvish girl."

"Her? I'd forgotten her already," I lied.

"And the moon is made of green cheese."

"That's what the experts say. But as long as you bring her up, what'd she have to say?"

"I couldn't get specific because I didn't want her to know what we were up to. She might tell Hester. I think you're right. One of the girls sounds like her. Polly doesn't like her. Polly is kind of a prude."

"A what?" I laughed.

"It's all look-and-don't-touch on the premises there, Garrett. Polly says her regulars just want to talk to somebody who's easy on the eyes. Somebody who can listen and talk back, and who isn't any kind of threat. She never actually sees any of them. She says some of them must be important men but she doesn't know who they are. She never sees them outside. Some of the other girls do. Polly claims she's a virgin."

Maya found that hard to swallow. I didn't want to think about it.

It was a strange setup but I could see how it could be a gold mine—without extortion. The one thing the movers and shakers lack is somebody they can relax with and talk to without risking betrayal.

That was the essence of the racket. Polly harvested enough in tips to satisfy herself. But some of her coworkers wanted more.

"It's because she's elvish," Maya guessed. "She doesn't have to hurry. She can trade on her looks for a long time. Human women only get a few years." Hint, hint. Nudge, nudge. The girl had her own talent for distraction. Had to be inborn. How would she learn it running with a street gang?

We got to Morley's place. Maya reaped a harvest of appreciative looks. Nobody paid any attention to me. So that was the secret of getting in without the gauntlet of hostile stares—bring a woman to distract them.

Slade was behind the counter. He lifted the speaking tube and pointed upstairs. We took the hint. I knocked on the office door. Morley let us in.

"Your taste has improved, Garrett." He ogled Maya.

I slipped my arm around her waist. "Didn't have time to get her into the disguise we use to protect her from characters like you."

His eyes popped. "You're the lady he was with the other night?"

She just smiled mysteriously.

"Miracles do happen," he said. And whined, "But they never happen to me."

At which point a gorgeous half-caste brunette stepped out of his back room and draped herself on his shoulder.

"I hope your luck turns, Morley. Saucerhead said you had some news for me."

"Yes. Remember the man whose name you mentioned to the kingpin? The one who visited you the night you got into your mess?"

I presumed he was being cagey about naming Peridont. "That religious character?"

"The very one."

"What about him?"

"Somebody sent him to his reward. Put a poisoned quarrel in his back.

About four blocks from your place, I figure he was going to see you. He wouldn't have any other reason to be around there dressed like somebody's gardener."

Maybe. "Damn! Who did it?"

Morley spread his hands wide and gave a blank look. "I suppose one of the same fun-loving bunch. It went down in broad daylight, in front of fifty witnesses. Farmer-looking guy just steps out of a doorway behind him and lets him have it."

"Being a wizard ain't everything." I'd developed an itch between my shoulder blades. That could happen to anybody at any time. If somebody wants you bad enough, they'll get you. "I don't know if I wanted to know that."

"We'll tighten up around you, Garrett. We'll make them work for it."

"That's a comfort, Morley." Peridont getting it bothered me bad. I had this feeling I'd lost my last best ally.

"You think I want to go tell Chodo I blew it?"

I knew what he wanted to say, but he was saying it so clumsily it was worse than if he hadn't said anything. For Morley, the actual expression of concern or friendship is next to impossible.

"Never mind," I told him. "Quit while you're ahead. Was there anything else?" His friend was tickling his neck with a fingernail. He wouldn't keep his mind on business long.

"No. Go home and stay there. We won't have to pick up pieces of Garrett if you keep your head down."

"Right. I'll think about it."

"Don't think. Do."

"Come on, Maya. Let's go home."

Morley and I both knew I wouldn't give it a thought.

40

I t started when we were two blocks from my house, a roaring and grumbling hurrying up from the south. Lightning zigged around it. I pulled Maya into a doorway.

"What is it?"

"Something we don't want to notice us." A big red nasty bobbed in the middle of the cloud.

People stuck their heads out windows, got a look, and decided they didn't want to know.

The microstorm headed straight for my place.

Wouldn't you know it?

This time there was no roof busting. A nasty red spider strutted down out of the night—and something swatted it right back.

"Old Chuckles is going to pay his rent tonight," I muttered.

"You're shaking."

I was, worse than if I'd been in the thick of it. Yet my mind wasn't working right. I didn't think about Dean or the Dead Man. All I could think about was what might happen to my house. It was all I had in the world. I'd gone through hell to get the money to pay for it. I was getting too long in the tooth to start over.

The storm whooped and hollered. The spider headed in again, scarlet swords of fire leaping from its eyes. Bam! They hit an invisible wall. The spider bounced back.

"I didn't know he had it in him."

The Dead Man had a lot more than I'd suspected. He never tried to hurt the spider, but he turned every assault. The more its efforts were stymied, the more ferocious the monster became. It didn't worry about damaging the neighborhood.

This was going to make me popular with my neighbors.

You can only stay keyed up so long. When I began to settle down I had a thought. "This doesn't make sense. I may have been a pain in the ass to those guys, but not this big a pain. There's something else going on."

The flash and fury distressed Maya less than it did me. Maybe it was her lack of experience with sorcery. "Analyze it, Garrett. This is the second time your place has been attacked. You weren't home either time. Maybe it doesn't matter if you are. Maybe it's the house."

"Or something in it."

"Or something in it. Or someone."

"Besides me? Nobody . . ." The Dead Man? But he'd been dead too long to have enemies left. "Know what I think? I got started on the wrong foot at the beginning. I've been trying to get it to make sense."

Maya looked at me weird. "What the hell are you yapping about?"

"I'm trying to make sense of something that isn't rational. I knew from the beginning that religion was involved. Several religions, maybe. You can try from now until the end of the world and you're not going to make sense out of that. I shouldn't be attacking it that way. I should be going with it, going after who's doing what to who and not trying to figure out why."

Her look got weirder. "Did you get hit on the head? You're raving."

Maybe I was. And maybe somewhere in my nonsense there was a kernel of wisdom. That business down the street looked like a good argument for reassessing my place in the excitement. "Ever been to Leifmold, kid?"

"What?"

"I'm starting to think the smart thing would be to get out of town. Let this thing take care of itself."

She didn't believe me for a moment. And she was right. Maybe it's a lack of common sense. Maybe I just have a feeble survival instinct. I'd hang in until the end.

I mean, what kind of reputation would I get if I backed off just because that was the safe thing to do? Somebody hires you, he wants you to stick. You want to work, you got to do that—at least until moral revulsion forces you out. You don't let a little thing like fear slow you down.

The thing with eight limbs was on the ground now, stomping around the house, making the earth shake, roaring, grabbing up cobblestones and throwing them. I told Maya, "Every living city flunky will be around to pester me now." I didn't look forward to that. I'm not at my best with those people.

One of my angels darted through the shifting witch light. I recognized Wedge.

"Remind me I don't want to get into your line of work, Garrett." He looked up the street. "What the hell is going on?"

"You got me. I'm not sure I want to know."

The eight-limbed thing tore chunks out of a couple of houses, and flung them at my place. They bounced back. The Dead Man was showing unnecessary patience. The monster jumped up and down like an angry child. It looked to me like he and the Dead Man had a standoff. I was amazed. I couldn't picture my boarder holding his own against the avatar of a god.

"I didn't sign on for this, Garrett," Wedge told me. "I ain't no chickenshit, but saving your ass from demons is a little too much."

I could empathize with that. "Saving my ass from demons is a little too much for me, too, Wedge. You want to do a fade you won't hear me cry. I didn't beg Morley for any guardian angels."

"You didn't. Chodo did. If you did he'd have told you to go tongue-kiss a ghoul. Bye, Garrett. Good luck."

"Yeah." Candyass. When the going gets tough, the smart get going and the stupid keep heading toward trouble. Garrett didn't have enough sense to follow Wedge's example. He hung on where he was.

Maya asked, "We going to do something?"

"Find a tavern and hang out till it's over."

She knew a wisecrack when she heard one. "We hang around here and the Watch will scoop us up. They must be awake by now."

She had a point. Something this loud would force those guys to come out so their asses would be covered when questions were asked later. In that way having the spider get held off was worse than having the house get smashed. This was a hurrah that couldn't be ignored.

"Hell!" I spat. "Enough is enough." I stepped out of the doorway, trotted up the street, stopped a hundred fifty feet from home, eyeballed the spider, wound up and let my last bottle fly like it was a flat rock. It didn't hit the spider but it did smash between the monster's legs. Whatever was inside splashed.

The thing jumped about forty feet high and shrieked like the world's biggest stuck hog. It turned in the air. It picked me out of the crowd, which wasn't all that tough. It started its charge before it hit the ground.

Now what, genius?

I shoved Maya into a breezeway and scooted in after her. The spider smashed into the buildings as though trying to bull right through. It let out a big bass whoop of frustration, then started ripping materials out of its way. One hairy leg kept reaching for me.

There were greenish spots on the leg where Peridont's stuff had splattered it. Every little bit it paused to scratch those. In five minutes it was scratching more than it was trying to get us.

The breezeway was a dead end. We were caught good. I didn't waste the five minutes it took the spider to become preoccupied with itself. I tested two doors and attacked the weakest. I got it open just as the spider started spending most of its time scratching.

"Come on." I pushed into the darkened interior, part of someone's home. Maya stumbled around behind me. When I paused I heard rapid, frightened breathing. There were people in there, trying to keep quiet and not be noticed.

We got through without killing ourselves on unseen furniture, found a window in back, got it open and slithered through.

"Slick, Garrett," Maya said. "You'd better hope they didn't recognize you."

"Yeah." I already had enough trouble getting along with my neighbors.

"What now?"

We took half a block along an alleyway, toward home, to where I could check on the spider.

For a god it wasn't very bright. It was still trying to tear its way into that breezeway, when it wasn't scratching. Doing a fair job, too. "When I say go, we head for the front door. And pray Dean lets us in before that thing catches up."

"I think maybe going to Leifmold was a better idea."

"Maybe. Ready?"

"Yes."

"Go."

That damned spider wasn't as fixated as I hoped. It spotted us and began bouncing in our direction before we'd gone ten steps.

We wouldn't make it in time.

Maya pounded the door with both fists. I bellowed at Dean. The spider galloped toward us. I spotted a human skull-type face where the thing's head was, sort of like it had been painted over the usual spider face. Spreading mandibles made that skull look like it was grinning.

Chains and bolts rattled on the other side of the door.

We had gotten Dean's attention.

But it was too late. The spider was on us—

It hit something. Or something hit it. There was a sound like crunching gravel. The monster went tumbling back the way it had come, trailing another of its bellows of frustration. "The Dead Man is still on the job," I gasped at Maya. "Come on, Dean!"

The monster was charging again before the old man got the door open. We plunged inside, trampling him, then tumbled over one another trying to bolt up. Though a fat lot of good bolts and bars would do against that thing.

"What's going on, Mr. Garrett?" Dean was pale and rattled.

"I don't know. I was just going to call it a night when that thing dropped out of the sky."

"Like the thing you saw at the kingpin's place?"

"Same kind of thing in a different shape."

"I don't think I want to be involved anymore, Mr. Garrett. Things like this don't happen in your regular cases. I think I want to go home until it's over."

"I don't blame you. But first we have to get that thing to go away." I peeked out. It had quieted down. I thought it might be getting ready to try something nasty.

It was standing in the street, balanced on three legs. It scratched itself with the other five. The green spots on its legs had grown and now shed a phosphorescent light. The more it dug at those the more they irritated it.

Good. Maybe it would forget us altogether.

It pounced at my place like it meant to take us by surprise. Off it went with a howl, slapped away. It stood up unsteadily, scratched vigorously. I told Maya, "I'm going to have a chat with my dead buddy. Why don't you help Dean in the kitchen?" Hint, hint.

It took the old boy a while. But he got it after I told him to bring me a pitcher.

The house shook again. Storms of rage played around outside. I went into the Dead Man's room, settled into the chair we kept there for me, and considered the old mountain of blubber. Despite the excitement he looked no more animated than usual. You couldn't tell if he was asleep or awake if it wasn't for a sort of electric radiation bleeding off him. "Whenever you have a minute or two," I told him.

He wasn't himself. *Go ahead, Garrett.* He was saving his irritation for the thing outside.

"Got any idea what that thing is?"

I have begun to develop a suspicion. I have not yet gathered evidence enough to establish a certainty. I do not like the suspicion. If that thing is what I fear. . . .

He wasn't going to say, but then he never let anything out of the bag until he was sure he wouldn't contradict himself later. I knew what sort of answer I'd get, but I asked anyway. "And what's that?" Maybe he'd be distracted enough to let something slip.

Not yet.

"Can you at least get it to go away?"

I do not have that power, Garrett. You seem to have done what was needed to discourage it, though it is losing its determination very slowly.

Not sure what he meant, I took a peek outside. The spider was more involved in scratching itself and less interested in my place. I went back. "You going to contribute something now or are you just going back to sleep?"

Though I am certain you brought this upon yourself and deserve any villainies visited upon you, it seems—

"Don't get wise, Old Bones. That thing didn't come to see me. Neither did those firebombers. I wasn't home either time. So you tell me—"

Quiet. I must reflect. You are correct. I have failed to see the obvious, that you are too small a mouse to interest this cat.

"I think you're special, too."

Quiet.

He reflected. He batted that spider away. I got tired of waiting. "You better not take forever. It won't be long before we're up to our hips in people who want to know what's going on. Hill-type people."

Correct. I have foreseen that. I do not have enough information. You must tell me all that has happened since you became involved. Spare me no detail.

I protested.

Hurry. The thing will accept defeat soon. The minions of the state will bestir themselves. It will be to your advantage to be absent when they arrive. You will not be absent if you do not hasten.

That was true, though maybe it wasn't his full concern. I played along, anyway. I started at the beginning and gave him everything to the moment I'd gotten in a step ahead of the spider. The telling took a while.

He took a while longer to digest everything. I was pretty antsy when Dean stuck his head in. "Mr. Garrett, that thing gave up."

I hurried to the front door and peeked out. Dean was right. It was staggering down the street, not even trying to walk on air, spending more energy scratching than going. I bounced back into the Dead Man's room. "It's headed out, Chuckles. We don't have much time." I leaned back into the hall. "Dean, tell Maya we've got to get out of here."

He scowled at me. He muttered and cursed and made it damned clear he thought I had no business putting Maya at risk.

The Dead Man said, *If I can have your attention?*

"You got it, Smiley."

Your sense of humor never rises above the juvenile. Pay attention. First, it is probable that you are correct. The attacks upon this house were not launched either to get you or because the place belongs to you. For a moment I considered it possible that I was their target. That seemed reasonable under the assumption that this trouble springs from the source I suspect. But that source should not be aware of my presence, considering its prior indifference to researching the nature of its adversaries. So its focus, its interest, must be something within the house.

Say what? He knew who was stirring all the commotion?

Have you bothered to examine the guest room? You did not mention having done so, yet I cannot imagine any protégé of mine having been so lax as to have overlooked the obvious.

He was going to bounce right up on his high horse. He loves it when he nails me.

Damn it, I'd thought about this before and I hadn't bothered to see if Jill had left something.

Sometimes you get too busy to think.

Now, with him sitting there smirking, I began to wonder if Jill hadn't set me up.

"Dean! Go upstairs and see if Jill left anything in the guest room. Maya can help you look. If you don't find anything, look wherever she could've gotten to while she was here. If you still don't find anything, look where she couldn't have gotten. There must be something."

Better late than never.

"Right. I'm sure the neighbors will agree when they try to figure out why their houses got torn up."

He understood. If he'd gotten off his mental duff back when, we might not have this mess now.

Let us not fall to bickering, Garrett. Time has been wasted. Let us waste no more.

"Check. So let's get at it. You think you know what's going on? Do you know anything about these Sons of Hammon?"

I recall them. A vicious and nihilistic cult. For them all life is sorrow and misery and punishment and shall continue to be till their Devourer has been unchained to scour the world clean. The many shall be consumed and the True Believers, the Faithful, who serve without cavil, who help release the Devourer and set the Devastation in motion, shall be rewarded with perpetual bliss. Their paradise resembles the adolescent paradise of the Shades cults. Milk and honey, streets of gold, an inexhaustible supply of suppliant virgins.

"That part doesn't sound so bad."

To you it would not.

I waited for him to tell me more.

The cult's roots reach back to the time of your prophet Terrell. It was declared heretic and a persecution launched against it a thousand years ago. Till then it was just one of countless Hanite cults. The heretics fled into various nonhuman areas. A colony formed in Carathca, where its doctrines became polluted by dark-elvish nihilism, then fell under the sway of devil-worshipers who brought it around to its present philosophical form three hundred years ago. About that time its high priests began claiming direct revelations from heaven, revelations the laity could feel themselves. The cult began acting politically, trying to hasten the Devastation.

They were persecuted, Garrett. First in the power games of empire and churches, then because the masters of Carathca grew afraid of them and wanted to drive them out.

The cult faded into the human population, which supported it because humans were not well treated in Carathca. It deployed all the instruments of terror. After two generations it mastered Carathca. The dark-elfin nobility survived only as puppets. The countryside for fifty miles around fell under cult sway. Fanatic assassins went out to silence the Devastator's enemies. The cult became so dangerous, so vicious, that the early Karentine Kings had no choice but war or submission. They chose war, as humans always do, determined to exterminate the cult. For a time it seemed they had succeeded. King Beran declared them extinct only to be assassinated by a branch which had established itself in TunFaire under another name. His son Brian continued the fight and, it appeared, succeeded in extinguishing the cult's last lights a century and a half ago. Do you follow?

"Well enough. I don't understand, but I don't have to understand to deal with them, do I?"

You need understand only that they are more dangerous than anyone you have ever battled, excepting perhaps vampires defending their nest. They do not just believe, they know. Their devil god has spoken to each of them directly and has given each of them a look into a paradise where they will spend eternity. They will do anything because they know there is no penalty to compare with their coming reward. They fear nothing. They are saved and will be born again, and concrete evidence has been given them for this. They need take the word of no one but their god himself.

I got a really creepy feeling. "Just wait up, Old Bones. What the hell? I don't need this. I'm a nonbeliever. You trying to tell me there's no side of the angels, that there really is a god and he's really a devil and—"

Hold! Enough!

I calmed down a little, though I was still pretty shaky. Think about stepping up face-to-face with possible proof that something you find completely repellent is the law of the universe.

We Loghyr have never found proof of the existence of any gods. Neither have we disproved their existence, although logic militates against it. They are not necessary to explain anything. Nature does not provide that which is not needed.

He'd never spent half a year trying to survive in a swamp infested with five hundred parasitic species. Were gods some sort of psychic or spiritual parasites?

However, proof or lack thereof is unnecessary to the mind that must believe. And that mind becomes doubly narrow and doubly dangerous when it is given what it perceives as proof. Then it can begin to create that in which it believes.

Hanging out with him wasn't all a dead waste. "You mean somebody is running a game on the Sons of Hammon, making like he's their god? Fooling them into doing his dirty deeds?"

Someone was back when the cult ruled Carathca and its environs. We who brought about his downfall believed we had destroyed him. Perhaps we failed. Or perhaps another has taken his place, though what other there could be is a greater puzzle than how the one we fought could have escaped to nurture his wickedness in secret.

I was on a roll. "We're talking another dead Loghyr here, aren't we?" It didn't take much imagination to see how my old buddy here could kick ass if he wasn't so damned lazy.

We are. We are speaking of the only Loghyr ever to have gone mad. We are speaking of a true son of the Beast, if you will, who did great evils while he lived, in the guises of several of your history's bloodiest villains, and who strove to do greater evils still after the righteous slew him.

We chattered back and forth. He convinced me that not only could a live Loghyr pass for human, but that it had been done countless times—and some of the worst men of olden times and a couple of *saints* hadn't been human at all. But he couldn't make me understand why, even though we humans are notorious meddlers. Loghyr are supposed to stand outside and observe and look down their noses.

"Interesting as hell. I'm learning things about Loghyr I never suspected. We'll have to have a long chat someday. But we don't have time right now. We have to make moves and make them fast, or all the machineries of the state will have us under siege and we won't be able to do a thing."

You may be right.

"You figure there's a Loghyr out there somewhere who's revived the old cult? I'll buy that. But why the hell are they tearing up TunFaire?"

I must confess, that has me baffled. It is my guess that Magister Peridont could have told us. The Craight woman might know. She was trusted more than any rational man should trust a woman. Peridont may have revealed himself. Find her, Garrett. Bring her to me.

"Right. Like snapping my fingers."

Also find, or at least identify, the man who was in that apartment opposite hers. I have a hunch he is as important as the Craight woman. Perhaps more so.

A *hunch*? The Dead Man? That flabby-lump of pure reason? It couldn't be.

Dean came in. "We couldn't find anything, Mr. Garrett."

"Keep looking. There's got to be something."

Not necessarily, Garrett. All there needs be is the perception that there is something.

I'd thought that myself but I didn't like it. "She set us up as a diversion?"

There is that possibility. It gains weight if we presume Magister Peridont told her something that would be of interest to those who are plaguing us.

"I just might break both her kneecaps next time I see her." I could see her siccing those guys on us in hopes they'd get into it with the Dead Man. It was the kind of stunt I might have tried if I wanted somebody off my back.

A troop of the Watch is coming, Garrett. You would be wise to absent yourself now. I will deal with them. Bring me that woman.

I ducked out the back way, leaving Dean to bolt up behind me, mumbling and grumbling and secretly pleased to be close to the heart of things.

Maya stuck with me again. There was no arguing her into going back to the Doom.

"At least let them know you're alive and healthy. I don't want Tey Koto ambushing me because she thinks I've trifled with you."

She burst out laughing. I guess I would have, too, if somebody had tossed "trifle" at me. "You're too much, Garrett. How can somebody in your business have so many little blind spots and naïvetés?"

It was a question you would expect from someone beyond her age. But the young aren't stupid and sometimes they're more perceptive than us old cynics with our arsenals of preconceptions. I told her the truth.

"I nurture them. There are poetic truths as well as scientific truths. They maybe look silly to you, but I think they deserve to be sustained."

She laughed but there was no mockery in it, just pleasure. "Good for you, Garrett. Now you know why I love you. Inconsistencies and all."

The little witch sure knew how to rattle a guy.

42

Back about a thousand years ago the other evening, Morley had made a crack about how I might be better off if everybody thought I was dead. I didn't know how to make that look believable, but I figured I could do the next best thing and disappear. Wedge and my angels had taken off. Though the neighborhood was in a state of ferment, with what looked like the whole damned population of TunFaire in the streets wanting to know what had happened, I didn't think anybody else would be watching. It seemed the right time to get lost.

"Where can we go?" Maya asked.

"Good question." There had to be somewhere nobody would think to look, someplace we could get in and out of without anybody noticing. Someplace we could live awhile without the regular business of life giving us away. I couldn't think of anywhere perfect, though I had a few morally indebted ex-clients who might put me up.

Maya asked, "How about that apartment across from Hester's? She's gone and everybody's sacked her place, so nobody ought to be interested in the building. And you know that squeenky little guy isn't going to come back."

"Squeenky?"

"Yeah. You know. Dorky and creepy at the same time."

She was right. The place was as decent a hideout as we were likely to find. We headed over there. We had no more trouble getting inside than we'd had before. It must be nice having the kingpin holding an umbrella over your head.

Sometimes. Hadn't done me that much good, had it?

We barely got inside before Maya started grumbling. "I'm hungry."

"I saw some stuff in the kitchen when I tossed the place."

The apartment hadn't been set up for living. The stores consisted mostly of stuff that couldn't be put together into a decent meal. As we did our best, I asked, "Why didn't you have Dean feed you before you left?"

"Why didn't you?"

"Point. I had too much on my mind." I stirred some goop and wondered why Dean hadn't been able to find anything Jill had left. The note she had left here indicated that what the Sons of Hammon wanted was safe. There would be no safer place than with the Dead Man, so I couldn't see her taking it out of the house.

I wondered how she'd planned to collect it later if that had been her plan. I wondered what the hell it was. The missing Terrell Relics Peridont had wanted me to find? Possibly. But it didn't seem likely the Relics would get a heretical cult so excited they'd risk destruction to glom them.

Once again I was back to a need for research. Thanks to Dean and the Dead Man I knew what the cult was and what it wanted, but that information was pretty spare. I had to know more about what they believed and why they believed it. A lot more.

Though if I could lay hands on Jill, that might not be necessary.

"Look, I found some wine," Maya said. She seemed pleased, so I was pleased for her, but the discovery didn't excite me.

"Good. Put it on the table." I went on thinking, about the kingpin. His people had been quiet for a while; probably lying low until the outrage died down. It would. It always does in TunFaire. Who could stay exercised about the deaths of a bunch of weird strangers?

The wine wasn't bad as wines go. Whoever laid in the stock had expensive tastes. It helped the rest of an absurd meal go down with less difficulty.

I said, "Dean's gotten me spoiled. I'm getting so I expect decent food all the time."

"We could eat out."

I gave her a sharp look. She was teasing. But she added, "You promised."

I did? That's not the way I remembered it. "Maybe after this is over. If you can stand getting fixed up." It had been a while since Dean's niece had worked her over. She'd begun to look a little ragged. But hadn't I, too? "I'm shot. I've got to get some sleep. We'll hit the Tenderloin again after breakfast."

I carried a lamp around to check the possibilities. I could make do in the parlor. I made sure the windows were covered so nobody would see a light moving around, then took my shoes off and started arranging a place to lie down. Suddenly I had about as much energy as a vampire at high noon.

Maya came in. "You take the bed, Garrett. I can sleep in here."

Old Noble said, "No. I'll be fine here."

"Garrett, you need the comfort more than I do."

Oh boy, here came the old-timer routine. "I don't play polite games, Maya. Somebody makes me an offer, I only give them one chance to back down, then I take them up on it."

"Don't get yourself in an uproar. I meant it. You're a lot more tired than I am. And I'm used to sleeping on floors and sidewalks. This is luxury for me." But there was the ghost of something like a twinkle in her eyes, like she was up to something.

"You asked for it, you got it." I headed for the bedroom. Maybe it was just because I was so damned tired, but I couldn't fathom what she had in mind.

I found out about six hours later.

I usually sleep in the raw. In deference to the fact that somebody might walk in, I sacked out wearing my underclothes. I lay there tossing and turning, worrying the case, for maybe seven seconds before I passed out. Next thing I knew I wasn't alone. And the someone with me was very warm, very naked, and very female. And very determined. And I sure don't have much willpower.

There are limits to the nobility of even the best of us good guys. When she turned on the heat, Maya didn't have any trouble getting past mine.

It turned out to be one truly amazing morning.

had Maya slicked down and spiffed up in some clothes I'd swiped from Jill's apartment. I swear, the girl grew more beautiful by the minute—the woman, I should say. There was no doubt about that now. What she lacked in experience she made up for in enthusiasm.

I helped her with her hair and with a touch of makeup. She was going to need grooming lessons. When she got a hold on that she'd be deadly.

"I hate to do it, but I'm going to have to destroy the whole effect," I told her after I showed her herself in a mirror. "I can't take you outside looking like that."

"Why not?" She liked what she saw, too.

"Because you'd attract too damned much attention. Come here." When I finished she didn't look like Maya at all. "Pity we can't do as much for me."

"Do we *really* need to disguise ourselves?"

"Probably not. But there are people out there who want to kill us. It can't hurt. And we can't be hurt if nobody can find us." I didn't have the means to change my own appearance much. I thought about Pokey Pigotta and some of the tricks he'd used, like putting a rock in his shoe, walking stoop-shouldered, carrying a couple different hats and changing them randomly, and so forth. The hat trick I could do. There were several in the walk-in here. And everybody who knew me knew I'd wear a hat only when I had to to keep from freezing my ears off.

I picked the most absurd topper, one people who knew me knew I wouldn't wear at swordpoint. "How do I look?"

"Like a buzzard nested on your head."

It did look a bit like a tricornered haystack. I'm glad sartorial display is a vice confined to the better classes. I'd hate to try to keep up with fashion.

There were a few odds and ends of clothing, too, but all for a man so much shorter there was no using them for anything. So I had Maya use touches of lampblack to give my cheeks and eyes a hollow look, practiced a stoop and slight limp, asked, "You ready?"

"Whenever you are." She gave it a double meaning. The child seemed happier than ever I'd seen before.

You devil, Garrett. How do you get into these things?

You give in to yourself and you undertake a contract no matter how casual the collision. This was more than casual because this was somebody I cared about, independent of the body that had moved with mine. . . .

Damn it, sex *always* complicates things.

We hit the street looking like poor folks. Like almost everybody else out there. I did my limp and stoop to perfection, I thought, and invented a history to explain it if anybody asked. I had been wounded at Yellow Dog Mesa. Nobody asked what you did in the war. The fact that you'd gotten out alive was commentary enough.

I wondered what Glory Mooncalled was doing. There had been no talk for days. That meant nothing, of course. That's the way war works. Long periods of inaction sandwich brief, intense periods of combat. But I had a feeling something interesting would happen soon. I wondered how the Dead Man was dealing with the bureaucratic siege. If he was as impatient with them as he was with me, they were going to regret bothering him.

We stopped at a third-rate place and ate, then ambled down to the Tenderloin. It was noon when we got there. The noon hour is one of the district's secondary peaks. Those who can't get away in the evening escape work for an hour to appease their hungers. Maya and I planted ourselves on the same bench we'd used before to watch the players parade. The day people were more furtive than those at night. Quite a few made some effort to disguise themselves. Once again I spent some time pondering the curiosities of human nature. What a species.

"I think we're some kind of practical joke on the part of the gods," I told Maya.

She laughed. She understood without me having to explain. I liked that. In fact, I was beginning to like a lot of things about her, in ways I hadn't when she'd been a charitable project.

She sensed that, too. She touched my hand and gave me a big "I told you so" smile.

Whoa! This wasn't going my way at all. I didn't even understand it. Garrett doesn't get involved. He makes friends and leaves them smiling. But he doesn't get caught up inside any commitment.

Damn it, this was a raggedy-ass kid I'd saved from abuse and exploitation. This was a project. . . .

I smiled at myself. You have to do that when you're wriggling on a hook of your own device.

I watched the barker across the way. "I think we have a small problem."

"What?"

"I need to talk to that guy. I can't without letting him know it's me. And that cancels out my disappearance."

"You must be getting senile, Garrett. You just tell him Chodo says forget he ever talked to you. He'll forget."

She was right. The man would chomp down on what he knew until somebody twisted him good. Nobody ought to have a reason. "You're right. I am getting senile."

"Or maybe you're just worn out. You did real good for an old guy."

I spat into the gutter. It's a wonder I didn't hit my mind. "You just aren't used to a real man."

"Maybe." There was a sort of soft purr in her voice. "You want me to go tell him you want to see him?"

"Sure."

I kept one eye on the place we'd visited last night. One old guy came out. Nobody went inside. I was surprised there wasn't more traffic. It seemed the kind of place that would appeal to the crowd that came down during the day. I still thought the guy who came up with the idea was a genius. We all need somebody to talk to. I did myself.

I sort of spread it out among Dean, the Dead Man, Tinnie, and Playmate, maybe opening up more to Playmate than the others because I have no relationship with him other than friendship. And there are things I don't feel comfortable telling him because I value his good opinion.

Maya sat back down. "He'll be here in a minute. At first he didn't believe it was you."

"But you convinced him."

"I can be pretty convincing."

"No lie." I hadn't stood a chance once she went to work on me seriously. But that's my weak spot.

The barker settled beside me a few minutes later. He leaned forward to look into my face. "It is you."

"Last I looked. What's happening is, I've disappeared. Maybe run out of town. You aren't seeing me. You're seeing some guy who came down here to gawk."

He lifted an eyebrow. Damn, I hate it when people steal my tricks.

"It's getting tight. The organization is under pressure. Some of us are turning invisible till we make it ease up."

"What's going on, anyways? Tied up here, all I hear is crazy rumors."

"You haven't heard anything as crazy as the truth." I told him some of that, including a few details of the attack on Chodo's place. He didn't want to believe me, but the story was so outrageous he accepted it.

"That's weird," he said. "They must be really sick. I'm ready to help. We all are down here. But I don't see what I can do."

"Near as we can figure, there are two people who know what we need to put this mess away. One is the woman I was asking about. I can't give you a name because she uses about a hundred, but I'm pretty sure she's working that place over there."

He looked at it and sneered. "Doyle's wimp house. All that gorgeous pussy and half of them don't put out. You figure it, paying just to look."

"Takes all kinds to make a horserace. If people weren't strange, you and I wouldn't be in business."

"You got a point. What do you need to know?"

"Have you seen an outstanding blonde in and out of that place?"

"Several of them. You're going to have to be more specific."

I couldn't be. Jill Craight, for all her looks, had had a sort of nebulous quality, like she really was a whole gang of people, each one a little different from the others. "Forget her. I'll assume she's working that place. I'll get to her if she is. I'll just sit here till I spot her. How about that guy I came charging out after last night? When you didn't have time to talk?"

"What guy was that? I was pretty busy."

"Maya, you describe him. You got a better look."

"Not that good. He was short, kind of chunky, had a big nose that looked like it got broken once. His skin was kind of dark. He was bald but you couldn't tell that if he was wearing a hat. He was dressed in real dark clothes both times. Kind of sloppy, even though the clothes were good ones. Like he wasn't used to wearing them." And so on. And so on. I wished I had an eye as quick and sharp.

The barker said, "Come to think of it, I did see a guy like that before you came roaring up. Only reason I noticed was he was headed out like a demon was chewing his ass."

"So?"

"So that's all I can tell you. He lit out."

That was what I'd expected to hear. "Did you recognize him?"

"You mean, do I know who he is? No. But I've seen him around. Hits the Tenderloin every four, five days. Used to come in for the shows. He's mostly dropped that and the joyhouses since Doyle come up with his silly talk house."

"Don't seem so silly when you think about it."

"No. Guess not. The old fart is cleaning up. I tell you, I'll never understand the freaks that come down here."

I thought he understood them all too well, but I didn't say so. If guys like him didn't understand, they wouldn't be successful catering to people who needed the comforts of a Tenderloin.

I shrugged. "I guess that's that. I don't know what else I could ask."

The barker got up. "Always glad to help the kingpin. Hey. For what it's worth, the little bald gink with the big honker, I think he's some kind of high-powered priest."

Maybe I jumped. Maybe something below conscious level was excited. "You sure?"

"No. It's just the way he snuck around and at the same time acted like people ought to bend the knee. I seen other priests act that way. Don't want to be seen. But the bigger they are, the worse habit they have of expecting special treatment. Get what I mean?"

"Yeah. Thanks. I'll mention how you helped. Maybe a bonus will come tumbling down."

"I could use it."

"Couldn't we all?" I watched him cross to his post. "A priest," I muttered. "Another big-time priest, maybe. With a place in the same building where Jill was shacking up with Magister Peridont. That sound any alarms?"

Maya said, "It doesn't sound like a coincidence. You think it's important?"

I hadn't told her everything about Peridont. I decided to trust her now. I laid it out from the beginning.

She didn't speak for a while. When she did, she said, "I know what you're thinking. It's too outrageous."

"You're probably right. But . . . things tend to tie together. Even when they're outrageous. And the first time Peridont visited me, he wanted me to find Warden Agire and the Terrell Relics."

"Pure speculation, Garrett. Gossamer. Almost whimsy."

"Maybe. We could sink it quick with a description of the Warden that doesn't match that guy."

She nodded.

"Let me run with it. Tell me where the holes are."

"All right."

"Jill Craight works over there, listening to sad tales of woe. She's a little greedy so sometimes she meets her clients outside, when she's off duty. Maybe she's not completely honest and tries to find out who they are. Maybe it just comes to her by accident. But she finds out she has both the Grand Inquisitor and the Warden among her regulars. Maybe she gets an idea she can make a big hit. Maybe she gets idealistic.

"Whatever, she gets some kind of underground dialogue going. Maybe they're actually working something out. Then the Sons of Hammon hit town. They're after the Relics for some reason. Agire goes on the lam. He slips the Relics to Jill to take care of while he leads the baddies somewhere else. Peridont doesn't know what's going on, he only knows that Agire and the Relics have disappeared.

"Meantime, Peridont makes a connection with Jill and finds out what's up with Agire and the Relics. So he doesn't bother bringing that up anymore. Now he wants to find out more about the Sons, only he doesn't tell me that. Being a typical client, he knows what he gives me to work with will give away something about him, so he wants to send me out blind and let me thrash around till I kick up something he can use.

"After that, because he wants to cover his ass and because he's got Church politics to deal with, things go from bad to worse. When he finally decides he's in so deep he's got to come clean (so I can dig him out), he gets ambushed as he's coming to see me. I'm not convinced the man who killed him was one of the Sons of Hammon."

It was about the longest continuous speech I've ever made, just sort of blurting out and not stopping. When I did turn myself off, Maya didn't say anything. Maybe she needed a little coaxing.

"Well? What do you think?"

"I think you're trying it out on the wrong person. I can't knock a hole in it. You should lay it out for the Dead Man. He'd tell you why it couldn't be that way."

"You don't think it was?"

"I don't want it to be. And don't ask me why. It's just an emotional thing. Actually, I'm scared you're right."

Why should that scare her? Because it might come out and give the scandal hunters a boost?

Intellectually I saw danger. The Sons of Hammon going public with an ascetic lifestyle and a god who really talked at a time when the two major Hanite denominations could be shown to be conniving and powerless and riddled with corruption . . .

No. The people of TunFaire wouldn't go for something as crazy as the Hammon cult right now.

They hadn't chosen their time well. They should have waited for the war's end. Come into the city with any kind of a crazy promise then and I'd bet money, marbles, or chalk dust you could win battalions of converts. I thought about that for a long time. I conjured me a grim future, decided me and the Dead Man would have to have a serious discussion about how to make things easier on ourselves. Maybe I'd have to take up Weider's offer of a job as chief head thumper at the brewery. The brewery business prospers in hard times.

Maya just snuggled up and purred. For all I could tell there was nothing going on inside her head. Time drifted away.

I had a thought, which happens occasionally. "Think Jill would recognize you if she passed you in the street?"

"No."

"I think we ought to spread out, then. I can't fool her. She sees me, she's going to hightail it."

"You really think so?"

"I think she'll panic. I think she's gotten so far into this changing names that she thinks all she has to do to disappear is call herself something else. If somebody turns up that knows her some other way, she'll lose her confidence and overreact. It won't matter who she spots."

Maya frowned and gave me a searching look. "I don't know. But you're more an expert on people than I am."

I snorted. Me an expert? I can't even figure me out, let alone the rest of the world.

44

Part of my job is to remain patient. I probably do more waiting than anybody but a soldier. It ought to be second nature after five years in the Marines and all those since in this investigation racket. But I never was very good at sitting still, especially in the cold.

I needed to get up and prowl. That would make me easier to spot but my aching butt and stiffening muscles wouldn't listen to common sense.

I told Maya, "I'm going to stroll around the block and see how many ways there are to get out of that building."

"What if she decides to come out when you're gone?"

"There isn't much chance of that. Won't take me three minutes."

"You're the expert."

The way she kept saying that made it sound like she had some doubts.

I walked away, forgetting my act for a dozen steps because I was conscious of her questioning look.

I didn't find out anything that I hadn't reasoned out sitting with Maya. There was a back way out, down an outside stair into an alley behind the place. That had to be there because we'd seen no access to the second floor while we'd been inside. Hell.

Well, I got the kinks out, anyway.

I headed for the bench and my girl.

What girl? Maya was gone.

I gaped like a cretin for maybe fifteen seconds, then looked around, jumping to see over the heads of the crowd. There was no sign of Maya. I scuttled over to my friend the lanky barker. "You see what happened to the gal I was with? Over on the bench?"

He sneered a sneer that questioned my competence.

"Yeah, man. This time I caught the action. Your blond fluff came galloping past right after you left. Your twitch took off after her. They went that way." He pointed uphill, which meant back toward the heart of the city, whence we had come, and whence most everyone else came, too.

"The blonde was in a hurry?"

"Running. My guess is, she'd made you and was waiting for a chance to run."

"Thanks." I took off, ignoring the curses of those I jostled. I wondered how Jill could have recognized us from over there. . . .

Damnation! How dumb can a guy be? She probably didn't recognize us at all. But she sure as hell could've recognized the clothes Maya had borrowed.

How come we never thought of that when we were being so clever about changing who we were?

I kicked up the pace as the people thinned out. Once I was out of the Tenderloin I couldn't do anything but guess which way Jill was headed.

I saw nothing.

I wondered why I bothered. I wondered if Maya would hang on. I wondered what Jill would do if she couldn't shake Maya. I wondered how Maya would get in touch if she did run Jill to ground.

I looked down cross streets as I passed them. I questioned street-side vendors. Some told me to get the hell away from them. Some just looked blank. Here, there, one gave me a straight answer. One of those actually had noticed Jill.

She was still headed toward the heart of town.

I wasn't going to get much cooperation just being Garrett. So I swallowed my pride and started alluding to Chodo Contague. That kicked the level of cooperation up a few notches. A man with a sausage cart on a corner needs the goodwill of the kingpin. Else somebody's liable to put him out of business.

That kept me on the trail until I got out of the area where there was anyone to ask, by which time Jill's course had shifted southward.

I wished I knew more about her. Where could she run? But I'd had no time to research her. In any of her guises, let alone all of them. More than ever I felt that things were moving too fast.

I'm a plodder. I get to the end of the trail through sheer stubbornness, just keeping on until I get there, doing what I have to do. I hadn't had a minute to catch my breath since Jill first turned up on my doorstep.

When you're moving like that sometimes you don't have time to think. Your mind works on things out of sight and you come up with hunches. Three minutes after Jill's trail turned southward I had one.

She was headed for the Dream Quarter.

She did have that one resource. That little gink who used the apartment across from the one Peridont provided. If he was who I thought he was . . . But Warden Agire had disappeared. I'd heard nothing about him turning up again. But I'd been too busy to stay in touch with that situation.

"Bet the long odds," I told myself. I adjusted my course and increased my pace. Ten minutes later I got to Playmate's stable.

He was about to close his main gate. But he brightened like a rising sun when he saw me. He always does. He is the one grateful former client I can count on anytime. "Garrett. Been wondering about you. Where've you been?"

"Working. I've got a real mind-twister going. You been keeping up with the scandals?"

"Not much to keep up with lately. Too much other excitement. That your place where the demon turned up last night?"

"Yes. Part of what I'm working on."

"You're playing with fire this time, then."

"The hottest. You don't know the half. I'll tell you about it sometime."

"In a hurry?"

"Aren't I always?"

"Usually. What do you need?"

"A horse so I can make up some time on somebody I'm chasing. And some info. The horse shouldn't be one of your damned Lightnings or Firebrands, either. I want one that will run but won't play games." Horses and I don't get along. I don't know why but the whole damned tribe is out to get me. They think it's great fun making my life miserable.

"You always say that. I can't figure a guy your age being scared of horses. But since you are I picked up a nag so docile and stupid even you'll be satisfied."

Grumble grumble. He led me into the stable. While we walked I asked, "You heard anything about Warden Agire and the Terrell Relics?"

"Funny you should ask. Agire turned up last night. Minus the Relics."

"Ha!" I'd guessed right, more or less. But there wasn't time to congratulate myself. I had to move. "I need the beast fast. I have to get to the Dream Quarter before somebody who's already way ahead of me."

Playmate threw a saddle blanket on a monster that didn't look docile to me. There were moments when he surrendered to a nasty sense of humor. This was no time for that. I jumped him as he started cinching the saddle.

"No joke, Garrett. The animal is a pussycat."

"Yeah?" I didn't like the way it looked at me, like it had heard of me and was determined to make a liar out of Playmate.

I have that kind of trouble with women, too, and have never understood it.

"Here we go."

"Thanks." I grabbed the horse by the bridle and looked it in the eye. "I got work to do. I don't got time to mess around. You want to play games, just remember that around here you're never more than a couple miles from the glue works."

It just looked back at me. I went around and mounted up. In a moment I was pounding through the streets. People cussed me. Some threw things. What I was doing was against the law because it was so damned dangerous. But there was no one to stop me. I had several narrow misses. The horse slipped and slid on sections that were cobbled, and a couple times I thought we were going down. As we neared the Dream Quarter I began to feel foolish. I was ready to bet that I'd outguessed myself and was going to find nothing.

Wrong. They were there. I spotted Jill first, from three blocks away, passing Chattaree, blond hair flying. She was in a sprint for the Orthodox complex. Maya was right behind her and looked like she'd decided to catch her. Jill glanced over her shoulder. She didn't see me.

I booted the horse into an all-out gallop.

A gallop wasn't good enough. Jill reached the gates. Ordinarily those were open and unguarded, but not today and not since the scandals had begun. Jill spoke to the guards, glanced at Maya, then spotted me.

Maya reached Jill when I was still a block away.

The guards grabbed both women, flung them inside, and closed up.

I reined in outside. Though I could make out no specific words, I heard the women and a man arguing inside the gatehouse. The gate the women had gone through was a small pedestrian entrance now shut. I eyed those steel bars, then the coach gate beside it. A guard looked at me nervously. He was unarmed but determined. I didn't have to talk to him to know he wasn't going to let me in or, probably, even answer me.

I wasn't exactly heavily armed, either. I had a couple of knives and my head knocker tucked away, but nothing I could intimidate anyone with while they were on that side of the gate and I was on the street side.

The coach gate wasn't quite five feet high in the middle.

Maya let out a squeal. Three men dragged her out of the gatehouse, headed toward the center of the grounds, which was concealed behind vegetation. Jill walked along with them. She glanced back, eyes huge, looking almost apologetic.

All right. That did it.

I backed my horse away, took him across the street, faced the gate, and kicked him into a gallop. He ought to clear that gate easily.

Let's just say he wasn't a jumper.

He skidded to a stop. I yelled as I went over his head, crashed into the gate, and fell on my face. About ten guys lined up inside. They had no weapons but they weren't going to let me in without somebody getting hurt. I was hurt enough already—especially my pride.

I peeled myself off the cobblestone. Still on hands and knees, I looked at that damned horse. I tell you, he was grinning. He'd scored big for his tribe in its old war against Garrett. "You've had it, beast." I stumbled to my feet, limped toward him. He ambled away, moving just fast enough to stay ahead of me.

The guys behind the gate had a lot of fun at my expense. They were going to be real unhappy because they'd done that.

A kindly passerby took pity and held the horse until I could take charge. I walked the son of a bitch back to Playmate's.

Playmate—my old buddy—took the damned horse's side. "Every animal has its limitations, Garrett. A jumper has to be trained. You don't just climb on a horse and tell it to take a leap."

"Damn it, I understand that. I placed my bet and took my chances. I lost. I accept that." Like hell. "What I'm griping about is the way he laughed at me afterward. He did it on purpose."

"Garrett, you got an obsession. You're always complaining about how horses are out to get you. They're just dumb beasts. They can't be out to get anybody."

Shows you how much he knew. "Don't tell me. Tell them." They sure had him fooled.

"What happened? Eh? You'd be laughing about the whole thing if something else hadn't gone wrong."

So I told him how Maya had gotten herself grabbed and the reason I tried the jump was that I wanted to get her loose.

"You going to try again?"

"Damned straight, I am. And it's not going to be any nice guy going in after her, either. I'm out of patience with these superstitionmongers."

He gave me a little of my own raised eyebrow. "Girl means enough to get you upset, eh? What about Tinnie?"

"Tinnie is Tinnie. Leave her out of it. She isn't part of this."

"If you say so. Need some help?"

He meant it. And if it came to a slugfest he might be handy, being nine feet tall and strong enough to lift the horses he tended. But he wasn't a fighter by nature. He'd get himself hurt because he was too damned kindly. "You stay out of it. You did enough, letting me use that four-legged snake. Sell the damned thing for dog food."

Playmate laughed. He gets a kick out of my feud with the equine species. "Sure you don't want some help?"

"No. You do what you do best. I need a hand I'll get somebody who does it for a living." I'd shot hell out of my disappearing act. "You really want to do something, go by the house and see how Dean and the Dead Man are doing. I'll get back with you in the morning." If I was alive in the morning.

"Sure, Garrett."

I knew what I was going to do next. I was going to make a lot of people unhappy. I'd be the unhappiest of all if I got caught.

45

Crask was staked out at a table in Morley's place, alone. He looked like he'd been there a long time. He didn't look happy. I didn't spot him until I was halfway to the serving counter. Then it was too late to duck out.

He summoned me with a gesture. I held my temper, joined him. From the corner of my eye I saw Slade talk into the speaking tube connecting with Morley's office. "What you need?"

"Chodo's getting impatient for results."

I gave him a blank look. "I missed something. The way I hear, he's getting results right and left. The city ratmen are working overtime picking up the bodies."

"Don't get wise, Garrett. He owes you but that don't mean he's gonna let you mess him around."

"Crask, I'm farther at sea every time you say something. How could I mess him around?"

"You were supposed to catch a broad for him. Where is she?"

I looked over my shoulder, back to Crask. "Me? Catch somebody for him? I don't remember it that way. What I heard was we were going to join forces, let each other know what we knew. And that's the way I'm playing it."

"Chodo Contague ain't a guy you want mad at you, Garrett."

I agreed. "You're right. He isn't. But he isn't a guy I want trying to run me, either. The deal I made is the only deal. Exactly the way it was worded. No hidden meanings. Understand?"

Crask rose. "I'll tell him. I don't think he's going to be pleased."

"I don't care if he's pleased. Far as I'm concerned I stuck to my half of the bargain."

He gave me an evil look. I knew what he was thinking. Someday he was going to pull my toes off one at a time.

"One more thing. Everywhere I go I get this load of crap from people who think I work for Chodo. I don't. I work for Garrett. If somebody is putting it out that I'm on the kingpin's payroll, tell them to stop. I don't work for him. And I won't."

He sneered, sort of, which is the most emotion I'd ever seen him show. He stalked out.

I headed for the bar. My hands were shaking. That damned Crask really put the hoodoo on me. He came on like a natural force, distilled menace and intimidation.

Slade said, "Morley says come straight up."

I went. Morley wasn't alone but both he and his guest had their clothes on, which was all I could ask, I guess. The woman was the same one I'd seen before—record setter. I'd never seen him with the same one twice. Maybe he was settling down.

"Had a run-in with Crask?"

"Sort of. Chodo's working on me. Trying to recruit me through the back door. Crask is irritated because I won't cooperate."

"Heard you had some excitement at your place last night."

"Some. The Dead Man took care of it."

"Remind me not to get on his bad side. What's up?"

"I need somebody to cover my back on a break-and-enter gig. Targets aren't going to be easy. People won't be understanding if we get caught."

He frowned. "Sensitive?"

"Like a ripe boil. One wrong word in the wrong place afterward could get a bunch of people killed."

"Right. I know the man to give you a hand. Wait downstairs. I'll take you to him myself."

Good. He had the idea. Don't let the woman know any more than she'd heard already.

Though I'd be the engineer on this, I'd still have to be careful. Morley would volunteer himself. Once he found out what I intended he'd get real nervous. If *he* was to pull a stunt like this he'd get rid of his backup man afterward, just to make sure nobody ever found out, even twenty years down the line. Though he tried to understand me he still didn't really believe, in his heart, that I didn't secretly think the way he did. He might get so jumpy we'd have a problem.

He came downstairs as I was draining a brandy Slade had slipped me. Slade was one employee of Morley's who wasn't devoted to the vegetable cause. He kept the real stuff hidden out handy. Morley pretended he didn't smell it. "Let's hit the street. Not so many ears out there."

We went out. Before he asked, I said, "I'm going into Chattaree. I want to break into Peridont's office."

Morley grunted. He was impressed. "You have a good reason?"

"Somebody grabbed Maya again. To have a shot at getting her loose I have to steal something from Peridont's office."

Providing the Church guys hadn't messed everything up there, now the Grand Inquisitor had gone to his guaranteed reward. I couldn't see that Sampson character not trying to move in.

Morley walked half a block with me before he said, "Tell me straight. Not with your heart. Can it be done?"

"I was in there the other day. There isn't any internal security. They flat don't expect anything. They don't think they have reason to expect anything. I'm not worried about doing the job." Liar. "I'm worried about pulling it without anybody finding out who did it. I don't want every member of the Church after me for the rest of my life."

"You're up to something."

"I told you that."

"No. I know you, Garrett. You're not just going to steal something. You're going to make it look like something it isn't."

If I could. I didn't deny that. I didn't agree, either. I had some ideas. Maybe they'd work out, maybe they wouldn't. The way my life was going they wouldn't. Morley didn't need to know what those ideas were.

"You play them too damned close to your chest, Garrett. What's the other target?"

I shook my head, which he couldn't see in the dark, so I said, "We don't worry about that till we've handled the first one. If I don't get what I need from Peridont's office, I can't make another move anyway."

"Too close to your chest, Garrett."

"Did you let me in on anything that time we ended up going after those vampires?"

"That was different."

"Sure it was. It was you moving me like a pawn without ever telling me you were doing it. You in or not?"

"Why not? You're a pretty dull guy yourself but interesting things happen where you're at. And I've never been inside Chattaree. They say it's magnificent."

He'd never been in because his kind were banned. According to Church doctrine he had no soul despite having human blood which was not a smart stance in a world where nonhuman races added up to half the total sentient population. And the Church didn't talk it up much here in TunFaire, where so many would be quick to take offense.

"Yeah," Morley said, evidently thinking about that. "I'd like to get into Chattaree for a while."

"Let's don't go grinding any axes."

"Right." We walked away, toward the Dream Quarter. Then he said, "You're taken with that Maya gal, aren't you?"

"She's a nice kid. She got herself in trouble because of hanging around with me. I owe her."

"Got you."

I glanced at him. He was grinning.

"She's just a kid I know, Morley."

The trouble with Morley is, he does understand.

'd been hustling so much lately the weather had had little chance to gain my attention. Sitting in a deep shadow opposite Chattaree, watching, getting a feel for the night, it got plenty of opportunity.

"Damned cold," I muttered.

Morley glanced up. It was too dark to tell anything except that there were no stars out. "Might snow."

"That's all we need."

There'd been something going on at Chattaree when we arrived, just breaking up. It was a holy day but I couldn't remember which one. Morley didn't know. He didn't keep track of human superstitions.

I asked, "Think we've waited long enough?" We'd given them an hour to settle down inside.

"Give it a while yet." He wasn't comfortable with the adventure anymore. He was trying to recall if anyone had invaded the temple recently. I'd never heard of anybody trying. People in there ought to be lax. But Morley suspected safeguards that fixed it so invaders were not heard from again.

I said, "Any guy who can go into a vampire nest shouldn't have problems with this."

He snorted. "That was do or die."

We gave it fifteen minutes. Morley stared at Chattaree with obsessive concentration. I wondered if he was mongoose or cobra. His night vision was better than mine. If there was anything to see he'd see it.

"Give me the layout again," he said. I did. He said, "Let's do it."

It was a good time. There was no one in sight. But I found myself reluctant to go. I went anyway.

I was puffing when we reached the temple door. Morley looked at me and shook his head. He raised an eyebrow, barely discernible in wan light from inside the temple. Ready? I nodded.

He walked through the doorway. I ducked out of sight.

"Hey! Where the hell you going?"

I peeked. Morley had darted past the guard, who *was* awake. I wondered if that was a common occurrence. Morley turned to face the man, who was as wide as he was tall.

I wound up two-handed and stepped into it, whacking him behind the ear with my stick. He went down.

I let out a big breath. "I didn't think I could put him down."

"I worried, too, the way you've let yourself go."

"Let's get him put away."

We used materials at hand, bound and gagged the guy and tucked him out of sight inside his post. Hopefully anybody who came by would figure he'd gone AWOL.

I led the way. We'd chosen our time well. They'd closed up shop except for one sleeping priest at the main altar. Passing through in the far shadows we didn't disturb his slumber. Morley made less noise than a tiptoeing roach. I found the stairway descending into the catacombs.

"We have a problem," I whispered, halfway down. It was tomb-dark. We hadn't brought a light. I didn't think I could negotiate the maze without one.

"I'll go steal a candle," Morley said.

He could be a ghost when he wanted. He went right up to the main altar and lifted a votive candle. The priest on duty never missed a snore.

He came back grinning. He'd been showing off. He hadn't had to snatch a light from disaster's jaws.

We descended into the catacombs. They seemed more claustrophobic than on my previous visit. A dwarf would have felt at home, but humans weren't made to inhabit mole holes. I worked up a bad case of the creeps.

Morley did, too. He didn't have anything to say, just tagged along quietly, so alert you could smell it.

The old memory was cooking. I made only one false turn and corrected that before I'd gone a step. I marched right up to Peridont's door.

"This place gives me the creeps," Morley whispered.

"Me, too." It was as quiet as a grave in there. I would have been happier if there'd been some guy howling down the way. Thinking just made the creeps worse.

The door was locked but the lock was of ancient vintage. It didn't take me half a minute to open it. We stepped inside.

The room was unchanged, though there was more litter on the big table. I told Morley, "Light a couple of lamps."

"Hurry," he suggested.

"It shouldn't take long." I moved to the cabinet from which Peridont had taken the bottles he'd given me. Morley fired up a couple of lamps and posted himself beside the door.

The cabinet doors weren't latched, let alone locked. Sometimes you have to wonder about people. I mean, the stuff stored there was as dangerous as you could get, yet it was just sitting there waiting to be taken. Just because you don't want to think somebody would rob you doesn't mean you shouldn't take precautions.

I used the votive candle for light. I saw green and blue and red bottles (only one of the latter), plus lemon, orange, amber, indigo, turquoise, lime, and clear, and one that looked like bottled silver dust.

The temptation was to take the lot, a fortune in useful tricks. But I had no idea what would happen if an unfamiliar bottle was used. You don't mess with the unknown when you're dealing with sorcery. Not if you want to stay healthy.

I wasn't shy about grabbing all the green and blue bottles. I dithered over the red one, then recalled how effective it had been at Chodo's. I might run into that ape again. I pocketed the bottle, but this time with more respect. I padded it with cotton I found on the bottom shelf of the cabinet.

"What're you doing?" Morley asked.

The look in his eye said he had a damned good idea. And he'd love to lay hands on some of those bottles. "Putting tricks up my sleeve. I don't know what these others will do so I'm not taking them."

"You done? We ought to get while our luck's holding."

He was right. I checked the cabinet, closed it up. It wasn't obviously disturbed. Let them go crazy wondering why somebody bopped the guard. "Done. Let's . . ."

"Damn!" Morley jerked a thumb at the door.

He'd left it cracked so he could listen for footsteps. I heard nothing but that meant nothing. Someone was coming. Wavering light shone through the crack.

I jumped, extinguished the lamps, blew out the candle, and ducked under the table as the door swung inward.

It was that creepy Sampson. He held a lantern up and glared around. Morley stood behind the door, ready to cut him down if he came inside. Sampson sniffed, frowned, finally shrugged and backed out, shutting the door behind him.

I slithered through the darkness, listening but hearing nothing. The light leaking under the door weakened, presumably because Sampson was moving away. He'd pulled the door all the way shut but he hadn't locked it. I was surprised he hadn't been more suspicious, finding it unlocked and ajar.

I opened up slowly so I'd make no sound, then put my eye to the crack. Sampson was twenty feet away, his back to me, about to turn a corner. He scratched his head, a man who had a feeling something was wrong but who couldn't put his finger on it. He might any minute. "You ready?" I breathed at Morley.

He didn't reply.

Sampson shrugged again and moved on out of sight.

"Come on. Let's get while we can." I hoped I could manage without a light. I had no way to get the candle going again.

Again Morley didn't answer. I heard the faintest sound, like a fairy's wing beat. It didn't come from where Morley was, though in the dark sounds are confusing.

I spoke a little louder. "Let's go! He knows there's something wrong. He just hasn't figured it out yet."

"Right." He was there after all.

I opened the door, slipped out, extended my hand to the wall, walked slowly. "You behind me?"

"Yes."

"Close the door tight."

"I did."

That Sampson had to be an insomniac or something. We'd lucked out getting in without bumping into him. We almost ran into him twice before we reached the steps leading upward. We almost got lost, having to adjust our route to keep from colliding with him.

But get out of the catacombs we did, and exit we did, without incident—until we reached the guard station.

Four guys jumped me. They'd found the guard and had set an ambush. A fifth, inside, sounded an alarm.

I spun away from the rush. They didn't see Morley, who had lagged, eyeballing the treasures of the altar, probably figuring how much trouble it would be to get them out. I thumped a guy, my back against a wall. They had their hearts set on bloodshed. I thought I was dead. They kept me too busy to shove a hand into a pocket.

Morley just walked up, jumped in the air, and literally kicked the side of a man's head in. He ripped another's throat out with his bare hand. I whacked the same guy over the head with my club. The remaining attacker and the guy who had sounded the alarm got a case of the big eyes. One tried to run. Morley folded him up with a groin kick. I put the other one down with my stick.

"Let's go!" There was all kinds of racket in the depths of the temple. The gods knew who or what lived in those twisty ways beyond the main worship gallery. It sounded like we'd have a hundred men after us in a minute.

"We're not finished." Morley indicated the three men still alive. "They can identify us."

He was right. They would know what faces to look for and the Church was known for holding a grudge. Hell, they were still trying to get even for things that happened a thousand years ago. "I can't."

"You'll never learn."

He used a thin-bladed knife to still three hearts as quick as you could blink.

I've seen a lot of guys killed. I've had to do a few myself. I've never liked it and I've never gotten used to it. I almost puked. But I didn't stop thinking. I got out the coin I'd taken from Jill's place a thousand years ago and stuffed it under a body. When Morley was past me I smashed a couple blue bottles in the entryway, hoping their contents would slow the pursuit.

We ran like hell until we were a block away, hidden in shadows.

"Now what?" Morley asked.

"Now we go after the real target." And I told him how Maya and Jill had disappeared into the Orthodox compound.

●●●47

Men with lanterns poured from Chattaree. It looked like they'd dragged out every damned priest in the place. Morley said, "Better move out. You have a plan?"

"I told you the plan."

"Get the women out? That's a plan?"

"It's the one I've got."

We were across the street from the gate where the women had entered the Orthodox compound. A group of Church priests were set to head our way. I dashed across the street. Morley stayed at my heels. "Even if they saw us I don't think they'd come in after us," I whispered.

"Shit. You're such a goddamned genius."

I vaulted the coach gate. Morley followed. He had more difficulty because he was shorter. I'd barely landed when a couple of guys came out of the gatehouse. They weren't armed but they were looking for trouble. I gave it to one with my stick. The other dove for an alarm bell. Morley landed on his back.

We'd barely gotten them inside when the Church bunch roared up. I stepped outside. "What's going on?"

"Thieves. Murderers. Invaded the temple." They all wore priestly garb. I, as an Orthodox employee, should have no trouble knowing what temple they were from. "See anybody go by here?"

"No. But I heard somebody run past a minute ago. Going like crazy. That's why I came out."

"Thanks, brother." Off the gang went.

"Good thinking, Garrett," Morley said when I stepped back inside. I didn't look for the guards. Morley was nothing if not certain about covering his ass. Those guys weren't going to come to, get themselves loose, and raise an alarm. "You ever been here before? Know your way around?"

"Once when I was a kid. They used to let you wander around the grounds."

"You're a wonder. Don't you ever plan anything?"

In the circumstances it was hard to argue with him. I didn't waste my breath. "You can back out anytime."

"I wouldn't miss it. Let's go."

Needless risk-taking isn't like Morley Dotes. He wouldn't do this sort of thing unless he had an angle somewhere.

No skin off my nose. If somebody looted the temple or this place, I'd have my suspicions but I wouldn't be heartbroken. Morley would just look at me blankly, baffled, if I suggested he'd had anything to do with it.

We found a whole complex of buildings behind the first stand of trees. The biggest was the main Orthodox basilica in TunFaire. It was as grand as Chattaree but had no name except something generic like All Saints. Morley and I slipped into some shrubbery and reviewed everything we'd heard about the compound, which wasn't much. We could identify only three of the cluster of seven buildings, the basilica itself and two structures housing monks and nuns. Those had featured prominently in the scandals.

"Isn't there supposed to be an orphanage and a seminary?" Morley asked.

"Yeah. I think so." That would identify two more buildings. But which two?

"Logic would suggest a building with kitchens and whatnot to feed all the people."

"Unless each has its own."

"Yeah."

"How's this sound? If you grabbed a couple women wouldn't you maybe stash them in the nunnery?"

"Maybe. Unless they have jail cells or something."

"Yeah. But I've never heard a rumor like that." Short of searching the complex, building by building, I had no idea what to do. I hadn't thought this part out. Like Morley said, I tend to jump without looking.

"Hey."

Somebody was doing a sneak from shadow to shadow. It was too dark to tell much but he came close enough to identify as a monk. Morley suggested, "Let's follow him."

That seemed as good an idea as any.

I let Morley lead since he could see better and walk more softly. In a minute he reached back and stopped me. "He's checking to see if anybody's watching."

I froze. After a minute Morley tugged at my sleeve. We didn't go twenty steps before Morley stopped again and urged me into some shrubbery.

The man had climbed steps to a side door of the building I thought was the nunnery—which explained his sneaking.

He tapped a code. The door opened. He embraced somebody, then slipped inside. The door closed.

"Think that would work for us?" Morley asked.

"If we had somebody waiting."

"Let's check that door."

It took only a second to discover that it was barred inside. It took only a few minutes to learn that all the building's four entrances were barred. The ground-floor windows were masked by steel lattices.

Morley muttered, "See what happens when you bull ahead with no research? We don't have the equipment we need."

I didn't argue. I went around to that one side door and tapped the code the visitor had used earlier. Nothing happened. Morley and I got into a brisk discussion about my tendency to act without thinking. I didn't put up much of a defense. As Morley was getting irked enough to walk, I tapped the door again.

And to our astonishment it opened.

We gaped. The woman said, "You're early . . ." then started to yell when she saw we weren't who she was expecting. We jumped her, and managed to keep her quiet. We dragged her into the little hall behind the door, which was about six feet long and four wide and lighted by a single candle on a tiny stand. Morley yanked the door shut behind us. I let him take the woman, then I darted to the end of the hallway and looked both ways, but saw nothing.

I turned. "Let's make it quick."

Morley grunted.

I told the nun, "Two women came in today. A blonde, middle twenties, and a brunette, eighteen, both attractive. Where are they?"

She didn't want to play.

Morley placed a knife at her throat. "We want to know. We aren't worried about the sin of murder."

Now she couldn't answer because she was too scared. I said, "Cooperate and you'll be all right. We don't *want* to hurt anybody. But we won't mind if we have to. Do you know the women we want?"

Morley pricked her throat. She nodded.

I asked, "Do you know where they are?"

Another nod.

"Good. Take us there."

"Mimphl murkle mibble" came from behind Morley's hand.

"Let her talk," I said. "Kill her if she tries to yell."

We were convincing because Morley would have done it. She said, "They put the blond woman in the guesthouse. They put the other one in the dining-hall wine cellar. It was the only place they could lock her up."

"That's fine," I said.

"Dandy," Morley agreed. "You're doing wonderfully. Now take us to them. Which one first?" That to me.

"The brunette."

"Right. Show us this wine cellar."

Somebody knocked on the door, just a gentle tippy-tap. Morley whispered, "How long before he gives up."

She shrugged. "I don't know. I've never not shown up."

"Been late?"

"No."

I suggested, "We could use another door. Which building do you use for a dining hall?"

She was reasonably calm now, and pliant. She explained. Morley said, "Let's go. And quietly."

"I have no wish to die. Why are you doing this? The Holy Fathers won't tolerate it. They'll have you hunted down."

"The Holy Fathers won't have time. We approach the Hour of Destruction. We have entered the Time of the Devastator. The heretic will be devoured." I couldn't get much passion into it because it sounded so silly but I doubted she was calm enough to hear that. "Show us the way."

She balked. Morley pricked her. I said, "We *will* have those women, with or without you. You have only one chance to see the sun rise. Move."

She moved.

We went out another secondary door. The dining hall proved to be a one-story affair between the nunnery and monks' quarters and behind the main temple. A seminary, occupied by yet another bunch of people, stood behind the dining hall. Maximum convenience. I asked about the other buildings in the complex. Stables and storage, she told us. The guesthouse, orphanage, and a few other buildings, like homes for several of the Holy Fathers (four of Karenta's twelve lived in TunFaire), were scattered around the grounds, in semi-seclusion. I thought it must really gall the Church to be stuck with one oversized block while the Orthodox maintained a whole city estate. But that's the way it goes when you're number two.

We reached the dining hall without incident. It wasn't locked. Morley muttered something about moving too slow, that sooner or later there was going to be a change of guard at the gate and an alarm would sound.

I tried to hurry the nun.

48

The nun seemed a little old for clandestine assignations. I guessed she had fifteen years on me. But maybe we never get tired of the great game.

"There'll be a guard," Morley whispered. "Let me go first."

I didn't argue. He was better at that sort of thing. "Don't cut him if you don't have to."

"Right." He went down the stair like a ghost. It wasn't a minute before he called up, "Clear." I herded the nun down. Morley waited at the bottom. "I'll watch her. Get the girl."

Thoughtful of him.

The guard slumped on a stool in front of a massive oak door strapped with iron, hung on huge hinges. There was no opening in it. It was secured by a wooden peg through a hasp. Effective enough, I guessed.

I touched the guard's throat. His pulse was ragged but it was there. Good for Morley. I opened the door, and saw nothing but darkness. I used the guard's lamp to give me light.

I found Maya curled in a corner on burlap sacks, asleep, filthy. The dirt on her face had been streaked by tears. I dropped to my knees, placed a hand over her mouth, and shook her. "Wake up."

She started violently, almost broke loose. "Don't say a word till we get home. Especially don't name any names. Understand?"

She nodded.

"Promise?"

She nodded again.

"All right. We're going out. We'll collect Jill, then run like hell. We don't want these people to know who we are."

"I got it, Garrett. Don't pound it in with a hammer."

"You think somebody just heard you? Maybe somebody we forced to show us where you were? Somebody we'd have to kill so they won't repeat it?"

She got a little pale. Good. "Come on."

I stepped out and told Morley, "I got her. Watch her while I put this guy away." The nun didn't look like she'd heard anything.

I dragged the guard inside, stepped out and shoved the peg home, then told the nun, "Lead on to the guesthouse."

She led on. Maya kept her mouth shut. Some notion of the stakes had gotten through.

There were lights on the second floor of the guesthouse, a cozy two-story limestone cottage of about eight rooms. Morley checked for guards. I watched the women. "Just a few minutes more," I promised the nun.

She shook. She thought her minutes were numbered. I kept on with the dialectic of nihilism, filling her with arrows pointing at the Sons of Hammon. I wouldn't let Morley do what he'd want to do after we used her up. I wanted one live, primed witness left behind. I wanted the Orthodox Holy Fathers to foam at the mouth when they thought of the Sons.

The trouble was, there would be some right to Morley's argument. The nun had had too many chances to get a good look at us.

Maya caught on. She put on a damned good act, pretending to be terrified. She kept whispering tales about her previous stay with the Sons of Hammon.

Maya knew most everything I did. She was able to lay it on thick.

Morley came back. "Guards front and back. One for each door."

"Any problem?"

"Not anymore. They weren't very alert."

I grunted. "Let's go," I told the women. "Sister, behave for a couple more minutes and you're free."

We'd gone maybe fifty feet toward the house when Morley said, "There it is."

"It" was the alarm we'd anticipated.

Bells rang and horns blew. Signal lights and balls of fire arced through the night. "They do get excited, don't they?" I grabbed the nun's habit to make sure she didn't stray.

We stepped over a guard. The door he'd watched was locked but the top half was a leaded glass window, Terrell with a halo. I bashed it in and lifted the inner bar. We shoved inside. I said, "Put her to sleep." Morley slugged the nun behind the ear. He understood what I was doing.

Someone shouted a question downstairs. A man. I started up. Morley was right behind me. Maya was behind him, armed with a knife she'd taken off the guard as soon as the nun went down.

The hurrah outside got louder.

The stairs took a right-angle turn at a landing twelve steps up. A man in a nightshirt met me there. He made a noise that sounded like "Gork!"

"Not me, brother."

He was the guy I'd seen at the talk-talk place, the little gink with the nose. I grabbed him by the back of the nightshirt before he could run for it. I softened him up with my stick and shoved him at Morley. "Bonus prize."

Morley grabbed him. I went on. Maya followed me.

That Jill was a quick mover. When I charged in she had a window open and was shoving a leg through. It wasn't wide enough for a fast exit. I got to her while she was still trying to scrunch up small enough to fit. I grabbed an arm and pulled. She popped out like a cork. "Anybody'd think you weren't thrilled to see me. After all the trouble I've gone through to rescue you."

She regained her balance and dignity, then gave me a lethal look. "You've got no right."

I grinned. "Maybe not. But here I am. And there you are. And here we go. You've got one minute to get dressed. You're not ready then, you take it through the streets like that."

The proverbial jaybird wore more than she had on. I couldn't help admiring the landscape. Maya said, "Put your eyes back in, Garrett. You'll have me suspecting you of immoral thoughts."

"The gods forfend. Jill?"

Maya moved between Jill and the window. I gave her an approving smile and retreated to the door to check Morley and the bald gink. "We've got her. She's got to get dressed."

"Don't waste time. The whole place is awake."

"Speaking of. See if you can wake him up. He's going with us."

Morley scowled.

"If anybody knows the answers, he does."

"If you say so. Find something we can put on him. Can't drag him around like this."

I looked around. The little man's clothes were on a chair, neatly folded. Jill was almost ready. She hadn't bothered with underwear. Maya was giving her some song and dance about us telling the nun that she'd been sent ahead to soften up the little guy for the grabbing. I raised an eyebrow, then winked. The girl could think on her feet.

I said, "Jill, carry your friend's clothes. He's going with us."

"I'm sorry I ever came to you."

"So am I, sweetheart. Let's go."

We stepped out of the room, me first, Maya last and brandishing her knife. She was having fun.

Morley had the little guy organized enough to stumble along. They were halfway down the stair. We caught up at the bottom. Morley said, "We'd better head for the nearest fence."

"Right." Though that would put us on the side of the Dream Quarter farthest from where I wanted to be.

We went out the door we'd entered. It faced the center of the grounds. There was all kinds of excitement over there. Some was moving our way fast.

Morley came up with a piece of cord. He slipped a loop around the little man's neck. "One peep and I choke you. We didn't come after you so we won't be brokenhearted if we kill you. Got me?"

The little man nodded.

Morley headed due south. Maya and I followed with Jill between us. Maya threatened to stab Jill in the behind if she didn't move faster.

She *was* having a good time.

I'd like to turn the whole thing into high drama with harrowing near misses, ferocious battles with fanatic priests, and a skin-of-the-teeth getaway when all seemed lost, but it didn't work that way. We never came close to getting caught. A dozen priests with torches thundered up to the house as we fled, but they didn't see us. We were at the enclosure wall, with Morley and Maya and Jill and the little gink perched on top and me reaching for Morley's hand, before the gang charged out of the house again. We were gone before they found a trail.

We got ourselves lost in the alleys of the industrial district south of the Dream Quarter and made the little guy get dressed. He didn't have much to say. No threats, no bluster. Once he'd taken stock he remained calm, silent, and cooperative.

We spent the rest of the night working around the Dream Quarter the long way, out to the western parts of the city, beyond the Hill, then back down to my place. I was damned tired when home hove into view.

I was pleased with myself, too. I'd pulled off a grand stunt and it'd proven easier than I'd expected. The raid on Chattaree hadn't been necessary. I still had all my little bottles in my pockets.

49

There was a problem. The Watch had the house surrounded. And it was light out. There'd be no sneaking past them.

We hadn't talked much but I'd mentioned my notion of getting Jill and Warden Agire together with the Dead Man. The little guy had proven to be exactly whom I'd suspected. I'd gotten that from Jill, not him. She'd been the one to try bluster, dropping his name. It hadn't done her any good.

Morley said, "What now, genius? Want to hide them out at my place?"

"We'll get in. We just need a distraction."

"Better come up with it quick. Five of us hanging around is going to catch somebody's eye."

"Right. Maya. Could I buy a little help from the Doom?"

She was surprised. "What kind?"

"Like maybe have Tey run to the door and tell Dean to tell the Dead Man we're out here. Better, have her send one of the young ones. They wouldn't do anything to a kid."

"All right." She sounded doubtful but she trotted off.

Those Watchmen were on their best behavior. TunFaire is a funny city some ways. One way is a popular determination to protect the common-law sanctity of the home. Our worst tyrants haven't dared overstep people's rights within their homes. An invasion of a home without a lot of legal due process will stir up a riot quick. People will put up with almost anything else but will shed blood in an instant over their right to retreat into and remain inviolate within their castles. It's odd.

Those Watchmen would be under close scrutiny and they would be intensely aware of it. The whole neighborhood might come boiling out if they made a wrong move.

So there was a good chance an unknown could stroll right to my door without interference. They might try a grab once they saw where the messenger was headed but I was sure Dean would be alert. Once the messenger got inside there'd be nothing the Watch could do.

Maya wasn't gone long. She looked bleak when she came back.

"What's the matter?" I asked.

"I had to pay a price."

She was upset. I took her hand without knowing why. She squeezed hard. "Tell me about it."

"You got what you need. They're sending a girl. But she made me pay."

Oh-oh. I had a feeling Maya had given more than she should have. "What?"

"I had to step out. Leave the Doom. Give her warchief."

"Maya! We could've worked something else out."

"It's all right. You said it. I'm getting too old. It's time I grew up."

It was all true, but I felt guilty because she'd done it for me, not for her.

They sent the ragamuffin in a gunnysack who let me in that time I visited Maya. Tey would make a deadly warchief. That kid was perfect. Every one of those Watchmen stared and thought filthy, shameful thoughts, and not one considered interfering until she pounded on the door. By the time somebody reacted she was making her pitch to Dean.

Dean let her in.

Morley muttered, "That kid is a witch." He'd felt it, too.

I said, "Some are at that age. Even when they don't know what they're doing."

"She knows," Maya said. "She *is* a witch. She'll own the Doom before she's sixteen."

The Watchmen snapped to attention. I felt the lightest touch from the Dead Man as they presented arms. "Time to go, kids."

Jill and Agire balked.

Agire refused to move. Morley cured that with a quick kick to the foundation of his dignity. Jill wanted to yell. Maya laid a roundhouse on her nose. "That's for the way Garrett looked at you."

"Take it easy." I knew she was spending her disappointment.

"Sorry." She didn't mean it and apologized to me instead of Jill. I let it slide. Jill had decided to cooperate.

We walked over to the house. Near as I could tell the Watchmen didn't see us. Dean let us in, croggled by the numbers. I told him, "Breakfast for all. In with his nibs."

"Not me," Morley said. "I did my part. You have it under control. I have to see if there's anything left of my place."

I thought he was in an awful hurry but I didn't argue. He'd done his share and hadn't tried to hit me with an inflated fee. He had something on his mind. I didn't want to interrupt.

Dean let him out after I had Jill and Agire installed with the Dead Man. Jill was frightened. Agire was terrified. He clung to self-control by concentrating on offenses to his dignity.

I trust there is some significance to the presence of these people, the Dead Man thought at me.

"Yep. How'd it go with the civil servants?"

They kept losing track of what they were doing and wandered off to drink beer or indulge other vices.

"What about those Watchmen? They going to call down the wrath of the Hill?"

They believe one of the stormwardens just went past. Once Mr. Dotes is out of sight they will return to their duties unaware that anyone has come or gone.

The little witch from the Doom was gone, too. I hadn't seen her go. Dean must have planted her in the front parlor, then hustled her out behind me.

These two? the Dead Man reminded me.

I made the introductions and suggested we might tie things up if he'd help out for a few minutes. He could, after all, plunder their minds if he wanted.

He astounded me by agreeing without being bullied. He went after Agire first. The Warden let out a squeal of panic. He yelled, "You have no right! What's going on is none of your business."

"Wrong. I have two paying clients and a personal interest. A friend of mine got caught in your game. It killed him. One of my clients died, too. Magister Peridont. Heard of him? His death doesn't end the commitment. And my other client is too damned nasty to walk out on. His name is Chodo Contague. He took offense at the Sons of Hammon. He's after scalps. If you know anything about him, you know you don't want to get on his bad side."

Agire knew something. He got rockier.

I said, "We don't have to be enemies. But my friend and I want to know what's going on so we can get ourselves out of a bind and maybe put the crazies out of their misery."

That is enough, Garrett. Say nothing more. He is considering his position and options and the probability that you are telling the truth. You are?

"The whole and nothing but." I glanced at Jill. Gone was the cool. She had a bad case of the fidgets. Her eyes wouldn't stay still. She might have tried to run if Maya hadn't been between her and the door.

We waited on Agire. Agire waited on divine inspiration.

Dean brought a small side table from the kitchen. "I'll set up a buffet," he said.

"Fine. As long as there's plenty of it." I was hungry and tired and impatient with my guests.

The Dead Man cautioned, *They are thinking, Garrett. That is enough.*

"Anything interesting?"

A great deal. We now know, for example, why Dean and your young friend could not locate what the woman concealed here. She is trying too hard not to think of it.

"What?"

My backchat disturbed my guests. I told myself to can it. I helped Dean when he brought a tray of goodies. I wasn't polite. I helped myself immediately. "Breakfast," I told the others.

After a pause calculated to have me panting with suspense, the Dead Man said, *She hid it here while I was sleeping.*

"I know." I went to the case on the short wall where we keep our maps and references, searched the shelf that kept drawing Jill's eye, and found a big copper key. It looked like it had been lying around turning green for a couple hundred years.

The Dead Man was irked. I had stolen his thunder. Jill looked like she was going to cry. Agire couldn't take his eye off the key.

It was six inches long and the heaviest key I'd ever hefted. It excited Agire but I knew there was no key among the Terrell Relics. It was squared off flat on the sides. There was an inscription under the verdigris. I scraped at it.

"My, my." It was the very slogan on those old temple coins. I chunked it under the Dead Man's chair, collected my plate, and started stuffing myself. Maya followed my lead. My guests were too nervous to partake. If they didn't get busy, I'd get their share.

50

Patience paid. Agire cracked.

"The Hammon cult has been making war on us. Its object is recovery of that key, which can unlock the Tomb of Karak, where legend has the Devourer imprisoned. The cult can't free him any other way. It's only been a few months since they found out who had the key, although they've known for decades that it was in TunFaire.

"For three decades they've slipped men into the priesthoods here. Sometime this year one of them reached a level of trust where he could find out the key is kept with the Terrell Relics.

"The cult's leaders brought men to TunFaire. Using sources inside my church, they began a whisper campaign meant to rip us apart. They might've succeeded, but a minor player defected. He told me what he knew. I tried to take steps but learned that the hierarchy was riddled with traitors.

"I shared some of this with my friend." He indicated Jill. "I didn't realize she knew who I was, nor that she had a relationship with Magister Peridont. Nor, for that matter, was I aware that my peccadillo was known to my enemies.

"I mentioned my informant in front of the wrong man, resulting in an attempt on my life and an effort to steal the Relics. By Orthodox monks. I fled to the one person I could trust." He indicated Jill again. "But I chose a bad time. She was entertaining her friend from the Church."

Pain showed for a moment. "I should have known she couldn't afford a place like that." Another pause. "Later she arranged for me to hide in the apartment opposite hers. She urged me to take Magister Peridont into my confidence. The threat to the Orthodox Church was a threat to all Hanites. I was stubborn. She says she dropped hints to Peridont. Those set him moving along the course you know. I didn't yield to her till too late. I gave her permission to speak to Peridont after she saw you that first time, hoping you could protect her from men watching her in hopes of tracing me. When she tried to tell Peridont he was too rushed to get the full story and didn't understand that she could bring us together. He tried to hire you to find me.

"Then he made the mistake I did—talking in front of someone who had infiltrated the Church. The enemy immediately suspected that she knew where the Relics were."

He seemed to think that explained everything. Maybe it did, in some ways. But it ignored why I'd received so much attention. I asked.

Jill confessed. "I set you up, sort of. You have a reputation for stumbling around turning over rocks and getting away with it. You scared them. They tried to get rid of you without being connected to it. You got the best of the kids they hired. They panicked. Everything just escalated."

Really? It made a crazy sense. Maybe perfect sense to somebody in the religion business.

"You telling me there really is a Devastator? And that this character can destroy the world but can't bust himself out of a tomb? Come on. You might as well stuff him in a bag made of cobwebs."

Agire looked at me like I was a mental defective. Make that spiritually handicapped.

"I know you priests believe six impossible things every day before breakfast," I said. "Some of you, anyway. I think most of you are parasites who live off the gullible, the ignorant, and the desperate. I don't think any of you who get ahead believe what you preach. You sure never practice it. Convince me you're an honest man and a believer, Warden."

Garrett.

I thought he was going to caution me about pushing the man.

True, the man does find some dogma a useful fiction. He manipulates the laity cynically and he is devoted to improving his place in the hierarchy. But he believes in his god and his prophet.

"That's absurd. He's an intelligent man. How can he buy something so full of contradictions and revisions of history?"

Agire smiled sadly, as though he had overheard the Dead Man and pitied me my blindness. I hate it when priests do that. Like their pity is all the proof they need.

You believe in sorcery.

My brain was in better shape than it should have been, tired as I was. I got his argument.

"I see sorcery at work every day. It's absurd but I see concrete results."

Agire said, "Mr. Garrett, you appear to be the sort who needs to be cut to believe in swords. I understand that mentality better than you think. Do you comprehend the idea of symbol? You say you accept sorcery. The very root of sorcery is manipulation of symbol in a way that affects referent. And that's the root of religion, too.

"Say there never was a Terrell. Or that Terrell was the villain portrayed by some. In the context of symbol and faith the Terrell who lived is irrelevant. The Terrell of faith is a symbol that must exist to fulfill the needs of a large portion of mankind. Likewise the creator.

"Hano must be because we need him to be. He was before we were. He will be after we're gone. Hano may not fulfill your prescription for such a being. So call him Prime Mover or just the force that set time and matter in motion.

"He must be because we need him to be. And he must be *what* we need him to be. It is a philosophical argument difficult to grasp for we who live among obdurately hard surfaces and sharp edges that ignore our wishes, but the observer invariably affects the phenomenon. In this context, God—by whatever name—is, and is constrained to be, whatever we believe him to be. The Hano of Terrell's time isn't the Hano of today. The Hano of the Orthodox denominations isn't the Hano of the Sons of Hammon. But he exists. He was what he was and he is what he's believed to be now. Do you follow? Hano is even what you believe him to be, in that infinitesimal fraction of himself that is yours alone."

I understood that they always have an argument. "You're saying we rule and create God as much as God creates and rules us."

"Ultimately. And that's how we get a fragment of God called the Devourer that can be locked in a tomb even though he can destroy the world. He can't get out because nobody believes he can get out—except by unlocking the door from outside. In fact, you might be able to argue that *nobody* wants him out—not even his followers—so the tomb becomes a total constraint."

"Too spooky for me. I'll keep thinking you're a bunch of crooks." I punctuated with a grin, telling him I knew what he'd say next.

"And the vast majority of people would as soon keep thinking in the symbols to which they're accustomed."

"All of which doesn't get us a step closer to cleaning this mess up before those guys turn TunFaire into a battleground. Symbols haven't been getting killed."

"The crux. Always the crux. The practicalities of everyday life. The early kings did what they had to when they exterminated an insidious and vicious enemy. Only a handful survived to rebuild. That solution is impractical today because we couldn't convince the agencies of the state that a threat exists. Symbolism again. A threat must be perceived to exist before the Crown will act. We have bodies all over the city? So the lower orders are slaughtering each other again. So what?"

I glanced at the Dead Man. He seemed amused. "Old Bones, you were going on about a rogue Loghyr the other day. This guy hasn't said anything about that."

He does not know, Garrett. The possibility of a true, cynical manipulation of men and their beliefs has not occurred to him, except in his own feeble way.

Ah! There is no contradiction, as you are about to protest. I am aware that I mentioned a great evil being created because some people needed it to exist. That is what the Warden has been saying. The rogue created a god in order to manipulate men. Men then created that god with their belief. Agire is right. There is a thing in a tomb. It can be released. It could destroy the world. It is a product of the imagination that has taken on life. Now it rules the rogue who imagined it. It has sent him to find the key.

"But . . ."

To end this you must find the rogue. You must destroy him.

"Oh boy." I glanced at Agire and Jill. The Dead Man had let them listen in. Jill seemed lost, Agire just frightened. "And how do we pull that off? How do you put an end to a Loghyr when even death doesn't slow him down?"

We will discuss that later. You are too tired to act, let alone think. I will consider means while you sleep.

Just dandy.

The Dead Man must not have let Dean rest while I was sawing logs. When I went downstairs the place was a zoo. The most exotic animals in TunFaire were there. They included Chodo Contague (who never leaves his estate) and his top two lifetakers, Morley, a man I didn't know who was obviously off the Hill, several species of priest old enough to have gray hair or no hair, and—wonder of all wonders—that character Sampson who'd been Peridont's assistant. At least fifteen people united in a conspiracy to exhaust my food and potables.

Were they talking about how to get shut of the Sons of Hammon? No. All they had on their minds was Glory Mooncalled, whose latest stunt had come earlier than expected and had people reeling everywhere. He had won his biggest victory yet, his slickest, and his most treacherous.

He let himself be discovered by the last Warlords of Venageta. He led their three armies a merry chase until they ran him to ground and he caught them. At the same time his agents guided even vaster Karentine armies into the same area. Those jumped right in figuring to end the war with a single day's bloodwork. They killed all three Warlords and most of their men. But the victory didn't turn out the way they hoped. Glory Mooncalled extricated himself early, engaged only to keep the Venageti from fleeing. The night after the battle he attacked the Karentine camp and killed all the officers, commanders, witches, warlocks, stormwardens, firelords, and what have you. He sent surviving enlisted men to Full Harbor with word that the Cantard's nonhuman peoples had declared it an independent state. Any Karentine or Venageti presence would be considered an act of war.

The man's audacity was amazing.

The Dead Man had gotten the news.

"You don't seem as smug as you should be. What did he do that you didn't predict?"

He declared creation of an independent republic. I had foreseen him turning on Karenta, as you know, but never considered the possibility that he had such lofty ambitions.

"The way I read it he just wants to be the warlord of the Cantard republic."

A convenient fiction. He permits the creation of an assembly representing the various sentient races of the Cantard. But who owns the power? Who controls the hearts of every veteran capable of wielding a weapon? Today he is not just a king or emperor or even a dictator. He is a demigod. If Karenta and Venageta continue to make claims to the Cantard, his power will not wane while he lives.

There was no "if" about what Karenta and Venageta would do. There were vast silver deposits in the Cantard. They were what the war was about. Sorcerers need silver to fuel their sorceries. Sorcerers are the true, hidden masters of both kingdoms. The war would continue with Karenta and Venageta as tacit allies until Glory Mooncalled's republic collapsed.

So it goes.

"What's this hungry horde I have filling up every nook and cranny? I've gained a few marks in this mess but at the rate they're going they'll eat up the profits."

Bring them in. I suggest you bring Mr. Sadler, Mr. Crask, and Mr. Chodo first and place them near the door, then bring the others, then come yourself with Mr. Dotes and Miss Stump. There could be some excitement when those priests realize they are in the presence of a Loghry. Caution Mr. Chodo and his associates.

I didn't have any idea what he was up to. I decided to humor him. It was pleasure enough to see him awake and working without carping.

When Sadler heard my warning he asked what was up. I told him I didn't know. He wasn't pleased, but what could I do? Chodo was more understanding— on the surface. He would await events before making judgments.

Morley and I stood to either side of the door as the others filed in. All I detected was a rising note of excitement. Then Sampson strode by. He looked at me like I was something with a hundred legs he'd discovered crawling in his breakfast.

He started violently when he saw the Dead Man. He turned, saw me and Morley blocking the doorway, and turned back again.

We went in, me frowning, looking at the Dead Man as though he might give me some physical clue. Maya closed the door behind us. She didn't look pretty today. She looked mean, like the street kid she'd been so long.

Garrett, ask Mr. Sampson to disrobe. Mr. Contague, would you lend us the aid of Mr. Crask and Mr. Sadler in the event Mr. Sampson is reluctant?

Everyone but Chodo looked at Sampson. Chodo looked at me and his henchmen, lifted a finger granting permission. I said, "Sampson?"

He headed for the door. Maya knocked him upside the head with a brass goblet. That slowed him down. Crask and Sadler held his arms while I hoisted the skirt of his habit and yanked down his pants. Morley leaned against the wall and made a crude remark about human perversion.

Mr. Sampson of the Church, heir to the Grand Inquisitor, had a bald crotch.

If you dress him in peasant garb and put him into a doorway I believe witnesses would swear he was the man who assassinated Magister Peridont. I believe he is the only one of his kind present.

"Good enough for me," I said. "Pity there's no one else from the Church here. It would save us the trip to turn him over."

We will keep him here. He knows who in each denomination is what you call a ringer.

Sampson went rigid as a stone post. I had Crask and Sadler set him to one side. I glanced at the Dead Man. Did he have an ulterior motive for having invited Chodo? Like wanting him to see how much aggravation he could get if he ever decided to push us? That kind of thinking ahead wasn't beyond him.

Gentlemen. As you know, the death of a Loghyr stills the flesh only. Many centuries can pass before the spirit separates from the flesh. In some cases, where the spirit is unwilling, Passing can be delayed almost indefinitely. In the ancient days of your race, when mine was more numerous, many of your local gods and devils were the departed of my species. It was the fashion to while away the Passing protecting or plaguing the primitives. Most of those animistic spirits have faded from memory, as my race has faded from the world. That game has lost its jest, so that now most Loghyr prefer to go to Khatar Island for their Passing. But there is one ancient, malignant presence among you. He has been known by many names in many times. He always attaches himself to dark, nihilist cults. In recent ages he has shown himself less because the rest of us took an oath to end his torment. He is the motive force behind the Sons of Hammon. And he is in TunFaire now.

He made a mistake coming here. But he did not know of my presence. He did not discover his mistake until he attacked this house in an effort to obtain the key that will unlock the tomb of the Devastator. I had suspected his presence earlier, based on reports from Mr. Garrett. His attack confirmed it.

Gentlemen, this ancient wickedness is most vulnerable at this moment. It is never likely to be this exposed again. Its adventures lately have stripped it of all allies but a handful hidden inside the priesthoods. A dead Loghyr is not very mobile. Without cohorts to remove it to safety, it can do nothing but await its fate, be that rescue or despair at your hands.

Determine among you what course to pursue. Though we of this house have done our share already we will continue to lend our support.

Thanks a bunch, Old Bones. If there was no more profit in it I wasn't that excited about staying involved. Who wants to duke it out with a dead Loghyr who's had several thousand years to practice being nasty? My own pet devil was bad enough. He's only been at it a few centuries and claims he's a friend. He doesn't create eight-armed demons out of whole cloth or send them calling in their own private thunderstorms.

He sent a personal message. These priests have the power to make thousands forget their temples were profaned.

And there were stormwardens and firelords and whatnot on the Hill who could turn into real pests if we kept attracting their attention. The priests could dissuade them. Maybe there was a profit after all.

Two hours of politicized yak passed before Chodo Contague asked the critical question. He'd gotten fed up with their bickering over precedence.

"Do you know where this thing is?"

That was the key question. If you're going after rats it helps to know where the rathole is.

Yes.

"Then this chatter is pointless. Mr. Sadler and Mr. Crask will tend to the matter. Are there special needs they should be aware of before they start?"

The Dead Man was amused. Within seconds the arguments collapsed. Everybody wanted to be right behind the kingpin. It didn't seem like that bad a spot, either. Better still would be behind his boys and the whole religious bunch. Then there would be nobody to trip over when I made a run for it.

The target had picked a spot.

Copperhead Bar is a long, skinny island that starts where the river bends as it passes the southern city limit. It's a mile long and maybe seventy yards wide at its widest. It's covered with scrub growth that has anchored the sand and silt that make up the bar. Forty yards of channel separate it from the mainland. It's a hazard and an eyesore and the only reason it isn't dredged out of there is that it belongs to the Church, deeded over in early imperial times. Way back they tried to establish a monastery on it but the footings were too infirm and the floods too frequent. There's nothing left but a tumble of creeper-covered building stone.

The Dead Man said our target was hiding under that rockpile.

He might as well have been in another dimension.

We had a good crowd gathered just south of the city wall, in an area kept barren by an eccentric owner. Chodo had sent a dozen street soldiers to back Crask and Sadler. The various denominations had contributed several hundred vigorous young priests. The guy who had come off the Hill, whose name I never did get, had juice enough to borrow a company of the Watch. Morley and I kind of stood off by ourselves, with Maya, wondering what was going to happen.

An ecumenical delegation had gone to Chattaree in hopes of recruiting a Magister or two. We were waiting on the Church's reply.

The drop-off to the river was about twelve feet, a sort of miniature bluff. Morley and Maya and I were on a knoll fifty yards back. Everyone else was between us and the river but kind of hanging back, not wanting to get any closer than they had to. I wondered if the thing on the island was aware of us.

I wondered, too, if I had some score to settle with Jill Craight. She and her pal Agire were standing separate, thirty yards south of anyone else. I'd been keeping an eye on them. They weren't talking and didn't seem very friendly. Maybe Agire was having trouble coping with being seen in a whore's company. It was too late for him to make it look like anything but what it was.

Maya noted my interest. She was too nervous to tease me. "What're they doing here?" she asked.

"I don't know."

The only men who had dared the lip of the bluff were Crask and Sadler. Now they headed our way. I was excited about that.

Crask came up, said, "Garrett, you were the Marine. How do we get over there?"

"I don't think we do, you want the truth."

He scowled.

"Remember the thing that came to Chodo's place? That's what we're up against." That and a lot more. This Loghyr had been polishing his tricks for ages. He'd lived through these things before. In fact, the Dead Man said this particular Loghyr was supposed to have been scrubbed after the fall of Carathca. "An attack will just get us all killed."

Neither Crask nor Sadler was known for subtle solutions to problems. Sadler asked, "Then what're we doing out here?"

"We're here because the people who tell us what to do don't understand what we're up against."

"All right, smart guy," Crask said. "You live with one of these things. How would you take it out?"

I'd hoped that wouldn't come up. I didn't want to give anybody something he could use against me and the Dead Man.

"We should wear him down. First thing, set up a kind of siege."

"A line here, and somebody on the river, to keep its people from rescuing it. After that I'd just collect mice and rats and bugs and float them to the island on rafts. For as long as it took."

"What?" They both looked lost.

"All right. First thing you got to realize, this thing *is* dead. But its spirit is tied to its body. No body, the spirit has to go away." Or so the Dead Man claimed. "There's nothing on that island for vermin to eat except that Loghyr body. The Loghyr knows that, too. He'll be watching for bugs and stuff. But if there are a lot of them, it'll be hard for him to spot them all and take care of them. Also, a dead Loghyr has to spend a lot of time sleeping. That's when they develop the energy they use when they pull their stunts. This one is probably sleeping right now. When he's asleep he can't keep track of vermin. They could work him over good. He wouldn't feel them biting because he's dead."

Crask snorted, disgusted. But Sadler nodded, seeing it. "Take a while, though."

"It would. But I don't know of any more certain, less risky way to handle it."

"We'd have to check with Chodo. He wants results quick." Chodo had retired to his estate.

"He'll pay dear for that if he insists."

Crask jerked his head at Sadler. They went off to talk it over. Morley asked, "Why not ring in a firelord or two? They could burn it out there, couldn't they?"

"Maybe. But a sorcerer wouldn't be safer from it than you or me."

"Garrett," Maya said softly, scared, "I don't think it's asleep."

She had a flair for understatement.

I saw nothing but a glow from where we stood but something was happening on the island. Those nearer the edge began yammering and backing away.

Then a spot of black cloud formed above the island, maybe fifty feet high. It grew quickly, spinning like a whirlpool. Everybody watched it, which was a mistake.

Sudden as lightning three guys in antique armor jumped over the lip of the bluff. Glowing, they charged the crowd. They hurled spears of fire.

A six-armed woman formed inside the spinning cloud. She grew huge. She wore nothing, was a polished black, and had a skull for a face and teats like a dog.

Priests screamed. The Watch company decided they weren't getting paid enough to deal with this.

Crask and Sadler and their boys were willing to take on the armored guys but couldn't get to them through the panicky mob.

The armored guys went to work. Pieces of body flew.

"Damn!"

I glanced at Morley but kept most of my attention on the black thing. It seemed especially interested in Jill and Agire. Morley dipped into a pocket.

I caught a glimpse of something lemon-colored. He threw it at the armored men.

Damn him, he'd managed to sneak himself some of Peridont's goodies while the lights were out that night.

The bottle broke on a man's breastplate. For a moment I thought nothing was happening. When it did start it wasn't what Morley had in mind.

The guy started laughing. In a minute he was laughing so hard he rested his sword tip on the ground and leaned on the weapon, having one hell of a good time.

"Shit," Morley grumbled. "That was a bust." He threw a couple more bottles, other colors, at the other two armored figures. Those had even less obvious effect.

The yellow bottle wasn't a complete bust. Crask forced his way through the crowd, took the sword away from the laughing villain, used it to carve him up. Then he got the giggles himself.

One down. But the other two were slaughtering everybody they could catch. And the thing in the air was after Agire and Jill.

I threw my red bottle.

I didn't want to do that. In the back of my mind I'd hoped to get to the island and use it on the dead Loghyr.

The results were the same as they'd been at Chodo's place. The monster melted and evaporated. But I didn't have time to watch. Two armored guys were headed my way and, except for Chodo's troops, everybody was opting for discretion.

One of Morley's bottles began to take effect. One of the attackers started having trouble keeping his balance. He slipped, staggered, and as he got closer fell to his knees.

Neither was throwing sorceries anymore. Though maybe that was because the thing on the island was distracted by what was happening to its monster.

Crask got behind the staggering character, ran a spear through him. So then there was one. All of a sudden it was at the heart of a circle of unfriendlies including Morley and myself, Sadler and most of Chodo's boys, and maybe a dozen priests and Watchmen with more than average nerve. The guy was like a giant thunder lizard surrounded by little hunters. We couldn't hurt him head-on but his back was always turned to somebody.

He didn't last long.

When it was over I glanced at the thing that had been in the air. It lay on the ground twitching, half devoured by the stuff eating it, black fog boiling off. Sadler stepped over. "I get the point you were making, Garrett. That thing can hack away anytime it wants."

Somebody pulled the helmet off a suit of armor and discovered that the man inside had been a corpse longer than a few seconds. He had drowned days ago. Fish and corruption had been working on him.

I nodded to Sadler. "It has to rest sometimes, but this's what we can expect, or maybe worse, if we try to go over there." I thought about how the Dead Man could make people forget, could make them do things they didn't want to do. This could get rough.

Actually, though, I was surprised by the level of violence. I'd figured the Loghyr wouldn't want to attract attention from the Hill. Sorcerers could get real interested in this kind of show.

Morley said, "We'd better take care of the dead and get the wounded to help."

Two kinds of guys had run from the excitement, those who were so ashamed that they never came back and those that did come back looking sheepish. They helped sort the mess out.

Maya hadn't run. I don't know why not. She couldn't have done anything but get hurt. Fifteen minutes into the cleanup she grabbed my arm. "Agire bought it. And Hester is gone."

For a moment I felt sorry for Jill. She deserved more of life . . . Then suspicion raised its snoot. "Where's Agire?"

"Over where they were."

I walked that way, keeping one eye on the smoldering black thing. Its flesh—if flesh it could be called—was almost consumed.

I found the Warden and knelt. Maya dropped to her knees opposite me. "Been hard on religious bigwigs lately," I said. And on littlewigs, too, as the cults and denominations stripped their priests and monks to see how well they were hung.

Blood had run from Agire's mouth. He was lying on his back. There was no wound visible. I rolled him over, grunted.

A minute later I told Sadler, "Far as I can see I've done my part here. You guys know how to handle it. I'm going home."

Morley stayed. Maya tagged along with me. She had nowhere else to go. We had to do some serious thinking about her future now. She said, "You've got something on your mind. What is it?"

"Jill."

"What upset you?"

"She killed Agire. While we were distracted she stuck a knife in his back. Couldn't have been anyone else because the excitement never got to them."

"But why?" She didn't claim Jill couldn't do a thing like that.

"The Terrell Relics, I think. Agire gave them to her to hide. He never said he got them back. The only thing she left at our house was that key. That could've gotten her killed if she'd kept it. Hell. Maybe she was out to snatch the Relics from the beginning."

"Why?"

"She's fond of money and nice things. How much would the Church pay for the Relics? How about some other cult?"

Maya just nodded. After we'd walked a few blocks, she said, "We should be headed for the Tenderloin."

Maybe. But I'd wanted to ask the Dead Man if it was really any of my business.

t *was* my business. I'd been hired by Peridont and I'd made a point of
claiming he was still my client, dead or not.

Maya was pleased. I wasn't so sure I was. It had started to snow earlier
than I'd expected, heavier than I'd anticipated. The wind was nippy. If I'd
let it go I'd be home, toasty warm, sipping a beer, wondering how I could
get Dean out of the house and the Dead Man to go to sleep so Maya and I
could . . .

We walked into a Tenderloin like a ghost town. The first snowfall always
has that effect on TunFaire. Everyone gets in out of it and stays. We went
around the side of the talk house, into the alley.

"Too late," Maya said. There were tracks in the snow on the steps to the
second floor, downward bound.

"Maybe." I hustled upstairs, went inside, hurried along a hallway not
unlike the one downstairs. One door stood open. I stuck my head in.

Jill's, all right. I recognized the clothing scattered around. It included
what she'd worn to the festivities down south. I cursed and headed out.

Maybe I was a little loud. A door opened. The elvish woman Polly looked
out. "What're you doing?" she asked.

I fell in love all over again. I gulped. "I came to tell you how much . . . I'd
better go. I'm making a fool of myself." Not bad for off the cuff, Garrett. I
got out.

I rejoined Maya. "She's gone. Let's get after her before her tracks disappear."

As we moved out I glanced up. The elvish woman was at the top of the steps looking down, wearing a puzzled smile.

Jill wasted no time but the snowfall betrayed her. We gained ground. Her tracks became fresher. The snowfall tapered off. Visibility improved. The street we were following entered a square. A figure shuffled across it ahead of us.

"That's an old woman," Maya said. "Look at her. She's old enough to be Hester's mother."

I could see that, just the way the woman moved. She wore a lot of black, the way old women do, and moved slowly. "Damn it!" How had I confused trails? I thought back.

I hadn't. This trail hadn't crossed any other. That woman was the one who had come out of the talk house. And she was carrying a bundle she hugged to her breast. "Come on." I began to trot.

The snow and wind muted our footsteps till we were a half dozen yards from the woman.

She whirled.

No old woman moved like that.

"Hello, Jill."

She straightened up, stopped pretending. "Garrett."

Maya moved around to cut her off if she ran. I said, "I can't let you get away."

She sighed. "I know. That's the way you are." She shrugged. "I didn't think you'd catch on so quick."

"It was pure chance."

"Suppose I turned them over voluntarily? Would that be enough?"

"I don't think so. There's a saying. Any man's death diminishes me. You shouldn't have killed Agire. You didn't have to."

"I know. It was stupid. I did it without thinking. The opportunity was there and I grabbed it. I knew it was a mistake before he fell. But that's not something you can take back."

"Let's go." I believed her. Maya didn't. She stayed behind us throughout a walk all the way to the Dream Quarter. And as I walked beside Jill, in silence, shivering, I did a lot of reflecting, most of it on the fact that, though none had by my own hand, seven men had died the night we rescued Maya from the Orthodox complex. I could rationalize however I wanted but I was the guy who had taken Morley along.

As we approached the gate I told Jill, "Just hand them the casket. Don't say anything. Don't answer any questions."

She looked at me oddly, her eyes as old as she was dressed. And that's the way she did it. A guard came to see what she wanted. She pushed the casket into his hands and turned away, looked at me to see what next.

I said, "Good-bye," and walked into a quickening snowfall, holding Maya's arm. We pushed into the wind with our heads down and our cheeks biting cold, saying nothing. Crystals of ice formed at the corners of my eyes.

54

The Dead Man was pleased with himself. He was cocky as hell. Even mention of his miscalculation regarding Glory Mooncalled didn't let the wind out of his sails. While Maya watched him nervously, unsure where she stood in his bachelor household, he crowed at me and I tried to shut him out.

I emptied my pockets, putting little bottles onto the shelf where the dread key had been hidden. We would do the obvious with that. There were no protective spells on it, only charms meant to fit it to the lock it served. I would cut it up and scatter the pieces among several scrap dealers. It would be no problem once it was melted down. That should've been done in the old days.

I placed the coin from the Blue Bottle on a shelf with memorabilia from other cases. I wished I had the one from Jill's place instead. It would've meant more and would've reminded me more strongly of our fallibility. I wondered what she would do.

She'd survive. She was a survivor. In a way, I wished her well. I wished her free of the burden of her past.

As I lifted an iron chain and rock pendant from around my neck I hit the point where I'd had enough of the Dead Man. "You blew it on Jill, Old Bones. She sucked you up. You were so damned proud because you spotted that key that you never looked at what she was hiding behind her worry."

You can shut him out or hide your thoughts from him if you concentrate.

Obviously, Jill had kept the whereabouts of the Relics from him by worrying about the key, which was of no value to her anyway.

That slowed him down. But instead of confessing a shortcoming he changed the subject. *Why have you been wearing that rock? Have you joined one of the cults?*

"Not hardly." I grinned. "Sadler gave me this little gizmo. It keeps the thunder lizards away. In all the excitement that night he forgot to take it back. I didn't remind him. It might come in handy someday."

He gave me a big dose of that mental noise which serves him as laughter. *It might at that. It might at that.* I got a hint that his thoughts had turned to Maya. He sent, *I have stretched myself unreasonably rescuing you from the consequences of your actions this time. I am going to take a nap.*

That was as close as he could get to saying he approved of a female friend of mine.

I went into the kitchen and told Dean he had his nights off to go home again, starting immediately, and hastened him out the door over his protests.

The city buzzed for days about the reappearance of the Terrell Relics. Once that became old news, though, it looked like we were in for a quiet winter.

Then somebody raided Chattaree, stealing a fortune in gold and silver and gems from the altars. No villains were identified. The Church suspected darko-breed street gangs because of profane graffiti left at the scene.

I stayed away from Morley's place. My contacts told me the Chattaree raiders had used a variety of nuisance spells to neutralize the priests who responded to the initial alarm. I didn't want to be in the place if a gang of unhappy Churchmen turned up. From what Saucerhead told me, though, I gathered Morley didn't change his lifestyle.

When Chodo Contague decides to do something he sticks with it till it gets done. For eight months he masterminded and underwrote the siege of Copperhead Bar, employing a full-time staff of temporary employees numbering as many as a hundred. By the end of that eighth month he'd thrown damned near every rat, mouse, and bug in TunFaire at the island. He'd foiled four rescue attempts by the Sons of Hammon. He'd survived several attacks by eight-limbed devils conjured by the dead Loghyr. A very stubborn man, Chodo Contague.

He had a purpose behind his purpose, of course. He wasn't just settling a score; he was making a high-profile effort to show the world what you were in for if you pissed him off. I didn't look forward to that inevitable day when our careers pushed along irreconcilable paths. But for the moment he owed me and would do most anything for me.

For me it was a quiet, lazy winter for about ten days.